D0187565

"Tautly written, wickedly sexy, and just plain fun."
—Lisa Gardner, *New York Times*
bestselling author of *Hide*

"J. R. Ward's unique band of brothers is to die for. I love this series!" —*New York Times* bestselling author
Suzanne Brockmann

"Utterly absorbing and deliciously erotic.... The Brotherhood is the hottest collection of studs in romance. I can't wait for the next one!"
—*USA Today* bestselling author Angela Knight

PRAISE FOR THE
BLACK DAGGER BROTHERHOOD SERIES

Lover Avenged

"While the story line is tortured and gut-wrenching, the unfolding love story is hopeful and healing. Plenty of action, intrigue, and betrayal ensure edge-of-seat entertainment."
—*Romantic Times*

"J. R. Ward does—unlike some other authors I might name when they made the leap to hardcover—step up to the plate to deliver a bigger, meatier book ... a worthy book that I think many readers will enjoy."
—All About Romance

"The latest Brotherhood vampire romantic suspense is an excellent entry in one of the great sagas on the market today." —The Best Reviews

Lover Enshrined

"Ward has outdone herself with this latest Brotherhood novel." —*Publishers Weekly* (starred review)

"Ward's fans have come to expect stories jam-packed with complex ongoing story lines, and her newest is no exception." —*Booklist*

continued ...

Lover Unbound

"The newest in Ward's ferociously popular Black Dagger Brotherhood series bears all the marks of a polished storyteller completely at home in her world. . . . This fix will give Brotherhood addicts a powerful rush."

—*Publishers Weekly*

"Graphic and powerful. Ward pulls no punches and delivers an extraordinary paranormal drama."

—*Romantic Times* (top pick, 4½ stars)

Lover Revealed

"These erotic paranormals are well worth it, and frighteningly addictive. . . . It all works to great page-turning effect. The . . . series [has] earned Ward an Anne Rice–style following, deservedly so." —*Publishers Weekly*

"It's tough to keep raising the bar in a series, but the phenomenal Ward manages to do just that! . . . The world of the Black Dagger Brotherhood continues to grow and become more layered, ramping up the tension, risk, and passion . . . awesome stuff." —*Romantic Times* (top pick, 4½ stars)

Lover Awakened

"A raw, gritty tour de force . . . a tale that sparks enough plot stunners to keep readers fascinated for years to come."

—*Booklist* (starred review)

"Compelling. Ward pulls no punches in this dark, dangerous, and at times tragic series."

—*Romantic Times* (top pick, 4½ stars)

Lover Eternal

"Hold on tight for an intriguing, adrenaline-pumping ride . . . [that] leaves readers begging for more. Fans of L. A. Banks, Laurell K. Hamilton, and Sherrilyn Kenyon will add Ward to their must-read list." —*Booklist*

J. R. WARD

LOVER
AVENGED

A NOVEL OF THE BLACK DAGGER BROTHERHOOD

A SIGNET BOOK

SIGNET
Published by New American Library, a division of
Penguin Group (USA) Inc., 375 Hudson Street,
New York, New York 10014, USA
Penguin Group (Canada), 90 Eglinton Avenue East, Suite 700, Toronto,
Ontario M4P 2Y3, Canada (a division of Pearson Penguin Canada Inc.)
Penguin Books Ltd., 80 Strand, London WC2R 0RL, England
Penguin Ireland, 25 St. Stephen's Green, Dublin 2,
Ireland (a division of Penguin Books Ltd.)
Penguin Group (Australia), 250 Camberwell Road, Camberwell,
Victoria 3124, Australia (a division of Pearson Australia Group Pty. Ltd.)
Penguin Books India Pvt. Ltd., 11 Community Centre, Panchsheel Park,
New Delhi - 110 017, India
Penguin Group (NZ), 67 Apollo Drive, Rosedale, North Shore 0632,
New Zealand (a division of Pearson New Zealand Ltd.)
Penguin Books (South Africa) (Pty.) Ltd., 24 Sturdee Avenue,
Rosebank, Johannesburg 2196, South Africa

Penguin Books Ltd., Registered Offices:
80 Strand, London WC2R 0RL, England

Published by Signet, an imprint of New American Library, a division of
Penguin Group (USA) Inc. Previously published in a New American Library hardcover edition.

First Signet Mass Market Printing, December 2009
10 9 8 7 6 5 4 3 2 1

DEDICATED TO *YOU*:

Good *and* bad *have never been more relative terms*

than when applied to the likes of you.

But I agree with her. To me, you have always been a hero.

ACKNOWLEDGMENTS

With immense gratitude to the readers of the Black Dagger Brotherhood and a shout-out to the Cellies!

Thank you so very much: Steven Axelrod, Kara Cesare, Claire Zion, Kara Welsh, and Leslie Gelbman.

Thank you, Lu and Opal, as well as our Mods and all our Hall Monitors, for everything you do out of the goodness of your hearts!

As always with many thanks to my Executive Committee: Sue Grafton, Dr. Jessica Andersen, and Betsey Vaughan. And with much respect to the incomparable Suzanne Brockmann and the ever-fabulous Christine Feehan (and family).

To D.L.B.—to say I look up to you would be self-obvious but there you go. Love u xxx mummy

To N.T.M.—who is always right, and still manages to be loved by all of us.

To LeElla Scott—who *owns* it, baby, yeah, she so does.

To Kaylie-girl and her momma—'cuz I love them so.

None of this would be possible without: my loving husband, who is my adviser and caretaker and visionary; my wonderful mother, who has given me so much love I couldn't possibly ever repay her; my family (both those of blood and those by adoption); and my dearest friends.

Oh, and with love to the better half of WriterDog, as always.

GLOSSARY OF TERMS AND PROPER NOUNS

ahstrux nohstrum (n.) Private guard with license to kill who is granted his or her position by the king.

ahvenge (v.) Act of mortal retribution, typically carried out by a male loved one.

Black Dagger Brotherhood (pr. n.) Highly trained vampire warriors who protect their species against the Lessening Society. As a result of selective breeding within the race, Brothers possess immense physical and mental strength, as well as rapid healing capabilities. They are not siblings, for the most part, and are inducted into the Brotherhood upon nomination by the Brothers. Aggressive, self-reliant, and secretive by nature, they exist apart from civilians, having little contact with members of the other classes except when they need to feed. They are the subjects of legend and the objects of reverence within the vampire world. They may be killed by only the most serious of wounds, e.g., a gunshot or stab to the heart, etc.

blood slave (n.) Male or female vampire who has been subjugated to serve the blood needs of another. The practice of keeping blood slaves has recently been outlawed.

chrih (n.) Symbol of honorable death in the Old Language.

the Chosen (n.) Female vampires who have been bred to serve the Scribe Virgin. They are considered members of the aristocracy, though they are spiritually rather than temporally focused. They have little or no interaction with males other than the Primale, but can be mated to Brothers at the Scribe Virgin's direction to further propagate their class. Some have the ability to prognosticate. In the past, they were used to meet the blood needs of unmated members of the Brotherhood, and that practice has been reinstated by the Brothers.

cohntehst (n.) Conflict between two males competing for the right to be a female's mate.

doggen (n.) Member of the servant class within the vampire world. *Doggen* have old, conservative traditions about service to their superiors and follow a formal code of dress and behavior. They are able to go out during the day, but they age relatively quickly. Life expectancy is approximately five hundred years.

Dhunhd (pr. n.) Hell.

ehros (n.) A Chosen trained in the matter of sexual arts.

exhile dhoble (n.) The evil or cursed twin, the one born second.

the Fade (pr. n.) Nontemporal realm where the dead reunite with their loved ones and pass eternity.

First Family (pr. n.) The king and queen of the vampires, and any children they may have.

ghardian (n.) Custodian of an individual. There are varying degrees of *ghardians*, with the most powerful being that of a *sehcluded* female.

glymera (n.) The social core of the aristocracy, roughly equivalent to Regency England's ton.

granhmen (n.) Grandmother.

hellren (n.) Male vampire who has been mated to a female. Males may take more than one female as mate.

leahdyre (n.) A person of power and influence.

leelan (adj.) A term of endearment loosely translated as "dearest one."

Lessening Society (pr. n.) Order of slayers convened by the Omega for the purpose of eradicating the vampire species.

lesser (n.) De-souled human who targets vampires for extermination as a member of the Lessening Society. *Lessers* must be stabbed through the chest in order to be killed; otherwise they are ageless. They do not eat or drink and are impotent. Over time, their hair, skin, and irises lose pigmentation until they are blond, blushless, and pale eyed. They smell like baby powder. Inducted into the society by the Omega, they retain a ceramic jar thereafter into which their heart was placed after it was removed.

lewlhen (n.) Gift.

lheage (n.) A term of respect used by a sexual submissive to refer to her dominant.

lys (n.) Torture tool used to remove the eyes.

mahmen (n.) Mother. Used both as an identifier and a term of affection.

mhis (n.) The masking of a given physical environment; the creation of a field of illusion.

nalla (n. f.) or **nallum** (n. m.) Beloved.

needing period (n.) Female vampire's time of fertility, generally lasting for two days and accompanied by intense sexual cravings. Occurs approximately five years after a female's transition and then once a decade thereafter. All males respond to some degree if they are around a female in her need. It can be a dangerous time, with conflicts and fights breaking out between competing males, particularly if the female is not mated.

newling (n.) A virgin.

the Omega (pr. n.) Malevolent, mystical figure who has targeted the vampires for extinction out of resentment directed toward the Scribe Virgin. Exists in a nontemporal realm and has extensive powers, though not the power of creation.

pherarsom (adj.) Term referring to the potency of a male's sexual organs. Literal translation something close to "worthy of entering a female."

princeps (n.) Highest level of the vampire aristocracy, second only to members of the First Family or the Scribe Virgin's Chosen. Must be born to the title; it may not be conferred.

pyrocant (n.) Refers to a critical weakness in an individual. The weakness can be internal, such as an addiction, or external, such as a lover.

rahlman (n.) Savior.

rythe (n.) Ritual manner of assuaging honor granted by one who has offended another. If accepted, the offended chooses a weapon and strikes the offender, who presents him- or herself without defenses.

the Scribe Virgin (pr. n.) Mystical force who is counselor to the king as well as the keeper of vampire archives and the dispenser of privileges. Exists in a nontemporal realm and has extensive powers. Capable of a single act of creation, which she expended to bring the vampires into existence.

sehclusion (n.) Status conferred by the king upon a female of the aristocracy as a result of a petition by the female's family. Places the female under the sole direction of her *ghardian*, typically the eldest male in her household. Her *ghardian* then has the legal right to determine all manner of her life, restricting at will any and all interactions she has with the world.

shellan (n.) Female vampire who has been mated to a male. Females generally do not take more than one mate due to the highly territorial nature of bonded males.

symphath (n.) Subspecies within the vampire race characterized by the ability and desire to manipulate emotions in others (for the purposes of an energy exchange), among other traits. Historically, they have been discriminated against and, during certain eras, hunted by vampires. They are near to extinction.

the Tomb (pr. n.) Sacred vault of the Black Dagger Brotherhood. Used as a ceremonial site as well as a storage facility for the jars of *lessers*. Ceremonies performed there include inductions, funerals, and disciplinary actions against Brothers. No one may enter except for members of the Brotherhood, the Scribe Virgin, or candidates for induction.

trahyner (n.) Word used between males of mutual respect and affection. Translated loosely as "beloved friend."

transition (n.) Critical moment in a vampire's life when he or she transforms into an adult. Thereafter, they must drink the blood of the opposite sex to survive and are unable to withstand sunlight. Occurs generally in the mid-twenties. Some vampires do not live through their transitions, males in particular. Prior to their transitions, vampires are physically weak, sexually unaware and unresponsive, and unable to dematerialize.

vampire (n.) Member of a species separate from that of Homo sapiens. Vampires must drink the blood of the opposite sex to survive. Human blood will keep them alive, though the strength does not last long. Following their transitions, which occur in their mid-twenties, they are unable to go out into sunlight and must feed from the vein regularly. Vampires cannot "convert" humans through a bite or transfer of blood, though they are in rare cases able to breed with the other species. Vampires can dematerialize at will, though they must be able to calm themselves and concentrate to do so and may not carry anything heavy with them. They are able to strip the memories of humans, provided such memories are short term. Some vampires are able to read minds. Life expectancy is upward of a thousand years, or in some cases even longer.

wahlker (n.) An individual who has died and returned to the living from the Fade. They are accorded great respect and are revered for their travails.

whard (n.) Equivalent of a godfather or godmother to an individual.

All kings are blind.
The good ones see this and use more than their eyes to lead.

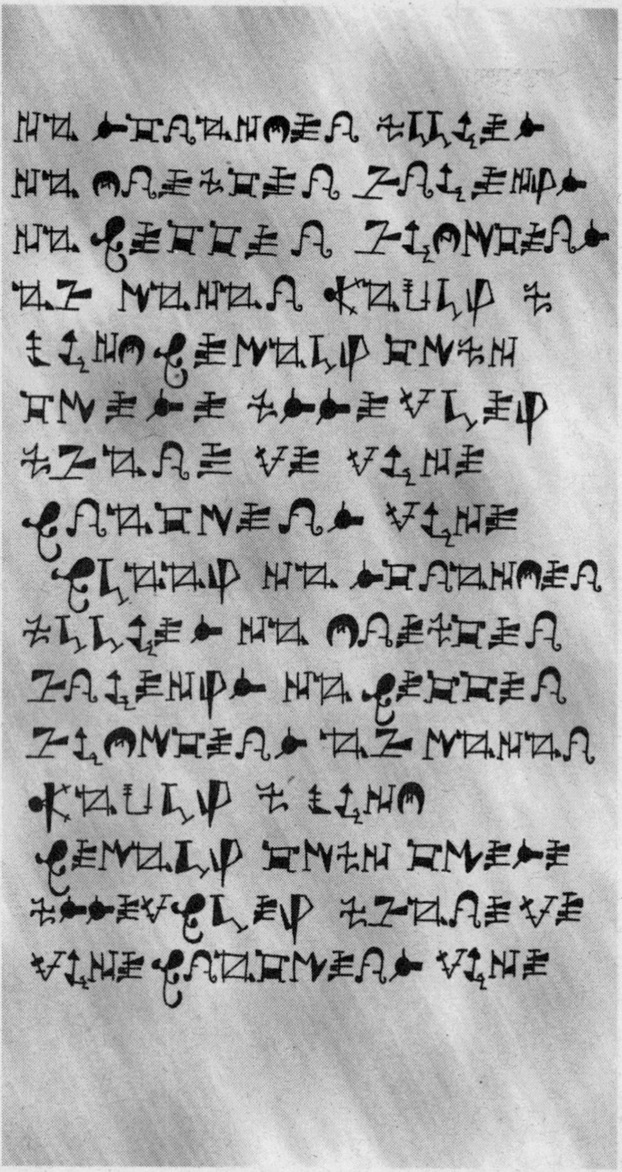

ONE

"The king must die."

Four single-syllable words. One by one they were nothing special. Put together? They called up all kinds of bad shit: Murder. Betrayal. Treason.

Death.

In the thick moments after they were spoken to him, Rehvenge kept quiet, letting the quartet hang in the stuffy air of the study, four points of a dark, evil compass he was intimately familiar with.

"Have you any response?" Montrag, son of Rehm, said.

"Nope."

Montrag blinked and fiddled with the silk cravat at his neck. Like most members of the *glymera*, he had both velvet slippers firmly planted in the dry, rarified sand of his class. Which meant he was just plain precious, all the way around. In his smoking jacket and his natty pin-striped slacks and . . . shit, were those actually spats? . . . he was right out of the pages of *Vanity Fair*. Like, a hundred years ago. And in his myriad condescensions and his bright frickin' ideas, he was Kissinger without a president when it came to politics: all analysis, no authority.

Which explained this meeting, didn't it.

"Don't stop now," Rehv said. "You've already jumped off the building. The landing isn't getting any softer."

Montrag frowned. "I fail to view this with your kind of levity."

"Who's laughing."

A knock on the study's door brought Montrag's head to the side, and he had a profile like an Irish setter: all nose. "Come in."

The *doggen* who followed the command struggled under the weight of the silver service she carried. With an ebony tray the size of a porch in her hands, she humped the load across the room.

Until her head came up and she saw Rehv.

She froze like a snapshot.

"We take our tea here." Montrag pointed to the low-slung table between the two silk sofas they were sitting on. "*Here.*"

The *doggen* didn't move, just stared at Rehv's face.

"What *is* the matter?" Montrag demanded as the teacups began to tremble, a chiming noise rising up from the tray. "Place our tea here, now."

The *doggen* bowed her head, mumbled something, and came forward slowly, putting one foot in front of the other like she was approaching a coiled snake. She stayed as far away from Rehv as she could, and after she put the service down, her shaking hands were barely able to get the cups into the saucers.

When she went for the pot of tea, it was clear she was going to spill the shit all over the place.

"Let me do it," Rehv said, reaching out.

As the *doggen* jerked away from him, her grip slipped off the pot handle and the tea went into free fall.

Rehv caught the blistering-hot silver in his palms.

"What have you done!" Montrag said, leaping off of his sofa.

The *doggen* cringed away, her hands going to her face. "I am sorry, master. Verily, I am—"

"Oh, shut up, and get us some ice—"

"It's not her fault." Rehv calmly switched his hold to the handle and poured. "And I'm perfectly fine."

They both stared at him like they were waiting for him to hop up and shake his bumper to the tune of *ow-ow-ow*.

He put the silver pot down and looked into Montrag's pale eyes. "One lump. Or two?"

"May I . . . may I get you something for that burn?"

He smiled, flashing his fangs at his host. "I'm perfectly fine."

Montrag seemed offended that he couldn't do anything, and turned his dissatisfaction on his servant. "You are a total disgrace. Leave us."

Rehv glanced at the *doggen*. To him, her emotions were a three-dimensional grid of fear and shame and panic, the interlocking weave filling out the space around her as surely as her bones and muscles and skin did.

Be of ease, he thought at her. *And know I'll make this right.*

Surprise flared in her face, but the tension left her shoulders and she turned away, looking much calmer.

When she was gone, Montrag cleared his throat and sat back down. "I don't think she's going to work out. She's utterly incompetent."

"Why don't we start with one lump." Rehv dropped a sugar cube into the tea. "And see if you want another."

He held the cup out, but not too far out, so that Montrag was forced to get up again from his sofa and bend across the table.

"Thank you."

Rehv didn't let go of the saucer as he pushed a change of thought into his host's brain. "I make females nervous. It wasn't her fault."

He released his hold abruptly and Montrag scrambled to keep hold of the Royal Doulton.

"Oops. Don't spill." Rehv settled back onto his sofa. "Shame to get a stain on this fine rug of yours. Aubusson, is it?"

"Ah ... yes." Montrag parked it again and frowned, like he had no idea why he felt differently about his maid. "Er ... yes, it is. My father bought it many years ago. He had exquisite taste, didn't he? We built this room for it because it is so very large, and the color of the walls was chosen specifically to bring out the peach tones."

Montrag looked around the study and smiled to himself as he sipped, his pinkie out in the breeze like a flag.

"How's your tea?"

"Perfect, but won't you have some?"

"Not a tea drinker." Rehv waited until the cup was up to

the male's lips. "So you were talking about murdering Wrath?"

Montrag sputtered, Earl Grey dappling the front of his bloodred smoking jacket and hitting Daddy's peachy-keen rug.

As the male batted at the stains with a limp hand, Rehv held out a napkin. "Here, use this."

Montrag took the damask square, awkwardly patted at his chest, then swiped the rug with equal lack of effect. Clearly, he was the kind of male who made messes, not cleaned them up.

"You were saying," Rehv murmured.

Montrag ditched the napkin on the tray and got to his feet, leaving his tea behind as he paced around. He stopped in front of a large mountain landscape and seemed to admire the dramatic scene with its spotlit colonial soldier praying to the heavens.

He spoke to the painting. "You are aware that so many of our blooded brethren have been taken down in the raids by the *lessers*."

"And here I thought I'd been made *leahdyre* of the council just because of my sparkling personality."

Montrag glared over his shoulder, his chin cocked in classic aristocratic fashion. "I lost my father and my mother and all of my first cousins. I buried each one of them. Think you that is a joy?"

"My apologies." Rehv put his right palm over his heart and bowed his head, even though he didn't give a shit. He was not going to be manipulated by the recitation of losses. Especially when the guy's emotions were all about greed, not grief.

Montrag turned his back to the painting, his head taking the place of the mountain the colonial soldier was on . . . so that it looked like the little man in the red uniform was trying to climb up his ear.

"The *glymera* has sustained unparalleled losses from the raids. Not just lives, but property. Houses raided, antiques and art taken, bank accounts disappearing. And what has Wrath done? *Nothing.* He's given no response to repeated inquiries ·about how those families' residences were found . . . why the Brotherhood didn't stop the attacks . . . where all those assets went. There is no plan to make sure it never happens again. No assurance that, if what few remaining members of the aristocracy return to Caldwell proper, we are protected." Montrag really got on a roll, his voice rising and bouncing off the crown molding and gilded ceiling. "Our race is *dying* out and we need real leadership. By law, though, if Wrath's heart beats within his chest, he is king. Is the life of one worth the lives of many? Search your heart."

Oh, Rehv was looking into it, all right, black, evil muscle that it was. "And then what."

"We take control and do what is right. During his tenure, Wrath has restructured things. . . . Look at what has been done to the Chosen. They are now allowed to tally on this side—unheard of! And slavery is outlawed, along with *sehclusion* for females. Dearest Virgin Scribe, next thing you know there'll be someone wearing a skirt in the Brotherhood. With us in charge, we can reverse what he has done and recast the laws properly to preserve the old ways. We can organize a new offensive against the Lessening Society. We can triumph."

"You're using a lot of *we*s here, and somehow I don't think that's exactly what you are thinking."

"Well, of course there needs to be an individual who is first among equals." Montrag smoothed the lapels of his smoking jacket and angled his head and body as if he were posing for a bronze statue or maybe a dollar bill. "A chosen male who is of stature and worth."

"And in what manner is this paragon going to be picked?"

"We're going to move to a democracy. A long-overdue democracy that shall replace the unjust and unfair convention of monarchy . . ."

As a whole lot of blah-blah-blahing got its groove on, Rehv eased back, crossed his legs at the knees, and steepled his fingers. Sitting on Montrag's fluffy sofa, the two halves of him warred, the vampire and the *symphath* clashing.

The only bene was that the internal shouting match droned out the sound of all that nasally I-know-everything.

The opportunity was obvious: Get rid of the king and seize control of the race.

The opportunity was unthinkable: Kill a fine male and a good leader and . . . a friend of sorts.

"... and we would choose who leads us. Make him accountable to the council. Ensure that our concerns are responded to." Montrag returned to the couch he'd been on, sitting down and getting comfortable as if he could hot-air it about the future for hours. "The monarchy is not working and democracy is the only way—"

Rehv cut in, "Democracy typically means that everyone gets a vote. Just in case you're unfamiliar with the definition."

"But we would. All of us who serve on the council would be on the electoral board. Everyone would be counted."

"FYI, the term *everyone* encompasses a couple more folks over and above 'everyone like us.'"

Montrag shot over a load of *oh-please-do-be-serious*. "Would you honestly trust the race to the lower classes?"

"Not up to me."

"It could be." Montrag brought his teacup up to his mouth and looked over the brim with eyes that were sharp. "It absolutely could be. You are our *leahdyre*."

Staring at the guy, Rehv saw the path as clearly as if it were paved and lit with halogen beams: If Wrath were killed, his royal line would end, because he had yet to sire young. Societies, particularly those at war as the vampires were, abhorred leadership vacuums, so a radical shift from monarchy to "democracy" wouldn't be as unthinkable as it would have in another, saner, safer time.

The *glymera* might be out of Caldwell and hiding in their safe houses throughout New England, but that bunch of effete motherfuckers had money and influence and had wanted to take over forever. With this particular plan, they could clothe their ambitions in the vestments of democracy and make like they were taking care of the little people.

Rehv's dark nature seethed, a jailed criminal impatient for probation: Bad acts and power plays were a constitutional compulsion for those of his father's blood, and part of him wanted to create the void ... and step into it.

He cut into Montrag's self-important driveling. "Spare me the propaganda. What exactly are you suggesting."

The male made elaborate work of putting down his teacup, as if he wanted to appear as if he were corralling his words. Whatever. Rehv was willing to bet the guy knew exactly what he was going to say. Something of this nature wasn't the kind of thing you just pulled out of your ass, and there were others in on it. Had to be.

"As you well know, the council is to meet in a couple of days in Caldwell specifically for us to have an audience with the king. Wrath will arrive and . . . a mortal event will occur."

"He travels with the Brotherhood. Not exactly the kind of muscle you can easily work around."

"Death wears many masks. And has many different stages on which to perform."

"And my role is . . . ?" Even though he knew.

Montrag's pale eyes were like ice, luminescent and cold. "I know what kind of male you are. So I know exactly what you are capable of."

This was not a surprise. Rehv had been a drug lord for the past twenty-five years, and though he hadn't announced his avocation to the aristocracy, vampires did hit his clubs regularly, and a number of them were in the ranks of his chemical customers.

No one but the Brothers knew about his *symphath* side—and he would have kept it from them if he'd had the choice. For the past two decades he'd been paying his black-mailer well to make sure the secret was his to keep.

"That is why I come to you," Montrag said. "You will know how to take care of this."

"True enough."

"As *leahdyre* of the council, you would be in a position of enormous power. Even if you are not elected as president, the council is going nowhere. And let me reassure you about the Black Dagger Brotherhood. I know your sister is mated to one of them. The Brothers will not be affected by this."

"You don't think it's going to piss them off? Wrath is not just their king. He's their blood."

"Protecting our race is their primary mandate. Whither we go they must follow. And you have to know that there are many who feel they have been doing a poor job of late. Methinks perhaps they require better leadership."

"From you. Right. Of course."

That would be like an interior decorator trying to command a tank platoon: a shitload of noisy chirping until one of the soldiers offed the lightweight flash in the pan and churned over the body a couple of times.

Perfect plan there. Yup.

And yet . . . who said Montrag had to be the one elected? Accidents happened to both kings and aristocrats.

"I must say unto you," Montrag continued, "as my father always said unto me, timing is everything. We need to proceed with haste. May we rely on you, my friend?"

Rehv got to his feet and towered over the other male. With a quick tug on his jacket cuffs, he straightened his Tom Ford, then reached for his cane. He felt nothing in his body, not his clothes or the weight shifting from his ass to his soles or the handle against the palm he'd burned. The numbness was a side effect of the drug he used to keep his bad side from coming out in mixed company, the prison in which he jailed his sociopathic impulses.

All he needed to get back to basics was one missed dose, though. An hour later? The evil in him was alive and kicking and ready to play.

"What say you?" Montrag prompted.

Wasn't that the question.

Sometimes in life, from out of the myriad of prosaic decisions like what to eat and where to sleep and how to dress, a true crossroads is revealed. In these moments, when the fog of relative irrelevancy lifts and fate rolls out a demand for free will, there is only left or right—no option of four-by-fouring into the underbrush between two paths, no negotiating with the choice that has been presented.

You must answer the call and pick your way. And there is no reverse.

Of course, the problem was, navigating a moral landscape was something he'd had to teach himself to do to fit in with the vampires. The lessons he'd learned had stuck, although only to a point.

And his drugs only kind of, sort of worked.

Abruptly, Montrag's pale face became cast in variations of pastel pink and the male's dark hair went magenta and his smoking jacket became the color of ketchup. As a red wash tinted everything, Rehv's visual field flattened out so it was like a movie screen of the world.

Which perhaps explained why *symphaths* found it so easy to use people. With his dark side taking over, the universe had all the depth of a chessboard, and the people in it were pawns to his omniscient hand. Every one of them. Enemies . . . and friends.

"I'll take care of it," Rehv announced. "As you said, I know what to do."

"Your word." Montrag put forward his smooth palm. "Your word that this shall be carried out in secret and in silence."

Rehv let that hand hang in the breeze, but he smiled, once again revealing his fangs. "Trust me."

TWO

As Wrath, son of Wrath, pounded down one of Caldwell's urban alleys, he was bleeding in two places. There was a gash along his left shoulder, made by a serrated knife, and a hunk out of his thigh, thanks to the rusty corner of a Dumpster. The *lesser* up ahead, the one he was about to gut like a fish, had been responsible for neither: The asshole's two pale-haired, girlie-smelling buddies had done the damage.

Right before they'd been reduced to a matched set of mulch bags three hundred yards and three minutes ago.

This bastard up ahead was the real target.

The slayer was hauling ass, but Wrath was faster—not just because his legs were longer, and despite the fact that he was leaking like a corroded cistern. There was no question the third would die.

It was an issue of will.

The *lesser* had chosen the wrong path tonight—although not in picking this particular alley. That had been the only right and just thing the undead had probably done for decades, because privacy was important for fighting. Last thing the Brothers or the Lessening Society needed was for human police to get involved in anything so much as a nose blow in this war.

No, the bastard's *I'm-sorry-that's-not-the-correct-answer* had happened when he'd killed a male civilian about fifteen minutes ago. With a smile on his face. In front of Wrath.

The scent of fresh vampire blood had been how the king had first found the trio of slayers, catching them in the act as they tried to abduct one of his civilians. They'd clearly known he was at least a member of the Brotherhood, because this *lesser* up ahead had killed the male so he and his squadron could be hands-free and fully focused for the fight.

The sad part was, Wrath's arrival had spared his civilian a long, slow, tortured death in one of the Society's persuasion camps. But it still burned his ass to see a terrified innocent sliced open and dropped like an empty lunch box onto the icy, cracked pavement.

So this motherfucker up here was going down.

Eye-for-an-eye-and-then-some–style.

At the alley's dead end, the *lesser* did a pivot-and-prepare, spinning around, planting his feet, bringing up his knife. Wrath didn't slow. In midstride, he slipped free one of his *hira shuriken* and sent the weapon out with a flick of his hand, making a show of the throw.

Sometimes you wanted your opponent to know what was coming at him.

The *lesser* followed the choreography perfectly, shifting his balance, losing his fighting form. As Wrath closed the distance, he winged another throwing star and another, driving the *lesser* into a crouch.

The Blind King dematerialized right on the motherfucker, striking from above with fangs bared to lock into the back of the slayer's neck. The stinging sweetness of the *lesser*'s blood was the taste of triumph, and the chorus of victory was not long in coming either as Wrath grabbed onto both of the bastard's upper arms.

Payback was a snap. Or two, as it were.

The thing screamed as both bones popped out of their sockets, but the howl didn't travel far after Wrath clapped his palm over its mouth.

"That's just a warm-up," Wrath hissed. "It's important to get loose before you're worked out."

The king flipped the slayer over and stared down at the thing. From behind Wrath's wraparounds, his weak eyes were sharper than usual, the adrenaline cruising along his highway of veins giving him a shot at visual acuity. Which was good. He needed to see what he killed in a way that had nothing to do with ensuring the accuracy of a mortal blow.

As the *lesser* strained for breath, the skin of its face sported an unreal, plastic sheen—as if the bone structure had been upholstered in the shit you made grain sacks out of—and the eyes were popping wide, the sweet stench of the thing like the sweat of roadkill on a hot night.

Wrath unclipped the steel chain that hung from the shoulder of his biker jacket and unwound the shiny links from under his arm. Holding the heavy weight in his right hand, he wrapped his fist, widening the spread of his knuckles, adding to their hard contours.

"Say 'cheese.'"

Wrath struck the thing in the eye. Once. Twice. Three times. His fist was a battering ram, the eye socket below giving way like it was nothing more than a pocket door. With every cracking impact, black blood burst up and out, hitting Wrath's face and jacket and sunglasses. He felt all the spray, even through the leather he wore, and wanted more.

He was a glutton for this kind of meal.

With a hard smile, he let the chain uncoil from his fist, and it hit the dirty asphalt on a seething, metallic laugh, as if it had enjoyed that as much as he had. Below him, the *lesser* wasn't dead. Even though the thing was no doubt developing massive subdural hematomas on the front and back of its brain, it would still live, because there were only two ways to kill a slayer.

One was to stab it in the chest with the black daggers the Brothers wore strapped to their chests. This sent the POS back to its maker, the Omega, but was only a temporary fix, because the evil would just use that essence to turn another human into a killing machine. It was not death, but delay.

The other way was permanent.

Wrath got out his cell phone and dialed. When a deep male voice with a Boston accent answered, he said, "Eighth and Trade. Three down."

Butch O'Neal, a.k.a. the *Dhestroyer*, descended of Wrath, son of Wrath, was characteristically phlegmatic in his response. Real middle-of-the-road. Easygoing. Leaving so much room for interpretation in his words:

"Oh, for fuck's sake. Are you kidding me? Wrath, you

have *got* to stop this moonlighting shit. You're the king now. You're not a Brother any—"

Wrath clipped the phone shut.

Yup. The other way to get rid of these sonsabitches, the permanent way, was going to be here in about five minutes. With his mouth riding shotgun. Unfortunately.

Wrath sat back on his heels, re-coiled the chain on his shoulder, and looked up at the squat box of night sky that was visible above the rooftops. As his adrenaline ebbed, he could only slightly differentiate the rising dark torsos of the buildings against the flat plane of the galaxy, and he squinted hard.

You're not a Brother anymore.

The hell he wasn't. He didn't care what the law said. His race needed him to be more than a bureaucrat.

With a curse in the Old Language, he got back with the program, going through the slayer's jacket and pants, looking for ID. In an ass pocket, he found a thin wallet with a driver's license and two dollars in it—

"You thought . . . he was one of yours. . . ."

The slayer's voice was both reedy and malicious, and the horror-movie sound triggered Wrath's aggression once more. In a rush, his vision sharpened, bringing his enemy into semifocus.

"What did you say to me?"

The *lesser* smiled a little, seeming not to notice that half its face had the consistency of a runny omelet. "He was always . . . one of ours."

"What the fuck are you talking about?"

"How . . . do you think"—the *lesser* took a shuddering breath—"we found . . . all those houses this summer—"

A vehicle's arrival cut off the words, and Wrath's head shot around. Thank fuck it was the black Escalade he was hoping for and not some human with a cell phone cocked and loaded with a 911 call.

Butch O'Neal stepped out from behind the wheel, his gum-flapping in full swing. "Have you lost your damn mind? What are we going to do with you? You're gonna give . . ."

As the cop kept riding the Holy Hell Trail, Wrath looked back at the slayer. "How did you find them? The houses?"

The slayer started laughing, the weak wheeze the kind

of thing you heard out of the deranged. "Because he'd been in them all . . . that's how."

The bastard passed out, and shaking him didn't help bring him back. Neither did a palm slam or two.

Wrath got to his feet, frustration triggering the rise. "Do your business, cop. The other two are back behind the Dumpster on the next block."

The cop just stared at him. "You're not supposed to fight."

"I'm the king. I can do whatever the fuck I want."

Wrath started to walk away, but Butch grabbed onto his arm. "Does Beth know where you are? What you're doing? You tell her? Or is it only me you're asking to keep this secret?"

"Worry about that." Wrath pointed to the slayer. "Not me and my *shellan*."

As he pulled free, Butch barked, "Where are you going?"

Wrath marched up into the cop's grille. "I thought I would pick up a civilian's dead body and carry it to the Escalade. You got a problem with that, son?"

Butch held his ground. Just one more way their shared blood showed. "We lose you as king and the whole race is fucked."

"And we got four Brothers left in the field. You like that math? I don't."

"But—"

"Do your business, Butch. And stay out of mine."

Wrath stalked the three hundred yards back to where the fighting had started. The beaten slayers were right where he'd left them: moaning on the ground, their limbs at wrong angles, their black blood seeping out into filthy slush puddles beneath their bodies. They were no longer his concern, though. Going around behind the Dumpster he looked at his dead civilian and found it hard to breathe.

The king knelt down and carefully brushed the hair back from the male's beaten-to-shit face. Clearly, the guy had fought back, taking a number of hits before getting stabbed through the heart. Brave kid.

Wrath cupped the nape of the male's neck, slid his other arm under the knees, and slowly rose. The weight of the dead was heavier than the pounds of the body. As he stepped away from the Dumpster and started for the Escalade, Wrath felt as though he held his whole race aloft in his arms, and he was glad he had to wear sunglasses to protect his weak eyes.

His wraparounds hid the sheen of tears.

He passed Butch as the cop jogged off toward the broken slayers to do his thing. After the guy's footfalls halted, Wrath heard a long, deep inhale that sounded like the hiss of a balloon slowly deflating. The retching that followed was much louder.

As the suck and gag was repeated, Wrath laid the dead out in the back of the Escalade and went through the pockets. There was nothing . . . no wallet, no phone, not even a gum wrapper.

"Fuck." Wrath pivoted around and sat on the SUV's back bumper. One of the *lessers* had cleaned him out already in the course of the fighting . . . and that meant that as all the slayers had just been inhaled, the civilian's ID was ashed.

As Butch came weaving down the alley toward the Escalade, he was like an alkie on a bender and the cop didn't smell like Acqua di Parma anymore. He stank of *lesser*, as if he'd lined his clothes in Downy dryer sheets, taped a pair of fake-vanilla car fresheners under his armpits, and done a dog roll in some dead fish.

Wrath got up and shut the Escalade's back.

"You sure you can drive?" he asked as Butch carefully eased himself behind the wheel, looking like he was about to throw up.

"Yeah. Good to go."

Wrath shook his head at the hoarse voice and glanced around the alley. There were no windows going up the buildings, and having Vishous come right away to heal the cop wouldn't take a lot of time, but between the fights and the cleanup there had been a lot going on here for the last half hour. They needed to get out of the area.

Originally, Wrath's plan had been to take a picture of the slayer's ID with his camera phone, enlarge it enough so he could read the address, and go after the jar of that fucker. He couldn't leave Butch on his own, though.

The cop seemed surprised when Wrath got into the Escalade's shotgun seat. "What are you—"

"We'll take the body to the clinic. V can meet you there and take care of you."

"Wrath—"

"Let's fight on the way, shall we, cousin mine?"

Butch put the SUV in gear, reversed out of the alley, and turned around at the first cross street they came to. When he hit Trade, he took a left and headed for the bridges that stretched over the Hudson River. As he drove, he white-knuckled the steering wheel—not because he was scared, but because he was no doubt trying to hold down the bile in his gut.

"I can't keep lying like this," Butch mumbled as they got to the other side of Caldwell. A little gag was followed by a cough.

"Yeah, you can."

The cop looked over. "It's killing me. Beth needs to know."

"I don't want her to worry."

"I get that—" Butch made a choking sound. "Hold on."

The cop pulled over onto the iced-up shoulder, popped open the door, and dry-heaved like his liver had received evacuation orders from his colon.

Wrath let his head fall back, an ache setting up shop behind both his eyes. The pain was so not a surprise. Lately he had migraines the way allergy sufferers had sneezes.

Butch reached back and patted around the center console, his upper body still arched out of the Escalade.

"You want the water?" Wrath asked.

"Ye—" Retching cut off the rest of the word.

Wrath picked up a Poland Spring bottle, cracked it open, and put the thing in Butch's hand.

When there was a break in the throwing up, the cop glugged some water, but the shit didn't stay down.

Wrath took out his phone. "I'm calling V now."

"Just give me a minute."

It took more like ten, but eventually the cop got himself back in the car and put them on the road again. They both were silent for a couple miles, Wrath's brain racing while his headache got worse.

You're not a Brother anymore.

You're not a Brother anymore.

But he had to be. His race needed him.

He cleared his throat. "When V shows up at the morgue, you're going to say you found the civilian's body and did the nasty with the *lessers*."

"He'll want to know why you're there."

"We'll tell him that I was on the next block meeting with Rehvenge at ZeroSum and I sensed that you needed help." Wrath leaned across the front seat and locked a hand on the guy's forearm. "No one is going to find out, understand?"

"This is not a good idea. This is *so* not a good idea."

"The fuck it isn't."

As they fell silent, the lights from cars on the other side of the highway made Wrath wince, even though his lids were down and his wraparounds in place. To cut the glare, he turned his face to the side, making like he was staring out his window.

"V knows something is up," Butch muttered after a while.

"And he can keep wondering. I need to be out in the field."

"What if you get hurt?"

Wrath put his forearm over his face in hopes of blocking out those goddamn headlights. Man, now *he* was getting nauseated.

"I won't get hurt. Don't worry."

THREE

You ready for your juice, Father?"
When there was no response, Ehlena, blooded daughter of Alyne, paused in the process of buttoning her uniform. "Father?"

From down the hall, she heard over the dulcet strings of Chopin a pair of slippers moving across bare floorboards and a soft waterfall of tumbling words, like a deck of cards being shuffled together.

This was good. He was up on his own.

Ehlena pulled her hair back, twisted it, and put a white scrunchie on to hold the knot in place. Halfway through her shift, she was going to have to redo the bun. Havers, the race's physician, required his nurses to be as pressed and starched and well-ordered as everything in his clinic.

Standards, he always said, were critical.

On the way out of her bedroom, she picked up a black shoulder bag she'd gotten from Target. Nineteen bucks. A steal. In it was the shortish skirt and the knockoff Polo sweater she was going to change into about two hours before dawn.

A date. She was actually going on a date.

The trip upstairs to the kitchen involved only one flight of stairs, and the first thing she did when she emerged from the basement was head over to the old-fashioned Frigidaire. Inside, there were eighteen small bottles of Ocean Spray CranRaspberry in three rows of six. She took one from the front, then carefully moved the others forward so that they were all lined up.

The pills were located behind the dusty stack of cookbooks. She took out one trifluoperazine and two loxapine and put them in a white mug. The stainless-steel spoon she used to crush them up was bent at a slight angle, and so were all the others.

She'd been crushing pills like this for close to two years now.

The CranRas hit the fine white powder and swirled it away, and to make sure the taste was adequately hidden, she put two ice cubes in the mug. The colder the better.

"Father, your juice is ready." She put the mug down on the small table, right on top of a circle of tape that delineated where it needed to be placed.

The six cupboards across the way were as orderly and relatively empty as the fridge, and out of one she grabbed a box of Wheaties, and from another she got a bowl. After pouring herself some flakes she grabbed the milk carton, and as soon as she was finished using it, she put the thing right back where it went: next to two more of its kind, the Hood labels facing out.

She glanced at her watch and switched into the Old Language. *"Father? I must take my leave."*

The sun had set, and that meant her shift, which started fifteen minutes after dark, was about to kick off.

She glanced at the window over the kitchen sink, although it wasn't as if she could measure how dark it was. The panes were covered with sheets of overlapping aluminum foil that were duct-taped to the molding.

Even if she and her father hadn't been vampires and unable to handle daylight, those Reynolds Wrap blinds would have had to be in place over each window in the house: They were lids on the rest of the world, sealing it out, containing it so that this crappy little rented house was protected and insulated . . . from threats only her father could sense.

When she was finished with the Breakfast of Champions, she washed and dried her bowl with paper towels, because sponges and dishcloths weren't allowed, and put it and the spoon she'd used back where they belonged.

"Father mine?"

She propped her hip against the chipped Formica counter and waited, trying not to look too closely at the faded wallpaper or the linoleum floor with its worn tracks.

The house was barely more than a dingy shed, but it was all she could afford. Between her father's doctor visits and his meds and his visiting nurse there just wasn't much left over from her salary, and she'd long ago used up what little was left of the family money, silver, antiques, and jewelry.

They were barely staying afloat.

And yet, as her father appeared in the cellar's doorway, she had to smile. His fine gray hair radiated out of his head, a halo of fluff making him look like Beethoven, and his overly observant, slightly frantic eyes also gave him the look of a mad genius. Still, he seemed better than he had in a long while. For one thing, he had his fraying satin robe and silk pajamas on right—everything facing forward, with the top and bottom matching and the sash done up. He was clean, too, freshly bathed and smelling like bay rum aftershave.

It was such a contradiction: He needed his environment spotless and precisely ordered, but his personal hygiene and what he wore were not an issue at all. Although perhaps it made sense. Caught up in his tangled thoughts, he got too distracted by his delusions to be self-aware.

The meds were helping, though, and it showed as he met her eye and actually saw her.

"*Daughter mine,*" he said in the Old Language, "*how fare thee this night?*"

She responded as he preferred, in the mother tongue. "*Well, my father. And you?*"

He bowed with the grace of the aristocrat he was by blood and had been by station. "*As always I am charmed by your greeting. Ah, yes, the* doggen *has put out my juice. How good of her.*"

Her father sat with a swish of his robes, and he picked up the ceramic mug as if it were fine English china. "*Whither thou goest?*"

"*To work. I am going to work.*"

Her father frowned as he sipped. "*You are well aware I do not approve of your industry outside of the home. A lady of your breeding should not be tendering her hours as such.*"

"*I know, father mine. But it makes me happy.*"

His face softened. "*Well, that is different. Alas, I do not understand the younger generation. Your mother managed the household and the servants and the gardens, and that was plenty to engage her nightly impulses.*"

Ehlena looked down, thinking that her mother would weep to see where they had ended up. "*I know.*"

"*You shall do as you will, though, and I shall love you e'ermore.*"

She smiled at the words she'd heard all of her life. And on that note . . . "*Father?*"

He lowered the mug. "*Yes?*"

"*I shall be a bit late in getting home this evening.*"

"*Indeed? Why for?*"

"*I am going to have coffee with a male—*"

"*What is that?*"

The change in his tone brought her head up, and she looked around to see what— *Oh, no . . .*

"*Nothing, Father, verily, it is nothing.*" She quickly went over to the spoon she'd used to crush the pills and picked it up, rushing for the sink like she had a burn that needed cold water stat.

Her father's voice quavered. "*What . . . what was it doing? I—*"

Ehlena quickly dried the spoon and slipped it in the drawer. "*See? All gone. See?*" She pointed to where it had been. "*The counter is clean. There's nothing there.*"

"*It was there . . . I saw it. Metal objects are not to be left . . . It's not safe to . . . Who left it . . . Who left it out . . . Who left the spoon—*"

"*The maid did.*"

"*The maid! Again! She must be fired. I have told her— nothing metal is left out nothing metal is left out nothing metal is left out-they-are-watching-andtheywillpunishthose whodisobeytheyarecloserthanweknowand—*"

In the beginning, when her father's attacks had first occurred, Ehlena had reached out to him as he got agitated, thinking a pat on the shoulder or a comforting hand in his own would help. Now she knew better. The less sensory input into his brain, the faster the rolling hysteria slowed: On the advice of his nurse, Ehlena pointed out the reality to him once and then didn't move or speak.

It was hard, though, to watch him suffer and be unable to do anything to help. Especially when it was her fault.

Her father's head shook back and forth, the agitation frothing his hair up into a fright wig of crazy frizz, while in his wobbling grip, CranRas jumped out of the mug, splashing on his veined hand and the sleeve of the robe and the pitted Formica tabletop. From his trembling lips, the staccato beats of syllables increased, his internal record getting played at an ever-higher speed, the flush of madness riding up the column of his throat and flaring in his cheeks.

Ehlena prayed this wasn't going to be a bad one. The attacks, when they came, varied in intensity and duration, and the drugs helped shrink both metrics. But sometimes the illness bested the chemical management.

As her father's words became too crowded to comprehend and he dropped the mug on the floor, all Ehlena could do was wait and pray to the Scribe Virgin that this would pass soon. Forcing her feet to stay glued to the crappy linoleum, she closed her eyes and wrapped her arms around her rib cage.

If she had just remembered to put the spoon away. If she had just—

When her father's chair scraped back and crashed to the floor, she knew she was going to be late for work. Again.

Humans really were cattle, Xhex thought as she looked over all the heads and shoulders packed in tight around ZeroSum's general-population bar.

It was like some farmer had just grained up a trough and the milking stock was jockeying for muzzle space.

Not that the bovine characteristics of Homo sapiens were a bad thing. The herd mentality was easier to manage from a security point of view, and in a way, like cows, one could feed off of them: That crush around those bottles was all about wallet purge, with the tide flowing only one way—into the coffers.

Liquor sales were good. But the drugs and sex had even higher profit margins.

Xhex walked by the bar's outer rim slowly, dousing the hot speculation of heterosexual men and homosexual women with hard looks. Man, she didn't get it. Never had. For a female who wore nothing but muscle shirts and leathers and had hair cut short as a infantryman's, she caught attention as much as the half-dressed prostitutes up in VIP area did.

Then again, rough sex was in fashion these days, and volunteers for autoerotic asphyxiation and ass-crack whippings and three ways with handcuffs were like the rats in Caldwell's sewer system: everywhere and out at night. Which resulted in over a third of the club's profits every month.

Thank you very much.

Unlike the working girls, however, she never took money for sex. Didn't really do the sex thing at all. Except for Butch O'Neal, that cop. Well, that cop and . . .

Xhex came up to the VIP section's velvet rope and took a glance inside the exclusive part of the club.

Shit. He was here.

Just what she needed tonight.

Her libido's favorite eye candy was sitting in the far back at the Brotherhood's table, his two buddies flanking him and thus buffering him from the three girls who were also crowded into the banquette. Damn, he was big in that booth, all decked out in an Affliction T-shirt and a black leather jacket that was built half biker, half flak.

There were weapons under it. Guns. Knives.

How things had changed. The first time he'd made an appearance, he'd been the size of a bar stool, packing barely enough muscle to bench-press a swizzle stick. But that was not the case anymore.

As she nodded to her bouncer and went up the three graduated steps, John Matthew lifted his stare from his Corona. Even through the dimness, his deep blue eyes glowed when he saw her, flashing like a set of sapphires.

Man, she could pick 'em. The son of a bitch was just out of his transition. The king was his *whard*. He lived with the Brotherhood. And he was a damned mute.

Christ. And she'd thought Murhder had been a bad idea? You'd have figured she'd learned her lesson over two decades ago with that Brother. But noooooooooooooo . . .

Thing was, as she looked at the kid, all she could picture was him spread out naked on a bed, thick cock in his hand, palm going up and down . . . until her name left his lips on a soundless groan and he came all over his tight six-pack.

The tragedy was that what she saw wasn't a fantasy.

Those fist pneumatics actually happened. Often. And how did she know? Because, like an asshole, she'd read his mind and caught the Memorex, good-as-live version.

Sick to shit of herself, Xhex went deeper into the VIP section and stayed away from him, checking in with the floor manager of the working girls. Marie-Terese was a brunette with great legs and an expensive look. One of the big earners, she was a strict professional and therefore exactly the kind of HBIC you wanted: She never fell into catty crap, always showed up for her shifts on time, and never brought whatever was wrong in her personal life to work. She was a fine woman in a horrible job, making money hand over fist for a damn good reason.

"How we doing?" Xhex asked. "You need anything from me and my boys?"

Marie-Terese glanced around at the other working women, her high cheekbones catching the dim light, making her look not just sexually alluring, but downright beautiful. "We're good for now. Two in the back at the moment. It's been business as usual, except for the fact that our girl is not here."

Xhex snapped her brows down. "Chrissy again?"

Marie-Terese inclined her head of long, black, and lovely. "Something needs to be done about that gentleman caller of hers."

"Something was, but it didn't go far enough. And if he's a gentleman, I'm Estée fucking Lauder." Xhex fisted both hands. "That son of a bitch—"

"Boss?"

Xhex looked over her shoulder. Past the mountain of bouncer who was trying to get her attention, she caught another full-on of John Matthew. Who was still staring at her.

"Boss?"

Xhex refocused. "What."

"There's a cop here to see you."

She didn't move her eyes from her bouncer. "Marie-Terese, tell the girls to relax for ten."

"I'm on it."

The head bitch in charge moved fast while seeming to just saunter in her stillies, going to each of the girls and tapping them on the left shoulder, then knocking once on each of the private bathroom doors down the dark hall to the right.

As the place emptied of prostitutes, Xhex said, "Who and why."

"Homicide detective." The bouncer handed over a card. "José de la Cruz, he said his name was."

Xhex took the thing and knew exactly why the guy was here. And Chrissy was not. "Park him in my office. I'll be there in two."

"Roger that."

Xhex brought her wristwatch up to her lips. "Trez? iAm? We've got heat in the house. Tell the bookies to chill and Rally to stop the scales."

When confirmation came through her earpiece, she did a quick double check that all the girls were off the floor; then she headed back to the open part of the club.

As she left the VIP section, she could feel John Matthew's eyes on her and tried not to think about what she had done two dawns ago when she got home . . . and what she was likely going to do when she was by herself at the end of tonight as well.

Fucking John Matthew. Ever since she'd barged into his brain and saw what he'd been doing to himself whenever he thought about her . . . she'd been doing likewise.

Fucking. John Matthew.

Like she needed this shit?

Now, as she went through the human herd, she was rough, not caring when she hard-elbowed a couple of dancers. She almost hoped one complained so she could toss them out on their ass.

Her office was up on the mezzanine floor in the back, as far away as you could get from where the sex-for-hire happened and from where the beat-downs and the deals rolled out in Rehvenge's private space. As head of security, she was the primary interface with the police, and there was no reason to bring the blue unis closer to the action than they had to be.

Scrubbing the minds of humans was a handy tool, but it had its complications.

Her door was open and she sized up the detective from behind. He wasn't too tall, but he had a thick build she approved of. His sports coat was Men's Wearhouse, his shoes were Florsheim. Watch peeking out of his cuff was Seiko.

As he turned to look at her, his dark brown eyes were Sherlock-smart. He might not be making a lot of paper, but he was no dummy.

"Detective," she said, shutting the door and going past him to take a seat behind her desk.

Her office was all but naked. No pictures. No plants. Not even a phone or a computer. The records in the three locked fireproof filing cabinets pertained only to the legitimate side of the business, and the wastepaper basket was a shredder.

Which meant Detective de la Cruz had learned absolutely nothing about anything during the 120 seconds he'd spent alone in the room.

De la Cruz took his badge out and flashed it. "I'm here about one of your employees."

Xhex pretended to lean across and look at the shield, but she didn't need the ID. Her *symphath* side told her all she had to know: The detective's emotions were the correct mix of suspicion, concern, resolve, and pissed off. He took his job seriously, and he was here on business.

"Which employee?" she asked.

"Chrissy Andrews."

Xhex eased sat back in her chair. "When was she killed?"

"How do you know she's dead?"

"Don't play games, Detective. Why else would someone from Homicide be asking about her?"

"Sorry, I'm in interrogation mode." He slipped his shield back into his inside breast pocket and sat in the hard-backed chair across from her. "Tenant below her apartment woke up to a bloodstain on his ceiling and the guy called the police. No one in the apartment building will admit to knowing Ms. Andrews, and she has no next of kin that we can locate. While we were going through her place, though, we found tax returns listing this club as her employer. Bottom line, we need someone to identify the body and—"

Xhex stood up, the word *motherfucker* banging around her skull. "I'll do it. Let me get my men organized so I can leave."

De la Cruz blinked, like he was surprised she was so quick. "You . . . ah, you want a ride down to the morgue?"

"St. Francis?"

"Yup."

"I know the way. I'll meet you there in twenty."

De la Cruz got to his feet slowly, his eyes sharp on her face, as if he were searching for signs of trepidation. "I guess it's a date."

"Don't worry, Detective. I'm not going to faint at the sight of a dead body."

He looked her up and down. "You know ... somehow that doesn't concern me."

FOUR

As Rehvenge drove into the Caldwell city limits, he wished like hell he were going directly to ZeroSum. He knew better, though. He was in trouble.

Since leaving Montrag's Connecticut safe house, he'd pulled his Bentley over to the side of the road and shot himself up with dopamine twice. His miracle drug, however, was failing him again. If he'd had more of the shit in the car, he'd have fired up another syringe, but he was out.

The irony of a drug dealer having to go to *his* dealer at a dead run was not lost, and it was a damn shame there wasn't more of a demand for the neurotransmitter on the black market. As it stood now, Rehv's only supply was through legitimate means, but he was going to have to fix that. If he was smart enough to funnel X, coke, weed, meth, OxyC, and heroin through his two clubs, surely he could figure out how the hell to get his own vials of dopamine.

"Ah, come *on*, move your ass. It's just a goddamned exit ramp. You've seen one before."

He'd made good time on the highway, but now that he was in town, traffic slowed his progress, and not just because of congestion. With his lack of depth perception, judging bumper distances was tricky, so he had to go far more carefully than he liked.

And then there was this fidiot in his twelve-hundred-year-old beater and his overactive braking habits.

"No . . . no . . . by all that is holy don't change lanes. You can't even see out your rearview mirror as it is—"

Rehv punched on the brakes because Mr. Timid was actually thinking he belonged over in the fast lane and seemed to think the way to get into it was to come to a dead stop.

Usually, Rehv loved to drive. He even preferred it to dematerializing because it was the only time when he was medicated that he felt like he was himself: fast, nimble, powerful. He drove a Bentley not just because it was chic and he could afford one, but for the six hundred horses under the hood. Being numb and relying on a cane for balance made him feel like an old, crippled male a lot of the time, and it was good to be . . . normal.

Of course, the no-feeling thing had its benes. For example, when he banged his forehead into the steering wheel in another couple minutes, he was just going to see stars. The headache? No prob.

The vampire race's stopgap clinic was about fifteen minutes past the bridge he was just getting on, and the facility was not sufficient for the needs of its patients, being little more than a safe house converted into a field hospital. Still, the Hail Mary solution was all the race had at the moment, a bench player brought in because the quarterback's leg was snapped in half.

Following the raids over the summer, Wrath was working with the race's physician to get a new permanent location, but like everything it was taking time. With so many places sacked by the Lessening Society, no one thought it was a good idea to use real estate currently owned by the race, because God only knew how many other locales had been leaked. The king was looking to buy another place, but it had to be secluded and . . .

Rehv thought of Montrag.

Had the war really come down to murdering Wrath?

The rhetorical, initiated by his mother's vampire side, rippled through his mind, but triggered no emotion whatsoever. Calculation carried his thoughts. Calculation unencumbered by morality. The conclusion he'd reached as he'd left Montrag's did not waver, his resolution only growing stronger.

"Thank you, dearest Virgin Scribe," he muttered as the beater slid out of his way and his exit presented itself like a gift, the reflective green sign a tag with his name on it.

Green . . . ?

Rehv looked around. The red wash had started to drain out of his vision, the other colors of the world reappearing through the two-dimensional haze, and he took a deep breath of relief. He didn't want to go juiced to the clinic.

As if on schedule, he started to feel cold, even though the Bentley was no doubt a balmy seventy degrees, and he reached forward and cranked the heat. The chills were another good, if inconvenient sign the medication was starting to work.

For as long as he had been alive, he'd had to keep secret what he was. Sin-eaters like him had two choices: They either passed as normals or they got sent upstate to the colony, deported from society like the toxic waste they were. That he was a half-breed didn't matter. If you had any *symphath* in you, you were considered one of them, and with good reason. The thing about *symphaths* was, they liked the evil in themselves too much to be trusted.

For fuck's sake, look at tonight. Look at what he was prepared to do. One conversation and he was pulling the trigger—not even because he had to, just because he wanted to. *Needed* to, was more like it. Power plays were oxygen for his bad side, both undeniable and sustaining. And the whys behind his choice were typically *symphath*: They served him and no one else, not even the king who was a friend of sorts.

This was why, if an everyday, average vampire knew of a sin-eater who was out and about in the gen pop, by law they had to report the individual for deportation or face criminal action: Regulating the whereabouts of sociopaths and keeping them away from the moral and the law-abiding was a healthy survival instinct for any society.

Twenty minutes later, Rehv pulled up to an iron gate that was downright industrial in its function over form. The thing was without any grace whatsoever, nothing but solid shafts bolted together and topped with a curly wig of barbed-wire coil. To the left there was an intercom, and as he put down his window to hit the call button, security cameras focused on the grille of his car and the front windshield and the driver's-side door.

So he was not surprised at the tense tone of the female

voice that answered. "Sire . . . I was not aware that you had an appointment?"

"I don't."

Pause. "As a nonemergency walk-in, the wait time could be rather long. Perhaps you would like to schedule—"

He glared into the closest camera eye. "Let me in. Now. I have to see Havers. And this is an emergency."

He had to get back to the club and check in. The four hours he'd blown already this evening were a lifetime when it came to managing the likes of ZeroSum and the Iron Mask. Shit didn't just happen in places like those, it was SOP, and his fist was the one with *Buck Stops Here* tatted on the knuckles.

After a moment, those ugly-ass, rock-solid gates slid free, and he didn't waste time on the mile-long driveway.

As he came around the last turn, the farmhouse up ahead didn't warrant the kind of security it had, at least not if you took it at face value. The two-story clapboard was barely a colonial, and it was totally pared-down. No porches. No shutters. No chimneys. No plantings.

Compared to Havers's old crib and clinic setup it was the poor relation to a garden shed.

He parked opposite the detached bank of garages where the ambulances were kept and got out. The fact that the cold December night made him shiver was another good sign, and he reached into the Bentley's backseat to take out his cane and one of his many sable dusters. Along with numbness, the downside of his chemical mask was a drop in core temperature that turned his veins into air-conditioning coils. Living out his nights and days in a body he couldn't feel or warm was not a party, but it wasn't as if he had a choice.

Maybe if his mother and his sister hadn't been normals, he might have Darth Vadered himself and embraced the dark side, living out his days fucking with the minds of his comrades-in-harm. But he'd put himself in the position of being head of his household, and that kept him in this stretch of neither here nor there.

Rehv walked around the side of the colonial, pulling the sable in close to his throat. When he came up to a nothing-looking door, he rang the button that was tacked onto the aluminum siding and stared into an electronic eye. A moment later, an air lock popped with a hiss, and he pushed his way into a white room the size of a walk-in closet. After he stared into a camera's face, another seal popped free, a hidden panel shifted back, and he descended a set of stairs. Another check-in. Another door. And then he was in.

The reception area was every clinic's patient-and-family parking lot, with rows of chairs and magazines on little tables and a TV and some plants. It was smaller than the one at the old clinic, but it was clean and well-ordered. The two females sitting in it both stiffened as they saw him.

"Right this way, sire."

Rehv smiled at the nurse who came around the reception desk. For him, a "long wait" was always one in an exam room. The nurses didn't like him spooking the folks in those rows of chairs, and they didn't like him around themselves, either.

Worked for him. He wasn't the socializing kind.

The exam room he was led down to was located on the nonemergency side of the clinic, and it was one he'd been in before. He'd been in all of them before.

"The doctor is in surgery and the rest of the staff are with other patients, but I'll have a colleague come take your vitals as soon as I can." The nurse left him like somebody had just coded down the hall and she was the only one with paddles.

Rehv got up on the table, keeping his coat on and his cane in his palm. To pass the time, he closed his eyes and let the emotions in the place seep into him like a panoramic vista: The walls of the basement dissolved away and the emotional grids of each individual emerged from out of the darkness, a host of different vulnerabilities and anxieties and weaknesses exposed to his *symphath* side.

He held the remote to all of them, instinctually knowing what buttons to push on the female nurse next door who was worried that her *hellren* wasn't attracted to her anymore . . . but who had still had too much to eat at First Meal. And the male she was treating who had fallen down the stairs and cut his arm . . . because he'd been into the booze. And the pharmacist across the hall who up until recently had been lifting Xanax for his personal use . . . until he'd found the hidden cameras put in place to catch him.

Self-destruction in others was a *symphath*'s favorite reality show to watch, and it was especially good when you
were the producer. And even though his vision was now
back to "normal" and his body was numb and cold, what he
was at his core was just banked, not spent.

For the kind of shows he could put on, there was an endless source of inspiration and funding.

"Shit."

As Butch parked the Escalade in front of the clinic's garages, Wrath's mouth did some more pull-ups on the curse
bar. In the headlights of the SUV, Vishous was spotlit like
some frickin' calendar girl, all sprawled out on the hood of
a very familiar Bentley.

Wrath unclipped his seat belt and opened his door.

"Surprise, surprise, my lord," V said as he straightened
and knocked on the sedan's hood. "Musta been a short
meeting downtown with our buddy Rehvenge, huh. Unless
that guy's figured out how to be in two places at once. In
which case, I need to know his secret, true?"

Mother. Fucker.

Wrath got out of the SUV and decided the best course
was to ignore the Brother. Other options included trying to
reason his way out of the lie, which would suck because of
all V's failings, none were intellectual; or in the alternative,
instigating a fistfight, which would be only a temporary diversion and would waste time when they both had to get
their Humpty Dumptys put back together.

Going around, Wrath opened the rear door of the Escalade. "Heal your boy. I'll deal with the body."

As he lifted the civilian's lifeless weight up and turned,
V's stare locked on a face that was beaten beyond
recognition.

"Goddamn it," V breathed.

At that moment, Butch stumbled out from behind the
wheel looking like a hot mess. As the smell of baby powder
wafted over, his knees went loose and he barely caught the
door for support in time.

Vishous flashed over and took the cop into his arms,
holding him close. "Shit, man, how you doing?"

"Ready . . . for anything." Butch clung to his best friend.
"Just need to be under the heat lamp for a bit."

"Heal him," Wrath said as he started for the clinic. "I'm going in."

As he walked off, the doors of the Escalade shut one after the other, and then there was a glow like clouds had broken free of the moon. He knew what the two were doing inside the SUV, because he'd seen the routine once or twice: They were wrapped around each other, the white light of V's hand suffusing them both, the evil that Butch had inhaled leaching out into V.

Thank God there was a way to cleanse that shit out of the cop. And being a healer was good for V, too.

Wrath came up to the first door of the clinic and just stared up into the security camera. He was buzzed in immediately, and the instant the air lock had resealed, the hidden panel to the stairs popped open. It took no time at all to get down into the clinic.

The king of the race with a dead male in his arms wasn't stopped for a nanosecond.

He paused at the landing as the last door lock was sprung. Looking into the camera, he said, "Get a gurney and a sheet first."

"We're coming right now, my lord," said a tinny voice.

No more than a second later, two nurses opened the door, one turning a sheet into a privacy curtain while the other rolled a gurney right up to the bottom of the stairs. With strong and gentle arms, Wrath laid out the civilian as carefully as if the male had been alive and had every bone in his body fractured; then the nurse who'd handled the gurney flapped another sheet out of its folded square. Wrath stopped her before she draped the body.

"I do that," he said, taking it from her.

She gave the thing over to him with a bow.

Speaking sacred words in the Old Language, Wrath turned the humble cotton sheath into a proper death shroud. After he was done praying for the male's soul and wishing it a free and easy carry unto the Fade, he and the nurses had a moment of silence before the body was draped.

"We don't have ID on him," Wrath said quietly as he smoothed out the edge of the sheet. "Do either of you recognize his clothes? The watch? Anything?"

Both nurses shook their heads, and one murmured,

"We'll put him in the morgue and wait. It's all we can do. His family will come looking for him."

Wrath hung back and watched as the body was rolled away. For no particular reason, he noticed the wheel on the front right wiggled as it went along, like it was new on the job and worried about its performance . . . although this was not because he saw the thing clearly, but rather from the soft whistle of its miscalibration.

Out of whack. Not pulling its weight.

Wrath could so relate.

This fucking war with the Lessening Society had gone on too long, and even with all the power he had and all the resolve in his heart, his race wasn't winning: Holding steady against your enemy was just a case of losing by increments, because innocents kept dying.

He turned around toward the stairs and smelled the fear and awe of the two females sitting in the plastic chairs of the waiting area. With a mad shuffle, they got to their feet and bowed to him, the deference resounding in his gut like a kick in the balls. Here he was delivering the latest, but far from the last, casualty in the fight, and these two still paid him respect.

He bowed back to them, but couldn't marshal any words. The only vocabulary he had at the moment was full of George Carlin's best, and all of it was directed at himself.

The nurse who'd been on shield duty finished folding up the sheet she'd used. "My lord, perhaps you would have a moment to see Havers. He should be out of surgery in about fifteen minutes? It appears you are wounded."

"I have to get back to the—" He stopped himself before the word *field* slipped out. "I've got to get going. Please let me know about that male's family, okay? I want to meet with them."

She bowed at the waist and waited, because she wanted to kiss the massive black diamond that rested on the middle finger of his right hand.

Wrath squeezed his weak eyes shut and held out what he was seeking to pay homage to.

Her fingers were cool and light on his flesh, her breath and her lips the barest of brushes. And yet he felt flayed.

As she righted herself, she said with reverence, *"Fare thee well this night, my lord."*

"And you with your hours as well, loyal subject."

He wheeled around and jogged up the stairs, needing more oxygen than there was in the clinic. Just as he hit the final door, he ran into a nurse who was coming in as fast as he was busting out. The impact knocked her black shoulder bag off, and he barely caught her before she hit the ground along with it.

"Oh, fuck," he barked, dropping to his knees to get her stuff. "Sorry."

"My lord!" She bowed deeply to him and then obviously realized he was picking up her things. "You mustn't do that. Please, let me—"

"No, it's my fault."

He shoved what seemed to be a skirt and a sweater back into the bag and then nearly cracked her with a head butt as he shot to his feet.

He grabbed onto her arm once more. "Shit, sorry. Again—"

"I'm fine—honest."

Her bag changed hands in a messy scramble, going from someone who was in a rush to someone who was flustered.

"You got it?" he said, ready to start begging the Scribe Virgin to get outside.

"Ah, yes, but . . ." Her tone shifted from reverent to medical. "You're bleeding, my lord."

He ignored the comment and took his hand away from her experimentally. Relieved that she stood steady on her feet, he bade her good night and farewell in the Old Language.

"My lord, shouldn't you see—"

"Sorry I plowed into you," he called out over his shoulder.

He punched open the last door and sagged as the fresh air seeped into him. Deep breaths cleared his head, and he allowed himself to lean back against the aluminum siding of the clinic.

As the headache started up behind his eyes again, he popped his wraparounds up off his face and rubbed the bridge of his nose. Right. Next stop . . . the addy that had been listed on the *lesser's* fake ID.

He had a jar to collect.

Dropping the glasses back into place, he straightened and—

"Not so fast, my lord," V said, materializing smack in front of him. "We've got to talk, you and me."

Wrath bared his fangs. "Not in a conversating kind of mood, V."

"Tough. Shit."

FIVE

Ehlena watched the king of the species turn away and nearly break the door in half on his way out.

Man, he was big and scary-looking. And nearly getting mowed down by him put the final frazzle candle on the drama cake.

Smoothing her hair and dragging her shoulder bag up into place, she started down the stairs after passing the interior checkpoint. She was only an hour late to work because—miracle of miracles—her father's nurse had been free and able to come early. Thank the Virgin Scribe for Lusie.

As bad attacks went, her father's hadn't been as horrible as it could have been, and she had a feeling it was because he'd downed the meds right before it hit. Before the pills, the worst of his spells had lasted all night long, so in one sense, tonight had been a sign of progress.

Still broke her damn heart, though.

As she came up to the final camera, Ehlena felt the weight of her bag grow heavier. She'd been prepared to cancel her date and leave the change of clothes at home, but Lusie had talked her out of it. The question the other nurse had asked struck deep: *When was the last time you were out of this house for anything except work?*

Ehlena hadn't answered because she was private by nature . . . and drawing a complete blank.

Which was Lusie's point, wasn't it. Caregivers had to

take care of themselves, and part of that meant having a life beyond whatever illness had put them in their role. God knew Ehlena told this to the family members of her chronically sick patients all the time, and the advice was both sound and practical.

At least when she gave it to others. Turned on herself, it felt selfish.

So ... she was waffling on the date. With her shift ending close to dawn, it wasn't as if she had time to go home and check on her father first. As it was, she and the male who'd asked her out would be lucky to get even an hour of chatting at the all-night diner before encroaching sunlight put an end to things.

And yet she had been looking forward to going out with a desperation that made her feel guilty as hell.

God ... how typical. Conscience pulling her one way, loneliness another.

In the reception area, she beelined for the nursing supervisor, who was at the front desk computer. "I'm so sorry I'm—"

Catya stopped what she was doing and reached out a hand. "How is he?"

For a split second, Ehlena could only blink. She hated that everyone at work knew about her father's problems and that a few had even seen him at his worst.

Though the illness had stripped him of his pride, she still had some on his behalf.

She did a quick pat on her boss's hand and stepped out of range. "Thanks for asking. He's calmed down and his nurse is with him now. Fortunately, I'd just given him his meds."

"Do you need a minute?"

"Nope. Where are we?"

Catya's smile was more grimace than grin, as if she were biting her tongue. Again. "You don't have to be this strong."

"Yes, I do." Ehlena looked around and kept her wince to herself. More of the staff were coming at her from down the hallway, a ten-strong posse riding shotgun on a truckload of concerned purpose. "Where do you need me?"

She had to get free of— No luck.

Soon all but the OR nurses who were busy with Havers had formed a circle around her, and Ehlena's throat closed up as her colleagues threw out a chorus of how-are-yous. God, she was as claustrophobic as a pregnant female stuck in a hot elevator.

"I'm fine, everyone, thanks—"

The last of the staff came over. After expressing her sympathy, the female shook her head. "I don't mean to bring up work. . . ."

"Please do," Ehlena blurted.

The nurse smiled with respect, like she was impressed by Ehlena's fortitude. "Well . . . *he*'s back in an exam room. Should I get out a quarter?"

Everybody groaned. There was only one *he* out of the legions of male patients they treated, and coin bingo was typically how the staff decided who had to deal with *him*. Farthest from the date lost.

Generally speaking, all of the nurses kept a professional distance from their patients, because you had to, or you'd burn out. With *him*, though, the staff stayed separate for reasons other than job-related ones. Most of the females got nervous around him—even the toughest ones.

Ehlena? Not so much. Yes, the guy had some *Godfather* in him, those black pin-striped suits and his cropped mohawk and his amethyst eyes throwing off a don't-f-with-me-if-you-want-to-keep-breathing vibe. And it was true, when you were shut into an exam room with him, there was the impulse to keep your eye on the exit in case you needed to use it. And there were those tattoos on his chest . . . and the fact that he kept his cane with him as if it were not just an aid for walking, but a weapon. And . . .

Okay, so the guy made Ehlena nervous, too.

And yet she cut through an argument over who got to have the year 1977. "I'll do it. It'll make up for my being late."

"Are you sure?" someone asked. "Seems like you've already paid your dues tonight."

"Just let me get some coffee. What room?"

"I parked him in three," the nurse said.

Amid a cheer of, "Attagirl," Ehlena went to the staff room, put her things in her locker, and poured herself a mug of hot, steaming perk-your-ass-up. The coffee was strong enough to be considered an accelerant and did the job nicely, wiping her mental slate clean.

Well, mostly clean.

As she sipped, she stared at the banks of buff-colored lockers and the pairs of street shoes tucked here and there and the winter coats hanging on pegs. In the luncheon area, folks had their favorite mugs on the counter and the snacks they liked on the shelves, and sitting on the round table there was a bowl full of . . . what was it tonight? Little packs of Skittles. Above the table was a bulletin board covered with flyers for events and coupons and stupid comic-strip jokes and pictures of hot guys. The shift roster was next to it, the whiteboard marked with a grid of the next two weeks that was filled in with names in different colors.

It was the detritus of normal life, none of which seemed significant in the slightest until you thought about all those people on the planet who couldn't keep jobs or enjoy an independent existence or spare the mental energy on little distractions—like, say, the fact that Cottonelle toilet paper was fifty cents off if you bought the twelve-pack of the double rolls.

Taking it all in, she was reminded yet again that going out into the real world was a luck-of-the-draw privilege, not a right, and it bothered her to think of her father holed up in that awful little house, wrestling with demons that existed only in his head.

He'd once had a life, a big life. He'd been a member of the aristocracy and had served on the council and been a scholar of note. He'd had a *shellan* he adored and a daughter he'd been proud of and a mansion renowned for its celebrations. Now all he had were delusions that tortured him, and though they were only perception, never reality, the voices were a jail no less ironclad for the fact that no one else could see the bars or hear the warden.

As Ehlena rinsed out her mug, she couldn't help thinking of the unfairness of it all. Which was good, she supposed. Even with all she saw on her job, she hadn't gotten used to suffering, and she prayed she never did.

Before she left the locker room, she did a quick check in the full-length mirror next to the door. Her white uniform was perfectly pressed and clean as sterile gauze. Her stockings were without runs. Her crepe-soled shoes were smudge- and scuff-free.

Her hair was as frazzled as she felt.

She did a quick pull-free, retwist, and scrunchie-up, then headed out for exam room three.

The patient's chart was in the clear plastic holder mounted on the wall by the door, and she took a deep breath as she picked it out and opened it up. The thing was thin, considering how often they saw the male, and there was almost no information listed on the front, just his name, a cell phone, and a next of kin who was a female.

After she knocked, she walked into the room with confidence she didn't feel, her head up, her spine straight, her unease camo'd by a combo of posture and professional focus.

"How are you this evening?" she said, as she looked the patient right in the eye.

The instant his amethyst stare met hers, she couldn't have told a soul what had just come out of her mouth or whether he replied. Rehvenge, son of Rempoon, sucked the thought right out of her head, sure as if he'd drained the tank of her brain's generator and left her with nothing to catch a mental spark off of.

And then he smiled.

He was a cobra, this male; he truly was . . . mesmerizing because he was deadly and because he was beautiful. With that mohawk and his hard, smart face and his big body, he was sex and power and unpredictability all wrapped up in . . . well, a black pin-striped suit that clearly had been made for him.

"I'm good, thank you," he said, solving the mystery as to what she'd asked him. "And you?"

As she paused, he smiled a little, no doubt because he was fully aware that none of the nurses liked being in the same enclosed space with him, and evidently he enjoyed this fact. At least, that was how she read his controlled, hooded expression.

"I asked how you were doing?" he drawled.

Ehlena put his chart down on the desk and took her stethoscope out of her pocket. "I'm very well."

"You sure about that."

"Absolutely positive." Turning to him, she said, "I'm just going to take your blood pressure and your heart rate."

"My temperature, too."

"Yes."

"Do you want me to open my mouth for you now?"

Ehlena's skin flushed, and she told herself it was not because that deep voice of his made the question seem as sexual as a lazy stroke over a naked breast. "Er . . . no."

"Pity."

"Please take off your jacket."

"What a great idea. I totally take back the 'pity.' "

Good plan, she thought, or she was liable to feed the word back to him with the thermometer.

Rehvenge's shoulders rolled as he did what she'd asked him to, and with a casual flick of the hand, he tossed what was clearly a piece of menswear art onto the sable coat he'd carefully draped over a chair. It was odd: No matter what the season was, he always had one of those furs on.

Things were worth more than the house Ehlena rented.

As his long fingers went to the diamond cuff link on his right wrist, she stopped him.

"Could you please roll up the one on the other side?" She nodded toward the wall beside him. "More space for me on your left."

He hesitated, then went to work on his opposite sleeve. Taking the black silk up past his elbow and onto his thick biceps, he kept his arm turned into his torso.

Ehlena took the blood pressure equipment from a drawer and ripped it open as she approached him. Touching him was always an experience, and she rubbed her hand on her hip to get ready. Didn't help. When she came in contact with his wrist, as usual the current that licked up her arm landed in her heart, James Browning the damn thing until the shimmy-shimmies had her sucking back a gasp.

With a prayer that this wouldn't take long, she moved his arm into position for the cuff and—"Good . . . *Lord.*"

The veins running up through the crook of his elbow were decimated from overuse, swollen, black-and-blue, as ragged as if he'd been using nails, not needles on himself.

Her eyes shot to his. "You must be in such pain."

He rolled his wrist out of her grasp. "Nope. Doesn't bother me."

Tough guy. Like she was surprised? "Well, I can understand why you wanted to come in to see Havers."

Pointedly, she reached out and rotated his arm back

around, gently prodding at a red line that was traveling up his biceps, heading in the direction of his heart.

"There are signs of infection."

"I'll be fine."

All she could do was raise her eyebrows. "You ever hear of sepsis?"

"The indie band? Sure, but I wouldn't think you'd have."

She shot him a look. "Sepsis as in an infection of the blood?"

"Hmm, you want to lean over the desk a little and draw me a picture?" His eyes drifted down her legs. "I think I'd find that . . . very educational."

If any other male had pulled that kind of line, she'd have slapped them down until they saw stars. Unfortunately, when it was that heavenly bass voice doing the talking and that amethyst stare doing the walking, she didn't really feel leched upon.

She felt caressed by a lover.

Ehlena resisted the urge to V8 her forehead. What the hell was she doing? She had a date tonight. With a nice, reasonable, civilian male who'd been nothing but nice, reasonable, and very civil.

"I don't have to draw you a picture." She nodded down at his arm. "You can see for yourself right there. If you don't treat this, it's going to go systemic."

And even though he wore fine clothes like every tailor's dream mannequin, death's cold gray cloak would not look good on him.

He held his arm against his tight abs. "I'll take that under advisement."

Ehlena shook her head and reminded herself that she couldn't save people from their own stupidity just because she had a white coat hanging from her shoulders and the letters RN at the end of her name. Besides, Havers was going to see that in all its gory glory when the doctor examined him.

"Fine, but let's take your reading on the other arm. And I'm going to have to ask you to take your shirt off. The doctor's going to want to see how far up that infection goes."

Rehvenge's mouth lifted in a smile as he reached for his top button. "You keep this up and I'll be naked."

Ehlena looked away fast and wished like hell she found him sleazy. She could sure use an injection of righteous indignation to help fend him off.

"You know, I'm not shy," he said in that low voice of his. "You can watch if you like."

"No, thank you."

"Pity." In a darker tone, he added, "I wouldn't mind you watching me."

As the sound of silk moving against flesh rose up from the exam table, Ehlena made busywork going through his chart, double-checking things that were absolutely correct.

It was weird. From what the other nurses had said, he didn't pull this lothario stuff with them. In fact, he barely talked to her colleagues, and that was part of the reason they were anxious around him. With a male this big, silence read as menacing. Fact of life. And that was before you added the tat/mohawk chaser.

"I'm ready," he said.

Ehlena pivoted around and kept her eyes pinned on the wall next to his head. Her peripheral vision, however, worked just fine, and it was hard not to be grateful. Rehvenge's chest was magnificent, the skin a warm golden brown, with muscles that were defined even though his body was relaxed. On each of his pecs he had a five-pointed red star tattooed on the upper part, and she knew he had more ink.

On his stomach.

Not that she'd looked.

Right, because actually, she'd been gawking.

"Are you gong to examine my arm?" he said softly.

"No, that's for the doctor." She waited for him to say, "Pity," again.

"I think I've used that word enough around you."

Now her eyes shifted to his. It was the rare vampire who could read his own species' minds, but somehow it didn't surprise her that this male was among that small, rarified group.

"Don't be rude," she said. "And I do not want you to do that again."

"I'm sorry."

Ehlena slipped the cuff around his biceps, plugged her stethoscope into her ears, and took his blood pressure. With the little *piff-piff-piff* of the balloon inflating the sleeve until it was tight, she felt the edge in him, the tense power, and her heart tripped over itself. He was particularly sharp tonight, and she wondered why.

Except that was not her business, was it.

As she released the valve and the cuff let out a long, slow hiss of relief, she took a step back from him. He was just . . . too much, all the way around. Especially right now.

"Don't be frightened of me," he whispered.

"I'm not."

"Are you sure?"

"Absolutely positive," she lied.

SIX

She was lying, Rehv thought. She was definitely frightened of him. And talk about a pity.

This was the nurse Rehv hoped he would get each time he came in. This was the one who made these visits even partially bearable. This was his Ehlena.

Okay, so she wasn't his in the slightest. He knew her name only because it was on the blue-and-white pin on her coat. He saw her only when he came to be treated. And she didn't like him at all.

But he still thought of her as his, and that was just the way of it. The thing was, they had something in common, something that crossed species lines and eclipsed social stratifications and bonded them together even though she would have denied it.

She was lonely, too, and in the same way he was.

Her emotional grid had the same footprint his did, Xhex's did, and Trez's and iAm's did: Her feelings were surrounded by the disconnected void of someone separated from her tribe. Living among others, but essentially apart from it all. A shutout, a castaway, one who had been expelled.

He didn't know the whys, but he sure as fuck knew what life was like for her, and that was what had first gotten his attention when he met her. Her eyes and her voice and her scent had been next. Her intelligence and quick mouth had sealed the deal.

"One sixty-eight over ninety-five. That's high." She ripped the cuff's lip free with a quick jerk, no doubt wishing it were a strip of his skin. "I think your body's trying to fight off the infection in your arm."

Oh, his body was fighting something off, all right, but it had fuck-all to do with whatever was cooking in his needle sites. With his *symphath* side battling the dopamine, the impotent state he usually existed in when fully medicated had yet to report in for work.

Result?

His cock was stiff as a bat in his slacks. Which, contrary to popular opinion, was actually not a good sign—especially tonight. Coming off that convo with Montrag, he was feeling hungry, driven . . . a little crazy from the inner burn.

And Ehlena was just so . . . beautiful.

Although not in the way his working girls were, not in that obvious, over-the-top, injected, implanted, sculpted way. Ehlena was naturally lovely, with fine small features and that strawberry blond hair and those long, lean limbs. Her lips were pink because they were pink—not from some eighteen-hour, glossy, frosted grease coat. And her toffee-colored eyes were luminescent because they were yellow and red and gold all mixed together—not from a whole lot of paint-by-numbers shimmery shadow and slathered-on mascara. And her cheeks were flushed because he was getting under her skin.

Which, even though he sensed she'd had a hard night, didn't bother him at all.

But that was a *symphath* for you, wasn't it, he thought with derision.

Funny, most of the time he didn't care that he was what he was. His life as he'd always known it had been a constantly shifting mirage of lies and deceptions and that was that. Around her, though? He wished he were normal.

"Let's see what your temperature is," she said, bringing an electronic thermometer over from the desk.

"It's higher than usual."

Her amber stare flipped up to his. "Your arm."

"No, your eyes."

She blinked, then seemed to shake herself. "I seriously doubt that."

"Then you underestimate your appeal."

As she shook her head and clicked one of the plastic covers onto the silver wand, he caught a whiff of her scent.

His fangs elongated.

"Open." She brought the thermometer up and waited. "Well?"

Rehv stared into those amazing tricolored eyes of hers and dropped his jaw. She leaned in, all business as usual, only to freeze. As she looked at his canines, her scent surged with something dark and erotic.

Triumph singed in his veins as he growled, "Do me."

There was a long moment, during which the two of them were bound together by invisible strings of heat and longing. Then her mouth flattened out.

"Never, but I will take your temperature, because I have to."

She jabbed the thermometer in between his lips, and he had to clamp his teeth together to keep the thing from deflating one of his tonsils.

S'all good, though. Even if he couldn't have her, he turned her on. And that was more than he deserved.

There was a beep, an interval, and another beep.

"One oh nine," she said as she stepped back and released the plastic cover into the biohazard bin. "Havers will be with you as soon as he's able."

The door clapped shut behind her with the hard syllabic smack of the f-word.

Man, she was hot.

Rehv frowned, the whole sexual attraction thing reminding him of something he didn't like to think about.

Someone, rather.

What erection he had instantly limped out as he realized it was Monday night. Which meant tomorrow was Tuesday. The first Tuesday of the last month of the year.

The *symphath* in him tingled even as every inch of skin he had tightened like his pockets were full of spiders.

He and his blackmailer had another one of their dates tomorrow night. Christ, how was it possible another month had gone by? It seemed like every time he turned around it was the first Tuesday again and he was making the drive upstate to that godforsaken cabin for another command performance.

The pimp becoming the whore.

Power plays and hard edges and base fucking were the currency of the meetings with his blackmailer, the basis of his "love" life for the past twenty-five years. It was everything dirty and wrong and evil and degrading, and he did it over and over again to keep his secret safe.

And also because his dark side got off on it. It was *Love, Symphath Style*, the only time he could be how he was with no holds barred, his one slice of horrible freedom. After all, much as he medicated himself and tried to fit in, he was trapped by his dead father's legacy, by the evil blood in his veins. You couldn't negotiate with your DNA, and though he was a half-breed, the sin-eater in him was dominant.

So when it came to a female of worth like Ehlena, he was always going to be on the far side of the glass, nose pressed up hard, palms spread with need, never getting close enough to touch. It was only fair to her. Unlike his blackmailer, she didn't deserve what he brought to the table.

The morals he'd taught himself told him at least that much was true.

Yay. Rah. Go, him.

Next tat he got was going to be of the frickin' halo over his head.

As he looked down at the mess running up his left arm, he saw what festered there with total clarity. It wasn't just a bacterial infection from him deliberately using needles that weren't sterile on skin that hadn't been hit with an alcohol rub. It was a slow suicide, and that was why he was damned if he was showing it to the doctor. He knew exactly what would happen if that poison got deep into his bloodstream, and he wished it would get off its ass and take over.

The door swung open and he glanced up, ready to tango with Havers—except it wasn't the doc. Rehv's nurse was back, and she didn't look happy.

Matter of fact, she looked exhausted, like he was one more hassle in her castle and she didn't have the energy to deal with the shit he pulled when she was around.

"I spoke with the doctor," she said. "He's closing in the OR now, so it's going to be a while. He would like me to draw some blood—"

"I'm sorry," Rehv blurted.

Ehlena's hand went up to the collar of her uniform and she pulled the two halves closer together. "Excuse me?"

"I'm sorry for playing you. You don't need that from a patient. Especially on a night like tonight."

She frowned. "I'm fine."

"No, you're not. And no, I'm not reading your mind. You just seem tired." Abruptly, he knew how she felt. "I'd like to make it up to you."

"Not necessary—"

"By treating you to dinner."

Okay, he hadn't meant to say that. And given that he'd just gotten all self-congratulatory on keeping his distance, he'd also made a hypocrite out of himself.

Clearly his next tat needed to be more along the lines of a donkey.

'Cuz he was acting like an ass.

In the wake of the invitation, it was entirely unsurprising that Ehlena stared at him like he was insane. Generally speaking, when a male behaved like he did, the last thing any female wanted to do was spend *more* time with him.

"I'm sorry, no." She didn't even tack on an obligatory, *I never date patients.*

"Okay. I understand."

While she got the blood-drawing supplies ready and snapped on a pair of rubber gloves, Rehv reached over to his suit jacket and took out his card, hiding it in his big palm.

She was quick with the procedure, working on his good arm, filling up the aluminum vials fast. Good thing they weren't glass and Havers did all the testing himself. Vampire blood was red. *Symphath* ran blue. The color of his was somewhere in between, but he and Havers had an arrangement. Granted, the doctor was unaware of how things worked between them, but it was the only way to be treated without compromising the race's physician.

When Ehlena was finished, she capped the vials with white plastic stoppers, snapped off the gloves, and went for the door like he was a bad smell.

"Wait," he said.

"Do you want some pain meds for the arm?"

"No, I want you to take this." He held out his card. "And call me if you're ever in the mood to do me a favor."

"At the risk of sounding unprofessional, I'm never going to be in the mood for you. Under any circumstances."

Ouch. Not that he blamed her. "The favor is forgiving me. Got nothing to do with a date."

She glanced down at the card, then shook her head. "You'd better keep that. For someone who might ever use it."

As the door shut, he crushed the card in his hand.

Shit. What the hell had he been thinking, anyway? She probably had a nice little life in a tidy house with two doting parents. Maybe she had a boyfriend, too, who would someday become her *hellren*.

Yeah, his being your friendly neighborhood drug lord, pimp, and enforcer really fit in with the Norman Rockwell routine. Totally.

He tossed his card into the wastepaper basket by the desk, and watched as the rim shot circled, then dropped in amid the Kleenex and the wadded-up papers and an empty Coke can.

As he waited for the doctor, he stared at the discarded trash, thinking that to him most of the people on the planet were just like that stuff: things to use up and throw away with no compunction whatsoever. Thanks to both his bad side and the business he was in, he'd broken a lot of bones and cracked a lot of heads and been the cause of a lot of drug overdoses.

Ehlena, on the other hand, spent her nights saving people.

Yeah, they had shit in common, all right.

His efforts kept her in business.

How. Perfect.

Outside the clinic in the frosty air, Wrath was chest-to-chest with Vishous.

"Get out of my way, V."

Vishous, of course, was having none of the back-off. Not a surprise. Even before the little news flash about the Scribe Virgin having birthed him, the fucker had been a total free agent.

A Brother'd have better luck giving orders to a rock.

"Wrath—"

"No, V. Not here. Not now—"

"I saw you. In my dreams this afternoon." The ache in that dark voice was the kind normally associated with funerals. "I had a vision."

Wrath spoke without wanting to. "What did you see?"

"You standing in a dark field alone. We were all around your periphery, but no one could reach you. You were gone from us and us from you." The Brother reached out and grabbed hard. "Because of Butch, I know you're going out into the field alone and I've kept my mouth shut. But I can't let you do this anymore. You die and the race is fucked, to say nothing of what it'll do to the Brotherhood."

Wrath's eyes strained to focus on V's face, but the security light over the door was a fluorescent and the glow from the thing stung like a bitch. "You don't know what the dream means."

"And neither do you."

Wrath thought of the weight of that civilian in his arms. "It could be nothing—"

"Ask me when I first had the vision."

"—but a fear you have."

"Ask me. When I had the vision first."

"When."

"Nineteen oh nine. It's been a hundred years since I saw it first. Now ask me how many times I've had it this past month."

"No."

"Seven times, Wrath. This afternoon was the final straw."

Wrath broke out of the Brother's hold. "I'm leaving now. If you follow me, you're going to find a fight."

"You can't go out alone. It's not safe."

"You're kidding me, right." Wrath glared through his wraparounds. "Our race is failing and you want to bust my balls for going after our enemy? Fuck that for a laugh. I'm not getting stuck behind some bitch-ass desk pushing papers while my brothers are out there actually doing something—"

"But you're the king. You're more important than us—"

"The hell I am! I'm one of you! I was inducted, I drank of the Brothers and they of me, I want to fight!"

"Look, Wrath . . ." V assumed a tone that was so reasonable it made a guy want to knock all his teeth out. With an ax. "I know exactly what it's like not to want to be who you're born as. You think I get off on having these fucked-

up dreams? You think this lightsaber of mine is a party?"
He held up his gloved hand as if the visual aid was a value-
add to their "discussion." "You can't change who you are.
You can't undo the coupling of whatever parents you had.
You're the king, and the rules apply differently to you, and
that's the way it is."

Wrath did his best to cop to V's calm, cool, and collected.
"And I say I've been fighting for over three hundred years,
so I'm not exactly a greenhorn out there in the field. I'd
also like to point out that being king doesn't mean I lose
the right to choose—"

"You have no heir. And from what I hear from my *shellan*, you shut Beth down when she told you she wanted to
try for one when she has her first needing. Shut her down
hard. How did she say you put it? Oh . . . right. 'I don't want
any young in the foreseeable future . . . if at all.'"

Wrath's breath exhaled in a rush. "I can't believe you
just went there."

"Bottom line? You end up dead? The fabric of the race's
society is going to unravel, and if you think that's going to
help in the war, you've got your head so far up your ass
you're using your colon as a mouthpiece. Face it, Wrath.
You are the beating heart of all of us . . . so, no, you can't
just go out there and fight alone because you want to. Shit
don't work like that for you—"

Wrath grabbed onto the Brother's lapels and slammed
him against the clinic. "Watch it, V. You're walking a damn
fine line of disrespect here."

"If you think roughing me up is going to change things,
have at me. But I'll guarantee you that after the punches
are over and we're both bleeding on the ground, the situation will be exactly the same. You can't change who you're
born."

In the background, Butch stepped out of the Escalade
and jacked up his belt like he was getting ready to break up
a fistfight.

"The race needs you above ground, asshole," V said.
"Don't make me pull the trigger on you, because I will."

Wrath shifted his weak eyes back to V. "I thought you
wanted me alive and kicking. Besides, shooting me would
be treason and punishable by death. No matter whose son
you are."

"Look, I'm not saying you shouldn't—"

"Shut it, V. For once, just shut your damn mouth."

Wrath let go of the guy's leather jacket and stepped back. Jesus Christ, he had to leave or this confrontation was going to escalate into exactly what Butch was bracing himself for.

Wrath jammed a finger in V's face. "Don't follow me. We clear? You don't follow me."

"You stupid fool," V said with total exhaustion. "You're the king. We *all* must follow you."

Wrath dematerialized with a curse, his molecules scrambling across town. As he traveled, he couldn't believe V had thrown Beth and the baby thing under the bus. Or that Beth had shared that kind of private stuff with Doc Jane.

Talk about having your head up your ass, though. V was crazy if he thought Wrath was putting his beloved's life at risk by impregnating her when she went into her needing a year or so from now. Females died on the birthing table, more often than not.

He would give his own life for the race if he had to, but no fucking way was he putting his *shellan*'s at risk like that.

And even if she were guaranteed to live through it, he didn't want his son ending up right where he was . . . trapped and choiceless, serving his people with a heavy heart as one by one they died in a war he could do little if anything to end.

SEVEN

The St. Francis Hospital complex was a city all unto itself, the sprawling conglomeration of architectural blocks erected from different eras, each component forming its own mini-neighborhood, the parts connected to the whole by a series of winding drives and sidewalks. There was the McMansion-style administration section and the suburban simplicity of the ranch-level outpatient units and the apartment-like inpatient high-rises with their stacked windows. The sole unifying feature on the acreage, which was a godsend, was the red-and-white directional signs with their arrows pointing left and right and straight ahead depending on where you wanted to go.

Xhex's destination was obvious, however.

The emergency department was the newest addition to the medical center, a state-of-the-art, glass-and-steel facility that was like a brilliantly lit, constantly humming nightclub.

Hard to miss. Hard to lose sight of.

Xhex took form in the shadow of some trees that had been planted in a circle around some benches. As she walked toward the ER's bank of revolving doors, she was at once in the environment and utterly away from it. Though she altered her path around other pedestrians and smelled the tobacco from the designated smokers' hut and felt the cold air on her face, she was too distracted by a battle within herself to notice much.

As she entered the facility, her hands went clammy and cold sweat bloomed on her forehead, the fluorescent lights and the white linoleum and the staff milling around in their surgical scrubs paralyzing her.

"You need some help?"

Xhex wheeled around and brought her hands up, snapping into fighting position. The doctor who'd spoken to her held his ground, but seemed surprised.

"Whoa. Easy, there."

"Sorry." She dropped her arms and read the lapel of his white coat: MANUEL MANELLO, M.D., CHIEF OF SURGERY. She frowned as she sensed him, smelled him.

"You okay?"

Whatever. None of her biz. "I need to go to the morgue."

The guy didn't seem shocked, as if someone with her kind of moves might well know a couple of toe-tagged stiffs. "Yeah, okay, that hallway over there? Take it all the way back. You'll see a sign for the morgue on the door. Just follow the arrows from there. It's in the basement."

"Thanks."

"You're welcome."

The doctor walked out the revolving door she'd come in, and she went through the metal detector he'd just passed through. Not a peep, and she shot a tight smile at the rent-a-cop who was once-overing her.

The knife she carried at the small of her back was ceramic and she'd replaced her metal cilices with ones made of leather and stone. No probs.

"Evenin', Officer," she said.

The guy nodded her along, but kept his hand on the butt of his gun.

Down at the end of the hallway, she found the door she was looking for, punched through it, and hit the stairs, tracking the red arrows like the doctor had said. When she hit a stretch of whitewashed concrete wall she figured she was getting close, and she was right. Detective de la Cruz was standing farther down the corridor, next to a pair of double stainless-steel doors marked with the words MORGUE and AUTHORIZED STAFF ONLY.

"Thank you for coming," he said as she got closer. "We're going into the viewing room farther down. I'll just tell them you're here."

The detective pushed open one side of the doors, and through the crack she saw a fleet of metal tables with blocks for the heads of the dead.

Her heart stopped, then roared, even though she told herself over and over again that this wasn't her damage. She wasn't in there. This wasn't the past. There was no one with a white coat standing over her doing things "in the name of science."

And besides, she'd gotten over all of that, like, a decade ago—

A sound started off softly and grew in volume, echoing from behind her. She spun around and froze, fear so strong it stuck her feet to the floor. . . .

But it was just a janitor coming around the corner, pushing a laundry bin the size of a car. He was leaning forward against the rim, throwing his back into it, and he didn't look up as he passed.

For a moment, Xhex blinked and saw another rolling cart. One full of tangled, unmoving limbs, the legs and arms of the dead bodies overlapping like kindling.

She rubbed her eyes. Okay, she had gotten over what had happened . . . as long as she wasn't in a clinic or a hospital.

Jesus Christ . . . she had to get the fuck out of here.

"You okay to do this?" de la Cruz asked from right next to her.

She swallowed hard, and manned up, doubting the guy would understand that what was spooking her was a pile of sheets on a ride, not the corpse she was about to see. "Yup. Can we go in now?"

He stared at her for a moment. "Listen, you want to take a minute? Have some coffee?"

"Nope." When he didn't move, she headed to the door marked PRIVATE VIEWING herself.

De la Cruz scooted in front of her and opened the way. The anteroom beyond had three black plastic chairs and two doors and it smelled like chemical strawberries, the result of formaldehyde mixing with a Glade PlugIn. Over in the corner, away from the seats, there was a short table with a pair of paper cups half-filled with what looked like mud-puddle coffee.

Apparently, you had pacers and sitters, and if you were

a sitter, you were expected to balance your vending-machine caffeine on your knee.

As she looked around, the emotions that had been felt in the space lingered, like mold left after fetid water. Bad things happened here for people who walked through that door. Hearts were broken. Lives were shattered. Worlds were never the same.

Coffee was not what you should feed these folks before they did what they'd come here to do, she thought. They were nervous enough.

"This way."

De la Cruz took her into a narrow room that was wall-papered in flocked claustrophobia as far as she was concerned: The thing was pint-size with almost no ventilation, had fluorescent lights that hiccuped and flickered, and its one window hardly looked out over a meadow of wildflowers.

The curtain hanging on the far side of the glass was pulled across, blocking the view.

"You okay?" the detective asked again.

"Can we just do this."

De la Cruz leaned to the left and hit a doorbell button. At the sound of the buzz, the drapes parted down the middle in a slow swish, revealing a body that was covered by the same kind of white sheet that had been in the laundry bin. A human male in pale green scrubs stood at the head, and when the detective nodded, the man reached forward and folded the shroud back.

Chrissy Andrews's eyes were closed, her lashes down on cheeks that were the pale gray of December's clouds. She did not look peaceful in her perma-repose. Her mouth was a slash of blue, her lips cracked from what might have been a fist or a frying pan or a doorjamb.

The folds of the sheet resting on her throat mostly hid the strangulation marks.

"I know who did this," Xhex said.

"Just so we're clear, you are identifying her to be Chrissy Andrews?"

"Yup. And I know who did this."

The detective nodded at the clinician, who covered Chrissy's face and closed the drapes. "The boyfriend?"

"Yup."

"Long history of domestic violence calls."

"Too long. Course, that's over now. Motherfucker finally got the job done, didn't he."

Xhex went out the door and into the anteroom, and the detective had to hustle to keep up with her.

"Hold up—"

"I have to go back to work."

As they burst out into the basement corridor, the detective forced her to a stop. "I want you to know that the CPD is conducting a proper murder investigation, and we'll be handling any suspects in an appropriate, legal manner."

"I'm sure you will."

"And you've done your part. Now you have to let us take care of her and see this thing through. Let us find him, okay? I don't want you pulling a vigilante move."

The image of Chrissy's hair came to mind. The woman had been fussy about the stuff, always backbrushing it, then smoothing the top layer out and spraying it in place till it was like the top on a chess pawn.

Total *Melrose Place* rerun, Heather Locklear golden-helmet time.

The hair under that shroud had been flat as a cutting board, mashed in on both sides, no doubt from the body bag she'd been transported in.

"You've done your part," de la Cruz said.

Not yet she hadn't.

"Have a good evening, Officer. And good luck finding Grady."

He frowned, then seemed to buy the I'll-be-a-good-girl act. "Do you need a ride back?"

"No, thanks. And really, don't worry about me." She smiled tightly. "I won't do anything stupid."

On the contrary, she was a very smart assassin. Trained by the best.

And an *eye for an eye* was more than just a catchy little phrase.

José de la Cruz was not a rocket scientist or a Mensa member or a molecular geneticist. He was also not a betting man, and not just because of his Catholic faith.

No reason to bet. He had instincts like a fortune-teller's crystal ball.

So he knew exactly what he was doing as he followed Ms. Alex Hess out of the hospital at a discreet distance. When she got past the revolving doors, she didn't go left to the parking lot or right toward the three taxis parked by the entrance. She went straight ahead, walking between the cars picking up and dropping off patients and around the cabs that were free. After stepping up on the curb, she hit the frozen lawn and kept right on going, crossing the road and going into the trees the city had planted a couple of years ago to green up downtown.

Between one blink and the next she was gone, as if she had never been.

Which was, of course, impossible. It was dark and he'd been up since four a.m. two nights before, so his eyes were as sharp as they were when he was underwater.

He was going to have to watch that woman. He knew firsthand how hard it was to lose a colleague, and it was clear she cared about the dead girl. Still, this case did not need a wild-card civilian breaking laws and maybe even going so far as to murder the CPD's prime suspect.

José headed for the unmarked he'd left around back where the ambulances were cleaned up and the medics waited on standby breaks.

Chrissy Andrews's boyfriend, Robert Grady, a.k.a. Bobby G, had been renting an apartment month-to-month since she'd thrown him out over the summer. The hovel had been empty of inhabitants when José had knocked on the door around one o'clock this afternoon, and a search warrant based on the 911 calls that Chrissy had been making about her boyfriend for the past six months had allowed him to order the landlord to unlock the place.

Lot of rotting food in the kitchen and dirty plates in the living room and laundry all over the bedroom.

Also a number of cellophane Baggies with white powder which—OMG!—had been heroin. Go. Fig.

Boyfriend had been nowhere to be seen. Last sighting of him at the apartment had been the night before at around ten. Next-door neighbor had heard Bobby G shouting. Then a door slam.

And records already obtained from the guy's cell phone service provider had indicated that a call had been made to Chrissy's phone at nine thirty-six.

Plainclothes surveillance had been set up immediately, and the detectives were checking in regularly, with no news whatsoever. But José didn't think there was going to be any from that front. Chances were good that the place was going to stay a ghost town.

So there were two things on his radar: Find the boyfriend. And put a trail on ZeroSum's head of security.

And his instincts told him it would be best for everyone if he found Bobby G before Alex Hess did.

EIGHT

While Havers was in seeing Rehvenge, Ehlena re-stocked one of the supply closets. Which just happened to be outside of exam room three. She stacked Ace bandages. Made a tower of plastic-wrapped gauze rolls. Created a Modigliani-esque arrangement from boxes of Kleenex, Band-Aids, and thermometer covers.

She was running out of things to organize when the door to the exam room opened with a click. She put her head out into the hall.

Havers truly looked like a physician, with his tortoise-shell glasses and his precisely parted brown hair and his bow tie and the white coat. He also carried himself like one, always calmly and thoughtfully in charge of his staff, his facilities, and, most of all, his patients.

But he didn't seem himself as he stood in the corridor, frowning as if confused, rubbing his head like his temples hurt.

"Are you all right, Doctor?" she asked.

He glanced over, his eyes unusually vacant behind his lenses. "Er . . . yes, thank you." Shaking himself, he handed her a prescription slip from on top of Rehvenge's medical record. "I . . . ah . . , Would you be so kind as to bring the dopamine to this patient, as well as two doses of scorpion antivenin? I'd do it myself, but I do believe I need to have something to eat. I am feeling rather hypoglycemic."

"Yes, Doctor. Right away."

Havers nodded and put the patient's file back into the holder beside the door. "Thank you so kindly."

The doctor drifted away as if in a partial trance.

The poor male had to be exhausted. He'd been in the OR for most of the past two nights and days, tending to a birthing female, a male who had been in a car accident, and a small child who had been badly burned when he'd reached for a pot of boiling water on the stove. And that was on top of the fact that he hadn't taken any time off in the two years she'd worked at the clinic. He was always on call, always there.

Kind of like she was with her father.

So, yeah, she knew exactly how tired he must be.

At the pharmacy, she handed the prescription to the pharmacist, who never made small talk and didn't break with tradition today. The male went into the back and returned with six boxes of dopamine bottles and some antivenin.

As he handed the meds to her, he flipped a sign that said, BE BACK IN 15 MINUTES and stepped through the cutout door in the counter.

"Wait," she said, struggling to hold the load. "This can't be right."

The male had his cigarette and his lighter already in his hands. "It is."

"No, this is . . . Where's the slip?"

Greater wrath faced no female than that she obstruct the path of a smoker finally getting his break. But she didn't give a crap.

"Get me the slip."

The pharmacist grumbled his way back through the counter, and there was an inordinate amount of paper rustling, as if he were hoping maybe to start a fire by rubbing prescriptions together.

"'Dispense six boxes dopamine.'" He flipped the script to face her. "See?"

She leaned in. Sure enough, six boxes, not six vials.

"It's what the doctor always gives this guy. That and the antivenin."

"Always?"

The male's expression was all c'mon-lady-gimme-a-break, and he spoke slowly, as though she weren't fluent in

English. "Yes. The doctor usually comes for the order himself. You satisfied or you want to bring this up with Havers?"

"No . . . and thank you."

"You're *so* welcome." He tossed the slip back into the pile and beat feet out of there as if he were afraid of her coming up with more bright ideas for research projects.

What the hell kind of condition required 144 doses of dopamine? And antivenin?

Unless Rehvenge was taking a looooooooong trip out of town. To a hostile place that had scorpions like something out of *The Mummy.*

Ehlena went down the hall to the exam room, playing spinning plate with the boxes: As soon as she corralled one that was slipping free, she had to go after another. She knocked on the door with her foot and then nearly dominoed the load as she turned the knob.

"Is that all of it?" Rehvenge said in a hard tone.

Like he wanted a pallet of the stuff? "Yes."

She let the boxes tumble onto the desk and quickly arranged them. "I should get you a bag."

"That's okay. I'm good."

"Do you need any syringes?"

"I have plenty of those," he said wryly.

He was careful as he got off the exam table and drew that fur coat on, the sable widening the great width of his shoulders until he loomed even from across the room. With his eyes on her, he took his cane and came over slowly, as if he were unsure of his balance . . . and his reception.

"Thank you," he said.

God, the words were so simple and so commonly spoken, and yet, coming from him, they meant more than she was comfortable with.

Actually, it was less how he expressed himself than his expression: There was a vulnerability in that amethyst stare, buried deep within it.

Or maybe not.

Maybe she was the one feeling vulnerable and was seeking commiseration from the male who had put her in that state. And she was very weak at the moment. As Rehvenge stood close to her, taking the boxes one by one from the table and putting them in hidden pockets within the fur folds, she was naked though uniformed, unmasked though she had had nothing hiding her face.

She looked away and saw only that stare.

"Take care of yourself. . . ." His voice was so deep. "And like I said, thanks. You know, for taking care of me."

"You're welcome," she said to the exam table. "Hope you got what you needed."

"Some of it . . . at any rate."

Ehlena didn't turn back around until she heard the door click shut. Then, with a curse, she sat down on the chair at the desk and wondered again whether she had any business going on the date tonight. Not just because of her father, but because . . .

Oh, right. There was some good thinking. Why didn't she push away a sweet, normal guy just because she was attracted to a total no-go from another planet where people wore clothes worth more than cars. Perfect.

If she kept it up she might win the Nobel Prize for stupidity, a life goal she was simply panting to accomplish.

Her eyes drifted around as she pep-talked herself back to reality . . . until they locked on the wastepaper basket. On top of a Coke can, in an unfurled wad, was a cream-colored business card.

REHVENGE, SON OF REMPOON

There was only a number underneath, no address.

She bent down and picked the thing up, smoothing it flat on the desk. As she ran her palm down the face a couple of times, there was no raised pattern marring the surface, just a slight indent. Engraved. Of course.

Ah, Rempoon. She knew that name, and now Rehvenge's next of kin made sense. Madalina, who was listed, was a fallen Chosen who had taken to spiritually counseling others, a well-loved female of worth whom Ehlena had heard of though never met personally. The female had been mated of Rempoon, a male from one of the oldest and most prominent bloodlines. Mother. Father.

So those sable coats were not just flash cash laid down by a nouveau riche climber. Rehvenge was from where Ehlena and her family used to belong, the *glymera*—the highest level of vampire civilian society, the arbiters of taste, the bastion of civility . . . and the cruelest enclave of know-it-alls on the planet, capable of making Manhattan muggers look like people you'd rather have in for dinner.

She wished him well among that bunch. God knew she and her family hadn't had a good time with them: Her father had been double-crossed and kicked to the curb, sacrificed so a more powerful branch of the bloodline could survive financially and socially. And that had been just the start of the ruinations.

As she left the exam room, she tossed the card back into the trash and picked the medical chart out of the holder. After checking in with Catya, Ehlena went to registration to fill in for the nurse on break and to enter Havers's brief notes on Rehvenge and the prescriptions given into the system.

No mention of the underlying disease. But maybe it had been treated for so long it had been in only the earlier records.

Havers didn't trust computers and did all his work on paper, but fortunately, Catya had insisted three years ago that they keep an electronic copy of everything—as well as have a team of *doggen* transfer the medical files of every single current patient into the server in their entirety. And thank the Virgin Scribe. When they'd moved to this new facility after the raids, all they'd had were the e-files on patients.

On impulse, she scrolled up through the most recent part of Rehvenge's record. The dosage for the dopamine had been increasing over the last couple of years. And the antivenin.

She logged out and settled back in the office chair, crossing her arms over her chest and staring hard at the monitor. When the screen saver kicked in, it went all *Millennium Falcon* light speed, a sprinkle of stars shooting out from deep inside the monitor.

She was going on that damn date, she decided.

"Ehlena?"

She looked up at Catya. "Yes?"

"We have a patient coming in by ambulance. ETA, two minutes. Drug overdose, unknown substance. Patient intubated and bagged. You and I are assisting."

As another staff member appeared to handle check-ins, Ehlena sprang out of the chair and jogged behind Catya down the corridor to the emergency bays. Havers was already there, quickly finishing what looked like a ham sandwich on rye.

Just as he gave his clean plate over to a *doggen*, the patient came in through the underground tunnel that ran from the ambulance garages. The EMTs were two male vampires who were dressed the same as their human counterparts were, because blending in was mission critical.

·   The patient was out cold, being kept alive only by the medic near his head who was fisting a bag in a slow, steady rhythm.

"We were called in by his friend," the male said, "who promptly left him passed out in the cold in the alley next to ZeroSum. Pupils nonresponsive. Blood pressure sixty-two over thirty-eight. Heart rate thirty-two."

What a waste, Ehlena thought as she went to work.

Street drugs were such an unconscionable evil.

Across town, in the part of Caldwell known as Minimall Sprawlopolis, Wrath found the dead *lesser*'s apartment easily enough. The development it was in was called Hunter-bred Farms, and the setup of two-story buildings carried an equine theme that was about as authentic as the plastic tablecloths in a cheap Italian restaurant.

No such thing as a hunter-bred horse. And the word *farm* was not usually associated with one hundred one-bedroom units sandwiched in between a Ford/Mercury dealership and a supermarket shopping center. Agrarian? Yeah, right. Grass patches were losing the ground battle against the asphalt by a four-to-one margin and the one pond there was had clearly been man-made.

Damn thing had cement edges like a pool, and its thin ice cover was the color of piss, like there was a chemical treatment going on.

Considering how many humans lived in the units, it was a surprise that the Lessening Society would put troops in such a conspicuous place, but maybe this was just temporary. Or maybe the whole fucking thing was filled with slayers.

Each building had four apartments clustered around a communal stairwell, and the numbers mounted on the outside wall were spotlit from the ground. He solved the visual challenge using the tried and true touch-and-decipher method. When he found a row of upraised digits that felt like *Eight Twelve* in cursive letters, he willed off the security lights and dematerialized to the staircase's top landing.

The lock on unit eight twelve was flimsy and easily manipulated with his mind, but he wasn't taking anything for granted. Standing flat against the wall, he turned the horseshoe-shaped knob and opened the door only a crack.

He closed his useless eyes and listened. No movement, just the hum of a refrigerator. Considering his hearing was acute enough to hear a mouse breathe through its nose, he figured it was clear and palmed a throwing star, then slipped inside.

Chances were good there was a security system blinking somewhere in the place, but he didn't plan on being here long enough to tango with the enemy. Besides, even if a slayer showed up there could be no fighting. Place was crawling with humans.

Bottom line, he was looking for jars and that was it. After all, the feeling of wetness down his leg wasn't because he'd hit a slush puddle on the way in. He was bleeding into his boot from the fighting back in that alley, so, yeah, if anyone who smelled like a coconut-cream pie laced with cheap shampoo appeared, he was outtie.

At least . . . that was what he told himself.

Shutting the door, Wrath inhaled, long and slow . . . and wished he could power-wash the inside of his nose and the back of his throat. Still, although his gag reflex started churning, the news was good: There were three distinct sweet smells interwoven in the stale air, which meant three *lessers* stayed here.

As he headed for the back, where the cloying stenches were concentrated, he wondered what the hell was going on. *Lessers* rarely lived in groups because they fought with one another—which was what happened when you recruited only homicidal maniacs. Hell, the men the Omega picked couldn't shut off their inner Michael Myers just because the Society felt like saving a little on rent overhead.

Maybe they had a strong *Fore-lesser* in place, though.

After the raids of the summer, it was hard to believe the *lessers* were tight on cash, but why else consolidate troops? Then again, the Brothers, and Wrath on the QT, had been

seeing less sophisticated shit in those holsters. It used to be
when you fought the slayers you had to be prepared for any
special modification out on the market for any kind of
weapon. Lately? They had been going up against old-school
switchblades, brass knuckles, and even—gasp—a frickin'
billy club last week—all cheap weapons that didn't require
bullets or upkeep. And now they were playing *The Waltons*
here at Hunter-poser Farms? What the fuck?

The first bedroom he came up to was marked by a pair
of perfumes, and he found two jars next to the sheetless,
blanketless twin beds.

The next crip likewise smelled of a variant of old lady . . .
that and something else. A quick sniff told Wrath it was . . .
Christ, Old Spice.

Go. Fig. With the way those fuckers smelled, like you'd
want to add anything to the mix—

Holy shit.

Wrath inhaled hard, his brain filtering out anything remotely sweet.

Gunpowder.

Following the metallic bite in the air, he went over to a
closet that had the kind of flimsy doors you'd expect on a
dollhouse. As he opened them up, the eau d'ammo bloomed,
and he leaned down, feeling around with his hands.

Wooden crates. Four of them. All nailed shut.

The guns inside had definitely been fired, but not recently, he thought. Which suggested this might well have
been a CPO purchase.

Certified preowned by who, though.

Whatever, he wasn't leaving them behind. This stash was
going to be used by the enemy against his civilians and his
brothers, so he'd blow up the whole apartment before letting those weapons get palmed in the war.

But if he called this in to the Brotherhood? His secret
would be revealed. Trouble was, dragging the crates out by
himself was a yeah-right sitch: He had no car, and there was
no way of dematerializing with that kind of weight on his
back, even if he cut it up into smaller loads.

Wrath backed out of the closet and took stock of the
bedroom, using touch as much as sight. Oh, good. There
was a window over on the left.

He took out his phone with a curse and flipped it open—

Someone was coming up the stairwell.

He froze, closing his eyes to concentrate even further. Human or *lesser*?

Only one mattered.

Wrath bent to the side and put the two jars he'd macked on a dresser, finding, natch, both the third one and the bottle of Old Spice. Palming his forty, he stood with his shit-kickers planted and his gun pointed down the short hallway, directly at the unit's front door.

There was a jangle of keys, then a clang, as if they'd fallen out of a hand.

The curse was a woman's.

As his body eased up, he let his gun fall to his thigh. Like the Brotherhood, the Society admitted only males into its ranks, so that was no slayer playing pick-up sticks with those keys.

He heard the door to the apartment across the way close, and abruptly a surround-sound TV came on loud enough so he could hear the rerun of *The Office*.

He liked this epi. It was the one where the bat got loose—

A bunch of screams rippled over, generated by the sitcom.

Yup. The bat was flying around now.

With the woman safely occupied, he refocused but stayed where he was, praying the coming-home bit was a theme song the enemy would pick up and carry. Staying statue and breathing shallow didn't improve the ratio of *lessers* in the place, however. Some fifteen, maybe twenty minutes later, he was still completely surrounded by no slayers.

But it wasn't a total loss. He was copping a nice little comedy contact buzz from Dwight's head- and bat-bagging scene in the Office's kitchen.

Time to get a move on.

He hit up Butch, gave the Brother the address, and told the cop to drive like his foot was made of stone. Wrath wanted to get the guns out before anyone came, yes. But if he and his brother could get the crates out quickly, and Butch could ghost the shit, Wrath might still be able to hang around the premises for another hour or so.

To pass the time, he hunted through the apartment, patting surfaces down with his palms in an attempt to find computers, extra phones, more goddamn guns. He'd just returned to the second bedroom when something ricocheted off the window.

Wrath unholstered his forty again and back-flatted it on the wall next to the window. With his hand, he sprang the lock and pushed the sheet of glass open a crack.

The cop's Boston accent was about as subtle as a loud-speaker. "Yo, Rapunzel, you going to let down your frickin' hair, there?"

"Shh, you wanna wake the neighbors?"

"Like they can hear anything over that TV? Hey, this is the bat epi . . ."

Wrath left Butch to talk to himself, putting his gun back on his hip, pushing the window wide, then heading for the closet. The only warning he gave the cop as he winged the first two-hundred-pound crate out of the building was, "Brace yourself, Effie."

"Jesus Ch—" A grunt cut off the swearing.

Wrath poked his head out of the window and whispered, "You're supposed to be a good Catholic. Isn't that blasphemy?"

Butch's tone was like someone had pissed out a fire on his bed. "You just threw half a car at me with nothing but a quote from *Mrs.* fucking *Doubtfire.*"

"Put on your big-girl pants and deal."

As the cop cursed his way over to the Escalade, which he'd managed to park under some pine trees, Wrath headed back to the closet

When Butch returned, Wrath heaved again. "Two more."

There was another grunt and a rattle. "Fuck me."

"Not on your life."

"Fine. Fuck you."

When the last crate was cradled like a sleeping baby in Butch's arms, Wrath leaned out. "Buh-bye."

"You don't want a ride back to the mansion?"

"No."

There was a pause, as if Butch were waiting for the low-down on how Wrath intended to spend what little was left of the night hours.

"Go home," he told the cop.

"What do I tell the others?"

"That you're a fucking genius and you found the gun crates when you were out hunting."

"You're bleeding."

"I'm getting sick of people telling me that."

"Then word up, stop being an ass and go see Doc Jane."

"Didn't I already 'bye' you?"

"Wrath—"

Wrath shut the window, went over to the dresser, and put the three jars in his jacket.

The Lessening Society wanted to claim the hearts of their dead as much as the Brothers did, so as soon as the slayers heard a man of theirs was down, they reconnoitered and headed to the *lesser*'s addy. Surely one of those bastards he'd killed tonight had called for backup in the process. They had to know.

They had to come back here.

Wrath chose the best defensive position there was, which was in the back bedroom, and angled his click-click-bang-bang at the front door.

He wasn't leaving until he absolutely had to.

NINE

Caldwell's outskirts were either farm or forest, and the farms likewise came in two varieties, being either dairy or corn—with dairy predominating, given the short growing season. The forests were also binary, with a choice between the pines that led up the flanks of mountains or the oaks that led into the spun-off swamps of the Hudson River.

No matter what the landscape, *naturalis* or *industrialis*, you had roads that were less traveled and houses spaced by miles and neighbors who were just as reclusive and trigger-happy as someone reclusive and trigger-happy himself could want.

Lash, son of the Omega, sat at a beat-up kitchen table in a single-room hunting cabin in one of the stretches of forest. Across the weathered pine surface in front of him he'd spread every Lessening Society financial record he'd been able to find or print out or call up on his laptop.

This was such bullshit.

He reached over and picked up an Evergreen Bank statement that he'd read a dozen times. The Society's largest account had one hundred twenty-seven thousand five hundred forty-two dollars and fifteen cents in it. The others, which were housed among six other banks, including Glens Falls National and Farrell Bank & Trust, had balances of between twenty bucks and twenty thousand.

If this was all the Society had, they were teetering on the crumbling ledge of bankruptcy.

The raids over the summer had yielded some good re-sellables in the form of looted antiques and silver, but realizing those funds was proving complicated, because it involved a lot of human contact. And there had been some financial accounts that had been seized, but again, siphoning off money from human banks was a complicated mess. As he'd learned the hard way.

"Y'all want some more coffee?"

Lash looked up at his number two and thought it was a miracle Mr. D was still around. When Lash had first entered this world, reborn by his true father, the Omega, he had been lost, the enemy now his family. Mr. D had been his guide, although like all tourist maps, Lash had assumed the bastard would wear out his usefulness as the new locale was internalized by the driver.

Not so. The little Texan who had been Lash's entrée was now his disciple.

"Yeah," Lash said, "and how about food?"

"Y'sir. Got you some good ol' fatback bacon, right chere, and that cheese you like."

The coffee was poured nice and slow into Lash's mug. Sugar was next, and the spoon used to stir made a soft clinking sound. Mr. D would have cheerfully wiped Lash's ass if asked, but he wasn't a pussy. The little fucker could kill like no one's business, the Chucky doll of slayers. Great short-order cook, too. Made pancakes that were a mile high and fluffy as a pillow.

Lash checked his watch. The Jacob & Co. had diamonds all over it, and in the dim light from the computer screen they were a thousand points of light. But the thing was a replacement faker he'd gotten off eBay. He wanted another real one except . . . holy Christ . . . he couldn't afford it. Sure, he'd kept all the accounts of his "parents" after he'd killed the pair of vampires who'd raised him as their own, but though there was a good load of green in those baskets, he was leery of spending any of it on frivolous shit.

He had bills to pay. Like for mortgages and weapons and ammo and clothes and rent and car leases. *Lessers* didn't eat, but they consumed a lot of resources, and the Omega didn't care about cash. But then, he lived in hell and had the ability to conjure out of thin air anything from a hot meal to the Liberace cloaks he liked to jack his black shadow body into.

Lash hated to admit it, but he had the feeling his true father was a little light in the loafers. No real man would be caught dead in that sparkly shit.

As he lifted his coffee cup, his watch glimmered and he frowned.

Whatever, that was a status symbol.

"Your boys are late," he bitched.

"They be comin'." Mr. D went over and opened the seventies-era refrigerator. Which not only had a squeaking door and was the color of a rotten olive, but drooled like a dog.

This was ri-fucking-diculous. They needed to upgrade their cribs. Or if not all, at least one for his HQ.

At least the coffee was perfect, although he kept that to himself. "I don't like waiting."

"They be comin'—don'tchu worry. Three eggs in your omelet?"

"Four."

As a series of crack and splits radiated through the cabin, Lash tapped the tip of his Waterman on the Evergreen statement. Expenses for the Society, including cell phone bills, Internet hookups, rent/mortgages, weapons, clothes, and cars ran easily fifty grand a month.

When he'd first been getting a feel for his new role, he'd been damn sure someone in the ranks was peeling skin off the apple. But he'd been watching things carefully for months, and there was no Kenneth Lay going on that he could find. It was a simple matter of accounting, not fudging the books or embezzlement: Costs were higher than revenues. Period.

He was doing his best to arm his troops, even stooping so low as to buy four crates of guns from bikers he'd met in jail over the summer. But it wasn't enough. His men needed better than rehabbed Red Ryders to take out the Brotherhood.

And while he was at the wish list, he had to have more men. He'd thought the bikers would be a good pool to recruit from, but they were proving too cohesive. Based on his dealings with them, his intuition told him he had to bring them all on or none—because sure as shit if he cherry-picked, the ones chosen would return to their clubhouse and tell their buddies about their fun new job killing vampires. And if he took them all, then he was running the risk of their splitting off from his authority.

One-by-one recruiting was going to be the best strategy, but it wasn't like he'd had time to do any of it. Between the training sessions with his father—which, in spite of his issues with Daddy-o's wardrobe, were proving monstrously helpful—and his monitoring the persuasion camps and looting repositories, and trying to get his men to focus on the job at hand, he had not even an hour left in the day.

So shit was getting critical: To be a successful military leader required three things, and resources and recruits were two of them. And although being the son of the Omega gave him loads of benes, time was time, stopping for no man, no vampire, and no scion of evil.

Considering the state of the accounts, he knew he had to start with resources first. Then he could go about getting the other two.

The sound of a car pulling up to the cabin had him palming a forty and Mr. D going for his .357 Magnum. Lash kept his heat under the table, but Mr. D was all Times Square about his, holding the piece straight out, his arm extended in a line directly from his shoulder.

When there was a knock, Lash said sharply: "You'd better be who I think you are."

The *lesser*'s answer was the right one. "It's me 'n' Mr. A 'n' your pickup."

"Come on in," Mr. D said, ever the good host, even though his .357 was still up and ready for action.

The two slayers who walked through the door were the last of the pale ones, the final pair of old-timers who had been in the Society long enough to have lost their individual hair and eye coloring.

The human who was dragged in with them was a six-foot stretch of nothing particularly interesting, a twenty-something white boy with an average face and a hairline that would be giving up the ghost in another couple years. The guy's Wonder-bread, who-cares looks no doubt explained why he dressed the way he did: He had a leather jacket with an eagle embossed on the back, a Fender Rock

& Roll Religion shirt, chains hanging from his jeans, and kicks by Ed Hardy.

Sad. Truly sad. Like putting twenty-fours on a Toyota Camry. And if the boy was armed? No doubt it was with a Swiss Army knife that got used mostly for the toothpick.

But he didn't have to be a fighter to be useful. Lash had those. From this POS he needed something else.

The guy looked at Mr. D's welcome Magnum and glanced back at the door as if he were wondering if he could outrun a bullet. Mr. A solved the issue by closing them all in together and staying right in front of the exit.

The human looked at Lash and frowned. "Hey ... I know you. From jail."

"Yeah, you do." Lash stayed seated and smiled a little. "So you want to know what the good and bad thing is about this meeting?"

The human swallowed and went back to focusing on Mr. D's muzzle. "Yeah. Sure."

"You were easy to find. All my men had to do was go to Screamer's and stand around and ... there you were." Lash eased back in his chair, the cane seat creaking. As the human's stare flicked over, there was a temptation to tell the guy to forget about the sound and worry about the forty under the table that was aimed at his family jewels. "You been staying out of trouble since I saw you in jail?"

The human shook his head and said, "Yes."

Lash laughed. "You want to try that again? You're not in sync."

"I mean, I'm still keeping up my business, but I haven't been cuffed."

"Well, good." As the guy's eyes flipped back to Mr. D, Lash laughed. "If I were you, I'd want to know why I was brought here."

"Ah ... yeah. That would be cool."

"My troops have been watching you."

"Troops?"

"You do steady business downtown."

"I make paper okay."

"How'd you like to make more?"

Now the human stared at Lash, a smarmy, greedy look narrowing his eyes. "How much more."

Money really was the great motivator, wasn't it.

"You do okay for a retailer, but you're small-time right now. Fortunately for you, I'm in the mood to make an investment in someone like yourself, someone who needs backing to take him to the next level. I want to make you not just a retailer, but a middleman with the big boys."

The human brought a hand up to his chin and ran it down his neck as if he had to jump-start his brain by massaging his throat. In the quiet, Lash frowned. The guy's knuckles were skinned and his cheapo Caldwell High School ring was missing the stone.

"That sounds interesting," the human murmured. "But . . . I need to chill a little."

"How so." Man, if this was a negotiating tactic, Lash was more than ready to point out that there were a hundred other dime-bagger dealers who'd jump at this kind of deal.

Then he was going to nod at Mr. D and the slayer was going to cap Eagle Jacket right under that receding hairline.

"I, ah, I need to lie low in Caldie. For a little bit."

"Why."

"It's not related to the drug dealing."

"Have anything to do with your roughed-up knuckles?" The human quickly tucked his arm behind his back. "Thought so. Question. If you need to keep on the DL, what the hell were you doing in Screamer's tonight?"

"Let's just say I wanted to make a purchase of my own."

"You're an idiot if you do what you sell." And not a good candidate for what Lash had in mind. He didn't want to try to do business with a junkie.

"Wasn't drugs."

"Was it a new ID?"

"Maybe."

"Did you get what you were looking for? At the club?"

"No."

"I can help you with that." The Society had its own laminating machine, for fuck's sake. "And here's what I propose. My men, the ones to your left and behind you, will work with you. If you can't be the front man on the street, you can get the merchandise and they can move it after you show them the ropes." Lash glanced over at Mr. D. "My breakfast?"

Mr. D put his gun down next to the cowboy hat he took off only when indoors and then he popped up a flame under a pan on the little stove.

"What kind of money are we talking about?" the human asked.

"Hundred grand for the first investment."

The guy's eyes made like slot machines, all *ding-ding-ding* excited. "Well . . . shit, that's enough to play ball. But what's in it for me?"

"Profit sharing. Seventy for me. Thirty for you. Of all sales."

"How do I know I can trust you?"

"You don't."

As Mr. D laid some bacon out on the heat, the sizzle and hiss filled the room and Lash smiled at the sound.

The human looked around, and you could practically read his thoughts: cabin out in the middle of nowhere, four guys facing off at him, at least one of whom had a gun capable of blowing a cow into hamburger patties.

"Okay. Yeah. All right."

Which was, of course, the only answer.

Lash put the safety back on his weapon, and when he put his autoloader on the table, the human's eyes bugged. "Come on, like you didn't think I had you covered? Please."

"Yeah. Okay. Right."

Lash stood up and came around to the guy. As he stuck his hand out, he said, "What's your name, Eagle Jacket?"

"Nick Carter."

Lash laughed hard. "Try again, dickhead. I want your real one."

"Bob Grady. They call me Bobby G."

They shook and Lash squeezed hard, crunching those bruised knuckles together. "Glad to do business with you, Bobby. I'm Lash. But you can call me God."

John Matthew scanned the people in ZeroSum's VIP section not because he was looking for tail, as Qhuinn was, and not because he was wondering who Qhuinn was going to want to get with, as Blay was.

No, John had his own fixations.

Xhex usually came around every half hour, but after her

bouncer had approached her and she'd left in a hurry a while ago, she'd been missing.

As a redhead eased on by, Qhuinn shifted in the banquette, his combat boot tapping it out under the table. The human woman was about five-ten and had the legs of a gazelle, long and fragile and lovely. And she wasn't a professional—she was on the arm of a business-type guy.

Didn't mean she wasn't giving it up for money, but it was in a more legal fashion called a relationship.

"Shit," Qhuinn muttered, his mismatched eyes predatory.

John tapped his buddy on the leg and in American Sign Language said, *Look, why don't you just go back with someone. You're driving me crazy with the twitching.*

Qhuinn pointed to the tear that was tattooed under his eye. "I'm not supposed to leave you. Ever. That's the point of having an *ahstrux nohstrum.*"

And if you don't have some sex soon, you're going to be useless.

Qhuinn watched as the redhead arranged her short skirt so she could sit down without flashing what was no doubt nothing but a Brazilian wax.

The woman looked around without interest . . . until she got to Qhuinn. The moment she saw him, her eyes lit up like she'd found a good deal at Neiman Marcus. This was not a surprise. Most women and females did the same, and it was understandable. Qhuinn dressed simply, but with plenty of the hard-core: black button-down tucked into dark blue Z-Brands. Those black combat boots. Black metal studs running all the way up one ear. Hair set in black spikes. And he'd recently pierced his lower lip in the center with a black hoop.

Qhuinn looked like the kind of guy who kept his leather jacket in his lap because he carried his guns in it.

Which he did.

"Nah, I'm cool," Qhuinn muttered before finishing off his Corona. "I'm not into redheads."

Blay looked away sharply, taking an abrupt, feigned interest in a brunette woman. Truth was, he was into only one person, and that person had shut him down as kindly and solidly as a best friend could.

Qhuinn evidently really, truly didn't do redheads.

When was the last time you were with anyone? John signed.

"I dunno." Qhuinn signaled for another round of beers. "A while."

John tried to think back and realized it hadn't been since . . . Christ, back in the summer, with that chick at Abercrombie & Fitch. Considering Qhuinn was usually good for at least three people a night, it was a hell of a dry spell, and it was hard to imagine that a steady diet of one-handed get-offs was going to hold the guy. Shit, even when he fed from the Chosen, he'd been keeping his hands to himself, in spite of the fact that his erections strained until he cold-sweated it. Then again, the three of them fed from the same female at the same time, and as much as Qhuinn had no problem whatsoever with an audience, his pants stayed on in deference to Blay and John.

Seriously, Qhuinn, what the hell is going to happen to me? Blay's here.

"Wrath said always with you. So I need to be. Always. With. You."

I think you're taking that too seriously. Like, way too seriously.

Across the VIP section, the redheaded gazelle moved around in her seat so that her below-the-waist assets were on full display, her smooth legs out from under the table and in full view of Qhuinn.

This time when the guy shifted, it was pretty obvious he was rearranging something hard in his lap. And it wasn't one of his weapons.

For fuck's sake, Qhuinn, I'm not saying it should be her. But we have to get you taken care of—

"He said he's tight," Blay interjected. "Just leave him be."

"There is one way." Qhuinn's mismatched eyes shifted over to John. "You could come with me. Not that we would do anything, 'cuz I know you don't fly like that. But you could have someone, too. If you wanted. We could do it in one of the private bathrooms, and you could have the stall so I wouldn't be able to see you. You just say the word, 'kay? I won't bring it up again."

As Qhuinn looked away all casual and shit, it was hard not to like the guy. Consideration, like rudeness, came in a lot of different variations, and the gentle offer of a cozy double sex session was a sort of kindness: Qhuinn and Blay both knew why, even eight months past John's transition, he hadn't been with a female. Knew why and still wanted to hang with him.

Dropping the bomb John had been hiding had been Lash's final fuck-you before he died.

Had been the reason Qhuinn had killed the guy.

When the waitress brought freshies, John glanced over at the redhead and, to his surprise, she smiled at him when she caught him looking.

Qhuinn laughed quietly. "Maybe I'm not the only one she likes."

John brought his Corona up to his mouth and took a drink to hide his blush. Thing was, he wanted sex and, like Blay, wanted it with someone in particular. But having already lost an erection in front of a naked, willing female, he was in no hurry to do that again, especially not with the person he was interested in.

Hell. No. Xhex wasn't the kind of female you wanted to choke on a hot wing around. Going limp because you were chicken to do the deed? His ego would never be the same—

Unrest in the crowd had him ditching the poor-mes and straightening in the banquette.

A wild-eyed guy was being escorted through the VIP section by two enormous Moors, each with a hand on his upper arm. He was tap-dancing with his expensive shoes, his feet barely touching the ground, and his mouth was likewise pulling some kind of Fred Astaire, although John couldn't hear what he was saying over the music.

The trio went into the private office in the back.

John tipped his Corona and stared at the door as it closed. Bad things happened to people who were taken in there. Especially if they were being hovercrafted by that pair of private guards.

Abruptly, a hush dimmed all the talk in the VIP section, making the music seem very loud.

John knew who it was before he turned his head.

Rehvenge walked in through a side door, his entrance quiet but as obvious as a grenade going off: In the midst of all the sharp-dressed patrons with their arm candy and the working girls with their assets out for hire and the waitresses hustling trays, the guy shrank the size of the space, not just because he was a huge male dressed in a sable duster, but because of the way he looked around.

His glowing amethyst eyes saw everyone and cared about no one.

Rehv—or the Reverend, as the human clientele called him—was a drug lord and a pimp who didn't give a shit about the vast majority of people. Which meant he was capable of, and frequently did, anything the fuck he wanted to.

Especially to types like that tap dancer.

Man, the night was going to end badly for that guy.

As Rehv passed by, he nodded to John and the boys, and they all nodded back, raising their Coronas in deference. Thing was, Rehv was an ally of sorts with the Brotherhood, having been made *leahdyre* of the *glymera*'s council after the raids—because he was the only one of those aristocrats with the balls to stand his ground in Caldwell.

So the guy who cared about very little was in charge of a hell of a lot.

John turned toward the velvet rope, not even bothering to be smooth about it. Surely this meant Xhex had to be . . .

She appeared at the head of the VIP section, looking like a billion bucks, as far as he was concerned: As she leaned into one of her bouncers so the guy could whisper in her ear, her body was so tight her stomach muscles showed through the second skin of her muscle shirt.

Talk about shifting in the seat. Now he was the one with the rearrangement issues.

As she marched through to Rehv's private office, though, his libido went on ice. She was never the type who smiled much, but as she went by, she was grim. Just as Rehv had been.

Clearly, something was doing, and John couldn't help the knight-in-shining-armor impulse that lit up in his chest. But come on, Xhex didn't need a savior. If anything, she was the type who would be on the horse, fighting the dragon.

"You look a little tight there," Qhuinn said quietly as Xhex went into the office. "Keep my offer in mind, John. I'm not the only one hurting, am I."

"Will you excuse me," Blay said, getting to his feet and taking out his red Dunhills and his gold lighter. "I need some fresh air."

The male had started smoking recently, a habit Qhuinn despised in spite of the fact that vampires didn't get cancer. John understood it, though. Frustration had to be worked out, and there was only so much you could do alone in your bedroom or with your boys in the weight room.

Hell, they'd all gained muscle weight over the last three months, their shoulders and arms and thighs outpacing their clothes. Made a guy think fighters had a point about no sex before matches. They kept adding hard pounds like this, they were going to look like a pack of pro wrestlers.

Qhuinn stared down into his Corona. "You want to get out of here? Please tell me you want to get out of here."

John glanced at the door to Rehv's office.

"Stay it is," Qhuinn muttered as he signaled to a waitress, who came right over. "I'm going to need another of these. Or maybe a case."

TEN

Rehvenge shut the door to his office and smiled tightly, to keep his fangs from making an appearance. Even without the show of canines, though, the bookie hanging between Trez and iAm was smart enough to know he was in deep shit.

"Reverend, what's this all about? Why you calling me in like this?" the guy said in a staccato rush. "I was just working my business for you and suddenly these two—"

"I heard something interesting about you," Rehv said, going around behind his desk.

As he sat down, Xhex came into the office, her gray eyes sharp. After she closed the door, she leaned back against it, better than any Master Lock when it came to keeping cheating sports bookies inside and prying eyes outside.

"It was a lie, a total lie—"

"You don't like to sing?" Rehv leaned back in his chair, his numbed-out body finding a familiar position behind his black desk. "That wasn't you popping a little Tony B for the crowd at Sal's the other night?"

The bookie frowned. "Well, yeah . . . I got me some pipes."

Rehv nodded at iAm, who was, as always, stone-faced. Guy never showed emotion, except when it came to a perfect cappuccino. Then you got a little bit of the bliss out of him. "My partner over here . . . he said you sang real well. Real crowd-pleaser. What did he sing, iAm."

iAm's voice was all James Earl Jones, low and gorgeous. "'Three Coins in the Fountain.'"

The bookie did a *well-you-know* jack-up of his slacks. "I got range. I got rhythm."

"So you're a tenor like good ol' Mr. Bennett, huh?" Rehv shrugged out of his sable. "Tenors are my favorite."

"Yeah." The bookie glanced at the Moors. "Look, you mind telling me what this is about?"

"I want you to sing for me."

"You mean, like, for a party? 'Cuz I'd do anything for you, you know that, boss. All you had to do was ask ... I mean, this weren't necessary."

"Not for a party, although all four of us will enjoy hearing the performance. It's to repay me for what you skinned off last month."

The bookie's face drooped. "I didn't skin—"

"Yeah, you did. See, iAm is a fantastic accountant. Every week, you give him your reports. How much in on what teams and which spreads. Do you think no one does the math? Based on the games last month, you should have paid in—what was the figure, iAm?"

"One hundred seventy-eight thousand four hundred eighty-two."

"What he said." Rehv nodded a quick thanks to iAm. "But instead you came in at ... What was it?"

"One hundred thirty thousand nine eighty-two," iAm shot back.

The bookie started in immediately. "He's wrong. He's added—"

Rehv shook his head. "Guess what the difference is— not that you don't already know. iAm?"

"Forty-seven thousand five hundred."

"Which happens to be twenty-five grand on a ninety percent vig. Isn't that right, iAm?" As the Moor nodded once, Rehv punched his cane into the floor and got to his feet. "Which in turn is the courtesy rate charged by the Caldie mob. Trez then went and did a little digging, and what did you find?"

"My boy Mike says he loaned twenty-five large to this guy right before the Rose Bowl."

Rehv left his cane on the chair and came around the desk, keeping one hand on the surface to steady himself.

The Moors stepped back into position, crowding the bookie, holding his upper arms again.

Rehv stopped right in front of the guy. "And so I ask you once more, did you think no one was going to double-check the math?"

"Reverend, boss . . . please, I was going to pay you back—"

"Yeah, you are going to make good on it. And you're paying my vig for fucktards who try to play me. One hundred and fifty percent due at the end of this month or your wife's going to see you mailed back to her in pieces. Oh, and you're fired."

The guy burst into tears, and they weren't the crocodile kind. These were real, the sort that made the man's nose run and his eyes puff up. "Please . . . they were going to hurt me—"

Rehv snapped his hand out and clamped on between the guy's legs. The poodle yelp told him that even though he couldn't feel anything, the bookie could, and the pressure was in the right spot.

"I don't like being stolen from," Rehv said into the man's ear. "Cranks my shit right out. And if you think what the mob was going to do to you was bad, I will *guarantee* you that I am capable of worse. Now . . . I want you to sing for me, motherfucker."

Rehv twisted hard and the guy screamed for all he was worth, the sound loud and high, echoing in the low-ceilinged room. When the shriek began to trail off because the bookie had exhausted his air supply, Rehv relented and gave him a chance to refresh those pipes with some gasping. And then it was—

The second scream was louder and higher than the first, proving that vocalists did do better after a little warm-up.

The bookie jerked and jangled in the hold of the Moors, and Rehv kept at it, his *symphath* side watching raptly, like this was the best show on television.

It took about nine minutes until the guy lost consciousness.

After it was lights-out, Rehv let go and returned to his chair. One nod and Trez and iAm took the human through the back way, into the alley, where the cold would revive him eventually.

As they left, Rehv had a sudden image of Ehlena balancing all those boxes of dopamine in her arms as she came into the exam room. What would she think of him if she knew what he did to keep his business running? What would she say if she knew that, when he told a bookie he either paid up or his wife got FedEx packages that leaked blood on her doorstep, it wasn't a threat? What would she do if she knew that he was fully prepared to do the slice-and-dice himself or order Xhex, Trez, or iAm to do it for him?

Well, he already had the answer, didn't he.

Her voice, that clear, lovely voice, replayed in his mind: *You'd better keep that. For someone who might ever use it.*

Sure, she didn't know the particulars, but she was smart enough to turn down his business card.

Rehv focused on Xhex, who hadn't moved from her position against the front door. As silence stretched out, she stared down at the short-napped black carpet, her boot heel making a circle around herself.

"What," he said. When she didn't look up at him, he sensed her struggling to collect herself. "What the fuck happened?"

Trez and iAm came back into the office and settled against the black wall across from Rehv's desk. As they crossed their arms in front of their huge chests, they kept their mouths shut.

Silence was characteristic of Shadows ... but coupled with Xhex's tight expression and the protractor routine she was pulling with that boot, shit had gone down.

"Talk. Now."

Xhex's eyes flipped up to his. "Chrissy Andrews is dead."

"How." Even though he knew.

"Beaten and strangled to death in her apartment. I had to go down to the morgue and ID the body."

"Son of a bitch."

"I'm going to take care of it." Xhex wasn't asking permission, and no matter what he said, she was going to go after that piece-of-shit boyfriend. "And I'm going to do it fast."

Generally speaking, Rehv was in charge, but he wasn't standing in her way on this. To him, his working girls weren't just a revenue center.... They were employees who he cared about and identified with intimately. So if one got hurt, whether it was by a john or a boyfriend or a husband, he took a personal interest in payback.

Whores deserved respect, and his were going to get it.

"Teach him a lesson first," Rehv growled.

"Don't you worry about that."

"Shit . . . I blame myself," Rehv murmured as he reached forward and picked up his envelope opener. The thing was in the shape of a dagger and as sharp as a weapon, too. "We should have killed him sooner."

"She seemed as if she was better."

"Maybe she was just *hiding it* better."

The four of them sat in the quiet for a bit. There were a lot of losses in their profession—people turning up dead was hardly a news flash—but for the most part, he and his crew were the minus signs in the equations: They did the taking out. A loss of their own by someone else sat badly.

"You want the update on tonight?" Xhex asked.

"Not yet. Got a little news of my own to share." Forcing his head into gear, he looked at Trez and iAm. "What I'm about to say will make things very messy, and I want to give you both a chance to leave. Xhex, you don't get that option. Sorry."

Trez and iAm stayed put, which did not surprise him in the slightest. Trez also popped a middle finger at him. Not a shocker either.

"I went to Connecticut," Rehv said.

"You also went to the clinic," Xhex added. "Why?"

GPS sucked sometimes. Hard to have any privacy. "Forget the fucking clinic. Listen, I need you to do a job for me."

"Job as in . . . ?"

"Think of Chrissy's boyfriend as a cocktail before dinner."

This got a cold smile out of her. "Tell me."

He stared at the point of the envelope opener, thinking that he and Wrath had laughed because they both had one: The king had come in to visit after the raids during the summer, to discuss council business, and had seen the thing out on the desk. Wrath had joked that in their day jobs they both led by the blade, even if they had a pen in their hands.

Wasn't that the truth. Although Wrath had morality on his side and Rehv had only self-interest.

So it was not with virtue that he'd made his decision and chosen the course. It was, as usual, what benefited him most.

"It's not going to be easy," he murmured.

"The fun ones never are."

Rehv focused on the sharp point of the opener. "This one . . . is not for fun."

With the night closing down and her shift ending, Ehlena was antsy. Date time. Decision time. The male was supposed to come and pick her up at the clinic in twenty minutes.

God, she was back to waffling again.

His name was Stephan. Stephan, son of Tehm, although she didn't know him or his family. He was a civilian, not an aristocrat, and he'd come in with his cousin, who'd cut his hand splitting logs for firewood. While she'd been doing the discharge paperwork, she'd talked to Stephan about the kinds of things single people talked about: He liked Radiohead; she did, too. She liked Indonesian food; he did, too. He worked in the human world, doing computer programming, thanks to virtual commuting. She was a nurse, duh. He lived at home with his parents, the only son in a solidly civilian family—or at least they'd sounded solidly civilian, his father doing construction for vampire contractors, his mother teaching the Old Language freelance.

Nice, normal. Trustworthy.

Considering what the aristocrats had done to her father's sanity, she figured that all seemed like a good bet, and when Stephan had asked her out for a coffee, she'd said yes, they'd agreed on tonight, and exchanged cell phone numbers.

But what was she going to do? Call him and say she couldn't because of a family situation? Go anyway, and worry about her father?

A quick call to Lusie from the locker room, though, and the news from home was favorable: Ehlena's father had

had a long rest and was now calmly working on his papers at his desk.

Half an hour at an all-night diner. Maybe a shared scone. What was the harm?

As she decided to go once and for all, she didn't appreciate the image that flashed through her mind. Rehv's bare chest with those red star tattoos on it was not what she needed to be thinking about as she resolved to go on a date with another male.

What she needed to concentrate on was getting out of her uniform and at least nominally improving her appearance.

With the overday staff funneling in and those who had been on during the night leaving, she changed from her uniform into the skirt and sweater she'd brought with her—

She'd forgotten her shoes.

Great. White crepe soles were so sexy.

"What's wrong?" Catya said.

She turned around. "Any chance these two white boats on my feet don't totally ruin this outfit?"

"Er . . . honestly? They're not that bad."

"You so don't lie well."

"I gave it a shot."

Ehlena packed her uniform into her bag, redid her hair, and checked the makeup situation. Of course, she'd forgotten her eyeliner and mascara as well, so the cavalry was out of horses on that front, so to speak.

"I'm glad you're going," Catya said as she erased the night roster from the whiteboard.

"Considering you're my boss, that makes me nervous. I'd rather have you happy to see me coming into the clinic."

"No, it's not about work. I'm glad you're going out tonight."

Ehlena frowned and looked around. By some miracle, they were alone. "Who says I'm going anywhere but home?"

"A female going home doesn't change out of her uniform here. And she doesn't worry about how her footwear goes with her skirt. I'll spare you the who-is-he."

"That's a relief."

"Unless you want to volunteer?"

Ehlena laughed out loud. "No, I'd rather keep it private. But if it goes anywhere . . . I'll spill."

"And I'll keep you to that." Catya went over to her locker and just stared at it.

"You okay?" Ehlena said.

"I hate this damn war. I hate having the dead come in here, and seeing the pain they went through on their faces." Catya opened the locker and got busy getting her parka out. "Sorry, don't mean to be a downer."

Ehlena went over and put her hand on the female's shoulder. "I know just how you feel."

There was a moment between them as their eyes clung to each other's. And then Catya cleared her throat.

"Right, off you go. Your male awaits."

"He's picking me up here."

"Ohhh, maybe I'll just hang around and have a cigarette outside."

"You don't smoke."

"Drat, foiled again."

On her way to the exit, Ehlena checked in at the registration desk to make sure there was nothing else she needed to do with the handoff to the new shift. Satisfied everything was in order, she went through the doors and up the stairs until she was finally free of the clinic.

The night was out of the cool zip code and into chill city, the air smelling blue to her, if the color did indeed have a scent: There was just something so fresh and icy and clear as she breathed deep and exhaled in soft clouds. With each inhale, she felt as if she were taking the sapphire sprawl of the heavens above into her lungs and that the stars were sparks skipping through her body.

As the last of the nurses departed, dematerializing or driving off, depending on what they had planned, she said good-bye to the stragglers. Then Catya came and went.

Ehlena stamped her feet and checked her watch. The male was ten minutes late. No big deal.

Leaning back against the aluminum siding, she felt her blood sing in her veins, an odd freedom swelling in her chest as she thought about going out somewhere with a male on her own—

Blood. Veins.

Rehvenge hadn't had his arm treated.

The thought slammed into her head and lingered like the echo of a big noise. He hadn't dealt with that arm. There had been nothing in the record about the infection, and Havers was as scrupulous about his notes as he was about the staff uniforms and the cleanliness of the patient rooms and the organization of the supply closets.

When she'd come back from the pharmacy with the drugs, Rehvenge had had his shirt on and done up at the cuffs, but she'd assumed that was because the examination had been finished. Now she was willing to bet he'd put it on right after she'd finished taking the blood.

Except . . . it was none of her business, was it. Rehvenge was an adult male well within his rights to make poor decisions about his health. Just like that drug overdose who had barely survived the night, and just like the any number of patients who nodded a lot when the doctor was in front of them, but who went home and were noncompliant about their prescriptions or their aftercare.

There was nothing she could do to save someone who didn't want to be rescued. Nothing. And that was among the biggest tragedies in her work. All she could do was present options and consequences and hope the patient chose wisely.

A breeze rolled in, shooting right up her skirt and making her envy Rehvenge's fur coat. Leaning out from the side of the clinic, she tried to see down the drive, looking for headlights.

Ten minutes later, she checked her watch again.

And ten minutes after that, she lifted her wrist once more.

She'd been stood up.

It wasn't a surprise. The date had been so hastily thrown together, and they didn't really know each other, did they.

As another cold breeze tackled her, she took out her cell phone and texted: *Hi, Stephan—sorry to have missed you tonight. Maybe some other time. E.*

She put her phone back in her pocket and dematerialized home. Instead of going right in, she burrowed into her cloth coat and paced up and back on the cracked sidewalk that ran down the side of the house to the rear door. As the frigid wind kicked up again, a blast hit her face.

Her eyes stung.

Turning her back to the gust, wisps of her hair feathered forward as if they were trying to flee the chill, and she shivered.

Great. Now when her vision got watery, she didn't have the excuse of the stiff breeze.

God, was she crying? Over what could just be some misunderstanding? With a guy she barely knew? Why did it matter so much to her?

Ah, but it wasn't him at all. The problem was her. She hated that she was where she had been when she'd left the house: alone.

Trying to get a grip, literally, she reached out for the handle of the back door, but couldn't bring herself to go in. The image of that crappy, too-ordered kitchen, and the remembered sound of those creaky stairs going to the cellar, and the dusty, papery smell of her father's room were as familiar as her reflection in any mirror. Tonight it was all too clear, a brilliant flashlight nailing her in both eyes, a roaring sound in her ears, an overwhelming stench bombarding her nose.

She dropped her arm. The date had been a get-out-of-jail-free card. A raft off the island. A hand reached over the cliff she was hanging off of.

The desperation snapped her into focus like nothing else could. She had no business going out with anyone if that was her attitude. It wasn't fair to the guy or healthy for her. When Stephan hit her up again, if he did, she was just going to say she was too busy—

"Ehlena? You okay?"

Ehlena jumped back from the door that had evidently just opened wide. "Lusie! Sorry, just . . . just thinking too much. How's Father doing?"

"Fine, honestly fine. He's sleeping again now."

Lusie stepped out of the house and closed off the escaping heat from the kitchen. After two years, she was an achingly familiar figure, her boho clothes and her long salt-and-pepper hair comforting. As usual, she had her medicine bag in one hand and her big purse hanging off her opposite shoulder. Inside the medicine bag there was a standard-issue blood pressure cuff, a stethoscope, and some low-level medications—all of which Ehlena had seen put to use. Inside the purse there was the *New York Times*

crossword puzzle, some Wrigley's spearmint gum she liked
to chew, a wallet, and the peach lipstick she slipped across
her lips on a regular basis. Ehlena knew about the crossword puzzle because Lusie and her dad did them together,
the gum because of the wrappers that went into the trash,
and the lipstick was self-evident. She was guessing on the
wallet.

"How are you?" Lusie waited, her gray eyes clear and
focused. "You're back a little early."

"He stood me up."

The way Lusie's hand landed on Ehlena's shoulder was
what made the female a great nurse: With one touch she
conveyed comfort and warmth and empathy, all of which
worked to reduce blood pressure and heart rate and
agitation.

All of which helped the mind unscramble.

"I'm sorry," Lusie said.

"Oh, no, it's better this way. I mean, I'm looking for too
much."

"Really? You sounded pretty levelheaded to me when
you told me about it. You were just going for coffee—"

For some reason she spoke the truth: "Nope. I was looking for a way out. Which won't ever happen, because I will
never leave him." Ehlena shook her head. "Anyway, thank
you so much for coming—"

"It doesn't have to be an either-or situation. Your father
and you—"

"I really appreciate your coming early tonight. It was
good of you."

Lusie smiled in the way Catya had earlier in the evening,
tightly, sadly. "Okay, I'll drop it, but I'm right on this. You
can have a relationship and still be a good daughter to your
father." Lusie glanced over at the door. "Listen, you're going to have to watch that sore on his leg. The one he did on
that nail? I put a new dressing on, but I'm worried about it.
I think it's getting infected."

"I will, and thank you."

After Lusie dematerialized, Ehlena went into the
kitchen, locked the door and bolted it, and headed down to
the basement.

In his room, her father was asleep in his huge Victorian
bed, the massive carved headboard like the framing arch of

a tomb. His head was against a stack of white silk pillows, and the bloodred velvet duvet was folded precisely halfway down his chest.

He looked like a king in repose.

When the mental illness had really grabbed hold of him, his hair and beard had gone white, causing Ehlena to worry that the end-of-life changes were going to start in on him. But after fifty years, he still looked the same, his face unwrinkled, his hands strong and steady.

It was so hard. She couldn't imagine life without him. And she couldn't imagine having a life with him.

Ehlena closed his door partway and went into her own room, where she showered and changed and stretched out on her bed. All she had was a twin with no headboard, one pillow, and cotton sheets, but she didn't care about the luxury stuff. She needed a place to lay her tired bones each day and that was it.

Usually she read a little before falling asleep, but not today. She just didn't have the energy. Reaching to the side, she turned off the lamp, crossed her feet at the ankles, and laid her arms out straight.

With a smile, she realized she and her father slept in exactly the same position, didn't they.

In the dark, she thought about Lusie and the way she followed through about her father's cut. Good nursing was about being concerned for the welfare of patients, even after they left. It was about coaching family members as to what follow-up care was needed, and being a resource.

It wasn't the kind of job you just dumped because your shift was over.

She turned the lamp back on with a click.

Getting up, she went over to the desktop she'd gotten for free from the clinic when the IT systems had been upgraded. The Internet was slow to connect, as always, but eventually she was able to access the clinic's medical files database.

She signed in with her password, performed one search . . . then another. The first was a compulsion, the second a curiosity.

Saving them both, she shut down the laptop and picked up her phone.

ELEVEN

At the razor's edge of dawn, just before the light began to gather in the eastern sky, Wrath took form in the dense woods at the northern side of the Brotherhood's mountain. No one had showed back at Hunterbred, and the day's imminent rays had forced him to leave.

Small sticks cracked loudly under his shitkickers, the thin pine fingers brittle in the cold. There was not yet snow to muffle the sounds, but he could smell it in the air, feel that frosty bite deep in his sinuses.

The hidden entrance to the Black Dagger Brotherhood's sanctum sanctorum was at the ass end of a cave, far in the back. His hands located the trigger on the stone door by feel, and the heavy portal slid behind the rock wall. Stepping onto smooth black marble pavers, he followed them forward as the door closed behind him.

At his will, torches flamed up on either side of him, extending far, far, far into the distance and illuminating the massive iron gates that had been installed in the late eighteenth century, when the Brotherhood had turned this cave into the Tomb.

As he got closer, the gate's thick slats seemed to his blurry vision to be a lineup of armed sentries, the flickering flames animating what did not in fact move. With his mind, he parted the two halves and continued on, down a long hall fitted from floor to forty-foot ceiling with shelving.

Lesser jars of all types and kinds were stacked side by

side, a display that marked generations of kills made by the Brotherhood. The oldest jars were nothing but crude, hand-thrown vases that had been brought over from the Old Country. With each yard farther, the vessels grew more modern, until you got to the next set of gates and found mass-produced shit made in China and sold at Target.

There wasn't a lot of space left on the shelves and he was depressed by that. He had helped build with his own hands this repository of the enemy's dead, along with Darius and Tohrment and Vishous, the bunch of them laboring for a month straight, working during the day, sleeping on the marble pavers. He had been the one to decide how far down into the earth to go, and he had extended the shelving corridor yards and yards past what he had thought was needed. When he and his brothers had finished erecting everything, and had stacked the older jars, he'd been convinced that they wouldn't need so much storage space. Surely by the time they had filled even three-quarters of this, the war would be over.

And here he was, centuries later, trying to find enough room.

With a dreaded sense of portent, Wrath measured with his bad eyes the last remaining spaces on the original set of shelving. It was hard not to take it as evidence that the war was coming to an end, that the vampire equivalent of the finite Mayan calendar was on these rough-hewn stone walls.

It was not with victory's glow of success that he envisioned the final jar being set up next to the others.

They were either going to run out of race to protect or run out of Brothers to do the protecting.

Wrath took the three jars out of his jacket and placed them together in a little group; then he stepped back.

He had been responsible for a lot of these jars. Before he'd become king.

"I already knew that you have been out fighting."

Wrath's head shot around at the sound of the Scribe Virgin's commanding voice. Her Holiness was hovering just inside the iron gates, her black robes about a foot off the stone floor, her light shining out from beneath the hems.

It had once been blindingly bright, that glow of hers. Now it barely cast shadows.

Wrath turned back to the jars. "So that's what V meant. About pulling the trigger on me."

"My son came to me, yes."

"But you already knew. And that's not a question, by the way."

"Yeah, she hates those."

Wrath looked over and watched V step through the gates.

"Well, check this shit out," Wrath uttered. "The mother and son reunion . . . is only a moment away." He let the paraphrased lyric drift. "Not."

The Scribe Virgin came forward, moving slowly past the jars. Back in the old days—or, hell, as recently as the year before—she would have assumed control of the conversation. Now she just floated along.

V made a disgusted noise, like he'd waited long enough for his Mommie Dearest to no-more-wire-hanger his king, and wasn't impressed that she hadn't manned up. "Wrath, you didn't let me finish."

"And you think I will now?" He reached up and fingered the lip of one of the three jars he'd added to the collection.

"You will let him finish," the Scribe Virgin said, her tone disinterested.

Vishous strode forward, his shitkickers solid against the floor he himself had helped lay. "My point was, if you're going to go out, do it with backup. And tell Beth. Otherwise you're a liar . . . and you have a better chance of leaving her a widow. Damn it to hell, ignore my vision, fine. But at least be practical."

Wrath paced up and back, thinking that the setting for this convo was too fucking perfect: He was surrounded by evidence of the war.

Eventually, he stopped in front of the three jars he'd gotten tonight. "Beth thinks that I'm going upstate to meet with Phury. You know, to work with the Chosen. The lying sucks. But the idea we only have four Brothers in the field? Worse."

There was a long silence, during which the chattering flicker of the torch flames was the only sound.

V broke the quiet. "I think you need to have a meeting with the Brotherhood, and come clean with Beth. Like I said, if you're going to fight, fight. But do it with full disclosure, true? That way you're not out alone. And neither are any of us. Right now when rotation hits, someone ends up fighting without a partner. Your coming in legit would solve that."

Wrath had to smile. "Christ, if I'd thought you would agree with me, I might have said something sooner." He looked over at the Scribe Virgin. "But what about the laws. Tradition."

The mother of the race turned to face him and in a distant voice said, "So much has changed. What is one more. Be well, Wrath, son of Wrath, and Vishous of mine womb."

The Scribe Virgin disappeared like breath in the cold night, dissipating into the ether as if she'd never been.

Wrath leaned back against the shelving, and as his head started to pound, he popped up his sunglasses and rubbed his useless eyes. When he stopped, he shut his lids and grew as still as the stone that surrounded him.

"You look beat," V murmured.

Yes, he was, wasn't he. And how sad was that.

Drug dealing was a very lucrative business.

In his private office at ZeroSum, Rehvenge went over the night's receipts at his desk, meticulously checking off the amounts to the penny. iAm was doing the same over at Sal's Restaurant, and the first order of business at each nightfall was to meet here and compare results.

Most of the time they came up with the same total. When they didn't, he defered to iAm.

Between the alcohol, drugs, and sex, gross receipts were over two hundred and ninety thousand for ZeroSum alone. Twenty-two people worked at the club on salary, including ten bouncers, three bartenders, six prostitutes, Trez, iAm, and Xhex; costs for them all ran about seventy-five grand a night. Bookies and authorized floor dealers, meaning those drug pushers he allowed to sell on his premises, were on commission, and whatever was left after they'd taken their cut was his. Also, every week or so, he or Xhex and the Moors executed major product deals with a select number of distributors who had their own drug networks either in Caldwell or in Manhattan.

All told, and after personnel costs, he had roughly two

hundred thousand a night to pay the cost of the drugs and alcohol that he sold, cover heat and electricity and capital improvements, and take care of the cleaning crew of seven that came in at five a.m.

Every year he cleared about fifty million from his businesses—which sounded obscene, and it was, especially considering he paid taxes on only a fraction of it. The thing was, drugs and sex were risky businesses, but the profit potential was enormous. And he needed money. Badly. Keeping his mother in the lifestyle to which she was accustomed and well deserving of was a multimillion-dollar proposition. Then he had his own homes, and every year he traded his Bentley in as soon as the new models were available.

By far, however, the single highest personal expense he had came in small black velvet bags.

Rehv reached out over his spreadsheets and picked up the one that had been couriered up from the Big Apple's diamond district. The deliveries arrived on Mondays now—used to be the last Friday of the month, but with the Iron Mask opening up, ZeroSum's closed day had switched to Sundays.

He pulled the satin cord loose and opened the bag's throat, dumping out a glittering palmful of rubies. Quarter of a million dollars in blood stones. He poured them back into the pouch, tied the cording in a tight knot, and looked at his watch. About sixteen hours before he had to go up north.

First Tuesday of the month was ransom time, and he paid the princess off in two ways. One was gemstones. The other was his body.

He made it cost her, though.

The thought of where he was going and what he was going to have to do made the back of his neck tingle, and he wasn't surprised when his vision began to change, dark pinks and bloodreds replacing the blacks and whites of his office, his visual field bulldozing out into a flat plane.

Popping open a drawer, he took out one of his lovely new boxes of dopamine and grabbed the syringe he'd used the last couple of times he'd shot up in the office. Rolling up the sleeve of his left arm, he tourniqueted the middle of his biceps out of habit, not necessity. His veins were so swollen it was as if moles had burrowed under his skin, and he felt a stab of satisfaction at the mess they were in.

There was no cap on the needle's head to take off, and he filled the syringe's belly with the practice of a habitual user. It took him a while to find a vein that was viable, pushing the tiny steel shaft into himself again and again without feeling a thing. He knew he finally hit the right spot when he drew back on the plunger and saw blood mix with the clear solution of the drug.

As he freed the tourni and started to push his thumb home, he stared at the rot in his arm and thought of Ehlena. Even though she didn't trust him and didn't want to be attracted to him and would clearly move heaven and earth not to go out with him, she still wanted to be a savior. She still wanted what was best for him and his health.

That was what you called a female of worth.

He was halfway through the injection when his cell phone went off. A quick glance at the screen showed that the number wasn't one he recognized, so he let the call go. The only people who had his digits were ones he wanted to talk with, and that was a damn short list: his sister, his mother, Xhex, Trez, and iAm. And the Brother Zsadist, his sister's *hellren*.

That was it.

As he pulled the needle out of his vascular cesspool, he cursed as a beep indicated that voice mail had been left. He got those every once in a while, people leaving bits and pieces of their lives in his little corner of technospace, thinking it was someone else's. He never called them back, never texted them with a, *This is not who you think it is.* They'd figure it out when whoever they thought they were calling didn't return the favor.

Closing his eyes and easing back in his chair, he tossed the syringe onto the spreadsheets and couldn't care less if the drug worked.

Sitting alone in his den of iniquity, in the quiet hour after everyone had left and before the cleaning staff came in, he just didn't give a shit whether the flat plane of his vision returned to three dimensions. Didn't care if the full-color spectrum reappeared. Didn't wonder with each passing second whether or not he was going to get back to "normal."

This was a change, he realized. Up until now he'd always been desperate for the drug to work.

What had turned the tide?

He let the question hang as he picked up his cell phone and palmed his cane. With a groan, he stood up carefully and walked into his private bedroom. The numbness was coming back fast in his feet and legs, quicker than during the ride in from Connecticut, but then, that was par for the course. The less his *symphath* urges were triggered, the better the drug worked. And gee, funny, getting tapped to cap the king had riled him up.

Whereas sitting by himself in a home, of sorts, didn't.

The security system was already on in the office, and he triggered a second one for his private quarters, then shut himself in the windowless bedroom he crashed in from time to time. The bathroom was across the way and he dumped his sable duster on the bed before going in and turning the shower on. As he moved around, bone-deep cold settled into his body, emanating from the inside out, as if he'd injected himself with Freon.

This he did dread. He hated always being cold. Shit, maybe he should have just let himself go. It wasn't like he was going to be interacting with anyone.

Yeah, but if he got too far behind in his doses, the catch-up was a bitch.

Steam billowed free from behind the glass shower door, and he stripped naked, leaving his suit and tie and shirt on the marble counter between the two sinks. Stepping under the spray, he shivered hard, his teeth rattling.

For a moment, he collapsed back against the smooth marble walls, keeping himself in the center of the four showerheads. As hot water he couldn't feel cascaded down his chest and abs, he tried not to think about what the following night was bringing and failed.

Oh, God . . . did he have it in him to do it again? Go up there and whore himself out to that bitch?

Yeah, and the alternative was . . . her reporting him as a *symphath* to the council and getting his ass deported up to that colony.

The choice was clear.

Fuck that; there was no choice. Bella didn't know what he was, and it would kill her to find out the family lie. And she wouldn't be the only casualty. His mother would fall apart. Xhex would be livid and get herself murdered trying to save him. Trez and iAm would do the same.

The whole house of cards would fall.

Compulsively, he grabbed a bright gold bar of soap from the ceramic holder mounted on the wall and worked a froth up between his palms. The shit he used on himself wasn't some kind of fancy milled stuff. It was rotgut Dial, a disinfectant that was like a pavement grader over the skin.

His whores used the same. It was what he stocked in their shower rooms, at their request.

His rule was three times. Three times he went up and down his arms and his legs, his pecs and his abs, his neck and his shoulders. Three times he dipped between his thighs, soaping up his cock and sac. The ritual was stupid, but such were compulsions. He could have used up three dozen Dial bars and still felt vile.

Funny, his whores were always surprised at the way they got treated. Each time a new one came on, they expected to have to sex him up as part of their employment, and they were always prepared to be beaten. Instead, they got their own private dressing room with a shower, reliable hours, security that never, ever touched them, and this thing called respect—which meant they chose their johns, and if the fuckers who paid for the privilege of being with them messed up even a hair of theirs, all they had to do was say the word and a mountain of shit fell on the offender.

More than once, he'd had one of the women show up at his office door and ask to speak with him privately. It usually happened about a month into her tenure, and what she said was always the same and always spoken with a kind of confusion that, had he been a normal, would have broken his heart:

Thank you.

He wasn't big on hugging, but he'd been known to pull them into his arms and hold on to them for a short breath. None of them knew that it wasn't because he was a nice guy; it was because he was one of them. The hard reality was that life had put them all where they didn't want to be, namely on their backs for people they didn't want to be fucking. Yes, there were some who didn't mind the job, but like everyone, they didn't always want to be working. And God knew the johns always showed up.

Just like his blackmailer.

Getting out of the shower was pure, undiluted hell, and he put off the deep freeze as long as he could, huddling under the spray while he argued with himself over the evac. As the debate continued, he heard the water tinkling against the marble and chattering down the brass drain, but his numbed-out body felt nothing except a slight easing of his inner Alaska. When the hot water ran out, he knew only because his shivering got worse and the beds of his fingernails went from pale gray to deep blue.

He toweled off on the way to the bed and shot under the mink duvet as fast as he could.

Just as he was yanking the covers up to his throat, his phone beeped. Another voice mail.

Fucking Grand Central with his phone tonight.

Checking his missed calls, he found the latest was from his mother, and he sat up quickly, even though the vertical shift meant his chest went bare. Lady that she was, she never called, not wanting to "interrupt his work."

He hit some buttons, put in his password, and got ready to delete the wrong number's confused message which would come up first.

"Your call from 518-blah-blah-blah..." He hit the pound key to shoot past the ID shit and got ready to punch seven to get rid of the thing.

His finger was on the way down just as a female voice said, "Hi, I—"

That voice ... that voice was ... *Ehlena?*

"Fuck!"

Voice mail was inexorable, however, and didn't give a shit that a message from her was the last thing he'd choose to erase. As he cursed, the system churned on until he heard his mother's soft voice in the Old Language.

"Greetings, dearest son, I hope you fare well. Please excuse the intrusion, but I was wondering if you might stop by the house for a moment over the next couple of days? There is a matter about which I must speak to you. I love you. Good-bye, mine blooded firstborn."

Rehv frowned. So formal, the verbal equivalent of a

thoughtful note written in her beautiful hand, but the request was out of character, and that gave it an urgency. Except he was screwed—bad choice of words. Tomorrow evening was a no-go because of his "date," so it would have to be the night after, assuming he was well enough.

He called the house, and when one of her *doggen* picked up, he told the maid he'd be there Wednesday night as soon as the sun went down.

"Sire, if I may," the servant said. "Verily, I am glad you are coming."

"What's going on?" When there was a long pause, his inner chill got worse. "Talk to me."

"She is . . ." The voice on the other end grew rough. "She is as lovely as ever, but we are all glad you are coming. If you will excuse me, I shall deliver your message."

The line went dead. In the back of his mind, he had a sense as to what it was, but he studiously ignored the conviction. He just couldn't go there. Absolutely couldn't.

Besides, maybe it was nothing. Paranoia, after all, was a side effect of too much dopamine, and God knew he was doing more than his fair share. He would go to the safe house as soon as he was able, and she would be fine— Wait, the winter solstice. That had to be what it was. No doubt she wanted to plan festivities that included Bella and Z and the young, as it would be Nalla's first solstice ritual, and his mother took that kind of thing very seriously. She might live on this side, but the Chosen traditions she had been born into were still very much a part of her.

That was totally it.

Relieved, he put Ehlena's number into his addy book and hit her back.

All he could think about as the phone rang, aside from, *Pick up, pick up, pick up,* was that he hoped like hell she was okay. Which was nuts. Like she would ever call him if she were in trouble?

So why had she—

"Hello?"

The sound of her voice in his ear did something the hot shower, the mink throw, and the eighty-degree ambient air temperature couldn't. Warmth spread out from his chest, beating back the numbness and the cold, suffusing him with . . . life.

He extinguished the lights so he could concentrate all he had on her.

"Rehvenge?" she said after a moment.

He eased back down onto his pillows and smiled in the dark. "Hi."

TWELVE

There's blood on your shirt ... and—oh, God—your pant leg. Wrath, what happened?"

Standing in his study at the Brotherhood mansion, facing his beloved *shellan*, Wrath pulled the two halves of his biker jacket more tightly across his chest, and thought, well, at least he'd washed the *lesser* blood from his hands.

Beth's voice dropped. "How much of what I'm looking at is yours."

She was as beautiful as she had always been to him, the one female he wanted, the only mate for him. In her jeans and her black turtleneck, with her dark hair down around her shoulders, she was the most attractive thing he'd ever seen. Still.

"Wrath."

"Not all of it." The cut on his shoulder had no doubt leaked all over his wife-beater, but he'd held the civilian male to his chest as well, so the male's blood had no doubt mixed with his own.

Unable to keep still, he walked around the study, going from the desk to the windows and back. The rug his shit-kickers crossed was blue, gray, and cream, an Aubusson whose colors matched the pale blue walls and whose curvilinear swirls played off the delicate Louis XIV furniture, fixtures, and swirly moldings.

He'd never really appreciated the decor. And he didn't start now.

"Wrath . . . how did it get there." Beth's hard tone told him she knew the answer already, but was hoping there was another explanation.

Manning up, he turned to face the love of his life across the expanse of the frilly-ass room. "I'm fighting again."

"You're what?"

"I'm fighting."

As Beth went silent, he was glad the study door was closed. He saw the math she was doing in her head and knew the sum of what she was pulling together added up to one and only one thing: She was thinking about all those "nights up north" with Phury and the Chosen. All those times he'd worn long-sleeved, bruise-hiding shirts to bed because he had "a chill." All the "I'm limping because I worked out too hard" excuses.

"You're fighting." She plugged her hands into the pockets of her jeans, and even though he couldn't see a hell of a lot, he knew damn well that black turtleneck was a perfect complement to her stare. "Just to clarify. Is this as in, you're going to start fighting. Or have *been* fighting."

That was a rhetorical, but clearly she wanted him to present the full lie. "Have been. For the last couple of months."

Anger and hurt rolled off her, spilling toward him, smelling to him of scorched wood and burned plastic.

"Look, Beth, I have to—"

"You *have* to be honest with me," she said sharply. "That's what you have to do."

"I didn't expect to be going out for more than a month or two—"

"A month or two! How the hell long—" She cleared her throat and lowered her voice. "How long have you been doing this?"

When he told her, she went quiet again. Then, "Since August? August."

He wished she would let loose with her temper. Yell at him. Call him a cocksucker. "I'm sorry. I . . . Shit, I'm really sorry."

She didn't say anything else, and the scent of her emotions drifted away, dispersed by the hot air blowing up through the heating vents on the floor. Out in the hall, a *doggen* was vacuuming, the sound of the carpet attachment whirring up and back, up and back. In the silence between them, that normal, everyday sound was something he clung to—the kind of thing you heard all the time and rarely noticed because you were busy dealing with paperwork, or distracted by the fact that you were peckish, or trying to decide whether you wanted to decompress by watching TV or hitting the gym. . . . It was a safe sound.

And during this devastating moment in his mating, he hung on to the Dyson's lullaby with a death grip, wondering if he was ever going to be lucky enough to ignore it again.

"It never occurred to me . . ." She cleared her throat once more. "It never occurred to me that there was something you couldn't talk to me about. I've always assumed that you were telling me . . . everything you could."

As she stopped talking, he was chilled to the bone. Her voice was now the one she used to answer wrong numbers on the phone: She addressed him as if he were a stranger, without warmth or particular interest.

"Look, Beth, I have to be out there. I have to—"

She shook her head and raised her hand to stop him. "This isn't about you fighting."

Beth stared up at him for a heartbeat. Then she turned and went for the double doors.

"*Beth.*" Was that strangled croak his voice?

"No, leave me alone. I need some space."

"Beth, listen; we don't have enough fighters in the field—"

"It's not the fighting!" She wheeled around and faced off at him. "You lied to me. *Lied.* And not just once, but for four months straight."

Wrath wanted to argue, to defend himself, to point out that he'd lost track of time, that those 120 nights and days had flown by at the speed of light, that all he'd been doing was putting one foot in front of the other in front of the first, going minute by minute, hour by hour, trying to keep the race afloat, trying to keep the *lessers* back. He hadn't meant it to go on for so long. He hadn't set out to deceive her for that long.

"Just answer me one thing," she said. "One thing. And it had better be the truth or, so help me, God, I'm going to . . ." She put her palm to her mouth, catching a soft sob in her gentle hand. "Honestly, Wrath ... did you honestly think you were going to stop? In your heart, did you truly think you were going to—"

He swallowed hard as her words choked off.

Wrath took a deep breath. In the course of his life, he had been wounded many, many times. But nothing, no pain ever inflicted upon him, hurt a fraction of what answering her felt like.

"No." He inhaled again. "No, I don't think ... I was going to stop."

"Who talked to you tonight. Who was the one who made you decide to tell me."

"Vishous."

"I should have known. He's probably the only person other than Tohr who could have. ..." Beth crossed her arms around herself, and he would have given his dagger hand to have him being the one holding her. "Your being out there fighting scares the shit out of me, but you forget something. ... I mated you without knowing that the king isn't supposed to be in the field. I was prepared to stand by you even though it terrified me ... because fighting in this war is in your nature and in your blood. You fool—" Her voice cracked. "You fool, I would have let you do it. But instead—"

"Beth—"

She cut him off. "Remember that night you went out at the beginning of the summer? When you stepped in to save Z and then stayed downtown and fought with the others?"

He sure as hell did. When he'd come back home, he'd chased her up the stairs and they'd had sex on the rug in the second-floor sitting room. A number of times. He'd kept the cutoffs he'd ripped from her hips as a souvenir.

Jesus ... come to think of it ... that was the last time they had been together.

"You told me only for one night," she said. "One night. Only. You swore to it, and I trusted you."

"Shit ... I'm sorry."

"Four months." She shook her head, her gorgeous dark hair swinging around her shoulders, catching the light so beautifully even his piss-poor eyes registered its glory. "You know what hurts the most? That the Brothers knew and I didn't. I've always accepted this secret-society stuff, understood that there are things I can't know—"

"They didn't have a clue either." Okay, Butch had known, but there was no reason to throw him under the bus. "V only found out tonight."

She wobbled, steadying herself against the pale blue walls. "You've been going out *alone*?"

"Yes." He reached out for her arm, but she tore it away from him. "Beth—"

She yanked open the door. *"Don't touch me."*

The thing clapped shut behind her.

Rage at himself had Wrath spinning toward his desk, and the instant he saw all the papers, all the requests, all the complaints, all the problems, it was like someone hooked jumper cables up to his shoulder blades and hit him with a charge. He shot forward, swept his arms across the top, and sent the shit flying everywhere.

As papers fluttered down like snow, he took off his sunglasses and rubbed his eyes, a headache spearing into his frontal lobe. Robbed of breath, he stumbled around, finding his chair by feel and collapsing into the damn thing. With a ragged grunt, he let his head fall back. These stress headaches were becoming a daily occurrence lately, wiping him out and lingering like a flu that refused to be cured.

Beth. His Beth . . .

When he heard a knock, he gave the f-word a workout.

The knock came again.

"What," he barked.

Rhage put his head around the jamb, then froze. "Ah . . ."

"What."

"Yeah, well . . . Ah, going by the door slamming—and, wow, the stiff wind that clearly just blew by your desk—do you still want to meet with us?"

Oh, God . . . how was he going to get through another one of these conversations.

Then again, maybe he should have thought about that before he'd decided to lie to his nearest and dearest.

"My lord?" Rhage's voice became gentle. "Do you want to see the Brotherhood?"

No. "Yes."

"You need Phury on speakerphone?"

"Yeah. Listen, I don't want the boys in this meeting. Blay, John, Qhuinn . . . they're not invited."

"Figured. Hey, how about I help you clean up?"

Wrath looked down at the carpet of paperwork. "I'll deal with it."

Hollywood proved he had half a brain by not offering again or pulling an are-you-sure. He just ducked out and shut the door.

Across the way, the grandfather clock in the corner tolled. It was yet another familiar sound Wrath didn't hear on a regular basis, but now, as he sat alone in the study, the chimes rang out as if they were broadcast over concert speakers.

He dropped his hands onto the arms of the spindly, fragile chair, and they dwarfed the supports. The piece of furniture was more on the scale of something a female would perch on to take off her stockings at the end of the night.

It was not a throne. Which was why he used it.

He hadn't wanted to accept the crown on many levels, having been king by birthright but not inclination or actuality for three hundred years. But then Beth had come along and things had changed and he'd finally gone to the Scribe Virgin.

That had been two years ago. Two springs and two summers and two autumns and two winters.

He'd had great plans back then, in the beginning. Great, wonderful plans for bringing the Brotherhood together, getting everyone under one roof, consolidating forces, shoring up against the Lessening Society. Winning.

Saving.

Reclaiming.

Instead, the *glymera* had been slaughtered. More civilians were dead. And there were even fewer Brothers.

They hadn't made progress. They'd lost ground.

Rhage poked his head in again. "We're all still out here."

"Goddamn it, I told you I needed some—"

The grandfather clock chimed again, and as Wrath listened to the number of beats, he realized he'd been sitting by himself for an hour.

He rubbed his aching eyes. "Give me another minute."

"Whatever you need, my lord. Just take your time."

THIRTEEN

As Rehvenge's *hi* came through the phone, Ehlena sat up from the pillow she'd been lying against and swallowed back a *holy crap* . . . except then she wondered why she was so surprised. She'd called him, and the textbook way people handled those kind of things was . . . well, hey, they called you back. Wow.

"Hi," she said.

"I didn't answer your call only because I didn't know the number."

Man, his voice was sexy. Deep. Low. Like a male's should be.

In the silence that followed, she thought, *and she had called him why?* Oh, right. "I wanted to follow up about your appointment. When I did your discharge papers, I noticed that you received nothing for your arm."

"Ah."

The pause that followed was one she couldn't interpret. Maybe he was pissed she was interfering? "I just want to make sure you're okay."

"Do you do this with patients a lot?"

"Yes," she lied.

"Havers know you're checking his work?"

"Did he even look at your veins?"

Rehvenge's laugh was low. "I would rather you had called for a different reason."

"I don't understand," she said tightly.

"What? That someone might want to have something to do with you outside of work? You're not blind. You've seen yourself in mirrors. And surely you know you're smart, so it's not all just pretty window dressing."

As far as she was concerned, he was speaking in a foreign language. "I don't understand why you're not taking care of yourself."

"Hmmm." He laughed softly, and she felt the purr as well as heard it in her ear. "Oh . . . so maybe this is a pretense just so I can see you again."

"Look, the only reason I called was—"

"Because you needed an excuse. You shut me down in the exam room, but really wanted to talk to me. So you called about my arm to get me on the phone. And now you have me." That voice dropped even lower. "Do I get to pick what you do with me?"

She stayed quiet. Until he said, "Hello?"

"Are you finished? Or do you want to run around in circles a little longer, reading into what I'm doing here?"

There was a beat of silence, and then he broke out in a rich baritone belly laugh. "I knew there was more than one reason I liked you."

She refused to be charmed. And was anyway. "I called about your arm. Period. My father's nurse just left, and she and I were talking about his . . ."

She clammed up as she realized what she'd revealed, feeling like she'd tripped on the conversational equivalent of an untacked carpet edge.

"Go on," he said with gravity. "Please.

"Ehlena? Ehlena . . .

"Are you there, Ehlena?"

Later, much later, she would reflect that those four words were the precipice. *Are you there, Ehlena?*

Truly it was the beginning of everything that followed, the starting line of a harrowing journey disguised in the form of a simple question.

She was glad she didn't know where it would take her. Because sometimes the only thing that got you through hell was that you were in too deep to pull out.

While Rehv waited for a response, his fist tightened on the cell phone so hard, it cranked in toward his cheek and one of the keys let out a beep of, *Hey, man, lay off a little.*

The electronic curse seemed to break the spell for them both.

"Sorry," he muttered.

"It's okay. I, ah . . ."

"You were saying?"

He didn't expect her to answer, but then . . . she did. "My father's nurse and I were talking about a cut he's having trouble with, and that's what made me think of your arm."

"Your father is ill?"

"Yes."

Rehv waited for more, trying to decide whether prompting her would shut her up—but she solved the issue.

"Some of the medications he takes make him unsteady, so he bumps into things and doesn't always know he's hurt himself. It's a problem."

"I'm sorry. Caring for him must be hard on you."

"I'm a nurse."

"And a daughter."

"So it was clinical. When I called you."

Rehv smiled. "Let me ask you something."

"Me first. Why won't you get your arm looked at? And don't tell me Havers saw those veins. If he had, he would have prescribed you antibiotics, and if you refused them there would have been a note in your chart that you'd pulled an AMA. Look, all you need to treat it is some pills, and I know you're not medicine phobic. You take a hell of a lot of dopamine."

"If you were worried about my arm, why didn't you just talk to me at the clinic?"

"I did, remember."

"Not like this." Rehv smiled in the dark and ran his hand up and down the mink duvet. He couldn't feel it, but he imagined the pelts were as soft as her hair. "I still think you wanted to get me on the phone."

The pause that followed made him worry she was going to pull out of the call.

He sat up, like getting vertical would keep her from hitting her *end* button. "I'm only saying . . . well, shit, my point is, I'm glad you called. Whatever the reason."

"I didn't talk to you at the clinic about it any further because you left before I entered Havers's notes into the computer. That's when it all sank in."

He still wasn't buying that the call was completely professional. She could have e-mailed him. She could have told the doctor. Could have turfed it to one of the day nurses to follow up.

"So there's no chance you feel bad for slamming me down as hard as you did?"

She cleared her throat. "I am sorry for that."

"Well, I forgive you. Totally. Completely. You looked like you were not having a great night."

Her exhale was exhaustion made manifest. "Yeah, it wasn't my best."

"Why?"

Another long pause. "You are much better over the phone, you know that?"

He laughed. "Much better how?"

"Easier to talk to. You're actually . . . pretty easy to talk to."

"I do okay with the one-on-one."

Abruptly he frowned, thinking of the bookie he'd tuned up out in the office. Shit, that poor bastard was just one in a huge number of drug dealers and Vegas lackeys and bartenders and pimps he'd beaten into conversating over the years. His philosophy had always been that confession was good for the soul, especially when it came to scumbags who thought he wouldn't notice they were fucking him. His management style also sent an important message in a business where weakness got you killed: Back-alley commerce required a strong hand, and he'd always believed that was just the reality in which he lived.

Now though, in this quiet time, with Ehlena so close, he felt like his "one-on-ones" were something to apologize for and conceal.

"So why was tonight not so good?" he asked, desperate to shut himself the fuck up.

"My father. And then . . . well, I got stood up."

Rehv frowned so hard he actually felt a slight sting between his eyes. "For a date?"

"Yeah."

He hated the idea of her out with another male. And yet

envied the motherfucker, whoever he was. "What an ass. I'm sorry, but what an ass."

Ehlena laughed, and he loved everything about the sound, especially the way his body warmed a little more in response. Man, to hell with a hot shower. That soft, quiet chuckle was what he needed.

"Are you smiling," he said softly.

"Yeah. I mean, I guess. How did you know?"

"Was just hoping you were."

"Well, you can be kind of charming." Quickly, as if to cover up the compliment, she said, "The date wasn't a big deal or anything. I didn't know him that well. It was just coffee."

"But you ended the night on the phone with me. Which is so much better."

She laughed again. "Well, I won't ever know what it's like to go out with him."

"You won't?"

"I just . . . well, I thought about it, and I don't think dating is a good idea for me right now." His surge of triumph was sacked when she tacked on, "With anyone."

"Hm."

"Hm? What does *hm* mean?"

"It means I have your phone number."

"Ah, yes, you do—" Her voice caught as he shifted around. "Wait, are you . . . in bed?"

"Yeah. And before you go any farther, you don't want to know."

"I don't want to know what?"

"How much I'm not wearing."

"Er . . ." As she hesitated, he knew she was smiling again. And probably blushing. "I so won't ask."

"Wise of you. It's just me and the sheets—oops, did I just spill that?"

"Yes. Yes, you did." Her voice got a little lower, as if she were imagining him naked. And not minding the mental pinup in the slightest.

"Ehlena . . ." He stopped himself, his *symphath* urges giving him the self-control to slow down. Yes, Rehv wanted her as naked as he was. But even more than that, he wanted her on the phone.

"What?" she said.

"Your father . . . has he been ill for long?"

"I, ah . . . yes, yes, he has. He's schizophrenic. We've got him on meds now, though, and he's better."

"God . . . damn. That's got to be really difficult. Because he's there but he's not there, right."

"Yes . . . that's exactly what it feels like."

It was kind of the way he went through life, his *symphath* side a constant, other reality that dogged him as he tried to get through the nights as a normal.

"So do you mind if I ask," she said with care, "what you need the dopamine for? There's no immediate diagnosis in your medical record."

"Probably because Havers has been treating me forever."

Ehlena laughed awkwardly. "Guess that must be why."

Shit, what the hell did he tell her.

The *symphath* in him said, *Whatever, just lie to her.* Trouble was, from out of nowhere there was another competing voice in his brain, one that was unfamiliar and faint, but utterly compelling. Because he had no idea what it was, however, he led with his routine.

"I have Parkinson's. Or the vampire equivalent of it, as it were."

"Oh . . . I'm sorry. That's the cane you use, then."

"My balance is bad."

"The dopamine's doing you well, though. You have almost no tremors."

That quiet voice in his head morphed into an odd ache in the center of his chest, and for a moment he dropped pretense and actually spoke the truth. "I have no idea what I would do without that drug."

"My father's medications have been a miracle."

"Are you his sole caretaker?" When she *mm-hm*ed, he asked, "Where is the rest of your family?"

"It's just him and me."

"So you're carrying a hell of a burden."

"Well, I love him. And if the roles were reversed, he would do the same. It's what parents and children do for each other."

"Not always. Clearly you come from good people." Before he could stop himself, he continued, "But that's why you're lonely, isn't it. You get guilty if you leave him even for an hour, except if you stay home you can't ignore the fact that your life is passing you by. You're trapped and screaming, but you wouldn't change a thing."

"I have to go."

Rehv squeezed his eyes shut, that ache in his chest spreading through his whole body like wildfire across dry grass. He willed a light on as the darkness became too symbolic of his own existence.

"It's just . . . I know what it's like, Ehlena. Not for the same reasons . . . but I get that whole separated thing. You know, the idea that you're watching everybody else go through life. . . . Oh, fuck, whatever. I hope you sleep well—"

"That is how I feel a lot of the time." Her voice was gentle now, and he was glad she got what he'd been trying to say, even though he'd been as eloquent as an alley cat.

Now he was the one who grew awkward. He wasn't used to talking like this . . . or feeling as he did. "Listen, I'm going to let you get some rest. I'm glad you called."

"You know . . . so am I."

"And, Ehlena?"

"Yes?"

"I think you're right. It's not a good idea for you to get involved with anyone right now."

"Really?"

"Yup. Good day."

There was a pause. "Good . . . day. Wait—"

"What?"

"Your arm. What are you going to do about your arm?"

"Don't worry, it'll be fine. But thank you for the concern. It means a lot."

Rehv hung up first and put the phone down on the mink duvet. Closing his eyes, he left the light on. And didn't sleep at all.

FOURTEEN

Back at the Brotherhood compound, Wrath gave up the idea that he was going to feel better about the situation with Beth anytime soon. Hell, he could spend the next month stewing on his spindly chair, but that would only get him a numb ass.

And meanwhile, the rolling stones out in the hall were getting mossy and cranky.

He willed the double doors wide and as a unit his brothers came to attention. As he looked across the pale blue expanse of the study to their big, hard bodies out by the balcony, he knew them not by face or clothing or expression, but by the echo of each one in his blood.

The ceremonies in the Tomb that had bound them all together resonated no matter how long ago they had been done.

"Don't just stand there," he said as the Brotherhood stared back at him. "I didn't open those fuckers to turn myself into a zoo exhibit."

The brothers came in on their heavy boots—except for Rhage, who was in flip-flops, his standard house footwear no matter the season. Each of the warriors took up his usual station in the room, with Z going over to stand by the fireplace and V and Butch parking it on a recently reinforced pencil-legged sofa. Rhage came over to the desk in a series of *flip-flip-flips* and hit *speaker* on the phone, letting his fingers do the walking to get Phury on the horn.

No one said anything about all the papers on the floor. No one tried to pick them up. It was as if the mess weren't there, and that was how Wrath preferred it.

As he shut the doors with his mind, he thought of Tohr. The brother was in the house, just down the hall of statues by only a few doors, but he was on a different continent. Inviting him wasn't an option—more like a cruelty, given where his head was at.

"Hello?" came Phury's voice out of the phone.

"We're all here," Rhage said before unwrapping a Tootsie Pop and *flip-flip-flip*ping it over to an ugly-ass green armchair.

The monstrosity was Tohr's, moved up from the office for John Matthew to sleep in back after Wellsie had been murdered and Tohrment had disappeared. Rhage tended to use the thing because at his weight, it was really the safest option for his ass, steel-bolted sofas included.

With everyone settled, the room went quiet except for the crunching grind of Hollywood's molars on that cherry thing he had in his piehole.

"Oh, for fuck's sake," Rhage finally groaned around his lollipop. "Just tell us. Whatever it is. I'm getting ready to scream over here. Is someone dead?"

No, but it sure as shit felt like he'd killed something.

Wrath glanced in the brother's direction, then looked at each one of them. "I'm going to be your partner, Hollywood."

"Partner? As in . . ." Rhage glanced around the room as if checking to see whether everyone else had heard what he had. "You ain't talking about gin rummy, are you."

"No," Z said quietly. "I don't believe he is."

"Holy. Shit." Rhage took another lollipop out of the pocket of his black fleece. "Is this legal?"

"It is now," V muttered.

Phury spoke up from the phone. "Wait, wait . . . is this to replace me?"

Wrath shook his head even though the Brother couldn't see him. "It's to replace a lot of people we've lost."

Conversation bubbled up like a can of Coke had just been cracked open. Butch, V, Z, Rhage all started talking at once until a tinny voice cut through the chatter:

"I want to come back, too, then."

Everyone looked at the phone—except for Wrath, who stared over at Z in order to gauge the guy's reaction. Zsadist had no trouble showing anger. Ever. But he hid concern and worry like the stuff was loose money and he was surrounded by muggers: As his twin's statement resonated, he was in full self-protection mode, tightening up, emitting absolutely nothing in terms of emotion.

Ah, right, Wrath thought. The tough-skinned bastard was scared cockless.

"You sure that's a good idea," Wrath said slowly. "Maybe fighting isn't what you need right now, my brother."

"I haven't toked up in nearly four months," Phury said through the speaker. "And I've got no plans to go back to the drugging."

"Stress won't make that shit any easier."

"Oh, but sitting on my ass while you're out there will?"

Wonderful. The king and the Primale in the field for the first time in history. And why? Because the Brotherhood was on its last gasp.

Great record to break there. Kind of like winning the fifty-meter ass-stroke in the Loser-lympics.

Christ.

Except then Wrath thought of that dead civilian. Was that a better outcome? No.

Leaning back in his delicate chair, he stared hard at Z.

As if he felt the eyes on him, Zsadist stepped free of the mantel and stalked around the study. They all knew what he was picturing: Phury ODed on a bathroom floor, an empty heroin syringe next to him on the tile.

"Z?" came Phury's voice over the phone. "Z? Pick up the handset."

When Zsadist got on with his twin, his face, with its jagged scar, drew into such a nasty frown even Wrath could see the glare. And the expression didn't improve as he said, "Uh-huh. Yeah. Uh-huh. I know. Right." There was a long, long pause. "No, I'm still here. Okay. All right."

Pause. "Swear to me. On my daughter's life."

After a moment, Z hit the speaker again, put the handset back in place, and returned to the fireplace.

"I'm in," Phury said.

Wrath shifted in the pansy chair, wishing so many things were different. "You know, maybe in another time, I might have told you to back off. Now, I'll just say . . . When can you start."

"Nightfall. I'll leave Cormia in charge of the Chosen while I'm out in the field."

"Your female going to be tight with this?"

There was a pause. "She knows who she mated. And I'm going to be honest with her."

Ouch.

"Now I have a question," Z said softly. "It's about the dried blood on your shirt, Wrath."

Wrath cleared his throat. "I've been back for a while now, actually. With the fighting."

The temperature in the room dropped. Which was Z and Rhage getting pissed off that they hadn't known.

And then suddenly, Hollywood cursed. "Wait . . . wait. You two knew . . . you knew before us, didn't you. 'Cause neither of you look surprised."

Butch cleared his throat like he was getting glared at. "He needed me on cleanup. And V's tried to change his mind."

"How long ago did this start, Wrath?" Rhage bit out.

"Since Phury stopped fighting."

"Are you kidding me."

Z stalked over to one of the floor-to-ceiling windows, and even though the shutters were down, he stared at the thing as if he could see the grounds beyond. "Good goddamn thing you didn't get yourself killed out there."

Wrath bared his fangs. "You think I fight like a pussy just because I'm behind this desk now?"

Phury's voice rose up from the phone. "Okay, everyone just relax. We all know now, and things are going to be different going forward. No one's going to fight alone, even if we go in threes. But I need to know, is this going to be common knowledge? Are you going to announce it at the council meeting the night after tomorrow?"

Man, that happy little face-to-face was not something he was looking forward to. "I think we'll keep it quiet for now."

"Yeah," Z bit out, " 'cuz really, why be honest."

Wrath ignored that. "I'm going to tell Rehvenge, though. I know there are members of the *glymera* who are grumbling about the raids. If it gets to be too much, he'll be able to calm things down with that kind of intel."

"Are we done here," Rhage said in a flat tone.

"Yeah. That's it."

"I'm outtie then."

Hollywood stalked from the room, and Z was right behind him, two more casualties of the bomb Wrath had dropped.

"So how'd Beth take it?" V asked.

"How do you think." Wrath got to his feet and followed the example set by the pair who had left.

Time to go find Doc Jane and get stitched up, assuming the slices hadn't already closed.

He needed to be ready to go out and fight again tomorrow.

In the cold, bright morning light, Xhex dematerialized past a high wall and into the bare branches of a stout maple tree. The mansion beyond rested in its landscaped acreage like a gray pearl in a filigree setting, wiry winter-stripped specimen trees rising up around the old stone manse, anchoring it to its rolling lawn, holding it to the earth.

The weak December sun poured down, making what would have been dour at night seem merely venerable and distinguished.

Her sunglasses were nearly black, the one concession she needed to make to her vampire side if she went out during the day. Behind the lenses, her vision remained acute, and she saw every motion detector and every security light and every leaded-glass window that was covered by a shutter.

Getting in was going to be a challenge. The panes of those fuckers were no doubt reinforced with steel, which meant dematerializing in even if the shutters were up was a no-go. And with her *symphath* side, she sensed there were a lot of people inside: The staff in the kitchen. The ones sleeping upstairs. The others moving around. It was not a happy house, the emotional grids left by the people inside full of dark, heavy feelings.

Xhex dematerialized to the roof of the main section of the mansion, throwing out a *symphath* version of *mhis*. It wasn't a complete erase, more like she became a shadow among the shadows thrown by the chimneys and the HVAC shit, but it was enough to buy her a pass of the motion detectors.

Approaching a ventilation duct, she found a steel mesh plate thick as a ruler that was bolted into the metal sidewalls. Chimney was the same. Capped with stout steel.

Not a shocker. They had very good security here.

Her best shot at penetration was going to be at night, using a small, battery-operated Sawzall against one of the windows. The servants' quarters in the back would be a good place for entry, given that the staff would be on duty and that part of the house would be quieter.

Get in. Find the target. Eliminate.

The instructions from Rehv were to leave a loud corpse, so she wouldn't bother hiding or disposing of the body.

As she walked across the small pebbles that covered the roof, the cilices around her thighs bit into her muscles with each step, the pain draining her of a measure of energy and providing a necessary focus—both of which helped keep her *symphath* urges chained in her brain's backyard.

The barbed strips would not be on when she went out to do the job.

Xhex paused and looked up at the sky. The dry, slicing wind promised snow, and soon. Winter's deep freeze was coming to Caldwell.

But had been in her heart for ages.

Down beneath her, under her feet, she sensed the people again, reading their emotions, feeling them. She would kill them all if she was asked to. Slaughter them without thought or hesitation as they lay in their beds or went about their staff duties or copped a midday snack or rose for a quick piss before going back to sleep.

The messy, sloppy residue of demise, all that blood, didn't bother her, either, any more than an H&K or a Glock would give a shit about carpet stains or smudges on tile or leaking arteries. The color red was the only thing she saw when she went about her work, and besides, after a while all bulging, horrified eyes and mouths that choked on last breaths looked the same anyway.

That was the great irony. In life, everyone was a snowflake of separate and beautiful proportion, but when death came in and grabbed hold, you were left with anonymous skin and muscle and bone, all of which cooled and decayed at predictable rates.

She was the gun attached to her boss's forefinger. He

pulled her trigger, she shot, the body dropped, and in spite of the fact that some lives were forever changed, the sun still came up and went down the next day for everyone else on the planet, including her.

Such was the course of her jobligation, as she thought of it: half employment, half obligation for what Rehv did to protect them both.

When she returned to this place at nightfall, she would do what she was there to do and leave with a conscience as intact and secure as a bank vault.

In and out and never to be thought of again.

Such was the way and the life of an assassin.

FIFTEEN

Allies were the third prong in the wheel of war.

Resources and recruits gave you the tactical engine that allowed you to meet, engage, and reduce the size and strength of your enemies' forces. Allies were your strategic advantage, people whose interests were aligned with your own, even if your philosophies and ultimate goals might not intersect. They were just as important as the first two if you wanted to win, but they were a little less controllable.

Unless you knew how to negotiate.

"We been drivin' for a while," Mr. D said from behind the wheel of Lash's adoptive dead father's Mercedes.

"And we're going to drive a little longer." Lash glanced at his watch.

"You ain't told me where we're going."

"Nope. I haven't, have I."

Lash stared out the sedan's window. The trees at the side of the Northway looked like pencil drawings before the leafy bits had been sketched in, nothing but barren oaks and spindly maples and twiggy birches. The only thing with any green were the stumpy coniferous stalwarts, the numbers of which had been increasing as they went farther into the Adirondack Park.

Gray sky. Gray highway. Gray trees. It was like New York State's landscape had come down with the flu or some shit, looking about as healthy as someone who hadn't had his pneumonia shot in time.

There were two reasons Lash hadn't been up-front about where he and his second in command were headed. The first was straight-up pussy, and he could barely admit it to himself: He wasn't sure whether he was going to go through with the meeting he'd set up.

The issue was that this ally was complicated, and Lash knew he was poking a hornet's nest with a stick by even approaching them. Yes, there was potential for a great alliance, but if loyalty was a good attribute in a soldier, it was mission critical in an ally, and where they were headed, loyalty was as unknown a concept as fear. So he was kind of fucked on both ends and that was why he wasn't talking. If the meeting didn't go well, or his sniff test didn't work, he wasn't going to proceed, and in that case, Mr. D didn't have to know the ins and outs of who they were dealing with.

The other reason Lash was tight-lipped was because he wasn't certain whether the other party was going to show. In which case, he again didn't want a record of what he'd been contemplating.

At the side of the road, a small green sign with white reflective print read: U.S. BORDER 38.

Yup, thirty-eight miles and you were out of the country . . . and that was why the *symphath* colony had been located all the way up here. The goal had been to get those psychotic motherfuckers as far away from the civilian vampire population as you could, and goal accomplished. Any closer to Canada and you'd have to say *fuck off and die* to them in French.

Lash had made contact thanks to his adoptive father's old Rolodex, which, like the male's car, had proven very useful. As a former *leahdyre* of the council, Ibix had had a way of contacting the *symphaths* in the event that one was found hiding in the general population and needed to be deported. Of course, diplomacy between the species had never been in the cards. That would have been like offering a serial killer not only your own exposed throat, but the Henckels to cut it with.

Lash's e-mail to the king of the *symphaths* had been short and sweet, and in the brief rundown, he identified himself as who he really was, not who he'd been raised to think himself to be: He was Lash, head of the Lessening Society. Lash, son of the Omega. And he was seeking an alliance against the vampires that had discriminated against and shunned the *symphaths*.

Surely the king wanted to avenge the disrespect showed to his people?

The response he'd received had been so gracious he'd nearly hurled, but then he recalled from his training days that *symphaths* treated everything like a chess match— right down to the moment they captured your king, turned your queen into a whore, and burned down your castles. The reply from the colony's leader had indicated that a collegial discussion of mutual interest would be welcome, and would Lash be so kind as to come up north, as the exiled king's travel options, by definition, were limited.

Lash had taken the car because he'd imposed a condition of his own, and that was Mr. D's attendance. Truth was, he put out the requirement for no other reason than equity of demands. They wanted him to come to them; fine, he was bringing one of his men. And as the *lesser* couldn't dematerialize, the drive was necessary.

Five minutes later, Mr. D took an exit off the highway and eased through an urban center the size of just one of Caldwell's seven city parks. Here there were no skyscrapers, just four- and five-story brick buildings, such that it seemed as if the harsh winter months had stunted the growth not only of the trees, but the architecture as well.

At Lash's direction, they headed west, passing leafless apple orchards and fenced-in cow farms.

As he had on the highway, he ate up the scenery. It was still amazing to him to be witness to milky December sunlight throwing shadows on sidewalks or house roofs or over the brown ground beneath barren tree limbs. Upon his rebirth, he had been given purpose anew from his true father, along with this gift of daylight, and he enjoyed both immensely.

The Mercedes' GPS conked out a couple minutes later, the reading going all-over wonky. He figured this meant they were getting close to the colony, and sure enough the road they were looking for presented itself. Ilene Avenue was marked by only a tiny street sign. And avenue, his ass; it was nothing but a dirt lane that intersected cornfields.

The sedan did its best over the uneven trail, its shocks absorbing the craters created by puddles, but the trip would

have been easier in a fucking four-wheeler. Eventually,
though, a thick collar of trees appeared in the distance, and
the farmhouse that formed the head around which they
were crowded was in pristine condition, all brilliant white
with dark green shutters and a dark green roof. Like something off a human's Christmas card, smoke eased from two
of its four chimneys, and the porch was set with rocking
chairs and evergreen topiaries.

As they drew closer, they passed a discreet sign in white
and dark green that read: TAOIST MONASTICAL ORDER, EST.
1982.

Mr. D brought the Mercedes to a halt, killed the engine,
and made the sign of the cross over his chest. Which was so
fucking dumb. "This don't feel right."

The thing was, the little Texan had a point. In spite of the
fact that the front door was open with sunlight spilling onto
warm cherry floorboards, something wrong lurked behind
the homey facade. It was just too perfect, too calculated to
set a person at ease and thus weaken his defensive instincts.

This was a pretty girl with an STD, Lash thought.

"Let's go," he said.

They both got out, and whereas Mr. D palmed his Magnum, Lash didn't bother to reach for his gun. His father had
given him many tricks, and unlike those instances when he
dealt with humans, he had no problem bringing out his special skills in front of a *symphath*. If anything, putting on a
show might help them see him in his proper light.

Mr. D positioned his cowboy hat. "This really don't feel
right."

Lash narrowed his eyes. Lace curtains hung in front of
every one of the windows, but as Clorox bright as the fabric
was, the shit was creepy. . . . Whoa, was it moving?

At that moment, he realized it wasn't lace, but spider-
webs. Populated by white arachnids.

"Them's . . . spiders?"

"Yup." Wouldn't be Lash's decor choice, for real, but he
didn't have to live here.

The two of them paused at the first of the three steps
up onto the front porch. Man, some open doors were
not welcoming, and that was so the case here—less *hi-
how're-ya*,more*come-in-so-your-skin-can-be-used-to-make-a-
superhero-cape-for-one-of-Hannibal-Lecter's-patients*.

Lash grinned. Whoever was in this house was so his peeps.

"You be wantin' me to go up and ring the doorbell?" Mr. D said. "If there is one?"

"Nope. We wait. They will come to us."

And what do you know, someone appeared at the far end of the front hall.

What came down toward them had enough robes hanging from its head and shoulders to give a Broadway stage a run for its money. The fabric was an odd, shimmering white, one that caught the light and refracted it in the thick folds, and the weight of it all was captured by a stout brocaded white belt.

Very impressive. If you were into the monarch-as-priest thing.

"Greetings, friend," came a low, seductive voice. "I am the one whom you seek, the leader of those cast away."

The Ss were strung out until they were almost their own words, the accent sounding a lot like the warning tremble of a rattler's tail.

A thrill went through Lash, tingling down into his cock. Power was, after all, better than Ecstasy as a turn-on, and this thing that came to stand between the jambs of the front door was all about authority.

Long, elegant hands reached up to the hood and eased the white folds back. The face of the *symphaths'* anointed leader was as smooth as his spectacular robing, the planes of the cheeks and chin cast in elegant, soft angles. The gene pool that had spawned this gorgeous, effete killer was so refined that the sexes were almost as one, male and female characteristics blending, with a preference toward the female.

The smile was stone-cold, though. And the flashing red eyes were shrewd to the point of malevolence.

"Won't you please come in?"

The snake's lovely voice blended those words into one another, and Lash found himself liking the sound.

"Yeah," he said, making his mind up on the spot. "We will."

As he stepped forward, the king raised his palm.

"One moment, if you will. Please tell your associate to fear not. Nothing will harm you here." The statements were

kind enough on the surface, but the tone was hard—which
Lash took to mean that they weren't welcome in the house
if Mr. D's heat was in his hand.

"Put the gun away," Lash said softly. "I've got us covered."

Mr. D holstered the .357, his *y'sir* unspoken, and the
symphath moved out of the way of the door.

As they went up the steps, Lash frowned and looked
down. Their heavy combat boots made no sound on the
wood, and the same happened on the porch slats as they
approached the doorway.

"We prefer things quiet." The *symphath* smiled, revealing even teeth, which was a surprise. Evidently, the fangs of
these creatures, who had once been closely related to vampires, had been bred right out of their mouths. If they did
still feed, it couldn't be very often, not unless they liked
knives.

The king swept his arm out to the left. "Shall we adjourn
to the sitting room?"

The "sitting room" could more accurately have been described as the "bowling alley with rocking chairs." The expanse was nothing but glossy floorboards, and walls hung
only with white paint. Across the way, four Shaker chairs
were clustered in a semicircle around the lit fireplace like
they were afraid of all the emptiness and had huddled together for support.

"Won't you sit down," the king said as he swept his robing up and out and took a seat in one of the spindly chairs.

"You stay standing," Lash said to Mr. D, who obligingly
took up res behind where Lash parked it.

The flames made no cheery crackle as they ate at the
logs that birthed and sustained them. The rockers made no
creak as the king and Lash settled their weight. The spiders
were silent as each fell into the center of its web, as if they
were prepared to be witnesses.

"You and I have a common cause," Lash said.

"So you seem to believe."

"I thought your kind would find vengeance attractive."

As the king smiled, that odd thrill shot down into Lash's
sex. "You would be misinformed. Vengeance is but a crude,
emotional defense against a given slight."

"And you're telling me that's beneath you?" Lash leaned

back and set his chair in motion, going back and forth.
"Hmm ... I may have misjudged your kind."

"We are more sophisticated than that, yes."

"Or maybe you're just a bunch of dress-wearing pussies."

That smile disappeared. "We are far superior to those who believed they imprisoned us. In truth, our preference is for our own company. Do you think we did not engineer this outcome? Foolish of you. Vampires are the crass basis of where we evolved from, chimps to our higher reasoning. Would you care to remain among animals if you could live in civility with your own kind? Of course not. Like finds like. Like requires like. Those of common and superior minds shall be fed only by those of commensurate status." The king's lips lifted. "You know this to be true. You have not remained where you began, either, have you."

"No, I have not." Lash flashed his fangs, thinking his brand of evil hadn't fit in among the vampires any better than the sin-eaters' did. "I am where I need to be now."

"So you see, had we not desired the very end result we obtained in this colony, we might have taken not vengeance, but corrective action such that our destiny was favorable to our interests."

Lash stopped rocking. "If you weren't interested in an alliance, you could have just told me in a fucking e-mail."

An odd light flashed in the king's eyes, one that made Lash even hotter, but also disgusted him. He didn't fly with the homosexual shit, and yet ... well, hell, his father liked the males; maybe some of that was in him, too.

And wouldn't that give Mr. D something to pray over.

"But if I had e-mailed you, I wouldn't have had the pleasure of your acquaintance." Those ruby red eyes swept down Lash's body. "And that would have been a robbery to my senses."

The little Texan cleared his throat, like he was gagging on his tongue.

As the disapproving choke faded, the king's chair started moving up and back soundlessly. "There is something you could do for me however ... which would in turn obligate me to provide you with what you are looking for—and it's locating vampires, isn't it. That has long been the struggle of the Lessening Society. Finding vampires within their hidden homes."

The bastard hit the nail on the head. Lash had known where to raid over the summer because he had been to the estates of the ones he'd killed, having attended the birthday parties of his friends and the weddings of his cousins and the balls of the *glymera* at those mansions. Now, though, what was left of the vampire elite had scattered out of town or to out-of-state safe houses, the addys of which he didn't know. And civilians? He didn't have a clue where to start there, because he'd never socialized with the proletariat.

Symphaths, however, could sense others, humans and vampires alike, seeing them through solid walls and underground basement foundations. He needed that kind of insight if he were going to make progress; it was the one thing that was missing from all the tools his father was giving him.

Lash pushed his combat boot into the floor again and fell into the same rhythm as the king.

"And what exactly might you need from me," he drawled.

The king smiled. "Couplings are our fundamental congregations, are they not. A male and a female bound together. And yet within these intimate relationships discord is common. Promises are made, but not kept. Vows are given and yet discarded. Against these transgressions, measures must be taken."

"Sounds like you're talking vengeance, there, big guy."

That smooth face shifted into a self-satisfied expression. "Not vengeance, no. Corrective action. That a death would be involved . . . is merely what the situation requires."

"Death, huh. So *symphaths* don't believe in divorce?"

Ruby eyes flashed with contempt. "In the case of a faithless mate whose actions outside of the bed run contrary to the core of the relationship, death is the only divorce."

Lash nodded. "I get the logic. So who's the target?"

"Are you committing yourself to act?"

"Not yet." It wasn't clear to him exactly how far he was willing to go. Getting his hands dirty inside the colony had not been part of his original plan.

The king stopped rocking and got to his feet. "Think of it, then, and be sure. When you are ready to receive from us what you need for your war, come unto me again and I shall show you the way to proceed."

Lash stood up as well. "Why don't you just kill your mate yourself."

The king's slow smile was like that on a corpse, rigid and cold. "My dearest friend, the insult to which I most object is less the disloyalty, which I would expect, but rather the arrogant assumption that I would never know the deceit. The former is a trifle. The latter inexcusable. Now . . . shall I see you to your car?"

"Nope. We'll walk ourselves out."

"As you wish." The king extended his six-fingered hand. "Such a pleasure . . ."

Lash reached forward and felt electricity lick up his arm as their palms met. "Yeah. Whatever. You'll be hearing from me."

SIXTEEN

She was with him . . . oh, God, she was finally back with him.

Tohrment, son of Hharm, was naked and pressed against the flesh of his beloved, feeling her satin skin and hearing her gasp as his hand went to her breast. Red hair . . . red hair everywhere on the pillow he'd rolled her back against and on the white sheets that smelled like lemons . . . red hair wrapped around his thick forearm.

Her nipple was tight against his circling thumb and her lips soft beneath his own as he kissed her deep and slow. When she was begging for him, he was going to roll onto her and take her from above, driving into her hard, holding her down.

She liked the weight of him. She liked the feel of him covering her. In their life together, Wellsie was an independent female with a strong mind and a stubborn streak to rival a bulldog's, but in bed, she liked him on top.

He dropped his mouth to her breast, sucking her nipple in, rolling it around, kissing it.

"Tohr . . ."

"What, *leelan*? More? Maybe I'll have you wait. . . ."

But he couldn't. He nursed at her and stroked her stomach and her hips. As she writhed, he licked up to her neck and raked his fangs across her jugular. He couldn't wait to feed. For some reason, he was starved for blood. Maybe he'd been fighting a lot.

Her fingers dug into his hair. "Take my vein. . . ."

"Not yet." The sting of delay was just going to make it better—the more he wanted it, the sweeter the blood.

Moving up to her mouth, he kissed her harder than before, his tongue penetrating her as he deliberately rubbed his cock against her thigh, a promise of another, deeper invasion down below. She was thoroughly aroused, her scent rising up through the lemony sheets, making his fangs pound in his mouth and the tip of his sex weep.

His *shellan* had been the only female he'd ever known. They'd both been virgins on their mating night—and he'd never wanted anybody else.

"Tohr . . ."

God, he loved the low sound of her voice. Loved everything about her. They had been promised to each other before they'd been born, and it had been love at first sight the moment they'd met. Destiny had been so kind to them.

He swept his palm down onto her waist, and then . . .

He stopped, realizing something was wrong. Something . . .

"Your belly . . . your belly is flat."

"Tohr . . ."

"Where's the young?" He pulled back in a panic. "You were with young. Where's the young? Is he okay? What happened to you . . . are you all right?"

"Tohr . . ."

Her eyes opened, and the stare he had looked into for over a hundred years focused on him. Sadness, the kind that made you wish you'd never been born, drained the sexual flush from her beautiful face.

Reaching up to him, she put her hand on his cheek. "Tohr . . ."

"What happened?"

"Tohr . . ."

The sheen over her eyes and the quaver of her lovely voice snapped him in half. And then she began to drift away, her body disappearing under his touch, her red hair, her exquisite face, her despairing eyes fading so that only the pillows remained before him. Then in a final blow, the lemony smell of the sheets and her naturally clean scent left his nose, replaced by nothing—

Tohr jacked upright off the mattress, his eyes spilling over with tears, his heart aching as if he'd had nails driven into his chest. Breathing raggedly, he clutched at his breast-bone and opened his mouth to scream.

No sound came. He didn't have the strength.

Falling back against the pillows, he wiped his wet cheeks with hands that shook and tried to calm the hell down. When he finally caught his breath, he frowned. His heart was skipping in his rib cage, not so much beating as flutter-ing, and no doubt because of the erratic spasms, dizziness spun his head in a tight circle.

Pulling up his T-shirt, he stared down at his deflated pecs and his shrunken torso and willed his body to keep failing. The spells had been coming with increasing regularity and strength, and he wished to hell they'd just get organized and help him wake up dead. Suicide was not an option if you wanted to get into the Fade and be with your deceased loved ones, but he was operating under the assumption that you could effectively neglect yourself to death. Which wasn't technically suicide, like eating a bullet or throwing a noose around his neck or doing a slit-the-wrist special would be.

The scent of food from out in the hallway had him look-ing at the clock. Four in the afternoon. Or was it morning? The drapes were drawn, so he didn't know whether the shutters were up or down.

The knock that sounded was soft.

Which, thank fuck, meant it wasn't Lassiter, who just came in whenever he wanted. Evidently fallen angels weren't big on manners. Or personal space. Or boundaries of any kind. Clearly the great, glowing nightmare had been booted out of heaven because God hadn't liked his com-pany any more than Tohr did.

The quiet knock was repeated. So it must be John.

"Yeah," Tohr said, letting his shirt fall as he pushed him-self up on the pillows. His arms, once strong as cranes, struggled under the weight of his wilted shoulders.

The boy, who was no longer a boy, came in bearing a tray heavily laden with food, and a face full of baseless optimism.

Tohr glanced over as the burden was put on the bedside table. Herbed chicken and saffron rice and green beans and fresh rolls.

The shit might as well have been roadkill wrapped in

barbed wire, for all he cared, but he picked up the plate and rolled out the napkin and took the fork and the knife and put them to use.

Chew. Chew. Chew. Swallow. More chewing. Swallow. Drink. Chew. Eating was as mechanical and autonomic as his respiration, something he was only dimly aware of, a necessity, not a pleasure.

Pleasure was a thing of the past . . . and a torture within his dreams. As he recalled his *shellan* up against him, naked, in lemony sheets, the fleeting image lit up his body from the inside out, making him alive, and not just living. The strike of his mortal match head faded quick, though, a flame with no wick to sustain it.

Chew. Cut. Chew. Swallow. Drink.

As he ate, the boy sat down in a chair by the closed drapes, elbow on knee, fist on chin, a living, breathing Rodin's *The Thinker*. John was always like that lately, always with something on his mind.

Tohrment knew damn well what it was, but the solution that was going to end John's sad preoccupation was going to hurt the kid like a bitch first.

And Tohr was sorry about that. Very sorry.

Christ, why couldn't Lassiter have just left him where he'd lain in that forest? That angel could have kept right on going, but no, His Lordship Halogen had to be a hero.

Tohr shifted his eyes over to John and his gaze locked on the kid's fist. The thing was huge, and the chin and jaw that rested on it were strong, masculine. The boy had turned out to be a handsome guy; then again, as Darius's son, he'd had a good gene pool. One of the best.

Come to think of it . . . he really looked like D, a carbon copy, actually, except for the blue jeans. Darius wouldn't have been caught dead in blue jeans, even fancy designer-distressed ones like the kind John was sporting.

Matter of fact . . . D had often assumed that exact position when he'd been stewing over life, pulling the Rodin, all frown and churn—

A flash of silver winked from John's free hand. It was a quarter, and the kid was weaving the coin in and out and around his fingers, his version of a nervous twitch.

Tonight was more than John's usual silent perching. Something had happened.

"What's doing?" Tohr asked, his voice a rasp. "You okay?"

John's eyes shot over in surprise.

To avoid the stare, Tohr looked down, speared some chicken, and put it in his mouth. Chew. Chew. Swallow.

Going by the shifting sounds, John was uncurling himself from his wood-burning routine slowly, as if he were afraid that sudden movements would spook away the question hanging between them.

Tohr glanced over again, and when he waited, John put the quarter in his pocket and signed with economy and grace, *Wrath is out fighting again. V just told me and the guys.*

Tohr was rusty with American Sign Language, but not that rusty. Surprise lowered his fork. "Wait . . . he's still king, right?"

Yeah, but he told the Brothers tonight that he's going back on rotation. Or I guess he's been on rotation and kept it to himself. I think the Brotherhood's pissed at him.

"Rotation? Can't be. The king's not allowed to fight."

He is now. And Phury's coming back, too.

"What the fuck? The Primale's not supposed to . . ." Tohr frowned. "Is there some change in the war? Something going on?"

I don't know. John shrugged and settled back into the chair, crossing his legs at the knee. Another thing Darius always did.

In the pose, the son seemed as old as the father had been, although that was less about the way John's limbs were arranged and more about the exhaustion in his blue eyes.

"It's not legal," Tohr said.

Is now. Wrath met with the Scribe Virgin.

Questions started to buzz in Tohr's head, his brain struggling with the unaccustomed load. In the midst of the disjointed swirl, it was hard to think coherently, and he felt as if he were trying to hold a hundred tennis balls in his arms; no matter how hard he tried, ones slipped through and bounced around, creating a mess.

He gave up trying to make sense of anything. "Well, that's a change. . . . I wish them luck."

John's low exhale pretty much summed it all up as Tohr

unplugged from the world and went back to eating. When he was finished, he folded up the napkin neatly and took a final drink from the water glass.

He turned the TV on to CNN, because he didn't want to think and he couldn't handle the quiet. John stayed for about a half hour, and when he clearly couldn't stand being still any longer, he got to his feet and stretched.

I'll see you at the end of the night.

Ah, so it was afternoon. "I'll be here."

John picked up the tray and left with no pause, no hesitation. There had been plenty of both at first, as if each time he hit the door, he hoped that Tohr would stop him and say, *I'm ready to face life. I'm going to soldier on. I'm better enough to give a shit about you.*

But hope didn't spring eternal.

When the door was shut, Tohr pulled the sheets off his stick legs and shuffled his feet over the edge of the mattress.

He was ready to face something, all right, but it wasn't his existence. With a groan and a lurch, he stumbled into the bathroom, went to the toilet, and popped up the porcelain throne's seat. Bending over, he gave the command and his stomach evacuated the meal without a fuss.

In the beginning, he'd had to cram his finger down his throat, but no more. He just clenched his diaphragm and up it all came, like rats fleeing an overflowing sewer.

"You gotta cut that shit out."

Lassiter's voice harmonized with the sound of the toilet flushing. Which so made sense.

"Christ, don't you ever knock?"

"It's Lassiter. L-A-S-S-I-T-E-R. How is it possible you're still getting me confused with someone else? Do I need a nametag?"

"Yes, and let's put it over your mouth." Tohr sagged onto the marble and dropped his head into his hands. "You know, you can go home. You can leave anytime."

"Get your flat ass in gear, then. 'Cuz that's what'll do it."

"Now, there's a reason to live."

There was a soft chiming sound, which meant, tragedy of tragedies, the angel had just popped himself up onto the countertop. "So, what are we doing tonight? Wait, let me guess, sitting in morose silence. Or, no . . . you're mixing it up. Brooding with soulful intensity, right? What a fucking wild child you are. Whoo. Hoo. Next thing you know, you'll be opening for Slipknot."

With a curse, Tohr stood up and went over to turn on the shower, hoping that if he refused to look at the loudmouth, Lassiter would get bored more quickly and move on to ruin someone else's afternoon.

"Question," the angel said. "When are we going to cut that rug that's growing out of your head? Shit gets any longer, we're going to have to mow it down like hay."

As Tohr stripped out of his T-shirt and boxers, he enjoyed the only consolation to be had in suffering Lassiter's company: He flashed the motherfucker.

"Man, flat ass is right," Lassiter muttered. "You're sporting a pair of deflated basketballs back there. Makes me wonder . . . Hey, I'll bet Fritz has a bicycle pump. I'm just saying."

"You don't like the view? You know the door. It's the one you never knock on."

Tohr didn't give the water time to warm up; he just got under the spray, and he cleaned himself for no good reason he knew of—he had no pride, so he didn't give a shit what anyone thought of his hygiene.

The throwing up had a purpose. The showering . . . maybe it was simply habit.

Closing his eyes, he parted his lips and stood facing the nozzle. Water licked into his mouth, whisking away the bile, and as the sting left his tongue, a thought walked into his brain.

Wrath was out fighting. Alone.

"Hey, Tohr."

Tohr frowned. The angel never used his proper name. "What."

"Tonight is different."

"Yeah, only if you leave me alone. Or hang yourself in this bathroom. Got six showerheads to choose from in here."

Tohr picked up the bar of soap and went over his body, feeling the hard, jabbing thrusts of his bones and joints coming through his thin skin.

Wrath out alone.

Shampoo. Rinse. Turn back to the spray. Open mouth.
Out. Alone.

He ended the shower, and the angel was front and center with a towel, all manservant and shit.

"Tonight is different," Lassiter said softly.

Tohr looked at the guy truly, seeing him for the first time,
even though they had been together for four months. The
angel had black-and-blond hair that was as long as Wrath's,
but he was no cross-dresser in spite of all the Cher dripping
down his back. His wardrobe was straight-up army/navy,
black shirts and camo pants and combat boots, but he
wasn't all soldier. Fucker was pierced like a pincushion and
accessorized like a jewelry box, with gold hoops and chains
hanging from holes in his ears and wrists and eyebrows.
And you could bet the mountings were on his chest and
below the waist—which was something Tohr refused to
think about. He didn't need help throwing up, thank you
very much.

As the towel changed hands, the angel said with gravity,
"Time to wake up, Cinderella."

Tohr was about to point out that it was Sleeping Beauty
when a memory came to him as if it had been injected into
his frontal lobe. It was the night he'd saved Wrath's life
back in 1958, and the images came to him with the clarity of
the actual experience.

The king had been out. Alone. Downtown.

Half-dead and bleeding into the sewer.

An Edsel had nailed him. A piece-of-shit Edsel convert-
ible the color of a diner waitress's blue eye shadow.

As near as Tohr could figure out later, Wrath had been
on foot in pursuit of a *lesser* and barrel-assing around a
corner when the boat of a car had plowed into him. Tohr
had been two blocks away and heard the screeching brakes
and the impact of some sort, and he'd been prepared to do
absolutely nothing.

Human traffic accidents? Not his problem.

But then a pair of *lessers* had run past the alley he'd
been standing in. The slayers had been hauling nut through
the fall drizzle like they were being pursued, except there
was no one riding their bumpers. He'd waited, expecting to
see one of his brothers. None had come pounding along.

Didn't make any sense. If a slayer had been hit by a car

in the company of his cronies, they wouldn't have left the scene. The others would have killed the human driver and any passengers, then packed their dead up in the trunk and driven off from the scene: The last thing the Lessening Society wanted was an incapacitated *lesser* leaking black blood on the street.

Maybe it was just coincidence, though. A human pedestrian. Or someone on a bike. Or two cars.

Only one set of squealing breaks though. And none of that would explain the pair of paled-out flip-heels who'd passed him like they were arsonists running from a fire they'd lit.

Tohr had jogged onto Trade and around the corner and caught sight of a human male in a hat and trench coat crouched over a crumpled body twice his size. The guy's wife, who had been dressed in one of those petticoated, frothy fifties numbers, stood just beyond the headlights, huddled into her fur.

Her brilliant red skirt had been the color of streaks on the pavement, but the scent of the spilled blood hadn't been human. It was vampire. And the one who'd been struck had long dark hair . . .

The woman's voice had been shrill. "We need to take him to the hospital—"

Tohr had stepped in and cut her off. "He's mine."

The man had looked up. "Your friend . . . I didn't see him. . . . Dressed in black—he came out of nowhere—"

"I'll take care of him." Tohr had stopped explaining himself at that point and just willed the two humans into a stupor. A quick thought suggestion sent them back into their car and on their way with the impression that they had hit a trash can. He'd figured the rain would take care of the blood on the front of their car, and the dent they could fix on their own.

Tohr's heart had been going as fast as a jackhammer as he'd leaned over the body of the heir to the race's throne. Blood had been everywhere, leaking fast from a gash in Wrath's head, so Tohr had shrugged out of his jacket, bit into the sleeve, and ripped off a strip of leather. After wrapping up the heir's temples and tying the makeshift bandage as tight as he could, he'd flagged down a passing truck, pulled a gun on the greaser behind the wheel, and been chauffeured by the human out to Havers's neighborhood.

He and Wrath had ridden in the back bed, with him keeping pressure on Wrath's head wound, and the rain had been cold. A late-November rain, maybe December. Good thing it hadn't been summer, though. No doubt the chill had slowed Wrath's heart and eased his blood pressure.

Quarter of a mile from Havers's, in the ritzy part of Caldwell, Tohr had told the human to pull over and brain-washed him on his way.

The minutes it had taken Tohr to walk to the clinic had been among the longest of his life, but he'd gotten Wrath there, and Havers had closed what had turned out to be a temporal artery slice.

It had been touch and go that next day. Even with Marissa there to feed Wrath, the king had lost so much blood, he hadn't rebounded as expected, and Tohr had stayed for the duration, sitting in a chair by the bedside. As Wrath had lain so still, Tohr had felt as if the whole of the race were tipping between life and death, the only one who could take the throne locked into a sleep that was only a few firing neurons off a permanent vegetative state.

Word had gotten out and people had come undone. The nurses and the doctor. The other patients who had stopped by to pray over the king who would not serve. The Brothers, who had used rotary phones to call every fifteen minutes.

The collective sense was that without Wrath, there was no hope. No future. No chance.

Wrath had lived, however, waking up with the kind of crankiness that made you sigh in relief . . . because if a patient had the energy to be that pissy, he was going to pull through.

The following nightfall, after having been out cold for twenty-four hours straight and having scared the shit out of everyone around him, Wrath had unplugged the IV, dressed himself, and left.

Without a word to any of them.

Tohr had expected . . . something. Not a thank-you, but an acknowledgment or . . . something. Hell, Wrath was a gruff son of a bitch now, but back then? He'd been downright toxic. Even so . . . nothing? After he'd saved the guy's life?

Kinda reminded him of the way he'd been treating John. And his brothers.

Tohr wrapped the towel around his waist and thought about the more important point of the memory. Wrath out there fighting alone. Back in '58, it had been a stroke of luck that Tohr had been where he had and found the king before it was too late.

"Time to wake up," Lassiter said.

SEVENTEEN

As night settled in for the duration, Ehlena prayed that she wouldn't be late to work again. With the clock ticking, she waited upstairs in the kitchen with the CranRas and the crushed drugs. She'd been meticulous about cleanup: She'd put the spoon away. Double-checked all the surfaces. Even made sure the living room was ordered properly.

"Father?" she called down the stairs.

While she listened for sounds of shuffling movement and quiet words spoken without sense, she thought of the bizarre dream she'd had during the day. She'd imagined Rehv in the dark distance with his arms hanging to the sides. His magnificent, naked body had been spotlit as if on display, his muscles bunching up in a powerful show, his skin a warm, golden brown. His head had been angled down, his eyes closed as if in repose.

Captivated, summoned, she had walked across a cold stone floor to him, saying his name over and over again.

He had not responded. He had not lifted his head. He had not opened his eyes.

Fear had whistled through her veins and kick-started her heart, and she had rushed to him, but he had stayed ever distant, a goal never realized, a destination never reached.

She had awoken with tears in her eyes and a body that trembled. As the choking trauma had receded, the meaning was clear, but really, she didn't need her subconscious to tell her what she already knew.

Snapping herself out of it, she called down the stairs again, "Father?"

When there was no reply, Ehlena took her father's mug and walked down to the cellar. She went slowly, although not because she was afraid of spilling bloodred CranRas on her white uniform. Every once in a while her father didn't rouse himself and she had to make this descent, and each time she took the steps in this way, she wondered if it had finally happened, if her father had been gathered up unto the Fade.

She wasn't ready to lose him. Not yet, and no matter how hard things were.

Putting her head through the doorway into his room, she saw him seated at his hand-carved desk, shaggy stacks of papers and unlit candles surrounding him.

Thank you, Virgin Scribe.

As her eyes adjusted to the dimness, she worried over how the lack of light might damage her father's vision, but the candles were going to stay as they were, because there were no matches or lighters in the house. The last time he'd gotten his hands on a match had been back at their old place—and he'd lit the apartment on fire because his voices told him to.

That had been two years ago, and the reason he'd been put on meds.

"Father?"

He looked up from the mess and seemed surprised. *"Daughter mine, how fare thee this night?"*

Always the same question, and she always gave him the same answer in the Old Language. *"Well, my father. And you?"*

"As always I am charmed by your greeting. Ah, yes, the doggen *has put out my juice. How good of her."* Her father took the mug. *"Wither goest thou?"*

This led to their verbal pas de deux over him not approving of her working and her explaining that she did it because she liked to and him shrugging and not understanding the younger generation.

"Verily I am departing now," she said, *"but Lusie shall arrive in a matter of moments."*

"Yes, good, good. In truth, I am busy with my book, but I shall entertain her, as is proper, for a time. I must needs get about my work, though." He waved his hand around the physical representation of the chaos in his mind, his elegant sweep at odds with the ragged sheaves of paper that were filled with nonsense. *"This needs tending to."*

"Of course it does, Father."

He finished the CranRas and, as she went to take it from him, he frowned. *"Surely the maid will do that?"*

"I should like to help her. She has many duties." Wasn't that the truth. The *doggen* had to follow all the rules for objects and where they belonged, as well as do the shopping and earn the money and pay the bills and watch after him. The *doggen* was tired. The *doggen* was worn out.

But the mug absolutely had to go up to the kitchen.

"Father, please let go of the mug so that I may take it upstairs. The maid fears disturbing you, and I should like to spare her the concern."

For a moment, his eyes focused on her the way they used to. *"You have a beautiful and generous heart. I am so proud to call you daughter."*

Ehlena blinked fiercely and in a rough voice said, *"Your pride means everything to me."*

He reached out and squeezed her hand. *"Go, my daughter. Go to this* 'job' *of yours, and come home to me with stories of your night."*

Oh . . . God.

Just what he had said to her way back when she'd been in private school and her mother had been alive and they lived among the family and the *glymera* like people who mattered.

Even though she knew that by the time she got home likely as not he would have no memory of asking her his old lovely question, she smiled and ate up the tasty crumbs of the past.

"As always, Father mine. As always."

She left to the sound of shifting pages and the *tink-tink-tink* of a quill nib on the edge of a crystal ink bottle.

Upstairs, she rinsed out the mug, dried it, and put it in the cupboard, then made sure that everything in the refrigerator was where it needed to be. When she received the text that Lusie was on her way, she ducked out the door, locked it, and dematerialized to the clinic.

As she came in to work, she felt such a relief at being like everyone else, showing up on time, putting things in her locker, talking about nothing in particular before the shift started.

Except then Catya came up to her when she was at the coffeepot, all smiles. "So . . . last night was . . . ? Come on, do tell."

Ehlena finished filling her mug and hid a wince behind a deep first draw that burned her tongue. "I think 'no-show' would cover it."

"No-show?"

"Yup. As in, he didn't show."

Catya shook her head. "Damn it."

"No, it's fine. Really. I mean, it's not like I had much invested." Yeah, only a whole fantasy about the future that included things like a *hellren*, a family of her own, a life worth living. Nothing much at all. "It's fine."

"You know, I was thinking last night. I have a cousin who is—"

"Thanks, but no. With my dad the way he is, I shouldn't be dating anyone." Ehlena frowned, recalling how quickly Rehv had agreed with her on that. Even though you could argue that it made him some kind of gentleman, it was hard not to be a little annoyed.

"Caring for your father doesn't mean—"

"Hey, why don't I go man the front desk during the shift change?"

Catya stopped, but the female's light eyes were sending plenty of messages, most of which could be filed under, *When Is This Girl Going to Wake Up?*

"I'll head out there now," Ehlena said, turning away.

"It doesn't last forever."

"Of course not. Most of our shift is already here."

Catya shook her head. "That wasn't what I meant, and you know it. Life doesn't last forever. Your father has a serious psychological condition, and you're very good with him, but he could stay like this for a century."

"In which case I will still have about seven hundred years left. I'll be at the front. 'Scuse me."

Out in the reception, Ehlena took up res behind the computer and logged in. There was no one in the waiting room because the sun had only just gone down, but the patients would start coming in soon enough, and she couldn't wait for the distraction.

Reviewing Havers's schedule, she saw nothing unusual. Checkups. Patient procedures. Surgical follow-ups . . .

The exterior doorbell chimed, and she glanced at a security monitor. There was a walk-in outside, a male who was huddled into his coat against the cold wind.

She hit the intercom button and said, "Good evening. How may I help you?"

The face that looked up into the camera was one she had seen before. Three nights ago. Stephan's cousin.

"Alix?" she said. "It's Ehlena. How are—"

"I'm here to see if he's been brought in."

"He?"

"Stephan."

"I don't think so, but let me check while you come down." Ehlena hit the lock release and went to the in-house patient list on the computer. One by one she reviewed the names as she released the series of doors for Alix.

No mention of Stephan as an inpatient.

As Alix walked into the waiting room, her blood ran cold the instant she saw the male's face. The vicious dark circles under his gray eyes were about so much more than lack of sleep.

"Stephan didn't come home last night," he said.

Rehv lamented December, and not just because the cold in upstate New York was enough to make him want to go stuntman with the pyrotechnics just to get warm.

Night came early in December. The sun, that fucking work-shy, bone-idle pansy, gave up its efforts as early as four thirty in the afternoon, and that meant Rehv's first-Tuesday-of-the-month date-mares started early.

It was just ten o'clock as he entered Black Snake State Park after a two-hour drive north from Caldwell. Trez, who always dematerialized up, was no doubt already in position around the cabin, making himself scarce and preparing to act as a guard.

As well as a witness.

The fact that the guy who was arguably his best friend had to watch the whole thing was just part of the cluster-fuck carousel, an added ball crusher. The trouble was, after it was all over, Rehv needed help getting back home, and Trez was good at that kind of shit.

Xhex wanted the job, of course, but you couldn't trust her. Not around the princess. If he turned his back for one second the cabin would end up with a fresh new paint job on its walls—of the gruesome variety.

As always, Rehv parked in the dirt lot that was around the dark side of the mountain. There were no other cars, and he expected the trails fanning out from the lot's ass to be empty also.

Staring out of the windshield, everything was red and flat to his eyes and though he despised his half sister and hated looking at her and wished that this dirty fucking business of theirs would just stop, his body was not numb and cold, but alive and humming: In his slacks, his hard cock was primed and ready for what was going to happen.

Now if only he could make himself get out of the car.

He put his hand on the door release, but couldn't pull the lever back.

So quiet. Only the gentle, ticking sounds of the Bentley's cooling engine disturbed the silence.

For no good reason, he thought of Ehlena's lovely laughter, and that was what got him to open the door. With a quick lunge, he shoved his head out of the car just as his stomach clenched up tight as a fist and he nearly threw up. As the cold settled his nausea, he tried to get Ehlena out of his mind. She was so clean and honorable and kind that he couldn't bear even having her in his thoughts when he was about to do this.

Which was a surprise.

Protecting someone from the cruel world, from the deadly and dangerous, from the tainted, the obscene, and the revolting wasn't part of his hardwiring. But he'd taught himself to do just that when it came to the only three normal females in life. For the one who had borne him and the one he had raised as his own and the young his sister had recently birthed, he would level all manner of threats, kill with bare hands anything that would hurt them, seek out and destroy even the slightest menace.

And somehow the cozy conversation he'd had with Ehlena in the early hours had put her on that very, very short list.

Which meant he had to shut her out. Along with those other three.

He'd been fine living as a whore, because he exacted an expensive price out of the one he fucked, and besides, prostitution was nothing better than he deserved, considering the way his true father had forced his conception on his mother. But the buck stopped with him. He alone went into the cabin and made his body do what it did.

Those few normals in his life had to stay far, far away from this whole thing, and that meant wiping them out of his thoughts and his heart when he came up here. Later, after he'd recovered and showered and slept, then he could go back to remembering Ehlena's toffee-colored eyes and the way she smelled of cinnamon and how she had laughed in spite of herself when they talked. For now, he shut her and his mother and his sister and his beloved niece out of his front lobe, packing up every memory he had into a separate section of his brain and locking them down.

The princess always tried to get into his skull, and he didn't want her to know anything about those he cared for or about.

When a bitter gust nearly slammed the door on his head, Rehv drew his sable loosely around himself, got out, and locked the Bentley. As he walked to the trailhead, the ground beneath his Cole Haans was frozen, the dirt crunching under his soles, hard and resistant.

Technically the park was now closed for the season, a chain hanging across the widemouthed path that took you past the map of the mountain and the cabins that were for rent. The weather, rather than the Adirondack Park Service, was more likely to keep people away, though. After stepping over the links, he bypassed the sign-in sheet that hung on a clipboard even though no one was supposed to be using the trails. He never left his name.

Yeah, 'cuz human rangers really needed to know what was doing between two *symphaths* in one of those cabins. Riiiiiiiiiiiiight.

One good thing about December was that the forest was less claustrophobic in the winter months, its oaks and maples nothing but skinny trunks and branches that let in plenty of the starry night. All around them, the evergreens were having a ball, their fluffy boughs an arboreal fuck you to their now-naked brethren, payback for all the showy fall foliage the other trees had just sported.

Penetrating the tree line, he followed the main trail as it gradually narrowed. Smaller trails broke off on the left and the right, marked with rough wooden signs with names like Hobnob's Walk, Lightning Strike, Summit Long, and Summit Short. He kept on going straight, his breath leaving his lips in puffs, the sound of his loafers on the frozen ground seeming very loud. Overhead, the moon was brilliant, a knife-edged crescent that, with his *symphath* urges firmly not in check, was the color of his blackmailer's ruby eyes.

Trez made an appearance in the form of an icy breeze rolling down the trail.

"Hey, my man," Rehv said quietly.

Trez's voice floated into his head as the guy's Shadow form condensed into a shimmering wave. MAKE IT QUICK WITH HER. SOONER WE GET YOU WHAT YOU NEED AFTERWARD THE BETTER.

"It is what it is."

SOONER. BETTER.

"We'll see."

Trez cursed him and dissolved back into a cold gust of wind, shooting forward out of sight.

Truth was, as much as Rehv hated coming here, sometimes he didn't want to leave. He liked hurting the princess, and she was a good opponent. Smart, fast, cruel. She was the only outlet for his bad side, and, like a runner starved for a workout, he needed the exercise.

Plus, maybe it was like his arm: The festering felt good.

Rehv took the sixth left, walking on a footpath that was wide enough for only one, and soon enough, the cabin came into view. In the bright moonlight, its logs were a color of something like rosé wine.

As he got to the door, he reached forward with his left hand, and as he gripped the wooden toggle, he thought of Ehlena and how she had cared enough to call him about his arm.

For a brief, lapsing moment, the sound of her voice in his ear came back to him.

I don't understand why you're not taking care of yourself.

The door whipped out of his hold, opening so fast it slammed against the wall.

The princess stood in the center of the cabin, her brilliant red robes and the rubies at her throat and her bloodred eyes all the color of hatred. With her stark hair twisted up off her neck, and her pale skin, and the live albino scorpions she wore as earrings, she was an exquisite horror, a Kabuki doll constructed by an evil hand. And she was evil, her darkness coming at him in waves, emanating from the center of her chest even as nothing about her moved and her moonlike face remained unmarred by a frown.

Her voice, likewise, was slick as a blade. "No beach scene tonight in your mind. No, no beach this night."

Rehv covered Ehlena up quickly by picturing a glorious Bahaman stereotype, all sun and sea and sand. It was one he'd seen on TV years ago, a "getaway special," as the announcer had said, with people in swimsuits strolling hand in hand. Given its vividness, the image was the perfect jockstrap over his gray matter's 'nads.

"Who is she?"

"Who is who?" he said as he stepped inside.

The cabin was warm, thanks to her, a little trick of molecular agitation of the air that was enhanced by her being pissed off. The heat she generated was not cheery like that from a fire however—more like the kind of hot flash you got along with a case of the shits.

"Who is the female in your mind."

"Just a model from an ad on TV, my dearest bitch," he said as smoothly as she did. Without turning his back on her, he shut the door quietly. "Jealous?"

"To be jealous, I would have to be threatened. And that would be absurd." The princess smiled. "But I think you need to tell me who she is."

"That all you want to do? Talk?" Rehv deliberately let his coat fall open and cupped his hard cock and heavy sac. "Usually you want me for more than conversation."

"True enough. Your highest and best use is for what humans call . . . a dildo, is it not? A toy for a female with which to pleasure herself."

"*Female* is not necessarily the word I would use to describe you."

"Indeed. *Beloved* will do nicely."

She lifted a hideous hand to her chignon, her bony, triple-jointed fingers skipping over the careful construction, her wrist thinner than a handle on a wire whisk. Her body was no different: All *symphaths* were built like chess players, not quarterbacks, which followed their preference to battle with the mind, not the body. In their robing, they were neither male nor female, but rather a distilled version of both sexes, and this was why the princess wanted him as she did. She liked his body, his muscle, his obvious and brutal maleness, and she usually wanted to be physically restrained during sex—something she sure as shit wasn't getting at home. As far as he understood it, the *symphath* version of the act was no more than some mental posturing followed by two rubs and a gasp on the male's part. Plus he was willing to bet their uncle was hung like a hamster, and had balls the size of pencil erasers.

Not that he'd ever checked—but come on, the guy was not exactly a paragon of testosterone.

The princess moved around the cabin as if she were showing off her grace, but there was a purpose as she went from window to window and looked out.

Damn it to hell, always with the windows.

"Where is your watchdog tonight?" she said.

"I always come alone."

"You lie to your love."

"Why ever would I want anyone to see this?"

"Because I am beautiful." She stopped in front of the panes closest to the door. "He is over to the right, by the pine."

Rehv didn't need to lean to one side and look out to know she was right. Of course she could sense Trez; she just couldn't be exactly sure where or what he was.

Still, he said, "There is nothing but trees."

"Untrue."

"Afraid of shadows, Princess?"

As she looked over her shoulder, the albino scorpion hanging from her earlobe made eye contact with him as well. "Fear is not the issue. Disloyalty is. I do not abide by disloyalty."

"Unless you're practicing it, of course."

"Oh, I am quite faithful to you, my love. Except for our father's brother, as you know." She turned and lifted her shoulders to her full height. "My mate is the only one apart from you. And I come here alone."

"Your virtues abound, although as I've said, please take more into your bed. Take a hundred other males."

"None would compare to you."

Rehv wanted to throw up every time she paid him a false compliment, and she knew it. Which naturally was why she insisted on saying shit like that.

"Tell me," he said to change the subject, "since you brought up our uncle, how does the motherfucker fare?"

"He still believes you dead. So my half of our relationship remains honored."

Rehv put his hand in the pocket of his sable coat and took out the two hundred and fifty thousand dollars in cut rubies. He tossed the happy little packy onto the floor at the hem of her robe and removed his fur. His suit jacket and his loafers were next. Then it was his silk socks and his slacks and his shirt. No boxers to take off. Why bother.

Rehvenge stood before her fully erect, feet planted, breath easing in and out of his heavy chest. "And I'm ready to complete our transaction."

Her ruby eyes went down his body and stopped at his sex, her mouth parting, her split tongue running over her lower lip. The scorpions in her ears twirled their clawed limbs in anticipation, like they were responding to her sexual flush.

She pointed to the velvet bag. "Pick this up and give it to me properly."

"No."

"*Pick it up.*"

"You like to bend over in front of me. Why should I rob you of your favorite hobby."

The princess tucked her hands into the long sleeves of her robe and came to him in the smooth manner of *symphaths*, all but floating over the wooden floor. As she approached, he held his ground, because he would be dead and decayed before he took a step back for the likes of her.

They stared at each other, and in the deep, vicious silence, he felt a terrible communion with her. They were like of like, and though he hated it, there was a relief in being his true self.

"Pick it—"

"No."

Her crossed arms unfurled and one of her six-fingered hands came tearing through the air at his face, the slap hard and sharp as her ruby eyes. Rehv refused to let his head kick back on impact while the cracking sound reverberated loud as a plate breaking.

"I want your tithe handed to me properly. And I want to know who she is. I have sensed your interest in this one before—when you are away from me."

Rehv kept that beach ad pinned to his frontal lobe and knew she was bluffing. "I don't bow down to you or anybody else, bitch. So if you want that bag, you're going to have to touch your toes. And as for what you think you know, you're wrong. There is no one for me."

She slapped him again, the sting flickering down his spinal cord and pulsing into the head of his cock. "You bow down to me every time you come here with your pathetic payment and your hungry sex. You need this, you need me."

He pushed his face closer to hers. "Don't flatter yourself, Princess. You are a chore, not a choice."

"Wrong. You live to hate me."

The princess took his cock in her hand, her graveyard fingers wrapping around him tightly. As he felt her grip and her stroking, he was revolted . . . and yet his erection wept at the attention even as he couldn't bear it: although he didn't find her attractive at all, his *symphath* side was fully engaged in the battle of wills, and that was the erotic thing.

The princess leaned into him, her forefinger rubbing over the barb at the base of his arousal. "Whoever that female is in your head, she can't compete with what we have."

Rehv put his hands up to the sides of his blackmailer's neck and pressed in with his thumbs until she gasped. "I could snap your head off your spine."

"You won't." She moved her red, glossy lips over his throat, the crushed-pepper lipstick she wore burning him. "Because we couldn't do this if I were dead."

"Don't underestimate the appeal of necrophilia. Especially where you're concerned." He grabbed onto the back of her chignon and yanked hard. "Shall we get down to business?"

"After you pick up—"

"*Not going to happen.* I don't bow." With his free hand, he ripped the front of her robe open, exposing the fine mesh weave of the bodysuit she always wore. Spinning her around, he forced her face-first into the door, fishing up through the folds of red satin as she gasped. The weave she wore over herself was soaked in scorpion venom, and as he worked toward her core, the poison soaked in through his skin. Hopefully, he could fuck her for a while with her robes still on—

The princess dematerialized out of his grip and re-formed right at the window Trez could see through. In a shifting rush, her robes left her, removed by her will, her flesh revealed. She was built like the snake she was, sinewy, and altogether too thin, her shimmering bodysuit giving the impression of scales as the moonlight reflected off its interlocking threads.

Her feet were planted on either side of the bag of rubies.

"You're going to worship me," she said, her hand going in between her thighs and stroking her slit. "With your mouth."

Rehv came over and got down on his knees. Looking up at her, he said with a smile, "And you will be the one who picks up that bag."

EIGHTEEN

Ehlena stood just outside the clinic's morgue, arms banded around her chest, heart in her throat, prayers leaving her lips. In spite of her uniform, she was not waiting in any kind of professional capacity, and the STAFF ONLY sign that was at eye level barred her as much as it would have anyone in regular clothes. As the minutes passed slow as centuries, she stared at the letters as if she'd forgotten how to read. The word *staff* was on one half of the doors, the *only* on the other. Big red block print. Underneath the English was a translation in the Old Language.

Alix had just gone through them, with Havers at his side.

Please . . . not Stephan. Please let the John Doe not be Stephan.

The wail that filtered through the STAFF ONLY doors had her shutting her eyes hard enough to make her head spin.

She hadn't been stood up after all.

Ten minutes later, Alix came out, his face white, the stretch underneath both eyes red from his having wiped away many tears. Havers was right behind him, the physician looking equally heartbroken.

Ehlena stepped forward and took Alix into her arms. "I am so sorry."

"How . . . how can I tell his parents . . . They didn't want me to come down here. . . . Oh, God . . ."

Ehlena held the male's shuddering body until Alix straightened and dragged both hands across his face. "He was looking forward to going out with you."

"And I with him."

Havers put his hand on Alix's shoulder. "Do you want to take him with you?"

The male looked back at the doors, his mouth flattening into a slash. "We're going to want to get started on the ... death ritual ... but ..."

"Would you like me to wrap him?" Havers said softly.

Alix closed his eyes and nodded. "We can't let his mother see his face. It would kill her. And I would do it except ..."

"We'll take excellent care of him," Ehlena said. "You can trust us to take care of him with respect and reverence."

"I don't think I could. ..." Alix looked over. "Is it bad of me?"

"No." She held both his hands. "And I promise you, we'll do it with love."

"But I should assist—"

"You can trust us." As the male blinked quickly, Ehlena gently led him away from the morgue doors. "I want you to go wait in one of the family rooms."

Ehlena walked Stephan's cousin down the corridor to the hallway that had patient rooms running off it. As another nurse passed by, Ehlena asked that he be taken to a private waiting room, and then she returned to the morgue.

Before she entered, she took a deep breath and straightened her shoulders. Pushing inside, she smelled herbs and saw Havers standing by a body covered by a white sheet. Ehlena's stride faltered.

"My heart is heavy," the physician said. "So heavy. I didn't want that poor boy to see his blooded family like this, but he insisted after he identified the clothes. He had to see."

"Because he had to be sure." It was what she would have needed in the same situation.

Havers lifted the sheet, folding it back to the chest, and Ehlena clapped a palm over her mouth to keep her gasp in.

Stephan's beaten, mottled face was nearly unrecognizable.

She swallowed once. And again. And a third time.

Dearest Virgin Scribe, he'd been alive twenty-four hours ago. Alive and downtown and looking forward to seeing her. Then a wrong choice to go one way and not another and he ended up here, lying on a cold, stainless-steel bed, about to be prepared for his death ritual.

"I'll get the wraps," Ehlena said roughly as Havers took the sheet completely off the body.

The morgue was small, with only eight refrigerated units and two examination tables, but it was well stocked with equipment and supplies. The ceremonial wraps were kept in the closet by the desk, and as she opened the door, a fresh waft of herbs drifted out. The linen strips were three inches wide and came in rolls that were the size of two of Ehlena's fists. Soaked in a combination of rosemary, lavender, and sea salt, they let out a pleasant enough smell that nonetheless made her recoil every time she caught a whiff of it.

Death. It was the smell of death.

She took out ten rolls and stacked them in her arms, then returned to where Stephan's body was fully exposed, only a cloth over his loins.

After a moment, Havers came out of a changing room in the back wearing a black robe tied with a black sash. Around his neck, suspended on a long, heavy silver chain, was a sharp-edged, ornate cutting tool that was so old, the filigree work on the handset had blackened nooks within its curvilinear design.

Ehlena bowed her head as Havers said the requisite prayers to the Scribe Virgin for Stephan's peaceful rest within the tender embrace of the Fade. When the doctor was ready, she handed him the first of the scented rolls and they started with Stephan's right hand, as was proper. With every gentleness and care, she held the cold, gray limb aloft as Havers wrapped the flesh tightly, doubling up the linen strip upon itself. When they worked their way up to his shoulder, they moved to the right leg; then it was left hand, left arm, left leg next.

As the loincloth was lifted, Ehlena turned away, as was required because she was female. In the event of a female body, she would not have had to, although a male assistant would have done so out of respect. After the hips were wrapped, the torso was bound up to the chest and the shoulders covered.

With each pass of the linen, the scent of the herbs hit her nose anew until she felt like she couldn't breathe.

Or maybe it wasn't the smell in the air; it was more the thoughts in her head. Had he been her future? Would she have known his body? Could this have been her *hellren* and the father of her young?

Questions that would never be answered.

Ehlena frowned. No, actually, they had all been answered.

Each one of them with a no.

As she handed another roll to the race's physician, she wondered whether Stephan had lived a full, satisfying life.

No, she thought. He'd been gypped. Totally gypped.

Cheated.

The face was the last to get covered, and she held up Stephan's head as the doctor slowly wound the linen around and around. Ehlena's breath was hard in coming, and just as Havers covered the eyes, one tear left her own and landed on the white wrap.

Havers put his hand on her shoulder briefly and then finished the job.

The salt in the fibers of the linen worked as a sealant so no fluids seeped through the weave, and the mineral also preserved the body for entombment. The herbs served an obvious function in the short term to mask any odor, but they were also emblematic of the fruits of the earth and cycles of growth and death.

With a curse, she went back to the closet and retrieved a black shroud, which she and Havers used to wrap Stephan up. The outer black was to symbolize the corruptible mortal flesh, the inner white the soul's purity and incandescence within its eternal home in the Fade.

Ehlena had once heard that rituals served important purposes beyond the practical. They were supposed to aid in psychological healing, but standing over Stephan's dead body she felt as if that were such bullshit. This was a false closure, a pathetic attempt to contain the exigencies of cruel fate with sweet-smelling cloth.

Nothing but a fresh slipcover over a bloodstained couch.

They stood for a moment of silence at Stephan's head and then pushed the gurney out the back of the morgue and into the tunnel system that ran underground to the garages. There, they put Stephan into one of the four ambulances that were made up to look exactly like the ones humans used.

"I'll drive them both to his parents' home," she said.

"Do you need to be accompanied?"

"I think Alix would do better without any more of an audience."

"You will be of care, though? Not just with them, but your own safety?"

"Yes." Each of the ambulances had a pistol under the driver's seat, and as soon as Ehlena had started working at the clinic, Catya had shown her how to shoot: Without a doubt, she could handle whatever came her way.

As she and Havers shut the ambulance's double doors, Ehlena glanced at the tunnel entrance. "I think I'm going to go back to the clinic across the parking lot. I need the air."

Havers nodded. "And I shall do the same. I find I need the air as well."

Together they walked out into the cold, clear night.

Like the good whore he was, Rehv did everything he was asked to do. The fact that he was rough and unkind was a concession to his free will—and again, part of the reason the princess liked their business.

When it was all over and they were both spent—she from having orgasmed so much, he because the scorpion venom was deep in his bloodstream—those fucking rubies remained where he'd thrown them. On the floor.

The princess was sprawled against the windowsill, panting hard, her three-knuckled fingers splayed, likely because she knew they creeped him out. He was across the cabin, as far as he could get from her, weaving on his two feet.

As he tried to breathe, he hated the way the cabin air smelled of dirty sex. Likewise, her scent was all over him, coating him, suffocating him such that even with the *symphath* blood in his veins, he felt like throwing up. Or maybe that was the venom. Who the fuck knew.

One of her bony hands lifted and pointed to the velvet bag. "Pick. Them. Up."

Rehv's eyes locked on hers, and he shook his head back and forth slowly.

"Better get back to our uncle," he said in a rasp. "I'm willing to bet if you're gone too long he gets suspicious."

He had her on that one. Their father's brother was a calculating, suspicious sociopath. Just like the two of them.

All in the family, as they said.

The princess's robes lifted from the floor and floated over to her, and as they hung in the air beside her, she took a wide red sash out of an inner pocket. Slipping it between her legs, she bound up her sex, keeping what he'd left behind inside of her. Then she clothed herself, covering up the half of the robe he'd torn by making it wrap under the top layer. The gold—or at least he assumed it was gold, given the way it reflected light—belt was next.

"Send my uncle my regards," Rehv drawled. "Or . . . not."

"Pick . . . them . . . up."

"You're either bending over to get that bag, or you're leaving it behind."

The princess's eyes flashed with the kind of nastiness that made murderers so much fun to spar with, and they glared at each other for long, hostile minutes.

The princess cracked. Just as he'd said she would.

To his ever-loving satisfaction, she was the one who did the retrieving, and her capitulation nearly made him come again, that barb of his threatening to engage even though there was nothing for it to lock in against.

"You could be king," she said, holding out her hand, the velvet bag with the rubies lifting from the floor. "Kill him and you could be king."

"Kill you and I could be happy."

"You will never be happy. You are a breed apart, living a lie among inferiors." She smiled, true joy reflecting in her face. "Except here with me. Here, you can be honest. Until next month, my love."

She blew him a kiss with her hideous hands and dematerialized, dissipating in the manner his breath had outside the cabin, eaten up by the thin night air.

Rehv's knees gave out and he collapsed to the floor, landing in a heap of bones. Lying on the rough-hewn planks, he felt everything: the twitching muscles of his thighs, the tickle at the tip of his cock as his foreskin eased back into place, the compulsive swallows which were caused by the scorpion venom.

As the warmth in the cabin leached out, nausea rolled into him on a fetid, oily tide, his stomach curling into a fist, a whole lot of we're-outta-here tightening up his throat. His gag reflex followed orders and he popped open his mouth, but nothing came out.

He knew better than to eat before he had a date.

Trez came through the door so quietly that it wasn't until the guy's boots were in front of Rehv's face that he noticed his best friend was with him.

The Moor's voice was gentle. "Let's get you out of here."

Rehv waited for a break in the heaving to try to push himself up off the floor. "Let me . . . get dressed."

The scorpion poison was barreling through his central nervous system, jamming up his neuro-highways and -byways, making it so that dragging his body over to his clothes involved an embarrassing display of weakness. The trouble was, the antivenin had to stay in the car, because the princess would have found it, and showing a core weakness like that was like handing over your loaded weapon to the enemy.

Trez clearly lost patience with the show, because he went over and picked up the coat. "Just put this on so we can get you treated."

"I . . . get dressed." It was whore's pride.

Trez cursed and knelt down with the coat. "For fuck's sake, Rehv—"

"No—" Wild wheezing cut him off and took him flat on the floor, giving him a quick close-up of the knots in the pine boards.

Man, it was bad tonight. The worst it had ever been.

"Sorry, Rehv, but I'm taking over."

Trez ignored his pathetic attempts to fend off help, and after the sable was wrapped around him, his friend picked him up and carried him out like a broken piece of equipment.

"You can't keep doing this," Trez said as his long legs took them quickly to the Bentley.

"Watch . . . me."

To keep him and Xhex alive and out in the free world, he had to.

NINETEEN

Rehv woke up in his bedroom in the Adirondack Great Camp he used as a safe house. He could tell where he was by the floor-to-ceiling windows, the cheery fire across the way, and the fact that the footboard on the bed had putti carved in the mahogany. What he wasn't clear on was how many hours had passed since his date with the princess. One? A hundred?

Across the dim room, Trez was sitting in an oxblood club chair, reading in the dim yellow light of a goosenecked lamp.

Rehv cleared his throat. "What book is that?"

The Moor looked up, his almond-shaped eyes focusing with a sharpness Rehv could have done without. "You're awake."

"What book?"

"It's *The Shadow Death Lexicon*."

"Light reading. And here I thought you were a Candace Bushnell fan."

"How're you feeling?"

"Fine. Great. Perky as shit." Rehv grunted as he pushed himself up higher on the pillows. In spite of his sable coat, which was wrapped around his naked body, and the quilts and throw blankets and down comforters on top of him, he was still cold as a penguin's ass, so Trez had obviously hit him with a lot of dopamine. But at least the antivenin had worked, so the wheezing and shortness of breath were gone.

Trez slowly closed the ancient book's cover. "I'm just getting ready, s'all."

"For going into the priesthood? I thought the whole king thing was up your alley."

The Moor put the tome on the low table next to him and rose to his full height. After a full-body stretch, he came over to the bed. "You want food?"

"Yeah. That'd be good."

"Gimme fifteen."

As the door shut behind the guy, Rehv fished around and found the sable's inside pocket. When he took out his phone and checked, there were no messages. No texts.

Ehlena hadn't reached out and touched him. But then, why would she have?

He stared at the phone and traced the keyboard with his thumb. He had a striking hunger to hear her voice, as if the sound of her could wipe away everything that had happened in that cabin.

As if she could wipe away the past two and a half decades.

Rehv went into his contacts and fired up her number on the screen. She was probably at work, but if he left a message, maybe she'd call him on her break. He hesitated, but then hit *send* and put the phone up to his ear.

The instant he heard ringing, he got a vivid, vile image of him having sex with the princess, his hips pounding away, the moonlight casting obscene shadows on rough floorboards.

He ended the call on a quick punch, feeling as if his body were coated in shit lotion.

God, there were not enough showers in the world for him to be clean enough to talk to Ehlena. Not enough soap or bleach or steel wool. As he pictured her in her pristine nurse's uniform, her strawberry blond hair back in a neat ponytail, her white shoes unscuffed, he knew that if he ever touched her he'd stain her for life.

With his numb thumb, he stroked the flat screen of the phone, as if it were her cheek, then let his hand fall down onto the bed. The sight of the brilliant red veins of his arm reminded him of a couple more things he'd done with the princess.

He'd never thought of his body as any particular gift. It

was big and muscular, so it was useful, and the opposite sex liked it, which meant it was an asset of sorts. And it functioned all right . . . well, except for the side effects it kicked out from the dopamine and the allergy to scorpion venom.

But really, who was counting.

Lying in his bed in the near-dark, with his phone in his hand, he saw more hideous scenes of his time with the princess . . . her blowing him, him bending her over and fucking her from behind, his mouth working between her thighs. He remembered what it felt like when his cock's barb engaged and the two of them were locked together.

Then he thought of Ehlena taking his blood pressure . . . and how she'd stepped away from him.

She was right to do that.

He was wrong to call her.

With deliberate care, he moved his thumb around the buttons and accessed her contact information. He didn't pause as he erased her out of his phone, and as she disappeared, an unexpected warmth filled his chest—and told him that according to his mother's side, he'd done the right thing.

He would ask for another nurse the next time he went to the clinic. And, if he saw Ehlena again, he would leave her alone.

Trez came in with a tray of oatmeal, some tea, and some dry toast.

"Yum," Rehv said without enthusiasm.

"Be a good boy and finish that. Next meal I'll bring you bacon and eggs."

As the tray was settled over his legs, Rehv tossed the phone on the fur and picked up a spoon. Abruptly, and for absolutely, positively no reason at all, he said, "You ever been in love, Trez?"

"Nah." The Moor returned to his chair in the corner, the curved lamp illuminating his handsome, dark face. "I watched iAm give it a try and decided it wasn't for me."

"iAm? Get the fuck out. I didn't know your brother ever had a chippie."

"He doesn't talk about her, and I never met her. But he was miserable for a while in the way only a female can make a guy."

Rehv swirled around the brown sugar that was sprinkled

on the top of his oatmeal. "You think you'll ever get mated?"

"Nope." Trez smiled, his perfect white teeth flashing. "Why the questions?"

Rehv brought the spoon to his mouth and ate. "No reason."

"Yeah. Right."

"This oatmeal's fantastic."

"You hate oatmeal."

Rehv laughed a little and kept on eating to shut himself up, thinking the subject of love was none of his business. But work sure as hell was.

"Anything happening at the clubs?" he asked.

"Smooth sailing so far."

"Good."

Rehv slowly polished off the Quaker Oats, wondering to himself why, if everything was going fine and dandy down in Caldwell, he had a sinking feeling in his gut.

Probably the oatmeal, he thought. "You told Xhex I was okay, right?"

"Yeah," Trez said, picking up the book he'd been reading. "I lied."

Xhex sat behind her desk and stared up at two of her best bouncers, Big Rob and Silent Tom. They were humans, but they were smart, and in their low-hanging jeans, they gave off the perfect, deceptively laid-back vibe she was looking for.

"What can we do for you, boss?" Big Rob asked.

Leaning forward in her chair, she took out ten folded bills from the back pocket of her leathers. She was deliberate in revealing them, splitting them into two piles, and sliding them toward the men.

"I need you to do some off-the-books work."

Their nods were as fast as their hands on those Benjis. "Anything you like," Big Rob said.

"Back over the summer, we had a bartender who we fired for skimming. Guy named Grady. You remember him—"

"I saw that shit about Chrissy in the paper."

"Fucking bastard," Silent Tom chimed in for once.

Xhex was not surprised they knew the whole story. "I

want you to find Grady." As Big Rob started cracking his knuckles, she shook her head. "Nope. The only thing you do is get me an address. If he sees you, you nod and walk it off. We clear? You do not so much as brush his sleeve."

Both of them smiled grimly. "No problem, boss," Big Rob murmured. "We'll save him for you."

"The CPD is looking for him as well."

"Bet they are."

"We don't want the police to know what you're doing."

"No problem."

"I'll take care of getting your shifts covered. Faster you find him, the happier I'll be."

Big Rob looked over at Silent Tom. After a moment, they took the bills she'd given them out of their pockets and slid them back across the table.

"We'll do right by Chrissy, boss. Don't you worry."

"With you guys on it, I won't."

The door closed behind them, and Xhex ran her palms up and down her thighs, forcing the cilices on her legs to go deeper into her flesh. She was burning with the need to get out there herself, but with Rehv up north and the deals that were going to be made tonight, she couldn't leave the club. Just as important, she couldn't do the legwork on Grady herself. That homicide detective was going to be watching her.

Shifting her eyes to the phone, she wanted to curse. Trez had called earlier to let her know that Rehv had made it through his business with the princess, and the sound of the Moor's voice had told her what his actual words had not: Rehv's body wasn't up for much more of the torture.

Yet another situation she was forced to ride out, sitting on her ass, waiting.

Powerless was not a state that worked for her, but when it came to the princess, she was used to feeling impotent. Way back over twenty years ago, when Xhex's choices had put them in this situation, Rehv had told her he would take care of things on one condition: She let him handle it his way without interfering. He'd made her swear to stay away, and though it killed her, she'd kept the promise and lived in the reality that Rehv had been forced into that bitch's hands because of her.

Goddamn it, she wished he'd lose it and lash out at her.

Just once. Instead, he kept on putting up with it, paying her debt with his body.

She'd turned him into a whore.

Xhex left her office because she couldn't stand to spend any more time with herself, and out in the club she prayed for a skirmish in the general pop, like a love triangle imploding, where one guy bitch-slapped another over a chick with fish lips and plastic tits. Or maybe a bathroom tryst gone sour in the men's room on the mezzanine floor. Shit, she was so desperate she'd even take a drunk getting pissy about his Patrón or some deep corner grind that crossed the line into penetration.

She needed to hit something, and her best chances were with the masses. If only there were—

Just her luck. Everyone was behaving themselves.

Miserable fuckers.

Eventually, she ended up in the VIP section because she was making the floor bouncers mental as she prowled around, trolling for a throw-down. And more to the point, she had to play muscle on a major deal.

As she walked past the velvet rope, her eyes went right to the Brotherhood's table. John Matthew and his buddies were not there, but then, this early, they'd be out hunting for *lessers*. Deep-throating Coronas would come later in the night, if at all.

She did not care whether John showed.

Whatsoever.

Walking up to iAm, she said, "We ready?"

The Moor nodded. "Rally's got the product ready. Buyers should be here in twenty minutes."

"Good."

Two six-figure deals for coke were being executed tonight, and with Rehv down for the count and Trez up north with him, she and iAm were in charge of the transactions. Although the money was going to change hands in the office, the product was going to be loaded into the cars in the back alley, because four kilos of pure South American dust wasn't the kind of thing she wanted dancing through the club. Shit, the fact that the buyers were coming in with cash in briefcases was enough of a problem.

Xhex was just at the office door when she caught sight of Marie-Terese easing up to a guy in a suit. The man was looking at her with awe and wonder, as if she were the female equivalent of a sports car someone had just given him the keys to.

Light glinted off the wedding band he wore as he reached for his wallet.

Marie-Terese shook her head and put her graceful hand out to stop him, then pulled the rapt guy to his feet and led the way to the private bathrooms in the back, where the cash would change hands.

Xhex turned around and found herself in front of the Brotherhood's table.

As she looked at where John Matthew usually sat, she thought about Marie-Terese's most current john. Xhex was willing to bet that SOB, who was about to shell out five hundred dollars to get sucked or fucked or maybe a thousand for both, didn't look at his wife with that kind of excitement and lust. It was the fantasy. He knew nothing about Marie-Terese, had no clue that two years ago her son had been abducted by her ex-husband and she was working off the cost of getting the kid back. To him, she was a gorgeous piece of meat, something to be played with and left behind. Neat. Clean.

All the johns were like that.

And so was Xhex's John. She was a fantasy to him. Nothing more. An erotic lie he called to mind to jerk off to—which actually wasn't something she blamed him for, because she was doing the same thing with him. And the irony was that he was one of the better lovers she'd ever had, although that was because she could do whatever she wanted to him for however long she needed to get sated, and there were never any complaints, reservations, or demands.

Neat. Clean.

iAm's voice came over her earpiece. "Buyers just walked in."

"Perfect. Let's do this."

She would get through both of the deals, and then she had a private job of her own to do. Now, that was something to look forward to. By the end of the night, she was going to get exactly the kind of release she needed.

Across town, in a quiet cul-de-sac in a safe neighborhood, Ehlena was parked in front of a modest colonial, going nowhere fast.

The key wouldn't go into the ambulance's ignition.

Having gotten what should have been the hardest part of the trip over with, having delivered Stephan safely into the arms of his blooded relations, it was a surprise that getting the goddamn key in the frickin' ignition was more difficult.

"*Come on. . . .*" Ehlena focused on steadying her hand. And ended up watching really closely as the slip of metal skipped around the hole it belonged in.

She sat back in the seat with a curse, knowing that she was adding to the misery in the house, that the ambulance parked right outside was just another loud, screaming declaration of the tragedy.

As if the family's beloved son's body weren't enough of one.

She turned her head and stared at the colonial's windows. Shadows moved around on the other side of gauze curtains.

After she'd backed into the driveway, Alix had gone inside and she'd waited in the cold night. A moment later, the garage door had trundled up, and Alix had come forward with an older male who looked a lot like Stephan. She had bowed and shaken his hand, then opened the ambulance's rear bay. The male had had to clamp a hand over his mouth as she and Alix wheeled the gurney out.

"My son . . ." he had moaned.

She would never forget the sound of that voice. Hollow. Hopeless. Heartbroken.

Stephan's father and Alix had carried him home, and just as at the morgue, moments later there had been a wail. This time, though, it had been a female's higher-pitched mourning call. Stephan's mother.

Alix had returned as Ehlena had pushed the gurney into the ambulance's belly, and he had been blinking fast, like if he was facing a stiff headwind. After paying her respects and saying good-bye to him, she'd gotten behind the wheel and . . . not been able to start the damn vehicle.

On the other side of the gauze curtains, she saw two shapes cleave together. And then it was three. And then more came.

For no evident reason, she thought of the windows in the house she rented for her and her father, all of them covered with aluminum foil, sealing out the world.

Who would stand over her wrapped body when her life ended? Her father knew who she was most of the time, but he wasn't connected to her more than rarely. The staff at the clinic were very kind, but that was work, not personal. Lusie was paid to come when she did.

Who would take care of her father?

She'd always assumed he would go first, but then, no doubt Stephan's family had thought along the same lines.

Ehlena looked away from the mourners and stared out the ambulance's front windshield.

Life was too short, no matter how long you lived. When it was their turn, she didn't think anybody was ready to leave their friends and their family and the things that made them happy, be they five hundred years old, like her father, or fifty years, like Stephan.

Time was an endless source of days and nights only for the galaxy at large.

It made her wonder: What the hell was she doing with the time she had? Her job gave her a purpose, sure, and she took care of her father, which was what one did for family. But where was she going? Nowhere. And not just because she was sitting in this ambulance with hands that shook so badly she couldn't work a key.

The thing was, it wasn't that she wanted to change everything. She just wanted something for herself, something that made her know she was alive.

Rehvenge's deep amethyst eyes came at her from out of nowhere, and like a camera pulling back, she saw his carved face and his mohawk and his fine clothes and his cane.

This time, when she reached forward with the key, the thing went in steadily, and the diesel engine came awake on a growl. As the heater blasted cold air at her, she turned down the fan, then put the gearshift in drive and left the house and the cul-de-sac and the neighborhood.

Which no longer seemed quiet to her.

Behind the wheel, she was driving and out of it at the same time, caught up in the image of a male she couldn't have, but at the moment needed like crazy.

Her feelings were wrong on so many levels. For God's sake, they were a betrayal of Stephan, even though she didn't really know him. It just seemed disrespectful to be wanting another male while his body was being mourned by his blood.

Except she would have wanted Rehvenge anyway.

"Damn it."

The clinic was all the way across the river, and she was glad, because she couldn't face work right away. She was too raw and sad and angry at herself.

What she needed was . . .

Starbucks. Oh, yeah, that was *exactly* what she needed.

About five miles away, in a square that was home to a Hannaford supermarket, a flower shop, a LensCrafters boutique, and a Blockbuster store, she found a Starbucks that was open until two a.m. She pulled the ambulance around to the side and got out.

When she'd left the clinic with Alix and Stephan, she hadn't thought to bring her coat, so she huddled into her purse and hotfooted it over the sidewalk and through the door. Inside, the place was as most of them were: red wooden trim, dark gray tile floor, with a lot of windows, stuffed chairs, and little tables. Over at the counter there were mugs for sale, a glass display of lemon squares and brownies and scones, and two humans in their early twenties manning the coffee machines. The smell in the air was hazelnut and coffee and chocolate, and the aroma wiped the lingering herbal bouquet of the death wraps from her nose.

"C'I help you?" the taller guy asked.

"Venti latte, foam, no whip. Double cup, double sleeve."

The human male smiled at her and lingered. He had a dark brush-cut beard and a nose ring, his shirt splashed with graphics that spelled out TOMATO EATER in drops of what could have been blood or, given the band's name, ketchup. "You like anything else? The cinnamon scones totally rock."

"No, thanks."

His eyes stayed on her as he worked her order, and to keep from having to deal with the attention, she went into her purse and checked her phone in case Lusie—

MISSED CALL. View now?

She hit *yes*, praying it wasn't something about her father—

Rehvenge's number came up, although not his name, because she hadn't put him in her phone. She stared at the digits.

God, it was like he'd read her mind.

"Your latte? Hello?"

"Sorry." She put her phone back, took what the guy held out to her, and thanked him.

"I double-cupped just like you wanted. The sleeve, too."

"Thanks."

"Hey, you work at one of the hospitals around here?" he said, eyeing her uniform.

"Private clinic. Thanks again."

She left quickly and didn't waste time getting into the ambulance. Back behind the wheel, she hit the locks on the doors, started the engine, and turned the heater on immediately, because the air coming out was still warm.

The latte was really good. Superhot. Tasted perfect.

She got her phone again and went into the received-calls log and fired up Rehvenge's number.

She took a deep breath and a long pull on the latte.

And hit *send*.

Destiny had a 518 area code. Who knew.

TWENTY

Lash parked the Mercedes 550 under one of Caldwell's bridges, the black sedan indistinguishable from the shadows thrown by the mammoth concrete supports. The digital clock on the dash told him that showtime was getting close.

Assuming there had been no fuckups.

As he waited, he thought about the meeting with the head of the *symphaths*. In retrospect, he really didn't like the way the guy made him feel. He fucked chicks. Period. No guys. Ever.

That kind of shit was for cock jockeys like John and his weak-ass crew.

Switching tracks in his mind, Lash smiled in the darkness, thinking he couldn't wait to reintroduce himself to those motherfuckers. In the beginning, right after he'd been brought back by his real father, he'd wanted to rush it. After all, John and his boys no doubt still hung out at Zero-Sum, so finding them wouldn't be a problem. But timing was everything. Lash was still figuring shit out with this new life of his, and he wanted to be solid when he crushed John and killed Blay in front of Qhuinn, then slaughtered the fucker who'd murdered him.

Timing mattered.

As if on cue, two cars pulled up between some pylons. The Ford Escort was the Lessening Society's, and the silver Lexus was Grady's wholesaler's car.

Sweet rims on the LS 600h. Very sweet.

Grady was the first to get out of the Escort, and when Mr. D and the other two *lessers* followed, it was like watching the evac of a clown car, given the amount of meat that had been stuffed inside.

As they approached the Lexus, two men wearing slick winter coats got out of the 600h. In sync, the human males both put their right hands into their jackets, and all Lash could think of was, *Better guns than badges coming out of those breast pockets.* If Grady had fucked up and those were undercover cops pulling a modern day Crockett and Tubbs, things were going to get complicated.

But no . . . no CPD shields, just some conversation on the part of the coats, no doubt along the lines of, *Who the fuck are those three ass-wipes you brought with you to a private business transaction?*

Grady looked back at Mr. D with out-of-his-league panic, and the little Texan took the reins, stepping forward with an aluminum briefcase. After he put the case on the trunk of the Lexus, he popped it open to reveal what appeared to be stacks of hundred-dollar bills. In reality, they were just bundles of ones with a single Benji on the top of each stack. The coats looked down—

Pop. Pop.

Grady jumped back as the dealers hit the ground like mops, and his mouth opened wide as a toilet bowl. Before he could get a whole lot of oh-my-God-what-did-you-do rolling, Mr. D stepped up into his grille and bitch-slapped his lid shut.

The two slayers put their guns back into their leather jackets as Mr. D closed the suitcase, went around, and got behind the wheel of the Lexus. While he drove off, Grady looked up into the faces of the pale men like he was waiting to get plugged himself.

Instead, they just headed back to the Escort.

After a moment of confusion, Grady followed in a sloppy jog like all his joints had been overoiled, but when he went to open the back door, the slayers refused to let him get in the car. As Grady realized he was getting left behind, he started to panic, his arms flopping, his mouth shouting. Which was pretty fucking dumb, considering he was standing fifteen feet away from two guys with bullets in their brains.

Quiet would be good right about now.

Evidently one of the slayers thought the same thing. With a calm hand, he outted his gun and leveled the muzzle at Grady's head.

Silence. Stillness. At least from the idiot.

Two doors shut and the Escort's engine turned over on a crank and a wheeze. With a buzz of tires, the slayers took off, speckling Grady's boots and shins with frozen dirt.

Lash hit the Mercedes' lights, and Grady spun around, arms going up to shield his eyes.

There was the temptation to mow him down, but for the moment, the guy's utility justified his heartbeat.

Lash started the Mercedes, pulled up to the SOB, and dropped his window down. "Get in the car."

Grady lowered his arms. "What the hell happened—"

"Shut the fuck up. Get in the car."

Lash closed the window and waited while Grady flopped into the passenger seat. As the guy put his belt on, his teeth were doing the castanets, and not from the cold. Fucker was the color of salt, and sweating like a tranny in Giants Stadium.

"You might as well have killed 'em in broad daylight," Grady stammered as they headed out onto the surface road that ran beside the river. "There are eyes all over the place—"

"Which was the point." Lash's phone rang, and he answered as he accelerated up a ramp and onto the highway. "Very nice, Mr. D."

"I think we done good," the Texan said. "'Cept I can't see no drugs. Must be in the trunk."

"They're in that car. Somewhere."

"We still meetin' back at Hunterbred?"

"Yes."

"Hey, ah, listen, y'all plannin' on doin' anything with this here car?"

Lash smiled in the darkness, thinking greed was a great weakness for a subordinate to have. "I'm getting it repainted and buying a VIN and tags for it."

There was silence, as if the *lesser* were waiting for more. "Oh, that'll be good. Y'sir."

Lash hung up on his disciple and turned to Grady. "I

want to know all of the other big retailers in town. Their
names, their territories, their product lines, everything."

"I don't know if I got all that—"

"You'd better find it out then." Lash tossed his phone
into the guy's lap. "Make the calls you need to. Do the digging. I want every single dealer in town. Then I want the elephant that's feeding them. The Caldwell wholesaler."

Grady's head fell back against the seat. "Shit. I thought
this was going to be, like . . . about my business."

"That was your second mistake. Start dialing and get me
what I want."

"Look . . . I don't think this is . . . I should probably go
home. . . ."

Lash smiled at the guy, revealing his fangs and flashing
his eyes. "You are home."

Grady shrank back in the seat, then started pawing for
the door handle, even though they were cruising down the
highway at seventy miles an hour.

Lash hit the locks. "Sorry, you're on the ride now, and
there's no getting off in the middle. Now dial the fucking
phone and do me right. Or I'm going to carve you up piece
by piece and enjoy every second of the screaming."

Wrath stood outside Safe Place in a ball-numbing wind, not
caring two shits about the nasty weather. Rising before him
like something out of a *Leave It to Beaver* Rockwell day-
dream, the house that was a haven to victims of domestic
violence was big and rambling and welcoming, the windows
covered with quilted drapery, a wreath on the door, the mat
on the top step reading WELCOME in cursive letters.

As a male, he couldn't go inside, so he waited like lawn
sculpture on the hard brown grass, praying that his beloved
leelan was inside—and willing to see him.

After having spent all day in the study hoping that Beth
would come to him, he'd finally gone through the mansion
searching her out. When he hadn't found her, he'd prayed
she was volunteering here, as she often did.

Marissa appeared on the back stoop and shut the door
behind herself. Butch's *shellan* and Wrath's former blood
mate looked typically professional in her black slacks and
jacket, her blond hair twisted into an elegant chignon, her
scent like the ocean.

"Beth just left," she said as he walked over to her.

"She go back home?"

"Redd Avenue."

Wrath stiffened. "What the ... Why's she over there?" Shit, his *shellan* out alone in Caldwell? "You mean at her old apartment?"

Marissa nodded. "I think she wanted to go back to where things started."

"Is she alone?"

"As far as I know."

"Jesus Christ, she's already been abducted once," he snapped. As Marissa recoiled, he cursed himself. "Look, I'm sorry. I'm not real rational right now."

After a moment, Marissa smiled. "This is going to sound bad, but I'm glad you're frantic. You deserve to be."

"Yeah, I was a shit. Big-time."

Marissa tilted her head up to the sky. "On that note, a word of advice when you go over to her."

"Hit me."

Her perfect face leveled again, and as she refocused on him, her voice grew rueful. "Try not to be angry. You look like an ogre when you're pissed, and right now, Beth needs to be reminded of why she should let her guard down around you, not why she shouldn't."

"Good point."

"Be well, my lord."

He nodded to her with a quick bob of the head and dematerialized directly to the Redd Avenue address where Beth had had an apartment when they'd first met. As he went, he got a good goddamn taste of what his *shellan* had to deal with every night he was out in the city. Dearest Virgin Scribe, how did she deal with the fear? The idea that everything might not be all right? The fact that there was more danger to be found out where he was than safety?

As he took form in front of the apartment building, he thought of the night he had gone to find her after her father's death. He'd been a reluctant, unsuitable savior, tasked by his friend's last will and testament to see her through her transition—when she hadn't even known what she was.

His first approach hadn't gone well, but the second time he'd tried to talk to her? That had gone *very* well.

God, he wanted to be with her again like that. Naked skin on naked skin, moving together, him deep inside of her, marking her as his.

But that was a long way off, assuming it ever even happened again.

Wrath walked around to the backyard; his shitkickers were quiet, his shadow large on the frosty ground beneath his feet.

Beth was huddled on a rickety picnic table he'd once sat on himself, and she was staring into the apartment straight ahead just as he had when he'd come for her. Cold wind blew her dark hair around, making it seem as if she were underwater and swimming amid strong currents.

His scent must have carried over to her, because her head snapped around. As she looked at him, she sat up straighter and kept her arms locked around the North Face parka he'd bought her.

"What are you doing here?" she said.

"Marissa told me where you were." He glanced at the apartment's sliding glass door, then back at her. "Mind if I join you?"

"Ah . . . okay. That's fine." She shuffled over a little as he came to her. "I wasn't going to be here long."

"No?"

"I was going to come see you. I wasn't sure when you were going out to fight and thought maybe there was time before . . . But then, I don't know, I . . ."

As she let the sentence drift, he got up on the table beside her, the supports squeaking as the thing accepted his heft. He wanted to put an arm around her, but hung back and hoped the parka was doing its job to keep her warm enough.

In the silence, words buzzed in his head, all of them of the apologetic variety, all of them bullshit. He'd already said he was sorry, and she knew he meant it, and it was going to be a long time before he stopped wishing there were more he could do to make it up to her.

On this cold night, as they sat suspended between their past and their future, all he could do was sit with her and stare at the darkened windows of the apartment she had once lived in . . . back before fate had put them together.

"I don't remember being especially happy in there," she said softly.

"No?"

She swept her hand across her face, clearing wisps of hair from her eyes. "I didn't like coming home from work and being there alone. Thank God for Boo. Without that cat? I mean, TV only does so much for a person."

He hated that she had been on her own. "So you don't wish you could go back?"

"Christ, no."

Wrath exhaled. "I'm glad."

"I was working for that leering asshole, Dick, at the paper, doing the jobs of three people, getting nowhere because I was a young woman and the good old boys didn't have a club—they were in a cabal." She shook her head. "But you know what the worst of it was?"

"What?"

"I was living with this sense that there was something going on, something important, but I didn't know what it was. It was like . . . I knew the secret was there, and it was a dark one, but I just couldn't reach it. Nearly drove me mad."

"So finding out you weren't just a human was—"

"These last months with you have been worse." She looked over at him. "When I think back over the fall . . . I knew something was wrong. In the back of my mind, I knew it, I could absolutely sense it. You stopped coming to bed regularly, and if you did, it wasn't to sleep. You couldn't settle. You didn't really eat. You never fed. The kingship always stressed you, but these last couple of months have been different." She went back to staring at her old apartment. "I knew it, but I didn't want to face the reality that you might actually be lying to me about something as significant and terrifying as you going out alone to fight."

"Shit, I didn't mean to do that to you."

Her profile was both beautiful and hard as she continued. "I think that's part of the head fuck I've got going on now. The whole thing takes me back to the way I used to live every day of my life. After I went through the change and you and I moved in with the Brothers, I was so relieved, because I finally knew for sure what I'd always wondered about. The truth was incredibly grounding. It made me feel safe." She turned back to him. "This thing with you? The lying? I don't feel like I can trust my reality again. I just don't feel safe. I mean, my whole world is about you. My *whole* world. It's all based on you, because our mating is the foundation of my life. So this is about so much more than you fighting."

"Yeah." Fuck. What the hell did he say?

"I know you had your reasons."

"Yeah."

"And I know you didn't mean to hurt me." This was spoken with a lift at the end, the words a question, rather than a statement.

"I absolutely didn't mean to."

"But you knew it would, didn't you."

Wrath put his elbows on his knees and leaned into his heavy arms. "Yeah, I did. That's why I haven't been sleeping. It felt wrong not to tell you."

"Were you afraid I'd refuse to let you go out or something? That I'd turn you in for violating the law? Or . . . ?"

"Here's the thing. . . . At the end of every night I came home and told myself I wasn't doing it again. And every sunset I found myself strapping on my daggers. I didn't want you to worry, and I told myself I didn't think it would continue. But you were right to call me on that. I had no plans to stop." He rubbed his eyes under his wraparounds as his head started to pound. "It was so wrong, and I couldn't face up to what I was doing to you. It was killing me."

Her hand went to his leg and he froze, her kind touch more than he deserved. As she stroked his thigh a little, he dropped his sunglasses back in place and carefully captured her hand.

Neither said a thing as they held on to each other, palm-to-palm.

Sometimes words were less valuable than the air that carried them when it came to getting close.

As the cold wind blew across the backyard, causing some brown leaves to crackle by in front of them, the lights went on in Beth's old place, illumination flooding the galley kitchen and the single main room.

Beth laughed a little. "They put their furniture right where mine was, the futon against that one long wall."

Which meant they had a full view of the couple who came stumbling into the studio and beelined for the bed. The humans were locked lip-to-lip, hip-to-hip, and they landed on the futon in a messy scramble, the man mounting the woman.

As if embarrassed by the show, Beth got off the table and cleared her throat. "I guess I'd better get back to Safe Place."

"I'm off rotation tonight. I'll be at home, you know, all night."

"That's good. Try to get some rest."

God, the distance was horrid, but at least they were talking. "You want me to see you back there?"

"I'll be fine." Beth burrowed into her parka, her face sinking into the down collar. "Man, it's cold."

"Yeah. It is." As the time for parting came, he was anxious about where they stood, and fear made his vision fairly clear. God, how he hated the lonely look on her face. "You can't know how sorry I am."

Beth reached up and touched his jaw. "I hear it in your voice."

He took her hand and placed it over his heart. "I'm nothing without you."

"Not true." She stepped out of his hold. "You are the king. No matter who your *shellan* is, you are everything."

Beth dematerialized into the thin air, her vital, warm presence replaced with nothing but frigid December wind.

Wrath waited for about two minutes; then he dematerialized to Safe Place. She had so much of his blood in her after all their time of feeding from each other that he sensed her presence inside the stout walls of the security-laden facility, and he knew she was protected.

With a heavy heart, Wrath dematerialized again and headed back to the mansion: He had stitches to get removed and a whole night to pass alone in his study.

TWENTY-ONE

An hour after Trez took the tray back down to the kitchen, Rehv's stomach was in full revolt. Man, if oatmeal was no longer a viable food afterward, what was he left with? Bananas? White rice?

Fucking Gerber baby gruel?

And it wasn't just his digestive tract that was screwed up. If he'd been able to feel anything, he was pretty sure he had a headache along with the tossing nausea. Anytime there was a light source, like when Trez came in to check on him, Rehv's eyes went on autoblink, flickering up and down in an uncoordinated, ocular version of the Safety Dance; then he'd start to salivate and swallow compulsively. So he had to be nauseated.

As his phone went off, he put his hand on it and brought it to his ear without turning his head. There was a lot going on at ZeroSum tonight, and he needed to keep tabs. "Yeah."

"Hi . . . you called me?"

Rehv's eyes shot to the bathroom door, which had a soft light glowing around the jambs.

Oh, God, he hadn't had a shower yet.

He was still covered with the sex he'd had.

Even though Ehlena was about a three-hour drive away and he wasn't on a Web cam, he felt absolutely nasty just talking to her.

"Hey," he said in a rough voice.

"Are you all right?"

"Yeah." Which was a total fucking lie, and the gravel in his voice made that obvious.

"Well, I, ah . . . I saw that you'd called me—" As a strangled sound came out of his mouth, Ehlena stopped. "You're sick."

"No—"

"For God's sake, please come to the clinic—"

"I can't. I'm . . ." God, he couldn't bear to speak to her. "I'm not in town. I'm upstate."

There was a long pause. "I'll bring the antibiotics to you."

"No." She couldn't see him like this. Shit, she couldn't see him ever again. He was filthy. A filthy, dirty whore who let someone he hated touch him and suck on him and use him, and force him to do the same to her.

The princess was right. He was a fucking dildo.

"Rehv? Let me come to you—"

"No."

"Goddamn it, don't you do this to yourself!"

"You can't save me!" he shouted.

In the aftermath of his explosion, he thought, Jesus . . . where had that come from? "I'm sorry . . . it's been a bad night for me."

When Ehlena finally spoke, her voice was a thin whisper. "Don't do this to me. Don't make me see you in the morgue. Don't do that to me."

Rehv squeezed his eyes shut. "I'm not doing anything to you."

"The hell you aren't." Her voice cracked on a sob.

"Ehlena . . ."

Her moan of despair came through the phone all too clearly. "Oh . . . Christ. Whatever. Kill yourself, fine."

She hung up on him.

"Fuck." He rubbed his face. *"Fuck!"*

Rehv sat up and fired the cell phone at the bedroom door. And just as it ricocheted off the panels and went flying, he realized he'd busted the only thing he had with her number in it.

With a roar and a messy scramble, he launched his body off the bed, quilts landing everywhere. Not a great move on his part. As his numb feet hit the throw rug, he went Frisbee, finding air briefly before landing on his face. On impact, a sound like a bomb had gone off rumbled through the floorboards, and he crawled for the phone, tracking the light that still glowed from its screen.

Please, oh, fucking please, if there is a God . . .

He was almost in range when the door swung open, narrowly missing his head and clipping the phone—which shot like a hockey puck in the opposite direction. As Rehv wheeled around and lunged for the thing, he shouted at Trez.

"Don't shoot me!"

Trez was in full fighting stance, gun up and pointed at the window, then the closet, then the bed. "What the *fuck* was that."

Rehv sprawled out flat to reach the phone, which was spinning under the bed. When he caught it, he closed his eyes and brought it close to his face.

"Rehv?"

"Please . . ."

"What? Please . . . what?"

He opened his eyes. The screen was flickering, and he pressed the buttons fast. Calls received . . . calls received . . . calls r—

"Rehv, what the hell is going on?"

There it was. The number. He stared at the seven digits after the area code as if they were the combination to his own safe, trying to get them all.

The screen went dark and he let his head fall down on his arm.

Trez crouched beside him. "You okay?"

Rehv pushed himself out from under the bed and sat up, the room spinning like a merry-go-round. "Oh . . . fuck me."

Trez holstered his gun. "What happened?"

"I dropped my phone."

"Right. Of course. Because it weighs enough to make that kind of— Hey, easy, there." Trez caught him as he tried to get up. "Now where are you going?"

"I need a shower. I need . . ."

More pictures of him with the princess hammered into his brain. He saw her back arched, that red mesh split free of her ass, him buried deep in her sex, pumping until that barb of his locked him inside of her so that his release would get way up into her.

Rehv pressed his fists into his eyes. "I need to . . ."

Oh, Jesus . . . He orgasmed when he was with his blackmailer. And not just once, usually three or four times. At least the whores in his club who hated what they did for the money could take solace in the fact that they didn't enjoy it. But a male's release said it all, didn't it.

Rehv's gag reflex tightened, and in a panic he Curlyshuffled into the bathroom. The oatmeal and the toast made a successful bid for liberation, and Trez was right there to hold him over the loo. Rehv couldn't feel the retching, but he was damn sure that his esophagus was getting torn, because after a couple of minutes of coughing and trying to breathe and seeing stars, blood started to come up.

"Lie back," Trez said.

"No, shower—"

"You're in no shape—"

"I have to get her off me!" Rehv's voice bellowed through not just his bedroom, but the whole house. "For fuck's sake . . . *I can't stand her.*"

There was a moment that positively smacked of *holy crap*: Rehv wasn't the type to ask for a life jacket even if he were drowning, and he never bitched about the arrangement with the princess. He got through it and did what he had to and paid the consequences, because it was all worth it to him to keep his and Xhex's secret.

And part of you likes it, an inner voice pointed out. *You get to be you without apology when you're in her.*

Fuck off, he told himself.

"I'm sorry I yelled at you," he said to his friend hoarsely.

"Nah, it's cool. Don't blame you." Trez gently lifted him up from the tile and tried to reposition him on the sinks. "It's about time."

Rehv lurched for the shower.

"Nope," Trez said, pushing him back. "Let me get the water warm."

"I won't feel it."

"Your core temperature has enough problems already. Just stay there."

As Trez leaned into the marble shower and turned on the water, Rehv stared down at his cock, which lay loose and long down his thigh. It seemed like the sex of someone else, and that was a good thing.

"You realize I could kill her for you," Trez said. "I could make it look like an accident. No one would know."

Rehv shook his head. "I don't want you sucked into this shithole. We got enough people down it already."

"The offer stands."

"Duly noted."

Trez reached in and put his hand under the spray. With his palm in the rushing water, his chocolate eyes drifted back and abruptly became white from anger. "Just so we're clear. You die? I'm going to skin that bitch alive in the s'Hisbe tradition and send the strips back to your uncle. Then I'm going to spit-roast her carcass and chew the meat from her bones."

Rehv smiled a little, thinking it wasn't cannibalism, because on a genetic level Shadows had as much in common with *sympaths* as humans did with chickens.

"Hannibal Lecter motherfucker," he murmured.

"You know how we do." Trez shook the water off his hand. "*Symphaths* . . . it's what's for dinner."

"You going to bust out the fava beans?"

"Nah, but I might have a nice Chianti with her, and some *pommes frites*. I gotta have some tater with my meat. Come on, let's get you under the water and wash that bitch's stank off."

Trez walked over and got Rehv up off the counter.

"Thank you," Rehv said quietly as they limped toward the shower.

Trez shrugged, knowing damn well they weren't talking about the visit to the bathroom. "You'd do the same for me."

"I would."

Under the spray, Rehv worked the Dial over himself until his skin was red as a raspberry, and got out of the shower only after he'd done his three-times-over wash. When he stepped free of the water, Trez handed him a towel, and he dried off as fast as he could without losing his balance.

"Speaking of favors . . ." he said, "I need your phone. Your phone and some privacy."

"Okay." Trez helped him back to bed and covered him up. "Man, good thing this duvet didn't land in the fire."

"So can I have your phone?"

"You going to play soccer with it?"

"Not as long as you leave my door closed."

Trez handed him a Nokia. "Take care of her. She's brand-new."

When he was alone, Rehv dialed carefully and hit *send* on a wing and a prayer, having no clue whether or not he got the number right.

Ring. Ring. Ring.

"Hello?"

"Ehlena, I'm so sorry—"

"Ehlena?" the female voice said. "Sorry, there isn't any Ehlena at this number."

Ehlena sat in the ambulance holding in her tears out of habit. It wasn't like anyone could see her, but the anonymity didn't matter. As her latte cooled in its double cup, double sleeve, and the heater ran intermittently, she kept herself together because that's what she always did.

Until the CB radio went off with a squawk and scared her out of her numb colds.

"Base to four," Catya said. "Come in, four."

As Ehlena reached for the handset, she thought, See, this was exactly why she could never let her guard down. If she'd been a wilted mess and had to answer? Not where she needed to be.

She hit the *talk* button with her thumb. "This is four."

"Are you okay?"

"Ah, yes. I just needed . . . I'm coming back right now."

"There's no hurry. Take your time. I only wanted to make sure you were okay."

Ehlena glanced at the clock. God, it was nearly two a.m. She'd been sitting out here, gassing herself by running the engine and the heater, for almost two hours.

"I'm so sorry, I had no idea what time it was. Do you need the ambulance for a pickup?"

"No, we were just worried about you. I know you assisted Havers on that body and—"

"I'm fine." She rolled down the window to let some air

in and put the ambulance in gear. "I'm coming back right away."

"Don't rush, and listen, why don't you take the rest of the night off."

"That's okay—"

"It's not a request. And I've switched the schedule around so you have tomorrow free as well. You need a break after tonight."

Ehlena wanted to argue, but she knew that would just come across as defensive, and besides, with the decision made, there was nothing to fight for.

"All right."

"Take your time coming back."

"I will. Over and out."

She hung up the handset and headed for the bridge that would take her across the river. Just as she was accelerating on the ramp, her phone went off.

So Rehv was calling her back, huh. Not a surprise.

She took out the phone only to confirm that it was him, not because she was intending to answer his call.

Unknown number?

She hit *send* and brought her cell to her ear. "Hello?"

"Is this you?"

Rehv's deep voice still managed to shoot through her on a warm thrill, even though she was pissed off at him. And herself. Basically at the whole situation.

"Yes," she said. "This isn't your phone number, though."

"No, it's not. My cell had an accident."

She rushed ahead before he got to any *sorry*s. "Look, it's none of my business. Whatever's going on with you. You're right, I can't save you—"

"Why do you even want to try?"

She frowned. If the question had been self-pitying or accusatory, she would have just ended the call and changed her number. But there was nothing but sincere confusion coming through in his voice. That and utter exhaustion.

"I just don't understand . . . the why," he murmured.

Her answer was simple and from the soul. "How can I not."

"What if I don't deserve it."

She thought of Stephan lying on that stainless steel, his

body cold and bruised. "Everyone with a beating heart deserves to be saved."

"Is that why you got into nursing?"

"No. I got into nursing because I want to be a doctor someday. The saving thing is just the way I see the world."

The silence between them lasted forever.

"Are you in a car?" he said eventually.

"An ambulance, actually. I'm going back to the clinic."

"You're out alone?" he growled.

"Yes, and you can cut the he-man crap. I've got a gun under the seat and I know how to use it."

A subtle laugh came through the phone. "Okay, that's a turn-on. I'm sorry, but it is."

She had to smile a little. "You drive me nuts, you know that. Even though you're all but a stranger to me, you drive me up the frickin' wall."

"And somehow I'm complimented." There was a pause. "I'm sorry about earlier. I've had a bad night."

"Yeah, well, me too. On both the sorry part and the bad night."

"What happened?"

"It's too much to go into. How about you?"

"Ditto."

As he shifted, a sheet rustled. "Are you in bed again?"

"Yes. And yes, you still don't want to know."

She smiled widely. "You're telling me I shouldn't ask what you're wearing again."

"You got it."

"We're so falling into a rut, you know that?" She grew serious. "You sound really sick to me. Your voice is hoarse."

"I'll be all right."

"Look, I can bring you what you need. If you can't make it to the clinic, I can bring the medicine to you." The silence on the other end was so dense, and went on for so long, she said, "Hello? You there?"

"Tomorrow night . . . can you meet me?"

Her hands tightened on the steering wheel. "Yes."

"I'm on the top floor of the Commodore. Do you know the building."

"I do."

"Can you be there at midnight? East side."

"Yes."

His exhale seemed one of resignation. "I'll be waiting for you. Drive safely, okay?"

"I will. And don't throw your phone anymore."

"How did you know?"

"Because if I'd had an open space in front of me instead of the dashboard of an ambulance, I would have done the same thing."

His laugh made her smile, but she lost the expression as she hit *end* and put the phone back in her purse.

Even though she was driving at a steady sixty-five and the road ahead of her was straight and free of debris, she felt as if she were totally out of control, careening from guardrail to guardrail, leaving a trail of sparks as she ground off parts of the clinic's vehicle.

Meeting him tomorrow night, being alone with him somewhere private, was exactly the wrong thing to do.

And she was going to do it anyway.

TWENTY-TWO

Wontrag, son of Rehm, hung up the phone and stared out the French doors of his father's study. The gardens and the trees and the rolling lawn, like the great mansion and everything in it, were his now, no longer a legacy he would one day inherit.

As he took in the grounds, he enjoyed the sense of ownership singing in his blood, but he was less than satisfied with the view. Everything was battened down for winter, the flower beds emptied, the blooming fruit trees blanketed with mesh, the maples and oaks without their leaves. As a result, one could see the retaining wall, and that was just not attractive. Better for those ugly security sorts of things to be covered.

Montrag turned away and walked over to a more pleasing vista, albeit one that was mounted on the wall. With a flush of reverence, he regarded his favorite painting in the manner he always had, for indeed Turner deserved veneration for both his artistry and his choices of subject. Especially in this work: The depiction of the sun setting over the sea was a masterpiece on so many levels, the shades of gold and peach and deep burning red a feast for eyes robbed by biology of the actual glowing furnace that sustained and inspired and warmed the world.

Such a painting would be the pride of any collection.

He had three Turners in this house alone.

With a hand that twitched in anticipation, he took hold

of the lower right-hand corner of the gilt frame and pulled the seascape from the wall. The safe behind it fit the precise dimensions of the painting and was inset into the lath and plaster. After twisting the combination on the dial, there was a subtle shifting that was barely audible, giving no hint that each of the six retracting pins was thick as a forearm.

The safe opened without a sound and an interior light came on, illuminating a twelve-cubic-foot space stacked with thin leather jewelry cases, bound bundles of hundred-dollar bills, and documents in folders.

Montrag brought over a needlepointed stepping stool and got up on its flowered back. Reaching far into the safe, going behind all the real estate deeds and stock certificates, he took out a strongbox and then put the safe and the painting back as they had been. With a feeling of excitement and possibility, he carried the metal box over to the desk and got the key from the lower left-hand drawer's secret compartment.

His father had taught him the combination of the safe and shown him the location of the hiding place, and when Montrag had sons, he would pass down the knowledge to them. That was how one made sure things of value were not lost. Father to son.

The lid of the strongbox did not open with the same well-calibrated, well-lubricated slide the safe did. This one came wide with a squeak, the hinges protesting the disturbance of their rest and reluctantly revealing what lay within its metal belly.

They were still there. Thank the Virgin Scribe they were still there.

As Montrag reached inside, he thought, so relatively worthless, these pages, valued by themselves at a fraction of a penny. The ink held within their fibers was worth but a penny, as well. And yet for what they spelled out, they were invaluable.

Without them he was at mortal risk.

He took out one of the two documents and it didn't matter which he removed, as they were identical. Between careful fingers, he held the vampire equivalent of an affidavit, a three-page, handwritten, signed-in-blood dissertation concerning an event that had happened twenty-four years ago. The notarized signature on the third page was sloppy, a scrawl in brown that was barely legible.

But then, it had been made by a dying man.

Rehvenge's "father," Rempoon.

The documents laid the ugly truth all out in the Old Language: Rehvenge's mother's abduction by the *symphaths*, his conception and birth, her escape and later marriage to Rempoon, an aristocrat. The last paragraph was as damning as everything else:

> *Upon my honor, and the honor of mine blooded ancestors and decedents, verily on this night did mine stepson, Rehvenge, fall upon me and cause to be rendered unto my body mortal wounds through the application of his bare hands upon my flesh. He did so with malice aforethought, having lured me into my study with the object of provoking an argument. I was unarmed. Following my injuries, he did go about the study and prepare the room for to appear to have been invaded by intruders from without. Verily, he did leave me upon the floor for death's cold hand to capture my corporeal form, and he did depart from the premises. I was roused briefly by my dear friend Rehm, who had come to visit for the purpose of business discussions.*
>
> *I am not expected to live. My stepson has killed me. This is my final confession on earth as an embodied spirit. May the Scribe Virgin carry me unto the Fade with her grace and all alacrity.*

As Montrag's father had later explained it, Rempoon had gotten it mostly right. Rehm had come on business and found not only an empty house, but the bloody body of his partner—and had done what any reasonable male would have: He'd rifled through the study himself. Operating under the assumption Rempoon was dead, he'd set about trying to find the papers on the business so that Rempoon's fractional interest would stay out of his estate and Rehm would own the going concern outright.

Having succeeded in his quest, Rehm had been on his way to the door when Rempoon had shown a sign of life, a name leaving his cracked lips.

Rehm had been comfortable being an opportunist, but

falling into the roll of accomplice to murder went too far. He'd called for the doctor, and in the time it took Havers to arrive, the mumblings of a dying male had spelled out a shocking tale, one worth even more than the company. Thinking quickly, Rehm had documented the story and the stunning confession about Rehvenge's true nature and had Rempoon sign the pages—thus turning them into a legal document.

The male had then lapsed into unconsciousness and been dead when Havers had arrived.

Rehm had taken both the business papers and the affidavits with him when he'd left and been touted as a valiant hero for trying to rescue the dying male.

In the aftermath, the utility of the confession had been obvious, but the wisdom of putting such information in play was less clear. Tangling with a *symphath* was dangerous, as Rempoon's spilled blood had attested. Ever the intellectual, Rehm had sat on the information and sat on it . . . until it was too late to do anything with it.

By law, you had to turn a *symphath* in, and Rehm had the kind of proof that met the threshold for reporting someone. However, in considering his options for so long, he found himself in the dicey position of arguably protecting Rehvenge's identity. If he'd come forward twenty-four or forty-eight hours later? Fine. But one week? Two weeks? A month . . . ?

Too late. Rather than squander the asset completely, Rehm had told Montrag about the affidavits, and the son had understood the father's mistake. There had been nothing that could be done in the short run, and only one scenario where it was still worth anything—and that had come to pass over the summer. Rehm had been killed in the raids and the son had inherited everything, including the documents.

Montrag couldn't be blamed for his father's choice not to reveal what was known. All he had to do was state that he'd stumbled upon the papers in his father's things, and in turning them and Rehv in, he was just doing what he was supposed to.

It would never come out that he'd known about them all along.

And nobody would ever believe that Rehv hadn't been

the one who'd decided to kill Wrath. He was, after all, a *symphath*, and nothing they said could be trusted. More to the point, his hand was either going to be on the trigger, or if he just ordered the murder of the king, he was the *leahdyre* of the council and in the position to profit from the death the most. Which was precisely why Montrag had had the male elevated into the role.

Rehvenge would do the deed with the king, and then Montrag would go to the council and prostrate himself before his colleagues. He would say that he didn't find the papers until he had properly moved into the Connecticut house a month after both the raids and after Rehv had been made *leahdyre*. He would swear that as soon as he found them he reached out to the king and revealed the nature of the issue over the phone—but Wrath had forced his silence because of the compromising position it put the Brother Zsadist in: After all, the Brother was mated to Rehvenge's sister, and that would make her related to a *symphath*.

Wrath, of course, could say nothing to the contrary after he was dead, and more to the point, the king was disliked already for the way he had ignored the *glymera*'s constructive criticism. The council was primed to embrace another fault of his, real or manufactured.

It was intricate maneuvering, but it was going to work, because with the king gone, the remnants of the council would be the first place the race would go looking for the murderer, and Rehv, a *symphath*, was the perfect scapegoat: Of course a *symphath* would do such a thing! And Montrag would help the motive assumption along by testifying that Rehv had come to see him before the murder and talked with bizarre conviction about change of an unprecedented variety. In addition, crime scenes were never completely clean. Undoubtedly, there would be things left behind that would tie Rehv to the death, whether because it was actually there or because everyone would be looking for exactly that kind of evidence.

When Rehv fingered Montrag? No one would believe him, primarily because he was a *symphath*, but also because, in the tradition of his father, Montrag had always cultivated a reputation for thoughtfulness and trustworthiness in his business dealings and social conduct. As far as his fellow members of the council knew, he was above reproach, incapable of deception, a male of worth from impeccable bloodlines. None of them had a clue that he and his father had double-crossed many a partner or associate or blood relation—because they had been careful to choose the ones they preyed upon so that appearances were maintained.

The result? Rehv would be brought up on charges of treason, arrested, and either put to death according to vampire law or deported to the *symphath* colony, where he would be killed for being a half-breed.

Either outcome was acceptable.

It was all set, which was why Montrag had called his closest friend just now.

Taking the affidavit, he folded it in on itself, and slid it into a thick, creamy envelope. Drawing a page of his personalized stationery from an embossed leather box, he penned a quick missive to the male who he would tap as his second in command, and cemented the stage for Rehvenge's fall. In the note, he explained that, as they'd discussed over the phone, this was what he had found in his father's private papers—and if the document was validated, he was concerned for the future of the council.

Naturally, the thing would be verified by the law office of his colleague. And by the time it was, Wrath would be dead and Rehv poised for blame.

Montrag lit a stick of red wax, dripped some of it on the envelope's flap, and sealed the affidavit in. On the front, he wrote the male's name, and in the Old Language spelled out *HAND DELIVERY ONLY*; then he closed up and locked the metal box, tucking it under his desk, and returning the key to its safe place in the secret drawer.

A button on the phone summoned the butler, who took the envelope and immediately headed off to complete the task of getting it into the correct hands.

Satisfied, Montrag took the lockbox over to the wall safe, pivoted the painting outward, put his father's combination to use, and returned the remaining affidavit to its home: Keeping one copy for himself was only prudent, a safeguard in the event something happened to the document that was on its way across the border into Rhode Island.

As he eased the Turner back into place, the landscape spoke to him as always, and for a moment, he allowed himself to step out of the bedlam he was creating with purpose and seep into the peaceful, lovely sea. The breeze would be warm, he thought.

Dearest Virgin Scribe, how he missed the summer during these cold months, but then, it was contrast that enlivened the heart. Without the cold of winter, one would not truly appreciate the sultry nights of July and August.

He pictured where he would be in six months when a full solstice moon rose o'er Caldwell's sprawling city. Come June, he would be king, an elected and respected monarch. If only his father had been alive to see—

Montrag coughed. Breathed in with a hiccup. Felt something wet on his hand.

He looked down. Blood was all over the front of his white shirt.

Opening his mouth to shout in alarm, he tried to draw in a deep breath, but there was only a gurgling sound—

His hands snapped up to his neck and found a geyser jumping free of his exposed carotid artery. Wheeling around, he saw a female standing before him with a man's haircut and black leathers. The knife in her hand had a red blade, and her face was a calm mask of detached disinterest.

Montrag fell to his knees before her and then pitched over to his right, his hands still trying to keep his lifeblood in his body and not all over his father's Aubusson.

He was still alive when she rolled him over, took out a rounded tool made of ebony, and knelt down to him.

As an assassin, Xhex's job performance was measured in two dimensions. First, did she get her target? Self-explanatory. Second, was it a clean kill? Meaning, was there no collateral damage in the form of other deaths to protect herself, her identity, and/or the identity of the individual who had tasked her with the job.

In this case, the first was going to be a snap, given the way Montrag's artery was doing the drainpipe. The second was still open to question, so she needed to work fast. She took the *lys* out of her leathers, bent over to the bastard, and didn't waste more than a nanosecond watching his eyes roll around.

She grabbed his chin and forced his face to hers. "Look at me. *Look* at me."

His wild stare shot to hers, and when it did, she brought the *lys* forward. "You know why I'm here and who sent me. It's not Wrath."

Montrag clearly had enough air still going to his brain, because his lips mouthed, *Rehvenge,* in horror, before those eyeballs of his started rolling again.

She let go of his chin and slapped him hard. "Pay attention, asshole. *Look at me.*"

With their stares locked and her grip back on his jaw, she peeled the upper and lower lids of his left eye even wider. "*Look at me.*"

As she took the *lys* and pressed it into the socket at the corner near his nose, she reached into his brain and triggered all sorts of memories. Ah . . . interesting. He'd been a conniving fucker for real, specializing in screwing people about money.

Montrag's hands slapped into the rug and dug in hard as he gurgled his way through a scream. The eyeball came out of the skull like a scoop of honeydew off its rind, as perfectly round and clean as you'd want. The right eye was just the same, and she put both of them in a lined velvet pouch as Montrag's arms and legs jerked and flopped on his expensive rug, his lips peeling back such that every single one of his teeth including his molars showed.

Xhex left him to his sloppy death, walking right out of the French door behind the desk and dematerializing to the maple she'd first cased the place from the day before. She waited there for about twenty minutes and then watched as a *doggen* entered the study, saw the body, and dropped the silver tray she was carrying.

As the teapot and the china bounced, Xhex cocked her phone open, hit *send,* and put the thing to her ear. When Rehv's deep voice answered she said, "It's done and they've found him. Kill was clean and I'm bringing you the souvenir. ETA ten minutes."

"Well-done," Rehv said in a husky voice. "Well-fucking-done."

TWENTY-THREE

$\mathcal{W}$rath frowned as he spoke into his cell phone. "Now? You want me to come upstate now?"

Rehv's voice was all about the I'm-not-fucking-around. "This has to be done in person, and I'm immobile."

Across the study, Vishous, who had been about to report on the work he'd been doing tracking those crates of guns, mouthed, *What the fuck?*

Which was exactly what Wrath was thinking. A *symphath* calls you two hours before dawn and asks you to come upstate because he has "something he needs to give you." Yeah, okay, the bastard was Bella's brother, but his nature was what it was and sure as shit, the "something" was not a fruit basket.

"Wrath, this is important," the guy said.

"Okay, I'm coming right now." Wrath clipped his phone shut and looked at Vishous. "I'm—"

"Phury's out hunting tonight. You can't go there alone."

"The Chosen are in the house." And had been staying off and on at Rehv's Great Camp since Phury had taken the reins as Primale.

"Not exactly the kind of protection I had in mind."

"I can handle myself, fuck you very much."

V crossed his arms over his chest, his diamond eyes flashing. "Are we going now? Or after you waste time trying to change my mind?"

"Fine. Whatever. I'll meet you in the foyer in five."

As they left the study together, V said, "About those guns? I'm still working on the trace. Right now, I've got nothing, but you know me. That ain't going to last, true. I don't care if the serial numbers are scrubbed, I'm going to find out where the hell they got them."

"Confidence is high, my brother. Confidence is very high."

After they were fully armed, the two of them traveled in a loose dance of molecules up north, zeroing in on Rehv's Great Camp in the Adirondacks and materializing on the shores of a quiet lake. Up ahead, the house was a huge rambler of a Victorian, shingled and diamond paned, with cedar-post porches on both stories.

Lot of corners. Lot of shadows. And a lot of those windows looked like eyes.

The mansion was spooky enough on its own, but with it surrounded by a force field of the *symphath* equivalent of *mhis*, a guy could credibly believe that Freddy, Jason, Michael Myers, and that redneck crew with all the chain saws lived inside: All around the place, dread was an intangible fence made of mental barbed wire, and even Wrath, who knew what was doing, was glad to get on the other side of the barrier.

As he forced his eyes to focus better, Trez, one of Rehv's personal guard, opened the double doors on the porch that faced the lake and raised his palm in greeting.

Wrath and V walked up the frosty, crunchy lawn and though they kept their weapons holstered, V took the glove off his glowing right hand. Trez was the kind of male you respected, and not just because he was a Shadow. The Moor had the muscled body of a fighter and the smart stare of a strategist, and his allegiance was to Rehv and Rehv only. To protect the guy? Trez would level a city block in the blink of an eye.

"So how you doing, big man," Wrath said he mounted the porch steps.

Trez came forward and they clapped palms. "I'm solid. You?"

"Tight as always." Wrath knocked the guy in the shoulder. "Hey, you ever want a real job, come soldier with us."

"I'm happy where I am, but thanks." The Moor grinned

and turned to V, his dark eyes flicking down to V's exposed hand. "No offense, but I'm not shaking that thing."

"Wise of you," Vishous said as he offered his lefty. "You understand, though."

"Abso, and I'd do the same for Rehv." Trez led the way to the doors. "He's in his bedroom waiting for you."

"He sick?" Wrath asked as they entered the house.

"You want anything to drink? Eat?" Trez said as they headed to the right.

As the question remained unanswered, Wrath glanced at V. "We're okay, thanks."

The place was decorated right out of Victoria and Albert's back pocket, with heavy Empire furniture and garnet and gold everywhere. True to the Victorian period's affection for collection, each room had a different theme to it. One sitting parlor was full of antique clocks ticking away, from grandfathers to brass windups to pocket watches in display cases. Another had shells and coral and centuries-old driftwood. In the library, there were stunning Oriental vases and platters, and the dining room was kitted out in medieval icons.

"I'm surprised there aren't more Chosen here," Wrath said as they went through empty room after empty room.

"The first Tuesday of the month, Rehv has to come up. He makes the females a little nervous, so most of them go back over to the Other Side. Selena and Cormia always stay, though." There was no small measure of pride in his voice as he tacked on, "They're very strong, those two."

They took a grand set of stairs up to the second floor and went down a long hall to a pair of carved doors that positively screamed *master of the house*.

Trez paused. "Listen, he is a little ill, okay. Nothing contagious. It's just . . . I want you both to be prepared. We've given him everything he needs and he's going to be fine."

As Trez knocked and opened both doors, Wrath frowned, his vision sharpening on its own as his instincts pricked.

In the midst of a carved bed, Rehvenge was lying still as a corpse, a red velvet duvet pulled up to his chin and sable folds draped over his body. His eyes were closed, his breathing shallow, his skin pasty and tinged with yellow. His close-cropped mohawk was the only thing that looked remotely normal . . . that and the fact that standing at his right hand was Xhex, that half-breed *symphath* female who looked like she performed castrations for fun and profit.

Rehv's eyes opened, and the amethyst color was dulled to a murky bruised purple. "It's the king."

"S'up."

Trez shut the doors, parking it to the side and not in the middle to block the way as a measure of respect. "I already offered them libations and eats."

"Thanks, Trez." Rehv grimaced and made a move to push himself off the pillows. When he just sagged, Xhex leaned in to help him, and he shot her a glare that smacked of don't-even-think-about-it. Which she ignored.

After he was settled upright, he pulled the duvet up to his neck, covering the red stars tatted on his chest. "So I have something for you, Wrath."

"Oh, yeah?"

Rehv nodded at Xhex, who reached into the leather jacket she was wearing. The instant she moved, V's gun muzzle flipped up quick as a blink, aimed square at the female's heart.

"You want to slow that roll?" she snapped to V.

"Not in the slightest. Sorry." V sounded about as sorry as a wrecking ball in midswing.

"Okay, let's just relax," Wrath said, and inclined his head toward Xhex. "Go ahead."

The female pulled free a velvet bag and tossed it in Wrath's direction. As it came at him, he heard the soft whistle of its flight and caught the thing not by sight, but by sound.

Inside were two pale blue eyes.

"So, I had an interesting meeting last night," Rehv drawled.

Wrath looked at the *symphath*. "Whose blank stare do I have in my palm."

"Montrag, son of Rehm. He came to me and asked me to kill you. You got deep enemies in the *glymera*, my friend, and Montrag's only one of them. I don't know who else was in on the plot, but I wasn't taking any chances at finding out before we took action."

Wrath put the eyes back in the bag and closed his fist around them. "When were they going to do it."

"At the council meeting, the night after tomorrow."

"Son of a bitch."

V put his gun away and crossed his arms over his chest. "You know, I despise those motherfuckers."

"Speaking to the choir," Rehv said before refocusing on Wrath. "I didn't come to you before I solved the problem because I'm kind of sweet on the idea of the king owing me something."

Wrath had to laugh. "Sin-eater."

"You know it."

Wrath jogged the bag in his hand. "When did this happen?"

"About a half hour ago," Xhex answered. "I didn't clean up after myself."

"Well, they'll certainly get the message. And I'm still going to that meeting."

"You sure that's wise?" Rehv said. "Whoever else is behind this will not come to me again, because they know where my loyalties appear to lie. But that doesn't mean they won't find someone else."

"So let them," Wrath said. "I'm down with mortal combat." He glanced at Xhex. "Montrag implicate anyone?"

"I slit his throat from ear to ear. Talk was tough."

Wrath smiled and glanced at V. "You know, it's kind of a surprise you two don't get along better."

"Not really," they said at the same time.

"I can postpone the council meeting," Rehv murmured. "If you want to do recon yourself to see who else was involved."

"Nope. If they had balls of any size, they'd have tried to kill me themselves, not get you to do it. So one of two things is going to happen. Since they don't know whether Montrag outted them before he became visually impaired, they're either going to go into hiding, because that's what cowards do, or they're going to shift the blame to someone else. So the meeting goes on."

Rehv smiled darkly, the *symphath* in him obvious. "As you wish."

"I want an honest answer from you, though," Wrath said.

"What's the question."

"For real, did you think about killing me? When he asked."

Rehv was a silent for a bit. Then he slowly nodded. "Yeah, I did. But like I said, you owe me now, and given my ... circumstances of birth, as it were ... that's far more valuable than what any smarmy-ass aristocrat can do for me."

Wrath nodded once. "That's logic I can respect."

"Plus, let's face it"—Rehv smiled again—"my sister's married into the family."

"That she has, *symphath*. That she has."

After Ehlena put the ambulance in the garage, she went across the parking lot and down into the clinic. She needed to get her things from her locker, but that wasn't what was driving her. Usually at this time of night, Havers would be doing charts in his office, and that was where she headed. When she came up to his door, she took her scrunchie out, smoothed back her hair, and tightly knotted it at the base of her neck. Her coat was still on, but even though it hadn't been that expensive, it was made of black wool and looked tailored, so she figured she looked okay.

She knocked on the jamb, and when a cultured voice called out, she went in. Havers's former office had been a splendid old-world study, filled with antiques and leather-bound books. Now that they were at this new clinic, his private workspace was no different from anyone else's: white walls, linoleum floor, stainless-steel desk, black rolling chair.

"Ehlena," he said as he glanced up from the charts he was reviewing. "How fare you?"

"Stephan is where he belongs—"

"My dear, I had no idea you knew him. Catya told me."

"I ... did." But maybe she shouldn't have mentioned that to the female.

"Dearest Virgin Scribe, why didn't you say?"

"Because I wanted to honor him."

Havers removed his tortoiseshell glasses and rubbed his eyes. "Alas, that is something I can understand. Still, I wish I had known. Dealing with the dead is never easy, but it is especially hard if they are of personal acquaintance."

"Catya has given me the rest of the shift off—"

"Yes, I told her to. You have had a long night."

"Well, thank you. Before I leave, though, I want to ask you about another patient."

Havers put his glasses back on. "Of course. Which one?"

"Rehvenge. He came in last evening."

"So I recall. Is he having some difficulty with his medications?"

"Did you by any chance see his arm?"

"Arm?"

"The infection in the veins on the right side."

The race's physician pushed his tortoiseshell glasses up on his nose. "He didn't indicate that his arm was giving him bother. If he wants to come back in and see me, I'll be happy to look at it. But as you know, I can't prescribe anything without examining him."

Ehlena opened her mouth to argue when another nurse poked her head in. "Doctor?" the female said. "Your patient is ready in exam room four."

"Thank you." Havers looked back at Ehlena. "Now do go home and have a rest."

"Yes, Doctor."

She ducked out of his office and watched the race's physician hurry off and disappear around the corner.

Rehvenge wasn't coming back in here to see Havers. No way. One, he'd sounded too sick to, and two, he'd already proven he was a hardheaded idiot when he'd deliberately hidden that infection from the doctor.

Stupid. Male.

And she was stupid as well, considering what was banging around in her head.

Generally speaking, ethics were never a problem for her: Doing the right thing didn't require thought or a negotiation of principles or a cost-and-benefit calculation. For example, it would be wrong to go into the clinic's supply of penicillin and lift, oh, say, eighty five-hundred-milligram tablets.

Especially if you were giving those tablets to a patient who had not been seen by the doctor for the ailment being treated.

That would just be wrong. All the way around.

The right thing would be to call the patient and persuade him to come into the clinic and get seen by the doctor, and if he wouldn't get his ass in gear? Then that was that.

Yup, not a lot of complications there.

Ehlena headed for the pharmacy.

She decided to leave it up to fate. And what do you know, it was cigarette-break time. The little BE RIGHT BACK clock read three forty-five.

She checked her watch. Three thirty-three.

Unlatching the counter door, she went into the pharmacy, beelined for the penicillin jugs, and shook out those eighty five-hundred-milligram tablets into the pocket of her uniform—exactly what had been prescribed for a patient with a similar issue three nights ago.

Rehvenge was not going to come back to the clinic anytime soon. So she would bring what he needed to him.

She told herself that she was helping a patient and that was the most important thing. Hell, she was probably saving his life. She also pointed out to her conscience that this was not OxyContin or Valium or morphine. As far as she was aware, no one had ever crushed up some 'cillin and snorted it for a high.

As she went into the locker room and picked up the lunch she'd brought but hadn't eaten, she didn't feel guilty. And as she dematerialized home, she felt no shame in going to the kitchen and putting the pills in a Ziploc bag and tucking them into her purse.

This was the course she was choosing. Stephan had been dead by the time she got to him, and the best she'd been able to do was help wrap his cold, stiff limbs in ceremonial linen. Rehvenge was alive. Alive and suffering. And whether he was the cause of it or not, she could still help him.

The outcome was moral even if the method was not.

And sometimes that was the best you could do.

TWENTY-FOUR

By the time Xhex got back to ZeroSum it was three thirty a.m., just in time to close the club. She also had a little work to do on herself, and unlike zeroing out the cash registers and sending the staff and the bouncers off into the night, she couldn't wait on her personal biz.

Before she'd left Rehv's Great Camp, she'd gone into a bathroom and put her cilices back on, but the fuckers weren't working: She was buzzing. Twitchy with power. Right on the edge. For all the good they were doing, she might as well have been wearing a pair of shoelaces tied around her thighs.

Slipping in the side door to the VIP section, she scanned the crowd, well aware that she was looking for one male in particular.

And he was there.

Fucking John Matthew. A job well-done always made her hungry, and the last thing she needed was proximity to the likes of him.

As if he felt her eyes on him, his head lifted and his deep blue marbles flashed. He totally knew what she wanted. And given the way he discreetly rearranged himself in his pants, he was ready to be of service.

Xhex couldn't stop herself from torturing them both. She sent him a mental scene, drilling the image right into his head: the two of them in a private bathroom, him up on the sink and leaning back, her with one foot planted on the counter, his sex deep in hers, the two of them panting.

While he stared across the crowded room, John's mouth parted, and the flush on his cheeks had nothing to do with embarrassment and everything to do with the orgasm that was no doubt pounding up his shaft.

God, she wanted him.

His buddy, the redhead, snapped her out of the madness. Blaylock came back to the table with three beers hanging from their necks, and as he took a look at John's hard, sexed-up face, he stopped short and glanced over at her in surprise.

Shit.

Xhex waved off the bouncers who were coming up to her and walked out of the VIP section so fast, she nearly bowling-pinned a waitress.

Her office was the only place that was safe, and she headed there at a dead run. Assassination was an engine that, once she turned it on, was hard to slow, and memories of the kill, of the sweet moment when she'd met Montrag's eyes with her own and then taken his sight from him, were juicing up her *symphath* side. Burning off that energy, taking herself back down, required one of two things.

Sex with John Matthew was definitely one of them. The other was much less pleasurable, but beggars couldn't be choosers, and she was about to take her *lys* out and go to work on all the humans in her way. Which wouldn't be good for business.

A hundred years later, she closed her door on the noise and the cattlelike crush of people, but there was no relaxing in her barren haven. Hell, she couldn't even calm herself enough to tighten her cilices. She paced around the desk, caged, ready to boil over, trying to get herself level so she could—

With a roar, the change thundered down upon her, her visual field flipping into shades of red like someone had just put a visor down over her eyes. All at once, the emotional grids of every single living thing in the club popped into her brain, walls and floors disappearing and being replaced by the vices and the desperations, the angers and the lusting wants, the cruelties and the pain that were as solid to her as the club's structure had once been.

Her *symphath* side had had it with the let's-play-nices

and was ready to make hides out of that herd of simpering, strung-out humans outside.

As Xhex took off like the dance floor was on fire and she was only one with an extinguisher, John sank back down into his banquette. After what he'd seen in his head dissipated, the pinprick tingles over his skin started to fade, but his erection was having none of the oh-well-maybe-another-time.

His cock was hard in his jeans, trapped behind the button fly.

Shit, John thought. Shit. Just . . . shit.

"Way to cock-block, Blay," Qhuinn muttered.

"I'm sorry," Blay said as he slid in and passed out the beers. "I'm sorry. . . . Shit."

Well, didn't that cover things perfectly.

"You know, she's really into you," Blay said with a hint of admiration. "I mean, I thought we came here just so you could stare at her. But I didn't know she was looking at you like that, too."

John ducked his head to cover up his cheeks as they waaaaay surpassed the red of Blay's hair.

"You know where her office is, John." Qhuinn's mismatched eyes stayed level as he tilted back his freshie and drank hard. "Go there. Now. At least one of us can get a little relief."

John eased back and rubbed his thighs, thinking exactly what Qhuinn was. But did he have the balls for that? What if he approached her and she turned him down?

What if he lost his hard-on again?

As he remembered what he'd seen in his head, though, he wasn't so worried about that. He was ready to orgasm right where he sat.

"You could go back into her office alone," Qhuinn continued softly. "I can wait at the head of the hall and make sure no one interrupts. You'll be safe, and it will be private."

John thought of the one and only time he and Xhex had been in an enclosed space alone together. It had been back in August in the men's bathroom on the mezzanine floor, and she'd found him careening out of a stall, drunk as shit.

Even as polluted as he'd been, one look at her and he'd been ready to go, desperate for her sex—and thanks to a boatload of Corona confidence, he'd had the colossal cojones to go up to her and write her a little message on a paper towel. It had been payback for what she herself had demanded of him.

Fair was fair. He wanted her to say his name when she got herself off.

Since then they'd kept apart at the club, but damn close in their beds—and he knew she'd been doing as he'd asked; he could tell by the way she looked at him. And tonight's little telepathic exchange about what she was thinking they should be doing in one of the bathrooms was proof positive that even she followed orders once in a while.

Qhuinn put a hand on John's arm, and when he looked over, the guy signed, *Timing is everything, John.*

Too true. She wanted him, and tonight it was not just in the fantasy, home-alone sense. John didn't know what had changed for her or what the trigger was, but his cock didn't give a shit about those kinds of details.

Outcome was all that mattered.

Literally.

Besides, for fuck's sake, was he going to stay a virgin for the rest of his life just because of something that had been done to him a lifetime ago? Timing *was* everything, and he was sick and tired of sitting on his hands, denying himself what he really wanted.

John rose to his feet and nodded once at Qhuinn.

"Thank fuck," the guy said as he slid out of the banquette. "Blay, we'll be back."

"Take your time. And, John, good luck, okay?"

John clapped his friend on the shoulder and jacked up his jeans before heading out of the VIP section. Qhuinn and he passed by the bouncers standing at the velvet rope and then the sweaty dancers grinding and the people making out and a crowd that was gathering for last call around the big bar. Xhex was nowhere to be found, and he wondered if she hadn't left for the night.

No, he thought. She had to be here to close up, because Rehv hadn't been seen around.

"Maybe she's already in her office," Qhuinn said.

As they went up the stairs to the mezzanine floor, he

thought of the first time he'd met her. Talk about wrong foot. She'd dragged him down this hallway and interrogated him after she'd caught him tucking a gun so Qhuinn and Blay could have some tail in peace. That was how she'd learned his name and his ties to Wrath and the Brotherhood, and the way she'd manhandled him had been a total turn-on . . . once he'd gotten over the conviction that she was going to tear him limb from limb.

"I'll be right here." Qhuinn stopped at the head of the corridor. "It's going to be fine."

John nodded and then put one foot after the other, after the other, the hall getting darker and darker as he went along. When he got to her door, he didn't pause to gather himself, too afraid he'd pull a pussy and bolt back to his buddy.

Yeah, and how ball-less would that look?

Besides, he wanted this. He *needed* this.

John lifted his knuckles to knock—and froze. Blood. He smelled . . . blood.

Hers.

Without thinking, he busted open the door and—

Oh. My. God, he mouthed.

Xhex's head snapped up from what she was doing, and the sight of her burned his eyes. Her leathers were off and draped on the edge of the chair, her legs streaked with her own blood . . . blood that welled from the barbed metal bands that were locked around both her thighs. She had one black boot up on the desk and was in the process of . . . tightening them?

"Get the fuck out of here!"

Why, he mouthed, coming at her, reaching out. *Oh . . . God, you have to stop.*

With a deep growl in her throat, she pointed at him. *"Don't come near me."*

John started to sign fast and sloppy, even though she didn't understand ASL. *Why are you doing that to yourself—*

"Get the fuck out of here. Now."

Why? he shouted at her silently.

As if in answer, her eyes flashed ruby red, like there were colored flashbulbs mounted in her skull, and John went utterly cold.

There was only one thing in the Brotherhood's world that did that.

"Go."

John spun around and fast-tracked to the door. As he reached for the knob, he saw that it was lockable from the inside, and with a quick twist of the stainless-steel ridge, he locked her in so no one else would see her.

As he came up to Qhuinn, he didn't stop. He just kept right on going, not caring whether his friend and personal guard was behind him.

Of all the things he could ever have learned about her, this was one he couldn't possibly have foreseen.

Xhex was a frickin' *symphath*.

TWENTY-FIVE

Across Caldwell, on a tree-lined street, Lash was sitting inside a brownstone apartment in a club chair that was slipcovered in dark velvet. Hanging beside him were the only other remnants of the stylish, wealthy humans who'd previously lived in the place: Swaths of beautiful damask drapery ran from floor to ceiling, accentuating the bay windows that bowed out over the sidewalk.

Lash loved the damn drapes. They were wine, gold, and black, and fringed with gold satin balls the size of marbles. In their lush glory, they reminded him of the way things had always been when he'd lived in that big Tudor mansion up on the hill.

He missed the elegance of that life. The staff. The meals. The cars.

He was spending so much time with the lower classes.

Shit, the *human* lower classes, considering the pool where *lessers* were drawn from.

He reached out and stroked one of the drapes, ignoring the blush of dust that bloomed in the still air as soon as he touched it. Lovely. So heavy and substantial with nothing cheap about it, not the fabric, not the dyes, not the hand-sewn hems or borders.

The feel of it made him realize he needed a good house of his own, and he thought maybe this brownstone could be it. According to Mr. D, the Lessening Society had owned this place for the last three years, the property having been purchased by a *Fore-lesser* who was convinced vampires were in the area. A two-car garage was tucked in the back alley, so there was privacy, and the home was as close to graceful as he was going to get anytime soon.

Grady came in with a cell phone up to his ear, on the final lap of the pacing trail he'd developed over the past two hours. As he talked, the guy's voice echoed up to the high, ornate ceilings.

Now properly motivated by his adrenal gland, the guy had coughed up the names of seven dealers and had been calling them one after another and schmoozing his way into meetings.

Lash glanced down at the piece of paper Grady had scribbled his list on. Whether all the contacts worked out only time would tell, but one of them was definitely solid. The seventh person, whose nomenclature was circled in black at the bottom, was someone Lash knew: the Reverend.

A.k.a. Rehvenge, son of Rempoon. Owner of ZeroSum.

A.k.a. territorial fucker who had booted Lash out of the club because he'd sold a few grams here and there. Shit, Lash couldn't believe he hadn't thought of it sooner. Of course Rehvenge would be on the list. Hell, he was the river that spawned all the streams, the guy the South Americans and the Chinese manufactures dealt with directly.

Didn't this make things even more interesting.

"Okay, I'll see you then," Grady said into the phone. As he hung up, he looked over. "I don't have the Reverend's number."

"But you know where to find him, right." Duh. Everybody in the drug trade from pushers to users to the police knew where the guy hung out, and for that reason it was a wonder the place hadn't been shut down long ago.

"That's going to be a problem, though. I'm banned from ZeroSum."

Join the club. "We'll work around that."

Although not by sending a *lesser* in to try to make a deal. They were going to need a human for that. Unless they could lure Rehvenge out of his den, which was unlikely.

"Am I done now?" Grady asked, glancing desperately at the front door, like he was a dog who badly needed to go out for a piss.

"You said you needed to stay under the radar." Lash smiled, flashing his fangs. "So you're going back with my men to their place."

Grady didn't argue, just nodded and crossed his arms over the front of that *fakakta* eagle jacket of his. His acquiescence was equal parts personality, fear, and exhaustion. Clearly, it had dawned on him that he was in much deeper shit than he'd first realized. No doubt he thought the fangs were cosmetic add-ons, but someone who thought he was a vampire could be almost as deadly and dangerous as someone who really was.

The butler's door from the kitchen opened, and Mr. D came in with two square packages wrapped in cellophane. The pair were each the size of a head, and Lash saw a whole lot of dollar signs as the *lesser* brought them over.

"I done found them in 'er quarter panels."

Lash took out his switchblade and punctured a small hole in each. A quick lick of the white powder and he was smiling again. "Good quality. We're going to cut the shit out of it. You know where to put it."

Mr. D nodded and went back into the kitchen. When he returned, the other two slayers were with him, and Grady wasn't the only one who looked beat. *Lessers* needed to recharge every twenty-four hours, and at last count, they had been going for, like, forty-eight straight. Even Lash, who could power up for days, was feeling drained.

Time to crash out.

Getting up from the chair, he drew on his coat. "I'm driving. Mr. D, you're going sit in the back of the Mercedes and make sure Grady enjoys being chauffeured. You other two, take the POS."

They all departed, leaving the Lexus in the garage with the plates off and the VIN stripped.

The trip over to the Hunterbred apartment complex didn't take long, but Grady managed to fit a nap in. In the rearview mirror, the fucker was out like a light, his head lying back against the seat, his mouth open as he snored.

Which bordered on disrespect, really.

Lash pulled up to the apartment where Mr. D and his pair of buddies stayed, and craned around, looking back at Grady.

"Wake up, asshole." As the guy blinked and yawned,

Lash despised the weakness, and Mr. D likewise seemed unimpressed. "Rules are simple. If you try to bolt, my men will either shoot you on the spot or call the police and tell them exactly where you are. Nod your dumb-ass head if you understand what I'm saying."

Grady nodded, although Lash had a feeling he would have done that no matter what he'd been told. Eat your own feet. Okay, sure, fine.

Lash released the locks. "Get the fuck out of my car."

More nodding as the doors were opened and the bitter wind shot in. As he stepped free of the Mercedes, Grady huddled into his coat, that stupid fucking eagle getting its wings crowded as the human curled around himself. Mr. D, on the other hand, wasn't as bothered by the cold—one of the benefits to already having died.

Lash reversed out of the parking lot and headed off to where he stayed in town. His place was just a shithole ranch in a development full of old people—with windows that only had drapes from, like, Target to shut out his walleyed, Depends-wearing neighbors. The only advantage was that no one in the Society knew what the address was. Although he slept at the Omega's for safety reasons, coming back to this side left him logy for a half hour or so, and he didn't want to be caught unawares by anyone.

Thing was, sleep was a misnomer for what he needed. He didn't so much close his eyes and snooze away; he all but passed out, which, according to Mr. D, was what happened when you were a *lesser*. For some reason, with his father's blood in them they were like cell phones that couldn't be used when they were charging.

As he thought about going back to the ranch, he got depressed and found himself driving into the wealthiest part of Caldwell instead. The streets here were as well-known to him as the lines of his own palm, and he found the stone pillars of his old house easily.

The gates were shut tight, and he couldn't see over the tall wall that went around the property, but he knew what was inside: the grounds and the trees and the pool and the terrace . . . everything perfectly kept.

Shit. He wanted to live like that again. This downmarket existence with the Lessening Society felt like a cheap suit of clothes. Not him. On any level.

He put the Mercedes in park and just sat there, staring at the drive. After murdering the vampires who'd raised him and burying them in the side yard here, he'd stripped the Tudor of everything that wasn't nailed down, the antiques being stored at various *lesser* houses around and outside of town. He hadn't been back since he'd gone to pick up this car, and he assumed that through his parents' wills, the property had passed to whatever blooded relative of theirs was left after the raids he'd performed on the aristocracy.

He doubted the estate was still in the race's name. After all, it had been infiltrated by *lessers* and was therefore permanently compromised.

Lash missed the mansion, though he couldn't have used it as HQ. Too many memories, and more to the point, it was too close to the vampire world. His plans and his accounts and the Lessening Society's intimate details were not the kind of shit he wanted to risk falling into Brotherhood hands.

There would be a time when he met up with those warriors again, but it would be on his terms. Since he'd been murdered by that mutant defective Qhuinn, and his true father had come for him, no one but that fucker John Matthew had seen him—and even with that mute-ass idiot it had been in only a hazy way, the kind of thing that, considering they'd all seen his dead body, someone would write off as a misperception.

Lash liked making big entrances. When he came out to the vampire world, it was going to be from a position of dominance. And the first thing he was going to do was avenge his own death.

His future plans made him miss the past a little less, and as he looked up at the leafless trees getting blown around in the stiff wind, he thought of the force of nature.

And wanted to be exactly that.

As his cell phone went off, he cocked it and put it to his ear. "What."

Mr. D's voice was all business. "We've had an infiltration, suh."

Lash's palms squeezed the wheel hard. "Where."

"Here."

"Mother*fucker*. What did they get?"

"Jars. All three of them. That's why we done know it was the Brothers. Doors are solid, windows, too, so no idea how they got in. Must have happened sometime in the last two nights, because we ain't been sleeping here since Sunday."

"Did they get into the apartment below?"

"No, that is secure."

At least they had one thing going for them. Still, lost jars were a problem.

"Why didn't the security alarm go off?"

"It was not engaged."

"Jesus *Christ*. You'd better fucking be there when I pull up." Lash ended the call and wrenched the steering wheel around. As he floored the Mercedes, the sedan shot toward the gates, the front bumper raking across the iron slates.

Fucking wonderful.

When he got to the apartment, he parked right by the stairwell entrance and nearly ripped the door off the car getting out. With ice-cold gusts blowing his hair around, he took the stairs two at a time and shot into the place, ready to cap someone.

Grady was sitting on a stool at the kitchen counter's overhang, his jacket off, his sleeves rolled up, a whole lot of I'm-so-staying-out-of-this on his puss.

Mr. D was coming out of one of the bedrooms in the middle of a sentence. ". . . don't get how they found this here—"

"Who were the fuckups?" Lash said, shutting out the howling wind. "That's all I care about. Who was the dumb-ass who didn't engage the alarm and compromised this address? And if someone doesn't man up, I'm holding you"—he pointed to Mr. D—"responsible."

"It weren't me." Mr. D stared hard at his men. "I weren't back here since two day ago."

The *lesser* on the left raised his arms, but typical to his breed, it wasn't in subjugation, but because he was ready to fight. "I got my wallet and I ain't talked to no one."

All eyes went to the third slayer, who got annoyed. "What the fuck?" He made a show of going into his back pocket. "I got my . . ."

He shoved his hand in farther, like that might help. Then he did a Three Stooges, checking every pocket he had among his pants, his jacket, and his shirt. No doubt the fucker would have opened his own ass up for a look-see if he'd thought there was a chance his billfold had worked its way up into his colon.

"Where's your wallet," Lash asked smoothly.

Light dawned on Marblehead. "Mr. N . . . that fucker. We got into an argument 'cause he wanted some green from me. We fought and he must have nicked my billfold."

Mr. D calmly walked up behind the slayer and nailed him in the side of the head with the butt of his Magnum. The force of impact sent the slayer spinning like a beer cap and slamming into the wall, a black smudge staining the linen-white paint as he slid down onto the cheap tan rug.

Grady let out a bark of surprise, like a terrier who'd gotten smacked with a newspaper.

And then the doorbell rang. Everyone looked to the sound, then at Lash.

He pointed to Grady. "You stay right where you are." When the bell came again, he nodded at Mr. D. "Answer it."

As the little Texan stepped over the downed slayer, he tucked his heat into his waistband at the small of his back. He opened the door only a crack.

"Domino's," a male voice said as a blast of wind blew in. "Oh—crap, watch it!"

It was a comedy of fucking errors, the kind of thing you'd see in a movie full of slapstick cock-ups. The stiff wind caught hold of the pizza box as the delivery guy took it out of his red insulated box-bag, and the pepperoni-and-something went flying toward Mr. D. Ever the good employee, flyboy with the Dom cap lunged forward to catch the thing—and ended up plowing over Mr. D and busting into the apartment.

Which Lash was willing to bet employees of Domino's were specifically instructed never to do, and with good reason. You cracked into someone's house, even if you were being a hero, and you could find all kinds of bad shit: Perverted porn on a TV. Fat hausfrau in her granny panties and no bra. A nasty-ass hovel with more cockroaches than people.

Or a member of the undead bleeding black blood from a head wound.

There was no way Pizza Guy wasn't going to see what

was doing across the way. And that meant he would have to be dealt with.

After having spent what was left of the night roaming around downtown Caldwell looking for a *lesser* to fight, John took form in the courtyard at the Brotherhood's mansion, next to all the cars that were parked in an orderly row. Bitter wind shoved at his shoulders, a bully wanting to knock him down, but he stood tall against the onslaught.

A *symphath*. Xhex was a *symphath*.

As his mind churned over the revelation, Qhuinn and Blay materialized beside him. To their credit, neither had asked him what the hell had happened back at ZeroSum. Both, however, continued to look at him like he was a beaker in a science lab, as if they were waiting for him to change colors or froth up all over himself or something.

I need some space, he signed without meeting either of their stares.

"No problem," Qhuinn replied.

There was a pause as John waited for them to go in the house. Qhuinn cleared his throat once. Twice.

Then in a choked voice, he said, "I'm sorry. I didn't mean to push you again. I—"

John shook his head and signed, *It's not related to sex. So don't worry, k?*

Qhuinn frowned. "Okay. Yeah, cool. Ah . . . you need us, we're around. Come on, Blay."

Blay followed, the two of them walking up the shallow stone steps and going into the mansion.

Standing alone, finally, John had no idea what to do or where to go, but dawn was coming soon, so short of a quick jog through the gardens, he had few outdoor options.

Although, God, he wondered whether he could even go inside. He felt contaminated by what he'd learned.

Xhex was a *symphath*.

Did Rehvenge know? Did anyone else?

He was well aware of what the law required him to do. He'd learned that in training: When it came to *symphaths*, you reported them for deportation or you were deemed an accomplice. Pretty damn clear-cut.

Except what happened then?

Yeah, no guessing at that. Xhex would be shipped off

like trash to a dump—and things would not go well for her. It was clear she was a half-breed. He'd seen photographs of *symphaths*, and she looked nothing like those tall, thin, creepy-ass SOBs. So chances were very good she'd be killed up in the colony, because from what he knew, *symphaths* were like the *glymera* when it came to discrimination.

Save for the fact that they liked to torture what they derided. And not in the verbal sense.

What the fuck did he do . . .

When the cold had him shivering under his leather jacket, he went into the house and directly up the grand staircase. The doors of the study were open, and he could hear Wrath's voice, but he didn't stop to see the king. He kept walking, going around the corner to the hall of statues.

He wasn't heading for his room, though.

John pulled up in front of Tohr's door and paused to stroke his hair flat. There was only one person he wanted to talk this through with, and he prayed that for once there would be something coming back to him.

He needed help. Badly.

John knocked softly.

No answer. He knocked again.

As he waited and waited, he stared at the panels of the door and considered the last two times he'd burst into rooms uninvited. The first had been over the summer when he'd barged into Cormia's bedroom and found her naked and curled on her side with blood on her thighs. Result? He'd pummeled the holy hell out of Phury for no reason, as the sex had been consensual.

The second had been Xhex, tonight. And look at the situation that had put him in.

John knocked harder, his knuckles banging loud enough to wake the dead.

No answer. Worse, no sounds at all. No TV, no shower, no voices.

He stepped back to see if there was a glow coming from under the door. Nope. So Lassiter wasn't in there.

Dread made him swallow hard, as he slowly opened the door wide. His eyes went first to the bed, and when Tohr wasn't lying there, John flat-out panicked. Racing across the Oriental rug, he shot through into the bath, fully ex-

pecting to find the Brother sprawled out in the Jacuzzi with
his wrists cut.

There was no one in either room.

A strange, giddy hope flared in his chest as he went back
into the hall. Looking left and right, he decided to start with
Lassiter's bedroom.

No answer, and, looking inside, he found a whole lot of
neat and tidy along with the dimming scent of fresh air.

This was good. The angel had to be with Tohr.

John hot-stepped it down to Wrath's study and, after he
knocked on the jamb, he put his head in, doing a quick review of the spindly sofa and the armchairs and the mantel
by the fireplace that the Brothers liked to lean against.

Wrath looked up from the desk. "Hey, son. What's
doing?"

Oh, nothing. You know. Just . . . excuse me.

John headed down the grand staircase at a jog, knowing
that if Tohr was having his first foray back into the world,
he wouldn't want to make a big deal out of it. He'd probably start simple, just going into the kitchen for food with
the angel.

Downstairs, John hit the foyer's mosaic floor, and when
he heard male voices to the right, he looked inside the billiards room. Butch was bent over the pool table about to
take a shot, and Vishous was behind him, heckling. The
wide-screen was showing a whole lot of ESPN, and only
two squat glasses were out, one with amber liquid in it, the
other with crystal-clear stuff that was not water.

Tohr wasn't there, but he'd never been big into games.
Besides, with the way Butch and V went after each other,
they were not the kind of company you'd want if you were
just dipping your feet in social waters again.

Turning away, John hurried through the dining room,
which had been set for Last Meal, and went into the kitchen,
where he found . . . *doggen* preparing three different kinds
of pasta sauces and taking homemade Italian bread out of
the oven and tossing salads and opening bottles of red wine
to breathe and . . . no Tohr.

Hope decanted out of John's chest, leaving behind a
sour tightness.

He went up to Fritz, butler extraordinaire, who greeted

him with a brilliant smile on his old, wrinkled face. "Hello, sire, how fare thee?"

John signed in front of his chest so no one else could see. *Listen, have you seen . . .*

Shit, he didn't want to make a panic in the household for no reason other than that he was jumping to conclusions. The mansion was huge and Tohr could be anywhere.

. . . anyone? he finished.

Fritz's fuzzy white eyebrows pulled together. "Anyone, sire? Do you refer to the ladies of the house or—"

Males, he signed. *Have you seen any of the Brothers?*

"Well, I have been here preparing dinner for much of the last hour, but I know that several have come home from the field. Rhage had his sandwiches as soon as he returned, Wrath is in the study, and Zsadist is with the young one in the bath. Let's see . . . oh, and I believe Butch and Vishous are playing pool, as one of my staff served them drinks in the billiards room just a moment ago."

Right, John thought. If a Brother who no one had seen out and about for, oh, say, four months had shown up, surely his name would have been at the top of the list.

Thanks, Fritz.

"Was there anyone in particular you were searching for?"

John shook his head and went back out into the foyer, this time moving with heavy feet. As he walked into the library, he didn't expect to find anyone, and what do you know. The room was full of books and completely devoid of any Tohr.

Where could—

Maybe he wasn't in the house at all.

John bolted from the library and skidded around the bottom of the grand staircase, the soles of his shitkickers squeaking as he turned the corner. Ripping open the hidden door beneath the steps, he took the underground tunnel away from the mansion.

Of course. Tohr would go to the training center. If he were going to wake up and start living, that would mean he was going back into the field. And that meant working out and getting his body back into shape.

As John emerged into the facility's office, he had fully

returned to hope-land, and when Tohr wasn't at the desk, he wasn't surprised.

That was where he had been told about Wellsie's death.

John hauled ass out into the corridor, and the dim sound of weights clanking together was a fucking symphony to his ears, relief blooming in his chest until his hands and feet tingled.

But he had to be cool. Approaching the workout room, he shook off his smile, and opened the door wide—

Blaylock glanced over from the bench. Qhuinn's head bobbed up and down on the StairMaster.

As John looked around, both stopped what they were doing, Blay resetting the weight bar, Qhuinn slowly sinking down to the floor.

Have you seen Tohr? John signed.

"No," Qhuinn said while wiping his face with a towel. "Why would he be in here?"

John left in a hurry and headed into the gym, where he found nothing but caged lights and glossy pine floors and bright blue mats. The equipment room had only equipment in it. PT suite was empty. Jane's medical clinic was the same.

He broke out in a run as he gunned back for the tunnel to the main house.

Once he got there, he went directly upstairs to the study's open doors, and he didn't knock on the jamb this time. He walked straight up to Wrath's desk and signed, *Tohr is gone.*

As the Domino's delivery guy fumbled to catch the pizza box, everyone else went stock-still.

"That was close," the human said. "Don't want to get it—"

The guy froze in a crouch as his eyes traced the black stain on the wall to the crumpled, moaning *lesser* who'd made it. "... on ... your ... carpet."

"Christ," Lash spat, grabbing the switchblade out of his breast pocket, triggering the blade, and going up behind the man. As Domino's got to his feet, Lash locked his arm around his neck and drove the knife straight into his heart.

As the guy shriveled and gasped, the pizza box landed

on the floor and busted open, the tomato sauce and pep-
peroni in the same color family as the blood that was leaking from the wound.

Grady jumped off his stool and pointed at the slayer
who was still on his feet. "He let me order the pizza!"

Lash pointed the tip of the knife in the idiot's direction.
"Shut the fuck up."

Grady sank back onto his bar stool.

Mr. D was vicious pissed as he went up to the remaining
slayer. "You let him order that there pizza? Didja?"

The *lesser* snarled back, "You asked me to go in and
guard the window in the back bedroom. That's how we
found out the jars were gone, remember? Ass-wipe on the
carpet over there was the one who let him call."

Mr. D didn't seem to care about the logic, and as fun as
it might have been to watch him go Jack Russell on that rat
of a *lesser*, there was not a lot of time. This human who'd
shown up with the 'za wasn't going back to make more deliveries, and his cronies in uniform were going to tweak to
that soon enough.

"Call reinforcements," Lash said, closing up his blade
and going over to the incapacitated *lesser*. "Have them
come with a truck. Then get the gun crates. We're evac'ing
here and downstairs."

Mr. D got on the horn and started barking orders while
the other slayer went into the far bedroom.

Lash looked over at Grady, who was staring at the pizza
as if he were seriously considering eating it off the rug.
"Next time you—"

"Guns are gone."

Lash turned his head to the *lesser*. "Excuse me."

"Gun crates are not in the closet."

For a split second, all Lash could think about was killing
something, and the only thing that saved Grady from being
that guy was that he ducked into the kitchen, getting out of
the visual field.

Logic took over emotion, however, and he looked over
at Mr. D. "You are responsible for the evac."

"Y'sir."

Lash pointed to the slayer on the ground. "I want him
taken to the persuasion center."

"Y'sir."

"Grady?" When there was no answer, Lash cursed and went into the kitchen to find the guy leaning into the refrigerator and shaking his head at the empty shelves. Fucker was either very tight in the head or truly self-involved, and Lash was betting it was the latter. "We're leaving."

The human shut the fridge door and came like the dog he was: quickly and without argument, moving so fast he left his coat behind.

Lash and Grady bolted out into the cold, and the Mercedes' warm interior was a relief.

As Lash slowly eased out of the complex, because hurrying might have gotten people's attention, Grady looked over. "That guy . . . not the pizza one . . . the one who died . . . he wasn't normal."

"Nope. He wasn't."

"Neither are you."

"Nope. I am divine."

TWENTY-SIX

After night fell, Ehlena dressed in her uniform even though she wasn't going into the clinic. This was for two reasons: One, it helped with her father, who didn't deal well with any changes in schedule. And two, she felt as though it would buy her a little distance when she met with Rehvenge.

She hadn't slept at all during the day. Images from the morgue and memories of the way Rehvenge's strained voice had sounded were a hell of a tag team, battering at her as she lay in the dark, her emotions spinning and flipping until her chest ached.

Was she really going to meet Rehvenge now? At his home? How had this happened?

It helped to remind herself that she was just going to deliver meds to him. This was caretaking on a clinical level, nurse to patient. For godsakes, he'd agreed she shouldn't be dating anyone, and it wasn't as if he'd asked her for dinner. She was going to drop off the pills and try to persuade him to go see Havers. That was it.

After checking on her father and giving him his meds, she dematerialized to the sidewalk in front of the Commodore building in the thick of downtown. Standing in the shadows, looking up at the high-rise's sleek flank, she was struck by its contrast to the dingy, low-to-the-ground place she rented.

Man . . . to live in all this chrome and glass cost money. A lot of money. And Rehvenge had a penthouse. Plus this had to be just one of the places he owned, because no vampire in his right mind would crash out during daylight hours surrounded by all those windows.

The divide between the normal and the rich seemed as wide as the distance between where she stood and where Rehvenge was supposedly waiting for her, and for a brief moment she entertained the fantasy that her family still had money. Maybe then she'd be wearing something other than her cheap winter coat and her uniform.

As she stood down below him on the street, it seemed impossible that she'd connected with him as she had, but then, the phone was virtual relating, one step up from being online. Both people were in their own environments, invisible to each other, only their voices mixing. It was false intimacy.

Had she really stolen pills for this male?

Check your pockets, moron, she thought.

With a curse, Ehlena materialized up to the terrace of the penthouse, relieved that the night was relatively still. Otherwise, with how cold it was, any wind this high up—

What . . . the *hell*?

Through innumerable panes of glass, the glow of a hundred candles turned the dark night into a golden fog. Inside, the walls of the penthouse were black, and there were . . . things hanging from them. Things like cat-o'-nine-tails made of metal, and leather whips, and masks . . . and there was a large, ancient-looking table that was— No, wait, that was a rack, wasn't it? With leather straps hanging at the four corners.

Oh . . . *hell, no*. Rehvenge was into *this* shit?

Right. Change of plan. She'd leave the antibiotics for him, sure, but it was going to be in front of one of those sliding doors, because there was no way she was going in there. No. Frickin'. Way—

A tremendous male with a goatee came out of a bathroom, drying off his hands and straightening his leathers as he went over to the rack. With one easy hop, he got up on the thing and then he started shackling his ankle.

This was just getting sicker. A *three-way*?

"Ehlena?"

Ehlena wheeled around so fast she jammed her hip

against the wall that ran around the rooftop. As she saw who it was, she frowned.

"Doc Jane?" she said, thinking this night was going from the oh-hell-nos straight into WTF? territory. "What are you—"

"I think you're on the wrong side of the building."

"Wrong side—oh, wait, this isn't Rehvenge's place?"

"No, it's Vishous's and mine. Rehv's on the east side."

"Oh ..." Red cheeks. Very red, and not because of the wind. "I'm so sorry, I got it wrong—"

The ghostly doctor laughed. "It's okay."

Ehlena glanced back at the glass, but then looked quickly away. Of course, that was the Brother Vishous. The one with the diamond eyes and the tattoos on his face.

"East side's what you want."

Which Rehv had told her, hadn't he. "I'll just go over there now."

"I'd invite you to cut through, but ..."

"Yeah. Better for me to take myself there."

Doc Jane smiled with a good dose of badass. "I think that's best."

Ehlena calmed herself down and dematerialized to the right part of the roof, thinking, Doc Jane a dominatrix?

Well, stranger things had happened.

As she regained her form, she was almost afraid to look through the glass, considering what she'd just seen. If Rehvenge had more of the same—or worse, stuff like ladies clothes in a male's size, or farm animals milling around—she didn't know if she could chill enough to dematerialize her ass out of there.

But no. No RuPaul. Nothing that needed a trough or a fence. Just a lovely, modern interior done in the kind of sleek, simple furniture that must have come from Europe.

Rehvenge came out from an archway and stopped as he saw her. When he lifted his hand, the sliding glass door in front of her opened because he willed it so, and she caught a wonderful scent coming out of the penthouse.

Was that ... roast beef?

Rehvenge came over to her, moving with a smooth gait in spite of the fact that he relied on his cane. Tonight, he wore a black turtleneck that was clearly cashmere and a stunning black suit, and in his fine clothes, he was something off the cover of a magazine, glamorous, seductive, ever out of reach.

Ehlena felt like a fool. Seeing him here in his beautiful home, it wasn't that she thought she was beneath him. It was just clear they had nothing in common. What kind of delusions had struck her when they'd talked or been at the clinic?

"Welcome." Rehvenge stopped at the door and extended his hand toward her. "I would have waited for you outside, but it's too cold for me."

Two totally different worlds, she thought.

"Ehlena?"

"Sorry." Because it would be rude not to, she put her hand in his and stepped into his penthouse. But in her mind, she had already left him.

As their palms met, Rehv was robbed, mugged, burgled, broken and entered: He felt nothing as their hands melded, and desperately wished he could sense Ehlena's warmth. Still, even though he was numb, just watching their flesh come together was enough to make his chest sparkle like it had been steel-wooled to a bright shine.

"Hi," she said in a husky way as he drew her in.

He shut the door and kept hold of her hand until she broke the contact, ostensibly to walk around and look at his place. He sensed, though, that she needed physical space.

"The view here is extraordinary." She stopped and stared out at the sprawling vista of the twinkling city. "Funny, it looks like a model from way up here."

"We are high, that's for sure." He watched her with obsessive eyes, absorbing her through his sight. "I love the view," he murmured.

"I can see why."

"And it's quiet." Private. Just them and no one else in the world. And alone with her here now, he could almost believe all the dirty things he'd done had been crimes committed by a stranger.

She smiled a little. "Of course it's quiet. They're using ball gags next door—er . . ."

Rehv laughed. "You get the wrong side of the building?"

"Did I ever."

That blush told him she had seen more than just inanimate objects from V's Bondage-R-Us collection, and suddenly Rehv was dead serious. "Do I need to say something to my neighbor?"

Ehlena shook her head at him. "It was totally not his fault, and fortunately he and Jane hadn't . . . er, started. Thank God."

"You're not into that kind of thing, I take it."

Ehlena went back to staring at the view. "Hey, they're consenting adults, so it's all good. But me personally? Not on your life."

Talk about bubble burst. If BDSM was too much for her, he guessed that meant she wouldn't understand the fact that he was fucking for ransom a female he hated. Who happened to be his half sister. Oh, and who was a *symphath*.

Like him.

His silence brought her head over her shoulder. "I'm sorry. Have I offended you?"

"I'm not into that either." Oh, not at all. He was a whore with standards—kinky crap was okay only if you were forced into it. Fuck the consensual shit V and his mate were into. Yeah, 'cuz that was just wrong.

Christ, he was beneath her.

Ehlena wandered around, her soft-soled shoes making no sound on his black marble floors. As he watched her, he realized that under her black wool coat she was in her uniform. Which was logical, he pointed out to himself, if she had to go to work after this.

Come on, he told himself. Did he really think she was going to stay the night?

"May I take your coat?" he said, knowing she must be warm. "I have to keep this place hotter than most people are comfortable with."

"Actually . . . I should just head off." She put a hand in her pocket. "I only came to give you the penicillin."

"I was hoping you'd stay for dinner."

"I'm sorry." She held out a plastic bag to him. "I can't."

Flashes of the princess tripped through Rehv's brain, and he reminded himself of how good it felt to do right by Ehlena—and erase her number from his phone. He had no business courting her. None at all.

"I understand." He took the pills from her. "And thank you for these."

"Take two four times a day. Ten days. Promise me?"

He nodded once. "Promise."

"Good. And try to go see Havers, will you?"

There was an awkward moment, and then she lifted her hand. "Okay . . . so, bye."

Ehlena turned away, and he opened the glass panel with his mind, not trusting himself to get too close to her.

Oh, please don't go. Please don't, he thought.

He just wanted to feel . . . clean for a little while.

Just as she walked out, she stopped and his heart pounded.

Ehlena glanced back, the wind ruffling the pale wisps around her lovely face. "With food. You need to take them with food."

Right. Medical information. "I've got plenty of that here."

"Good."

After he shut the door, Rehv watched her disappear into the shadows and had to make himself turn away.

Walking slowly and using his cane, he went down the wall of glass and around the corner into the glow of the dining room.

Two candles lit. Two place settings of silver. Two glasses for wine. Two glasses for water. Two napkins folded precisely and laid on top of two plates.

He sat down on the chair he'd been going to give to her, the one to his right, the position of honor. He rested his cane against his thigh and put the plastic bag down on the ebony table, smoothing it out so that the antibiotics were resting one next to another in a neat and orderly row.

He wondered why they hadn't come in a little orange bottle with a white label on it, but whatever. She had brought them to him here. That was the main thing.

Sitting in the silence, surrounded by candlelight and the scent of the roast beef he'd just taken out of the oven, Rehv stroked the plastic bag with his numb forefinger. Sure as shit he was feeling something, though. In the dead center of his chest, he had an ache behind his heart.

He'd done a lot of evil deeds over the course of his life. Big ones and small.

He'd set people up just to mess with them, whether they were rogue dealers infringing on his turf, or johns who didn't treat his whores right, or idiots who screwed around at his club.

He'd leveraged the vices of others to his benefit. Sold drugs. Sold sex. Sold death in the form of Xhex's special skills.

He'd fucked for all the wrong reasons.

He'd maimed.

He'd murdered.

And yet, none of that had bothered him at the time. There had been no second thoughts, no regrets, no empathy. Just more schemes, more plans, more angles to be discovered and exploited.

Here at this empty table, though, in this empty penthouse, he felt the ache in his chest and knew it for what it was: Regret.

It would have been extraordinary to deserve Ehlena.

But that was just one more thing he wasn't ever going to feel.

TWENTY-SEVEN

As the Brotherhood met in his study, Wrath kept an eye on John from his vantage point behind the frilly desk. Across the way, the kid looked like roadkill. His face was pale and his big body was still and he hadn't participated in the discussion at all. The scent of his emotions was the worst part of it, though: There was none. Not the stinging, nostril-bracing bite of anger. Not the acrid, smoky blow of sadness. Not even the lemony pitch of fear.

Nothing. As he stood among the Brothers and his two best friends, he was insulated by his nonresponsiveness and his numbed-out trance . . . with them, but not really.

Not good.

Wrath's headache, which like his eyes and his ears and his mouth seemed to be permanently attached to his skull, made a renewed assault into his temples, and he sat back in his pansy-ass chair in the hope that a spinal realignment might ease the squeeze.

No luck.

Maybe a cranial amputation would work. God knew Doc Jane was good with a saw.

Over in the ugly green armchair, Rhage bit down on a Tootsie Pop, breaking one of the many thumb-up-the-ass silences that had marked the meeting.

"Tohr couldn't have gone far," Hollywod muttered. "He's not strong enough."

"I checked the Other Side," Phury said from the speak-erphone. "He's not with the Chosen."

"How about we do a drive-by of his old house," Butch suggested.

Wrath shook his head. "I can't imagine he'd go there. So many memories."

Shit, not even the mention of that home John had spent time in elicited anything from the kid. But at least it was fi-nally dark so they could go out and look for Tohr.

"I'm going to stay here and see if he comes back," Wrath said as the double doors opened and V strode in. "I want the rest of you out searching for him in the city, but before you go, first let's get an update from our very own Katie Couric." He nodded at Vishous. "Katie?"

V's glare was the ocular version of a fully extended mid-dle finger, but he got on with it. "Last night, on the police blotter, there was a report filed by a Homicide detective. Dead body was found at the address where those gun crates came from. Human. Pizza delivery guy. Single knife wound through the chest. No doubt the poor bastard walked into something he shouldn't have. I just finished hacking into the case details and what do you know, I found a note in it about a black, oily stain on the wall next to the door." There was a grumble of curses, many of which included the f-word. "Yeah, well, here's the interesting part. Police noted that a Mercedes had been spotted in the parking lot about two hours before the Domino's manager called in that his employee hadn't returned to work after delivering to that addy. And one of the neighbors saw a blond man, natch, get into it with another guy who was dark haired. She said it was weird seeing that kind of flashy sedan in the area."

"A Mercedes?" Phury said from the phone.

Rhage, having ground another lollipop to its royal re-ward, pitched a little white stick into the wastepaper bas-ket. "Yeah, since when has the Lessening Society put that kind of cash into their wheels?"

"Exactly," V said. "Makes no damn sense. But here's the shit. Witnesses also reported seeing a suspicious-looking black Escalade there the night before ... with a man in black carrying off ... oh, gee, what was it ... crates, yeah, four fucking crates from the back of that quartet of apartments."

As his roommate stared pointedly at Butch, the cop shook his head. "But there was no mention that they got the plates on the E. And we switched the set we had on it as soon as I got back. As for the Merc? Witnesses mistake things all the time. The blond and the other guy could have had nothing to do with the murder."

"Well, I'm going to keep an eye on things," V said. "I don't think there's any chance the police are going to tie it to something involving our world. Hell, a lot of things leave black stains, but we want to be prepared."

"If the detective on it is the one I'm thinking of, he's a good one," Butch said quietly. "A very good one."

Wrath got to his feet. "Okay, sun's down. Get out of here. John, I want to talk to you privately for a moment."

Wrath waited for the doors to close behind the last of his brothers before he spoke. "We're going to find him, son. Don't worry." No response. "John? What's doing?"

The kid just crossed his arms over his chest and stared straight ahead.

"John . . ."

John unfurled his hands and signed something that looked to Wrath's piss-poor eyes to be, *I'm going to go out with the others.*

"The hell you are." That brought John's head around sharply. "Yeah, so not happening, given the fact that you're a zombie. And fuck off with the I'm-fines. If you think for even a split second that I'm going to let you fight, you are talking out your damn ass."

John walked around the study like he was trying to get hold of himself. Eventually he stopped and signed, *I can't be here right now. In this house.*

Wrath frowned and tried to interpret what had been said, but all the frowning just made his headache sing like a soprano. "I'm sorry, what was that?"

John wrenched open the door, and a second later Qhuinn came in. There was a lot of hand movement and then Qhuinn cleared his throat.

"He says he can't be in this house tonight. He just can't."

"Okay, then go to a club and get faced until you pass out. But no fighting." Wrath said a silent prayer of thanks that

Qhuinn was grafted to the kid's side. "And, John . . . I'm going to find him."

More signing, and then John turned to the door.

"What did he say, Qhuinn?" Wrath asked.

"Ah . . . he said it doesn't matter to him if you do."

"John, you don't mean that."

The kid pivoted and signed and Qhuinn translated. "He
says, yes, he really does. He says . . . he can't live like this
anymore . . . waiting, wondering every night and day when
he goes into that room whether Tohr has—John, slow down
a little—ah . . . whether the male has hanged himself or
taken off again. Even if he comes back . . . John says he's
done. He's been left behind too many times."

Hard to argue with that. Tohr hadn't been a great father
lately, his sole accomplishment on that front being the creation of the next generation of the living dead.

Wrath winced and rubbed his temples. "Look, son, I'm
not a rocket scientist, but you can talk to me."

There was a long, quiet stretch marked by an odd
scent . . . a dry, almost stale smell . . . regret? Yeah, that was
regret.

John bowed a little as if in thanks and then ducked out
the door.

Qhuinn hesitated. "I won't let him fight."

"Then you'll save his life. Because if he takes up arms in
the shape he's in right now, he'll be coming home in a pine
box."

"Roger that."

As the door shut, pain roared in Wrath's temples and
forced him to sit back down.

God, all he wanted to do was go to his and Beth's room
and get into their big bed and lay his head down on pillows
that smelled like her. He wanted to call her and beg her to
come join him just so he could hold on to her. He wanted to
be forgiven.

He wanted to sleep.

Instead, the king got back to his feet, picked up his
weapons from the floor beside his desk, and strapped all of
them on. Leaving the study with his leather jacket in his
hand, he went down the grand staircase, out the vestibule,
and into the bitter night. Way he saw it was, the headache

was going to be with him wherever he went, so he might as well be useful and go look for Tohr.

As he drew on his coat, he was struck by the thought of his *shellan* and where she had gone the night before.

Holy shit. He knew exactly where Tohr was.

Ehlena meant to leave Rehvenge's terrace right away, but while stepping into the shadows, she had to look back at the penthouse. Through the banks of glass, she watched Rehvenge turn away and walk slowly down the flank of the penthouse—

Her shin caught something hard. "Damn it!"

Hopping around on one foot and rubbing her leg, she shot a nasty look at the marble urn she'd nailed herself with.

As she straightened, she forgot about the pain.

Rehvenge had gone into another room and stopped in front of a table set for two. Candles glowed amidst a shimmer of crystal and silver, the long wall of glass showing her all the trouble he had gone to for her.

"Damn it . . ." she whispered.

Rehvenge sat down as slowly and deliberately as he walked, looking behind himself first, as if to make sure the chair was where it should be, then bracing both hands and lowering himself down. The Baggie of what she'd given him was placed on the table, and as he seemed to stroke it, his gentle fingers were at odds with those heavy shoulders and the dark power inherent in his hard face.

Staring at him, Ehlena no longer felt the cold or the wind or the pain in her shin. Bathed in the candlelight, with his head tilted down and his profile so strong and true, Rehvenge was incalculably beautiful.

Abruptly, his head snapped up and he looked right at her, even though she was in the darkness.

Ehlena stepped back and felt the terrace wall against her hip, but she did not dematerialize. Even as he plugged his cane into the floor and rose to his full height.

Even as the door before him parted at his will.

It would have taken a better liar than she was to pretend she just was looking off into the night. And she wasn't a coward, to bolt.

Ehlena walked up to him. "You didn't take a pill."

"Is that what you're waiting for?"

Ehlena crossed her arms over her chest. "Yes."

Rehvenge glanced back at the table and the pair of empty plates. "You said they had to be taken with food."

"Yes, I did."

"Well, it looks like you're going to watch me eat, then." The elegant sweep of his arm inviting her in was a prompt she didn't want to take. "Will you sit with me? Or do you want to stay out here in the cold? Oh, wait, maybe this will help." Leaning heavily on his cane, he went over and blew out the candles.

The curling weaves of smoke above the wicks seemed to her a lament for all the extinguished possibilities that had been: He'd prepared a nice dinner for them both. Made the effort. Dressed beautifully.

She stepped inside because she'd already ruined enough of his evening.

"Seat yourself," he said. "I'll be back with my plate. Unless . . . ?"

"I've already eaten."

He bowed slightly as she pulled out a chair. "Of course you have."

Rehvenge left his cane against the table and walked out, steadying himself on the backs of chairs and the sideboard and the jamb of the butler's door into the kitchen. When he returned a few minutes later, he repeated the pattern with his free hand and then lowered himself down into the armed chair at the head of the table with careful concentration. Picking up a sleek sterling-silver fork, he didn't say a word as he carefully sliced his meat and ate with restraint and manners.

Christ, she felt like the bitch of the week, sitting in front of an empty plate while fully buttoned up in her coat.

The sounds of silver tines on porcelain made the silence between them scream.

Stroking the napkin in front of her, she felt god-awful about so much, and though she wasn't much of a talker she found herself speaking because she simply couldn't keep everything in anymore. "The night before last . . ."

"Mmm?" Rehvenge didn't look at her, just stayed focused on his plate.

"I wasn't stood up. You know, on that date."

"Well, good for you."

"He was killed."

Rehvenge's head shot up. "What."

"Stephan, the guy I was supposed to meet ... he was killed by *lessers*. The king brought his body in, but I didn't know it was him until his cousin showed up looking for him. I ... ah, I spent my shift last evening wrapping his body and returning him to his family." She shook her head. "They'd beaten him. . . . You couldn't tell who he had been."

Her voice fractured and refused to go on, so she just sat there stroking the napkin, in hopes of soothing herself.

Two subtle clinks marked Rehv's fork and knife coming to rest on his plate, and then he reached out to her, putting his solid hand on her forearm.

"I'm so goddamned sorry," he said. "No wonder you're not into all this. If I had known—"

"No, it's okay. Really. I should have handled it better when I arrived. I'm just off tonight. Not myself at all."

He gave her a squeeze and settled back into his chair as if he didn't want to crowd her. Which was normally what she liked, but tonight she found it a pity—to use a word he enjoyed. The weight of his touch through her coat had been very nice.

Speaking of which, she was getting really warm.

Ehlena unbuttoned herself and took the wool from her shoulders. "Hot in here."

"Like I said before, I can cool things down for you."

"No." She frowned, glancing over at him. "Why are you always cold? Side effects from the dopamine?"

He nodded. "It's really more why I need the cane. I can't feel my arms, legs."

She hadn't heard of many vampires reacting in that way to the drug, but then, individual reactions were legion. And also the vampire equivalent of Parkinson's was a nasty disease.

Rehvenge pushed his plate away and the two of them sat in silence for a long while. In the candlelight, he seemed dimmed somehow, his usual energy dialed down, his mood very somber.

"You're not yourself, either," she said. "Not that I know you very well, but you seem ..."

"How."

"Like I feel. In a walking coma."

He chuckled in a short burst. "That is so apt."

"You want to talk about it—"

"You want something to eat—"

They both laughed and stopped.

Rehvenge shook his head. "Look, let me get you some dessert. It's the least I can do. And it's not date food. The candles are out."

"Actually, you know what?"

"You lied about having eaten before coming and now you're starving?"

She laughed again. "You got it."

As his amethyst eyes stared into hers, the air between them changed and she had the sense that he saw so much, too much. Especially as he said in a dark voice, "Will you let me feed you?"

Hypnotized, captivated, she whispered, "Yes. Please."

His smile revealed long, white fangs. "That is so the answer I was going for."

What would his blood be like in her mouth, she wondered in a rush.

Rehvenge growled deep in his throat, as if he knew exactly what she was thinking. But he took it no further, rising to his great height and going into the kitchen.

By the time he returned with her plate, she'd managed to pull herself together a little bit better, although as he put the food down in front of her, the whiff of spices that drifted around her was too delicious—and had nothing to do with what he'd cooked.

Determined to keep it together, Ehlena put the napkin in her lap and tried the roast beef.

"My *God*, this is fabulous."

"Thanks," Rehv said as he sat down. "It's the way the *doggen* in our household have always done it. You get the oven up to four seventy-five and you put the roast in, blast it for a half hour, then turn everything off and let it sit in there. You're not allowed to open the door to check it. That's the rule, and you have to trust the process. Two hours later?"

"Heaven."

"Heaven."

Ehlena laughed as the same word came out of both of their mouths. "Well, it's really good. Melts in the mouth."

"In the interest of full disclosure, lest you think I'm a chef, it's the only thing I know how to cook."

"Well, you do one thing perfectly, and that's more than some people can say."

He smiled and looked down at the pills. "If I take one of these now, are you going to leave right after dinner?"

"If I say no, will you tell me why you're so quiet?"

"Tough negotiator."

"Just making it a two-way street. I told you what's weighing on me."

Darkness shadowed his face, tightening his mouth and drawing his brows together. "I can't talk about it."

"Sure you can."

His eyes, now hard, flashed up to her. "Just like you can talk about your father?"

Ehlena dropped her stare to her plate and took special care cutting a piece of meat.

"I'm sorry," Rehv said. "I . . . Shit."

"No, it's okay." Even though it wasn't. "I push too hard sometimes. Great for being in health care. Not so hot when it comes to the personal stuff."

As silence flared again, she ate faster, thinking she'd go as soon as she finished.

"I'm doing something I'm not proud of," he said abruptly.

She glanced up. His expression was positively vile, anger and hatred turning him into someone who, if she hadn't known otherwise, she would have feared. None of the evil look was directed at her, though. It was a manifestation of what he was feeling toward himself. Or another.

She knew better than to press. Especially given his mood.

So she was surprised when he said, "It's an ongoing thing."

Was it business or personal, she wondered.

His eyes lifted to hers. "It involves a certain female."

Right. A female.

Okay, she had no right to feel a cold vise around her chest. It was none of her business that he was already with someone. Or that he was a player who threw together this roast beef dinner, candlelight, and seduction special for God knew how many different females.

Ehlena cleared her throat and put down her knife and fork. As she dabbed her mouth with her napkin, she said, "Wow. You know, I never thought to ask if you were mated. You don't have a name in your back—"

"It's not my *shellan*. And I don't love her in the slightest. It's complicated."

"Do you share a young?"

"No, thank God."

Ehlena frowned. "Is this a relationship, though?"

"I guess you could call it that."

Feeling like a total raving idiot for getting caught up in him, Ehlena put her napkin on the table beside her plate and offered a very professional smile as she got to her feet and picked up her coat.

"I should go now. Thanks for dinner."

Rehv cursed. "I shouldn't have said anything—"

"If your goal was to get me in bed, you're right. Bad move. Still, I'm glad you were honest—"

"I wasn't trying to get you into bed."

"Oh, of course not, because you'd be cheating on her." Christ, why was she getting so upset over this?

"No," he snapped back, "it's because I'm impotent. Believe me, if I could get hard, bed would be the first place I'd want to go with you."

TWENTY-EIGHT

pending time with you is like watching paint dry."
Lassiter's voice echoed up to the stalactites hanging
from the Tomb's high ceiling. "Except without the home
improvement—which is a tragedy, given how this place
looks. Do you guys always go for the gloom and doom?
You never hear of Pottery Barn?"

Tohr rubbed his face and glanced around the cave that
had served as the Brotherhood's sacred meeting place for
centuries. Behind the massive stone altar he was sitting
next to, the black marble wall with all the Brothers' names
on it stretched out across the back of the cave. Black candles on heavy stanchions threw flickering light over all the
carvings in the Old Language.

"We're vampires," he said. "Not fairies."

"Sometimes I'm not so sure about that. You see that
study your king hangs out in?"

"He's nearly blind."

"Which explains why he hasn't hanged himself in that
pastel train wreck."

"I thought you were bitching about the gloom-and-
doom decorating?"

"I free-associate."

"Clearly." Tohr didn't look at the angel, as he figured eye
contact would only encourage the guy. Oh, wait. Lassiter
didn't need help.

"You expecting that skull on the altar to talk to you or some shit?"

"Actually we're both waiting for you to finally take a breath." Tohr glared at the guy. "Anytime you're ready. *Any*time."

"You say the sweetest things." The angel sat his glowing ass down on the stone steps next to Tohr. "Can I ask you something?"

"Is 'no' really an option?"

"Nope." Lassiter shifted around and stared up at the skull. "That thing looks older than I am. Which is saying something."

It was the first Brother, the inaugural warrior who fought the enemy bravely and with power, the most sacred symbol of strength and purpose within the Brotherhood.

Lassiter stopped fucking around for once. "He must have been a great fighter."

"I thought you were going to ask me something."

The angel stood with a curse and shook out his legs. "Yeah, I mean . . . how in the fuck have you sat there for so long? My ass is killing me."

"Yeah, brain cramps are a bitch."

Although the angel did have a point about time having passed. Tohr had been sitting there, staring at the skull and at the wall of names beyond the altar, for so long his butt wasn't so much numb as indistinguishable from the steps.

He had come here the previous night, drawn by an invisible hand, compelled to seek inspiration, clarity, reconnection to life. Instead, he had found only stone. Cold stone. And a lot of names that had once meant something to him and now were nothing but a grocery list of the dead.

"It's because you're looking in the wrong place," Lassiter said.

"You can go now."

"Every time you say that, it brings a tear to my eye."

"Funny, mine too."

The angel leaned down, the scent of fresh air preceding him. "Neither that wall nor that skull will give you what you're looking for."

Tohr narrowed his eyes and wished he were strong enough to fight the guy. "They won't? Well, then they're making a liar out of you. 'Now is the time. Tonight everything changes.' You give portent a bad name, you know that? You are just so full of shit."

Lassiter smiled and idly adjusted the gold hoop that pierced his eyebrow. "If you think being rude is going to get my attention, you'll be really bored before I care."

"Why the fuck are you here?" Tohr's exhaustion crept into his voice, weakening it and pissing him off. "Why the hell didn't you just leave me where you found me?"

The angel mounted the black marble steps and paced up and down in front of the glossy wall with the carved names, stopping now and then to inspect one or two.

"Time is a luxury, believe it or not," he said.

"Feels more like a curse to me."

"Without time, you know what you got?"

"The Fade. Which was where I was headed until you came along."

Lassiter ran his finger over a carved line of characters and Tohr looked away quickly when he realized what they spelled out. It was his name.

"Without time," the angel said, "you have only the bottomless, shapeless mire of eternity."

"FYI, philosophy bores me."

"Not philosophy. Reality. Time is what gives life significance."

"Fuck you. Seriously . . . fuck you."

Lassiter's head tilted to the side, as if he had heard something.

"Finally," he muttered. "Bastard was doing my nut in."

"Excuse me?"

The angel came back over, leaned down right into Tohr's face, and said with clear diction, "Listen up, sunshine. Your *shellan*, Wellsie, sent me. That's why I didn't leave you to die."

Tohr's heart stopped in his chest just as the angel looked up and said, "What took you so long."

Wrath's voice was annoyed as his shitkickers thundered down toward the altar. "Well, next time tell someone where the fuck you are—"

"What did you say," Tohr breathed.

Lassiter was utterly unapologetic as he refocused. "That wall isn't what you need to be looking at. Try a calendar.

One year ago your Wellsie was shot in the face by the enemy. *Wake the fuck up and do something about it.*"

Wrath cursed. "Easy, there, Lassi—"

Tohrment lunged off the cave floor with something close to the old strength he'd once had, and he hit Lassiter like a linebacker in spite of the weight difference, taking the angel down hard onto the stone floor. Wrapping his hands around the guy's throat, he stared down into white eyes and squeezed, baring his fangs.

Lassiter just stared right back and thought his voice directly into Tohr's temporal lobe: *What are you going to do, asshole? Are you going to avenge her, or disrespect her by wasting away like this?*

Wrath's huge hand clamped on Tohr's shoulder like a lion's claw, digging in, pulling back. "Let go."

"Don't . . ." Tohr's breath came in punches. "Don't . . . ever . . ."

"Enough," Wrath spat.

Tohr was whipped backward onto his ass, and as he bounced like a stick dropped on the ground, he came out of the murder trance. Came awake, too.

He didn't know how else to describe it. It was as if some switch had been triggered and his bank of lights, which had been extinguished, suddenly went live with juice again.

Wrath's face came into view, and Tohr saw it with a clarity he hadn't had in . . . forever. "You okay, there?" his brother said. "You landed hard."

Tohr reached out and ran his hands over Wrath's heavy arms, trying to get a feel of reality. He glanced over at Lassiter, then stared at the king. "I'm sorry . . . about that."

"Are you kidding me? We've all wanted to strangle him."

"You know, I'm gonna get a complex over here," Lassiter coughed out as he caught his breath.

Tohr gripped his king's shoulders. "No one's said anything about her," he groaned. "No one's said her name, no one's talked about . . . what happened."

Wrath held on to the back of Tohr's neck and supported him. "Out of respect for you."

Tohr's eyes went to the skull on the altar and then to the etched wall. The angel had been right. There was only one name that could wake him up, and it wasn't inscribed up there.

Wellsie.

"How did you know where we were," he asked his king, still focused on the wall.

"Sometimes people need to go back to the beginning. To where everything started."

"It's time," the fallen angel said softly.

Tohr stared down at himself, at the withered body beneath his sagging clothes. He was a quarter of the male he'd once been, maybe even less. And that wasn't just because of all the weight he'd lost. "Oh, Christ . . . look at me."

Wrath's response was front and center. "If you're ready, we're ready to have you back."

Tohr looked over at the angel, noticing for the first time the golden aura that surrounded the guy. Heaven-sent. Wellsie-sent.

"I'm ready," he said to no one and everyone.

As Rehv stared across the table at Ehlena, he thought, Well, at least she wasn't beelining for the exit after he'd dropped the i-bomb.

Impotent wasn't a word you wanted to use around a female you were interested in. Unless it was used along the lines of, *Fuck, no, I'm* NOT *impotent.*

Ehlena sat back down. "You're . . . is it because of the medication?"

"Yeah."

Her eyes skirted away, as if she were adding figures in her head, and the first thought that hit him was, *My tongue still works and so do my fingers.*

He kept that to himself. "Dopamine has an odd effect with me. Instead of stimulating testosterone, it drains the shit out of me."

The corner of her mouth twitched up. "This is totally inappropriate, but considering how male you are, without it—"

"I'd be able to make love to you," he said quietly. "That's what I'd be like."

Her eyes shot to his, all *holy-shit-did-he-just-say-that?*

Rehv brushed a hand over his mohawk. "I'm not going to apologize for the fact that I'm feeling you, but I won't disrespect you by trying to do anything about it either. You want some coffee? It's already made."

"Ah ... sure." Like she was hoping it would clear her head. "Listen ..."

He paused in the midst of standing up. "Yeah?"

"I ... ah ..."

When she didn't continue, he shrugged. "Just let me bring you coffee. I want to wait on you. Makes me happy."

Fuck happy. As he headed back into the kitchen, a screaming satisfaction broke through his numbness. The fact that he was feeding her food he had prepared for her, giving her drink to relieve her thirst, providing shelter from the cold ...

Rehv's nose picked up an odd scent, and at first he thought it was the roast he'd left out, because he'd rubbed the outside of the piece of meat with spices. But no ... it wasn't that.

Figuring he had other things to worry about rather than his nose, he went over to the cabinets and got a teacup and saucer. After he poured the coffee, he went to straighten the lapels of his jacket—

And froze.

Lifting his hand to his nose, he breathed in deep and didn't believe what he was smelling. It couldn't possibly ...

Except there was only one thing that the scent could be, and it had nothing to do with his *symphath* side: The dark spices coming off of him were the bonding scent, the mark that male vampires left on the skin and sex of their females so that other males would know whose wrath they risked if they dared to get close.

Rehv lowered his arm and looked toward the butler's door, stunned.

When you got to a certain age, you didn't expect any more surprises out of your body. At least, not the good kind. Rickety joints. Wheezy lungs. Bad eyesight. Sure, when the time came. But really, for the nine hundred years or so after your transition, you had what you had.

Although *good* might not be the exact word he'd use for this development.

For no evident reason, he thought of the first time he'd had sex. It had been right after his transition, and when the deed was done, he'd been convinced that the female and he were going to get mated and live together and be happy for the rest of their lives. She'd been perfectly beautiful, a female who his mother's brother had brought to the house for Rehv to use when he'd gone into the change.

She'd been a brunette.

Christ, he couldn't remember her name now.

Looking back on it, with what he'd since learned about males and females and attraction, he knew he'd surprised her with how big his body had been after the change. She hadn't expected to like what she saw. Hadn't expected to want him. But she did and they mated and the sex had been a revelation, the feel of all that flesh, the addictive rush, the power he'd had as he'd taken control after the first couple of times.

He'd learned he'd had a barb, then—whereas she'd been so into him, he wasn't sure she'd noticed that they had to wait a little before he could withdraw from her.

In the aftermath, he'd been so at peace, so content. But there had been no happily-ever-after coming. With the sweat still drying on her body, she'd put on her clothes and hit the door. Just as she'd left, she'd smiled at him sweetly and told him that she wouldn't charge his family for the sex.

His uncle had bought her to feed him.

Funny, as he considered it now, was it really a surprise where he'd ended up? Sex as a commodity had been drilled into him pretty damn early—even though that first fuck or six had been on the house, so to speak.

So yeah, if this dark scent meant his vampire nature had bonded with Ehlena, it was not good news.

Rehv picked the coffee up and carried it carefully through the butler's door and out to the dining room. As he placed it in front of her, he wanted to touch her hair, but sat down instead.

She lifted the cup to her lips. "You make good coffee."

"You haven't tasted it yet."

"I can smell it. And I love the way it smells."

It's not the coffee, he thought. Not all of it, at any rate.

"Well, I love your perfume," he said, because he was a dolt.

She frowned. "I'm not wearing any. I mean, other than the soap and shampoo I use."

"Well, I like them, then. And I'm glad you stayed."

"Is this what you planned?"

Their eyes met. Shit, she was perfect. Radiant as the candles had been. "You making it all the way to the coffee? Yeah, I guess a date was what I was after."

"I thought you agreed with me."

Man, that breathless quality in her voice made him want to have her up against his naked chest.

"Agreed with you?" he said. "Hell, if it would make you happy, I'd say yes to anything. But what are you specifically referring to?"

"You said . . . I shouldn't date anyone."

Ah, right. "You shouldn't."

"I don't understand."

Fuck him, but he went for it. Rehv put his numb elbow on the table and leaned into her. As he closed the distance, her eyes got wider, but she didn't pull back.

He paused, to give her a chance to tell him to cut the shit. Why? He had no clue. His *symphath* side was into pauses only for analysis or to better capitalize on a weakness. But she made him want to be decent.

Ehlena didn't tell him to step off, however. "I don't . . . understand," she whispered.

"It's simple. I don't think you should date anyone." Rehv moved in even closer, until he could see the flecks of gold in her eyes. "But I'm not just anyone."

TWENTY-NINE

'm not just anyone.

As Ehlena stared into Rehvenge's amethyst eyes, she thought that was so right. In this quiet moment, with an explosive sexual vibe linking them and the scent of dark cologne in the air, Rehvenge was everybody and everything.

"You're going to let me kiss you," he said.

It wasn't a question, but she nodded anyway, and he closed the distance between their mouths.

His lips were soft and his kiss softer. And he pulled back too fast, in her opinion. Way too fast.

"If you want more," he said in a low, husky voice, "I want to give it to you."

Ehlena stared at his mouth and thought of Stephan—and all the choices he no longer had. Being with Rehvenge was something she wanted. It didn't make sense, but right now that didn't matter.

"Yes. I want more." Except then it dawned on her. He couldn't feel a thing, could he. So what would happen if they took this even further?

Yeah, how did you bring that up without making him feel handicapped? And what about this other female of his? Clearly, he wasn't sleeping with her, but there was something serious going on.

His amethyst eyes dropped to her lips. "You want to know what I get out of it?"

Man, that voice of his was pure sex.

"Yes," she breathed.

"I get to see you like you are now."

"What . . . am I like?"

He brushed a finger down her cheek. "You're flushed." His touch went over to her lips. "Your mouth is open because you're thinking about me kissing you again." He went lower with that soft stroke, going down over her throat. "Your heart is pumping. I can see it in your vein here." He stopped between her breasts, his own mouth falling open and his fangs elongating. "If I keep on going, I think I'd find your nipples are hard, and I bet there are other signs you're ready for me." He leaned into her ear and whispered, "Are you ready for me, Ehlena?"

Holy. Shit.

Her rib cage tightened hard around her lungs, a sweet, dizzying sensation of suffocation making the rush she suddenly felt between her thighs even more stunning.

"Ehlena, answer me." Rehvenge nuzzled her neck, running one sharp canine up her vein.

As her head fell back, she grabbed onto the sleeve of his fine suit, crushing the material. It had been so long . . . forever . . . since she'd been held by anyone. Since she'd been something other than a caregiver. Since she'd felt like her breasts and her hips and her thighs were anything other than parts to be covered up before she went out in public. And here this beautiful, not-just-anyone male wanted to be with her for the sole purpose of pleasing her.

Ehlena had to blink quickly, feeling as if he'd just given her a gift, and she wondered how far what they were about to start could go. Back before her family had fallen out of the *glymera*'s graces and been torn apart, she'd been promised to a ma.e and he to her. The mating ceremony had been scheduled, but didn't come to pass after her family's reversal of fortune.

When they had been together, she had lain with the male even though as a female of worth in the *glymera*, she shouldn't have because they had yet to be formally joined. Life had seemed too short to wait.

Now she knew it to be even shorter.

"You have a bed in this place," she said.

"And I would kill to take you there."

She was the one who stood up and put out her hand for
him to take. "Let's go."

What made it okay was that this was all about Ehlena.
Rehv's lack of sensation took him completely out of the
equation, freeing them both from the nasty implications
of him being involved.

Man, what a joy this was. He had to give the princess his
body. But he was choosing to give Ehlena . . .

Well, shit, he didn't know exactly, but it was a fuckload
more than just his cock. Worth so much more, too.

Palming his cane, because he didn't want to have to rely
on her for balance, he took her to the bedroom, with its
swimming pool–size bed and its black satin duvet and its
view.

He shut the door with his mind, even though there was
no one else in the penthouse, and the first thing he did was
turn Ehlena to face him and take her hair out of its twist tie.
The deep strawberry blond waves fell to just below her
shoulders, and though he couldn't feel the silken strands, he
could smell the light, natural bouquet of her shampoo.

She was clean and fresh, like a stream he could bathe
himself in.

He paused, an unfamiliar spike of conscience reining
him in. If she knew what he was, if she knew what he did for
a living, if she knew what he did with his body, she wouldn't
choose him. He was sure of this.

"Don't stop," she said, tilting her face up. "Please . . ."

With force of will, he compartmentalized himself, putting the bad things and the vicious life he led and the dangerous realities he faced away from the bedroom, locking
them out, shutting them down.

So that it was just the two of them.

"I won't stop unless you want me to," he said. And if she
did he would, no questions asked. The last thing he ever
wanted to do was make her feel the way he did about sex.

Rehv bent down, put his lips on hers, and kissed her
carefully. As he couldn't judge sensation, he didn't want to
grind on her, and he had the sense she would press herself
closer if she wanted more—

Ehlena did just that, wrapping her arms around him and
melding them hip-to-hip.

And ... shit, he felt something. From out of nowhere, a flare of sensation broke through his numbness, the radiating wave dim, but very definitely warmth he could sense. For a split second he pulled back, fear spearing into him ... but his vision stayed in three dimensions, and the only red he saw was from the glow of the digital clock on the nightstand.

"Is this okay?" she asked.

He waited a couple more heartbeats. "Yeah ... yeah, it totally is." His eyes traced her face. "Will you let me get you naked?"

Oh, God, did he just say that?

"Yes."

"Oh ... thank you ..."

Rehv unbuttoned the front of her uniform slowly, each inch of flesh a revelation, the act not so much dishabille, but an unveiling. And he was careful with his hands as he slid the top half of what she wore off her shoulders and down over her hips to the floor. When she stood before him in her white bra and her white stockings, with the hint of her white panties showing beneath the hose, he was strangely honored.

But that wasn't all. The scent of her sex lit off a buzz between his ears that made him feel like he'd been doing lines of coke for a week and a half straight. She wanted him. Almost as much as he wanted to serve her.

Rehv picked her up by wrapping his arms around her waist and hugging her to him. She weighed nothing at all, and he knew it by the fact that his breathing didn't change in the slightest as he carried her over and laid her out on the bed.

As he pulled back to look at her, Ehlena wasn't like the females he'd been with. She didn't stretch and part her legs, didn't play with herself, didn't arch up and do some whorish variant of come-and-get-me-big-boy.

She also didn't want to cause him pain and didn't have any interest in degrading him—there was no hot, erotic cruelty in her eyes.

She just stared up at him with wonder and honest anticipation, a female without artifice or calculation—who was one trillion times sexier than anyone he'd ever been with or been around.

"Do you want me clothed?" he said.

"No."

Rehv ditched his jacket like it was made of nothing more than shopping circulars, tossing the Gucci work of art to the floor without a care. Kicking off his loafers, he undid his belt and dropped his slacks, leaving them where they landed. His shirt came off quickly. So did the socks.

He hesitated at his boxers, his thumbs tucked into the waistband, ready to do the shuck, but failing to move.

His lack of an erection embarrassed him.

Rehv wouldn't have thought it mattered. Hell, arguably his limp cock was what made this possible. Still, he felt like less of a male.

Didn't feel very male at all, actually.

He took his hands out and put them over his flaccid sex. "I'm going to leave these on."

Ehlena reached for him, desire in her eyes. "I want to be with you any way you come."

Or didn't come, as the case was. "I'm sorry," he said quietly.

There was an awkward moment, because what could she possibly reply? And yet, he waited anyway, wanting . . . something from her.

Reassurance?

Christ, what the fuck was wrong with him. All these bizarre thoughts and reactions were crisscrossing the landscape of his temporal lobe, blazing trails to destinations he'd only heard others speak of, places like shame and sadness and worry. Insecurity, too.

Maybe the sexual hormones she was stirring up in him were like the dopamine, hitting him in the opposite way. Turning him into a chick.

"You are beautiful in this light," she said in a husky tone. "Your shoulders and chest are so big, I can't imagine what it would be like to be that strong. And your stomach . . . I wish mine were that flat and hard. Your legs are so powerful, too, all muscle, not an ounce of fat."

As he moved his hand upward over his six-pack to one of his pecs, he looked down at her softly rounded belly. "I think you're perfect just as you are."

Her voice grew serious. "And I feel the same about you."

Rehv dragged in a breath. "Yeah?"

"You are very sexy to me. Just looking at you . . . makes me ache."

Well . . . there you go. And yet it still took a strange kind of courage to slip his thumbs back into the waistband of his boxers and slowly draw them down his thighs.

As he stretched out next to her, his body was shaking, and he knew it because he could see his muscles tremble.

He cared what she thought about him. About his body. About what was going to happen on this bed. With the princess? He didn't give a rat's ass whether she enjoyed what he did to her. And those few times he'd been with his working girls, he hadn't wanted to hurt them, of course, but it had been a transaction of sex for money.

Xhex and he had simply been a mistake. Neither good or bad. Just was and never would be again.

Ehlena ran her hands up his arms and over his shoulders. "Kiss me."

Rehv locked eyes with her and did just that, bringing his lips to hers and stroking, then extending his tongue and licking over her mouth. He kept kissing her until she undulated on the bed and closed her hands on him so tightly that the strange echo of sensation flared in him again. The feeling made him pause and open his eyes to check his vision, but all was normal, untainted by red.

He went back to what he was enjoying, being careful because he couldn't mediate the pressure of the contact, letting her come to him so he didn't crush her with his mouth.

He wanted to go so much further . . . and she read his mind.

Ehlena was the one who undid her bra, releasing the front clasp and baring herself. Oh . . . fuck, *yeah*. Her breasts were perfectly proportioned and tipped with tight pink nipples—which he promptly sucked into his mouth one after the other.

The sound of her moans flared up his body, replacing the cold with life and energy, warmth and need.

"I want to go down on you," he growled.

Her, "Please," was more groan than voice, and her body gave him an even clearer answer. Now her thighs parted, her legs falling open, all the invitation he could ever have asked for.

Those stocking of hers had to come off before he chewed through them.

Rehv was as slow and deliberate as he could stand to be, stripping her flesh free of its thin binding, nuzzling her all the way down to her ankles, breathing in deep as he went.

He left the panties in place.

Rehvenge's gentleness was what surprised Ehlena the most.

In spite of his great size, he was as careful with her as he could be, moving gently over her body, giving her every chance to tell him no or divert him or stop things altogether.

She had no intention of doing any of those.

Especially as his big hand drifted up the inside of her bare leg and subtly, inexorably inched her thigh out even farther. As his fingers brushed her panties, a shot of electricity sizzled in her sex, the miniorgasm leaving her gasping.

Rehvenge pushed himself up and spoke into her ear on a growl. "I like that sound."

He took her mouth and stroked her sex over the top of the modest cotton that covered her. Deep tongue thrusts contrasted with butterfly brushes, and she threw her head back, getting utterly lost in him. Tilting her hips, she wanted him to go underneath the panties, and prayed he took the hint, as she was too breathless and desperate to talk.

"What do you want?" he said into her ear. "You want nothing between us?"

As she nodded, his middle finger slipped under the elastic, and then it was skin against skin and—

"Oh . . . *God*," she moaned as a release pounded through her.

Rehvenge smiled like a tiger as he stroked her while she orgasmed, helping her ride out the pulses. When she finally stilled, she felt embarrassed. She hadn't been with someone in so long, and never someone like him.

"You're incredibly beautiful," he whispered before she could say something.

Ehlena turned her face into his biceps and kissed the smooth skin over the tight muscle. "It's been a while for me."

A quiet glow came into his face.

"I like that. A lot." He dropped his head to her breast and

kissed her nipple. "I like that you respect your body. Not everyone does. Oh, and by the way, I'm not finished yet."

Ehlena dug her nails into the back of his neck as he tugged her panties down her thighs. The sight of his pink tongue teasing her breast arrested her, especially as his amethyst eyes met hers while he circled her nipple and flicked at it—like he was giving her a sneak peak at the attention she could expect down below.

She came again. Hard.

This time Ehlena let herself go with it completely, and it was a relief to just be in her skin and with him. As she recovered from the pleasure, she didn't even flinch as he started to kiss his way down past her stomach and to her—

She groaned so loudly there was an echo.

As with his fingers, the feel of his mouth on her sex was all the more vivid because he barely touched her. Soft strokes hovered over that vulnerable, hot place on her body, making her strain to feel him, turning each pass of his lips and his tongue into a source of both pleasure and frustration.

"More," she demanded, pushing her hips up.

His amethyst eyes lifted. "I don't want to be too rough."

"You won't be. *Please* . . . it's killing me. . . ."

With a growl, he dove down and sealed her sex with his mouth, sucking her, pulling her into him. She came again, this time in hard, shattering blows, but he did her right. He kept going, riding out her jerks and arches, the sound of lips against lips rising up with her guttural cries as he worked her and made her climax over and over again.

When God only knew how many times she released, she stilled and so did he. They were both panting, his glossy mouth on the inside of her thigh, his three fingers buried tight in her, their scents mingling in the heated air of the—

She frowned. Part of the heady fragrance in the room was . . . dark spices. And as she sniffed deeply, his eyes lifted to hers.

Her shocked expression must have shown exactly the conclusion she came to.

"Yeah, I'm catching the scent as well," he said roughly.

Except he couldn't have bonded with her, could he? Did it really happen that fast?

"For some males it does," he said. "Evidently."

Abruptly she realized he was reading her mind, but she didn't care. Considering where he'd been, getting into her brain didn't seem half as intimate.

"I didn't expect this," she said.

"Wasn't on my list either." Rehvenge withdrew his fingers from her and licked them clean with deliberate strokes of his tongue.

Which naturally teed her up all over again.

Her eyes stayed on his as he repositioned himself upon the pillows she had thrashed around on.

"If you have no clue what to say, join the club."

"We don't have to say anything," she murmured. "It just is."

"Yeah."

Rehvenge rolled over onto his back, and as they lay in the dark with about six inches between them, she missed him as if he'd left the country.

Turning on her side, she rested her head on the inside of her arm and stared at him as he stared at the ceiling.

"I wish I could give you something," she said, leaving the whole bonding thing for a later time. Too much talk was going to ruin what they'd just shared, and she wanted to keep it going for a little longer.

He glanced over. "Are you crazy? Do I need to remind you what we just did?"

"I want to give you something like that." She winced. "I don't mean to make it sound like something was missing . . . I mean . . . Crap."

He smiled and brushed her cheek. "It's sweet of you, don't feel awkward about it. And don't underestimate how much all that pleased me."

"I want you to know something. No one could have made me feel any better or more beautiful than you just did."

He turned to her and mirrored her position, resting his head on his thick biceps. "See why it was good for me?"

She took his hand in hers and kissed his palm, only to frown. "You're growing cold. I can feel it."

She sat up and pulled the duvet over his body, wrapping him up first, then cuddling into him, while lying on top of the covers.

They stayed like that for a century.

"Rehvenge?"

"Yes."

"Take my vein."

She could tell she'd shocked the shit out of him by the way his breath caught. "Excuse ... Wh-what?"

She had to smile, thinking that he wasn't the kind of male who stuttered much. "Take my vein. Let me give you something."

Through his parted lips she saw his fangs elongate, not so much inching as punching out of his skull.

"I'm not sure ... whether that would be ..." As his breath grew ragged, his voice got even deeper.

She put her hand to her neck and massaged her jugular slowly. "I think it's a great idea."

As his eyes glowed purple, she eased onto her back and cocked her head to the side, exposing her throat.

"Ehlena ..." His eyes traveled down her body and returned to her neck.

He was panting and flushed now, a fine sheen of sweat slicking up what portion of his shoulders showed from out of the covers. And that wasn't the half of it. The scent of dark spices flared until it saturated the air, his internal chemistry reacting to the need he had for her and what she wanted to do for him.

"Oh ... shit, Ehlena—"

Abruptly, Rehvenge frowned and looked down at himself. His hand, the one that had been tender on her cheek, disappeared under the covers and his expression changed: The heat and the purpose drained right out of it, leaving only a troubling kind of disgust.

"I'm sorry," he said hoarsely. "I'm sorry ... I can't ..."

Rehvenge scrambled off the bed and took the duvet with him, pulling it free from under her body. He moved fast—but not so quickly that she missed the fact that he had an erection.

He was hard. Big, long, hard as a thighbone.

And yet he disappeared into the bathroom and closed the door solidly.

Then locked it.

THIRTY

John told Qhuinn and Blay he was just going to crash in his room for the night, and when he was sure they'd bought the lie, he slipped out through the staff quarters of the house and went directly to ZeroSum.

He had to work fast, because sure as shit one of the two of them would check in on him and then form a damn search party.

Bypassing the front entrance of the club, he went around to the alley where he'd once seen Xhex crack the head of an asshole with a big mouth and a fistful of coke. Finding the security camera above the side exit, John tilted up his head and stared into the lens.

When the door opened, he didn't have to look over to know it was her.

"You want to come in," she said.

He shook his head, for once not bothered by the communication barrier. Shit, he didn't know what to say to her. Didn't know why he was here. He just had to come.

Xhex stepped out of the club and put her back against the door, crossing one steel-toed boot over the other. "You tell anyone?"

He met her eyes steadily and shook his head.

"You going to?"

He shook his head.

In a soft tone, one he'd never heard from her or expected to, she whispered, "Why?"

He just shrugged. Frankly, he was surprised she hadn't tried to take his memories from him. Neater. Cleaner—

"I should have taken your memories," she said, making him wonder if she was reading his mind. "I was just fucked in the head last night, and you left fast and I didn't do it. Of course, now they're long-term, so . . ."

This was why he came, he realized. He wanted to reassure her that he was going to keep quiet.

Tohr's departure had cemented the decision. When John had gone to talk with the Brother and found the guy had disappeared again, and without word *again*, something had shifted in him, like a boulder being rolled from one side of his yard to another, a permanent change in the landscape.

John was alone. And therefore his decisions were his own. He respected Wrath and the Brotherhood, but he wasn't a Brother and might well never be one. Sure, he was a vampire, but he'd spent most of his life outside of the race, so the *symphath* revulsion was something he'd never fully understood. Sociopaths? Hell, that shit started at home, as far as he was concerned, with the way Zsadist and V had acted before they'd mated.

John was not turning Xhex in to the king so she could get deported to that colony. No way.

Now her voice became hard. "So what do you want."

Given the kind of bottom-feeding, opportunistic, desperate people she had to deal with night in and night out, he was not at all surprised by the demand.

Holding her stare, he shook his head and made a cutting motion over his throat. *Nothing*, he mouthed.

Xhex looked at him with cold gray eyes, and he felt her get into his head, sensing the push against his thoughts. He let her probe to see where he was at, because that more than any words he might have spoken would be what reassured her most.

"You're one in a million, John Matthew," she said quietly. "Most people would leverage the shit out of this. Especially given the kind of vices I can get serviced here at the club."

He shrugged.

"So where you headed tonight? And where are your boys?"

He shook his head.

"You want to talk about Tohr?" As his eyes shot to hers, she said, "Sorry, but he's on your mind."

As John shook his head again, something touched his cheek and he looked up. Snow was starting to come down, little, tiny flakes swirling in the wind.

"First snowfall of the year," Xhex said, standing up away from the door. "And you without a coat."

He glanced down and realized all he had on was jeans and a Nerdz T-shirt. At least he'd remembered to put shoes on.

Xhex put her hand in her pocket and held something out to him. A key. A small brass key.

"I know you don't want to go home, and I have a place not far from here. It's secure and underground. Go there if you want, stay however long you need to. Get the privacy you're looking for until your shit's together."

He was about to shake his head no when she said in the Old Language, *"Let me do right by you in this way."*

He took the key without brushing her hand and mouthed, *Thank you.*

After she gave him the address, he left her in that alley with the snow drifting down from the night sky. As he got to Trade, he looked over his shoulder. She was still by the side door, watching him with arms crossed and boots planted solidly on the ground.

The delicate flakes landing in her short dark hair and on her bare, hard shoulders didn't soften her a bit. She was no angel doing a kindness to him for simple reasons. She was dark and dangerous and unpredictable.

And he loved her.

John lifted his hand in a wave and turned the corner, joining a parade of huddled humans who were walking quickly from bar to bar.

Xhex stayed where she was even as John's big body disappeared out of sight.

One in a million, she thought once again. That kid was one in a million.

As she went back in the club, she knew it was only a matter of time before his two buddies, or maybe members of the Brotherhood, showed up to try to find him. Her response was going to be that she hadn't seen him and didn't have a clue where he was.

Period.

He protected her; she protected him.

End of.

She was heading out of the VIP section when her earpiece went off. After her bouncer stopped talking she cursed and lifted up her watch to speak into the transistor. "Take him to my office."

After she was sure the floor was clear of the working girls, she entered the general-population part of the club and watched as Detective de la Cruz was led through the throng of clubbers.

"Yes, Qhuinn?" she said without turning around.

"Christ, you must have eyes in the back of your skull."

She glanced over her shoulder. "And you should keep that in mind."

John's *ahstrux nohstrum* was the kind of male most females wanted to fuck. And a lot of the guys, too. He had the black-on-black thing rocking, between his Affliction shirt and his biker jacket, but his style was all over the place. Grommet belt and the roll on the cuffs of his beat-to-shit jeans spanked of The Cure. The spiked black hair and the piercing of his lip and the seven black studs working their way up his left ear were emo. Four-inch-soled New Rocks were Goth. Tats on the neck were Hart & Huntington–ish.

As for the concealed weapons she knew damn well were packed under his arms? They were straight-up Rambo, and those fists hanging at his sides were all about the MMA.

The whole package, regardless of the derivation of the components, was sex, and from what she'd seen at the club, up until recently he'd capitalized on the appeal. To the point where those private bathrooms in the back had been like his home office.

After getting promoted to John's personal guard, though, he'd slowed his roll.

"What's doing," she said.

"John been in here?"

"No."

Qhuinn's mismatched eyes narrowed. "You haven't seen him at all."

"No."

As the guy stared at her, she knew he was picking up nothing. Lying was second to murder on her skill-set list.

"Goddamn it," he muttered, glancing around the club.

"If I see him, I'll tell him you're looking for him."

"Thanks." He refocused on her. "Listen, I don't know what the fuck happened between you two, and it's none of my biz—"

Xhex rolled her eyes. "Which clearly explains why you're bringing it up now."

"He's a good guy. Just keep that in mind, all right?" Qhuinn's blue and green stare was full of the kind of clarity only a really hard life gave a male. "Lot of people wouldn't be cool with him getting planted on his ass. Especially me."

In the silence that followed, she had to give Qhuinn credit: Most folks didn't have the balls to stand up to her, and the threat behind the level words was obvious.

"You're okay, Qhuinn, you know that. You're tight."

She clapped him on the shoulder, then headed for her office thinking the king had been smart in the choice of *ahstrum nohstrum* for John. Qhuinn was a perverted fucker, but he was a straight-up killer, and she was glad he was the one watching her boy.

Watching John Matthew, she meant.

Because he wasn't her boy. In the slightest.

When Xhex got to her door, she swung it open without hesitation. "Good evening, Detective."

José de la Cruz was sporting another downmarket two-piece, and he and his suit and the coat that was over it all looked equally tired.

"Evening," he said.

"What can I do for you?" She sat down behind the desk and motioned for him to take the chair he'd used last time.

He did not avail himself. "Would you be able to tell me where you were late last night?"

Not completely, she thought. Because at one point she'd been killing a vampire, and that was none of his bizniz.

"I was here at the club. Why?"

"Do you have some employees who could verify that?"

"Yup. You can talk to iAm or any of my staff. Provided you tell me what the hell is doing."

•

"Last night we found an article of clothing belonging to Grady at a murder scene."

Oh, man, if someone else had popped that motherfucker, she was going to be pissed. "But not his body?"

"No. It was a coat with an eagle on the back, something he was known to wear. His signature, as it were."

"Interesting. So why are you asking me where I was?"

"The jacket had blood splatterings on it. We're not sure whether it's his or not, but we'll find out tomorrow."

"And again, why do you want to know where I was."

De la Cruz planted his palms on her desk and leaned in, his chocolate brown eyes dead fucking serious. "Because I have a hunch you'd like to see him dead."

"I'm not into abusive men, true. But all you have is his jacket, no body, and more to the point, I was here last night. So if someone offed him, it wasn't me."

He straightened. "Are you giving Chrissy a funeral?"

"Yup, tomorrow. The notice went in the paper today. She might not have had a lot of relatives, but she was well liked on Trade Street. We're just one big, happy family here." Xhex smiled a little. "You going to wear a black armband for her, Detective?"

"Am I invited?"

"Free country. And you'd come anyway, wouldn't you."

De la Cruz smiled genuinely, his eyes losing most of their aggression. "Yeah, I would. You mind if I talk to your alibis? Get statements?"

"Not at all. I'll call them in right now."

As Xhex spoke into her watch, the detective looked around the office, and when she dropped her arm, he said, "You're not much for decorations."

"I like things stripped down to what I need and nothing more."

"Huh. My wife's into the decorating. She's got a knack for making places homey. It's nice."

"Sounds like a good woman."

"Oh, she is. Plus she makes the best queso I've ever had." He glanced over. "You know, I hear a lot about this club."

"Do you."

"Yup. Particularly from Vice."

"Ah."

"And I've done my homework on Grady. He was arrested over the summer on felony drug possession. Case is still pending."

"Well, I know he'll be brought to justice."

"He was fired from this club shortly before that arrest, wasn't he."

"For skimming cash from the bar."

"And yet you didn't charge him?"

"If I called the police every time one of my employees lifted some green, I'd have you guys on speed dial."

"But I heard that wasn't the only reason he was booted."

"Did you."

"Trade Street, as you said, is its own family—but that doesn't mean there isn't talk. And people are telling me that he was fired because he was dealing here at the club."

"Well, that follows, doesn't it. We'd never allow anyone to deal on our property."

"Because this is your boss's territory and he doesn't appreciate the competition."

She smiled. "There is no competition here, Detective."

And that was the truth. Rehvenge was top dog. Period. Any two-bit ass-wipe trying to pass small loads off under the club's roof got cracked. Hard.

"To be honest, I'm not sure how you've done it," de la Cruz murmured. "There's been speculation about this place for years, and yet no one's been able to get probable cause for a search warrant."

And that was because human minds, even those plugged into the shoulders of cops, were easily manipulated. Whatever was seen or talked about could be erased in the blink of an eye.

"Nothing shady happens here," she said. "That's how we do it."

"Your boss around?"

"No, he's out tonight."

"So he trusts you to run his business while he's gone."

"Like me, he's never gone for long."

De la Cruz nodded. "Good policy. On that note, I don't know if you heard, but there seems to be a turf war going on."

"Turf war? I thought the two halves of Caldwell were at peace with each other. The river isn't a divide anymore."

"Drug turf war."

"I wouldn't know about those."

"That's my other case right now. We found two dealers dead by the river."

Xhex frowned, thinking she was surprised she hadn't heard about that already. "Well, drugs are a rough business."

"They were both shot in the head."

"That'll do it."

"Ricky Martinez and Isaac Rush. You know them?"

"Heard of them, but then both have been in the papers." She put her hand on the copy of the *CCJ* that was neatly stacked on her desk. "And I'm a big reader."

"So you must have seen the article on them today."

"Not yet, but I was just about to take a break. Gotta have my Dilbert fix."

"Is that the one about the office? I was a Calvin and Hobbes fan for years. Hated to see that stop and haven't really gotten into any of the new ones. Guess I'm behind the times."

"You like what you like. Nothing wrong with that."

"That's what my wife says." De la Cruz's eyes drifted around again. "So, a couple people said both of them came into this club last night."

"Calvin and Hobbes? One was a kid and the other a tiger. Neither would have gotten past my bouncers."

De la Cruz grinned briefly. "No, Martinez and Rush."

"Ah, well, you walked through this club. We have a huge number of folks in here every night."

"True enough. This is one of the most successful clubs in town." De la Cruz put his hands in his hip pockets, his coat falling back, his suit jacket pouching out around his chest. "One of the junkies who lives under the bridge saw an oldish Ford along with a black Mercedes and a chromed-out Lexus leaving the area a little after those two got popped."

"Drug dealers can afford nice cars. Not sure what to make of the Ford."

"What does your boss drive? A Bentley, isn't it? Or did he get a new ride."

"No, he's still got the B."

"Expensive car."

"Very."

"You know anyone with a black Mercedes? 'Cuz witnesses also saw one hanging around the apartment Grady's eagle jacket was found in."

"Can't say as I know any Merc owners."

There was a knock on the door, and Trez and iAm came in, the two Moors making the detective look like a Honda parked between a pair of Hummers.

"Well, I'll leave you all to talk," Xhex said with absolute faith in Rehv's besties. "See you at the funeral, Detective."

"If not before then. Hey, you ever think of getting a plant for in here? Could make a difference."

"No, I'm too good at killing things." She smiled tightly. "You know where to find me. Later."

As she shut the door behind her, she stopped fronting and frowned. Turf wars were not good for business, and if Martinez and Rush got done, it was a sure sign that in spite of the December weather, Caldwell's underbelly was developing another heat rash.

Shit, that was the last thing they needed.

Vibrations coming from her pocket told her someone was reaching out to touch her, and she answered the call the instant she saw who it was.

"You find Grady yet," she asked softly.

Big Rob's deep voice was full of frustration. "Fucker must be in hiding. Silent Tom and me, we been to all the clubs. Been to his place and also a couple of his buddies'."

"Keep looking, but be careful. His jacket was just found at another murder scene. The cops are on him hard."

"We aren't giving up till we have a bead on him for you."

"Good man. Now get off this phone and get back on the trail."

"No problem, boss."

THIRTY-ONE

Inside his pitch-dark bathroom, Rehvenge banged into one of the marble walls, tripped across the marble floor, and ricocheted off the marble counter. His body was alive, sensation tingling through him, the pain of nailing his hip registering, the sawing breath in his lungs causing a burn, his heart thumping against his sternum.

He dropped the satin duvet, willed the lights on, and looked down.

His cock was stiff and thick, the tip glossy and ready to penetrate.

Holy . . . *shit*.

He glanced around. His vision was normal, the bathroom's colors black and steel and white, with the edge of the Jacuzzi rising up from the floor, its depth obvious. And yet even though nothing was flat or ruby red, his senses were utterly alive, his blood heated and thundering in his veins, his skin ready to be touched, the orgasm in the shaft of his erection screaming to get free.

He'd totally bonded with Ehlena.

And that meant—at least in this moment, when he was so desperate to have sex with her—his vampire side was winning out over the *symphath* part of him.

His need for her triumphed over the darkness in him.

It had to be the bonding hormones, he thought. Bonding hormones that had shifted his internal chemistry.

In recognizing his new reality, there was no soaring joy,

no sense of triumph, no impulse to throw himself on top of her and pump away hard. All he could do was stare down at his cock and think of where it had been last. What he'd done with it . . . and with the rest of his body.

Rehvenge wanted to snap the fucking thing off.

No way in hell was he sharing that with Ehlena. Except . . . he couldn't go back out there like this.

Rehv grabbed his arousal in his broad hand and stroked himself. Oh . . . fuck . . . that was good . . .

He thought of going down on Ehlena, of having her warmth in his mouth and down the back of his throat. He saw her spread thighs and her glistening softness and his fingers slipping in and out as she moaned and rocked her—

His balls tightened up hard as fists, and the small of his back rippled in a wave, and that disgusting barb of his triggered even though it had nothing to grab onto. A roar threatened to come up out of his throat, but he held it in by biting his lip until he tasted blood.

Rehv came all over his hand and kept working his sex anyway, propping himself on the counter. He orgasmed again and again, messing up the mirror and the sinks, and still needing more—as if his body hadn't released in, like, five hundred years.

When the storm finally passed, he realized . . . shit, he was draped against the wall, face shoved in hard to the marble, shoulders sagging, thighs twitching like there were jumper cables hooked up to his toes.

With shaky hands, he cleaned things up using one of the towels that was folded neatly on a rack, wiping off the counter and the glass and the sink. Then he flipped free another one and washed his hands and his cock and his stomach and his legs, because he'd gotten himself as dirty as the fucking bathroom.

When he finally reached for the doorknob, after what must have been nearly an hour, he half expected Ehlena to be gone, and he wouldn't blame her: A female whom he had essentially made love to offers him her vein and he runs like a pussy into the bathroom and locks himself in.

Because he gets a hard-on.

Jesus Christ. This evening, which hadn't even started out

so well, had turned into a sixteen-car pileup on the road to relationshipville.

Rehv braced himself and opened the door.

As light spilled into the bedroom, Ehlena sat up in the sheets, her face worried . . . and completely nonjudgmental. There was no condemnation, no calculation as if she were looking for what would make him feel even worse. Just honest-to-God concern.

"Are you okay?"

Well, wasn't that the question.

Rehvenge dropped his head and for the first time wanted to unburden everything to another person. Even with Xhex, who had been through more than he had, he had no interest in doing the sharing shit. But with Ehlena's toffee-colored eyes so wide and warm in her lovely, perfect face, he wanted to confess every single dirty, shitty, scheming, mean, nasty thing he'd ever done.

Just to be honest.

Yeah, but if he dumped his life out on the table, where would that leave her? In a position of having to report him as a *symphath* and likely fearing for her very life. Great outcome. Perfect.

"I wish I were different," he said, which was as close as he could get to speaking the truth that would separate them forever. "I wish I were a different male."

"I don't."

That was because she didn't know him. Not truly. And yet he couldn't handle the idea of never seeing her after this night they'd had together.

Or that she would be terrified of him.

"If I asked you to come here again," he said, "and let me be with you, would you?"

There was no hesitation. "Yes."

"Even if things couldn't be . . . normal . . . between us? Sexually speaking."

"Yes."

He frowned. "This is going to come out wrong. . . ."

"Which is fine, because I've already put my foot in it with you back at the clinic. We'll just be even."

Rehv had to smile, but the expression didn't stick. "I have to know . . . why. Why would you come back."

Ehlena lay back down against the pillows and, in a slow sweep, moved her hand up over the satin sheet that covered her stomach. "I have only one answer to that, but I don't think it's going to be what you want to hear."

The cold numbness, which was returning as the remnants of those orgasms he'd had dissipated, sped up its reclamation of his body.

Please let it not be *pity*, he thought. "Tell me."

She was quiet for a long while, her stare shifting out toward the blinking, glowing view of Caldwell's two halves.

"You ask me why I would come back?" she said softly. "And the only answer I have is . . . how could I not." Her eyes flipped to his. "It doesn't make sense to me on some level, but then, feelings don't make sense, do they? And they don't have to. Tonight . . . you gave me things I not only haven't had for a long time, but I don't think I've *ever* felt." She shook her head. "I wrapped up a body yesterday . . . a body of someone my own age, a body of someone who likely as not had headed out of his house the evening he was killed with no clue that it was his last night. I don't know where this"—she gestured back and forth between them—"thing with us is going. Maybe it's just a night or two. Maybe it's a month. Maybe it's longer than can be measured by a decade. All I know is, life is too short not to come back here and be with you like this again. Life is just too short, and I like being with you too much for me to give a crap about anything other than having another moment like this."

Rehvenge's chest swelled as he stared at her. "Ehlena?"

"Yeah?"

"Don't take this the wrong way."

She drew in a deep breath and he saw her bare shoulders tighten. "Okay. I'll try not to."

"You keep showing up here? Being who you are?" There was a pause. "I'm going to fall in love with you."

John found Xhex's place easily enough because it was only ten blocks from ZeroSum. Even still, the neighborhood might as well have been in a different zip code entirely. The brownstones on the street were elegant and old-world, with the curlicue shit around all the bay windows making him think they were Victorian—although how he knew that with such surety he hadn't a clue.

Hers wasn't a whole building, but a basement apartment in one particularly attractive walk-up. Underneath the stone stairs that led up from the sidewalk there was an alcove, and he slipped in and used the key on a strange copper-colored lock. A light came on as he stepped through, and he saw nothing exciting: Red-washed floor made of stone slabs. Whitewashed walls made of concrete blocks. At the far end there was another door with another odd lock.

He'd expected Xhex to live someplace exotic and filled with weapons.

And plenty of French stockings and stillies.

But that was fantasy for you.

Down at the far end of the hallway, he opened the other door and more lights flared. The room beyond was windowless and empty except for a bed, and the nondecor was no surprise, considering what the basement hall was like. There was a bathroom across the way, but no kitchen, no phone, no TV. The only color in the room came from the floor of old-fashioned pine boards that were finished to a fresh honey glow. Walls were whitewashed, like the corridor, but made of brick.

The air was surprisingly fresh, but then he saw the vents. Three of them.

John took off his leather jacket and laid it out on the floor. Then he removed his boots, keeping his thick black socks on.

In the bathroom, he used the toilet and splashed his face with water.

No towels. He used the tail ends of his heavy black shirt.

Stretching out on the bed, he kept his weapons on, although not because he was afraid of Xhex.

God, maybe that made him stupid. The first thing he had been taught in the Brotherhood's training program was that you never trusted *symphaths*, and here he was, risking his life by staying in the home of one—likely through the day, without having told anyone where he was.

Yet it was exactly what he needed.

When night fell again, he was going to decide what to do. He didn't want out of the war—he liked fighting too much. It felt . . . right, and on more than just a defend-the-species kind of level. It felt like it was what he was supposed to be doing, what he had been born and bred to do.

But he wasn't sure he could go back to the mansion and live there.

After a while, the lights went off when he didn't move, and he just stared into the darkness. As he lay on the bed with his head on one of the two rather stiff pillows, he realized it was the first time he had been truly alone since he'd been picked up from his shitty apartment by Tohr in that big-ass black Range Rover.

With total clarity, he remembered what it had been like to live in that hell-hole of a studio in not the wrong part of town, but the downright dangerous section of Caldie. He'd been terrified every night because he'd been scrawny and weak and defenseless, drinking only Ensure because of his bad gut, weighing less than a vacuum cleaner. The door that had separated him from the drug users and the prostitutes and the rats that were the size of donkeys had seemed thin as paper.

He had wanted to do good in the world. Still did.

He had wanted to fall in love and be with a woman. Still did.

He had wanted to find a family, have a mother and a father, be a part of a clan.

Didn't anymore.

John was beginning to understand that emotions in the heart were like tendons in the body. You could pull them and pull them and pull them and feel the pain of the distortion and the stretching . . . and up to a point, the joint would still function and the limb would bend and support weight and remain useful after the stress was off. But it wasn't an infinite kind of thing.

He'd snapped. And he was damn sure there was no emotional equivalent of arthroscopic surgery.

To help ease his mind into rest so he didn't drive himself nuts, he concentrated on what was going on around him. The room was quiet, except for the heat blower, but that didn't make much noise. And the building was empty above him, with no sounds of anyone moving around.

Closing his eyes, he felt safer than he probably should have.

Then again, he was used to being on his own. The time he'd spent with Tohr and Wellsie and then with the Brotherhood was an anomaly. He'd been born in that bus stop alone, and he'd been alone in the orphanage even as he'd been surrounded by an ever-shuffling deck of kids. And then he'd been out in the world by himself.

He'd been brutalized and gotten over it without help. Been sick and healed himself. Made his way as best he could and done an okay job of it.

Time to get back to basics.

And the core of himself.

That time with Wellsie and Tohr ... and the Brothers ... was like a failed experiment—something that had seemed to have potential, but that, ultimately, was a failure.

THIRTY-TWO

Night or day, it didn't bother Lash.

As he and Mr. D pulled into the parking lot of an abandoned mill and the Mercedes' headlights swung around in a fat arc, it didn't matter to him whether he met the king of the *symphaths* at noon or midnight, as he somehow wasn't intimidated by the motherfucker anymore.

He locked up the 550 and walked with Mr. D across a decaying asphalt stretch to a door that was very sturdy, considering the shape the mill was in. Thanks to the light snow that was falling, the setting seemed like something out of an ad for quaint Vermont vacations, as long as you didn't look too closely at the sagging roofline or the ragged siding.

The *symphath* was already inside. Lash knew it sure as he felt the flurries on his cheeks and heard loose stones crunch under his combat boots.

Mr. D opened the door and Lash stepped inside first to show he didn't need a subordinate to clear the way. The interior of the mill was nothing but a lot of cold air, the rectangular building having long ago been stripped of anything useful.

The *symphath* was waiting down at the far end, near the massive wheel that still sat in the river like an old fat woman in a cooling bath.

"My friend, how nice to see you once more," the king said, that snake voice rippling along the rafters.

Lash walked over to the guy nice and slow, taking his time, checking and double-checking the shadows thrown by the glass windows. Nothing but the king. This was good.

"Have you considered my proposal?" the king said.

Lash was not in a fucking-around mood. After the shit with the Domino's delivery guy the night before and the fact that there was another drug dealer to pick off in about an hour, now wasn't the time to play.

"Yeah. And you know what? I'm not sure I need to do you any favors. I'm thinking either you give me what I want, or . . . maybe I just send my men north to slaughter you and all the other freaks up there."

That flat, pale face broke into a serene smile. "But how would that work for you? It would be destroying the very tools with which you wish to best your enemy. Not a logical step for any ruler to take."

Lash's cock tingled at the tip, respect turning him on, though he refused to acknowledge the fact. "You know, I wouldn't think the king would need help. Why can't you just do the killing yourself?"

"There are extenuating circumstances, and benefits to making it appear as if the demise occurred outside of my influence. You will learn, over time, that machinations in the background are at times far more effective than those you conduct in full view of your population."

Point taken, though again, Lash wasn't going to give props.

"I'm not as young as you think," he said instead. Fuck it, he'd aged about a billion years in the last four months.

"And you are not as old as you believe. But that is another conversation for a different time."

"I'm not looking for a therapist."

"Which is a shame. I'm rather good at getting into the heads of others."

Yeah, Lash could see that. "This target of yours. Is it a male or a female."

"Would it matter?"

"Not in the slightest."

The *symphath* positively beamed. "It is a male. And as I said, there are unusual circumstances."

"How so?"

"He will be difficult to get to. His private guard is rather fierce." The king floated over to a window and looked out. After a moment, his head turned as an owl's would, rotating on the spine until it was nearly facing backward, and then his white eyes flared red for a moment. "Do you think you can handle such a penetration?"

"Are you a homo?" Lash blurted.

The king laughed. "You mean, do I prefer lovers of my same sex?"

"Yeah."

"Would that make you uncomfortable?"

"No." Yes, because it would mean that he kinda sorta had the hots for a guy who swung that way.

"You don't lie very well," the king murmured. "But it will come with age."

Fuck that. "And I don't think you're as powerful as you think you are."

When the sexual speculation disappeared Lash knew he'd hit a sore spot. "Beware the waters of confrontation—"

"Spare me the two-bit, fortune-cookie bullshit, Your Highness. If you were filling out that robe with a good set of balls, you'd get rid of this guy yourself."

Serenity returned to the king's face, as if Lash had just proven his inferiority with the outburst. "Yet instead I'm having someone else take care of it for me. Far more sophisticated, although I don't expect you to understand that."

Lash dematerialized right in front of the guy and locked his palms around that slender throat. With a single, brutal thrust, he forced the king up against the wall.

Their eyes locked, and as Lash felt a probe into his mind, he instinctively shut the entryway through his frontal lobe.

"You're not unlocking my trunk there, asshole. Sorry."

The king's stare grew red as blood. "No."

"No what?"

"I do not prefer lovers of my own sex."

It was the perfect shoe to drop, of course: the implication being that Lash was staying close because he was the one who liked cock out of the pair of them. He let go and stalked around.

The king's voice was now less snakelike and more factual. "You and I are rather well matched. I believe we shall both get what we want from this alliance."

Lash turned and faced the guy. "This male, the one you want dead, where do I find him."

"The timing must be correct. Timing . . . is everything."

Rehvenge watched Ehlena put her clothes back on, and though getting her back into that uniform wasn't exactly what he wanted, the show of her bending over and slowly smoothing her stockings up her leg wasn't half-bad.

Not. At. All.

She laughed as she picked her bra up and twirled it around her finger. "Can I put this on now?"

"Absolutely."

"You going to make me take my time again?"

"I just figured there was no rush on the hose." He smiled like the wolf he was feeling like. "I mean, those things run, don't they— Oh, fuck *me* . . ."

Ehlena didn't wait for him to finish talking, but arched her back and pulled the bra around her torso. The little shimmy she worked as she reclasped it in the front made him pant . . . and that was before she drew the straps over her shoulders, leaving the cups wedged under her breasts.

She came over to him. "I've forgotten how to work it. Can you help?"

Rehv growled and pulled her in close, sucking one nipple into his mouth and working the other with his thumb. Just as she gasped, he flipped the cups into place.

"I'm glad to be your lingerie engineer, but, you know, it looked better off you." As he jogged his eyebrows at her, her laugh was so free and easy his heart stopped. "I like that sound."

"And I like making it."

She stepped into her uniform and pulled it up and then fastened its buttons.

"Pity," he said.

"You want to know something silly? I wore this even though I don't have to go to work tonight."

"Did you? Why?"

"I wanted to keep things professional, and yet here I am, thrilled that it didn't work out that way."

He stood up and took her into his arms, not worried at all about being totally naked now. "Count me in on the thrilled part."

He kissed her softly, and as they parted, she said, "Thank you for a lovely evening."

Rehv tucked her hair behind her ears. "What are you doing tomorrow?"

"Working."

"When do you get off?"

"Four."

"Be here?"

She didn't pause. "Yes."

As they walked out of the bedroom and through the library, he said, "I'm going to see my mother now."

"You are?"

"Yeah, she called me and asked to see me. She never does that." It felt so right to be sharing details of his life. Well, some of them, at any rate. "She's been trying to make me more spiritual, and I'm hoping this isn't a bid to get me on some kind of retreat."

"What do you do, by the way? For work?" Ehlena laughed. "I know so little about you."

Rehv fixated on the view of the city over her shoulder. "Oh, a lot of different things. Mostly in the human world. I have only my mother to take care of, now that my sister is mated."

"Where's your father?"

In the cold grave, where the fucker belonged. "He's passed."

"I'm sorry."

Ehlena's warm eyes made a shot of what sure as shit felt like guilt go through his chest. He didn't regret killing his old man; he was sorry that he was obscuring so much from her.

"Thanks," he said stiffly.

"I don't mean to pry. About your life or your family. I'm just curious, but if you'd prefer—"

"No, it's just . . . I don't talk about myself much." Wasn't that the truth. "Is that . . . is that a cell phone ringing?"

Ehlena frowned and broke away. "Mine. In my coat."

She loped off into the dining room, and the tension in her voice as she answered was apparent. "Yes? Oh, hi! Yeah, no, I— Now? Of course. And the funny thing is I won't need to go change into my uniform because— Oh. Yes. Uh-huh. Okay."

He heard the phone clip shut as he got to the dining room's archway. "Everything all right?"

"Ah, yeah. Just work." Ehlena came over while pulling her coat on. "It's nothing. Probably just staffing stuff."

"You want me to drive you over?" God, he would love to take her to work, and not just because they could be together a little longer. A male wanted to do things for his female. Protect her. See to her—

Okay, what the fuck? It wasn't that he didn't like the thoughts he was having about her, but it was as if someone had switched his CD. And no, it wasn't to Barry fucking Manilow.

Although there was definitely some Maroon 5 on the bitch now.

Bleh.

"Oh, I'll just go, but thank you." Ehlena paused in front of one of the sliding doors. "Tonight has been such . . . a revelation."

Rehv stalked up to her, took her face in his hands, and kissed her hard. When he pulled back, he said darkly, "Only because of you."

She beamed then, glowing from within, and abruptly he wanted her naked again just so he could come inside of her: The marking instinct was screaming in him, and the only way he could placate it was by telling himself he'd left enough of his scent on her skin.

"Text me when you get to the clinic so I know you're safe," he said.

"I will."

One last kiss and she was through the door and off into the night.

As she left Rehvenge's, Ehlena was flying, and not just because she was dematerializing across the river to the clinic. To her, the night wasn't cold; it was fresh. Her uniform wasn't wrinkled from having been tossed on a bed and rolled around upon; it was artfully disheveled. Her hair wasn't a mess; it was casual.

The call to come into the clinic wasn't an intrusion; it was an opportunity.

Nothing could take her down from this incandescent elevation. She was one of the stars in the velvety night sky, unreachable, untouchable, above the strife of the earth-bound.

Taking form in front of the clinic's garages, though, she lost some of her rose-colored glow. It seemed unfair that she could feel as she did, considering what had happened the night before: She'd bet her life on the fact that Stephan's family wasn't rebounding back to any semblance of joy right now. They would have just barely finished the death ritual, for God's sake.... It would be years before they could feel anything even remotely like what sang in her chest as she thought of Rehv.

Or if ever. She had the sense his parents might never be the same.

With a curse, she walked swiftly across the parking lot, her shoes leaving little black prints across the dusting of snow that had fallen earlier. As a staff member, getting through the checkpoints down to the waiting room didn't take long, and when she came into the registration area, she shucked her coat and headed right for the front desk.

The nurse behind the computer looked up and smiled. Rhodes was one of the few males on the staff, and definitely a favorite at the clinic, the kind of guy who got along with everyone and was quick with the smiles and the hugs and the high fives.

"Hey, girlie, how you . . ." He frowned as she got closer to him, then pushed his chair back, putting space between them. "Er . . . hi."

Frowning, she looked behind her, expecting to see a monster, given the way he shrank from her. "Are you okay?"

"Oh, yeah. Totally." His eyes were sharp. "How are *you*?"

"I'm fine. Glad to come in and help. Where's Catya?"

"Waiting for you in Havers's office, I think she said."

"I'll head on back then."

"Yeah. Cool."

She noticed his mug was empty. "You want me to bring you a coffee when I'm done?"

"No, no," he said quickly, holding both hands up. "I'm fine. Thanks. Really."

"You sure you're okay?"

"Yup. Totally fine. Thanks."

Ehlena walked off, feeling like an absolute leper. Usually she and Rhodes were pally-pally, but not tonight—

Oh, my God, she thought. Rehvenge had left his scent on her. That had to be it.

She turned around . . . but what could she say, really?

Hoping Rhodes was the only one who'd pick up on it, she hit the locker room to ditch her coat and headed off, waving to staff and patients along the way. When she got to Havers's office, the door was open, the doctor sitting behind his desk, Catya in the chair with her back to the hall.

Ehlena knocked softly on the jamb. "Hi."

Havers looked up, and Catya glanced over her shoulder. They both seemed positively ill.

"Come in," the doctor said gruffly. "And shut the door."

Ehlena's heart started to beat fast as she did what he asked. There was an empty chair next to Catya, and she sat down because her knees were suddenly loose.

She'd been in this office a number of times, usually to remind the doctor to eat, because once he started in with patient charts he lost track of time. But this was not about him, was it.

There was a long silence, during which Havers's pale eyes would not meet hers as he fiddled with the earpieces of his tortoiseshell glasses.

Catya was the one who spoke, and her voice was tight. "Last night, before I left, one of the security guards who had been monitoring all the camera feeds brought it to my attention that you were in the pharmacy. Alone. He said he saw you take some pills and leave with them. I looked at the tape and checked the relevant shelves and it was penicillin."

"Why didn't you just bring him in?" Havers said. "I would have seen Rehvenge again immediately."

The moment that followed was like something in a TV soap, where the camera zoomed in on the face of a character: Ehlena felt as though everything pulled away from her, the office retreating into the far distance as she was abruptly spotlit and under microscopic scrutiny.

Questions rolled into her brain. Did she really think she was going to get away with what she'd done? She'd even known about the security cameras . . . and yet she hadn't thought about that when she'd gone behind the pharmacist's counter the night before.

Everything was going to change as the result of this. Her life, once a struggle, was going to become insupportable.

Destiny? No ... stupidity.

How the hell could she have done this?

"I'll resign," she said roughly. "Effective tonight. I should never have done it.... I was worried about him, overwrought about Stephan, and I made a horrible judgment call. I'm deeply sorry."

Neither Havers nor Catya said a thing, but they didn't have to. It was all about trust, and she had violated theirs. As well as a shitload of patient safety regulations.

"I'll clean out my locker. And leave immediately."

THIRTY-THREE

Rehvenge didn't get out to see his mother enough.

That was the thought that occurred to him as he pulled in front of the safe house he'd moved her into nearly a year ago. After the family mansion in Caldwell had been compromised by *lessers*, he'd gotten everyone out of that house and installed them at this Tudor mansion well south of town.

It had been the only thing good that had come of his sister's abduction—well, that and the fact that Bella had found herself a male of worth in the Brother who'd rescued her. The thing was, with Rehv having taken his mother from the city when he had, she and her beloved *doggen* had escaped what the Lessening Society had done to the aristocracy over the summer.

Rehv parked the Bentley in front of the mansion, and before he got out of the car, the door to the house opened and his mother's *doggen* stood in the light, huddled against the cold.

Rehv's wingtips had slick soles, so he was very careful as he came around on the dusting of snow. "Is she okay?"

The *doggen* stared up at him, her eyes misting with tears. "It's getting close to the time."

Rehv came inside, closed the door, and refused to hear that. "Not possible."

"I'm very sorry, sire." The *doggen* took out a white handkerchief from the pocket of her gray uniform. "Very ... sorry."

"She's not old enough."

"Her life has been far longer than her years."

The *doggen* knew well what had gone on in the house during the time Bella's father had been with them. She had cleaned up broken glass and shattered china. Had bandaged and nursed.

"Verily, I can't bear for her to go," the maid said. "I shall be lost without my mistress."

Rehv put a numb hand on her shoulder and squeezed gently. "You don't know for sure. She hasn't been to see Havers. Let me go be with her, okay?"

When the *doggen* nodded, Rehv slowly took the stairs up to the second floor, passing family portraits in oil that he had moved from the old house.

At the top of the landing, he went down to the left and knocked on a set of doors. *"Mahmen?"*

"In here, my son."

The response in the Old Language came from behind another door, and he backtracked and went into her dressing room, the familiar scent of Chanel No. 5 calming him.

"Where are you?" he said to the yards and yards of hanging clothes.

"I am in the back, my dearest son."

As Rehv walked down the rows of blouses and skirts and dresses and ball gowns, he breathed deeply. His mother's signature perfume was on all of the garments, which were hung by color and type, and the bottle it came from was on the ornate dressing table, among her makeup and lotions and powders.

He found her in front of the three-way full-length mirror. Ironing.

Which was beyond odd and made him take stock of her.

His mother was regal even in her rose-colored dressing gown, her white hair up on her perfectly proportioned head, her posture exquisite as she sat on a high stool, her massive pear-shaped diamond flashing on her hand. The ironing board she sat behind had a woven basket and a can of spray starch on one end and a pile of pressed handkerchiefs on the other. As he watched her, she was in midkerchief, the pale yellow square she was working on halved, the iron she wielded hissing as she swept it up and down.

"*Mahmen,* what are you doing?" Okay, obvious on one level, but his mother was the chatelaine. He couldn't remember ever seeing her do housework or laundry or anything of the sort. One had *doggen* for those things.

Madalina looked up at him, her faded blue eyes tired, her smile more effort than honest joy. "These were my father's. We found them when we were going through the boxes that had been brought over from the old house's attic."

The "old house" was the one they had lived in for almost a century in Caldwell.

"You could get your maid to do that for you." He came over and kissed her soft cheek. "She would love to help you."

"She said as much, yes." After she put her hand on his face, his mother went back to what she was doing, folding the linen square again, picking up the can of starch, misting over the kerchief. "But this is something I must do."

"May I sit?" he asked, nodding at the chair beside the mirror.

"Oh, of course, where are my manners." The iron went down and she started to get off the stool. "And we must get you something to—"

He held up his hand. "No, *Mahmen,* I've just eaten."

She bowed to him and rearranged herself on her perch. "I am grateful for this audience, as I know the busy nature of your—"

"I'm your son. How can you think I wouldn't come to you?"

The pressed kerchief was placed on top of its orderly brethren, and the last one was taken from the basket.

The iron exhaled steam as she smoothed its hot underbelly over the white square. As she moved slowly, he looked into the mirror. Her shoulder blades were prominent under the silk robe, her spine showing clearly at the back of her neck.

When he refocused on her face, he saw a tear drop from her eye onto the kerchief.

Oh . . . dearest Virgin Scribe, he thought. I'm not ready.

Rehv plugged his cane into the floor and came over to kneel before her. Turning the stool toward him, he removed the iron from her hand and put it aside, ready to take her to

Havers's, prepared to pay for whatever medicine would buy her more time.

"Mahmen, what ails you?" He took one of her father's pressed handkerchiefs and dabbed under her eyes. *"Speak unto your born son the weight of your heart."*

The tears were without end, and he caught them one by one. She was lovely even in her age and her crying, a fallen Chosen who had lived a hard life and nonetheless remained full of grace.

When she finally spoke, her voice was thin. "I am dying." She shook her head before he could speak. "No, let us be truthful with each other. My end has arrived."

We'll see about that, Rehv thought to himself.

"My father"—she touched the handkerchief Rehv had dried her tears with—"my father . . . it is odd that I think of him daily and nightly now, but I do. He was the Primale long ago, and he loved his children. His greatest joy was his blood, and though we were many, he had relationships with us all. These handkerchiefs? They were made out of his robes. Verily, the industry of sewing was of favor to me, and he knew this and he gave unto me some of his robes."

She reached over with a bony hand and smoothed the stack she'd ironed. "When I left the Other Side, he made me take a few of them. I was in love with a Brother and certain my life would be fulfilled only if I were with him. Of course, then . . ."

Yeah, it was the *then* part of her days that had caused her such pain: Then she was raped by a *symphath* and fell pregnant with Rehvenge and was forced to give birth to a half-breed monstrosity that somehow she had taken to her breast and loved as any son would have wanted to be loved. And all the while as she was imprisoned by the *symphath* king, the Brother she'd loved had searched for her—only to die in the process of getting her back.

And those tragedies hadn't been the end of it.

"After I had been . . . returned, my father called me unto his deathbed," she continued. "Of all the Chosen, of all his mates and his children, he'd wanted to see me. But I wouldn't go. I couldn't bear . . . I was not the daughter he knew." Her eyes met Rehv's, a deep pleading in them. "I didn't want him to know of me at all. I was befouled."

Man, he knew that feeling, but his *mahmen* didn't need

the burden of that. She had no clue about the kind of shit he was dealing with, and she would never know, because it was self-evident that the main reason he was whoring himself out was so she wouldn't endure the torture of having her son deported.

"When I refused the summons, the Directrix came unto me and said he was suffering. That he wouldn't go unto the Fade until I came to him. That he would stay on the painful brink of death for an eternity unless I relieved him. The following evening, I went with a heavy heart." Now his mother's stare grew fierce. "Upon my arrival at the Primale temple, he wanted to hold me, but I couldn't ... let him. I was a stranger with a beloved face, that was all, and I tried to speak of polite and distant things. It was then that he said something which afore now I could not fully understand. He said, 'The heavy soul will not pass though the body is failing.' He was imprisoned by what was unresolved with me. He felt as though he had failed in his role. That if he had kept me on the Other Side, my destiny would have been kinder than what had transpired after I left."

Rehv's throat got tight, a sudden, horrible suspicion parking in his brain's front lot.

His mother's voice was weak but forthright. "I approached the bed, and he reached for my hand, and I held his palm within mine own. I told him then that I loved my born son and that I was to be mated to a male of the *glymera* and that all was not lost. My father searched my face for the truth in the words I spoke, and when he was satisfied with what he saw, he closed his eyes ... and drifted away. I knew that if I hadn't come ..." She took a deep breath. "Verily, I cannot leave this earth the way things are."

Rehv shook his head. "Everyone's fine, *Mahmen.* Bella and her young are well and safe. I'm—"

"*Stop it.*" His mother reached up and grabbed onto his chin, the way she had when he'd been very young and prone to causing trouble. "I know what you did. I know you killed my *hellren*, Rempoon."

Rehv weighed whether it was better to keep up the lie, but given his mother's expression, the truth was out, and nothing he could say would dissuade her from it.

"How," he said. "How did you find out?"

"Who else would have? Who else could have?" As she released her hold and stroked his cheek, he yearned to feel the warm touch. "Do not forget, I saw this face of yours each time my *hellren* lost his temper. My son, my strong, powerful son. Look at you."

The honest, loving pride she had for him was something he'd never understood, given the circumstances of his conception.

"I also know," she whispered, "that you killed your birth father. Twenty-five years ago."

Now, that really got his attention. "You were not supposed to know. Any of this. Who told you about it?"

She took her hand from his face and pointed over to her makeup table, to a crystal bowl that he'd always assumed was for her manicures. "Old habits of a Chosen scribe, they die hard. I saw it in the water. Right after it happened."

"And you kept it all to yourself," he said with wonder.

"And could not any longer. Which was why I brought you here."

That horrible feeling resurged, the result of his being trapped between what his mother was going to ask him to do and his strong conviction that his sister wasn't going to benefit from knowing all her family's dirty, evil secrets. Bella had stayed protected from this nastiness all her life, and there was no reason to do a full disclosure now, especially if their mother was dying.

Which Madalina *wasn't*, he reminded himself.

"Mahmen—"

"Your sister must *never* be told."

Rehv stiffened, praying he'd heard her right. "Excuse me?"

"Swear to me you shall do everything in your power to ensure that she never knows." As his mother leaned forward and gripped his arms, he could tell she was really digging her fingers in by the way the bones in her hands and wrists stood out starkly. "I don't want her to carry these burdens. You were forced to, and I would have spared you this if I could have, but I couldn't. And if she doesn't know, then the next generation will not have to suffer. Nalla will not bear the weight either. It can die with you and me. *Swear to me.*"

Rehv stared up into his mother's eyes and never loved her more.

He nodded once. *"Look upon mine face and be assured, I so swear it. Bella and her issue shall never know. The past shall die with thee and me."*

His mother's shoulders eased under her dressing gown, and her shuddering sigh spoke loudly of her relief. "You are the son other mothers may only wish for."

"How can that possibly be true," he said softly.

"How can it not."

Madalina gathered herself up and took the kerchief from his hand. "I must needs do this one again, and then perhaps you will help me to my bed?"

"Of course. And I'd like to call Havers."

"No."

"Mahmen—"

"I should like my passing to be without medical intervention. None would save me now, anyway."

"You can't know that—"

She lifted her lovely hand with its heavy diamond ring. "I shall be dead before nightfall tomorrow. I saw it within the bowl."

Rehv's breath left him, his lungs refusing to work. *I'm not ready for this. I'm not ready. I'm not ready. . . .*

Madalina was so precise with the final kerchief, lining up its corners carefully, sweeping the iron back and forth slowly. When she was finished, she moved the perfect square over to the others, making sure that everything was lined up.

"It is done," she said.

Rehv leaned on his cane to rise and offered her his arm, and together they shuffled into her bedroom, both unsteady.

"Are you hungry?" he asked as he pulled back the covers and helped her lie down.

"No, I am well as I am."

Their hands worked together to arrange the sheets and the blanket and the duvet so that everything was folded precisely and lying directly across her chest. As he straightened, he knew she would not be getting out of bed again, and he couldn't bear it.

"Bella needs to come here," he said roughly. "She needs to say good-bye."

Her mother nodded and shut her eyes. "She must come now, and please have her bring the young."

Back in Caldwell, at the Brotherhood mansion, Tohr paced around his bedroom. Which was a joke, really, considering how weak he was. *Lurched* was about all he could pull off.

Every minute and a half he checked the clock, time passing at an alarming rate until he felt as if the world's hourglass had been shattered and seconds, like sand, were spilling all over the place.

He needed more time. More ... Shit, would that even help, though?

He just couldn't figure out how to get through what was about to happen and knew more stewing wasn't going to change that. For example, he couldn't decide whether it was better to have a witness. The advantage was that it was even less personal that way. The disadvantage was that if he cracked wide open, there was another person in the room to see.

"I'll stay."

Tohr glanced over at Lassiter, who was lounging on the chaise by the windows. The angel's legs were crossed at the ankles, and one combat boot ticked from side to side, another hateful measure of time.

"Come on," Lassiter said, "I've seen your sorry ass naked. What could possibly be worse than that."

The words were typical bravado, the tone surprisingly gentle—

The knock on the door was soft. So it wasn't a Brother. And given that there was no food aroma working its way under the door, it wasn't Fritz with a tray of eats destined for the porcelain throne.

The call to Phury had worked, evidently.

Tohr started to shake from head to toe.

"Okay, easy, there." Lassiter got up and came over fast. "I want you to park it over here. You're not going to want to do this anywhere near a bed. Come on—no, don't fight me. You know this is the drill. It's biology, not choice, so you need to take the guilt out of it."

Tohr felt himself getting pulled across to a stiff-backed

chair that was by the bureau, and right in fucking time: His knees lost interest in their calling, the pair of them falling loose so that he hit the woven seat so hard he bounced.

"I don't know how to do this."

Lassiter's gorgeous puss appeared right in front of his. "Your body's going to do it for you. Take your mind and your heart out of it and let your instinct do what needs to be done. This is not your fault. This is how you survive."

"I don't want to survive."

"You don't say. And here I thought all this self-destructive crap was just a hobby."

Tohr didn't have the strength to lash out at the angel. Didn't have the strength to leave the room. Didn't even have enough in reserve to cry.

Lassiter went over to the door and opened it. "Hey, thanks for coming."

Tohr couldn't bear to look at the Chosen who entered, but there was no ignoring her presence: Her delicate, flowery scent drifted over to him.

Wellsie's natural fragrance had been stronger than that, made not only of rose and jasmine, but the spice that reflected her backbone.

"My lord," a female voice said. "I am the Chosen Selena, here to serve you?"

There was a long pause.

"Go to him," Lassiter said softly. "We need to get this over with."

Tohr put his face in his hands, his head falling loose on his neck. It was all he could do to breathe in and out as the female settled on the floor at his feet.

Through his spindly fingers, he saw the white of her flowing robes. Wellsie hadn't been into dresses all that much. The only one she'd ever truly liked had been the red-and-black gown she'd mated him in.

An image from that sacred ceremony appeared in his mind, and he saw with tragic clarity the moment when the Scribe Virgin had clasped both his and Wellsie's hands and declared that it was a good mating, a very good mating indeed. He'd felt such warmth linked to his female through the mother of the race, and that sensation of love and purpose and optimism had increased a million times over as he'd stared into his love's eyes.

It had seemed as if they had a lifetime of only happiness and joy before them ... and yet now here he was on the other side of unthinkable loss, alone.

No, worse than alone. Alone and about to take another female's blood into his body.

"This is happening too fast," he mumbled behind his palms. "I can't ... I need more time. ..."

So help him, God, if that angel said one word about how now was the right moment, he was going to make that bastard wish his teeth were made out of safety glass.

"My lord," the Chosen said softly, "I shall come back if that is your wish. And come back anon if then is not right. And return and return once more until you are ready. Please ... my lord, verily I should only wish to help, not hurt you."

He frowned. She sounded very kind, and there wasn't a sultry note to any of the syllables that had left her lips.

"Tell me the color of your hair," he said through his hands.

"It is black as the night and bound tight as my sisters and I could make it. I took leave to wrap it in a turban as well, though you did not ask that of me. I thought ... perhaps it would help further."

"Tell me the color of your eyes."

"They are blue, my lord. A pale sky blue."

Wellsie's had been sherry colored.

"My lord," the Chosen whispered, "you need not even look upon me. Allow me to stand behind you, and take my wrist that way."

He heard the rustle of soft cloth, and the scent of the female shifted around until it came from behind him. Dropping his hands, Tohr saw Lassiter's long, jeans-clad legs. The angel's ankles were crossed again, this time as he leaned back against the wall.

A slender arm draped in white cloth appeared before him.

In slow tugs, the sleeve of the robing was gradually lifted higher and higher.

The wrist that was exposed was fragile, the skin white and fine.

The veins beneath the surface were light blue.

Tohr's fangs slammed down from the roof of his mouth

and a snarl came out of his lips. The bastard angel was right. Suddenly there was nothing on his mind; everything was his body and what he'd deprived it of for so long.

Tohr clamped a hard hand on her shoulder, hissed like a cobra, and bit the Chosen's wrist down to the bone, locking his fangs in place. There was a cry of alarm and a scramble, but he was gone as he drank, his swallows like fists on a rope, pulling that blood down into his gut so fast he didn't have time to taste it.

He nearly killed the Chosen.

And he knew this only later, after Lassiter finally peeled him free and knocked him out with a punch to the head—because the instant he'd been separated from the source of those nutrients, he'd tried to go for the female again.

The fallen angel had been right.

Horrible biology was the ultimate driver, winning over even the stoutest of heart.

And the most reverent of widowers.

THIRTY-FOUR

When Ehlena got home, she put on a fake face, sent Lusie off, and checked with her father, who was "making incredible strides" in his work. The second she could get free, though, she went into her room to hop online. She had to figure out how much money they had, down to the penny, and didn't think she was going to like what she came up with. After signing onto her bank account, she scrolled through the checks that had yet to clear and tallied up what was due the first week of the month. The good news was that she was still going to get her pay for November.

Their savings account had just under eleven grand in it.

There was nothing left to sell. And no fat on the monthly budget.

Lusie would have to stop coming. Which would suck, because she'd take on another client to fill the spot, so when Ehlena found a new job there'd be a nursing care hole to plug.

Although that was assuming she could get another position. Sure as hell it wasn't going to be in nursing. Getting fired for cause was not what any employer wanted to see on a résumé.

Why had she lifted those fucking pills?

Ehlena sat staring at the screen adding and readding all the little numbers until they blurred together, not even the sum of them registering anymore.

"Daughter mine?"

She quickly shut down the laptop, because her father didn't do well with electronics, and composed her face. "Yes? I mean, *yes*?"

"I wonder if you would care to read a passage or two of my work? You seem anxious, and I find such pursuits calm my mind." He shuffled to the side and gallantly extended his arm.

Ehlena stood up because sometimes all a person could do was accept the direction of others. She didn't want to read any of the gibberish he had committed to the page. Couldn't bear to pretend that everything was okay. Wished that, even if just for an hour, she could have her parent back so she could talk through the bad position she had landed them both in.

"That would be lovely," she said in a dead, elegant voice.

Following him into his study, she helped settle him into his chair and looked around at the sloppy stacks of paper. What a mess. There were black leather binders crammed to the point of breaking. File folders stuffed wide. Spiral-bound notebooks with pages lolling out of their confines like the tongues of dogs. White loose-leaf paper sprinkled here and there, as if the pages had tried to fly away and gotten only so far.

It was all his diary, or so he maintained. In reality, it was just pile after pile of nonsense, the physical manifestation of his mental chaos.

"Here. Sit, sit." Her father cleared off the seat next to his desk, moving over steno pads that were held together with tan rubber bands.

After she sat down, she put her hands on her knees and squeezed hard, trying not to lose it. It was as if the debris in the room were a spinning magnet that made her own thoughts and machinations rotate even faster, and that was absolutely not the help she needed.

Her father glanced around the office and smiled as if in apology. *"Such industry for a comparatively small yield. Rather like harvesting pearls. The hours I have spent herein, the many hours to fulfill my purpose . . ."*

Ehlena barely heard him. If she couldn't afford the rent here, where would they go? Was there anything even cheaper that didn't have rats and hissing cockroaches in it?

How would her father fare in an unfamiliar environment? Dearest Virgin Scribe, she'd assumed they'd hit bottom the night he'd burned down the proper house they'd been renting. What was lower than this?

She knew she was in trouble when everything got blurry.

Her father's voice continued on, marching across her panicked silence. *"I have endeavored to record with faithfulness all that I saw. . . ."*

Ehlena didn't hear much more.

She cracked in half. Sitting in the little side chair, swamped by her father's mindless, useless prattle, confronted by her actions and where a bad call had landed both of them, she wept.

It was about so much more than losing the job. It was Stephan. It was what had happened with Rehvenge. It was the fact that her father was an adult who couldn't comprehend the realities of their situation.

It was that she was so alone.

Ehlena held herself and wept, hoarse breaths barking out of her lips until she was too exhausted to do anything but sag into her own lap.

Eventually, she heaved a great sigh and wiped her eyes with the sleeve of the uniform she no longer needed anymore.

When she looked up, her father was sitting stock-still in his chair, his expression one of utter shock. *"Verily . . . my daughter."*

See, this was the thing. They might have lost all the monetary trappings of their previous station, but old habits died hard. The reserve of the *glymera* still defined their discourse—so a great wailing session was tantamount to her flipping onto her back at the breakfast table and having an alien bust out of her stomach.

"Forgive me, Father," she said, feeling like an utter fool. *"I believe I shall excuse myself."*

"No . . . wait. You were going to read."

She closed her eyes, her skin tightening up all over her body. On some level, her whole life was defined by his mental pathology, and though for the most part she saw her sacrifices as his due, tonight she was too raw to be able to

pretend the crucial importance of something as worthless
as his "work."

"*Father, I . . .*"

One of the desk drawers opened and shut. "*Here, daughter. Take into thy hands more than just a passage.*"

She dragged her lids open . . .

And had to lean forward to make sure she was seeing
things right. Between her father's two palms was a perfectly
aligned stack of white pages about an inch thick.

"*This is my work,*" he said simply. "*A book for you, mine
daughter.*"

Downstairs in the Tudor safe house, Rehv waited by the
windows in the living room, staring out over the rolling
lawn. The clouds had cleared, and a half-assed moon hung
winter-bright in the sky. In his numb hand, he held his new
cell phone, which he had just clipped shut with a curse.

He couldn't believe that above him his mother was on
her deathbed and that at this very moment his sister and
her *hellren* were speeding to beat the sunrise to get here . . .
and yet work was raising its ugly horned head.

Another dead drug dealer. Which made three in the last
twenty-four hours.

Xhex had been short and to the point, which was her
way. Unlike Ricky Martinez and Isaac Rush, whose bodies
had been found down by the river, this guy had turned up
in his car in a strip mall parking lot with a bullet through
the back of the skull. Which meant that the car had to have
been driven there with the body in it: No way anyone would
be stupid enough to pop a motherfucker in a place that undoubtedly had security-camera coverage. As the police
scanner hadn't reported anything further, though, they
were going to have to wait for the newspapers and the
morning news on TV tomorrow for more details.

But here was the problem, and the reason that he'd
cursed.

All three of them had made buys from him within the
last two nights.

Which was why Xhex had interrupted him at his mother's. The drug business was not merely deregulated, but totally *un*regulated, and the stasis point that had been reached

in Caldwell so that he and his high-level broker colleagues could make money was a very delicate kind of thing.

As a big player, his suppliers were a combination of Miami traffickers, New York harbor importers, Connecticut meth labbers, and Rhode Island X makers. They were all businessmen, just like him, and most of them were independents, i.e., unaffiliated with the mob here in the States. The relationships were solid, the men on the other end as careful and scrupulous as he was: what they did was simply a matter of financial transactions and product changing hands, just like any other legitimate segment of the economy. Shipments came into Caldwell to various residences and were transferred to ZeroSum, where Rally was in charge of the sampling and the cutting down and the packaging.

It was a well-oiled machine that had taken ten years to set up, and required a combination of well-reimbursed employees, threats of bodily harm, actual beatings, and constant relationship building to maintain.

Three dead bodies was enough to throw the whole arrangement into the shitter, causing not just an economic shortfall, but a power struggle on the lower levels that no one needed: Someone was picking off people on his turf, and his colleagues were going to wonder if he was doing a discipline or, worse, being disciplined himself. Prices would fluctuate, relationships would be strained, information would get twisted.

This needed tending to.

He had to make some calls to reassure his importers and producers that he was in control of Caldwell and that nothing was going to impede the sale of their goods. But Christ, why now?

Rehv's eyes shifted to the ceiling.

For a moment, he fantasized about giving it all up, except that was just bullshit. As long as the princess was in his life, he had to stay in business, because there was no way in hell he was going to let that bitch take down his family's fortunes. God knew Bella's father had done enough in that direction by making bad financial decisions.

As long as the princess was aboveground, Rehv would remain the drug lord of Caldie and he would make his calls—although not in his mother's house, not during this family time. Business could wait until family had been served.

Although one thing was clear. Going forward, Xhex, Trez, and iAm were going to have to keep an even tighter eye on things, because sure as shit, if someone was ambitious enough to try to knock off those middlemen, they were more than likely going to attempt a run at a fat boy like Rehv. Trouble was, it was going to be important for Rehv to be seen around the club. Showing face was critical during unsettled times, when his contacts in the biz would be looking to see if he was going to run and hide. Better to be perceived as the person who might be doing the killings than a pussy-ass who ducked out of his turf when the going got tough.

For no good reason, he opened his phone and checked for missed calls. Again. Nothing from Ehlena. Still.

She was probably just busy at the clinic, all caught up in the hustle. Of course she was. And it wasn't like the facility was in danger of being sacked. It was in a remote location and had plenty of security, and he would have heard something if anything bad had happened.

Right?

Damn it.

With a frown, he checked his watch. Time for two more pills.

He headed into the kitchen and was drinking a glass of milk and popping more penicillin when a pair of headlights hit the front of the house. As the Escalade pulled up in front and its doors opened, he put his glass down, plugged his cane into the floor, and went to greet his sister and her mate and their young.

Bella was already red-eyed as she came in, because he'd made it clear what was going on. Her *hellren* was right behind her, carrying their snoozing daughter in his huge arms, his scarred face grim.

"Sister mine," Rehv said as he took Bella into his arms. While holding her loosely, he clapped palms with Zsadist. "I'm glad you're here, my man."

Z nodded his skull-trimmed head. "Me too."

Bella pulled back and wiped her eyes quickly. "Is she up in bed?"

"Yeah, and her *doggen* is with her."

Bella took hold of her daughter, and then Rehv led the way upstairs. At the bedroom doors, he knocked on the jamb first and waited as his mother and her faithful servant got prepared.

"How bad is she?" Bella whispered.

Rehv looked down at his sister, thinking that this was one of the few situations where he could see himself not being as strong for her as he wanted to be.

His voice was hoarse. "It's time."

Bella's eyes squeezed together just as their *mahmen* said in a wobbly voice, "Come in."

As Rehv opened one side of the doors, he heard Bella's sharp inhale, but more than that he sensed her emotional grid: Sadness and panic intertwined with each other, doubling up and redoubling until a solid box was formed. It was a footprint of feelings that he saw only at funerals. And didn't that make tragic sense.

"*Mahmen,*" Bella said as she went to the bedside.

As Madalina held her arms out, her face was suffused with happiness. "My loves, my dearest loves."

Bella bent down and kissed their mother's cheek, then transferred Nalla's weight with care. As their mother didn't have the strength to hold the young, a spare pillow was positioned to support Nalla's neck and head.

Their mother's smile glowed. "Look at her face. . . . She shall be a great beauty, indeed." She lifted a skeletal hand toward Z. "And the proud papa, who looks after his females with such strength and fortitude."

Zsadist came over and clasped what was extended to him, bowing down and brushing her knuckles with his forehead, as was custom between mothers and sons-in-law. "I shall always keep them safe."

"Indeed. Of that I am well sure." Their mother smiled up at the fierce warrior who seemed totally out of place among the lace draped around the bed—but then her strength lagged and she let her head fall to the side.

"My greatest joy," she whispered as she stared at her grandchild.

Bella eased a hip onto the mattress and gently rubbed her mother's knee. The silence in the room became soft as down, a cocoon of quiet that eased over all of them and relieved the tension.

There was only one good thing in all this: An easy death that happened in the right order was as much a blessing as a long, easy life.

Their mother hadn't had the latter. But Rehv was going to keep his promise and make sure the peace in this room was kept well after she was gone.

Bella leaned into her daughter and whispered, "Sleepyhead, wake up for *Granhmen*."

When Madalina brushed the young's cheek softly, Nalla awoke with a coo. Yellow eyes as bright as diamonds focused on the old, lovely face before her, and the young smiled and reached out chubby hands. As the infant gripped her grandmother's finger, Madalina lifted her gaze and peered up over the next generation at Rehv. In her stare, she begged him.

And he gave her exactly what she needed. Putting his fist over his heart, he bowed ever so slightly, taking his vow once more.

His mother blinked, tears trembling on her lashes, and the wave of her gratitude reached him in a rush. Although he couldn't feel the warmth of it, he knew by the way he could allow his sable duster to fall open that his core temperature had just risen.

Knew also that he would do anything to keep his promise. A good death wasn't just quick and painless. A good death meant you were leaving your world in order, that you passed unto the Fade with the satisfaction that your loved ones were well cared for and safe, and that although they had to go through the mourning process, you were certain you had left nothing unsaid or undone.

Or nothing said, as was the case here.

It was the greatest gift he could give the mother who had raised him in a manner better than he deserved, the only way he could repay the circumstances of his cruel birth.

Madalina smiled and released a long, grateful breath.

And all was as it needed to be.

THIRTY-FIVE

John Matthew came awake with his H&K pointed at the opening door across Xhex's barren room. His heart rate was as calm as his steady palm, and even when the lights came on, he didn't blink. If he didn't like the looks of whoever had sprung the lock and twisted the knob, he was going to put a bullet right through whatever chest presented itself.

"Easy," Xhex said as she came inside and shut them in together. "It's just me."

He put the safety back on and lowered the muzzle.

"I'm impressed," she murmured as she leaned back against the jamb. "You wake up like a fighter."

Standing across the way, her powerful body relaxed, she was the most attractive female he had ever seen. Which meant that unless she wanted what he wanted, he had to go. Fantasies were fine, but flesh was better, and he didn't think he could keep himself away from her.

John waited. And waited. Neither of them moved.

Right. Time to leave before he made an ass out of himself.

He started to shift his legs off her bed, but she shook her head. "No, stay where you are."

Okaaaay. But that meant he needed some camo.

Reaching for his coat, he dragged the leather across his lap, because his gun wasn't the only thing ready for use. As usual, he had a hard-on, which was standard-issue for the wakey-wakey shit—as well as a problem whenever he was within range of her.

"I'll be right out," she said, dropping her black jacket and heading for the bathroom.

The door shut and his mouth slacked open.

Could this be . . . it?

He smoothed down his hair, tucked in his shirt, and quickly shifted around his cock. Which was now not just hard, but throbbing. Looking down at the length straining against the fly of his A&F jeans, he tried to point out to the thing that she might be staying, but that didn't necessarily mean she had any interest in using his hips for buck-off practice.

Xhex came back out a little later and paused by the light switch. "You have anything against the dark?"

He shook his head slowly.

The room plunged into black and he heard her moving toward the bed.

Heart pounding, cock on fire, John quickly hustled over, leaving her plenty of room. As she lay down, he felt every nuance of the mattress shifting, heard the soft brush of her hair as it hit the pillow, knew the scent of her deep in his nose.

He couldn't breathe.

Even as she sighed in relaxation.

"You're not afraid of me," she said quietly.

He shook his head even though she couldn't see him.

"You're hard."

Oh, God, he thought. Yes, he was.

Momentary panic flared, a jackal jumping out of the bush and snarling at him. Fuck him, but it was hard to decide what would be worse: Xhex reaching for him and him losing his erection—like he had with the Chosen Layla on the night of his transition. Or Xhex not reaching for him at all.

She settled the coin toss by turning toward him and putting her hand on his chest.

"Easy," she said as he jumped.

After he settled, her touch moved down his stomach, and when she cupped his cock through his jeans, he arched up off the bed, mouth opening to release a silent groan.

There was no preamble, but he didn't want any at all.

She undid the fly, sprang his arousal, and then there was shifting and the sound of her leathers hitting the floor.

She mounted him, planting her palms on his pecs, pushing him down into the mattress. As something warm and soft and wet rubbed against him, he didn't worry at all about going limp. His body was raging to get inside of her, nothing of the past coming through his mating instincts.

Xhex rose onto her knees, took him in her hand, and stood him up. When she sat down, he felt a delicious, tight pressure along the sides of his cock, the electric compression kicking off an orgasm that had him punching his hips up. Without thinking whether it was okay, he grabbed onto her thighs—

He froze as he felt metal, but then he was too far gone. All he could do was squeeze with his hands as he shuddered again and again, losing his virginity over and over.

It was the most amazing thing he'd ever felt. He knew from hand jobs. Had worked himself out a thousand times since his transition. But this blew all of what he'd done out of the park. Xhex was indescribable.

And that was before she started to move.

When he was finished with that first phantasmagasm, she gave him a minute to catch his breath, then started to roll her hips up and back. He gasped. The muscles inside of her gripped and released his cock, the alternating pressure getting his balls tight and ready once again.

He so totally and completely understood Qhuinn's drive to get naked now. This was incredible, especially when John let his body follow hers and they moved together. Even as the rhythm grew faster and faster, becoming urgent, he knew exactly what was happening and where every part of both of them was, from her palms on his chest to the weight of her on top of him to the friction of the sex to the way his breath was tearing in and out of his throat.

His body went rigid from head to toe as he came again, her name leaving his lips as it had when he fantasized about her—only more urgent.

And then it was done.

Xhex lifted herself free of him and his cock fell down onto his belly. Compared to the hot cocoon of her body, the soft cotton of the shirt he was wearing was like sandpaper, and the air temperature was freezing cold. The bed moved as she lay down beside him, and he turned to face her in the dark. He was breathing hard, but he yearned to kiss her in the break before they did that again.

John reached out and felt her stiffen as his palm landed on the far side of her neck, but she didn't pull away. God, her skin was soft . . . oh, so soft. Although the muscles that ran up from her shoulders were like steel, what covered them was satin smooth.

John was slow as he lifted his upper body off the bed and leaned over her, slipping his touch up to her cheek, cradling her face gently, finding her lips with his thumb.

He didn't want to fuck this up. She had done most of the work, and done it spectacularly. More than that, she had given him the gift of sex and had shown him that in spite of what had been done to him, he was still male, still capable of enjoying what his body had been born to do. If he was going to be the one making their first kiss happen, he was determined to get it right.

Dropping his head—

"That's not what this is about." Xhex pushed him back, got off the bed, and went into the bathroom.

The door shut, and John's cock shriveled up on his shirt as he heard water come on: She was washing him off her, getting rid of what his body had given her. With hands that shook, he stuffed himself back into his jeans, trying to ignore the wetness and the erotic scent.

When Xhex came out, she got her jacket, and went over to open the door. As light from the hall streamed in, she was a black shadow standing tall and strong.

"It's daylight outside, in case you haven't checked your watch." She paused. "And I appreciate your being discreet about my . . . situation."

The door closed behind her silently.

So that was the *why* behind the hookup. She'd given him the sex to thank him for keeping her secret.

Christ, how could he have thought it was more?

Fully clothed. No kissing. And he was pretty sure he was the only one who came: Her breathing hadn't changed, she hadn't cried out, there had been no sagging relief for her after it was done. Not that he knew anything about females and orgasms, but that was what happened to him when he had the release.

Not a pity fuck. A gratitude one.

John rubbed his face. He was so stupid. Thinking that it meant anything.

So very, very stupid.

Tohr woke up with a stomach that had been spray-painted in the color pain. The agony was so bad that in his dead-to-the-world, postfeeding sleep, he'd wrapped his arms around his belly and hunched into himself.

Unfurling from the tuck and shiver, he wondered if there had been something wrong with the blood—

The grumble that rose up was loud enough to rival a garbage disposal.

The pain . . . was hunger? He looked down at the concave pit between his hips. Rubbed at the hard, flat surface. Listened to another roar.

His body was demanding food, massive quantities of sustenance.

He glanced at the clock. Ten a.m. John hadn't come by with Last Meal.

Tohr sat up without using his arms and made it into the bathroom on legs that felt curiously steady. He used the toilet, but not to throw up, then washed his face, and realized he had no clothes to wear.

Slipping a terry-cloth robe on, he left his bedroom for the first time since he'd walked into it.

The lights along the hall of statues made him blink like he'd been spotlit on a stage, and he needed a minute to adjust to . . . everything.

Stretching up and down the corridor, the marble males in their various poses were just as he remembered them, so strong and graceful and static, and for no good reason, he remembered Darius buying them one by one, building up the collection. Back when D had been in acquisition mode, he'd sent Fritz to auctions at Sotheby's and Christie's in New York, and when each of the masterpieces had been delivered in its crate with all the shredded stuffing and those cloth wraps, the brother had had an unveiling party.

D had loved art.

Tohr frowned. Wellsie and his unborn child would always be his first and foremost loss. But he had more dead to avenge, didn't he. The *lessers* had taken not only his family, but his best friend.

Anger stirred deep in his gut . . . triggering another hunger. For war.

With a focus and determination that was both foreign and familiar, Tohr headed down toward the grand staircase and paused as he got to the mostly closed doors of the study. He sensed Wrath behind them, but he didn't really want to interact with anyone.

At least, he didn't think so.

Why then hadn't he just called down to the kitchen for an order of food?

Tohr peered in through the slit that was between the doors.

Wrath was asleep at his desk, his long, glossy black hair fanning out over paperwork, one forearm curled under his head as a pillow. In his free hand, he still gripped the magnifying glass he had to use if he wanted to try to read anything.

Tohr stepped into the room. Looking around, he saw the mantelpiece over the fireplace and could just picture Zsadist lounging against it, his scarred face serious, his eyes flashing black. Phury had always been close to him, usually parking it in the pale blue chaise by the window. V and Butch had tended to take that spindly-ass couch. Rhage chose different locales depending on his mood. . . .

Tohr frowned as what was next to Wrath's desk registered.

The ugly, ratty, avocado green armchair, with patches worn on its leather cushions . . . was Tohr's chair. The one his Wellsie had insisted be thrown out because it was a mess. The one he'd put in the office down in the training center.

"We moved it here so John would come back to the mansion."

Tohr's head whipped around. Wrath was lifting himself off his arm, his voice as groggy as his face appeared.

The king spoke slowly, as if he didn't want to spook his visitor. "After . . . what happened, John wouldn't leave the office. He refused to sleep anywhere but that chair. What a mess . . . He was acting out in training. Getting into fights. Eventually, I put my foot down, moved that stinker in here, and things got better." Wrath turned to the chair. "He used to like to sit there and watch me work. After his transition and the raids over the summer, he's been out fighting at night and crashing during the day, so he hasn't been here as much. I kind of miss him."

Tohr winced. He'd done such a head job on that poor kid. Sure, he'd been incapable of doing anything else, but John had suffered a lot.

Suffered still.

Tohr was ashamed of himself as he thought of his waking up in that bed each morning and every afternoon, John bringing that tray in and sitting while the food was eaten—then staying, as if the kid knew that he was throwing up most of whatever had been served as soon as he was alone.

John had had to deal with Wellsie's death by himself. Go through his transition by himself. Cross however many first times by himself.

Tohr sat down on V and Butch's couch. The thing felt surprisingly sturdy, more so than he remembered. Putting his palms on the cushions, he pushed.

"It was reinforced while you were gone," Wrath said quietly.

There was a long period of quiet, the question Wrath wanted to ask hovering in the air as loud as the echo of clanging bells in a private chapel.

Tohr cleared his throat. The only person he could have talked to about what was on his mind was Darius, but the brother was dead and gone. Wrath was the next person he was closest to though. . . .

"It was . . ." Tohr crossed his arms over his chest. "It went okay. She stood behind me."

Wrath nodded slowly. "Good idea."

"Hers."

"Selena's tight. Kind."

"I'm not sure how long it's going to take," Tohr said, not wanting to even talk about the female. "You know, until I'm ready to fight. I'm going to have to spar some. Hit the shooting range. Physically? No clue how my body's going to rebound."

"Don't worry about time. Just get yourself healthy."

Tohr looked down at his hands and curled up a pair of fists. There was no meat on the bones at all, so his knuckles poked through the skin like a relief map of the Adirondacks, nothing but jagged peaks and hollow valleys.

It was going to be a long trip back, he thought. And even once he was physically strong, his mental deck of cards was still missing all of its aces. No matter how much he weighed or how well he fought, nothing was going to change that.

There was a sharp knock and he shut his eyes, praying it wasn't one of his brothers. He didn't want to make a big deal out of returning to the land of living.

Yay. Rah. Whoo. Hoo.

"What's doing, Qhuinn?" the king asked.

"We found John. Kinda."

Tohr's lids popped wide and he shifted around, frowning up at the kid in the doorway. Before Wrath could speak, Tohr said, "Was he missing?"

Qhuinn seemed surprised to see him up and about, but the guy gathered himself quickly as Wrath demanded, "Why wasn't I told he was gone?"

"I didn't know he was." Qhuinn came in, and the redhead from the training classes, Blay, was with him. "He told both of us he was off rotation and going to crash out. We took him at his word, and before you fist my balls, I stayed in my room the entire time because I thought he was in his. As soon as I realized he wasn't there, we went in search of him."

Wrath cursed under his breath, then cut off Qhuinn's apology. "Nah, it's cool, son. You didn't know. Nothing you could do. Where the fuck is he?"

Tohr didn't hear the answer for the roar in his head. John out in Caldwell alone? Gone without telling anyone? What if something had happened?

He cut through the conversation. "Wait, where is he?"

Qhuinn held up his phone. "He won't say. His text is just that he's safe, wherever he is, and he'll meet us out tomorrow night."

"When's he coming home?" Tohr demanded.

"I guess"—Qhuinn shrugged—"he's not."

THIRTY-SIX

Rehvenge's mother passed unto the Fade at eleven eleven a.m.

She was surrounded by her son and her daughter and her sleeping granddaughter and her fierce son-in-law and attended by her beloved *doggen*.

It was a good death. A very good death. She closed her eyes, and an hour later she gasped twice and let out one long exhale, as if her body were sighing in relief as her soul flew free of its corporeal cage. And it was strange . . . Nalla woke up at that moment and the young focused not on her *granhmen*, but above the bed. Her little chubby hands reached high, and she smiled and cooed as if someone had just stroked her cheek.

Rehv stared down at the body. His mother had always believed she would be reborn unto the Fade, the roots of her faith planted in the rich soil of her Chosen upbringing. He hoped that was true. He wanted to believe she lived on somewhere.

It was the only thing that eased the pain in his chest even slightly.

As the *doggen* began crying softly, Bella embraced her daughter and Zsadist. Rehv stayed apart from them, sitting alone on the foot of the bed and watching the color drain out of their mother's face.

When a tingle bloomed in his hands and feet, he was reminded that his father's legacy, like his mother's, was ever with him.

He stood up, bowed to them all, and excused himself. In the bathroom off the room he stayed in, he looked under the sink and thanked the Virgin Scribe that he'd been smart enough to tuck a couple of vials of dopamine in the back. Turning the heat light in the ceiling on, he took off his sable duster and stripped his Gucci jacket from his shoulders. When the red glow from up above freaked his shit out, because he thought the stress of the death was bringing out his bad side, he shut the thing off, cranked the shower on, and waited until the steam rose up before continuing.

He swallowed another two penicillin pills as he tapped his loafer.

When he could stand it, he rolled up his shirtsleeve and studiously ignored his reflection in the mirror. After he filled a syringe, he used his LV belt to loop around his biceps, pulling the black leather over and holding it against his ribs.

The steel needle slipped into one of his infected veins and he hit the plunger—

"What are you doing?"

His sister's voice jacked his head up. In the mirror, she was staring at the needle in his arm and his red, rancid veins.

His first thought was to bark at her to get the fuck out. He didn't want her to see this, and not just because it meant more lying. It was private.

Instead, he calmly pulled the syringe free, capped it, and tossed it. As the shower hissed, he pulled his sleeve down, then put on his jacket and his sable coat.

He turned off the water.

"I'm diabetic," he said. Shit, he'd told Ehlena he had Parkinson's. Damn it.

Well, it wasn't like the two were going to meet anytime soon.

Bella lifted her hand to her mouth. "Since when? Are you okay?"

"I'm fine." He forced a smile. "Are you okay?"

"Wait, since when has this been going on?"

"I've been injecting myself for about two years now." At

least that wasn't a lie. "I see Havers regularly." *Ding! Ding!*
Another truth. "I'm managing it well."

Bella looked at his arm. "Is that why you're always
cold?"

"Bad circulation. It's why I need the cane. Bad
balance."

"I thought you said that was because of an injury?"

"The diabetes compromises how I heal."

"Oh, right." She nodded sadly. "I wish I'd known."

As she stared up at him with her big blue eyes, he hated
lying to her, but all he had to do was think of his mother's
peaceful face.

Rehv put his arm around his sister and led her out of the
bathroom. "It's no big deal. I'm on it."

The air was cooler in the bedroom, but he knew this
only because Bella wrapped her arms around herself and
hunkered in.

"When should we do the ceremony?" she asked.

"I'll call the clinic and have Havers come out here at
nightfall and wrap her. Then we have to decide where to
bury her."

"At the Brotherhood compound. That's where I want
her."

"If Wrath will let the *doggen* and me come, that's fine."

"Of course. Z's on the phone with the king now."

"I don't think there's much of the *glymera* left in town
who'd want to say good-bye."

"I'll get her address book from downstairs and put together
an announcement."

Such a factual, practical conversation, illustrating that
death was indeed part of living.

When Bella let out a soft sob, Rehv pulled her against
his chest. "Come here, sister mine."

As they stood together with her head on his chest, he
thought of the number of times he'd tried to save her from
the world. Life, however, had happened anyway.

God, when she had been small, before her transition, he
had been so certain he could protect her and take care of
her. When she was hungry, he made sure she had food.
When she needed clothes, he bought them for her. When
she couldn't sleep, he stayed with her until her eyes closed.
Now that she had grown up, though, he felt like his reper-

toire was restricted to nothing but placations. Although maybe that was the way it worked. When you were young, a good lullaby was all you needed to ease the stress of the day and make you feel safe.

Holding her now, he wished there were such a quick fix for grown-ups.

"I'm going to miss her," Bella said. "We weren't very much alike, but I always loved her."

"You were her great joy. Always."

Bella pulled back. "And you as well."

He tucked a stray hair behind her ear. "Would you and your family like to have a rest here?"

Bella nodded. "Where do you want us?"

"Ask *mahmen*'s *doggen*."

"Will do." Bella gave his hand a squeeze that he couldn't feel and left his room.

When he was alone, he went over to the bed and took out his cell phone. Ehlena never had texted him the night before, and as he retrieved the clinic's number from his address book, he tried not to worry. Maybe she had done the overday shift. God, he hoped she had.

Chances were small something bad had happened. Very small.

But he was calling her next.

"Hello, clinic," came the voice in the Old Language.

"This is Rehvenge, son of Rempoon. My mother has just passed, and I need to make arrangements for her body to be preserved."

The female on the other end gasped. None of the nurses liked him, but they had all adored his mother. Everyone did—

Everyone had, that was.

He rubbed his mohawk. "Is there any way Havers could come out to the house at nightfall?"

"Yes, absolutely, and may I say on behalf of all of us, we are deeply aggrieved at her passing and wish her safe passage unto the Fade."

"Thank you."

"Hold a moment." When the female came back on, she said, "The doctor will come immediately after sundown. With your permission, he will bring someone to assist—"

"Who." He wasn't sure how he'd feel about it being

Ehlena. He didn't want her to have to deal with another
body so soon, and the fact that it was his mother's might
make it even harder on her. "Ehlena?"

The nurse hesitated. "Ah, no, not Ehlena."

He frowned, his *symphath* instincts triggered by the female's tone. "Did Ehlena make it in last night?" Another
pause. "Did she?"

"I'm sorry, I cannot discuss—"

His voice dropped to a growl. "Did she come in or not.
Simple question. Did she. Or not."

The nurse became flustered. "Yes, yes, she came in—"

"And?"

"Nothing. She—"

"So what's the problem?"

"There isn't one." The exasperation in that voice told
him it was happy interactions like this that were part of
what made them all dislike him so much.

He tried to make his voice more even. "Clearly there is
a problem, and you're going to tell me what's doing or I'm
going to keep calling back until someone talks to me. And
if no one will, I'm going to show up at your front desk and
drive every single one of you insane until a member of the
staff cracks and talks to me."

There was a pause that vibrated with *you-are-such-an-
asshole.* "Fine. She doesn't work here anymore."

Rehv's breath sucked in on a hiss and his hand shot to
the plastic Baggie full of penicillin he'd been keeping in his
suit's breast pocket. "Why?"

"That I will not disclose to you no matter what you do."

There was a click as she hung up on him.

Ehlena sat upstairs at the crappy kitchen table, her father's
manuscript in front of her. She'd read it twice at his desk,
then put him to bed and come up here, where she'd gone
through it again.

The title was *In the Rain Forest of the Monkey Mind.*

Dearest Virgin Scribe, if she'd thought she had sympathy
for the male before, now she had empathy for him. The three
hundred handwritten pages were a guided tour through his
mental illness, a vivid, walk-a-mile-in-his-shoes study of
when the disease had started and where it had taken him.

She glanced over at the aluminum foil that covered the

windows. The voices in his mind that tortured him came from a variety of sources, and one way was through radio waves beamed down from satellites orbiting the earth.

She knew all this.

But in the book, her father described the Reynolds Wrap as a tangible representation of the psychosis: Both the foil and the schizophrenia kept the real world away, both insulated him . . . and with both in place he was safer than if they weren't around. The truth was, he loved his illness as much as he feared it.

Many, many years ago, after family had double-crossed him in business and ruined him in the eyes of the *glymera*, he no longer trusted his ability to read the intentions and motivations of others. He had put his faith in the wrong people and . . . it had cost him his *shellan*.

The thing was, Ehlena had figured her mother's death wrong. Right after the great fall, her mother had turned to laudanum to help her cope, and the temporary relief had bloomed into a crutch as life as she'd known it had crumbled . . . money, position, homes, possessions leaving her like lovely doves scattering from a field, going somewhere safer.

And then Ehlena's engagement had failed, the male distancing himself before publicly declaring that he was ending the relationship—because Ehlena had seduced him into her bed and taken advantage of him.

That had been her mother's last straw.

What had been a joint decision between Ehlena and the male had been spun into Ehlena's being a female without worth, a harlot hell-bent on corrupting a male who had had only the most honorable of intentions. With that known in the *glymera*, Ehlena would never marry, even if her family had had the station they'd lost.

The night the scandal had broken, Ehlena's mother had gone into her bedroom and they'd found her dead hours later. Ehlena had always assumed it had been a laudanum overdose, but no. According to the manuscript, she had slit her wrists and bled out on the sheets.

Her father had started hearing voices as soon as he saw his female deceased on their mated bed, her pale body framed by a halo of dark red spilled life.

As his mental disease had progressed, he had retreated

farther and farther into paranoia, but in a strange way he felt more secure there. Real life was fraught, in his mind, with people who might or might not betray him. The voices in his head, however, were all out to get him. With those crazy monkeys that flipped and tripped among the branches of the sickness's forest, raining sticks and hard nubs of fruit at him in the form of thoughts, he knew his enemies. He could see and feel and know them for what they were, and his weapons to combat them were a well-ordered refrigerator and tin over the windows and rituals of words and his writings.

Out in the real world? He was helpless and lost, at the mercy of others, with no defenses to judge what was dangerous and what wasn't. The illness, on the other hand, was where he wanted to be, because he knew, as he put it, the confines of the forest and the trails around the trunks and the tribulations of the monkeys.

There his compass held a true north.

To Ehlena's surprise? It wasn't all suffering for him. Before he had fallen ill, he'd been a litigator in matters of the Old Law, a male well-known for his affection for debate and his lust for strong opponents. In his illness, he found just the kind of conflict he had enjoyed while sane. The voices in his own head, as he put it with self-actualized irony, were every bit as intelligent and facile at debate as he was. To him, his violent episodes were nothing more than the mental equivalent of a good boxing match, and since he always came out of them eventually, he always felt victorious.

He was also aware he was never leaving the forest. It was, as he said in the final line of the book, his last address before he went unto the Fade. And his only regret was that there was room for just one inhabitant in there—that his sojourn among the monkeys meant he could not be with her, his daughter.

He was saddened by the separation and the burden he was on her.

He knew he was a lot to handle. He was aware of the sacrifices. He mourned her loneliness.

It was everything she had wanted to hear him say, and as she held the pages, it didn't matter that it was all written and not voiced. If anything it was better this way because she could read it over and over again.

Her father knew so much more than she thought.

And he was far more content than she ever could have guessed.

She smoothed her palm over the first page. The hand-writing, which was in blue, because a properly trained attorney never wrote in black, was as neat and orderly as the recitation of the past, and as elegant and graceful as the larger conclusions he drew and the insights he offered.

God . . . for so long, she had lived around him, but now she knew what he lived in.

And all people were like him, weren't they. Each in their own rain forests, alone no matter how many folk walked beside them.

Was mental health just a matter of having fewer monkeys? Maybe the same number, only nice ones?

The muffled sound of a cell phone going off brought her head up. Reaching across to her coat, she took the thing out of her pocket and answered it.

"Hello?" She knew in the silence who it was. "Rehvenge?"

"You got fired."

Ehlena put her elbow on the table and covered her forehead with her hand. "I'm fine. About to go to sleep. And you?"

"It was because of the pills you brought me, wasn't it."

"Dinner was really good. Cottage cheese and carrot sticks—"

"Stop it," he barked.

She dropped her arm and frowned. "I beg your pardon."

"Why did you do it, Ehlena? Why the hell—"

"Okay, you're going to rethink your tone or this conversation's getting the *end* button."

"Ehlena, you need that job."

"Don't tell me what I need."

He cursed some. Cursed some more.

"You know," she muttered, "if I add a sound track and some machine guns to this, we'd have a *Die Hard* movie. How did you find out, anyway?"

"My mother passed."

Ehlena gasped. "Wha . . . ? Oh, my God, when? I mean, I'm sorry—"

"About a half hour ago."

She slowly shook her head. "Rehvenge, I'm so sorry."

"I called the clinic to ... make arrangements." He exhaled with the kind of exhaustion she was feeling. "Anyway ... yeah. You never texted me that you'd gotten to the clinic safely. So I asked, and there it was."

"Damn it, I meant to but ..." Well, she was busy getting fired.

"But that wasn't the only reason why I wanted to call now."

"No?"

"I just ... I needed to hear your voice."

Ehlena took a deep breath, her eyes locking on the lines of her father's handwriting. She thought of all she had learned, good and bad, in those pages.

"Funny," she said, "I feel the same way tonight."

"Really? Like ... for real?"

"Absolutely, positively ... yes."

THIRTY-SEVEN

Wrath was in a bad mood, and he knew this because the sound of the *doggen* waxing the wooden balustrade at the top of the main staircase was making him want to light the whole fucking mansion on fire.

Beth was on his mind. Which explained why as he sat behind his desk his chest was killing him.

It wasn't that he didn't understand why she'd gotten upset with him. And it wasn't that he didn't think he deserved some kind of punishment. He just hated the fact that Beth wasn't sleeping at home and he had to text his *shellan* for permission to call her.

The fact that he hadn't slept in days had to be part of the pissed-off as well.

And he probably needed to feed. But like sex, it had been so long since he'd done it, he could barely remember what it was.

He glanced around the study and wished he could self-medicate the urge to scream by going out and fighting something: His only other options were hitting the gym or getting drunk, and he was just back from the former and not all that interested in the latter.

He checked his phone again. Beth hadn't returned his text, and he'd left it three hours ago. Which was fine. She was probably just busy, or sleeping.

The hell it was fine.

He got to his feet, slipped his RAZR into the back

pocket of his leathers, and headed for the double doors. The *doggen* just outside in the hall was putting a ton of elbow grease into the buff-and-polish routine, and the fresh smell of lemon that rose from his efforts was thick.

"My lord," the *doggen* said, bowing low.

"You're doing great work."

"As is my pleasure." The male beamed. "It is my joy to serve you and your household."

Wrath clapped a palm on the servant's shoulder and then jogged down the stairs. When he got to the foyer's mosaic floor, he went left, toward the kitchen, and he was glad that there was nobody inside. Opening up the refrigerator, he confronted all manner of leftovers and took out a half-eaten turkey with no enthusiasm whatsoever.

Turning toward the cabinets—

"Hi."

He jerked his head over his shoulder. "Beth? What are . . . I thought you were at Safe Place."

"I was. But I came back just now."

He frowned. As a half-breed, Beth was able to tolerate sunlight, but he stressed the fuck out every time she traveled during the day. Not that he went into it now. She knew how he felt, and besides, she was home, and that was all that mattered.

"I was making something to eat," he said, even though the turkey sitting on the butcher-block table was a dead giveaway. "You want to join me?"

God, he loved the way she smelled. Night-blooming roses. Homier to him than any lemon polish, more gorgeous than any perfume.

"How about I make something for both of us?" she said. "You look like you're about to fall down."

It was on the tip of his tongue to say, *Nah, I'm tight*, when he stopped. Even the smallest of half-truths was going to underscore the issues between them—and the fact that he was utterly exhausted wasn't even a little lie.

"That would be great. Thank you."

"Have a seat," she said, coming over to him.

He wanted to hug her.

He did.

Wrath's arms just snapped out, latched onto her, and pulled her against his chest. Realizing what he'd done, he went to let her go, but she stayed with him, keeping their bodies together. With a shudder, he dropped his head down into her fragrant, silky hair and gathered her up, molding her softness to the contours of his hard muscles.

"I've missed you so much," he said.

"I've missed you, too."

As she sagged against him, he wasn't a fool to think this moment was an instant cure-all, but he would take what he had been given.

Pulling back, he moved his wraparounds up onto the top of his head so she could see his useless eyes. To him, her face was blurry and beautiful, though the fresh-rain scent of tears didn't please him. He brushed both her cheeks with his thumbs.

"Will you let me kiss you?" he asked.

When she nodded, he cradled her face in his palms and brought his mouth down to hers. The cushioned contact was at once utterly, heartbreakingly familiar and yet something from the past. It seemed like forever since they had done more than peck—and that separation wasn't just what he'd done. It was everything. The war. The Brothers. The *glymera*. John and Tohr. This household.

Shaking his head, he said, "Life has gotten in the way of our life."

"You are so right." She smoothed her palm down his face. "It's also gotten in the way of your health. So I want you to sit down over there and let me feed you."

"It's supposed to be the other way around. The male feeds his female."

"You're the king." She smiled. "You make the rules. And your *shellan* would like to wait on you."

"I love you." He pulled her in tight again and just held on to his mate. "You don't have to say it back—"

"I love you, too."

Now he was the one sagging.

"Time for you to eat," she said, tugging him over to the country-style oak table and pulling a chair out for him.

When he parked it, he winced, shifted his hips up, and took his cell phone from his pocket. The thing skittered across the table, bumping into the salt and pepper shakers.

"Sandwich?" Beth asked.

"That'd be great."

"Let's make it two for you."

Wrath put his sunglasses back in place, because the overhead light was making his head pound. When that didn't go far enough, he closed his eyes, and although he couldn't see Beth move around, the sounds of her in the kitchen calmed him like a lullaby. He heard her opening drawers, the utensils in them rattling. Then the refrigerator cracked open with a gasp and there was shuffling, followed by glass knocking into glass. The bread drawer was slid out and the plastic wrap around the rye he liked rustled. There was the cracking of a knife going through lettuce....

"Wrath?"

The soft sound of his name brought his lids open and his head up. "Wha ... ?"

"You fell asleep." His *shellan*'s hand smoothed over his hair. "Eat. Then I'm taking you to bed."

The sandwiches were exactly the way he liked them: overstuffed with meat, light on the lettuce and the tomatoes, plenty of mayo. He ate both of them, and though they should have perked him up, the exhaustion that had a death grip on his body just pulled harder.

"Come on, let's go." Beth took his hand.

"No, wait," he said, rousing himself. "I need to tell you what's doing at nightfall tonight."

"Okay." Tension crept into her tone, like she was bracing herself.

"Sit. Please."

The chair pulled out from under the table with a squeak and she settled her weight slowly. "I'm glad you're being up front with me," she murmured. "Whatever it is."

Wrath smoothed her fingers with his, trying to calm her, knowing that what he had to say was only going to make her more worried. "Someone ... well, likely more than one, but at least one we know of, wants to kill me." Her hand tightened in his, and he kept on stroking her, trying to relax her. "I'm meeting with the *glymera*'s council tonight, and I'm expecting ... problems. All of the Brothers are going with me, and we're not going to be stupid, but I'm not going to lie and tell you this is a garden-variety sitch."

"This ... someone ... is obviously part of the council, right? So is it worth your going in person?"

"The one who started it all is a nonissue."

"How so?"

"Rehvenge had him assassinated."

Her hands tightened again. "Jesus . . ." She took a deep breath. And another. "Oh . . . dear God."

"The question we're all wondering now is, who else is in on it? That's part of the reason my showing up at that meeting is so important. It's also a show of strength, and that matters. I don't run. Neither do the Brothers."

Wrath braced himself for her to say, *No, don't go,* and wondered what he would do then.

Except Beth's voice was calm. "I understand. But I have a request."

His brows popped up over his wraparounds. "Which is?"

"I want you to wear a bulletproof vest. It's not that I doubt the Brothers—it's just that it would give me a little added comfort."

Wrath blinked. Then he brought her hands to his lips and kissed them. "I can do that. For you, I can absolutely do that."

She nodded once and rose from the chair. "Okay. Okay . . . good. Now, come, let's go to bed. I'm as exhausted as you look."

Wrath rose to his feet, tucked her against him, and together they walked out into the foyer, their feet crossing over the mosaic of an apple tree in bloom.

"I love you," he said. "I am so in love with you."

Beth's arm tightened around his waist and she put her face on his chest. The acrid, smoky scent of fear rose up from her, clouding her natural rose fragrance. And yet even so, she nodded and said, "Your queen doesn't run, either, you know."

"I know. I . . . totally know."

In his bedroom at his mother's safe house, Rehv pushed his body back until he was lying against the pillows. As he arranged his sable coat across his knees, he said into his cell, "I have an idea. How about we start this phone call over."

Ehlena's soft laugh made him feel strangely buoyant. "Okay. Are you going to call me again or . . ."

"Tell me this, where are you?"

"Upstairs in the kitchen."

Which might explain the slight echo. "Can you go to your room? Get relaxed?"

"Is this going to be a long conversation?"

"Well, I've rethought my tone, and check this out." He dropped his voice, going total lothario. "Please, Ehlena. Go to your bed, and take me with you."

Her breath caught and then she laughed again. "What an improvement."

"I know, right—lest you think I don't take direction well. Now, how about you return the favor. Go to your bedroom and get comfortable. I don't want to be alone, and I get the sense you don't either."

Instead of an, *It's true*, he heard the gratifying sound of a chair being pushed back. As she moved around, her dim footfalls were lovely, the creaking stairs not—because the sound made him wonder where exactly she lived with her father. He hoped it was an antique house with old, quaint boards, not something run-down.

There was the squeak of a door opening and a pause, and he was willing to bet she was checking on her father.

"Is he sleeping soundly?" Rehv asked.

The hinges rasped again. "How did you know?"

"Because you're good like that."

There was another door noise and then the click of a lock getting flipped into place. "Will you give me a minute?"

A minute? Shit, he'd give her the world if he could. "Take your time."

There was a muffled sound, as if she'd put the phone down on a duvet or a quilt. More door protests. Silence. Another squeak and the faded gurgle of a toilet flushing. Footfalls. Bedsprings. Rustling close by and then—

"Hello?"

"Comfortable?" he said, aware he was grinning like an idiot—except God, the idea that she was where he wanted her to be was fantastic.

"Yes, I am. Are you?"

"You'd better believe it." Then again, with her voice in his ear, he could have been in the process of getting his fingernails pulled off and still been all jolly-jolly.

The silence that followed was as soft as the sable of his coat, and just as warm.

"Do you want to talk about your mom?" she said gently.

"Yes. Even though I don't know what to say, other than that she went quietly and with her family around her, and that's all anyone can ask for. It was her time."

"You'll miss her, though."

"Yes. I will."

"Is there anything I can do?"

"Yes."

"Tell me."

"Let me take care of you."

She laughed quietly. "Right. How about I clue you in on something. In this kind of situation, you're the one who's supposed to be taken care of."

"But we both know that I was what cost you your job—"

"Hold up." There was another rustle, as if she'd just sat up from her pillows. "I made the choice to bring you those pills, and I'm an adult capable of making the wrong call. You don't owe me because I messed up."

"I disagree with you completely. But putting that aside, I'm going to talk to Havers when he comes here to—"

"No, you're not. Dear Lord, Rehvenge, your mother's just passed. You don't need to worry about—"

"What I can do for her is done. Let me help you. I can talk to Havers—"

"It's not going to make a difference. He's not going to trust me anymore, and I can't blame him."

"But people make mistakes."

"And some cannot be remedied."

"I don't believe that." Although as a *symphath*, he was not exactly anyone's go-to guy on moral shit. Not by a long shot. "Especially when it's you we're talking about."

"I'm no different from anybody else."

"Look, don't make me bust out my tone again," he warned. "You did something for me. I want to do something for you. It's simple barter and exchange."

"But I'm going to get another job, and I've been making things work for a long time on my own. It happens to be one of my core competencies."

"I don't doubt it." He paused for effect, playing the best card he had. "Here's the thing though, you can't leave me with this on my conscience. It's going to eat me up inside. Your bad choice was the result of mine."

She laughed softly. "Why does it not surprise me that you know my weakness? And I really appreciate it, but if Havers bends the rules for me, what kind of message does that send out? He and Catya, my supervisor, have already announced it to the rest of the staff. He can't go back now, nor would I want him to just because you strong-armed him."

Well, shit, Rehv thought. He'd been planning on manipulating Havers's mind, but that wouldn't take care of all the other folks who worked at the clinic, would it.

"Okay, then let me help you until you have your feet back under you."

"Thank you, but—"

He wanted to curse. "I have an idea. Meet me tonight at my place and we'll argue about it?"

"Rehv—"

"Excellent. I have to tend to my mother early in the evening, and I have a meeting to go to at midnight. How's three a.m. sound? Wonderful—I'll see you then."

There was a heartbeat of silence and then she chuckled. "You always get what you want, don't you."

"Pretty much."

"Fine. Three o'clock tonight."

"I'm *so* happy I changed my tone, aren't you?"

They both laughed, the tension draining from the connection as if it had been flushed out.

When there was a rustle again, he took it to mean she was lying back down and getting comfortable once more.

"So can I tell you what my father did?" she said abruptly.

"You can tell me that and then explain to me why you didn't eat more for dinner. And after that we're going to talk about the last movie you saw and the books you read and what you think about global warming."

"Really, all that?"

God, he loved her laugh. "Yup. We're in network, so it's free. Oh, and I want to know what your favorite color is."

"Rehvenge ... you really don't want to be alone, do you." The words were spoken gently and almost absently, as if the thought had snuck out of her mouth.

"Right now ... I just want to be with you. That's all I know."

"I wouldn't be ready, either. If my father passed tonight, I wouldn't be ready to let him go."

He closed his eyes. "That is . . ." He had to clear his throat. "That is exactly what I'm feeling. I'm not ready for this."

"Your father has also . . . passed. So I know it's extra hard."

"Well, yes, he's dead, although I don't miss him at all. She was always the one for me. And with her gone . . . I feel like I just drove up to my home to find someone's burned it down. I mean, I didn't see her every night or even every week, but I always had the potential of going over and sitting down and smelling her Chanel No. 5. Of hearing her voice and seeing her across a table. That potential . . . grounded me, and I didn't know it until I lost it. Shit . . . I'm not making sense."

"No, you totally are. For me it's the same. My mother's gone and my father . . . he's here but he's not. So I feel homeless, too. Adrift."

This was why people got mated, Rehv suddenly thought. Fuck the sex and the social position. If they were smart, they did it to make a house that had no walls and an invisible roof and a floor that no one could walk on—and yet the structure was a shelter no storm could blow down, no match could torch up, no passage of years could degrade.

That was when it hit him. A mated bond like that helped you through shit nights like this.

Bella had found that shelter with her Zsadist. And maybe her older brother needed to follow his sister's example.

"Well," Ehlena said awkwardly, "I can answer the question about my favorite color if you like. Might keep things from getting too heavy."

Rehv shook himself back into gear. "And what would it be?"

Ehlena cleared her throat a little. "My favorite color is . . . amethyst."

Rehv smiled until his cheeks hurt. "I think that's a great color for you to like. A perfect color."

THIRTY-EIGHT

There were fifteen people at Chrissy's funeral who knew her, and one who hadn't—and as Xhex scanned the windswept cemetery, she looked for a seventeenth person hiding among the trees and tombs and larger headstones.

No wonder the fucking graveyard was called Pine Grove. There were fluffy boughs all over the place, providing ample cover for someone who didn't want to be seen. Damn it to hell.

She'd found the cemetery in the Yellow Pages. The first two she'd called hadn't had any space left. The third had had space only in their Wall of Eternity, as the guy called it, for cremated bodies. Finally, she'd found this Pine Grove thing and purchased the rectangle of dirt they were all standing around.

The pink coffin had been about five grand. The plot another three. The priest, father, whatever humans called him, had indicated that a suggested donation of a hundred dollars would be appropriate.

No problem. Chrissy deserved it.

Xhex searched the frickin' pines again, hoping to find the asshole who'd murdered her. Bobby Grady had to be coming. Most abusers who killed the objects of their obsessions remained connected emotionally. And even though the police were looking for him, and he had to know that, the drive to see her put to rest was going to override logic.

Xhex refocused on the officiant. The human male was

dressed in a black coat, his white collar showing at his throat. In his palms, over Chrissy's pretty coffin, he held a Bible that he read from in a low, reverent voice. Satin ribbons were laid among the gold-leafed pages to demarcate whatever sections he used most, the ends trailing out the bottom of the book, waving red and yellow and white in the cold. Xhex wondered what his "favorites" list was like. Marriages. Baptisms—if she got that word right. Funerals.

Did he pray for sinners, she wondered. If she remembered the Christian thing right, she believed he had to—so although he didn't know Chrissy had been a prostitute, even if he had he would still have had to affect that respectful tone and expression.

This gave Xhex comfort, although she couldn't have said why.

From out of the north, a chilly breeze blew, and she resumed surveying the landscape. Chrissy wasn't staying here when they were done. Like so many rituals, this was for show. With the earth frozen, she was going to have to wait until spring, housed in a meat locker at the mortuary. But at least she had her headstone, pink granite, of course, set where she'd be buried. Xhex had kept the words of the inscription simple, just Chrissy's name and her dates, but there was a lot of nice scrollwork done around the edges.

This was the first human death ceremony Xhex had ever been to, and it was utterly foreign, all this entombing, first in the box, then under the earth. The idea of getting stuck beneath the ground was enough to make her tug at the collar of her leather jacket. Nope. Not for her. In this respect, she was solidly *symphath*.

Funeral pyres were the only way to go.

At the grave, the officiant bent down with a silver shovel and roughed up the ground, then he took a handful of the loose dirt and pronounced over the coffin, "Ashes to ashes, dust to dust."

The man let the granules of earth fly, and as the brisk wind took them, Xhex sighed, this part making sense to her. In the *symphath* tradition, the dead were raised upon wooden platforms and lit from below, the smoke wafting up and scattering just as this dirt did, at the mercy of the elements. And what remained? Ash that was left where it lay.

Of course, *symphaths* were burned because no one

trusted that they were actually dead when they "died." Sometimes they were. Sometimes they were just playing at it. And it was worth being sure.

But the elegant lie was the same in both traditions, wasn't it. Being swept away, free from the body, gone and yet part of everything.

The priest closed the Bible and bowed his head, and as everyone else followed his example, Xhex glanced around again, praying that fucker Grady was somewhere.

But as far as she could see or sense, he hadn't shown yet.

Shit, look at all the headstones . . . planted into rolling hills that were winter-brown. Although the markers were all different—tall and thin, or short and close to the ground, white, gray, black, pink, gold—there was a central plan to it all, the rows of the dead arranged like houses in a development, with asphalt lanes and stretches of trees winding among them.

One headstone kept drawing her eyes. It was a statue of a robed woman who was staring up to the heavens, her face and pose as serene and calm as the overcast sky she was focused on. The granite she was carved out of was pale gray, the same color as what loomed over her, and for a moment it was hard to tell what was the grave marker and what was the horizon.

Shaking herself, Xhex looked over at Trez and, when he met her eyes, he shook his head imperceptibly. Same with iAm. Neither of them had tweaked to Bobby's presence, either.

Meanwhile Detective de la Cruz was staring at her, and she knew it not because she returned the favor to him, but because she could feel his emotions change whenever those eyes of his landed on her. He understood how she felt. He truly did. And there was a part of him that respected her for her vengeance. But he was resolved.

As the priest stepped back and talk sprang up, Xhex realized the graveside service was over, and she watched as Marie-Terese was the first to break ranks, going up to the officiant and shaking his hand. She was spectacular in her funeral garb, her black lace head covering looking positively bridal, the beads and cross in her hands making her seem pious to the point of nun-ish.

Clearly, the priest approved of her dress and her serious,

beautiful face and whatever it was she said to him, because he bowed and held on to her hand. With the contact between them, his emotional grid shifted to love, pure, undiluted, chaste love.

That was why the statue stood out, Xhex realized. Marie-Terese looked exactly like the robed female. Weird.

"Nice service, huh."

She turned and looked at Detective de la Cruz. "Seemed fine. I wouldn't really know."

"You're not Catholic, then."

"Nope." Xhex waved at Trez and iAm as the crowd dispersed. The boys were taking everyone out to lunch before they all headed into work, as one more way of honoring Chrissy.

"Grady didn't come," the detective said.

"Nope."

De la Cruz smiled. "You know, you talk like you decorate."

"I like to keep things simple."

"'Just the facts, ma'am'? I thought that was my line." He glanced at the backs of the people walking off toward the three cars parked together in the lane. One by one, Rehv's Bentley, a Honda mini-van, and Marie-Terese's five-year-old Camry pulled out.

"So, where's your boss?" de la Cruz murmured. "I expected to see him here."

"He's a night owl."

"Ah."

"Look, Detective, I'm going to take off."

"Really?" He swept his arm around. "In what? Or do you like walking in this kind of weather."

"I parked somewhere else."

"Did you? You weren't thinking of sticking around? You know, seeing if there were any late arrivals."

"Now, why would I do that."

"Why, indeed."

Long, long, long pause, during which Xhex stared at the statue that reminded her of Marie-Terese. "You want to give me a ride to my car, Detective?"

"Yeah, sure."

The unmarked sedan was as serviceable as the detective's wardrobe, but like the guy's heavy coat, it was warm, and like what was in the detective's clothes, it was power-ful, the engine growling like something you'd find under the hood of a Corvette.

De la Cruz looked over as he gunned it. "Where am I going?"

"To the club, if you don't mind."

"That's where you left your car?"

"I got a ride here."

"Ah."

As de la Cruz drove them along the winding road, she stared out at the headstones and for a brief moment thought of the number of bodies she'd walked away from.

Including John Matthew's.

She'd done her best not to think about what they'd done and the way she'd left that big, hard body of his sprawled all over her bed. His eyes as he'd watched her go out the door had been full of a heartbreak she couldn't allow herself to internalize. It wasn't that she didn't give a shit; she cared too much.

That was why she'd had to leave, and why she couldn't afford to be caught alone with him again. She'd been down that road before, and the results had been beyond tragic.

"You okay?" de la Cruz asked.

"I'm just fine, Detective. You?"

"Good. Just fine. Thanks for asking."

The gates of the cemetery loomed up ahead, the iron latticeworks split and pulled to either side of the lane.

"I'm going to be coming back here," de la Cruz said as they braked and then surged forward onto the street be-yond. "Because I think Grady will show up eventually. He's going to have to."

"Well, you won't be seeing me."

"No?"

"Nope. Count on it." She was just too good at being hidden.

When Ehlena's phone made a beep in her ear, she had to take it away from her head. "What the— Oh. Battery's go-ing dead. Hold on."

Rehvenge's deep laughter had her pausing while she reached for the cord, just so she could hear every last rum-ble of the sound.

"Okay, I'm plugged in." She resettled against her pillows. "Now, where were we—oh, yeah. So I'm curious, exactly what kind of businessman are you?"

"A successful one."

"Which explains the wardrobe."

He laughed again. "No, my good taste explains the wardrobe."

"Then the successful part is how you pay for it."

"Well, my family's fortunate. We'll just leave it at that."

She deliberately focused on her duvet cover so she wouldn't be reminded of the low-ceilinged, ratty room she was in. Better yet ... Ehlena reached up and clicked off the light that sat on the milk crates she had stacked next to her bed.

"What was that?" he asked.

"The light. I, ah, I just turned it off."

"Oh, man, I've kept you on way too long."

"No, I just ... wanted it dark, is all."

Rehv's voice dropped so low she could barely hear it. "Why."

Yeah, like she was going to tell him it was because she didn't want to think about where she stayed. "I ... wanted to get even more comfortable."

"Ehlena." Need suffused his tone, changing the tenor of the conversation from flirtatious chitchat to ... something very sexual. And in an instant, she was back on his bed in that penthouse, naked, his mouth on her skin.

"Ehlena ..."

"What," she said hoarsely.

"Are you still in your uniform? The one I took off of you?"

"Yes." The word was more breath than anything else, and it went so much further than just an answer to the question he'd asked. She knew what he wanted, and she wanted it, too.

"The buttons on the front of it," he murmured. "Undo one for me?"

"Yes."

As she popped the first of them free, he said, "And another."

"Yes."

They kept at it until her uniform was open down the

front, and she was really glad the lights were off—not because she would have been embarrassed, but because it made him seem right there with her.

Rehvenge groaned, and she heard him lick his lips. "If I were there, you know what I would be doing? I'd be running my fingertips down to your breasts. I'd find a nipple and I'd draw circles around it so it was ready."

She did as he described and gasped when she touched herself. Then she realized . . . "Ready for what?"

He laughed long and low. "You want to hear me say it, don't you."

"I do."

"Ready for my mouth, Ehlena. Do you remember what that felt like? Because I remember exactly what you taste like. Leave your bra on and pinch yourself for me . . . as if I'm sucking on you though those pretty white lace cups of yours."

Ehlena squeezed her thumb and forefinger together, trapping her nipple in between the two. The effect was second-best to his warm, wet sucking, but it was good enough, especially with his having told her to do it. She repeated the pinch and arched up off the bed, moaning his name.

"Oh, Christ . . . *Ehlena*."

"Now . . . what . . ." As her breath shot out of her mouth, between her thighs she was throbbing, wet, desperate for whatever they were going to do.

"I want to be there with you," he groaned.

"You are with me. You are."

"Again. Squeeze for me." As she shuddered and called out his name, he was quick with the next command. "Take your skirt up for me. So it's around your waist. Put the phone down and do it fast. I'm impatient."

She let the phone fall onto the bed and swept her skirt past her thighs and over her hips. She had to pat around to find her cell and then she rushed it to her ear.

"Hello?"

"God, that sounded good . . . I could hear the cloth moving up your body. I want you to start with your thighs. Go there first. Keep the stockings on and stroke your way up."

The hose acted as a conductor of her touch, magnifying the sensation just as his voice did.

"Remember me doing that," he said in a dark voice. *"Remember."*

"Yes, oh, yes . . ."

She was panting so hard in anticipation, she nearly missed him growl: "I wish I could smell you."

"Higher?" she said.

"No." As his name left her lips in protest, he laughed the way a lover did, soft and low, with both satisfaction and promise. "Go up the outside of your thigh to your hip and around the back and then down again."

She did as he asked and he talked her through the caresses: "I loved being with you. I can't wait to go there again. You know what I'm doing?"

"What?"

"Licking my lips. Because I'm thinking of me kissing my way over your thighs and then running my tongue up and down where I'm dying to be." She moaned his name again and was rewarded. "Go down there, Ehlena. On top of the stockings. Go where I want to be."

As she did, she felt all the heat they'd generated through the thin nylon, and her sex responded by welling up even more.

"Take them off," he said. "The stockings. Take them off and keep them with you."

Ehlena put down the phone again and didn't care if she ran the hell out of the hose as she stripped them from her legs. Scrambling for the cell, she barely got it in range before she was demanding what was next.

"Slip your hand under your panties. And tell me what you find."

There was a pause. "Oh, God . . . I'm wet."

When Rehvenge moaned this time, she wondered if he was erect: She'd seen that he was capable of that, but then, impotence didn't mean that you couldn't get hard. It just meant that for whatever reason you couldn't finish.

Christ, she wished she could lay some commands on him, ones that were consistent with whatever sexual level he could function at. She just didn't know how far to take it.

"Stroke yourself and know it's me," he growled. "That's my hand."

She did as he asked and orgasmed hard, sprawling all

over her bed, his name leaving her lips in as quiet an explosion as possible.

"Get rid of the panties."

Roger that, she thought as she yanked them down her thighs and ditched them God only knew where.

She lay back down, looking forward to doing that again when he said, "Can you hold the phone against your ear with your shoulder?"

"Yes." Screw it; if he wanted her to turn herself into a vampire pretzel she was on board with the plan.

"Take the stockings between both hands, stretch them out taut, then run them in between your legs front to back."

She laughed with an erotic edge, then said sweetly, "You want me to work myself against them, do you?"

His breath shot into her ear. "Fuck, yes."

"Dirty male."

"A tongue bath from you might clean me up. What do you say?"

"Yes."

"I love that word on your lips." As she laughed, he said, "So what are you waiting for, Ehlena? You need to put those stockings to good use."

She cradled the cell phone in her neck, found a good position for it, and then, feeling like a harlot and loving it, she took her white stockings, rolled onto her side, and threaded the nylon length between her legs.

"Nice and tight," he said, panting.

She gasped at the contact, the hard, smooth line diving into her sex in all the right places.

"Move yourself against it," Rehvenge said with satisfaction. "Let me hear how good it feels."

She did exactly that, the stockings getting saturated and warming to match her core. She kept at it, riding the sensations and his stream of words until she came over and over: In the dark, with her eyes closed and his voice in her ear, it was almost as good as being with him.

When she was limp and lying in a heap, her breath laboring but in a very good way, she cuddled around the phone.

"You are so beautiful," he said softly.

"Only because you make me that way."

"Oh, you're so wrong about that." His voice dropped. "Will you come and see me earlier tonight? I can't wait until four."

"Yes."

"Good."

"When."

"I'll be with my mother and family here until about ten. Come then?"

"Yes."

"I have that meeting, but we'll get well over an hour of privacy."

"Perfect."

There was a long pause, one that she had the alarming sense might well have been filled with *I love you* on both sides if they'd had the courage.

"Sleep well," he breathed.

"You, too, if you can. And listen, if you can't sleep, call me. I'm here."

"I will. Promise."

There was another stretch of quiet, as if each were waiting for the other to hang up first.

Ehlena laughed, even though the idea of letting him go made her heart ache. "Okay, on the count of three. One, two—"

"Wait."

"What?"

He didn't answer for the longest time. "I don't want to get off the phone."

She closed her eyes. "I feel the same way."

Rehvenge released a breath, low and slow. "Thank you. For staying on with me."

The word that came to mind didn't make a whole lot of sense, and she wasn't sure why she spoke it, but she did:

"Always."

"If you want, you can close your eyes and imagine me next to you. Holding you."

"I will do just that."

"Good. Sleep well." He was the one who ended the call.

As Ehlena took the phone away from her ear and hit the *end* button, the keypad lit up, glowing bright blue. The thing was warm from where she'd held it for so long, and she smoothed her thumb over the flat screen.

Always. She wanted to be there for him always.

The keypad went dark, the light extinguished with a finality that made her panicky. But she could still call him, couldn't she? It would look pathetic and needy, but he remained on the planet even though he wasn't on her phone.

The potential for the call was there.

God, his mother had died today. And of all the people in his life who he could have passed the hours with, he had chosen her.

Pulling the sheets and the duvet up her legs, Ehlena curled herself around the phone, cradled it close, and passed out.

THIRTY-NINE

Marking time in the crappy ranch he'd decided to use as a drug house, Lash sat upright on a chair that in his old life he wouldn't have allowed his rottweiler to take a shit on. The thing was a Barcalounger, a cheap, fat padded POS that unfortunately was comfortable as fuck.

Not exactly the throne he was going for, but a damn good place to park his ass.

On the other side of his open laptop, the room beyond was fourteen by fourteen and decorated in low-income can't-afford-replacements, the sofas worn at the arms, the picture of a faded Jesus Christ hanging cockeyed, the stains on the pale carpet small and round—thus suggesting cat piss.

Mr. D was out cold with his back against the front door, gun in his hand, cowboy hat pulled down over his eyes. Two other *lessers* were parked in the archways of the room, each propped up against a jamb with their legs stretched out.

Grady was over on the couch, a Domino's Pizza box open beside him with nothing but grease spots and stripes of cheese in a spoke pattern left on the white cardboard. He'd eaten an entire large Mighty Meaty by himself and was now reading a day-old *Caldwell Courier Journal*.

The fact that the guy was so frickin' relaxed made Lash want to do an autopsy on him while the SOB was still breathing. What the hell? The son of the Omega deserved a little more anxiety out of his kidnap victims, fuck you very much.

Lash checked his watch and decided to give his men only another half hour of recharge. They had two other meetings with drug retailers set up today, and tonight was going to be the first time his men hit the streets with product.

Which meant that *symphath* king's business was going to have to chill until tomorrow—Lash was going to do the deed, but the financial interests of the Society had to come first.

Lash looked past one of his snoozing *lessers* into the kitchen, where a long folding table was set up. Scattered across its laminated top were tiny plastic bags, the kind you got with a pair of cheap earrings at the mall. Some had white powder in them, some small brown rocks; others contained pills. The diluting agents that had been used, like baking powder and talc, were in fluffy piles, and the cellophane wrappings the kilos had come in littered the floor.

Quite a haul. Grady thought it was worth about $250,000 and would move, with four men on the street, in about two days.

Lash liked that math, and he'd spent the last few hours examining his business model. Access to more product was going to present a supply issue; he couldn't keep up the pop-and-pinch routine forever, because he was going to run out of people to target. The issue was where to insert himself in the chain of commerce: There were the foreign importers, like the South Americans or the Japanese or the Europeans; then the wholesalers, like Rehvenge; then the larger retailers, like the guys Lash was picking off. Considering how hard it was going to be to get to the wholesalers, and how long it would take to develop relationships with importers, the logical thing was to become a producer himself.

Geography limited his choices, because Caldwell had a ten-minute growing season, but drugs like X and meth didn't require good weather. And what do you know, you could get instructions on how to build and work meth labs and X factories on the Internet. Of course, there were going to be problems securing the ingredients, because there were regulations and tracking mechanisms in place to monitor the sale of the various chemical components. But he had mind control on his side. With humans being so easily manipulated, there would be ways of dealing with those kinds of problems.

As he stared at the glowing screen, he decided that Mr. D's next big job was going to be setting up a couple of these producing facilities. The Lessening Society had enough real estate; hell, one of the farms would be perfect. Staffing was going to be an issue, but recruiting needed to be addressed anyway.

While Mr. D was pulling the factories together, Lash was going to clear the way in the marketplace. Rehvenge had to go down. Even if the Society dealt in X and meth only, the fewer retailers of those products the better, and that meant taking out the wholesaler at the top—although how to get at him was going to be a ball-scratcher. Zero-Sum had those two Moors and that she-male bitch and enough security cameras and alarm systems to give the Metropolitan Museum of Art a hard-on. Rehv also had to be a smart son of a bitch or he wouldn't have lasted as long as he had. The club had been open for what, like five years?

A loud rustle of paper refocused Lash's eyes over the top of the Dell. Grady had jacked up from his lounging sprawl and was gripping the *CCJ* in fists cranked tight as knots in boat rope, that class ring without a stone cutting into the flesh of his finger.

"What is it?" Lash drawled. "You read about how pizza causes high cholesterol or some shit?"

Not that the fucker was going to live long enough to worry about his coronary arteries.

"It's nothing . . . nothing, it's nothing."

Grady tossed the paper aside and collapsed into the couch's cushions. As his unremarkable face paled out, he put one hand over his heart, like the thing was doing aerobics in his rib cage, and with the other he brushed back hair that didn't need any help moving away from his forehead.

"What the fuck is wrong with you?"

Grady shook his head, closed his eyes, and moved his lips as if he were talking to himself.

Lash looked down at the computer screen again.

At least the idiot was upset. That was good enough.

FORTY

The following evening, Rehv walked carefully down the curving staircase of his family's safe house, leading Havers back to the grand door the race's physician had come through a mere forty minutes ago. Bella and the nurse who had assisted were following as well. No one said a thing; there was only the unusually loud sound of footfalls on padded carpet.

As he went, all he could smell was death. The scent of the ritual herbs lingered deep in his nostrils, like the shit had taken shelter from the cold in his sinuses, and he wondered how long it would be before he didn't catch a whiff of it every single time he inhaled.

Made a male want to take a sandblaster and go to town up there.

Truth be told, he was in desperate need of fresh air, except he didn't dare move any faster. Between his cane and the carved handrail, he was managing okay, but after seeing his mother wrapped in linen, he wasn't just numb of body; he was head numb, too. Last thing he needed was to do an ass-over-ears down to the marble foyer.

Rehv took the last step off the staircase, switched his cane to his right hand, and all but lunged to open the door. The cold wind that hustled in was a blessing and a curse. His core temperature went into a free fall, but he was able to take a deep, icy breath that replaced some of what plagued him with the stinging promise of coming snow.

Clearing his throat, he put his hand out to the race's physician. "You treated my mother with incredible respect. I thank you."

Behind his tortoiseshell glasses, Havers's eyes were not professionally compassionate, but honestly so, and he extended his palm as a fellow mourner. "She was very special. The race has lost one of its spiritual lights."

Bella stepped forward to hug the physician, and Rehv bowed to the nurse who had assisted, knowing that she would no doubt prefer not having to touch him.

As the pair went out the front door to dematerialize back to the clinic, Rehv took a moment to stare up into the night. Snow was indeed coming again, and not just the dusting sort of the night before.

Had his mother seen the flurries last evening, he wondered. Or had she missed what had proven to be her last chance to see delicate crystal miracles drift down from the heavens?

God, there were not a countless number of nights for anyone. Not an innumerable host of flurries to be seen.

His mother had loved falling snow. Whenever it appeared, she had gone into the sitting room, turned the outdoor lights on and the inside lights off, and sat there staring out at the night. She would stay for as long as it fell. For hours.

What had she seen, he wondered. In the falling snow, what had she seen? He had never asked her.

Christ, why did things have to end.

Rehv shut out the winter show and leaned back against the stout wooden panels of the door. Standing before him, beneath the overhead chandelier, his sister was hollow-eyed and listless as she cradled her daughter in her arms.

She hadn't put Nalla down since the death, but the young didn't mind. Daughter was asleep in mother's arms, brow tight in concentration, as if she were growing so fast, even in her repose she didn't get a break.

"I used to hold you like that," Rehv said. "And you used to sleep like that. So deep."

"Did I?" Bella smiled and rubbed Nalla's back.

The onesie tonight was white and black with an AC/DC LIVE tour logo on it and Rehv had to smile. It was so not a surprise that his sister had ditched the whole cutesy-cutesy ducky-and-bunny shit for a newborn wardrobe that was kick-ass. And God bless her. If he ever had any young—

Rehv frowned and put the brakes on that thought.

"What is it?" his sister asked.

"Nothing." Yeah, only the first time in his life he'd ever thought about having offspring.

Maybe it was his mother's death.

Maybe it was Ehlena, another part of him pointed out.

"You want something to eat?" he said. "Before you and Z head back?"

Bella glanced up at the stairs, where the sound of a shower running drifted downward. "I would."

Rehv put a hand on her shoulder and together they walked down a hall hung with framed landscapes, and through a dining room that had walls the color of merlot. The kitchen beyond, in contrast to the rest of the house, was plain to the point of utilitarian, but there was a nice table to sit at, and he parked his sister and her young in one of the chairs that had a high back and arms.

"What do you fancy?" he said, going to the fridge.

"You have any cereal?"

He went over to the cabinet where the crackers and the canned goods were kept, hoping that ... Frosted Flakes, *yes*. A big box of Frosted Flakes was standing shoulder-to-shoulder with Keebler Club crackers and some Pepperidge Farm croutons.

As he took the cereal out, he turned the box to face him and looked at Tony the Tiger.

Running a fingertip over the lines of the cartoon, he said softly, "You still like Frosted Flakes?"

"Oh, completely. They're my fave."

"Good. That makes me happy."

Bella laughed a little. "Why?"

"Don't you ... remember?" He stopped himself. "Why would you, though."

"Remember what?"

"It was a long time ago. I watched you eat some and ... it was just nice, is all. The way you liked them. I liked the way you liked them."

He got a bowl and a spoon and the skim milk and brought the lot over to her, making a little place setting in front of his sister.

While she shifted the young around so her right hand was free to work the spoon, he opened the box and the thin plastic bag and started pouring.

"Tell me when," he said.

The sound of the flakes hitting the bowl, the little clapping noise, was all about normal, daily life and it was much too loud. Like those footsteps down the stairs. It was as if the silence of his mother's beating heart had turned the volume up on the rest of the world until he felt like he needed earplugs.

"When," Bella said.

He traded the cereal box for the Hood milk carton and tipped a stream of white into the flakes. "Once more with feeling."

"When."

Rehv sat down as he flipped the spout shut and knew better than to ask her if she wanted him to hold Nalla. As awkward as it was to eat, she wasn't going to let that young go for a while, and that was okay. More than okay. To see her comfort herself with the next generation was a comfort to him.

"Mmm," Bella murmured on the first bite.

In the quiet between them, Rehv allowed himself to go back to another kitchen, another time, way back when his sister was much younger and he was considerably less dirty. He recalled the particular bowl of Tony's best that she didn't remember, the one that she finished and wanted more of, but had had to fight against everything that bastard father of hers had taught her about females needing to be thin and never have seconds. Rehv had cheered silently as she'd crossed the kitchen in the old house and brought the cereal box back to her chair—as she'd poured herself another serving, he'd cried his blood tears and had to excuse himself to the bathroom.

He had murdered her father for two reasons: his mother and Bella.

One of his rewards had been Bella's tentative freedom to eat more when she was hungry. The other had been knowing there would be no more bruises on his mother's face.

He wondered what Bella would think if she'd known what he'd done. Would she hate him? Maybe. He wasn't sure how much she recalled of all the abuse, particularly that which had been done to their *mahmen*.

"Are you okay?" she asked abruptly.

He rubbed his mohawk. "Yeah."

"You can be hard to read." She offered him a small smile, as if she wanted to be sure there was no sting in the words. "I never know if you're okay."

"I am."

She looked around the kitchen. "What are you going to do with this house?"

"Keep it for at least another six months. I bought it a year and a half ago from a human, and I need to hold it a little longer or I'm going to get screwed on capital gains."

"You always were good with money." She leaned down to take another spoonful into her mouth. "Can I ask you something?"

"Anything."

"Is there someone for you?"

"Someone how?"

"You know . . . a female. Or a male."

"You think I'm gay?" As he laughed, she turned brilliant red, and he wanted to hug the shit out of her.

"Well, it's okay if you are, Rehvenge." She nodded in a way that made him feel as if she'd patted his hand in reassurance. "I mean, you've never brought any females around, ever. And I don't want to presume . . . that you . . . ah . . . Well, I went to your room to check on you during the day and I heard you talking to someone. Not that I was eavesdropping—I wasn't. . . . Oh, crap."

"It's all right." He grinned at her and then realized there was no easy answer to her question. At least, to the part about whether he had someone, that was.

Ehlena was . . . What was she?

He frowned. The answer that came to mind went deep into him. Way deep. And given the superstructure of lies that his life was built on, he wasn't sure that kind of tunneling was a wise idea: His coal mountain was pretty damn unsteady to have shafts going so far below the surface.

Bella's spoon slowly lowered. "My God . . . you have somebody, don't you."

He forced himself to answer in a way that would decrease

the number of complications. Although that was like taking only one piece of garbage off the pile.

"No. No, I don't." He glanced at her bowl. "Do you want some more?"

She smiled. "I would." As he poured, she said, "You know, the second bowl is always the best."

"I couldn't agree more."

Bella patted the flakes down with the back of her spoon. "I love you, brother mine."

"And I you, my sister. Always."

"I think *Mahmen* is in the Fade watching over us. I don't know if you believe in that kind of thing, but she did, and I've come to after Nalla's birth."

He was aware that they had almost lost Bella on the delivery table, and he wondered what she had seen in those moments when her soul had been neither here nor there. He'd never thought much about where you ended up, but he was willing to bet she was right. If anyone could watch over her decedants from the Fade, it would be their lovely, pious mother.

It gave him comfort and purpose.

His mother was never going to have to worry from up above about her issue. Not on his account.

"Oh, look, it's snowing," Bella said.

He glanced out the window. In the light thrown by the gas lamps along the drive, little white dots drifted down.

"She would have loved this," he murmured.

"Mahmen?"

"Remember how she used to sit in a chair and watch the flakes fall?"

"She didn't watch them fall."

Rehv frowned and glanced across the table. "Sure she did. For hours, she would—"

Bella shook her head. "She liked what it looked like after they came down."

"How do you know?"

"I asked her once. You know, why did she sit and stare out for so long." Bella repositioned Nalla in her arms and smoothed a hand over the young's sprinkling of hair. "She said it was because when the snow covered the ground and the branches and the rooftops, she remembered being on the Other Side with the Chosen, where everything was right. She said ... after the snow fell, she was returned to before she had fallen. I never understood what that meant, and she never did explain that one."

Rehv looked back out of the window. At the rate the flakes were falling, it would take a while before the landscape went white.

No wonder his mother had watched for hours.

Wrath came awake in darkness, but it was the delicious, familiar, happy kind. His head was on his own pillow, his back was against his own mattress, his covers were pulled up to his chin, and his *shellan*'s scent was deep in his nose.

He had been blissfully asleep for a long time; he could tell by how much he needed to stretch. And his headache was gone. Gone ... God, he'd been living with the pain for so long, it was only in its absence that he realized how bad it had gotten.

With a massive sprawl, he tightened the muscles of his legs and arms until his shoulder cracked and his spine realigned and his body felt glorious.

Rolling over, he found Beth with his arm, slipping a hold around her waist from behind and curling himself into her so that his face was buried in the soft hair at the nape of her neck. She always slept on her right side, and the whole spooning thing was totally up his alley—he liked to surround her smaller body with his much larger one because it made him feel like he was strong enough to protect her.

He kept his hips back from her, though. His cock was rigid and full of the *I-wants*, but he was grateful just to lie with her—and not about to ruin the moment by making her feel awkward.

"Mmm," she said, stroking his arm. "You're awake."

"I am." And then some.

There was a shuffle as she eased around, moving in his arm until she faced him. "Did you sleep well?"

"Oh, yeah."

When there was a gentle tug on his hair, he knew she was playing with the curled ends, and he was glad he kept it as long as he did. Even though he had to tie the heavy black load back when he went out to fight, and the shit took forever to dry—so long, in fact, that he had to use a hair dryer, which was too frickin' girlie to believe—Beth loved the stuff. He could remember many a time she had fanned it out over her naked breasts. . . .

Right, slowing that train would be a good plan. Much more of that kind of thing and he'd have to mount her or lose his damn mind.

"I love your hair, Wrath." In the darkness, her quiet voice was like the touch of her fingers, delicate, devastating.

"I love your hands on it," he replied roughly, "in it, anything you like."

They passed God only knew how long just lying side by side, facing each other, her fingers twisting and turning in the thick waves.

"Thank you," she said quietly, "for telling me about tonight."

"I'd rather have some good news to bring to you."

"I'm still glad you told me. I'd rather know."

He found her face by touch, and as he ran his fingers over her cheeks and nose to her lips, he saw her with his hands and knew her with his heart.

"Wrath . . ." Her hand settled on his erection.

"Oh, *fuck* . . ." His hips jacked forward, his lower back going tight.

She laughed softly. "Your language of love does a trucker proud."

"I'm sorry, I—" His breath jammed in his throat as she stroked him over the boxers he'd worn for her modesty. "Fu—I mean—"

"No, I like it. It's you."

She rolled him over and mounted his hips—holy shit. He knew she'd gone to bed with a flannel nightgown on, but wherever the thing was, it wasn't covering her legs, because her sweet, hot core rubbed right on his hardness.

Wrath growled, and lost it. With a sudden surge he threw her on her back, shoved the Calvins he rarely wore down his thighs, and drove into her. As she cried out and scored his back with her nails, his fangs fully elongated and throbbed.

"I need you," he said. "I need this."

"Me, too."

He didn't spare her any of his power, but then, she liked

it like this sometimes, raw, wild, his body marking hers hard.

The roar when he came into her shook the oil painting that hung over their bed and rattled her perfume bottles over on the dresser and he kept right on going, more beast than civilized lover. But as her scent flooded his nose, he knew she wanted him just as he was—every time he orgasmed, she came with him, her sex gripping his and pulling at him, keeping him deep inside.

With breathless demand, she said, "Take my vein—"

He hissed like a predator and went for her neck, biting hard.

Beth's body jerked under his, and between their hips he felt a welling warmth that had nothing to do with what he'd left behind inside her. In his mouth, her blood was the gift of life, thick on his tongue and down his throat, filling his belly with a furnace of heat, lighting up his flesh from the inside out.

His hips took over as he drank, pleasuring her, pleasuring himself, and when he had his fill, he lapped at his bite marks, then went at her again, reaching down and stretching up one of her legs so he could get even deeper as he pounded hard. After he came in another rush, he palmed the back of her head and brought her lips to his throat.

He didn't get a chance to voice a demand. She bit him, and the instant her sharp points punctured his skin and he felt the sweet sting of pain, he orgasmed again, more brutally than all the others: The knowledge that he had what she needed and wanted, that she was living off of what beat through his veins, was erotic as fuck.

When his *shellan* was finished and had closed the wounds by licking them, he rolled over onto his back and kept them joined, hoping to—

Oh, yeah, he got good and ridden. As she became the master, he went to palm her breasts and found that she still had her nightgown on, so he whisked it over her head and tossed it to who-the-hell-cared. Finding her breasts again, the weights were so heavy and full in his palms that he had to arch up and take one of her nipples into his mouth. He suckled as she pumped them both off until it became too difficult to maintain the connection and he had to let his upper body fall back to the bed.

Beth cried out, and then he did, and then they were both coming together. Afterward, she collapsed off of him and they lay side by side, panting.

"That was amazing," she breathed.

"Fucking amazing."

He patted around in the dark until he found her hand, and they stayed there together for a while.

"I'm hungry," she said.

"Me, too."

"Here, let me go and get us something."

"I don't want you to leave." He tugged on her hand, drawing her to him, kissing her. "You are the best female a male could ever have."

"I love you, too."

As if they were plugged into the same outlet, both of their stomachs rumbled.

"Okay, maybe it is time to food up." Wrath let his *shellan* go as they laughed together. "Here, let me turn on the light so you can find your nightgown."

Instantly, he knew something was wrong. Beth stopped chuckling and went dead still.

"*Leelan?* Are you okay? Did I hurt you?" Oh, God ... he'd been so rough. "I'm sorry—"

She cut him off with a strangled voice. "My light was already on, Wrath. I was reading before you woke up."

FORTY-ONE

John took his fucking time in Xhex's shower, washing himself thoroughly not because he was dirty, but because he figured two could play at the whole wipe-the-slate-clean, what-happened-didn't-happen thing.

After she'd left however many hours and hours ago, his first thought had been a bad one. He wasn't going to lie: All he'd wanted to do was walk straight out into the sun and just be done with this loser-ass joke called life.

There were so many things he failed at. He couldn't talk. He sucked at math. His fashion sense, if left to its own devices, was anemic. He wasn't particularly good with emotions. He usually lost at gin rummy and always at poker. And there were a lot of other shortcomings.

But sucking at sex was the worst of them all.

As he'd lain in Xhex's bed and considered the merits of self-immolation, he'd wondered why the fact that he was a mess when it came to fucking seemed more important than any other deficiency.

Maybe it was because the newest chapter in his sex life had taken him into even rockier, more hostile territory. Maybe it was because the most recent disaster was so fresh.

Maybe it was because it was the last straw.

The way he saw it, he'd had sex twice, and both times he'd been taken, once violently and against his will and then however many hours ago with his total, full-bodied consent. The aftermath of the two experiences had sucked, and in the time he'd spent on Xhex's bed, he'd tried to stop replaying the hurts and mostly failed. Natch.

As night had fallen, however, he'd grown a set as it dawned on him that he was letting other people screw with his head. In neither case had he done anything wrong. So why the hell was he thinking about ending his own life when he wasn't the problem?

The answer was not to turn himself into the vampire equivalent of a s'more.

Shit, no. The answer was to never, ever be a victim again.

From now on, when it came to fucking, he was the one who was going to do the taking.

John got out of the shower, dried off his powerful body, and stood in front of the mirror, measuring his muscle and his strength. As he cupped his balls up around his cock, his heavy sex felt good in his hand.

Nope. No more being a victim of other people. Time to grow the fuck up.

John left the towel where it landed on the counter, dressed quickly, and felt taller somehow as he strapped his guns on and went for his phone.

He refused to be some weak-ass, crybaby motherfucker anymore.

His text to Qhuinn and Blay was short and sweet: *Mt me @ ZS. Am gttn drunk n expect u both 2 do same.*

After he hit *send*, he went through the call log. A lot of people had reached out and touched his phone during the day, mostly Blay and Qhuinn, who evidently had dialed up every couple of hours. There was also some unknown private caller who'd hammered in three times.

The end result was, he had two voice mails, and with no particular curiosity, he accessed his account and listened, expecting the unknown to be a human with a wrong number.

It wasn't.

Tohrment's voice was strained and low: "Hey, John, it's me, Tohr. Listen . . . I, ah, I don't know if you'll get this, but can you call me if you do? I'm worried about you. Worried about you, and I want to say that I'm sorry. I know I've been really fucking out-of-it for a while now, but I'm com-

ing back. I went . . . I went to the Tomb. That's where I was.
I had to go back and see . . . Shit, I don't know. . . . I had to
see where everything had started before I could shake myself back to reality. And then I, ah, I fed last night. For the
first time since . . ." The voice cracked and there was a brisk
breath. "Since Wellsie died. I didn't think I could get
through it, but I did. It's going to take me a while to
get—"

At that point the message cut off and the automated
voice asked him if he wanted to save or delete. He hit
pound to skip to the next one.

Tohr again: "Hey, sorry about that, I got cut off. I just
wanted to say that I'm sorry I fucked your head up. It
wasn't fair to you. You've been mourning her, too, and I
wasn't there to help you, and that's always going to weigh
on me. I abandoned you when you needed me. And . . . I'm
really sorry. I'm done with running, though. I'm not going
anywhere. I guess . . . I guess I'm here and that's where I
am. Fuck, I'm making no sense. Look, please call me and let
me know you're safe. Bye."

There was a beep and the automated voice cut in. "Save
or delete?" she prompted.

As John took the phone from his ear and stared down at
the thing, there was a moment of wavering as the child that
remained in him cried out for its father.

A text from Qhuinn flashed across the screen, snapping
him out of the immaturity.

John hit *delete* on Tohr's second v-mail, and when asked
if he wanted to review his first skipped message he said yes
and deleted that one as well.

Qhuinn's text was just: *W'll b thur.*

Good deal, John thought as he picked up his leather
jacket and left.

For someone who was jobless but had plenty of bills, Ehlena
had no business being in a good mood.

As she dematerialized out to the Commodore, though,
she was happy. Did she have problems? Yes, absolutely: If
she didn't find work fast, she and her father were in danger
of losing the roof over their heads. But she'd applied for a
housecleaning position with a family of vampires to tide
her over, and she was considering dabbling in the human

world. Medical transcription was an idea, the only problem being that she didn't have a human identity worth the laminated card it was printed on, and that was going to cost money to get. Still, Lusie was paid through the end of the week, and her father was delighted that his "story," as he called it, had pleased his daughter.

And then there was Rehv.

She didn't know where things were headed with him, but there was possibility between them, and the feeling of hope and optimism that created buoyed her in all parts of her life, even the holy-shit jobless stuff.

Taking form on the terrace of the correct penthouse, she smiled at the flurries that swirled around in the wind and wondered why it was that whenever they fell, the cold didn't feel as cold.

When she turned around, she saw a massive shape through the glass. Rehvenge had been waiting and watching for her, and the fact that he was looking forward to this as much as she was made her smile so wide, her front teeth tingled in the chill.

Before she could go over the door in front of him slid open, and he strode across the distance that seperated them, the winter wind catching his sable coat and sweeping it out from his body. His glowing amethyst eyes flashed. His stride was pure power. His aura was undeniably male.

Her heart leaped as he stopped before her. In the glow from the city, his face was hard and loving at the same time, and though it no doubt froze him to the bone, he opened his coat, inviting her to share what body heat he had.

Ehlena leaned in and wrapped her arms around him, holding him tight, breathing his scent deeply.

His mouth dropped to her ear. "I missed you."

She closed her eyes, thinking those three little words were as good as *I love you*. "I missed you, too."

As he laughed softly with satisfaction, she both heard the sound and felt it as his chest rumbled. And then he cuddled her closer. "You know, with you against me like this, I'm not cold."

"That makes me happy."

"Me, too." He turned them so they could both look out over the snow blanketed terrace and the skyscrapers of downtown and the two bridges with their stripes of yellow headlights and red taillights. "I've never gotten to enjoy this view up close and personal like this. Before you . . . I've only seen it through the glass."

Held within the cocooning warmth of his body and his coat, Ehlena had a sense of triumph that together they had bested the chill.

With her head lying on his heart, she said, "It's magnificent."

"Yeah."

"And yet . . . I don't know, only you feel real to me."

Rehvenge pulled back and tilted her chin up with one long finger. As he smiled, she saw that his fangs were longer, and instantly she was aroused.

"I was thinking the exact same thing," he said. "At this moment, I can't see anything but you."

His head dipped down and he kissed her and kissed her and kissed her some more while snowflakes danced around them as if the two of them were a centrifugal force, their own slowly spinning universe.

As she slid her arms around the back of his neck and they both got carried away, Ehlena closed her eyes.

Which meant she didn't see and Rehvenge didn't feel the presence that materialized on the top of the penthouse's roof. . . .

And glared at them with red, glowing eyes the color of freshly spilled blood.

FORTY-TWO

"Please don't wince if you can manage it—okay, that's good."

Doc Jane moved over to Wrath's left eye, flashing her penlight right into the back of his brain, as far as he could tell. While the spear bored into him, he had to fight the urge not to jerk his head back.

"You really don't like that," she murmured as she clipped the penlight off.

"No." He rubbed his eyes and put his wraparounds back on, unable to see anything but a pair of shiny black bull's-eyes.

Beth spoke up. "But that's not unusual. He's never been able to tolerate light."

As her voice drifted, he reached over and squeezed her hand to try to reassure her—which, if it worked, would reassure him by extension.

Talk about ruining the mood. After it had been clear that his eyes had taken a little unscheduled vacay, Beth had called Doc Jane, who had been down in the new clinic space, but more than willing to house-call it stat. Wrath, however, had insisted on going to where the doctor was. The last thing he wanted was for Beth to have to hear bad news in their marital chamber—and nearly as important, to him, that was sacred space. Apart from Fritz coming in to clean, no one was welcome in their bedroom. Even the Brothers.

Besides, Doc Jane was going to want to do tests. Doctors always wanted to do tests.

Persuading Beth had taken some time, but then Wrath had put on his sunglasses, wrapped his arm around his *shellan*'s shoulders, and together they had walked out of their chambers, down their private staircase, and onto the second-story balcony. Along the way, he'd stumbled a couple of times, catching his shitkickers on the corners of runners and misremembering where steps were, and the rough going was a revelation. He'd had no clue that he relied on his faulty vision as much as he apparently did.

Holy . . . dearest Virgin Scribe, he'd thought. What if he went permanently, totally blind?

He couldn't bear that. Just couldn't bear it.

Fortunately, halfway through the tunnel to the training center, his head had pounded a number of times, and suddenly the light glowing down from the ceiling pierced through his sunglasses. Or rather, his eyes registered it. He'd stopped and blinked and whipped off his wraparounds and immediately had to put them back on as he'd stared up at the fluorescent panels.

So all was not lost.

As Doc Jane stood before him, she crossed her arms, the lapels of her white coat bunching up. She was fully solid, her ghostly form as substantive as his or Beth's, and he could practically smell the wood burning as she considered his case.

"Your pupils are virtually nonresponsive, but that's because they are nearly contracted to begin with. . . . Damn it, I wish I'd done a baseline optical on you. You said the blindness came on suddenly?"

"I went to bed and woke up unable to see anything. I'm not sure when it happened."

"Anything different?"

"Other than the fact that I didn't have a headache?"

"Have you been getting them recently?"

"Yeah. It's stress."

Doc Jane frowned. Or at least he sensed that she did. To him, her face was a pale blur with short blond hair, the features of which were indistinct.

"I want you to get a CAT scan at Havers's."

"Why?"

"To see about a couple of things. So, wait, you just woke up and your sight was gone—"

"Why do you want the CAT scan?"

"I want to know if there's anything abnormal in your brain."

Beth's hand tightened on his as if she were trying to get him to chill, but panic made him impolite. "As in what? For fuck's sake, Doc, just talk to me."

"A tumor." As both he and Beth sucked in a breath, Doc Jane continued quickly, "Vampires do not get cancer. But there have been instances of benign growths and that might explain the headaches. Now tell me again, you woke up and . . . it was just gone. Was there anything unusual going on before you fell asleep? Afterward?"

"I . . ." Fuck. Shit. "I woke up and I fed."

"How long had it been since you'd last done that?"

Beth answered. "Three months or so."

"Long time," the doctor murmured.

"So you think that could be it?" Wrath said. "I didn't feed enough and lost it, but when I did take her vein, my vision came back and—"

"I think you need a CAT scan."

There was no nonsense coming from her, nothing to argue with. So as he heard a phone getting flipped open and being dialed, he kept his piehole shut even though it killed him.

"I'll see when Havers can get you in."

Which was going to be at the drop of a hat, no doubt. Wrath and the race's physician had had their differences, going way back to the Marissa days, but the male had always been front and center with the service when it was needed.

As Doc Jane started talking, Wrath cut in on her conversation. "Do not tell Havers what it's for. And you and only you see the results. We clear?"

Last thing they needed was any speculation on his fitness to rule.

Beth spoke up. "Tell him it's for me."

Doc Jane nodded and smoothly lied, and as she arranged everything, Wrath pulled Beth up against his side.

Neither of them said anything, because what kind of conversation was there to be had? They were both scared shitless—his vision was crap, but he needed what little he had. Without it? What the hell was he going to do?

"I have to go to that council meeting at midnight," he said softly. As Beth stiffened, he shook his head. "Politically speaking, I have to go. Things are too unstable right now for me to not show, or to try to move it to another night. I have to come from a position of strength."

"And what if you lose your sight in the middle of it?" she hissed.

"Then I'm going to fake it until I can get out of there."

"Wrath—"

Doc Jane clipped her phone shut. "He can see you right now."

"How long will it take?"

"About an hour."

"Good. I have somewhere I need to be at midnight."

"Why don't we see what the scan says—"

"I have to—"

Doc Jane cut him off with an authority that told him in this exchange he was a patient, not the king. "*Have to* is a relative term. We'll see what's doing in there and then you can decide just how much *have to* you've got."

Ehlena could have stayed on the terrace with Rehvenge for twenty years, but he whispered in her ear that he'd made them something to eat, and sitting across from him in candlelight sounded equally as great.

After a final, lingering kiss, they went inside together, her tucked against him, his arm around her waist, her hand up on his back between his shoulder blades. The penthouse was hot, so she took her coat off and draped it over one of the low-slung black leather couches.

"I thought we'd eat in the kitchen," he said.

So much for candlelight, but what did it matter? As long as she was with him, she glowed enough to light up the whole damn penthouse.

Rehvenge took her hand and drew her through the dining room and out the other side of a swinging butler's door. The kitchen was black granite and stainless steel, very urban and sleek, and at one end of the countertop, where there was an overhang, two place settings were arranged in front of a pair of stools. A white candle was lit, the flame lazy on top of its diminishing wax pedestal.

"Oh, this smells fantastic." She slid up onto one of the stools. "Italian. And you said you could only make one thing."

"Yeah, I really slaved over this." He turned toward the oven with a flourish and removed a flat pan with . . .

Ehlena burst out laughing. "French-bread pizza."

"Only the best for you."

"DiGiorno?"

"Of course. And I splurged on the supreme kind. I figured you could pick off what you don't like." He used a pair of sterling-silver tongs to transfer the pizzas onto the plates and then put the baking sheet back on the top of the stove. "I have red wine, too."

As he came over with the bottle, all she could do was stare up at him and smile.

"You know," he said as he poured some into her glass, "I like the way you're looking at me."

She put her hands over her face. "I can't help it."

"Don't try. It makes me feel taller."

"And you're not small to begin with." She tried to get a grip, but just felt like giggling as he filled his own glass, put the bottle down, and took a seat next to her.

"Shall we?" he said, picking up his knife and fork.

"Oh, my God, I'm glad you do that, too."

"Do what?"

"Eat pizza with a knife and fork. The other nurses at work give me such a hard . . ." She let the sentence drift. "Well, anyway, I'm glad there's someone like me."

There was the sound of crispy bread splintering under knife blades as they both worked on their dinner.

Rehvenge waited until she took her first bite and then said, "Let me see you through your job search."

He timed it perfectly, because she never talked with her mouth full, so he had plenty of airspace to continue. "Let me carry you and your father until you have another job that earns you as much as you made at the clinic." She started to shake her head, but he held up his hand. "Wait, think about it. Without my being an ass, you wouldn't have done what you did to get fired. So it's only fair that I make amends, and if it helps, think about it from a legal point of view. Under the Old Law I owe you, and I am nothing if not law-abiding."

She wiped her mouth. "It just feels . . . weird."

"Because someone's helping you for once instead of the other way around?"

Well, damn it, yes. "I don't want to take advantage of you."

"But I've offered, and believe me, I have the means."

True enough, she thought, looking at his coat and the heavy silverware he was eating with and the porcelain plate and the—

"You have lovely table manners," she murmured for no good reason.

He paused. "My mother's doing."

Ehlena put her hand on his huge shoulder. "Can I say I'm sorry again?"

He wiped his mouth with a napkin. "There's something better you can do for me."

"What?"

"Let me take care of you. So that your job search is more about finding something you want to do rather than a mad dash into any old thing just to pay the bills." He lifted his eyes to the ceiling and clasped his chest as if he had a case of the vapors. "That would relieve my suffering *so* much. You and you alone have the power to save me."

Ehlena laughed a little, but couldn't keep any semblance of joviality up. Beneath the surface of him, she sensed he was hurting, and the pain came out in the shadows under his eyes and the grim set of his jaw. Clearly, he was making an effort to be normal for her benefit, and though she appreciated it, she didn't know how she could get him to stop without putting pressure on him.

They really were strangers to each other still, weren't they? In spite of all the time they had spent together in the last couple of days, how much did she really know about him? His bloodline? When she was around him or they were on the phone, she felt as though she knew all she needed to, but realistically speaking, what did they have together?

He frowned as he dropped his hands and cut into his pizza again. "Don't go there."

"I'm sorry?"

"Wherever you are in your head. It's the wrong place for you and me." He took a drink of his wine. "I'm not going to be rude and read your mind, but I can sense what you're feeling, and it's distance. That's not what I'm after. Not when it comes to you." His amethyst eyes shifted over and stared straight into her. "You can trust me to take care of you, Ehlena. Don't ever doubt that."

Looking at him, she believed him one hundred percent. Absolutely. Positively. "I do. I do trust you."

Something flickered across his face, but he hid it. "Good. Now, finish your dinner and come to the realization that my helping you is the right thing."

Ehlena went back to eating, slowly working her way through her pizza. When she was finished, she put her silverware down on the right-hand edge of her plate, wiped her mouth, and took a sip of wine.

"Okay." She glanced over at him. "I'll let you help."

When he smiled broadly, because he was getting his way, she cut through his robin-breasted satisfaction. "But there are conditions."

He laughed. "You're putting restrictions on a gift given to you?"

"It's not a gift." She stared at him with dead seriousness. "It's only until I find some kind of work, not my dream job. And I want to pay you back."

He lost a little of his satisfaction. "I don't want your money."

"And I feel the same way about yours." She folded her napkin. "I know you're not hurting for cash, but that's the only way I'll be okay with this."

He frowned. "No interest, though. I won't accept even one penny in interest."

"Deal." She put her palm out and waited.

He cursed. And cursed again. "I don't want you to pay it back."

"Tough."

After his mouth performed some intricate f-bomb acrobatics, he put his hand in hers and they shook. "You drive a hard bargain, you know that," he said.

"But you respect me for it, right?"

"Well, yeah. And it makes me want to get you naked."

"Oh . . ."

Ehlena flushed from head to toe as he slid off his stool and towered over her, cupping her face in his hands. "You going to let me take you to my bed?"

Given the way those purple eyes of his were shining, she was willing to let him take her down on the damn kitchen floor if he asked. "Yes."

A growl rolled up out of his chest as he kissed her. "Guess what?"

"What?" she breathed.

"That was the right answer."

Rehvenge tugged her off her stool and kissed her quick and soft. With his cane in hand, he led her to the other side of the penthouse, through rooms she didn't see and past a twinkling view she didn't appreciate. All she knew was thick, pounding anticipation for what he was going to do to her.

Anticipation and . . . guilt. What could she give him? Here she was craving him sexually again, but there was no release for him. Even though he said he got something from it, she felt as if she were—

"What are you thinking about?" he said as they came into the bedroom.

She glanced over at him. "I want to be with you, but . . . I don't know. I feel like I'm using you or—"

"You're not. Trust me, I'm well familiar with being used. What happens between us here is nothing like that." He cut off her question. "No, I can't go into it, because I need . . . Shit, I need this time with you to be simple. Just you and me. I'm tired of the rest of world, Ehlena. I'm so fucking tired of it."

It was that other female, she thought. And if he didn't want whoever it was with them? Fine with her.

"I just need this to be okay," Ehlena said. "Between you and me. I want you to feel something, too."

"I do. I can't believe it myself sometimes, but I so do."

Rehv shut the door behind them, balanced his cane on the wall, and removed his sable coat. The suit underneath the duster was yet another exquisitely cut double-breasted masterpiece, this time a dove gray with black pinstripes. The shirt underneath was black with the top two buttons undone.

Silk, she thought. That shirt had to be made of silk. No other fabric gave off that luminescent glow.

"You are so beautiful," he said as he stared at her, "standing there in the light like that."

She glanced at her Gap black pants and her two-year-old knit turtleneck. "You must be blind."

"Why?" he asked, coming over to her.

"Well, I feel like such an ass for saying this." She smoothed the front of her off-the-rack-and-then-some slacks. "But I wish I had better clothes. Then I'd be beautiful."

Rehvenge paused.

And then shocked the crap out of her by kneeling before her.

As he looked up, he had a slight smile on his lips.

"Don't you get it, Ehlena." With gentle hands, he stroked down her calf and brought her foot forward, balancing it on his thigh. As he undid the laces on her cheapo Keds sneaker, he whispered, "No matter what you wear . . . to me, you will always have diamonds on the soles of your shoes."

As he slid her sneaker off and stared up at her, she studied his hard, handsome face, from those spectacular eyes of his to his thick jaw to his proud cheekbones.

She was falling in love with him.

And like any trip through thin air, there was nothing she could do to stop it. The leap had been made.

Rehvenge bowed his head. "I'm just glad you'll have me."

The words were so quiet and humble, at odds with the incredible breadth of his shoulders.

"How could I not?"

He shook his head back and forth slowly. "Ehlena . . ."

Her name was spoken roughly, as if there were a lot more words behind it, words he couldn't bear to speak. She didn't understand, but she knew what she wanted to do.

Ehlena took her foot from him, got down on her own knees, and wrapped her arms around him. She held him as he leaned into her, running one hand up the back of his neck to his mohawk's stripe of soft hair.

He seemed so fragile as he gave himself up to her, and she realized that if anyone tried to hurt him, even though he could more than take care of himself, she would commit murder. To protect him, she would kill.

The conviction was as solid as the bones beneath her skin:

Even the powerful needed protection sometimes.

FORTY-THREE

Rehv was the kind of male who took pride in his work, whether it was putting French-bread pizzas into the oven and cooking them to perfection or pouring wine . . . or pleasuring his Ehlena until she was nothing but a limp, resplendent stretch of utterly satisfied, naked female.

"I can't feel my toes," she murmured as he kissed his way up from between her thighs.

"Is that a bad thing?"

"Not. At. All."

As he paused to lick at one of her breasts, she undulated, and he felt the movement against his own body. By now, he was used to sensation breaking through his numb fog, and he relished the echoing warmth and friction, no longer concerned that his bad side might break out of its dopamine cage. Even though what registered wasn't as sharp as what he felt when he was unmedicated, it was enough so that his body became undeniably aroused.

Rehv couldn't believe it, but there were a number of times when he thought he might orgasm. Between her taste as he lollipopped her sex and the way her hips rocked into the mattress, he nearly lost it.

Except it was better to keep his cock out of the picture. Seriously, how was that going to work: *I'm not impotent, miracle of miracles, because you've triggered my marking instinct, so the vampire in me wins out over the symphath. Yay! Of course, this means you have to deal with my barb, along with where that piece of meat hanging between my legs has been on a regular basis for the last twenty-five years. But come on, that's hot, right.*

Yeah, he was in a big hurry to put Ehlena in that position.

Riiiiiight.

Besides, this was enough for him. To pleasure her, to serve her sexually, was enough—

"Rehv . . . ?"

He looked up from her breast. Given the husky tone in her voice and the erotic glaze in her eyes, he was prepared to agree to anything.

"Yes?" He licked at her nipple.

"Open your mouth for me."

He frowned, but did as she said, wondering why—

Ehlena reached out and touched one of his fully extended canines. "You said you liked pleasing me, and it shows. These are so long . . . and sharp . . . and white. . . ."

As she moved her thighs together like all of the above was turning her on, he knew where this was headed. "Yeah, but—"

"So it would please me if you used them on me. Now."

"Ehlena—"

The special glow started to leave her face. "Do you have something against my blood?"

"God, no."

"So why don't you want to feed from me." Sitting up, she put a pillow over her breasts, her strawberry blond hair falling down and shielding her face. "Oh. Right. Did you already feed from . . . her?"

"Christ, *no*." He'd rather suck blood out of a *lesser*. Fuck that, he'd drink out of the bloated carcass of a deer at the side of a highway before he'd take the vein of the princess.

"You don't take her vein?"

He looked Ehlena dead in the eyes and shook his head. "I do not. And I never will."

Ehlena sighed and swept her hair back. "I'm sorry. I don't know if I have the right to ask those kinds of questions."

"You do." He took her hand. "You totally do. It's not . . . that you can't ask. . . ."

As his words dangled, his worlds slammed into each

other, all kinds of rubble falling around him. Sure, she could ask . . . he just couldn't answer her.

Or could he?

"You are the one I want," he said simply, sticking with as much truth as he could reveal. "You are the only one I want to be in." He shook his head, realizing what he'd said. "With. I mean, with. Look, about the feeding. Do I want it from you? Fuck, *yes*. But—"

"Then there is no *but*."

The hell there wasn't. He had a feeling he was going to mount her if he took her vein. His cock was ready even now, and they were only talking about it.

"This is enough for me, Ehlena. Pleasing you is enough."

She frowned. "Then you must have some problem with my background."

"I'm sorry?"

"Do you think my blood's weak? Because for what it's worth, I can trace my line well into the aristocracy. My father and I may have fallen on hard times, but for generations and most of his life, we were members of the *glymera*." As Rehv winced, she got up off the bed, using the pillow to shield herself. "I don't know exactly where your people descend from, but I can assure you, what is in my veins is acceptable."

"Ehlena, that's not the point."

"You sure about that?" She went over to where he'd taken her clothes off. The panties and the bra went on first, and then she picked up her black slacks.

He couldn't fathom why serving his blood need was so important to her—because what could possibly be in it for her? But maybe that was the divide between them. She wasn't hardwired to take advantage of people, so her calculus wasn't locked on what she got out of things. To him, even when it came to pleasuring her, he was getting something tangible back: Watching her writhe under his mouth made him feel powerful and strong, a real male, not some sexless, sociopathic monster.

She wasn't like him. And that was why he loved her.

Oh . . . Christ. Did he . . .

Yeah, he did.

The realization had Rehv rising up from the bed, walking over to her, and taking her hand as she finished doing up her pants. She paused and looked up at him.

"It's not you," he said. "You can trust me on that."

He gave her a tug and drew her against his body.

"Then prove it," she said softly.

Pulling back, he stared at her face for a long time. His fangs were throbbing in his mouth; he knew that much. And he could feel the hunger in the pit of his stomach, grinding, demanding.

"Ehlena—"

"Prove. It."

He couldn't say no. Just didn't have the strength to turn her down. It was wrong on so many levels, but she was everything he wanted, needed, desired.

Rehv carefully brushed her hair away from her throat. "I'll be gentle."

"You don't have to be."

"I will anyway."

Cupping her face in his palms, he tilted her head to one side and exposed the fragile blue vein that ran to her heart. As she prepared herself for his strike, her pulse quickened; he saw the pumping get faster until it flickered.

"I don't feel worthy of your blood," he said, running his forefinger up and down her neck. "It has nothing to do with your line of descent."

Ehlena reached up to his face. "Rehvenge, what is it? Help me understand what's going on here. I feel like . . . when I'm with you, I feel closer to you than to even my own father. But there are huge holes. I know there's something in them. Talk to me."

Now would be the time, he thought, to unload everything.

And he was tempted. It would be such a relief to stop the lying. Trouble was, there was nothing more selfish he could do to her. If she knew his secrets, she'd be breaking the law along with him—either that or sending her lover to the colony. And if she chose the latter, he was blowing the shit out of his vow to his mother, because his cover would be totally blown.

He was wrong for her. He was very wrong for her, and he knew it.

Rehv meant to let Ehlena go.

He meant to drop his hands and step back and let her put her clothes all the way on. He was good at persuasion. He could bring her around and make her see that his not drinking was no big deal. . . .

Except his mouth parted. Parted as a hiss steamed up his throat and into the thin barrier of air that separated his fangs from her pumping, vital vein.

Abruptly she gasped, and the muscles that ran up from her shoulders tightened, as if he had cranked down on his hold of her face. Oh, wait, he had. He was hard-core numb, totally without sensation, but it wasn't about his medication. Every muscle in his body had gone rigid.

"I need you," he groaned.

Rehv struck hard and she cried out, her spine bending nearly in half as he caged her with his strength. Fuck, she was perfect. She tasted like thick, heavy wine and with dragging pulls of his mouth, he drank her down deep.

And moved her over to the bed.

Ehlena didn't stand a chance. Neither did he.

Triggered by the feeding, his vampire nature plowed over everything, a male's need to mark what he wanted, to establish sexual territory, to dominate, taking over and driving him to rip down her slacks, pull up one of her legs, position his cock at the threshold of her sex—

And push his way into her.

Ehlena let out another keening cry as he penetrated her. She was incredibly tight, and fearing he might hurt her, he fell still so her body could accommodate him.

"Are you okay?" he asked, his voice so guttural he didn't know if she could understand him.

"Don't . . . stop . . ." Ehlena wrapped her legs around his ass, angling herself so he could get in even deeper.

The growl that came out of him echoed around the bedroom—until he latched back onto her throat.

Although, even in the fury of the feeding and the sex, Rehv was careful with her—nothing like he was with the princess. Rehv slid in and out gently, making sure Ehlena was comfortable with his size. When it came to his black-mailer? He wanted to impart pain. With Ehlena? He'd castrate himself with a rusty knife before he hurt her.

Trouble was, she moved with him as he drank his fill of her, and the wild friction of their bodies soon overwhelmed

him, his hips no longer surging carefully but pounding—
until he had to release her vein or run the risk of tearing
her open at the neck. After a couple of laps at his puncture
marks, he dropped his head down into her hair and went
for it hard and deep and strong.

Ehlena orgasmed, and as he felt the draws gripping
along the shaft of his cock, his own release shot up from his
sac . . . which he couldn't let happen. Before his barb engaged, he pulled out, coming all over her sex and her lower
belly.

When it was over, he collapsed on top of her, and it was
a while before he could talk.

"Ah . . . shit . . . I'm sorry, I must be heavy."

Ehlena's hands slid up his back. "You're wonderful,
actually."

"I . . . orgasmed."

"Yes, you did." Her smile was in her tone. "You really
did."

"I wasn't sure that I . . . could, you know. Which was why
I pulled . . . I didn't expect to . . . yeah."

Liar. Fucking *liar*.

The happiness in her voice made him ill. "Well, I'm glad
you did. And if it happens again, that's great. And if not,
that's just fine. There's no performance pressure."

Rehv closed his eyes, his chest aching. He'd pulled back
so she didn't find out he had a barb—and because coming
inside of her was a betrayal, given all the things she didn't
know about him.

As she sighed and nuzzled him, he felt like a total, complete bastard.

FORTY-FOUR

The CAT scan was no big deal. Wrath just parked it on a cold slab and kept still as this white piece of medical equipment murmured and politely coughed its way around his head.

The bitch was the wait for the results.

During the scan, Doc Jane was the only one on the other side of the glass partition, and from what he could tell she spent the whole time frowning at a computer monitor. Now that it was over, she was still doing that. Meanwhile, Beth had come in and was by his side in the small tiled room.

God only knew what Doc Jane had found.

"I'm not scared of going under the knife," he said to his *shellan*. "As long as that female's got the handle of the damn thing."

"Would she do brain surgery?"

Good point. "I don't know."

He absently played with Beth's Saturnine Ruby, rolling the heavy stone around and around.

"Do me a favor," he whispered.

Beth's hold tightened on his hand. "Anything. What do you need?"

"Hum the *Jeopardy* theme."

There was a pause. Then Beth burst out laughing and swatted his shoulder. "Wrath—"

"Actually, take your clothes off and hum it while doing some belly grooves." As his *shellan* bent down and kissed his forehead, he looked up at her through his wraparounds. "You think I'm kidding? Come on, we both need the distraction. And I promise I'll tip well."

"You never carry cash."

He extended his tongue and swept it over his upper lip. "I plan on working it off."

"You are outrageous." Beth smiled down at him. "And I like it."

Staring at her, he got good and afraid. What would his life be like if he were totally blind? Never seeing his *shellan's* long dark hair or flashing smile was—

"Okay," Doc Jane said as she came in. "Here's what I know."

Wrath tried not to scream as the ghostly doctor put her hands in the pockets of her white coat and seemed to gather her thoughts.

"I see no evidence of a tumor or a hemorrhage. But there are abnormalities in the various lobes. I haven't looked at a CAT scan of a vampire brain before, so I have no idea what is structurally consistent within the range of 'normality.' I know you want only me to see it, but I can't call this, and I'd like to have Havers review the scan. Before you say no, I'll remind you that he's sworn to protect your privacy. He can't reveal—"

"Bring him in," Wrath said.

"This won't take long." Doc Jane touched his shoulder and then Beth's. "He's right outside. I asked him to wait in case there was a problem with the equipment."

Wrath watched the doctor go through the little monitoring room and out into the hall. A moment later, she returned with the tall, thin physician. Havers bowed to him and to Beth through the glass and then went over to the monitors.

Both of them assumed the identical pose: bent at the waist, hands in the pockets, brows down low over their eyes.

"Do they coach them to do that in medical school?" Beth said.

"Funny, I was wondering the same thing."

Long time. Long wait. Lots of that pair on the other side of the big bay window talking and gesturing at the screen with pens. The two eventually straightened and nodded.

They came in together.

"The scan is normal," Havers said.

Wrath exhaled so hard it was practically a wheeze. Normal. Normal was good.

Havers then asked a bunch of questions, all of which Wrath answered, none of which he was particularly aware of.

"With deference to your private physician," Havers said, with a bow toward Doc Jane, "I would like to take some blood from your vein for analysis and perform a brief examination."

Doc Jane chimed in, "I think it's a good idea. Second opinions are always good when things aren't clear."

"Work me up," Wrath said, giving Beth's hand a quick kiss before releasing it.

"My lord, would you be so kind as to remove your glasses?"

Havers was quick with the spearing-light-in-the-eyeball routine; then he moved around for an ear check, followed by a heart check. A nurse came in with blood-drawing shit, but Doc Jane did the pierce-and-pull on his vein.

When it was all done, Havers double-pocketed his hands again and sported another one of those doctor frowns. "Everything seems normal. Well, normal for you. Your pupils are nonresponsive, for all intents and purposes, but that's a protective mechanism because your retinas are so photophobic to begin with."

"So what's the bottom line?" Wrath asked.

Doc Jane shrugged. "Keep a diary of the headaches. And if the blindness happens again, we're all coming back here immediately. Maybe a CAT scan while it's occurring will help us pinpoint the issue."

Havers threw another bow to Doc Jane. "I'll let your physician know about the blood tests."

"Good deal." Wrath looked up at his *shellan*, prepared to go, but Beth was focused on the doctors.

"Neither of you seem very happy about this," she said.

Doc Jane spoke slowly and carefully, as if she were choosing her words with precision. "Anytime there's an impairment in function that we can't explain, I get twitchy. I'm not saying this is a dire situation. But I'm not convinced we're out of the woods yet just because the CAT scan was okay."

Wrath slid off the examination table and took his black leather jacket out of Beth's hold. It felt fan-fucking-tastic to pull the thing on and ditch the patient role his bitch-ass eyes had forced him into.

"I won't screw around with this," he told the coats. "But I'm going to keep working."

There was a chorus of you-need-to-chill-for-a-couple-of-days, which he blew off by leaving the examination room. The thing was, as he and Beth strode off down the corridor, an odd sense of urgency gripped him.

He had this unshakable sense that he had to act fast, because he didn't have a lot of time left.

John took his good goddamn time getting to ZeroSum. After he left Xhex's, he strolled over to Tenth Street and walked in the flurries down to the Tex/Mex place. Inside, he took a table next to a fire exit and, through pointing at pictures on the laminated menu, bought himself two plates of baby backs, a side of mashed, and a side of slaw.

The waitress who took his order and delivered the chow was wearing a skirt short enough to be considered underwear, and she seemed ready to serve him in more than just a dinner kind of way. He actually considered it. She had blond hair and not too much makeup and her legs were nice. But she smelled like barbecue, and he didn't appreciate the way she talked real slow around him, as if she thought he was dumb.

John paid cash, left a good tip, and hustled along before she could try to give him her number. Out in the cold, he took the long way down Trade. Which was to say he made a detour into each alley he came to.

No *lessers*. No humans doing bad shit, either.

Finally, he went into ZeroSum. As he walked through the steel-and-glass doors and caught a barrage of lights and music and shady people dressed up slick, his tough-man makeover slipped a little. Xhex would be here—

Yeah. So. Was he such a fucking nancy that he couldn't be in the same club with her?

Not anymore. John got his balls right and strode over to the velvet rope, past the stares of the bouncers, and up into the VIP lounge. In the back, at the Brotherhood's table, Qhuinn and Blay were sitting like a pair of quarterbacks stuck on a bench while their team was choking it out on the field: They were antsy and drumming their fingers, playing with the napkins that had come with their bottles of Corona.

As he walked over, they both looked up and stopped all movement, like someone had just freeze-framed their DVDs.

"Hey," Qhuinn said.

John sat down next to his buddy and signed, *Hey*.

"How you doing?" Qhuinn asked as the waitress came over with perfect timing. "Another three Coronas—"

John cut the guy off. *I want something different. Tell her . . . I want a lowboy of Jack Daniel's on ice.*

Qhuinn's eyebrows popped, but he put in the order and watched as the woman trotted over to the bar. "High-test, huh."

John shrugged and eyed a blonde two booths down. The second she caught him staring she went into full preen mode, sweeping her thick, shiny hair over onto her back and shoving her breasts out until they strained against her barely there LBD.

Bet she didn't smell like ribs.

"Um . . . John, what the fuck is doing with you?"

What do you mean, he signed to Qhuinn without taking his eyes off the woman.

"You're looking at that chick like you want to roll her up in a taco and put your hot sauce all over her."

Blay coughed a little. "You really don't have a way with words, you know that?"

"Just calling it like I see it."

The waitress came over and tabled the Jack and the beers, and John went for his booze hard-core, tossing the shit back and opening his throat so that it was nothing but a chute down into his belly.

"Is this going to be one of those nights?" Qhuinn murmured. "Where you end up in the bathroom?"

It sure as fuck is, John signed. *But not because I'm throwing up.*

"Then why would you . . . Oh." Qhuinn looked like someone had just goosed him in the ass with a two-by-four.

Yeah, *oh,* John thought as he scanned the VIP area in the event a better candidate presented herself.

Next door, there was a trio of businessmen, each of whom had a woman with him, all of whom looked like they were ready for their *Vanity Fair* close-up. Across the way, you had your basic six-pack of Eurotrash who kept blowing their noses a lot and going back to the bathrooms in pairs. Up at the bar were a pair of high-flyers with their jacked-up second wives, and another set of cokers who were eyeing the working girls.

He was still on scan mode when Rehvenge himself stalked into the VIP room. As everyone saw him, a ripple of thrill went through the place, because even if folks didn't know he owned the club, there were not a lot of six-foot-six guys who sported a red cane and a black sable coat and a brush-cut mohawk around.

Plus, even in the dim light, you could tell he had purple eyes.

As usual, he was flanked by two males who were the size of him and looked like they ate bullets for breakfast. Xhex was not with them, but that was fine. That was good.

"I so want to be that guy when I grow up," Qhuinn drawled.

"Just don't cut your hair," Blay said. "It's too beau— I mean, mohawks require a lot of upkeep."

As Blay fired back his beer, Qhuinn's mismatched eyes briefly touched on his best friend's face before hurrying away.

After signaling the waitress for another Jack, John cranked himself around and stared through the waterfall wall at the gen-pop section of the club. Out there on the dance floor, there were a ton of women looking for exactly what he wanted to give them. All he had to do was go out there and pick among the willing volunteers.

Great plan, except, for no good reason, he thought of *The Maury Show*. Did he really want to run the risk of impregnating some random human woman? You were supposed to know when they were ovulating, but what the fuck did he know from female anything?

Frowning, he turned back around, fisted his fresh Jack, and focused on the working girls.

Professionals. Who knew the kind of get-off game he was looking to get into. Much better.

He focused on a dark-haired female who had a face like

the Virgin Mary. Marie-Terese, he thought he'd heard her
name was. She was the boss of the working girls, but she
was also available for hire: At the moment, she was hip-out
and come-hithering a guy in a three-piece who seemed
very interested in her goods.

Come with me, John signed to Qhuinn.

"Where— Okay, gotcha." Qhuinn polished off his beer
and slid out. "Guess we'll be back, Blay."

"Yeah. Have . . . a good time."

John led the way over to the brunette, and her blue eyes
seemed surprised as the two of them came up to her. With
some kind of sultry apology, she stepped away from her
prospect.

"You need something?" she said, with no come-on what-
soever. She was friendly, though, because she knew that
John and the boys were special guests of the Reverend's.
Although naturally not why.

Ask her how much, he signed to Qhuinn. *For both of us.*

Qhuinn cleared his throat. "He wants to know how
much."

She frowned. "Depends on who you want. The girls
have—" John pointed to the woman. "Me?"

John nodded.

As the brunette's blue eyes narrowed and her red lips
pursed, John imagined her mouth on him and his cock liked
the picture, popping up an instant, cheering erection. Yeah,
she had a very nice mou—

"No," she said. "You can't have me."

Qhuinn spoke up before John's hands could go flying.
"Why? Our money's as good as anyone else's."

"I get to pick who I do business with. Some of the other
girls, they might feel differently. You can ask them."

John was willing to bet the shutdown had something to
do with Xhex. God knew there had been a lot of eye contact between him and the club's head of security and Marie-
Terese didn't want to get in the middle of that, no doubt.

At least, he told himself it was that, as opposed to the
fact that even a prostitute couldn't stand the idea of being
with him.

Okay, cool, John signed. *Who would you suggest?*

After Qhuinn spoke, she said, "I would suggest you go
back to your Jack and leave the girls alone."

Not going to happen, and I want a professional.

Qhuinn translated, and Marie-Terese's frown got even deeper. "I'll be honest with you. This feels like a fuck-you. Like you're sending a message. You want to get laid, go find some chippie on the dance floor or in one of these booths. Don't do it with someone who works with her, okay?"

Right. Totally was about Xhex.

The old John would have done what she suggested. Fuck that; the old John wouldn't be having this conversation in the first place. But things had changed.

Thanks, but I think we'll ask one of your colleagues. Take care.

John turned away as Qhuinn spoke, but Marie-Terese grabbed his arm. "Fine. You want to be an asshole, go talk to Gina over there in the red."

John bowed a little, then took the suggestion, going up to a black-haired woman who was dressed in red vinyl so bright, the shit nearly qualified as a strobe light.

Unlike Marie-Terese, she was on board with the plan before Qhuinn even got to the ask. "Five hundred," she said with a wide smile. "Each. I'm assuming this is to-gether?"

John nodded, a little astonished that it was so easy. Then again, that was what they were paying for. Easy.

"Shall we go into the back?" Gina positioned herself between him and Qhuinn, took each of them by an arm, and led them past Blay, who was fixated on his beer.

As they went down the hallway that led to the private bathrooms, John felt like he had a fever: Hot and disassociated from what was around him, he was bobbing along, tethered only to the thin arm of the prostitute he was about to pay to fuck.

If she were to let go, he was quite sure he would simply float away.

FORTY-FIVE

As Xhex came up the steps and into the VIP section, at first she wasn't sure what the hell she was seeing. It looked like John and Qhuinn were going into the back with Gina. Unless, of course, there happened to be another two guys just like them, one of whom had a tat in the Old Language on the back of his neck and another who had shoulders as big as Rehv's.

But that absolutely was Gina in her red-don't-mean-stop dress.

Trez's voice came through Xhex's earpiece. "Rehv is here and we're waiting for you."

Yeah, well, they were going to wait a little longer.

Xhex turned around and headed back for the velvet rope—at least until her path got blocked by a guy wearing wannabe Prada.

"Hey, baby, where you going so fast."

Dumb move on his part. The coked-up piece of Euro-irrelevance picked the wrong female to step in front of.

"Get out of my way before I move you."

"What's the matter?" He reached out for her hip. "Can't handle a real man— *Ow.*"

Xhex turned the guy's grope into a knuckle-crusher, twisting his hand in her fist until his arm flamingoed on him. "Right," she said. "About one hour and twenty minutes ago you bought seven hundred dollars' worth of coke. In spite of the amount you've been doing in the bathrooms,

I'm wagering you have enough left on you to get popped for possession. So get the fuck out of my way, and if you try to touch me again, I will break all these fingers, then go to work on your other hand."

She let him loose with a shove, sending him skipping into his buddies.

Xhex kept going, leaving the VIP area and striding past the dance floor. Under the stairs to the mezzanine floor, she went up to a door marked SECURITY STAFF ONLY and entered a code. The hallway on the other side led her by her staff's locker room and to her destination, the security office. After she entered another code, she walked into the twenty-by-twenty room where all the monitoring equipment dumped data into computers.

Everything on the property, except for Rehv's office and Rally's scale den, which were on a separate system, was digitally recorded here, and gray-blue screens showed pictures from all around the club.

"Hey, Chuck," she said to the guy behind the desk. "You mind if I have a minute alone?"

"No problem. Have to have a bathroom break anyway."

She traded places, sinking down into the Kirk chair, as the boys called it. "I don't need long."

"Neither do I, boss. You want something to drink?"

"I'm good, thanks."

As Chuck nodded and hulked out, she focused on the monitors that showed the bathrooms off the VIP section—

Oh . . . God.

The trio from hell were crowded in together, with Gina in the middle, John kissing his way down to her breasts, and Qhuinn, who was standing behind the woman, slipping his hands around to the front of her hips.

Pinned between the males, Gina did not look like she was working. She looked like she was a woman getting off in a big way.

Damn it.

Although at least it was Gina. Xhex had no particular relationship with her, as the woman had just come on staff, so it wasn't much different than if John had banged some chick from the dance floor.

Xhex eased back in the chair and forced herself to review the other monitors. People were all over the wall, flickering images of them drinking, doing lines, having sex, dancing, talking, staring off into the distance, filling her sight.

This was good, she thought. This was . . . good. John had lost his romantic delusions and was going elsewhere. This was good—

"Xhex, where are you?" came Trez's voice in her earpiece.

She yanked up her arm and spoke into her watch. "Give me a fucking minute!"

The Moor's response was typically calm. "You okay?"

"I . . . Look, I'm sorry. I'm coming now."

Yeah, and so was Gina. Christ.

Xhex stood up from the Kirk chair, her eyes going back to the screen she had pointedly not stared at.

Things had progressed. Fast.

John was moving his hips.

Just as Xhex winced and went to leave, he looked up into the security camera. Whether he knew it was there or whether that was just where his eyes ended up, it was hard to know.

Shit. His face was grim, his jaw set hard, his stare soulless in a way that saddened her.

Xhex tried not to see the change in him for what it was and failed. She had done this to him. Maybe she wasn't the only reason he'd turned to stone, but she was a big part of it.

He looked away.

She turned away.

Chuck put his head through the door. "You need more time?"

"No, thanks. I've seen enough."

She clapped her man on the shoulder and left, going out and to the right. At the end of the hall there was a reinforced black door. Entering yet another code, she took the passageway to Rehv's office, and when she came through his door, the three males around the desk all looked at her warily.

She took up res against the black wall across from them. "What."

Rehv leaned back in his chair, crossing his fur-clad arms

over his chest. "Are you getting ready to go into your needing."

As he spoke, Trez and iAm both made the Shadow hand motion for warding off disaster.

"God, no. Why do you ask?"

"Because, no offense, you're cranky as fuck."

"I am not." As the males looked at one another, she barked, "Stop that."

Oh, great, now they all just pointedly *didn't* look at each other.

"Can we get this meeting over with," she said, trying to moderate her tone.

Rehv unfurled his arms and sat forward. "Yeah. I'm about outtie to go meet with the council."

"You want us to come with you?" Trez asked.

"As long as we don't have any big deals scheduled after midnight."

Xhex shook her head. "The last one on the books for this week happened at nine and went off without a problem. Although I will say our buyer was extremely nervous, and that was before it came over the police scanner that another drug dealer's been found dead."

"So out of the six major subcontractors who buy from us, there are two left? Man, that's a turf war, right there."

"And whoever's pulling this shit is probably going to try to work his way up the food chain."

Trez spoke up. "Which is why iAm and I think you should have someone with you twenty-four/seven until this shit shakes out."

Rehv seemed annoyed but he didn't disagree. "We got any intel on who's leaving all those bodies around?"

"Well, duh," Trez said. "People think it's you."

"Not logical. Why would I kill off my own buyers?"

Now Rehv was the one getting the hairy eyeball from the peanut gallery. "Oh, come on," he said. "I'm not *that* bad. Well, okay, but only if someone fucks with me. And I'm sorry, but the four who've died? Straight-up businessmen. No bullshit. They were good customers."

"You talk to your suppliers?" Trez asked.

"Yup. Told them to hang tight and confirmed I was expecting to move the same amount of product. Those who

we lost will quickly be replaced by others, because dealers
are like weeds. They always grow back."

There was some discussion about the market and pric-
ing, and then Rehv said, "Before we run out of time, talk to
me about the club. What's going down?"

Right, great question, Xhex thought. And our survey
says? *Ding-ding-ding*: John Matthew, most likely. On his
knees in front of Gina.

"Xhex, are you growling?"

"No." She forced herself to focus and gave a quick over-
view of the incidents thus far tonight. Trez reported on the
Iron Mask, which he had been put in charge of, and then
iAm talked finances and about Sal's Restaurant, another of
Rehv's holdings. All in all, it was business as usual—
considering they were breaking the kind of human laws
that got you felony convictions if you were caught.

Still Xhex's head was only partially in the game, and
when it came time to leave, she was the first to hit the door,
even though she usually lingered.

She walked out of the office at the perfect time.

If she'd wanted to get kneed in the balls.

At just that moment, Qhuinn appeared at the head of
the hall of private baths, his lips swollen and red, his hair
tousled, the scent of sex and orgasms and dirty deeds done
with finesse preceding him.

She stopped, even though that was a dumb-ass idea.

Gina was next, and she looked like she needed a drink.
As in Gatorade. The woman was boneless, not because she
was in her deliberate trolling-for-sex mode, but because
she'd been worked out properly, and the soft smile on her
mouth was far too private and honest for Xhex's liking.

John was the last out, his head held high, his stare clear,
his shoulders back.

He had been magnificent. She was willing to bet . . . he had
been magnificent.

His head turned and he met her eyes. Gone was the shy
regard, the blush, the awkward fawning. He nodded once
and looked away, composed . . . and ready for more sex,
given the way he sized up another one of the prostitutes.

An uneasy, unfamiliar sorrow rippled through Xhex's
chest, screwing up the even beat of her heart. In her drive

to save him from the chaos her last lover had gone through,
she'd ruined something; in pushing him away, she'd stripped
him of something precious.

His innocence was gone.

Xhex put her wristwatch up to her mouth. "I need some
air."

Trez's response was straight-up approval. "Good idea."

"I'll be back right before you leave for the council
meeting."

When Lash returned from his father's lair, he gave himself
only about ten minutes to come fully back to life before he
got in the Mercedes and drove over to the shitty ranch
house where the drugs had been packaged. He was so
groggy he thought it was a wonder he didn't hit something,
and he almost did. While rubbing at his eyes and trying to
dial his phone, he didn't brake fast enough at a stoplight,
and it was only because the city of Caldwell's salting trucks
had been out earlier that his tires had anything worth grabbing hold of.

He put the phone down and concentrated on the behind-
the-wheel shit. Probably better not to speak to Mr. D anyway, given that he was in father fog, as he called it.

Shit, the heater was making him even logier.

Lash put down the windows and cut off the hot breeze
wafting into the sedan's front seat, and by the time he
pulled up to the piece-of-shit house, he was much more
alert. Parking around the back, so that the Merc was
shielded by the screened-in porch and the garage, he went
in through the kitchen door.

"Where are you?" he called out. "What's the update?"
Silence.

He put his head into the garage, and when he saw only
the Lexus, he figured Mr. D, Grady, and the other two were
probably on their way back from jumping that other dealer.
Which meant he had time to grab something to eat. As he
went to the fridge that was stocked for him, he called the
little Texan's phone. One ring. Two rings.

He was pulling out a deli-made turkey sandwich and
checking the date when D's voice mail kicked in.

Lash straightened and stared down at his phone. He
never went to voice mail. Ever.

Of course, maybe the meeting had been delayed and they were right in the middle of it.

Lash ate and waited, expecting to hear back right away. When he didn't, he went into the living room and fired up the laptop, accessing the GPS software that located every single Lessening Society phone on the map of Caldwell. He set the search for Mr. D's and discovered . . .

The guy was traveling fast and moving easterly. And the two other *lessers* were with him.

So why wasn't the guy answering his fucking phone?

Suspicious, Lash called again and walked around the shithole as the ringing went on and on. There was nothing out of place in the house as far as he could see. Living room was the same and the two bedrooms and the master were tight, with all the window frames bolted in place and the shades down.

He was calling the Texan a third time when he took the hall to the street side of the house—

Lash stopped in midstep and swiveled his head to the one door he hadn't opened—which had a cold breeze shooting out all around its jamb.

He didn't have to open the thing to know what had happened, but he cracked the fucker anyway. The window was shattered and there were black streaks—rubber, not the blood of slayers—around the sill.

A quick look out the gaper and Lash saw footsteps in the thin layer of snow that were headed in the direction of the street. No doubt the hotfoot routine hadn't lasted long. There were plenty of cars around to hot-wire in this quiet neighborhood, and that kind of shit was kindergarten for any criminal worth his cock.

Grady had done a runner.

And the move was a surprise. He was not the brightest diamond in the chain, but the police were after him. Why would he risk another set of motherfuckers gunning for him?

Lash went into the living room and frowned as he looked over at the couch, where Grady had left that greased-out Domino's box and . . . the *CCJ* he'd been reading.

Which was open to the obituaries.

Thinking of Grady's busted knuckles, Lash went over and picked up the paper—

He smelled something on the pages. Old Spice. Ah, so Mr. D had half a brain, and had looked at the thing, too....

Lash scanned down the listings. Bunch of humans in their seventies and eighties. One in her sixties. Two in their fifties. None of which had the name Grady listed either as sur or middle. Three out-of-towners with family here in Caldie ...

And then there it was: Christianne Andrews, age twenty-four. No cause of death listed, but the DOD was on Sunday, and the burial service had been today at Pine Grove Cemetery. The key? *In lieu of flowers, please send donations to the CPD's Victims of Domestic Violence Fund.*

Lash shot over to the laptop and checked on the GPS report. Mr. D's Focus was wheezing itself toward ... Well, what do you know. Pine Grove Cemetery, where the once-lovely Christianne was going to rest for eternity in the arms of angels.

Now Grady's story was clear: Asshole beats the shit out of his girl regularly until he pushes the hard loving too far one night. She kicks it and the police find her body and start looking around for the drug-dealing boyfriend who's taking his job stress home to the little woman. No wonder they were after the guy.

And love conquered all ... even the common sense of criminals.

Lash went outside and dematerialized to the cemetery, ready to do a meet-and-greet not only with that fool human, but the stupid fucking slayers who should have been watching the idiot better.

He materialized just ten yards from a parked car—which almost got him eyeballed by the guy sitting inside of the thing. Shifting quickly behind the statue of a robed woman Lash checked out what was doing in the sedan: A human was inside, going from the scent. A human with a lot of coffee.

Undercover cop. Who was no doubt hoping that SOB Grady did exactly what he was doing: namely pay respects to the girl he'd murdered.

Yeah, well, two could play at the wait-and-see game.

Lash took out his phone and shielded the bright screen

with his palm. The text he sent to Mr. D was a holdback that he hoped like fuck the guy got in time. With the police on-site Lash was going to handle Grady on his own.

And then he was going to throw down to whoever had left the human alone long enough so he could bust free.

FORTY-SIX

Standing at the foot of the grand staircase, Wrath finished prepping for the meeting with the *glymera* by drawing a Kevlar vest onto his shoulders. "It's light."

"Weight doesn't always do you better," V said as he fired up a hand-rolled and snapped his gold lighter shut.

"You sure about that."

"When it comes to bulletproof vests, I am." Vishous exhaled, the smoke momentarily shading his face before it floated upward to the ornate ceiling. "But if it'll make you feel better, we can strap a garage door on your chest. Or a car, for that matter."

Heavy footsteps from behind echoed up around the magnificent, jewel-colored foyer as Rhage and Zsadist came down together, a pair of straight-up killers with the daggers of the Brotherhood holstered handles-down on their chests. As they stepped in front of Wrath, there was a chiming noise from the vestibule, and Fritz shuffled over to let in Phury, who had dematerialized down from the Adirondacks, as well as Butch, who'd just walked across the courtyard.

Wrath felt a charge go through him as he looked at his brothers. Even though two of them were still not talking to him, he could feel the common warrior blood running through all their bodies, and he relished the collective need to fight the enemy, be it a *lesser* or one of their own race.

A soft sound from the stairs brought his head around.

Tohr was coming down from the second story with care, as if he weren't sure he trusted his thigh muscles to catch and hold his weight. From what Wrath could see, the brother was dressed in camos that were cinched onto hips the size of a boy's, and he had on a thick black turtleneck sweater that bagged under his armpits. There were no daggers on his chest, but he had a pair of guns hanging from that hope-and-a-prayer leather belt that was holding his pants up.

Lassiter was right beside him, but the angel for once wasn't pulling any smart-ass. Although he wasn't looking where he was going, either. For some reason, he was staring at the mural on the ceiling, at the warriors fighting in the clouds.

All the Brothers looked up at Tohr, and he didn't stop, didn't meet anyone's eye, just kept on coming until he reached the mosaic floor. Still no stopping. He passed the Brotherhood, went over to the door that led out into the night, and waited.

The only echo from what he'd once been was the set of his jaw. That hard shot of bone was parallel to the floor and then some. As far as he was concerned, he was going out and that was that.

Yeah, wrong.

Wrath walked over to him and said softly, "I'm sorry, Tohr—"

"There's no reason to be sorry. Let's go."

"No."

There was a whole lot of awkward shuffling, as if the other brothers were hating this as much as Wrath was.

"You're not strong enough." Wrath wanted to put his hand on Tohr's shoulder, but he knew that would lead to a violent shrug-off, given how Tohr's fragile body was tensing up. "Just wait until you're ready. This war . . . this fucking war is going to be around."

The grandfather clock in the study upstairs started to gong, the rhythmic sound drifting out of Wrath's office, over the gold-leafed balustrade, and falling to the ears of the assembled. It was eleven thirty. Time to head out if they wanted to scope the meeting locale before the *glymera* types arrived.

Wrath cursed under his breath and looked over his shoulder at the five black-clad fighters who were standing together in a unit. Their bodies hummed with power, their weapons not just what hung from holsters and harnesses, but also their hands and feet and arms and legs and minds. Their mental toughness was in the blood; the training and the brute strength in their flesh.

You needed both to fight. Will alone got you only so far.

"You're staying," Wrath said. "And that's final."

With a curse, he punched his way into the vestibule and out the other side. Leaving Tohr behind felt wrong, but there was no other choice. The Brother was compromised to the point of being a danger to himself, and he was a bad distraction. If he were on-site? Each one of the Brothers would have him on their minds, so the whole group would be head-fucked—not exactly what you wanted when you walked into a meeting where someone might try to assassinate the king. For, like, the second time this week.

As the outer doors of the mansion thundered shut, with Tohr on the other side, Wrath and the brothers stood in the bracing gusts that cut up the face of the compound's mountain, barreled across the courtyard, and weaved in and out of the assembled cars.

"Goddamn it," Rhage muttered as they focused on the horizon beyond.

After a while, Vishous turned his head to Wrath, his profile silhouetted against the gray sky. "We need to—"

The pop of a gunshot rang out, and the hand-rolled that was between V's lips was clipped from his mouth. Or maybe it was just vaporized.

"What the fuck!" V shouted as he recoiled.

They all wheeled around, going for their weapons even though there was no way in hell their enemies were anywhere near the great stone fortress.

Tohr was standing calmly in the mansion's doorway, his feet planted solidly, his two hands gripping the butt of the gun he'd set off.

V lunged forward, but Butch steel-barred him around the chest, keeping him from taking Tohr down to the ground.

Didn't stop V's mouth. *What the fuck are you thinking!*

Tohr lowered the muzzle. "I might not be able to fight hand-to-hand yet, but I'm the best shot out of all of you."

"You're fucking crazy," V spat. "That's what you are."

"Do you really think I'd put a bullet in your head?" Tohr's voice was even. "I've already lost the love of my life. Capping one of my brothers is not the kind of chaser I'm looking for. Like I said, I'm the best we've got with a gun, and that is not the kind of asset you want benched on a night like tonight." Tohr reholstered the SIG. "And before you *why* the hell out of me, I had to make a statement, and it was better than shooting your ugly-ass goatee off. Not that I wouldn't kill to give you the shave your chin is begging for."

There was a long pause.

Wrath busted out laughing. Which was, of course, insane. But the idea that he didn't have to deal with Tohr being left behind like some dog who wasn't allowed to come with the rest of the family was such a stunning relief, all he could do was bellow.

Rhage was the first to join in, throwing his head back, the lights from the mansion catching in his bright blond hair, his superwhite teeth flashing. As he laughed, his big hand came up and landed over his heart like he was hoping he didn't short the thing out.

Butch was next, the cop barking out loud and loosing his hold on his best friend's torso. Phury smiled for a second, and then his big shoulders started to quake—which set Z off until his scarred face was one big, wide grin.

Tohr didn't smile, but there was a glimmer of the way he used to be in the satisfaction with which he settled back on his heels. Tohr had always been a serious guy, the kind who was more interested in making sure everyone was chilled out and tight than cracking jokes and being a loudmouth. But that didn't mean he couldn't razz along with the best of 'em.

It was why he'd been so perfect as the Brotherhood's leader. Right skill set for a necessary job: tight in the head, warm in the heart.

In the midst of the laughing, Rhage looked over at Wrath. Without a word said, the two of them embraced, and when they pulled apart, Wrath gave his brother the male equivalent of an apology—which was a good knock of the shoulders. Then he turned to Z and Z nodded once. Which was Zsadist's shorthand of, *Yeah, you were a dick, but you had your reasons and we're cool.*

Hard to know who started it, but someone put his arms over the shoulders of someone else, and then another guy did it, and then they were in a football huddle. The circle they made in that cold wind was uneven, composed of different body heights and chest widths that varied and arm lengths that were not equal. But linked together they were a unit.

Standing hip-to-hip with his brothers, Wrath saw as very rare and special what he had once taken for granted: the Brotherhood together once again.

"Hey, you wanna share some of the bromance over here?"

Lassiter's voice brought their heads up. The angel was standing on the steps of the mansion, his glow casting a lovely, soft light into the night.

"Can I hit him?" V asked.

"Later," Wrath said, breaking up the clinch. "And many, many times."

"Not exactly what I had in mind," the angel muttered as one by one they dematerialized to the meeting, with Butch driving off to meet them.

Xhex took form in a stand of pines that was about a hundred yards from Chrissy's grave. She chose the locale not because she expected Grady to be standing over the headstone and sniffling into the arm of his eagle jacket, but because she wanted to feel even worse than she did already—and she couldn't think of a better place for that than where the girl was going to end up come spring.

To her surprise, though, she wasn't alone. For two reasons.

The sedan parked just around the bend, with a clear sight line to the grave, was undoubtedly de la Cruz or one of his subordinates. But there was someone else here, too.

A malevolent force, actually.

Every *symphath* urge she had told her to tread carefully. As far as she could tell, that thing was *lesser* with a nitrous oxide injection into its evil engine, and in a quick burst of self-protection, she insulated herself, blending into the landscape—

Well, well, well…another contingency heard from.

From the north, a group of men approached, two of whom were tallish and one who was much smaller. They were all dressed in black and were as fair in their coloring as Norwegians.

Great. Unless you had a new gang in town, one full of I'm-worth-it thugs who were into Preference by L'Oréal, that bunch of blondies were slayers.

The CPD, the Lessening Society, and something worse, all trolling around Chrissy's grave? What were the chances?

Xhex waited, watching the slayers splinter apart and find trees to shadow themselves behind.

There was only one explanation: Grady had fallen in with the *lessers*. Not a surprise, considering they recruited from criminals, especially the violent kind.

Xhex let the minutes tick by, Milk Dudding the sitch, just waiting for the burst of action that was inevitable, given a movie with this sort of cast. She was due back at the club, but shit was just going to have to roll there without her, because there was no way she was leaving.

Grady had to be on the way.

A little more time passed, and there were lots more cold wind and many more clouds drifting dark blue and bright gray across the face of the moon.

And then, just like that, the *lessers* walked off.

The malevolent presence dematerialized as well.

Maybe they had given up, but it didn't seem likely. From what she knew about *lessers* they were a lot of things, but ADD was not one of them. This meant either something more important had gone down, or they'd changed their—

She heard a rustle across the ground.

Glancing over her shoulder, she saw Grady.

He was huddling against the cold, his arms tucked into a black parka that was too big for him, his feet shuffling through the thin snow cover. He was looking all around, searching the graves for the newest one, and if he kept going, he was going to find Chrissy's soon enough.

Of course, that also meant he was going to see the cop in the unmarked. Or the cop was going to see him.

Right. Time to make a move.

Assuming the slayers stayed gone, Xhex could deal with the CPD.

She was not going to lose this opportunity. No fucking way.

Turning her phone off, she got ready to go to work.

FORTY-SEVEN

"Goddamn it, we have to go," Rehv said from behind his desk. As he ended yet another call to Xhex's cell, he tossed his new phone like it was nothing but a piece of junk, something which was clearly getting to be a bad habit. "I don't know where the hell she is, but we have to go."

"She'll come back." Trez pulled on a black leather trench coat and headed for the door. "And better to have her out than in, given her mood. I'll get with the shift supervisor and tell him to run any shit through me, then I'll go get the B."

As he left, iAm double-checked the two H&Ks under his arms with lethal efficiency, his black eyes calm, his hands steady. Satisfied, the male picked up a steel gray leather trench and put it on.

The fact that the brothers' coats were similar made sense. iAm and Trez liked the same things. Always. Though they weren't twins by virtue of birth, they dressed similarly and were always armed with identical weapons and consistently shared the same thoughts, values, and principles.

There was one way they were different, however. While iAm stood by the door, he was silent and still as a Doberman on duty. But his lack of chat didn't mean he wasn't as deadly as his brother, because the guy's eyes spoke volumes even as his mouth was screwed down tight: iAm never missed a thing.

Including, evidently, the antibiotics that Rehv took out

of his pocket and swallowed. As well as the fact that a sterilized needle made an appearance next and was put to use.

"Good," the male said, as Rehv rolled his sleeve back down and put on his suit coat.

"Good what."

iAm just stared across the office, all don't-be-an-ass-you-know-exactly-what-I'm-talking-about.

He did that a lot. In one glance he spoke volumes.

"Whatever," Rehv muttered. "Don't get a hard-on like I've turned over a new leaf."

He might be dealing with the infection in his arm, but there was still shit hanging like rotten fringe off all the sides of his life.

"You sure about that?"

Rehv rolled his eyes and got to his feet, slipping a bag of M&M's into the pocket of his sable. "Trust me."

iAm was all about the oh-really as his eyes dipped to the coat. "Melts in your mouth, not in your hand."

"Oh, shut it. Look, the pills have to be taken with food. You got a ham 'n' cheese on rye on you? I don't."

"I'da made you some linguine with Sal sauce and brought it over for you. Give me more notice next time."

Rehv headed out of the office. "You mind not being thoughtful. Makes me feel like shit."

"Your prob, not mine."

iAm spoke into his watch as they left the office, and Rehv didn't waste any time between the club's side door and the car. When he was in the B, iAm disappeared, traveling as a rolling shadow over the ground, disturbing the pages of a magazine, rattling a tin can that had been abandoned, ruffling loose snow.

He would get to the meeting location first and open the place while Trez drove over.

Rehv had set the meeting where it was for two reasons. One, he was the *leahdyre*, so the council had to go where he said and he knew they would squirm from viewing the location as beneath them. Always a pleasure. And two, it was an investment property he'd acquired, so it was on his turf.

Always a necessity.

Salvatore's Restaurant, home of the famous Sal sauce, was an Italian institution in Caldie, having been in business for over fifty years. When the original owner's grandson, Sal III, as he had been known, had developed a horrendous gambling habit and run up $120,000 in debt through Rehv's bookies, it had been a case of tit for tat: Grandson deeded the establishment over to Rehv, and Rehv didn't crack the third generation's compass.

Which, in laymen's terms, meant that the guy didn't have all his elbows and his knees shattered until they required joint replacements.

Oh, and the secret recipe for Sal's sauce had come with the restaurant—a requirement added by iAm: During the negotiations that had lasted all of a minute and a half, the Shadow had spoken up and said no sauce, no deal. And he'd demanded a taste test to make sure the intel was right.

Since that happy transaction, the Moor had been running the place, and what do you know, it was turning a profit. Then again, that was what happened when you didn't cleave off every spare dime and funnel it into piss-poor football picks. Traffic in the restaurant was up, food quality was back where it had been, and the place was getting a serious-ass face-lift in the form of new tables, chairs, linens, rugs, chandeliers.

All of which were replacements of exactly what had been there before.

You didn't fuck with tradition, as iAm said.

The only interior change was one nobody could see: A mesh of steel had been applied to every square inch of the walls and ceilings, and all the doors but one had been reinforced with the shit.

No one was dematerializing in or out unless management knew and approved.

Truth was, Rehv owned the place, but it was iAm's baby, and the Moor had reason to be proud of his efforts. Even the old-school Italian goombahs liked the food he cooked.

Fifteen minutes later, the Bentley pulled up under the porte cochere of the sprawling one-story stretch of trademark red-washed brick. The lights were off around the building, even the ones that lit up Sal's name, although the empty parking lot was illuminated with the orange glow from old-fashioned gaslights.

Trez waited in the dark with the engine running and the doors of the bulletproof car locked, clearly communicating with his brother in the Shadow way. After a moment he nodded and cut the motor.

"We're cool." He got out and walked around the Bentley, opening the rear door as Rehv palmed his cane and shifted his numb body off the leather seat. As the two of them crossed over the pavers and pulled wide the heavy black doors, the Moor's gun was out and at his thigh.

Stepping into Sal's was like walking into the Red Sea. Literally.

Frank Sinatra greeted them, his "Wives and Lovers" drifting down from speakers embedded in the red velvet ceiling. Underfoot, the red carpet had just been replaced, and it glowed with the same sheen and depth as freshly spilled human blood. All around, red walls were flocked with a black acanthus-leaf pattern and the lighting was what you'd find in a movie theater, i.e., mostly on the floor. During regular business hours, the hostess stand and the cloakroom were manned by gorgeous dark-haired women dressed in red and black short-and-tights, and all the waiters wore black suits with red ties.

Over to the side, there was a bank of public telephones from the fifties and two cigarette machines from the Kojak period, and as usual, the place smelled like oregano, garlic, and good food. In the background, there was also the lingering whiff of cigarettes and cigars—even though by law you weren't supposed to light up in this kind of establishment, in the back room, where the reserved tables were and the games of poker got dealt, management allowed people to light up.

Rehv had always been a little tight-balled at being around all the red, but he knew as long as he could look into the two dining rooms and see that the tables with their white linens and deep leather chairs receded properly, he was okay.

"The Brotherhood's already here," Trez said as they went down to the private suite where the meeting was going to be held.

When they walked into the room, there was no talk, no laughter, not even a throat cleared among the other males in the space. The Brothers were lined up shoulder-to-shoulder in front of Wrath, who was positioned in front of the one door that was not reinforced with steel—so he could dematerialize free in the blink of an eye if things came to that.

"Evening," Rehv said, choosing the head of the long, thin table that had been set with twenty chairs.

There was a patter of hi-how're-yas, but the tight knot of linebacker-and-then-some warriors was solely focused on the doorway he'd come through.

Yup, you fucked with their boy Wrath and you were going to get fed your future—right up your own ass.

And what do you know, they'd taken on a mascot, evidently. Off to the left, a glowing Oscar statue of a guy stood tall in combats, his blond-and-black hair making him look like an eighties headbanger looking for a backup band. Lassiter the fallen angel didn't seem any less fierce than the Brothers, however. Maybe it was his piercings. Or the fact that his eyes were all white. Fuck it, the guy's vibe was just hard-core.

Interesting. Given the way he was glaring at the doorway with the others, Wrath was clearly on the protected-species list with that angel.

iAm came in from the back, a pistol in one hand, a tray of cappuccinos on the palm of the other.

Several of the Brothers took what was offered, although all those dainty cups were going to become gum for their shitkickers' heels if they had to fight.

"Thanks, man." Rehv also took a cappuccino. "Cannoli?"

"Coming."

The instructions for the meeting had been spelled out clearly beforehand. Members of the council had to arrive at the front of the restaurant. If anyone even so much as jogged the handle of another door, they assumed the risk of getting shot. iAm would let them in and escort them down to the room. When they left, it would be through the front again, and cover would be provided for safe dematerialization. Ostensibly, the security measures were because of Rehv's "concern over *lessers.*" The truth was, it was all about protecting Wrath.

iAm came in with the cannoli.

Cannoli were eaten.

More cappuccino was brought out.

Frank did "Fly Me to the Moon." Then it was that song about the bar closing and him needing another for the road.

And the one about three coins in the fountain. And the fact that he had a crush on someone.

Over by Wrath, Rhage shifted his massive weight in his shitkickers, the leather of his jacket creaking. Next to him, the king rolled his shoulders and one of them popped. Butch cracked his knuckles. V lit up. Phury and Z looked at each other.

Rehv glanced at iAm and Trez, who were in the doorway. Looked back at Wrath. "Surprise, surprise."

Putting his cane to good use, he stood up and did a lap around the room, his *symphath* side respecting the offensive tactic of this unexpected no-show by the other council members. He didn't think they'd have the balls—

A *bing-bong* sound came from the front door of the restaurant.

As Rehv turned his head, he heard the soft metallic slide of the safeties coming off the guns in the Brothers' hands.

Across the street from the closed gates of Pine Grove Cemetery, Lash walked up to a Honda Civic that was parked in the shadows. When he put his hand on the hood, it was warm, and he didn't have to go around to the driver's side to know that the window was busted out of it. This was the car Grady had used to get to his dead ex's grave site.

As he heard the sound of boots approaching on asphalt, he palmed the gun in his breast pocket.

Mr. D was tugging his cowboy hat down as he came over. "Why'd you call us off—"

Lash calmly leveled his gun at the *lesser*'s head. "Tell me why I'm not blowing a hole in your motherfucking brain right now."

The slayers on either side of Mr. D stepped back. Way back.

"Because I done found out he was gone," Mr. D said in his Texas twang. "That's why. These two had no hide nor hair where he was at."

"You were in charge. You lost him."

Mr. D's pale eyes were steady. "I was counting y'all's

money. You want anyone else doing that? Don't believe so."

Shit, good point. Lash lowered his gun and looked at the other two. Unlike Mr. D, who was stick-steady, they were in full fidget. Which told him precisely who had lost the asset.

"How much money came in," Lash asked, still glaring at the men.

"Lot. It's right there in the Escort."

"Well, what do you know, my mood's improving," Lash murmured, putting his gun away. "As for why I called you off, Grady's about to go to jail with my fucking compliments. I want him to be someone's girlfriend a couple of times and enjoy life behind bars before I kill him."

"But what about—"

"We have the contacts for the other two dealers and we can sell the product ourselves. We don't need him."

The sound of a car approaching the iron gates from inside the cemetery brought all of their heads to the right. It was the unmarked that had been parked around the corner by that new grave and the POS came to a halt, steam rising from its tail pipe in puffs like the engine was farting. And a schlub with dark hair got out. After he unlocked the chain, he threw his back into wrenching aside one half of the Do Not Enters; then he drove through, got out again and closed the place back up.

There was no one in the car with him.

He went to the left, red lights fading as he took off.

Lash glanced back at the Civic, which was the only other way Grady was getting anywhere.

What the fuck had happened? The cop must have seen Grady, because he'd been walking right for the unmarked—

Lash stiffened and then pivoted on his boot, the salt that had been sprinkled on the road grinding under his thick sole.

Something else was in the cemetery. Something that had just chosen to reveal itself.

Something that registered exactly as that *symphath* had up north.

Which was why the cop had driven off. The guy had been willed to.

"Go back to the ranch with the money," he said to Mr. D. "I'll meet you there."

"Y'sir. Right away."

Lash didn't register the guy's response much. He was too captivated by what the fuck was going on around that dead girl's early grave.

FORTY-EIGHT

Xhex was glad the human mind was clay: It didn't take long for José de la Cruz's brain to register the command she gave, and as soon as it did, he put his cold coffee into a cup holder and started the unmarked car.

Over among the trees, Grady stopped his zombie march, looking like he was shocked as shit that the sedan had even been there. She wasn't worried the guy would lose his nerve, though. Aching loss and desperation and regret filled out the airspace around him and that grid would soon call him forward to the fresh gravestone with greater resolve than any thoughts she could plant into the fucker's frontal lobe.

Xhex waited as he waited . . . and sure enough, as soon as de la Cruz was gone, those boots that were meant for walking got back in the game, carrying Grady right where she wanted him.

As he came up to the granite marker, a choked sound left his mouth and it was the first sob of many. Like a pussy, he started to weep, his breath frothing in white clouds as he crouched down over where the woman he'd killed was going to spend the next century decomposing.

If he liked Chrissy so much, why didn't he think of that before he snuffed her.

Xhex stepped out from behind an oak and let her masking go, revealing herself to the landscape. As she approached Chrissy's murderer, she reached around to the

small of her back and unsheathed the stainless-steel blade
that she nicely holstered along her spine. The weapon was
as long as her forearm.

"Hi, Grady," she said.

Grady flipped himself around like he'd taken a stick of
dynamite up the ass and was hoping to extinguish the wick
in the snow.

Xhex kept the knife behind her thigh. "How you doing?"

"What . . ." He looked for both of her hands. When he
saw only one, he crabbed away from her on his hands and
feet, butt dragging over the ground.

Xhex followed, keeping a good yard between them. Going by the way Grady kept glancing over his shoulder, he
was getting ready to do a roll and bolt, and she was going to
stay in idle until he—

Bingo.

Grady lunged to the left, but she fell upon him, catching
his wrist at the top of its arc and letting his momentum
carry him against her hold. He ended up facedown with his
arm cranked behind his back, completely at her mercy.
Which of course she'd been born without. In a quick slash,
she knifed across one of his triceps, slicing through thick,
fluffy parka and thin, soft skin.

It was just to get him distracted, and it worked. He
howled and went to cover the wound.

Which gave her plenty of time to grab his left boot and
wrench it until he didn't care so much about what the hell
was up with his arm. Grady cried out and tried to relieve
the pressure by shifting around, but she planted a knee on
the small of his back and kept him in place as she broke his
ankle by twisting it until it snapped. Quick dismount and
another slash and she incapacitated his other side by slicing
the tendons of his thigh.

Cut the whining in half.

As Grady was tackled by pain, he lost his breath and
quieted down—until she started pulling him over to the
grave. He struggled the way he cried, though, with more
noise than effect. Once he was where she wanted him, she
slit the tendons in his other arm so that as much as he would
have loved to bat away her hands, he couldn't. Then she
flipped him over so he had a good view of heaven and
hauled up his parka.

She went for his belt at the same time she showed him her knife.

Men were funny. No matter how out of it they were, you got something long, sharp, and shiny anywhere near their primary brain and you got fireworks.

"No . . . !"

"Oh, yes." She brought the blade close to his face. "Very much yes."

He fought hard even with the pick-apart wounds she'd given, and she paused to enjoy the show.

"You're going to be dead before I leave you," she said as he flopped around. "But you and me are going to spend some quality time together before I take off. Not a lot, mind you. I have to go back to work. Good thing I'm quick."

She put her boot on his sternum to immobilize him, popped his button and fly, and yanked his pants down his thighs. "How long did it take for you to kill her, Grady? How long?"

In full panic, he moaned and thrashed, his blood staining the white snow red.

"How long, motherfucker?" She sliced through the waistband of his Emporio Armani boxers. "How long did she suffer?"

A moment later, Grady screamed so loudly, the sound wasn't even human; it was more the pealing cry of a black crow.

Xhex paused and looked over at the statue of the robed woman she'd spent so much time staring at during Chrissy's service. For a moment, the stone face seemed to have changed position, the lovely female looking not up to God, but across at Xhex.

Except that just wasn't possible, was it.

As Wrath stood behind his wall of Brothers, his ears tracked the distant sounds of the front door to Sal's opening and closing, isolating the subtle turn of hinges in between Sinatra's scooby-dooby-doos. Whatever they were waiting for had just shown up, and his body, his senses, his heart all downshifted like he was approaching a tight curve and preparing to power through.

His eyes cranked into better focus, the red room and the

white table and the backs of his brothers' heads becoming slightly clearer as iAm reappeared in the archway.

An extremely well-dressed male was with him.

Right, that guy had *glymera* stamped all over his natty ass. With his wavy blond hair parted on the side, he was rocking *The Great Gatsby*, his face so perfectly proportioned and balanced that he was downright beautiful. His black wool coat was tailored to fit a lean body, and in his hand, he carried a thin document case.

Wrath had never seen him before, but he seemed young for the situation he'd just walked into. Very young.

Nothing but a very expensive sacrificial lamb with a lot of style.

Rehvenge stalked over to the kid, the *symphath* palming his cane as if he might unsheathe the sword inside of it if Gatsby so much as took a deep breath. "You better start talking. Now."

Wrath stepped forward, shouldering between Rhage and Z, neither of whom was too happy about the position change. A quick slash of the hand stopped them from trying to maneuver in front of him.

"What's your name, son?" Last thing they needed was a dead body, and with Rehv nothing was ever certain.

The Gatsby lamb bowed somberly and straightened. When he spoke, it was in a voice that was surprisingly deep and sure, considering the number of autoloaders trained on his chest. "I am Saxton, son of Tyhm."

"I've seen your name before. You prepare bloodline reports."

"I do."

So, the council was really reaching down the bloodlines, weren't they? Not even the son of a council member.

"Who sent you, Saxton?"

"A dead man's lieutenant."

Wrath had no clue how the *glymera* had taken Montrag's death and he didn't care. As long as the message was out to anyone else in on the plot, that was all that mattered. "Why don't you say your piece."

The male put his case on the table and released the gold clip. The instant he did, Rehv pulled his red sword free and placed the point right against a pale throat. Saxton froze and looked around without moving his head.

"You might want to move slowly, son," Wrath murmured. "Lot of trigger-happy boys in this room, and you're everyone's favorite bull's-eye tonight."

That oddly deep and even voice spoke in measured words. "That's why I told him we had to do this."

"Do what." This came from Rhage, always the hothead—Rehv's sword notwithstanding, Hollywood was ready to jump on Gatsby whether or not any kind of weapon came out of those leather folds.

Saxton glanced at Rhage, then went back to focusing on Wrath. "The day after Montrag was assassinated—"

"Interesting word choice," Wrath drawled, wondering how much this guy knew, exactly.

"Of course it was an assassination. When you're murdered, usually you still have your eyes left in your skull."

Rehv smiled, revealing a matched set of oral daggers. "That depends on your murderer."

"Go on," Wrath prompted. "And, Rehv, relax with that sharpie of yours, if you don't mind."

The *symphath* backed off a little, but kept his weapon out, and Saxton eyed the guy before continuing. "The night Montrag was assassinated, this was delivered to my boss." Saxton opened his document case and took out a manila envelope. "It was from Montrag."

He put the thing facedown on the table to show that the wax seal had not been broken and stepped away.

Wrath looked at the envelope. "V, you mind doing the honors?"

V came forward and picked the thing up with his gloved hand. There was a soft tear and then a quiet whisper of papers sliding out.

Silence.

V replaced the documents, tucked the envelope into his waistband at the small of his back, and stared at Gatsby. "We supposed to think you didn't read this?"

"I didn't. My boss didn't. No one has since the chain of custody fell to him and me."

"Chain of custody? You a lawyer and not just a paralegal?"

"I'm apprenticing to be an attorney in the Old Law."

V leaned in and bared his fangs. "You are certain you did not read this, true?"

Saxton stared back at the Brother as if he were momentarily fascinated by the tattoos on V's temple. After a moment, he shook his head and spoke in that low voice. "I'm not interested in joining a list of people who've been found dead and eyeless on their carpets. Neither is my boss. The seal on that was made by Montrag's hand. Whatever he put in there hasn't been read since he let that hot wax drip."

"How you know it was Montrag who stuffed this?"

"It's his handwriting on the front. I know because I've seen a lot of his notes on documents. Plus it was brought to us by his personal *doggen* at his request."

As Saxton talked, Wrath read the male's emotions carefully, breathing through his nose. No deceit. Conscience was clean. Flyboy was attracted to V, but other than that? There was nothing. Not even fear. He was cautious, but calm.

"If you're lying," V said softly, "we will find out and find you."

"I don't doubt that for a second."

"What do you know, the lawyer has a brain." Vishous stepped back in line, palm returning to the butt of his gun.

Wrath wanted to know what was in the envelope, but he gathered that whatever was in there wasn't suitable for mixed company. "So where are your boss and his buddies, Saxton."

"None of them are coming." Saxton looked at the empty chairs. "They're all terrified. After what happened to Montrag, they are locked in their houses and staying there."

Good, Wrath thought. With the *glymera* displaying their talent for being cowards, he had one less thing to worry about.

"Thanks for coming, son."

Saxton took the dismissal for exactly what it was, reclipping his briefcase, bowing once again, and turning to go.

"Son?"

Saxton stopped and pivoted all the way around. "My lord?"

"You had to talk your boss into this, didn't you." Discreet silence was the response. "Then you give good advice, and I believe you—as far as you know, neither you nor your employer peeked in there and saw whatever it is. Word to the wise, though. I would find a new job. Things are going to get worse before they're better, and desperation makes shits out of even the most honorable of people. They've already sent you into the lion's mouth once. They will do it again."

Saxton smiled. "You ever need a personal lawyer, let me know. After all the trusts and estates and bloodline training I've had since this summer, I'm looking to branch out."

Another bow and the guy left with iAm, his head high and his stride even.

"What have you got there, V?" Wrath asked quietly.

"Nothing good, my lord. Nothing good."

As Wrath's vision dulled to its normal, unfocused uselessness, the last thing he saw with any clarity was V's icy eyes shifting over and locking on Rehvenge.

FORTY-NINE

As the unmarked police car left Pine Grove Cemetery, Lash became utterly focused on the *symphath* presence that had just revealed itself inside the gates.

"Get the fuck out of here," he told his men.

As he dematerialized, he went back toward the dead girl's grave in the rear corner of the—

The scream was out-of-control operatic, a soprano losing the grip on her voice, the pitch flying high above singing and into screeching. When Lash resumed his form, he was bitched that he'd just missed the fun and games . . . because it would have been worth seeing.

Grady was lying flat on his back with his pants wrenched down, bleeding from various places, most especially a fresh cut right across his esophagus. He was alive like a fly on the sill of a hot window, kinked arms and legs pinwheeling slowly.

Straightening up from a crouch was his killer: that butch bitch from ZeroSum. And unlike the dying fly, who was clueless to all but his own demise, she knew exactly when Lash came on the scene. She whipped around in a fighting stance, her face focused, the dripping knife in her hand steady, her thighs tight and ready to spring her hard body forward.

She was hot as fuck. Especially as she frowned in recognition.

"I thought you were dead," she said. "And I thought you were a vampire."

He smiled. "Surprise. And you've been keeping a secret of your own, haven't you."

"No, I never liked you, and that hasn't changed."

Lash shook his head and blatantly eyed her body. "You look really good in leather, you know that."

"You'd look better in a body cast."

He laughed. "Cheap shot."

"So's my target. Do the math."

Lash smiled and, with some vivid images, fanned his attraction into a full-blown hard-on because he knew she would sense it: He pictured her down on her knees in front of him, his cock in her mouth, his hands clamped on her head as he fucked her mouth until she gagged.

Xhex rolled her eyes. "Cheap. Porn."

"Nope. Future. Sex."

"Sorry, I'm not into Justin Timberlake. Or Ron Jeremy."

"We'll see about that." Lash nodded down at the human, whose writhing had slowed as if he were congealing in the cold. "So I'm afraid you owe me something."

"If it's a stab wound, I'm totally there."

"That"—he pointed to Grady—"was mine."

"You should upgrade your standards. That"—she echoed his stance—"is dog shit."

"Shit's good fertilizer."

"Then lemme lay you out under a rosebush and we'll see how you do."

Grady let out a moan and they both glanced at him. The bastard was in the final stages of death, his face the color of the frosted ground around his head, the blood flow from his wounds slowing.

Abruptly, Lash realized what had been shoved in his mouth and looked at Xhex. "Man . . . I could seriously go for a female like you, sin-eater."

Xhex drew her blade across the sharp edge of the headstone, Grady's blood getting transferred from the metal to the stone as if she were marking a payback. "You got balls, *lesser,* considering what I did to him. Or don't you want to keep your set?"

"I'm different."

"Smaller than him? Christ, how disappointing. Now, if you'll excuse me, I'm out of here." She lifted up her knife and waved, then disappeared.

Lash stared into the air where she had been, until Grady gurgled weakly like a drain on its last grab against a puddle of bathwater.

"Did you see her?" Lash said to the idiot. "What a female. I'm so getting some of that."

Grady's last breath came out the hole in his throat, because it had no other exit, given that his mouth was busy giving himself a blow job.

Lash put his hands on his hips and looked at the cooling body.

Xhex . . . he was going to have to make sure they crossed paths again. And he hoped she tried to tell the Brothers she'd seen him: An unsettled enemy was better than a collected one. He knew the Brotherhood would all wonder how in the hell the Omega had been able to turn a vampire into a *lesser*, but that was only a small part of the story.

He'd still get to serve up the punch line.

As Lash sauntered away into the cold night, he rearranged himself in his pants and decided he needed to go get laid. God knew he was in the mood.

While iAm was locking up Sal's front door, Rehvenge sheathed his red sword and looked at Vishous. The Brother was staring at him in a bad way.

"So what was in there?" Rehv said.

"You."

"Montrag try to say I was responsible for the plot to kill Wrath?" Not that it mattered if the guy had. Rehv had already proven which side he was on by having the motherfucker sliced.

Vishous shook his head slowly, then glanced over as iAm joined his brother.

Rehv spoke up sharply. "There is nothing they do not know about me."

"Well, then, here you go, sin-eater." V tossed the envelope onto the table. "Apparently, Montrag knew what you were. Which is undoubtedly why he went to you to try to kill Wrath. No one would believe it wasn't your idea and your idea alone, if what you are is revealed."

Rehv frowned and took out what looked to be an affidavit about how his stepfather had been killed. What. The. Fuck. Montrag's father had been in the house after the murder; that much Rehv knew. But the guy had gotten his mother's *hellren* not only to talk, but to testify? And then promptly done nothing with the intel?

Rehv thought back to a couple of days ago, to that meeting in Montrag's study ... and the guy's happy little comment that he knew what kind of male Rehv was.

He'd known, all right, and not about the drug dealing.

Rehv put the document back into the envelope. Shit, this got out and the promise he'd made to his mother was going to get blown to pieces.

"So what exactly's in there?" one of the Brothers asked.

Rehv tucked the envelope inside his sable. "Affidavit signed by my stepfather right before he died calling me out as a *symphath*. It's an original, going by the blood-inked siggy at the bottom. But how much you want to bet Montrag didn't send his only copy."

"Maybe it's faked," Wrath murmured.

Unlikely, Rehv thought. Too many details were correct about what had happened that night.

In a flash, he was back in the past, back to the night he had done the deed. His mother had had to be taken to Havers's clinic because she'd had one of her many "accidents." When it became clear she was going to be held for observation for a day, Bella had stayed with her, and Rehv had made up his mind.

He'd gone home, assembled the *doggen* in the staff quarters, and faced the collective pain of all who served his family. He could remember so clearly staring at the males and females of the house, meeting their eyes one by one. Many had come into the home because of his stepfather, but they stayed because of his mother. And they were looking to him to stop what had been going on for way too long.

He'd told them all to leave the mansion for an hour.

There had been no dissent, and each one had hugged him on the way out. They had all known what he was going to do, and it was their will, too.

Rehv had waited until the last *doggen* had left, and then he had gone into his stepfather's study and found the male poring over documents at his desk. In his fury, Rehv had taken care of the male the old-fashioned way, measuring blow for blow, exacting the pain inflicted upon his mother

first before ushering the son of a bitch to his royal, unde-
served reward.

When the front doorbell had rung, Rehv had assumed it
was the staff coming back and giving him notice so that
they could credibly state that they hadn't seen the killer at
work. Needing one last fuck-you, he'd fist-cracked his stepfather's skull hard enough to knock the bastard *shellan*-
beater's spine out of alignment.

Moving quickly, Rehv had stepped free of the body,
willed the front door to the mansion open, and left out of
the French doors in the back. Having the *doggen* come
home to "find" the body was perfect, as the subspecies was
by nature docile and would never be implicated in the violence. Besides, by that time, his *symphath* side was roaring,
and he'd needed to get himself under control.

Which, back in those days, hadn't included dopamine.
He'd had to use pain to tame the sin-eater in him.

Everything had seemed like it had fallen into place . . .
until he'd learned at the clinic that Montrag's father had
found the body. Turned out to be no big deal, though. As far
as the male had said at the time, Rehm had walked in, come
upon the scene, and called Havers. By the time the doctor
had arrived, the staff had returned, and blamed their group
absence on the fact that it was the summer solstice and they
had been out preparing for the ceremonies that would be
held that week.

Montrag's dad had played this well, and so had the son.
Any emotional disturbances Rehv had picked up either
back then or during that meeting mere days ago he'd
chalked up to fresh death and assassination, both of which
had been in the cards.

God, it was clear, so clear, what Montrag had been doing
in having Rehv arrange to kill Wrath. After the deed was
done, he'd been ready to come out with the affidavit exposing Rehv as both a murderer and a *symphath* so that when
Rehv was deported, he could assume control of not just the
council but the whole race.

Nice.

Too bad it didn't work out as he'd planned. Brought a
tear to the fucking eye, didn't it.

"Yeah, there's gotta be more affidavits," Rehv murmured.
"No one sends their only live copy out into the world."

"Would be worth a visit to that house," Wrath said. "Montrag's heirs and assigns get hold of something like this, we've all got problems, feel me?"

"He died without issue, but yeah, there's some of his bloodline around somewhere. And I'm going to make sure that they don't find out about this."

No way in hell anyone was making him break the vow he'd made to his mother.

Not gonna happen.

FIFTY

As Ehlena did her shopping at the twenty-four-hour Hannaford supermarket she always went to, she should have been in a better mood. Things couldn't have been left on a sweeter note with Rehv. When he'd had to go to his meeting, he'd taken a quick shower and let her pick out his clothes and even do up his tie. Then he'd wrapped his arms around her and they'd just stood together, heart-to-heart.

Eventually, she'd walked him outside into the hall and waited with him for the elevator to come. Its arrival had been announced on a chime and a slide of the double doors, and he'd held the things open to kiss her once, twice. A third time. Finally, he'd stepped back and as the twin doors shut, he'd held up his phone, pointed to it, and pointed to her.

The fact that he would be calling her made the good-bye much easier. And she loved the idea that the black suit and crisp white shirt and bloodred tie he had on were what she had chosen for him.

So, yeah, she should be happier. Especially because her financial squeeze had been eased a little with the loan from the First Rehvenge Bank & Trust Company.

But Ehlena was jumpy as hell.

She stopped in the juice aisle, in front of the neat rows of Ocean Spray Cran-everything-and-his-uncles, and looked over her shoulder. Just more juice on the left and arrangements of granola bars and cookies on the right. Farther down, there were the checkouts, most of which were closed, and beyond that, the dark glass windows of the store.

Someone was following her.

Ever since she'd gone back into Rehv's penthouse, gotten dressed herself, and dematerialized off the terrace after locking up.

Four CranRas bottles went into her cart, and then she headed for the cereal aisle and across to the paper towels and the toilet paper. In the meat department, she picked up a ready-made roasted chicken that looked like it had been taxidermied rather than cooked, but at this point, she just needed some protein she didn't have to oven-up herself. Then it was steak for her father. Milk. Butter. Eggs.

The only disadvantage to checking out after midnight was that all the U-Scans were closed, so she had to wait behind a guy with cart full of Hungry-Man frozen dinners. As the attendant swept the Salisbury steaks across the scanner, Ehlena stared out the glass storefront wondering whether she was losing her mind.

"You know how to cook these?" the guy asked her as he held up one of the thin boxes.

Evidently, he'd misread her forward fixation as having anything to do with him and was looking for someone to heat his meat, literally: The human's eyes were hot, and roaming over her, and all she could think of was what Rehvenge would do to the guy.

This made her smile. "Read the box."

"You could read it for me."

She kept her voice level and bored-sounding. "Sorry, I don't think my boyfriend would appreciate that."

The human seemed a bit crestfallen as he shrugged and handed his frozen dinner over to the girl behind the cash register.

Ten minutes later, Ehlena rolled her cart out of the electric doors and was greeted by a nasty, slapping cold that made her huddle up in her parka. Fortunately, the cab she'd taken to the store was right where it was supposed to be, and she was relieved.

"You need help?" the cabbie asked through the window he put down.

"No, thanks." She looked around as she put her plastic

bags in the backseat, wondering what in the hell the driver would do if a *lesser* jumped out from behind a truck and played Bad Santa on their asses.

When Ehlena got in next to the groceries and the driver hit the gas, she searched the eaves of the store and the half dozen cars that were parked as close to the entrance as you could get. Mr. Hungry-Man was farting around in his van, his interior light shining down on his face as he lit a cigarette.

Nothing. Nobody.

She forced herself to settle against the seat and decided she was nuts. No one was watching her. No one was after her—

Ehlena's hand went to her throat, a sudden dread overtaking her. Oh, God . . . what if she had what her father suffered from? What if this paranoia was the first of many episodes? What if . . .

"You okay back there?" the driver asked as he stared into the rearview mirror. "You seem shaky."

"Just cold."

"Here, lemme hit you with some hot air."

As a warm blast blew on her face, she glanced out the back window. No car in sight. And *lessers* couldn't dematerialize, so . . . she was schizophrenic?

Christ, she'd almost rather it be a slayer.

Ehlena had the driver drop her as close to the back of the rented house as possible and gave him a little extra in the tip for being so nice.

"I'll wait until you get inside," the guy said.

"Thanks." And man, she meant that.

With two plastic bags hanging from each hand, she walked quickly to the door and had to put her load down, because like an idiot she'd been so busy wigging out that she hadn't gotten her keys ready. Just as she put her hand into her purse to do the rummage-and-curse routine, the taxi took off.

She looked up as its taillights turned the corner. What the—

"Hello."

Ehlena froze. The presence was right behind her. And she knew exactly who it was.

As she pivoted around, she saw a tall female with black

hair and a lot of robes and glowing eyes. Ah, yes . . . this was Rehvenge's other—

"Half," the female finished. "I am his other half. And I am sorry your taxi driver had to leave so quickly."

On instinct, Ehlena covered her thoughts with the image of a display from Hannaford's: a five-foot-high, three-foot-wide display of red Pringles cans.

The female frowned as if she had no clue what she was finding in the cerebral cortex she was trying to invade, but then she smiled. "You have nothing to fear from me. I just thought I would share some things with you about that male you fucked back in his penthouse."

Screw the snack-food thought facade; that didn't go far enough. To keep calm, Ehlena needed all her professional training. This situation was a trauma case, she told herself. A bloody vampire body that had just been wheeled in before her, and she had to put aside all fear and all emotion to deal with the situation.

"Did you hear what I said?" the female drawled, her speech pattern nothing that Ehlena had ever heard before, the Ss extended into hisses. "I watched you through the glass, right until he pulled out at the end. Do you want to know why he did that?"

Ehlena kept her mouth shut and started wondering how she could get at the pepper spray in her pocketbook. Somehow, though, she didn't think that would have any effect—

Holy shit, were those . . . live scorpions in those earlobes?

"He's not like you." The female smiled with an evil satisfaction. "And not just because he's a drug lord. He's also not a vampire." When Ehlena's brows twitched, the female laughed. "You didn't know either of those?"

Evidently her Pringles and her training weren't completely doing the job. "I don't believe you."

"ZeroSum. Downtown. He owns it. You know the place? Probably not, as you don't seem like the type who would go there—which is no doubt why he likes to fuck you. Let me tell you what he sells. Human women. Drugs of all kinds. And you know why? Because he's like me, not you." The female leaned in close, her eyes flashing brightly. "And do you know what I am?"

A flaming bitch, Ehlena thought.

"I'm a *symphath*, little girl. That's what he and I are. And he's mine."

Ehlena started to wonder if she was going to die tonight, here on the back stoop with four bags of groceries at her feet. Although it wouldn't be because this lying female was actually a *symphath*—it would be because anyone who was crazy enough to suggest such a thing was absolutely capable of murder.

The female continued, her voice strident. "You want to really know him? Go to that club and find him there. Make him tell you the truth and know what you let into your body, little one. And remember this, he is all mine, emotionally, sexually, everything he is, is *mine*."

A three-knuckled finger brushed down Ehlena's cheek, and then just like that the female was gone.

Ehlena shook so badly she momentarily turned into a solid, the trembling so deep in her muscles she was rendered motionless. The cold was what saved her. As an icy blast shot down the sidewalk, it pushed her forward, and she caught herself before she teetered over onto her groceries.

The key to the house, when she finally found it, went into the lock no better than the one she'd tried to use on the ambulance. Skipping . . . skipping . . . skipping . . .

Finally.

She cranked the lock free, and all but threw the bags inside before slamming herself in and locking everything tight, including the interior dead bolts and the security chain.

On weak legs, she went and sat down at the kitchen table. When her father called up about the noise, she said it was the wind and prayed he wouldn't come up to see her.

In the ensuing quiet, Ehlena didn't feel any presence outside of the house, but the idea someone like that knew about her and Rehv and where she lived— Oh, God, that crazy female had *watched* them.

Bolting up, she rushed to the kitchen sink and ran the tap to cover the noise in case she got sick. Hoping to settle her stomach, she put her palms together, captured some cool water, and had a few swallows before washing her face.

The drink and rinse cleared her head a little.

The claims the female had made were totally and bizarrely outlandish, way far outside the realm of reality—and going by her glowing eyes, she clearly had an ax to grind.

Rehv wasn't any of those things. Drug lord. *Symphath*. Pimp. Come on.

Sure as hell you didn't take anything so much as what a male's favorite color was from some stalker ex-girlfriend type. Especially given that Rehv had made it clear the two weren't together, and intimated from the get-go that the chick was trouble. And no wonder he hadn't wanted to go into it. No one wanted to admit to somebody they were getting involved with that they had lurking in their past a bunny-boiling, I'm-not-going-to-be-*ignored*-Dan sort of psychotic.

So what did she do now? Well, that was obvious. She was going to tell Rehv. Not in a freaked-out, keep-the-drama-rolling kind of way, but more like, *Here is what happened and you need to be aware that this person is seriously unstable.*

Ehlena felt good with the plan.

Until she tried to get her phone out of her purse and realized she was still shaking. Her mind's response might be logical, her rationalizations might be fine and dandy, but her adrenaline was cooking along like crazy, and not really interested in all the sense she was talking into herself.

What was she doing? Oh . . . right. Rehvenge. Call Rehvenge.

As she hit his number, she started relaxing a little. They were going to work this out.

She was momentarily surprised when she got voice mail, but then remembered he'd had that meeting to go to. She almost hung up, but she wasn't the kind who beat around the bush, and there was no reason to wait.

"Hey, Rehv, I just got a visit from this . . . female. She was talking a lot of craziness about you. I just . . . well, I thought you should know. To be honest, she's freaky. Anyway, maybe you can call me and talk to me about this? I'd really appreciate it. Bye."

She hung up and stared at the phone, praying he got back to her fast.

* * *

Wrath had made a promise to Beth and he kept it. Even though it killed him.

When he and the Brothers finally left Sal's, he went straight home, along with his two thousand pounds of personal guard. He was twitchy and fist-hungry, teed up and pissed off, but he'd told his *shellan* he was not going to go out in the field after his little blind episode, and he wasn't.

Trust was something you had to build, and considering the hole he'd jackhammered into the foundation of their relationship, it was going to take him a lot of work just to get back to ground level.

Besides, if he couldn't fight, there was something else he could do to take the edge off.

As the Brotherhood walked into the foyer, the sound of boots echoed, and Beth shot out of the billiards room as if that were what she'd been waiting for. With a leap, she was in his arms before he could blink, and it was good.

After a quick hug, she stepped back and held him at arm's length, looking him over. "You're okay? What happened? Who showed? How—"

The Brothers all started talking at once, although not about the meeting that hadn't happened. The bunch of them were bidding over territory to hunt during the three hours they had left to be out and about.

"Let's go to the study," Wrath said over the din. "I can't hear myself think."

As he and Beth hit the stairs, he called out to his brothers, "Thanks for having my back once again."

The group stopped and turned to face him. After a beat of silence, they formed a half circle around the foot of the grand staircase, each making a thick fist with his weapon hand. With a great *whoomp!* of a war cry, they went down on their right knee and slammed their heavy knuckles into the mosaic floor. The sound was thunder and bass drums and bomb explosions, ricocheting outward, filling all the rooms of the mansion.

Wrath stared at them, seeing their heads bent, their broad backs curled, their powerful arms planted. They had each gone to that meeting prepared to take a bullet for him, and that would ever be true.

Behind Tohr's smaller form, Lassiter, the fallen angel, stood with a straight spine, but he wasn't cracking any jokes at this reaffirmation of allegiance. Instead, he was back to staring at the damn ceiling. Wrath glanced up at the mural of warriors silhouetted against a blue sky and could see nothing much of the pictures that he'd been told were there.

Getting back with the program, he said in the Old Language, *"No stronger allies, no greater friends, no better fighters of honor could a king behold than these assembled afore me, mine brothers, mine blood."*

A rolling growl of ascent lifted as the warriors got to their feet again, and Wrath nodded to each one of them. He had no more words to offer as his throat had abruptly choked, but they didn't seem to need anything else. They stared at him with respect and gratitude and purpose, and he accepted their enormous gifts with grave appreciation and resolve. This was the ages-old covenant between king and subjects, the pledges on both sides made with the heart and carried out by the sharp mind and the strong body.

"God, I love you guys," Beth said.

There was a lot of deep laughter, and then Hollywood said, "You want us to stab the floor for you again? Fists are for kings, but the queen gets the daggers."

"I wouldn't want you to take chips out of this beautiful floor. Thank you, though."

"Say the word and it's nothing but rubble."

Beth laughed. "Be still, my heart."

The Brothers came over and kissed the Saturnine Ruby that rode on her finger, and as each paid his honor, she gave him a gentle stroke of the hair. Except for Zsadist, who she smiled tenderly at.

"Excuse us, boys," Wrath said. "Little quiet time, feel me?"

There was a ripple of male approval, which Beth took in stride—and with a blush—and then it was time for some privacy.

As Wrath headed upstairs with his *shellan*, he was feeling like things were getting back to normal. Okay, yeah, there were assassination plots and political drama and *lessers* everywhere, but that *was* business as usual. And right now he had his brothers shoulder-to-shoulder and his beloved mate under his arm and the people and *doggen* he gave a shit about as safe as he could make them.

Beth laid her head on his pec and her hand on his waist. "I'm really glad everyone's okay."

"Funny, I was thinking the same thing."

He ushered her into the study and shut both doors, the warmth of the fire a balm ... and an enticement. As she walked over to the paper-strewn desk, he tracked the sway of her hips.

With a flick of the wrist, he locked them in together.

While he came over to her, Beth reached out to try to make some order of the documents. "So what hap—"

Wrath pressed his hips into her ass and whispered, "I need to be in you."

His *shellan* gasped and let her head fall back onto his shoulder. "Oh, God ... yes ..."

Growling, he slipped a hand around to her breast, and as her breath caught, he rolled his cock against her. "I don't want to take my time with this."

"Me neither."

"Lean on the desk."

Watching her tilt and arch her back nearly made him curse. And then she spread her feet apart and a *fuuuuck* slipped out.

Which was exactly what he was going to do.

Wrath canned the lamp on the desk so there was only the dancing golden light of the fire to illuminate them, and his hands were rough as he ran them over her hips in anticipation. Crouching behind her, he dragged his fangs down her spine and made her shift her weight onto one foot so he could pop off her stillie and shuck her Sevens free. He was too impatient to do the other side, though—especially as he looked up and saw her deliciously unfussy black panties.

Right. Change in plan.

The penetration was going to wait.

At least the one with his cock.

Staying on his haunches, he removed his weapons with both care and speed, making sure the safeties were in place on his guns and his blades were clipped into their holster. If the door wasn't locked, they would have been put in the combination gun closet, no matter how hard up he was for his female. With Nalla around, no one in the house was running the risk of Z and Bella's daughter picking up any kind of weapon. Ever.

Disarmed, he took off his wraparounds and tossed them onto the desk, then slid his hands up the backs of his mate's smooth thighs. Splitting her wide, he arched up and put himself between her legs, lifting his mouth to the cotton that covered the core he was going to be coming into very soon.

He pressed his mouth to her, feeling the heat through what she wore, her scent driving him wild, his cock kicking so hard in his leathers, he wasn't sure whether or not he'd just orgasmed. Nuzzling and then licking at her through the panties wasn't enough ... so he took the cotton between his teeth and rubbed at her sex with it, knowing damn well that lateral seam was massaging right at the spot he was dying to suck her off at.

There was a *thump-thump* as her palms repositioned on the desk and a rustle as papers flitted down to the floor.

"Wrath ..."

"What," he murmured against her, working her with his nose. "You don't like?"

"Shut up and get back to doing—"

His tongue slipping under the panties cut her off ... and made him have to slow himself down. She was so slick and wet and soft and willing, it was all he could do to keep himself from hauling her on the rug and going at her deep and hard.

And then they'd both miss out on the fun of anticipation.

Moving the cotton aside with his hand, he kissed her pink flesh, then delved in. She was oh, so ready for him, and he knew it because of the honey that he swallowed as he dragged upward in a long, slow lick.

But it wasn't enough, and holding the panties to the side was distracting.

With his fang, he punctured them, then split them apart right up the middle, leaving the two halves to hang off her hips. His palms went up to her ass and squeezed hard as he quit fooling around and got busy working out his female with his mouth. He knew exactly what she liked best, the sucking and the licking and the going in with his tongue.

Closing his eyes, he took it all in, the scent and the taste and the feel of her shuddering against him as she peaked and came apart. Behind the fly of his leathers, his cock was screaming for attention, the rasp of the buttons not nearly sufficient to satisfy what it was demanding, but tough shit. His erection was going to have to chill for a while, because this was too sweet to stop anytime soon.

When Beth's knees wobbled, he took her down to the floor and stretched one of her legs up, keeping to his pace while shoving her fleece to her neck and putting his hand under her bra. As she orgasmed again, she grabbed onto one of the desk legs, pulling hard and bracing her free foot into the rug. His pursuit pushed them both farther and farther beneath where he discharged his kingly duties until he had to crouch down to fit his shoulders.

Eventually her head was out the other side and she was gripping the pansy-ass chair he sat in and dragging it with her.

As she cried out his name once more, he prowled up her body and glared at the stupid, nancy chair. "I need something heavier to sit in."

Last coherent thing he said. His body found the entrance to hers with an ease that spoke of all the practice they'd had and . . . Oh, *yeah,* still as good as the first time. Wrapping his arms around her, he rode her hard, and she was right there with him as the storm rolling through his body gathered in his balls until they stung. Together, he and his *shellan* moved as one, giving, receiving, going faster and faster until he came and kept going and came again and kept going until something hit his face.

In full animal mode, he growled and swiped at it with his fangs.

It was the drapes.

He'd managed to fuck them out from under the desk, past the chair, and over to the wall.

Beth burst out laughing and so did he, and then they were cradling each other. Easing onto his side, Wrath held his mate against his chest, and tugged her turtleneck and fleece back into place so she wouldn't be cold.

"So what did happen at the meeting?" she said eventually.

"None of the council showed." He hesitated, wondering where the lines were with respect to Rehv.

"Not even Rehv?"

"He was there, but the others didn't make it up. Evidently, the council is scared of me, which is not a bad thing." Abruptly, he took her hands. "Listen, ah, Beth . . ."

Tension threaded through her reply. "Yes?"

"Honesty, right?"

"Right."

"Something did go down. It involves Rehvenge . . . his life . . . but I don't feel comfortable telling you the ins and outs because it's his biz. Not mine."

She exhaled. "If it doesn't involve you or the Brotherhood—"

"It does only because it puts us in a difficult position." And Beth would be in the same tight spot if she were in on the info. The thing was, protecting the identity of a known *symphath* was only half the problem. Last time Wrath had checked, Bella didn't have a clue what her brother was. So Beth would have to keep the secret from her friend, too.

His *shellan* frowned. "If I ask exactly how it presents an issue for you guys, I'm going to know what it is, right?"

Wrath nodded and waited.

She ran her hand down his jaw. "And you would tell me, wouldn't you."

"Yeah." He wouldn't like it, but he would. Without hesitation.

"Okay . . . I'm not going to ask." She leaned up to kiss him. "And I'm glad you gave me the choice."

"See, I'm trainable." He held her face and pressed his mouth to hers a couple of times, feeling the smile that lit her lips by the way the stroking sensation changed.

"Speaking of training, how'd you like some food?" she said.

"Oh, how I love you."

"I'll deliver."

"I think I'd better clean you up first." He whipped off his black shirt and carefully stroked up her thighs to her core.

"You're doing more than cleaning me up," she drawled as he let his hand rub between her thighs.

He surged up, making a move to mount her again. "Can you blame me? Mmmm . . ."

She laughed and held him back. "Food. Then more sex."

He nibbled at her mouth, thinking that eating was so overrated. But then her tummy rumbled, and he was instantly all about getting her fed, his instinct to protect and provide overriding the sexual one.

Putting his wide palm on her flat belly, he said, "Let me get it for—"

"No, I want to wait on you." She touched his face again. "Stay here. I won't be long."

As she got to her feet, he rolled onto his back and stuffed his well-used, but still very stiff cock in his leathers.

Beth bent down to pick up her jeans, giving him a hell of a view and causing him to wonder if he could wait even five minutes before getting into her again.

"You know what I feel like?" she murmured as she pulled her Sevens into place.

"Like you've been making love with your *hellren* and are about to do some more of that good ol' bump-and-grind?"

God, he loved making her laugh.

"Well, yes," she said, "but when it comes to food . . . I want homemade stew."

"Is it already made?" Please let it be—

"There's beef left over from— Look at that face!"

"Rather have less of you in the kitchen and more of you on my . . ." Okay, he so wasn't finishing that sentence.

She seemed to filled in the blank just fine, though. "Hmm, I'll be fast."

"You do that, *leelan*, and I'll give you a dessert that'll make your head spin."

She showed him some serious hip sway as she went across the room, a sexy little dance that left him growling, and in the doorway, she paused and looked back at him, the brighter light from the hall illuminating her.

And what do you know, his blurry vision gave him the loveliest parting gift: In the glow, he saw her long dark hair down over her shoulders and her flushed face and her tall body with all its curves.

"You are so beautiful," he said quietly.

Beth positively glowed at him, the scent of her joy and happiness intensifying until all he smelled was the fragrance of night-blooming roses that was hers alone.

Beth brought her fingertips to the mouth he'd ravished and blew him a soft, slow kiss. "I'll be right back."

"And I'll see you then." Although considering how

sexed-up he was, they were both likely to just see more under-the-desk time.

After she left, he lay for a bit, his keen ears listening to her going down the grand staircase. Then he dragged himself off the floor, put the pansy chair back where it had been, and parked his ass behind the desk. He reached for his wraparounds to spare his eyes the dim light of the fire and let his head fall back—

The knock on the door made his temples sting in frustration. Man, he couldn't get two seconds of peace, could he . . . and by the scent of Turkish tobacco, he knew who it was.

"Come in, V."

As the Brother entered, the scent of that tobacco joined the subtle smoke of hardwood burning across the room.

"We have a problem," Vishous said.

Wrath closed his eyes and rubbed the bridge of his nose, hoping like hell his headache wasn't pulling in for the whole night, like his brain was a TraveLodge. "Talk to me."

"Someone e-mailed us about Rehvenge. Gave us twenty-four hours to deliver him to the *symphath* colony or they're going blow his cover to the *glymera* and make it clear that you and all of us knew about his identity and failed to take action."

Wrath's eyes popped open. "What the fuck?"

"I'm already digging around on the e-mail addy. With some broken-field running through IT land, I should be able to access the account and find out who it is."

"Shit . . . so much for that document not being read by anyone else." Wrath swallowed hard, the pressure in his head making him nauseous. "Look, contact Rehv, tell him what was sent. See what he says. The *glymera*'s scattered and scared, but if that kind of shit gets out to them, we'd have no choice but to do something—otherwise we could have a riot on our hands not just of the aristocracy, but of the civilians as well."

"Roger that. I'll report back."

"Move fast."

"Hey, you okay?"

"Yeah. Go call Rehv. God*damn* it."

After the door closed again, Wrath groaned. The gentle

light of the fire made the agony at his temples worse, but he wasn't into putting the flames out: Total darkness was not an option, not after this afternoon's little wake-up call, when midnight was all he had.

Shutting his lids, he tried to get past the pain. Little rest. That was all he needed.

Just a little rest.

FIFTY-ONE

When Xhex returned to ZeroSum, she went in the back door to the VIP section and kept her hands in her pockets. Thanks to her vampire side, she didn't leave fingerprints, but bloody hands were bloody hands.

And she had Grady's shit on her pants as well.

But that was why, even in these modern times, the club had an old-fashioned, fire-breathing furnace in the basement.

She did not check in with anyone, just slipped into Rehv's office and headed through to his bedroom beyond. Fortunately, there was plenty of time to change and clean up, though, because it was going to take the CPD a while to find Grady. The command she'd given to de la Cruz was to leave for the whole night—although with a guy like him, it was possible that his conscience could override the thought she'd planted. Still, she had at minimum a couple of hours.

In Rehv's apartment, she locked the door and went directly to the shower. After she turned on the hot water, she disarmed and put all of her clothes and her boots down a chute that dumped directly into the furnace.

Fuck the Maytag man. That was the kind of laundry bin people like her needed.

She took her long blade under the water with her and washed her body and the knife with equal care. Her cilices were still on, the soap stinging where the barbed bands dug into her thighs, and she waited until the pain faded before releasing one and then the other—

The wet agony was so great it numbed her legs cold and shot up into her chest, causing her heart to palpitate. As an exhale barreled free of her mouth, she sagged against the marble, knowing there was a good chance she was going to pass out.

Somehow she kept conscious.

Watching all the red bloom around the drain beneath her feet, she thought of Chrissy's dead body. In that human morgue, the woman's blood had been black and brown under her mottled gray flesh. Grady's had run the color of wine, but sure as shit he was going to look just like the girl he killed in a couple of hours—dead on a stainless-steel table with what had once drummed through his veins setting like concrete.

She'd done her job well.

The tears came from nowhere and everywhere, and she despised them.

Ashamed of her weakness, Xhex covered her face with her hands, even though she was alone.

Someone had tried to avenge her death once.

Only she hadn't been dead—just wishing for it while her body was worked on with all kinds of "instruments." And the whole chivalrous, hero-on-a-white-horse act hadn't gone well for her avenger. Murhder had been driven mad. He'd thought he was rescuing a vampire, but surprise! He was actually risking his life to bring home a *symphath*.

Oops. Guess she forgot to tell her lover that little part.

She wished she had revealed herself. Considering what she was, he'd had a right to know, and maybe if he had, he'd still be in the Brotherhood. Maybe mated to a nice female. Definitely wouldn't have lost his sanity and taken off for God only knew where.

Avenging was dangerous business, wasn't it. In the case of Chrissy, it was fine. Everything had worked out. But sometimes what you sought to honor wasn't worth the effort.

Xhex hadn't been, and it hadn't just cost Murhder his mind. And Rehv was still paying for her mistakes.

She thought of John Matthew and wished like hell she hadn't fucked him. Murhder had been a casual thing for her. John Matthew? Going by the ache in the center of her chest every time she thought of him, she suspected he was a lot more than that—which was why she was trying to lock out of her mind what had happened between them back at her basement place.

The problem was how John Matthew had been with her. The tenderness he had shown threatened to crack her in half, his emotions everything that was soft and gentle and respectful . . . loving—even though he knew what she was. She'd had to shut him down hard because unless he'd cut that shit, she'd been in danger of pressing her lips to his and losing herself completely.

John Matthew was her well of soul, as the *symphaths* called it, or her *pyrocant*, to the vampires. Her essential weakness.

And she was very weak when it came to him.

With a wave of pain, she pictured him on that security monitor with his hands all over Gina. Like the barbed bands she wore, the image overwhelmed her with agony, and she couldn't help thinking that she deserved what it was going to be like to watch him drown himself in mindless, empty sex.

She turned off the shower, picked up her cilices and the knife from the slick marble flooring, and stepped out, dumping all her metal in a sink to drip-dry.

As she put one of Rehv's superluxurious black towels to use, she wished it—

"Were sandpaper, right?" Rehv drawled from the doorway.

Xhex paused with the towel across her back and looked into the mirror. Rehv was lounging against the jamb, his sable coat turning him into a great bear of a male, his mohawk and his sharp purple eyes testifying to his warrior side in spite of all the metrosexual clothes he wore.

"How did tonight go?" she asked, putting one foot up on the counter and running the black terry cloth down to her ankle.

"I might ask you the same thing. What the fuck's going on with you?"

"Nothing." She put her other leg up. "So how was the meeting?"

Rehv kept his eyes on hers, not because he was respecting the fact that she was buck-ass naked, but because he honestly didn't care one way or another. Hell, he'd be the same with Trez or iAm flashing their ass: She'd long ago ceased to be female to him even though they fed from each other.

Maybe that was what she liked about John Matthew. He'd looked at her and touched her and treated her like she was a female. Like she were precious.

Not because she wasn't as strong as he was, but because she was rare and special—

Christ. Spare her from the estrogen. And that would all be in the past tense now, anyway.

"The meeting?" she prompted.

"Fine. Be that way. As for the council? They didn't show, but this did." Rehv took a long flat envelope out of his breast pocket and tossed it onto the counter. "I'll let you read it later. Needless to say my secret's been known for quite some time. Stepdad blabbed on the way to the Fade, and it was a miracle the shit didn't get out before now."

"Son of a bitch."

"That's an affidavit, by the way. Not some kind of random scribble on the back of a napkin." Rehv shook his head. "I'm going to have to get into that house of Montrag's. See if there are any more copies around."

"I can do it."

Those amethyst eyes narrowed. "No offense, but I'll pass on the offer. You don't look right."

"That's just because you haven't seen me without clothes on in a while. Get me in leather and you'll be back to knowing I'm a hard-ass."

Rehv's eyes went down to the ragged wounds around her thighs. "Hard to imagine you got on me about what I was doing to my arm, considering what those pins of yours look like."

She covered herself up with the towel. "I'll go over to Montrag's place today."

"Why were you taking a shower?"

"Because I was all bloody."

The smile that stretched Rehv's mouth and revealed his fangs was all about the throw-down. "You found Grady."

"Yup."

"Niiiiiiice."

"We should expect a visit from the CPD sometime very soon."

"Looking forward to it."

Xhex patted dry her cilices and her knife, then walked past Rehv and went into the two square feet of his closet that were hers. Taking out a fresh pair of leathers and a black muscle shirt, she glanced over her shoulder.

"You mind giving me a little privacy."

"You're putting those damn things on again?"

"How's your dopamine supply?"

Rehv chuckled and headed for the door. "I'll take care of searching Montrag's place. You've done enough dirty work for other people lately."

"I can handle it."

"Doesn't mean you should have to." He reached into his pocket and took out his cell phone. "Fuck, I forgot to turn this thing back on."

When the screen lit up, he looked down and his emotions . . . flickered.

His emotions actually flickered.

Maybe it was because her cilices were off and her *symphath* side didn't take long to come forward, but she couldn't keep herself from focusing on him hard, the weakness he sported making her curious.

What she noticed, though, was not so much his emotional grid . . . but the fact that his scent was different.

"You've fed from someone," she said.

Rehv froze, giving himself away by the stillness of that big body of his.

"Don't even try to lie," she murmured. "I can smell it."

Rehv shrugged, and she got ready for a whole lot of no-big-dealing. He even opened his mouth, his hard face assuming the bored expression he used to distance people.

Except he didn't say a thing. Didn't seem to be able to muster the blow-off.

"Wow." Xhex shook her head. "Serious stuff, huh."

Ignoring the question was evidently the best he could do. "When you're ready, let's meet with Trez and iAm and do the status update before closing."

Rehv turned on his loafers and went back out into the office.

Funny, she thought to herself, as she picked up one of

the steel bands and got ready to crank it around her thigh, she'd never expected to see him like that. Ever.

Made her wonder who it was. And how much the female knew about him.

Rehv went to his desk and sat down, phone in his hand. Ehlena had called and left a message, but instead of wasting time to listen to it, he called up her contact info and—

The call that came through was the only one that would have diverted him from finishing the dial action. He answered and said, "Which Brother am I talking to?"

"Vishous."

"What's doing, man."

"Nothing good, true?"

The flat tone of the guy's voice made Rehv think of car accidents. Bad ones that required the Jaws of Life to free bodies. "Tell me."

The Brother talked and talked and talked. E-mail. Cover blown. Deportation.

There must have been a long stretch of silence at that point, because Rehv heard his name. "You there? Rehvenge? Yo, man?"

"Yeah, I'm here." Kind of. He was a little distracted by the dull roar in his head, like the building he was in was caving in all around him.

"Did you hear what I asked you?"

"Ah . . . no." The roaring sound grew so loud, he was sure the club had been bombed and the walls were crumbling and the roof coming down.

"I tried to trace the e-mail and I almost think it's coming from an IP address up north near the colony, if not actually within it. I really don't think this came from a vampire at all. Do you know anyone up there who might try to blow your cover?"

So the princess had lost interest in playing blackmail games. "No."

Now it was V's turn to be quiet. "Are you sure?"

"Yes."

The princess had decided to call him home. And if he didn't go, she would absolutely e-mail everyone in the *glymera* and implicate Wrath and the Brotherhood while she revealed Rehv's secret. Coupled with the affidavit that had been sprung tonight?

Life as he knew it was over.

Not that the Brotherhood needed to know that.

"Rehv?"

In a dead voice, he said, "It's just fallout from the Montrag shit. Don't worry about it."

"What the hell happened?"

Xhex's sharp voice from the bedroom doorway helped him focus, and he looked over at her. As he met her stare, her strong body and sharp gray eyes were as familiar to him as his own reflection, and the same was true with Kim for her . . . so she knew by the look on his face exactly what was doing.

The color slowly drained out of her cheeks. "What did she do? What did that cunt do to you?"

"I gotta go, V. Thanks for calling."

"Rehvenge?" the Brother cut in. "Look, buddy, why don't I keep trying to track it—"

"Waste of time. No one up there knows. Trust me."

Rehv ended the call, and before Xhex could jump in, he dialed voice mail and picked up Ehlena's message. He knew what she was going to say, though. Knew exactly—

"Hey, Rehv, I just got a visit from this . . . female. She was talking a lot of craziness about you. I just . . . well, I thought you should know. To be honest, she's freaky. Anyway, maybe you can call me and talk to me about this? I'd really appreciate it. Bye."

He deleted the message, hit *end*, and put the cell phone down on the desk, lining it up with the black leather blotter so that the LG was perfectly vertical.

Xhex came over, and as she did, there was a sharp knock and someone came in. "Give us a minute, Trez," he heard her say. "Take Rally with you, and don't let anyone in here."

"What hap—"

"Now. Please."

Rehvenge stared at the phone, only dimly aware of some shuffling and the door clicking shut.

"You hear that?" he said quietly.

"Hear what?" Xhex asked as she came and knelt down next to his chair.

"That sound."

"Rehv, what did she do?"

He looked over into her eyes and saw his mother on her deathbed instead. Funny, both females had the same kind of pleading in their stares. And both were people he wanted to protect. Ehlena was on that list. So was his sister. So were Wrath and the Brotherhood.

Rehvenge reached forward and cupped the chin of his second in command. "It's just Brotherhood stuff, and I'm really tired."

"The hell it was, and the hell you are."

"Can I ask you something?"

"What."

"If I asked you to take care of a female for me, would you make sure that happened?"

"Yes, fuck, yes. Christ, I've wanted to kill that bitch for over twenty years."

He dropped his hand, then put his palm out. "On your honor, swear it."

Xhex clasped his palm as a male would, not as a touch but as a vow. "You have my word. Anything."

"Thanks. Listen, Xhex, I'm going to crash—"

"But first you've got to give me a clue here."

"You'll lock up?"

She sat back on her heels. "What. The. Fuck. Is going on."

"Just Vishous with another hiccup in the road."

"Shit, is Wrath having more problems with the *glymera*?"

"As long as there is a *glymera*, he's going to have them."

She frowned. "Why are you thinking of a beach ad from the nineteen eighties?"

"Because chest medallions are coming back in style. I can just feel it. And quit trying to get into me."

There was a long silence. "I'm going to chalk this up to your mom's passing."

"Excellent plan." He pushed his cane into the floor. "Now, I'm going to get a little sleep. I've been up for, like, two days straight."

"Fine. But next time, try to block me with something a little less frightening than Deney Terrio in the Bahamas."

When he was alone, Rehv looked around. The office had seen a lot of action: Lot of money changing hands. Lot of drugs doing the same. Lot of wiseasses who'd fucked with him, bleeding.

Through the open door to the bedroom he stared at the apartment he'd spent a good number of nights in. He could just barely see the shower.

Back before he hadn't been able to handle the princess's venom, when he'd been able to go to her and take care of business and still been strong enough to get his own ass home, he'd always washed in that bathroom. He hadn't wanted to contaminate the family home with what was on his skin, and had needed plenty of soap and hot water and elbow grease before he could go back to see his mother and sister. The irony had been that whenever he'd arrive back at the house, his mother would invariably ask him whether he'd been to the gym, because he "had a healthy glow to his face."

He never had been clean enough. But then, ugly deeds were not like dirt—you couldn't wash them off.

He let his head fall back and walked through ZeroSum in his mind, picturing Rally's scale room and the VIP section and the waterfall wall and the open dance floor and the bars. He knew every inch of the club and all the things that happened in it, from what his girls did on their knees and their backs to how the bookies worked their odds to the number of ODs Xhex had dealt with.

So much dirty business.

He thought of Ehlena losing her job to bring him the antibiotics he was too much of a shithead to get at Havers's. See, that was a good act. And he knew this not just because of what he'd taught himself from being around his mother's people, but because of who he knew Ehlena to be. She was intrinsically good, and therefore she did good things.

What he had been doing here was not and never had been good, because that was who he was.

Rehv thought about the club. The thing was, the places of your life, like the clothes you wore and the car you drove and the friends and associates you had, were a product of the way you lived. And he lived dark and violent and seedy. Was going to die that way, too.

He deserved where he was going.

But on the way to the door, he was going to make things right. For once in his life, he was going to do all the right things for all the right reasons.

And he was going to do them for the short list of people he . . . loved.

FIFTY-TWO

Back across town at the Brotherhood's mansion, Tohr sat in the billiards room, his ass on the chair that he'd pulled over and angled out so he could see the vestibule's door. In his right hand, he held a brand-new black Timex Indiglo watch, which he was setting with the correct time and date, and at his left elbow he had a long/tall filled with a coffee-ice-cream milk shake. He was almost finished with the watch and only a quarter of the way through the shake.

His stomach wasn't handling the shitloads of food he'd thrown at it all that well, but he didn't give a rat's ass. He needed to put on weight fast, so his gut was just going to have to get with the program.

With a final beep, the watch was tight and he put it on his wrist, staring at the glowing 4:57 a.m. on the face.

He looked at the vestibule's door again. Fuck the watch and the eating. What he was really doing was waiting for John to walk through that damn thing with Qhuinn and Blay.

He wanted his boy home safe. Even though John wasn't a boy anymore and hadn't been his since he'd left the kid high and dry a year ago.

"You know, I can't believe you're not watching this."

Lassiter's voice made him pick up the glass and take a draw on the straw so he didn't lob another pipe-down-sonny at the fucker. The angel loved TV, but suffered from

ADD big-time. He was always changing channels. God only knew what he was watching now.

"I mean, she's a woman, going it alone in the world. She's cool, and the clothes are tight. It's a really good show."

Tohr looked over his shoulder. The angel was sprawled on the couch, remote in his hand, head propped up by a needlepoint pillow Marissa had done that said, *Fangs For The Memories.* And beyond him on the flat-screen was ...

Tohr nearly choked on his shake. "What the hell are you doing? That's Mary Tyler Moore, motherfucker."

"Is that who she is?"

"Yeah. And no offense, you should not be getting off on that show."

"Why?"

"It's, like, one step up from a Lifetime movie. You might as well be painting your toenails."

"Whatever. I like it."

The angel didn't seem to tweak to the fact that *MTM* on Nick at Nite was not like MMA on Spike. Any of the Brothers saw this and Lassiter's ass was going to get spanked.

"Yo, Rhage," Tohr called out to the dining room. "Come see what this Lava lamp is into on the tube."

Hollywood came in palming a plate piled high with mashed potatoes and roast beef. For the most part, he didn't believe in vegetables, considering them "a caloric waste of space," so the green beans that had come with First Meal were noticeably absent from his reheat.

"What's he watching— Oh, hey! Mary Tyler Moore. I love her." Rhage parked it in one of the club chairs next to the angel. "Great clothes."

Lassiter shot a see-I-told-ya in Tohr's direction. "And Rhoda's kind of hot."

The two pounded knuckles. "Feel you."

Tohr went back to his milk shake. "You are both an embarrassment to the male sex."

"Why, because we're not all about Godzilla?" Rhage shot back.

"At least I can hold my head up in public. The two of you should be watching that shit in a closet."

"I don't feel the need to hide my preferences." Rhage

arched his brows, crossed his legs, and extended his pinkie from his fork. "I am who I am."

"Please don't tempt with that kind of opening," Tohr muttered, hiding a smile by hitting his straw again.

When there was only silence, he glanced over, ready to keep up the—

Rhage and Lassiter were both staring at him, cautious approval on their faces.

"Oh, for fuck's sake, don't look at me like that."

Rhage recovered first. "I can't help it. You're just *so* sexy in those baggy-ass pants. I got to get me a pair, 'cause nothing says hotness like wearing what looks like two Heftys stitched together at your racket and balls."

Lassiter nodded. "Totally craptastic. Sign my sac up for some of that."

"You get that shit from Home Depot?" Rhage tilted his head to one side. "In the trash removal section?"

Before Tohr could hit back, Lassister jumped in. "Man, I only hope that I can pull off lookin' like I got a load in my shorts as well as you do. Did you get training? Or is it just a case of lack of ass?"

Tohr had to laugh. "I'm surrounded by asses. Trust me."

"Which would explain why you're so confident going without one."

Rhage tacked on, "Come to think of it, you're actually built like Mary Tyler Moore. So I'm surprised you don't like her more."

Tohr took a deliberate draw on the milk shake. "I'ma put on some weight just to throw you down for that."

Rhage's smile stayed in place, but his eyes went grave. "Looking forward to it. I'm so looking forward to that."

Tohr went back to focusing on the vestibule's door, closing himself up, ending the banter because abruptly it didn't feel right.

Lassiter and Rhage didn't follow the lead. The pair were a Chatty Cathy combo from hell, riffing off each other and whatever was on the TV and what Rhage was eating and where the angel was pierced and . . .

Tohr would have moved if he could have watched the front door from any other—

The security system let out a beep as the mansion's outer

door was opened. There was a pause and then another beep was followed by a gonging sound.

As Fritz raced to answer the summons, Tohr sat up straighter, which was pathetic, considering the shape his body was in. Torso height was not going to magically improve the fact that he weighed little more than the chair his nonexistent butt was parked in.

Qhuinn was the first to stride in, the kid dressed in black, the gunmetal piercings that ran up his left ear and marked his lower lip catching the light. Blaylock was next, dressed all Mr. Preppy in his high-necked cashmere sweater and his slacks. As the pair headed for the stairs, the expressions on them were as different as their clothes. Qhuinn had evidently had a really good night, going by the I-got-laid-and-then-some grin on his piehole. Blay, on the other hand, looked like he'd been to the dentist, his mouth set grimly, his eyes down on the mosaic floor.

Maybe John wasn't coming back. But where would he stay—

When John came into the foyer, Tohr couldn't help it: He rose from his seat, catching himself on the high back of the chair as he wobbled.

John's face had no expression on it at all. His hair was tousled, but not by the wind, and there was a series of scratches on the side of his neck, the kind made by a female's nails. The scent coming off him was of Jack Daniel's, multiple perfumes, and sex.

He looked about a hundred years older than when he'd been sitting by Tohr's bed doing *The Thinker* mere nights ago. This was not a kid. This was a full-grown male working off a hard edge in the time-tested ways most guys did.

Tohr sank back into the chair, expecting to be ignored, but when John reached the bottom step, he put his boot up and turned his head as if he knew someone was watching him. His expression didn't change at all as he met Tohr's stare. He just lifted his hand in a half-assed way and kept on going.

"I was worried you weren't coming home," Tohr said loudly.

Qhuinn and Blay halted. Rhage and Lassiter shut up. Mary's and Rhoda's voices filled the void.

John barely paused as he signed, *This isn't home. It's a house. And I need a place to stay.*

John didn't wait for a response, and the set of his shoulders suggested he wasn't interested in one. Clearly, Tohr could have talked until his tongue was worn to a stump about how the people here cared about John, but nothing would register.

As the three of them disappeared up the stairs, Tohr finished his milk shake, took the tall glass into the kitchen, and got the thing into the dishwasher without a *doggen* asking him if he wanted anything else to eat or drink. Beth, however, was stirring a pot of stew and looking as if she were hoping to slip him a bowl so he didn't stick around.

The trip up to the second floor was long and hard, but not because he was feeling weak physically. He'd fucked John up but good, and now he was reaping that crop of all the shutout he'd been laying, wasn't he. Damn it—

The crash and holler that came through the study's closed doors sounded like someone had been attacked, and Tohr's body, frail though it was, responded on instinct, hitting the door hard and throwing it open.

Wrath was crouched behind the desk, arms out in front of him, the computer and phone and paperwork scattered as if he'd pushed them away, his chair on its side. The wraparounds the king always wore were in one of his hands, his eyes staring straight ahead.

"My lord—"

"Are the lights on." Wrath was breathing hard. *"Are the fucking lights on."*

Tohr rushed around and grabbed onto one of his king's arms. "Out in the hall, yeah. And there's the fire. What's—"

Wrath's powerful body started to shake so badly, Tohr had to jack the Brother up. Which required more muscle than he had. Fuck, they were both going down if he didn't get help. Locking his mouth on his front teeth, he whistled loud and long and then got back with the job of trying not to lose hold of his king.

Rhage and Lassiter were the first to come running, and they burst through the door. "What the hell—"

"Turn the lights on," Wrath hollered again. *"Someone turn on the fucking lights!"*

As Lash sat in front of the granite counter at the brownstone's empty kitchen, his disposition improved greatly. It wasn't that he'd forgotten about the Brotherhood walking off with crates of guns and slayer jars. Or that the Hunter-bred apartments had been compromised. Or that Grady had escaped. Or that he had a *symphath* waiting for him up north who was no doubt cranking out because Lash hadn't gone up there to murder someone yet.

It was just that cash was distracting. And a lot of cash was very distracting.

He watched as Mr. D brought over another Hannaford paper bag. More stacks of bills came out, each bundle secured by a cheapy tan rubber band. When the *lesser* was finished, not a lot of granite showed.

Hell of a way to get him to calm his shit down, Lash thought as he looked up when Mr. D was finished hauling bags in.

"How much in total?"

"Seventy-two thousand, seven hundred forty. I done bundled it in hun'red-dollar lots."

Lash took one of the banded sets. This was not the neat and tidy currency that came from banks. This was dirty, wrinkled money, liberated from jeans pockets and mostly empty wallets and stained coats. He could practically smell the desperation wafting up from the bills.

"How much product do we have left?"

"Enough for another two nights like tonight, but no more. And there be only two more dealers left. 'Cept for the big one."

"Don't worry about Rehvenge. I'll take care of him. In the meantime, don't kill the other retailers—bring them to a persuasion center. We need their contacts. I want to know where and how they buy." Of course, likely as not they transacted with Rehvenge, but maybe there was someone else. A human who was more malleable. "First thing this morning, you go and get us a safety-deposit box and put this in there. This is seed money, and we're not losing it."

"Yessuh."

"Who sold the shit with you?"

"Mr. N and Mr. I."

Great. The fucktards who had let Grady bolt. Still, they had performed on the streets, and Grady had met a creative and uncomfortable end. Plus Lash had gotten to see Xhex in action. So all wasn't lost.

He was so going to be paying ZeroSum a visit.

And as for N and I, killing them was better than they deserved, but right now he needed those assholes out making paper. "At nightfall, I want those two *lessers* pushing product."

"I thought you'd want to—"

"First of all, you don't think. And secondly, we need more of this." He tossed the scrubby bills back amid the piles. "I have plans that cost money."

"Yessuh."

Abruptly reconsidering things, Lash leaned forward and picked up the bundle he'd thrown back. The shit was hard to let go of, even though all of it was his, and somehow, the war seemed less interesting all of a sudden.

Bending down, he grabbed one of the paper bags and filled it up. "You know that Lexus."

"Yessuh."

"Take care of it." He reached into his pockets and tossed Mr. D the keys to the thing. "That's your new ride. If you're going to be my street man, you have to look like you know what the fuck you're doing."

"Yessuh!"

Lash rolled his eyes, thinking that it took so little to motivate the stupid. "Don't fuck up anything while I'm gone, will you?"

"Where you be off to?"

"Manhattan. I'll be reachable on my cell. Later."

FIFTY-THREE

As a cold day dawned and clouds dappled across a milky blue sky, José de la Cruz drove through Pine Grove Cemetery's gates and wound around rows and rows of headstones. The tight, curving lanes reminded him of Life, that old board game his brother and he had played when they were kids. Each player got a little car with six holes and started with one peg to represent himself. As the game rolled on, you moved around the road track, picking up more pegs to represent a wife and kids. The goal was to acquire people and money and opportunity, to plug the holes in your car, to fill those voids you started out with.

He looked around, thinking that in the game called Real Life, you ended up plugging a dirt hole by yourself. Hardly the kind of thing you wanted your kids to know right out of the box.

When he came to where Chrissy's grave was, he parked his car in the same place where he'd been until around one a.m. the previous night. Up ahead, there were three CPD police cars, four uniforms in parkas, and a stretch of yellow crime scene tape that wound from gravestone to gravestone in a tight box.

He took his coffee with him even though it was lukewarm at best, and as he walked over, he saw the soles of a pair of boots through the circle of his colleagues' legs.

One of the cops looked over his shoulder, and the expression on the guy's face forewarned José about the condition of the body: If you'd offered the uni an airsick bag, he would have blown out the bottom of the damn thing. "Hey . . . Detective."

"Charlie, how we doing?"

"I'm . . . good."

Yeah, right. "You seem it."

The other guys glanced over and nodded, each one of them wearing an identical my-balls-are-in-my-lower-intestine look on his puss.

The crime scene photographer, on the other hand, was a woman known for having issues. As she bent down and started snapping, there was a little smile on her face, like she was enjoying the view. And maybe going to slip one of the candids into her wallet.

Grady had bitten it hard. Literally.

"Who found him?" José asked, crouching down to examine the body. Clean cuts. A lot of them. This had been done by a professional.

"Groundsman," one of the cops said. "'Bout an hour ago."

"Where's that guy now?" José got to his feet and stepped to the side so the cock-sogynist could keep doing her job. "I'm going to want to talk to him."

"Back in the shed having a cup of coffee. He needed it. Shook up bad."

"Well, I can understand that. Most of the bodies 'round here are not on top of the graves."

All four of the unis looked at him as if to say, *Yeah and not in this condition, either.*

"I'm done with the body," the photographer said as she put the cap on her lens. "And I already snapped the stuff in the snow."

José walked around the scene carefully so he didn't disturb the various prints or their little numbered flaggings or the path that had been made across the ground. It was clear what had happened. Grady had tried to run from whoever had gotten him and failed. Going by the blood streaks, he'd been injured, likely just to incapacitate him, and then moved over to Chrissy's grave, where he had been dismembered and killed.

José went back to where the body was and took a gander at the headstone, noticing a brown streak that ran from the top down the front. Dried blood. And he was willing to bet it had been put there on purpose and when it was warm: Some of the stuff had dripped down inside the inscribed letters that spelled out CHRISTIANNE ANDREWS.

"You get this?" he asked.

The photographer glared at him. Then uncapped, snapped, and recapped.

"Thank you," he said. "We'll call you if we need anything else." Or find any other guys hacked up like this.

She glanced back down at Grady. "My pleasure."

Obviously, he thought, taking a drink from his coffee and grimacing. Old. Cold. Nasty. And not just the photographer. Man, station-house java was the absolute worst, and if he hadn't been at a crime scene he would have ditched the swill and crushed the Styro cup.

José looked around the scene. Trees to hide behind. No lights other than on the road. Gates locked at night.

If only he'd stayed a little longer ... he could have stopped the killer before they castrated Grady, fed the SOB his last meal, and no doubt enjoyed watching him die.

"Goddamn it."

A gray station wagon with a county crest on the driver's door pulled up and stopped, a guy with a little black bag getting out and jogging over. "Sorry I'm late."

"No problem, Roberts." José clapped palms with the medical examiner. "We'd love to get an estimated time of death whenever you can."

"Sure thing, but it's only going to be rough. Maybe a four-hour window?"

"Whatever you can tell us would be great."

As the guy sat on his haunches and got to work, José looked around again, then went over and stared at the footprints. Three different kinds, one of which would match Grady's. The other two would have to be cast and researched by the CSI types who were due any moment.

One pair of the unknowns was smaller than the others.

And he would be willing to bet his house and car and the college funds of both his daughters that they would turn out to be a female's.

In the study at the Brotherhood mansion, Wrath was sitting upright in his chair with a death grip on both of the arms.

Beth was in the room with him, and he could tell by her scent that she was scared shitless. There were other people, too. Talking. Pacing.

He could see nothing but blackness.

"Havers's coming," Tohr announced from the double doors. His voice quieted the room like a mute button, cutting off every voice and all the sounds of movement. "Doc Jane's on the phone with him now. They're going to bring him in one of the ambulances that has a blackout screen, because its faster than Fritz picking him up."

Wrath had insisted on waiting for a couple of hours before even Doc Jane was called. He'd hoped his vision would come back. Was still hoping.

Praying was more like it.

Beth had been so strong, standing at his side, holding his hand as he struggled against the darkness. But a little bit ago, she'd excused herself. When she'd come back, he'd smelled her tears even though she'd no doubt wiped them clean.

That was what had made him pull the trig on the calling the white coats.

"How long?" Wrath asked roughly.

"ETA twenty minutes."

As silence reigned, Wrath knew the other Brothers were around him. He heard Rhage unwrap yet another Toostie Pop. And V light up with the rasp of flint and an exhale of Turkish tobacco. Butch was chewing gum, the subtle snaps coming rapid-fire, like his molars were tap shoes on a hardwood floor. Z was there, and Nalla was in his arms, her sweet, lovely smell and occasional coos coming from the far corner. Even Phury was with them, having elected to stay the day, and he was standing with his twin and his niece.

He knew they were all there . . . and yet, he was alone. Utterly alone, sucked down deeply into his body, imprisoned in blindness.

Wrath cranked down onto the chair's arms so he didn't scream. He wanted to be strong for his *shellan* and his brothers and his race. He wanted to drop a couple of jokes, laugh this off as an interlude that was going to pass soon, show that he still had his sac and shit.

He cleared his throat. But instead of something along

the lines of, *This man walks into a bar with a parrot on his shoulder* . . . what came out was, "Is this what you saw."

The words were guttural, and everyone knew who they were addressed to.

V's answer was low. "I don't know what you're talking about."

"Bullshit." Wrath was bathed in blackness, his brothers around him, no one able to reach him. It was what Vishous had seen. "Bull. Shit."

"You sure you want to do this now?" V said.

"Is it the vision." Wrath released the chair and slammed his fist onto the desk. *"Is it the fucking vision?"*

"Yes."

"The doctor's coming," Beth said quickly, her hand smoothing down his shoulder. "Doc Jane and Havers will talk. They'll figure this out. They will."

Wrath turned to where the sound of Beth's voice had come from. As he reached out for her hand, she was the one who found his palm.

Was this the future, he thought. Relying on her to take him when he needed to go somewhere? Lead him like a fucking cripple?

Keep it together. Keep it together. Keep it . . .

He said those three words over and over again until he didn't feel so much like he was going to explode.

And yet the impending detonation came right back when he heard Doc Jane and Havers enter the room. He knew who it was by the fact that everyone else once again stopped in the middle of what they were doing: No more smoking, no more chewing, no wrappers unfurling.

All quiet except for breathing.

And then the male doctor's voice. "My lord, may I examine your eyes?"

"Yes."

There was a shifting sound of clothes moving. . . . Havers was no doubt taking off his coat. And then a soft bump, like a weight had been put down on the desk. Metal against metal—the lock of a doctor's bag being released.

Havers's well-modulated voice came next: "With your permission, I'm going to touch your face now."

Wrath nodded, then flinched when the soft contact came, and for a moment, he had hope as he heard the click of a penlight. Out of habit, he tensed, preparing for the light to hit whatever retina Havers was going after first. God, ever since he had memories, he could remember squinting at light, and after his transition, it had gotten much worse. As the years had gone by—

"Doc, can you get on with the exam?"

"I've . . . my lord, I've finished." There was a click, presumably Havers turning off his light. "At least with this part."

Silence. Then Beth's hand gripping his harder.

"What's next?" Wrath demanded. "What can you do next."

More silence, which somehow made the darkness even blacker.

Right. Not a lot of options. Although why he was surprised he hadn't a clue. Vishous . . . was never wrong.

FIFTY-FOUR

As night fell, Ehlena crushed her father's pills into the bottom of his mug, and, when the powder was fine and consistent enough, she went to the refrigerator, got the CranRas, and poured. For once, she was grateful for the order that her father required, because her mind was not on what she was doing.

In her current state, she was lucky to know what state she was in. New York, right?

She checked the clock. Not much time. Lusie would be arriving in about twenty minutes, and so would Rehv's car.

Rehv's car. Not him.

About an hour after she had called and left her message about his ex, a voice mail had come back from him. Not a phone call. He'd dialed directly into the system, put her number in, and left the recording.

His voice had been low and serious: "Ehlena, I'm sorry that you were approached like that, and I'll make sure it never happens again. I'd like to see you at nightfall, if you're free. I'll send my car for you at nine unless I hear back from you that it doesn't work." Pause. "I'm so sorry."

She knew the message by heart because she'd listened to it about a hundred times. He sounded so different. Like he was speaking in another language.

Naturally she hadn't slept during the day, and in the end she figured there were two ways to take it: Either he was horrified she'd had to deal with the female at all, or he'd had a really shitty meeting.

Maybe it was a combination of both.

She refused to believe that nut with the crazy eyes had any credibility. Hell, the female reminded Ehlena too much of her father when he was in one of his delusional episodes: fixated, obsessive, in another reality. She had wanted to do damage and had calibrated her words accordingly.

Still, it would have been good to talk to Rehv. She could have used the reassurance, but at least she didn't have to wait any longer to see him.

After she was certain the kitchen was left in exactly the same arrangement as it had been when she'd come up, she took the stairs to the basement and went to her father's room.

She found him in bed with his eyes closed, his body still. "Father?" He didn't move. *"Father?"*

CranRas splashed as she all but threw the mug onto the table. "Father!"

Those eyes opened and he yawned. *"Verily, daughter mine, how fare thee?"*

"Are you all right?" She looked him over even though he was mostly covered by the velvet duvet. He was pale and his hair was all Chia Pet, but he seemed to be breathing easily. "Is there anything—"

"English is rather coarse on the ear, is it not?"

Ehlena paused. *"Forgive me. I just . . . Are you well?"*

"Indeed I am. I was up well into the day thinking of another project, which is why I dallied longer than usual upon this bed. I do believe I shall let the voices in my head wander onto the page. I believe I would benefit from giving them an outlet other than myself."

Ehlena allowed her knees to loosen and she sat without grace on the bed. *"Your juice, Father. Would you care for it now?"*

"Ah, lovely. The maid is so thoughtful to prepare it for you."

"Yes, she is very thoughtful." Ehlena handed him his meds and watched him drink, her heart rate slowing.

Lately, life had been nothing but a series of Batman BANG!s, POW!s, and CRACK!s, with her pinballing around her comic-book page until she was dizzy. Guess it was going to take some time before every little thing stopped getting blown up in her mind into mad drama.

When her father was finished, she kissed his cheek, told him she was going out for a bit, and took the mug back upstairs. By the time Lusie knocked about ten minutes later, most of Ehlena's brain was back where it needed to be. She was going to see Rehv, enjoy his company, then resume her job search when she got home. Everything was going to be okay.

As she opened the door, she straightened her shoulders with resolve. "How are you?"

"I'm fine." Lusie glanced over her shoulder. "Did you know there's a Bentley parked outside your door?"

Ehlena's brows shot up and she leaned around the jamb. There was indeed a brand-new, super-shiny, spectacular Bentley parked in front of her shitty little rental, looking as out of place as a diamond on the hand of a bag lady.

The driver's-side door opened and an incredibly beautiful, dark-skinned male rose from behind the wheel. "Ehlena?"

"Ah . . . yes."

"I'm here to pick you up. I'm Trez."

"I'll . . . I need a minute."

"Take your time." His smile revealed fangs and she was reassured. She didn't like being around humans. Didn't trust them.

She ducked back inside and put her coat on. "Lusie . . . would you be able to continue coming here? It looks like I'll be able to keep paying you."

"Of course. I'd do anything for your father." Lusie flushed. "I mean, both of you. Does this mean that you've found another job?"

"Money has loosened up a little bit more than I expected. And I hate his being here alone."

"Well, I'll take good care of him."

Ehlena smiled and wanted to hug the woman. "You always do. As for tonight, I'm not sure how long I'll be—"

"Take your time. He and I will be fine."

On impulse, Ehlena gave the female a quick embrace. "Thank you. Thank . . . you."

Grabbing her purse, she hit the door before she made a fool out of herself, and as she emerged into the cold, the driver came around to help her into the Bentley. Dressed in his black leather trench coat, he looked more like a hit man than a chauffeur, but when he smiled at her again, his dark eyes flashed an extraordinarily brilliant green.

"Don't worry. I'll get you there just fine."

She believed him. "Where are we going?"

"Downtown. He's waiting for you."

Ehlena felt awkward as the door was opened for her, even though she knew it was courtly manners among equals on his part and not anything to do with serving her. She was just out of practice at being attended to by a male of worth.

Jesus, the Bentley smelled good.

While Trez went around and got in behind the wheel, she stroked the fine leather of the seat and couldn't remember feeling anything so luxurious.

And as the car eased out of the alley and down onto the street, she barely felt the potholes that usually left her hanging on to the door handle in taxis. Smooth ride. Expensive ride.

Where were they going?

As a gentle, warm breeze suffused the backseat, that voice message from Rehv played over and over again in her head. Doubt flickered in her mind, like the brake lights of the cars in front of them, going off and on, slowing her everything's-okay roll.

It got worse. Downtown was not a place she knew very well, and she tensed up as they passed the part where the luxury high-rises were. Where she had met Rehv at the Commodore.

Maybe he was taking her out dancing.

Yeah, because you did that without telling the female to wear a dress.

The farther they went down Trade Street, the more she stroked the seat beside her, although not for the feel of it. Things got seedier and seedier, the lineup of all-right restaurants and the offices of the *Caldwell Courier Journal* giving way to tattoo parlors and bars that looked as if they'd have grizzled drunks on stools and dirty bowls of peanuts at their counters. Then it was the clubs, the loud, flashy kind she never, ever went to because she didn't like the noise, the lights, or the people in them.

As the black-on-black sign for ZeroSum came into view, she knew they were going to stop in front of it, and her heart dropped into her lower gut.

Strangely, she had the same reaction she'd had to seeing Stephan in the morgue: *This can't be right. This can't be happening. This is not how things are supposed to be.*

The Bentley didn't pull up in front of the club, though, and for a moment hope flared.

But of course. They went into the alley on the far side, stopping at a private entrance.

"He owns this club," she said in a dead voice. "Doesn't he."

Trez didn't touch the question, but he didn't have to. As he came around and opened the door for her, she sat frozen stiff in the back of the Bentley, staring at the brick building. Absently, she noted that there was grime dripping down its flank from the roof, and crud splashed up on it from the ground. Tarnished. Dirty.

She thought of standing at the foot of the Commodore and staring upward at all the sparkling-clean glass and chrome. That was the facade he had chosen to show her.

This one with the filth was what he had been forced to show her.

"He's waiting for you," Trez said gently.

The side door of the club opened wide, another Moorish male appearing. Behind him, everything was dim, but she heard the thumping bass.

Did she really need to see this, she wondered.

Well, she needed to tell Rehv off, that was for sure, assuming this train wreck was going in the direction it appeared to be. And then it dawned on her: If all this was true, she had a bigger problem. She'd had sex . . . with a *symphath.*

She'd let a *symphath* feed from her.

Ehlena shook her head. "I don't need this. Take me h—"

A female appeared, one who was built tough and hard as a male, and not just on the outside. Her eyes were icy cold and utterly calculating.

She came over and leaned into the car. "Nothing is going to hurt you inside here. I swear it."

Whatever—the hurt was already happening, Ehlena thought. She was getting chest pains like you would with a heart attack.

"He's waiting," the female said.

What got Ehlena out of the car was her backbone, and not just because it straightened her from a sitting position. The thing was, she didn't run. In all her life, she hadn't run from the hard stuff, and she was not starting now.

She walked in through the door and knew for sure that she was somewhere she wouldn't ever choose to be. Everything was dark, and the music banged into her ears like fists, and the smell of too much hot skin made her want to plug her nose.

The female led the way, and the Moors flanked Ehlena, their huge bodies carving a path through a human jungle she had no wish to be a part of. Waitresses dressed in tight black uniforms carried around endless variations on alcohol, and half-nude women rubbed up against men in suits, and every person Ehlena passed had eyes that were looking somewhere else, as if whatever they'd ordered or whoever was in front of them couldn't satisfy them.

She was led over to a reinforced black door, and after Trez spoke into his wristwatch, the thing opened and he stood to the side—as if he expected her to walk right in, like it was just someone's living room.

Yeah . . . *not.*

Staring into the darkness beyond, she saw nothing but a black ceiling and black walls and a shiny black floor.

But then Rehvenge stepped into her line of sight. He was exactly as she knew him to be, a big male dressed in a sable duster who had mohawked hair and amethyst eyes and a red cane.

He was, however, a total stranger.

Rehvenge stared at the female he loved and saw on her pale, strained face exactly what he had sought to put there.

Revulsion.

"Will you come in?" he said, needing to finish the job.

Ehlena glanced over at Xhex. "You're security, right?" Xhex frowned, but nodded. "Then you're coming in with me. I don't want to be alone with him."

As her words hit, Rehv might as well have been sliced through the throat, but he showed no reaction as Xhex came forward and Ehlena followed.

The door shut and the music was buffered away and the silence was as loud as a scream.

Ehlena looked at his desk, on which he'd deliberately left twenty-five thousand dollars in cash and a brick of cocaine that was wrapped in cellophane.

"You told me you were a businessman," she said. "Guess it was my fault for assuming it was legitimate."

All he could do was stare at her—his voice had left him, his shallow breath nothing that could sustain words. The only thing he could do, as she stood stiff and angry before him, was memorize her, from the way her strawberry blond hair was pulled back to her toffee-colored eyes to her simple black coat to the way she kept her hands in her pockets, as if she didn't want to touch a thing.

He didn't want this to be how he remembered her, but as it was the last time he would see her, he couldn't help but focus on every detail.

Ehlena's eyes flipped from the drugs and the cash back to his face. "So it's true? Everything your ex-girlfriend said."

"She is my half sister. And yes. Everything."

The female he loved took a step back from him, fear bringing her hand out of her pocket and up to her throat. He knew exactly what she was thinking of: him feeding from her vein, them being naked and alone in his penthouse. She was recasting the recollection, coming to terms with the fact that it hadn't been a vampire at her neck.

It had been a *symphath*.

"Why did you bring me down here?" she said. "You could have just told me over the phone—no, never mind. I'm going home now. Don't ever contact me again."

He bowed slightly and choked out, "As you wish."

She turned away and went to stand in front of the door. "Will someone please let me the fuck out of here."

After Xhex reached over and opened the way to freedom, Ehlena all but bolted away from him.

As the door shut, Rehv locked it with his mind and stood there, where she had left him.

Ruined. He was utterly ruined. And not because he was

turning himself and his body over to a sadistic sociopath who was going to enjoy every minute of torturing him.

When his vision clouded with red, he knew it wasn't his bad side coming out. Not a chance. He'd pumped enough dopamine in his veins over the last twelve hours to choke a horse, because otherwise he didn't trust himself to let Ehlena go. He'd needed to cage his bad side one last time . . . so he could do the right thing for the right reason.

So, no, this red wasn't going to be followed by flat vision and sensation returning all over his body.

Rehvenge took one of the handkerchiefs his mother had ironed out of the inside of his suit jacket and pressed the folded square beneath his eyes. The bloodred tears leaching out of him were for so much more than just Ehlena and himself. Bella had lost her mother no more than forty-eight hours ago.

And she was going to lose her brother by the end of the night.

He took a single, great breath, one so deep that his ribs strained. Then he tucked the handkerchief away and got on with putting his life into its grave.

One thing was certain: The princess was going to pay. Not for the shit she'd done to him and was going to do to him. Fuck that.

No, she had dared to approach his female. For that, he would cripple her, even if it killed him.

FIFTY-FIVE

*T*hat feel good? Shutting him down like that?"

Ehlena stopped at the club's side exit and looked over her shoulder at the female security guard. "As it is absolutely none of your business, I'm not answering the question."

"FYI, that male has put himself in a rat-hole situation for me, his mother, and his sister. And you think you're too good for him? Nice. Where the hell do you come from that's so perfect?"

Ehlena faced off with the female even though it wasn't a fair fight by a long shot, given how the security guard was built. "I never lied to him—how about that for *perfect*. Actually that's not perfect, it's *normal*."

"He does what he must to survive. That is very *normal*, not only for your kind but for *symphaths*, too. Just because you've had it easy—"

Ehlena got up in the female's face. *"You don't know me."*

"I don't want to."

"Right back at you." The *bitch* in that sentence was silent.

"Yeah, okay, whoa." Trez stepped in and separated them. "Let's just cool out on the catfight, 'kay? Lemme take you home. You"—he pointed to the other female—"go see if he's all right."

The security guard glared at Ehlena. "You watch yourself."

"Why? Because you're going to show up at my back door? Whatever—compared to that thing last night, you're a Barbie doll."

Both Trez and the female went still.

"What showed up at your door?" the security guard asked.

Ehlena stared up at Trez. "May I go home now?"

"What was it?" he asked.

"A Kabuki doll with a bad attitude."

As one, they said, "You need to move."

"Great suggestion. Thanks." Ehlena pushed past both of them and went to the door. When she tried the handle, of course, it was locked, so all she could do was wait to be let out again. Yeah, well, screw that. Biting down on her lower lip, she grabbed for the handle and wrenched at it, prepared to claw her way free.

Fortunately, Trez came over and sprang her like a bird from a cage, and out she flew from the club, into the cold air, away from the heat and the noise and the crowded desperation that choked her.

Or maybe the suffocation was a broken heart.

What did it matter.

She waited by another door, this one to the Bentley, wishing that she didn't need the car to get home, knowing it was going to be a long while before she was even halfway settled enough to breathe right, much less dematerialize.

On the trip back, she could remember none of the streets they passed or the lights they stopped at or the other cars around them. She just sat in the backseat of the Bentley, all but inanimate, her face turned to the window, her eyes seeing nothing as she was spirited away.

Symphath. Sleeping with his half sister. Pimp. Drug dealer. Killer, no doubt . . .

As they went farther and farther away from downtown, she had more difficulty breathing instead of less. The stinger was that she couldn't lose the image of Rehvenge kneeling before her, her cheap Keds in his hand, his amethyst eyes so soft and kind, his voice so lovely it was better than the music of a violin. *Don't you get it, Ehlena? No matter what you wear . . . to me, you will always have diamonds on the soles of your shoes.*

That was going to be one of two ghosts of him. She

would remember him down on that knee before her, and contrast it with the sight of him in that club just now, his truth revealed.

She had wanted to believe in the fairy tale. And she had. But like poor, young Stephan, the fantasy was dead, and the decay of it was horrific, a beaten, cold body that she would wrap in rationalizations and recastings that carried the scent not of herbs, but tears.

Closing her eyes, she leaned back against the butter-soft seat.

Eventually, the car slowed and stopped and she reached for the door handle. Trez got there first and opened her way.

"Can I say something?" he murmured.

"Sure." Because she wouldn't hear whatever it was. The fog around her was too thick, her world as her father sought to make his: restricted to only what was closest to her . . . and that was pain.

"He didn't do this without reason."

Ehlena looked up at the male. He was so earnest, so sincere. "Of course he didn't. He wanted me to believe in his lies, and his cover was blown. There was nothing to hide behind anymore."

"That's not what I meant."

"Would he have told me any of it if he hadn't been caught?" Silence. "So there you have it."

"There's more to this than you know."

"You think? Maybe there's just less of him than you need to believe there is. How about that."

She turned away and went through a door she could open and relock herself. Falling back against the jamb, she looked around at everything that was so dingy and familiar and wanted to break down.

She didn't know how to get past this. She really didn't.

After the Bentley took off, Xhex headed straight for Rehv's office. When she knocked once and wasn't answered, she punched in the code and opened the door.

Rehv was behind his desk, typing on a laptop. Next to him was his new cell phone, a plastic Baggie with some fat, chalky pills in it, and a bag of M&M's.

"Did you know the princess had been to see her?" Xhex

demanded. When he didn't answer, she cursed. "Why didn't you tell me?"

Rehv just kept typing, the soft sound of the keys like quiet chatter in a library. "Because it wasn't relevant."

"The hell it wasn't. I almost beat the female down for—"

Vicious purple eyes flipped up over the screen. "You don't *ever* touch Ehlena."

"Whatever, Rehv, she just dumped your ass hard. You think that was fun to watch?"

He pointed his finger at her. "Not your biz. And you never, ever touch her. We clear?"

As his eyes flashed in warning, like someone had shoved a Maglite up his ass and hit the switch, she thought, Well, okay . . . evidently she was staring over the lip of a cliff, and if she went any farther she was going to skydive without a parachute. "My point is, it might have been nice to know beforehand that you wanted her to dump you."

Rehv just went back to typing.

"So that was the call last night," she prompted. "That's when you found out your girlfriend had been paid a visit by the bitch."

"Yeah."

"You should have told me."

Before she got an answer, there was a squawk in her earpiece and then the voice of one of her bouncers: "Detective de la Cruz is here to see you."

Xhex lifted her wrist and spoke into the transistor. "Take him to my office. I'll be right there. And get the girls out of the VIP area."

"The CPD?" Rehv muttered while he typed.

"Yup."

"I'm glad you nailed Grady. I can't stand the wife-beater types."

"Is there anything I can do for you?" she asked stiffly, feeling shut out. She wanted to help, to ease, to take care of Rehv, but she wanted to do that shit on her mollycoddling terms: Fuck running him a bubble bath and getting him some hot chocolate; she wanted to murder the princess.

Rehv looked up again. "Like I said last night, I'm going to ask you to take care of someone."

Xhex had to hide her buzz kill. If he was going to ask her

to assassinate the princess, there would be no reason for him to drag his GF here, make a show of revealing what he'd lied to her about, and letting the female bin him off like he was week-old meat.

Shit, it had to be the GF. He was going to ask her to make sure nothing happened to Ehlena. And knowing Rehv, he was probably going to try to support the female financially, too—going by the chick's simple clothes and lack of jewelry and no-nonsense vibe, she didn't appear to come from cash.

Fun, fun, fun. Getting that one to take money from a male she hated was going to be a real party.

"Whatever you need," Xhex said tightly as she left.

Making her way through the club, she prayed no one rubbed her the wrong way, especially given that a badge was in the house.

When she finally got to her office, she reined her frustration in and opened the door, sticking a tight smile on her face. "Evening, Detective."

De la Cruz turned around. In his hand, he had a small ivy plant, one that was no bigger than his palm. "Got a present for you."

"I told you, I'm not good with living things."

He put it on the desk. "Maybe we'll just start you off slow, though."

As she sat on her chair, she stared at the fragile living thing and felt a flare of panic. "I don't think—"

"Before you say I can't give you anything because I work for the city"—he took a receipt out of his pocket—"it cost less than three dollars. Which is cheaper than a coffee from Starbucks."

He put the little white slip next to the dark green plastic pot.

Xhex cleared her throat. "Well, as much as I appreciate your concern for my interior decorating—"

"Got nothing to do with your furniture choice." He smiled and sat down. "Do you know why I'm here?"

"You found the man who murdered Chrissy Andrews?"

"Yeah, I did. And if you'll excuse my French, he was in front of her headstone with his cock cut off and stuffed in his mouth."

"Wow. Ouch."

"You mind telling me where you were last night? Or do you want to get an attorney first?"

"Why would I need one of those? I've got nothing to hide. And I was here all evening. Ask any of the bouncers."

"*All* evening."

"Yup."

"I found footprints around the crime scene. Smallish, combat boot–style ones." He looked down to the floor. "Kind of like what you wear."

"I've been to the grave. Of course I have. I'm mourning a friend." She put her soles up so he could see them, knowing they were a different make and manufacturer than the ones she'd worn the night before. Different size, too, with padding all along the interior making them a ten wide, not a nine medium.

"Hmm." After his inspection, de la Cruz leaned back and put his fingertips together, elbows resting on the stainless-steel arms of the chair. "Can I be honest with you?"

"Yup."

"I think you killed him."

"Do you."

"Yeah. It was a violent crime, the ins and outs of which suggest it was committed for the purpose of payback. See, the coroner believes, as I do, that Grady was alive when he was . . . shall we say, worked on. And this was no hatchet job. He was disabled in a professional way, like the murderer had been trained to kill."

"This is a tough neighborhood, and Chrissy had a lot of tough friends. Any one of them could have done it."

"There were mostly women at that funeral."

"And you don't think females are capable of something like that? Rather sexist, Detective."

"Oh, I know women can kill. Trust me. And . . . you look like the kind of female who could."

"You profiling me? Just because I wear black leather and work security in a club?"

"No. I was with you when you IDed Chrissy's body. I saw the way you looked at her, and that's what makes me think you did it. You have a revenge motive, and you had the opportunity, because anyone could slip out of this place for an hour, do the business, and get back here." He stood up and went to the door, pausing with his hand on the knob. "I would advise you to get a good lawyer. You're going to need one."

"You're barking up the wrong tree, Detective."

He shook his head slowly. "I don't think so. See, most people I go and talk to when there's a body involved, the first thing they tell me, whether it's true or not, is that they didn't do it. You haven't said anything even close to that."

"Maybe I don't feel the need to defend myself."

"Maybe you have no remorse because Grady was a shit-head who beat a young woman to death, and that crime sits no better with you than it does any of us." De la Cruz's eyes looked sad and exhausted as he turned the knob. "Why didn't you let us pick him up? We'd have nailed him. Put him away. You should have let us take care of it."

"Thanks for the plant, Detective."

The guy nodded, like the rules of the game had just been laid out and the playing field agreed upon. "Get that lawyer. Fast."

As the door shut, Xhex eased back in her chair and looked at the ivy. Nice green color, she thought. And she liked the shape of the leaves, the pointed symmetry pleasing to the eye, the little veins forming a pretty pattern.

She was so going to end up killing this poor, innocent thing.

A knock on the door brought her eyes up. "Come in."

Marie-Terese entered, smelling of Calvin Klein's Euphoria and wearing loose blue jeans and a white shirt. Obviously her shift hadn't started yet. "I just interviewed two girls."

"You like either of them?"

"One is hiding something. I'm not sure what. The other's okay, although she's had a botched boob job."

"Should we send her to Dr. Malik?"

"Think so. She's pretty enough to pull the Benjamins. You want to meet her?"

"Not right now, but yeah. How about tomorrow night?"

"I'll have her here, you just name the time—"

"Can I ask you something?"

Marie-Terese nodded without hesitation. "Anything."

In the silence that followed, it was on the tip of Xhex's tongue to bring up John and Gina's little bang sesh in the bathroom. But what was there to know? It had just been a business transaction that was common in the club.

"I was the one who sent him to Gina," Marie-Terese said quietly.

Xhex's stare flipped up to the woman. "Who?"

"John Matthew. I sent him to her. I figured it would be easier."

Xhex fiddled with the *Caldwell Courier Journal* on her desk. "I have no idea what you're talking about."

Marie-Terese's expression was all about the yeah-whatever, but to her credit she didn't take it any farther. "What time tomorrow night?"

"For what?"

"Meeting the new girl."

Oh, right. "Let's say ten o'clock."

"Sounds good." Marie-Terese turned away.

"Hey, do me a favor?" When the woman pivoted back around, Xhex held out the little ivy plant. "Take this home for me? And, like, I don't know . . . make it live."

Marie-Terese glanced at the thing, shrugged, and came over to get it. "I like plants."

"Which means that damn thing just won the lottery. Because I don't."

FIFTY-SIX

Rehvenge hit CTRL-P on his laptop and leaned back to pick up the papers spitting out of his printer one by one. When the machine let out a final whir and sigh, he brought the stack forward, separated the pages accordingly, initialed the top right of each, then signed his name three times. Same signature, same letters, same cursive scrawl.

He didn't call Xhex in to witness. Didn't ask Trez to do it.

iAm was the one who came, the Moor John Hancocking the name he'd assumed for human purposes on the appropriate lines to verify the will and the transfer of real property assets and the trust. After that was done, he went on to sign his true name on a letter that was written in the Old Language as well as a declaration of bloodline.

When it was all done, Rehv put everything in a black LV Epi briefcase and gave the lot to iAm. "I want you to take her out of here in thirty minutes. Take her even if you have to knock her ass cold. And make sure your brother is with you and all the staff is gone."

iAm didn't say anything. Instead, he took out the knife he kept at the small of his back, sliced open his palm, and reached out, his blood dropping thick and blue onto the laptop's keyboard. He was as steady as Rehv needed him to be, totally unblinking, and solid.

Which was why long ago he had been the one chosen for the rough shit.

Rehv had to swallow hard as he stood up and took the hand that was presented. They shook on the blood vow, and then their bodies met in a hard, tight embrace.

iAm said softly in the Old Language, *"I knew you well. I loved you as mine own flesh and bone. I will honor you e'er more."*

"Take care of her, okay? She's going to be wild for a while."

"Trez and I will do whatever we have to."

"None of this was her fault. Neither the beginning nor the end. Xhex is going to have to believe that."

"I know."

They parted and Rehv had a hard time letting go of his old friend's shoulder, mostly because this was the only good-bye he was going to make: Xhex and Trez would have fought what he was going to do, would have tried to negotiate other solutions as they clawed and grabbed for some other outcome. iAm was more fatalistic than that. More realistic, as well, because there was no other way.

"Go," Rehv said in a cracked voice.

iAm put his blooded palm over his heart, bowed down to the waist, then left without looking back.

Rehv's hands were shaking as he pulled back his cuff and checked his watch. The club was closing now at four. Cleaning people arrived at five a.m. on the dot. Which meant after everyone was gone he had about a half hour.

He picked up his phone and headed for his bedroom, hitting a number he called often.

As he locked the door, his sister's voice was warm on the line. "Hey, brother mine."

"Hey." He sat on the bed, wondering what to say.

In the background, Nalla whimpered in a little plaintive plea, and Rehv grew still. He could just picture the two of them together, the young held against his sister's shoulder, a fragile bundle of future wrapped up in a soft blanket edged with a satin ribbon.

For mortals, the only infinity you had was the young, wasn't it.

He would never have them.

"Rehvenge? Are you there? You okay?"

"Yeah. I just called because ... I wanted to say ..." Good-bye. "I love you."

"That is so sweet. It's hard, isn't it. Being without *Mahmen*."

"Yeah. It is." He squeezed his eyes shut, and as if on cue, Nalla started to cry properly, a howl warbling through the phone.

"Sorry about my little noise box," Bella said. "She won't sleep unless I'm walking around, and my feet are starting to give out."

"Listen . . . do you remember that lullaby I used to sing to you? Back when you were small."

"Oh, my God, the one about the four seasons? Yes! I haven't thought about that for years. . . . You used to do it when I couldn't sleep. Even when I was older."

Yes, that was it, Rehv thought. The one directly from the Old Myths about the four seasons of the year and of life, the one that had gotten both him and his sister through a lot of sleepless days, him singing, her resting.

"How did it go again?" Bella said. "I can't—"

Rehv sang awkwardly at first, the words tripping from rusty memory, the notes not perfect because his voice had always been too deep for the key it had been written in.

"Oh . . . that's it," Bella whispered. "Here, let me put you on speaker-phone. . . ."

There was a beep and then an echo, and as he sang on, Nalla's cries dried up, flames extinguished by a gentle rain of ancient words.

The spring's pale green cloak . . . the summer's bright-flowering veil . . . the fall's chilling weave . . . the winter's blanket of cold . . . Seasons not just of the earth but of every living thing, the peak to strive for and the victory of fruition, followed by the fall from the crest and the soft, white light of the Fade that was the eternal landing.

He sang the lullaby through twice, and his last trip through the words was his best. He stopped there, because he didn't want to risk that the next try wouldn't be as good.

Bella's voice was rocky with tears. "You did it. You put her to sleep."

"You could sing that for her if you like."

"I will. I definitely will. Thank you for reminding me of it. I don't know why I didn't think to give it a go before now."

"Maybe you would have. Eventually."

"Thank you, Rehv."

"Sleep thee well, sister mine."

"I'll talk to you tomorrow, 'kay? You sound off to me."

"I love you."

"Aw . . . I love you, too. I'll call you tomorrow."

There was a pause. "Take care. Take care of yourself and your young and your *hellren*."

"I will, dearest brother. Bye-bye."

Rehv hung up and sat with the phone in his hand. To keep the screen lit, he pressed the shift key every couple of minutes.

It killed him not to call Ehlena. Text her. Reach out. But she was in the place she needed to be: Better she hate him than mourn him.

At four thirty, he got the text from iAm he'd been waiting for. Just two words.

All clear.

Rehv stood up off the bed. The dopamine was wearing thin, but there was enough still in him so that without his cane he wobbled and he had to catch his balance. When he was convinced he was steady enough, he took off his sable coat and his jacket and disarmed himself, leaving the guns he usually kept under his arms right on the bed.

It was time to go, time to use the system he'd installed after he'd purchased the club's brick building and renovated it from cornerstone to rooftop.

The whole place was wired for sound. And not the Dolby kind.

He went back out into the office and sat behind the desk and unlocked the lowest right-hand drawer. Inside was a black box no bigger than a TV remote, and other than him, iAm was the only one who knew what it was and what it was for. iAm was also the only guy who knew about the bones that were tucked under Rehv's bed, bones that were human male in nature and roughly the size Rehv was. Then again, iAm had been the one who'd gotten them.

Rehv took the remote and got to his feet, looking around one last time. Neat piles of paperwork on the desk. Money in the safe. Drugs back in Rally's scale room.

He walked out of the office. The club was well lit now that it was after hours, and the VIP section had the detritus of the night all over it, like a whore too well used: There were footprints on the glossy black floor, circular water marks on the tables, napkins wadded up and left in the banquettes here and there. The waitresses cleaned up after each patron, but there was only so much you could see in the dark if you were a human.

Across the way, the waterfall was off, so there was a clear view to the general-pop section—which didn't look any better. The dance floor was scuffed up. There were swizzle sticks and lollipop wrappers everywhere, and even a pair of panties had been left behind in one corner. On the ceiling above, the laser lighting system's networks of girders and wires and lamp cups was exposed, and without music being played, the huge speakers hibernated like black bears in a cave.

In this state, the club was *The Wizard of Oz* made obvious: All the magic that went on here night after night, all the buzz and excitement, was really just a combination of electronics, booze, and chemicals, an illusion for the people who walked through the front doors, a fantasy that allowed them to be whatever they weren't in their day-to-day lives. Maybe they jonesed to be powerful because they felt weak, or sexual because they felt ugly, or chic and rich when they weren't, or young when they were gaining speed on middle age. Maybe they wanted to burn off the pain of a failed relationship or get revenge over being jilted or pretend they weren't searching for a mate when actually they were desperate for one.

Sure, they came out for "fun," but he was damn certain that underneath the surface of all the bright and shiny, there was a whole lot of dark and seedy.

The club as it was now was the perfect metaphor for his life. He had been the Wizard, fooling those closest to him for so long, fitting in with the normals through a combination of drugs and lies and subterfuge.

That time had passed.

Rehv took one last turn around and went out the front double doors. The black-on-black ZeroSum sign was not spotlit, indicating that they were closed for the night. Closed for good was more like it.

He glanced left and right. There was no one on the street, no cars or pedestrians in sight.

He walked over and checked the alley by the side entrance that led into the VIP section and then quickly went across and looked down the other alley. No homeless. No hangers-on.

Standing in the cold wind, Rehv took a moment to sense out the buildings around the club, searching for grids that indicated there were humans in them. Nothing. All clear was right.

Ready to go, he walked across the street and down two blocks, and then he paused, slid the top of the remote down, and entered an eight-digit code.

Ten . . . nine . . . eight . . .

They'd find the bones burned to a crisp, and he wondered for a brief moment whose they were. iAm hadn't said, and he hadn't asked.

Seven . . . six . . . five . . .

Bella was going to be okay. She had Zsadist and Nalla and the Brothers and their *shellans*. It was going to be brutal on her, but she would get through it, and better this than her learning the truth that would destroy her: She didn't need to ever know that her mother had been raped and her brother was half sin-eater.

Four . . .

Xhex would stay away from the colony. iAm would make sure of that, because he was going to force her to stick to the vow she'd made the night before: She'd promised to take care of someone, and the letter Rehv had written in the Old Language and made iAm witness had been the demand that she take care of herself. Yes, he'd tricked her into it. No doubt she assumed he was going to get her to kill off the princess, or maybe even watch after Ehlena. But he was a *symphath*, wasn't he. And she'd made the mistake of giving her word without knowing what she was committing to.

Three . . .

He traced the club's roofline with his eyes and imagined what the rubble was going to look like, not just around the club, but with what he was leaving behind in people's lives as he went up north.

Two . . .

Rehv's heart hurt like a bitch, and he knew it was because he was mourning Ehlena. Even though technically he was the one who was dying.

One . . .

The explosion that ignited under the main dance floor triggered two others, one under the VIP bar and one on the mezzanine's balcony. With a tremendous thunder and a bracing quake, the building was rocked to its core, a blast of brick and vaporized cement rushing outward.

Rehvenge staggered back and banged into the glass front of a tattoo parlor. After he caught his breath, he watched the fine mist of dust drift downward like snow.

Rome had fallen. And yet it was hard to leave.

The first of the sirens rang out no more than five minutes later, and he waited for the splashes of red flashers to come down Trade Street at a dead run.

When they did, he closed his eyes, calmed himself . . . and dematerialized up north.

To the colony.

FIFTY-SEVEN

hlena?" Lusie's voice came down the stairs. "I'm going to head out now."

Ehlena shook herself and glanced at the time in the lower corner of the laptop screen. It was four thirty? Already? God, it felt like ... well, she didn't know whether she'd been sitting at her makeshift desk for hours or days. The *Caldwell Courier Journal*'s help-wanted site had been up the whole time, but all she'd been doing was making circles with her forefinger on the mouse pad.

"Here I come." She stretched as she rose to her feet and headed for the stairs. "Thanks for cleaning up after Father's meal."

Lusie's head appeared at the top of the stairs. "You're welcome, and listen, there's someone here to see you."

Ehlena's heart flip-flopped in her chest. "Who?"

"A male. I let him in."

"Oh, God," Ehlena said under her breath. As she jogged up from the cellar, she thought, at least her father was sleeping soundly after he'd eaten. Last thing she needed to deal with right now was him getting upset over a stranger in the house.

As she came into the kitchen, she was prepared to tell Rehv or Trez or whoever it was to go to—

A blond male with a very rich vibe stood by the cheap table, a black briefcase in his hand. Lusie was next to him, pulling on her woolen coat and getting her patchwork satchel ready for her trip home.

"May I help you?" Ehlena said with a frown.

The male did a little bow thing, with his palm going gallantly to his chest, and when he spoke, his voice was unusually low and very cultured. "I'm looking for Alyne, blooded son of Uys. Are you his daughter?"

"Yes, I am."

"May I see him?"

"He's resting. What's this about, and who are you?"

The male glanced over at Lusie, then put his hand into his breast pocket and took out an ID in the Old Language. "I'm Saxton, son of Tyhm, an attorney hired by the estate of Montrag, son of Rehm. He's recently passed unto the Fade with no direct heirs, and according to my research of the bloodlines, your father is his next of kin and therefore his sole beneficiary."

Ehlena's brows shot up. "Excuse me?" When he repeated what he'd said, it still didn't sink in. "I ... ah ... what?"

As the lawyer took another shot at his message, her mind scrambled around, trying to connect the dots. Rehm was definitely a name she was familiar with. She'd seen it in her father's business records ... and in his manuscript. Not a nice guy. Not by a long shot. She had some vague memory of the son, but it was nothing specific, just a leftover from her days as a female of worth on the *glymera* debutante circuit.

"I'm sorry," she murmured, "but this is a surprise."

"I understand. May I speak with your father?"

"He's not ... receiving, actually. He's not well. I'm his legal guardian." She cleared her throat. "Under the Old Law, I had to have him declared incompetent due to ... mental issues."

Saxton, son of Thym, bowed a little. "I am sorry to hear that. May I ask, would you be able to present me with bloodline identification for you both? And the declaration of incompetence?"

"I have it all downstairs." She looked at Lusie. "I guess you need to go?"

Lusie glanced at Saxton and seemed to reach the same conclusion Ehlena did. The male seemed perfectly normal, and in his suit and coat and with that case in his hand, he positively screamed *lawyer*. His ID was legit, too.

"I can stay if you'd rather," Lusie said.

"No, I'll be fine, and besides, it's getting close to dawn."

"All right, then."

Ehlena walked Lusie out and then came back to the lawyer. "Will you excuse me a minute?"

"Take your time."

"Would you ... ah, like something to drink? Coffee?" She hoped he said no, as the best she could offer him was a mug, and he looked like the kind of guy who was more familiar with Limoges teacups.

"I'm fine, but thank you." His smile was genuine and not sexual in the slightest. Then again, no doubt he only went for the kind of aristocratic female she might have been if finances were different.

Finances ... and other things.

"I'll be right back. Please have a seat." Although those precision-pressed slacks of his might well rebel if he tried to take a load off on one of their grotty little chairs.

Down in her room, she went under her bed and got her lockbox out. Carrying it upstairs, she was numb, just totally fried from the drama that had been dropping around her life like flaming airplanes falling from the sky. Christ, the fact that a lawyer had turned up on her doorstep looking for lost heirs seemed ... ho-hum. Whatever. And she wasn't getting her hopes up at all. With the way things had been going, this "golden opportunity" was going to go in the direction everything else had lately.

Right into the shitter.

Back upstairs, she put the lockbox on the table. "I've got everything in here."

When she sat down, Saxton did as well, putting his briefcase on the pitted floor and focusing his gray eyes on the box. After putting in the combination, she flipped open the heavy top and took out a creamy business-size envelope and three rolled parchments, each of which had streaming satin ribbons flowing from their coiled insides.

"This is the incompetency paper," she said, opening the envelope and taking out a document.

After he looked the missive over and nodded, she unveiled her father's bloodline certificate, that illustrated a family tree in lovely, flowing black ink. At the bottom, the ribbons in yellow and powder blue and deep red were affixed with a black wax seal bearing the crest of her father's father's father.

Saxton got his briefcase, flipped it open, and took out a set of jeweler's glasses, sliding their weight onto his face and peering over every inch of the parchment.

"This is authentic," he pronounced. "The others?"

"My mother and myself." She unrolled each one and he did the same inspection.

When he was finished, he sat back in the chair and removed the specs. "May I look over the incompetency papers again?"

She passed them to him and he read, a frown tightening the space between his perfectly arched brows. "What is the precise medical situation with your father, if you don't mind my asking?"

"He suffers from schizophrenia. He's very ill and needs round-the-clock care, to be honest."

Saxton's eyes traveled slowly around the kitchen, noting the stain on the floor and the aluminum foil over the windows and the old, on-their-last-legs appliances. "Are you employed?"

Ehlena stiffened. "I don't see why that's relevant."

"Sorry. You're absolutely correct. It's just . . ." He opened his briefcase again and took out a fifty-page bound document and a spreadsheet. "Once I certify you and your father as Montrag's next of kin—and based on those parchments I'm prepared to do that—you're never going to have to worry about money again."

He turned the document and the legal-size spreadsheet toward her and took a gold pen out of his breast pocket. "Your net worth is now substantial."

With the nib of his pen, Saxton pointed to the final number in the lower right-hand corner of the sheet.

Ehlena glanced down. Blinked.

Then bent all the way over the table, until her eyes were no more than three inches away from the pen tip and the paper and . . . that number.

"Is that . . . How many digits am I looking at?" she whispered.

"That would be eight to the left of the decimal point."

"And it starts with a three?"

"Yes. There is an estate as well. In Connecticut. You can move in anytime you want after I finish the certification papers, all of which I'll draw up during the day and pass immediately on to the king for his approval." He sat back. "Legally, the money and real estate and personal effects, including the art and antiques and the cars, will be your father's until he passes unto the Fade. But with your conservatorship paper, you will be in charge of everything for his benefit. I'm assuming you're his heir vis-à-vis his will?"

"Ah . . . I'm sorry, what was the question?"

Saxton smiled gently. "Does your father have a will? Are you in it?"

"No . . . no, he doesn't. We don't have any assets anymore."

"Do you have any siblings?"

"No. It's just me. Well, him and me since *Mahmen* died."

"How would you like me to draw up a will for him in your favor? If your father dies intestate, it will all go to you anyway, but if we have that in place, it makes things easier for whatever solicitor you use, because you won't have to get the king's signature on the transfer of assets."

"That would be . . . Wait, you're expensive, right? I don't think we can—"

"You can afford me." He tapped the spreadsheet with his pen again. "Trust me."

In the long, dark hours after Wrath had lost his vision, he fell down the stairs—in front of everyone who had gathered in the dining room for Last Meal. The banana-peel move took him ass-over-headache all the way down to the mosaic floor of the foyer.

The only way it could have been more of a loser move was if he bled all over himself.

Oh . . . wait. As he put his hand up to his hair to push the shit back, he felt something wet and knew it wasn't because he was drooling.

"Wrath!"

"My brother—"

"What the fuck—"

"Holy—"

Beth was the first of the cast of thousands to get to him, her hands going to his shoulders as warm blood dripped down his nose.

Other hands reached him through the darkness, the hands of his brothers, the hands of the *shellans* in the house, all gentle, worried, compassionate hands.

In a furious punch, he shoved them all away and tried to get to his feet. Without any orientation to ground him, though, he ended up with one shitkicker up on the last stair—which pitched him wildly off balance. Grabbing for the handrail, he somehow managed to get his boots level and shuffled backward, unsure whether he was heading toward the front door or the billiards room or the library or the dining room. He was utterly lost in a space he knew very well.

"I'm okay," he barked. "I'm all right."

Everyone went silent around him, his commanding voice unmitigated by his blindness, his authority as king unassailable even though he couldn't see a fucking thing—

His back slammed against a wall and a crystal sconce above him twinkled from the impact, the delicate noise rising up into all the quiet.

Jesus . . . Christ. He couldn't go on like this, bumper-caring around, slamming into things, falling down. But it wasn't like he got a vote.

Ever since his lights had gone out, he'd been waiting for his eyes to start working again. As time passed, though, and Havers had no concrete answers, and Doc Jane was mystified, what he knew to be the truth in his heart started to make its way up to his brain: This darkness he found himself in was the new earth upon which he strode.

Or fell all over, as the case was.

As the sconce stilled above his head, every part of him was screaming, and he prayed that no one, even Beth, tried to touch him or talk to him or tell him everything was going to be all right.

It wasn't going to be all right ever again. He wasn't getting his vision back, no matter what the doctors might try to do to him, no matter how many times he fed, no matter how often he rested or how well he looked after himself. For shit's sake, even before V had laid out what he had foreseen, Wrath knew this was coming: His sight had been declining over the centuries, the acuity washing out gradually over time. And he'd been getting the headaches for years, with increasing severity over the last twelve months.

He'd known this was going to be where he ended up. His whole life, he'd known and ignored it, but the reality was here.

"Wrath." Mary, Rhage's *shellan*, was the one who broke the silence, her voice even and quiet and not at all frustrated or flustered. The contrast with the chaos in his mind had him turning toward the sound even though he couldn't say anything back to her because he had no voice. "Wrath, I want you to reach out your left hand. You'll find the doorjamb to the library. Move yourself over and take four steps backward into the room. I'm going to talk with you, and Beth is coming with me."

The words were so level and reasonable that they were like a map through a jungle of thorny growth, and he followed the directions with all the desperation of a lost traveler. He put his hand out . . . and yes, there was the uneven pattern of the molding around the doorway. Shuffling himself to the side, he used both hands to find his way beyond the jambs, and then he took four steps back.

There were quiet footfalls. Two sets. And the library doors were shut.

He sensed where the females were by the subtle sounds of their breathing, and neither of them crowded him, which was good.

"Wrath, I think we need to make some temporary changes." Mary's voice came from the right. "In the event that your sight doesn't return soon."

Smart packaging job, he thought.

"Like what," he muttered.

Beth answered, making him aware that the two had evidently already talked about this. "A walking stick to help with your balance, and a structure of staffing coverage in your study so you can get back to work."

"And perhaps some other kinds of help," Mary tacked on.

As he absorbed their words, the sound of his heartbeat roared in his ears, and he tried not to hear it so much. Yeah, good luck with that. When a cold sweat splashed over him, pooling on his upper lip and under his armpits, he wasn't sure whether it was from fear or the effort of keeping himself from breaking down in front of them.

Probably both. The thing was, not being able to see was bad, but what was really killing him was the claustrophobia. Without a sight reference, he was trapped in the tight, crowded space beneath his layer of skin, imprisoned in his body with no way out—and he didn't do well with shit like that. Reminded him way too much of being locked in a crawl space by his father when he had been young . . . locked in while he watched his parents get murdered by *lessers*. . . .

The piercing memory weakened his knees and he lost his balance, listing to the side until he started to topple off his boots. Beth was the one who caught him and gently eased him over so that when he collapsed it was on a sofa.

As he tried to breathe, he held her hand hard, and that contact was all that kept him from sobbing like a fucking lightweight.

The world was gone . . . the world was gone . . . the world was—

"Wrath," Mary said, "if you get back to work, it'll help, and we can make this easier on you in the interim. There are solutions that can make things safer and help you reacclimate to the . . ."

As she talked, he didn't hear her. All he could think of was no fighting again, ever. No easy way around the house, ever. No way to get even a blurry impression of what was on his plate, or who was at his table, or what Beth was wearing. He didn't know how to shave or find the clothes in his closet or see where the shampoo or the soap was. How would he work out? He wouldn't be able to get the weights he wanted or start the treadmill going or . . . shit, tie the laces on his running shoes—

"I feel like I've died," he choked out. "If this is the way it's going to be . . . I feel like the person I was . . . is dead."

Mary's voice came from directly in front of him. "Wrath, I've seen people get through exactly what you're struggling with. My autistic patients and their parents had to learn to look at things in a new way. But it was not over for them. There was no death, just a different kind of life."

As Mary spoke, Beth stroked the inside of his forearm, running her hand up and down the tattooed delineation of his bloodline. The touch made him think about the many males and females who had gone before him, their courage tested by challenges from within and without.

He frowned, abruptly embarrassed by his weakness. If his father and mother had been alive right now, he would have been ashamed for them to see the way he was acting. And Beth ... his beloved, his mate, his *shellan*, his queen, should not have to witness him like this, either.

Wrath, son of Wrath, should not be bowing under the weight that was laid upon him. He should be shouldering it. That was what members of the Brotherhood did. That was what a king did. That was what a male of worth did. He should be bearing up under the burden, rising above the pain and the fear, standing strong not just for those he loved, but for himself.

Instead, he was falling down the stairs like a drunk.

He cleared his throat. And had to clear it once more. "I need ... I need to go talk to someone."

"Okay," Beth said. "We can bring whoever it is to you—"

"No, I'll get there by myself. If you'll excuse me." He stood up and stepped forward ... right into the coffee table. Biting back a curse as he rubbed his shin, he said, "Would you just leave me here? Please."

"May I ..." Beth's voice broke. "May I clean up your face?"

Absently, he wiped his cheek and felt wetness. Blood. He was still bleeding. "It's fine. I'm okay."

There was a soft shuffle as the two females walked over to the door, then the click of the lock as one of them turned the handle.

"I love you, Beth," Wrath said quickly.

"I love you, too."

"It's ... going to be all right."

With another click, the door shut back into place.

Wrath sat down on the floor right where he was, because he didn't trust himself to circumnavigate the library to get in a better position. As he settled in, the crackle from the fire gave him some frame of reference ..., and then he realized he could picture the room in his mind.

If he reached out to the right ... yup. His hand brushed against one of the smooth legs of the table by the sofa. He rode the length up to the boxy bottom and patted across the surface of the thing to find ... yes, the coasters Fritz kept stacked neatly there. And a small leather book ... and the lamp base.

This was comforting. In some strange way, he had felt as if the world had disappeared just because he couldn't see it. But in fact everything was all there still.

Closing his eyes, he sent out a request.

It was a long while before it was responded to, a long, long while before he was spirited away and found himself standing on a hard floor, beside a fountain that chattered softly. He had wondered if he would be blind here on the Other Side as well, and he was. Still, as with the layout of the library, he knew what the place looked like, even if he couldn't see it. Over there to the right was a tree full of chirping birds, and in front of him, past the sprinkling fountain, would be the loggia with the columns that was part of the Scribe Virgin's private quarters.

"Wrath, son of Wrath." He did not hear the mother of the race approach, but then she levitated around such that her black robes never touched whatever floor was beneath her. "You have come unto me for what purpose."

She knew damn well why he was here, and he wasn't playing her game anymore. "I want to know if you did this to me."

The birds fell silent, as if shocked by his temerity.

"Did what to you." Her voice sounded the same as it had when she'd appeared at the Tomb with Vishous: distant and disinterested. Which kinda pissed a guy off when he was having trouble making it down his own stairs.

"My fucking sight. Did you take it away from me because I went out to fight?" He ripped his wraparounds off his face and tossed them across the slick floor. *"Did you do this to me."*

In days gone by she would have lashed him until he bled for that kind of insubordination, and as he waited to see what came at him, he almost hoped she licked his ass with a lightning bolt.

There was no smiting, however. "What was going to be was going to be. Your fighting had nothing to do with your loss of sight, and neither did I. Now go back to your world and leave me to mine."

He knew she had turned away, because her voice faded as she headed off in the opposite direction.

Wrath frowned. He'd come expecting a fight, and he wanted one. Instead? He got nothing to engage with, not even a row over his deliberate disrespect.

The radical shift in paradigm was so stark, for a moment he forgot all about his blindness. "What is wrong with you?"

He got no answer, just a door shutting softly.

In the Scribe Virgin's absence, the birds stayed quiet, the delicate sound of falling water all that grounded him. Until someone else approached.

On instinct, he turned to the footfalls and assumed his fighting stance, surprised to find that he wasn't as defenseless as he'd thought. In the absence of sight, his hearing filled out the picture that was no longer created by his eyes: He knew where the person was by the rustle of their robing and an odd *click, click, click* and . . . shit, he could even hear their heartbeat.

Strong. Steady.

What was a male doing here?

"Wrath, son of Wrath." Not a male voice. A female one. And yet the impression he had was masculine. Or maybe it was just powerful?

"Who are you?" he demanded.

"Payne."

"Who?"

"Doesn't matter. Tell me something, you plan on doing anything with those fists? Or are you just going to stand there?"

He dropped his arms immediately, as it was entirely inappropriate to raise a hand to a female—

The uppercut slammed into his jaw so hard, it whipped his head and shoulders around. Stunned, more out of surprise than pain, he fought to regain his balance. The second he did, there was a whizzing sound and he was pounded again, the next blow catching him under his jaw and kicking his skull back.

That was all she got in with the clean shots, though. His defensive instincts and his years of training responded even though he couldn't see anything, his hearing functioning as his eyes, telling him where things like arms and legs were.

He grabbed a surprisingly thin wrist and wrenched the female around—

Her heel made hard contact with his shin, the pain spearing up his leg and pissing him off as something like a rope swung into his face. He grabbed it and hoped it was a braid attached to the female's—

Yanking it hard, he felt her body torque backward. Yup, attached to her head. Perfect.

Getting her off-kilter was easy, but man, she was a strong motherfucker. With only one leg supporting her weight, she managed to jump and spin, clipping him in the shoulder with her knee.

He heard her land and start to scramble, but he kept a hold on her hair, reining her in. She was like water, though, always fluid, always moving, hitting him time and time again until he was forced to manhandle her onto the ground and pin her down.

It was a case of brute strength winning out over grace.

Panting, he looked into a face he couldn't see. "What the fuck is your problem?"

"I'm bored." With that, she head-butted him right in the goddamn nose.

Pain made him feel like he was on a merry-go-round, his hold briefly lessening. Which was all she needed to get free again. Now he was the one on the bottom, her forearm cranked around his throat and pulling back so hard, she must have had a grip on her wrist for greater leverage.

Wrath strained to get air down into his lungs. Holy shit, she was going to kill him if she kept this up. She really was.

Deep within himself, deep down into his very marrow, deep into the double helixes of his DNA, the response came. He was not going to die here and now. No fucking way. He was a survivor. He was a fighter. And whoever this bitch was, she was not going to issue him his ticket to the Fade.

Wrath let out a war cry in spite of the iron bar across his neck, and moved so fast he had no idea what he did. All he knew was that a split second later, the female was facedown on the marble with both her arms twisted up behind her back.

For absolutely no reason, he thought of however many nights ago, when he'd popped the arms off that *lesser* in the alley before he'd killed the fucker.

He was going to do exactly the same to her—

The laughter rippling up from underneath him was what stopped him. The female . . . was laughing. And not like someone who'd lost her mind. She was honestly having a good time, even though she must have known she was about to pass out from the kind of pain he was going to inflict on her.

Wrath loosened his hold only slightly. "You are a sick bitch, you know that?"

Her hard body quaked under his as she kept on laughing. "I know."

"If I let you go, are we going to just end up here again?"

"Maybe. Maybe not."

Strange, but he kind of liked those odds, and after a moment, he released her as he would have a stallion with a bad temper: quickly and with a fast out-of-the-way on his part. As he planted his feet, he was ready for her to come at him again, and sort of hoping she did.

The female stayed where she was, on the marble floor, and he heard that clicking again.

"What is that?" he asked.

"I have this habit of flicking my ring finger nail against the underside of the one on my thumb."

"Oh. Cool."

"Hey, are you going to come here again anytime soon?"

"I don't know. Why?"

"Because that was more fun than I've had since . . . a long time."

"Who are you again? And why haven't I seen you here before?"

"Let's just say She has never known what to do with me."

It was clear given the female's tone who the She was. "Well, Payne, I can come back for more of this."

"Good. Make it soon." He heard her get to her feet. "By the way, your glasses are right by your left foot."

There was a rustle and the quiet shutting of a door.

Wrath picked the wraparounds up and then let his legs have a time-out, taking a seat on the marble. Funny, he enjoyed the ache in his leg and the sting on his shoulder and

the pounding pulse points of each and every one of his
bruises. They were all familiar, part of his history and his
present, and what he was going to need in the unfamiliar,
frighteningly dark future.

His body was still his own. It still worked. He could still
fight, and maybe with practice he could get back to where
he had been.

He hadn't died.

He was still alive. Yes, he couldn't see, but he could still
touch his *shellan* and make love to her. And he could still
think and walk and talk and hear. His arms and legs worked
just fine, and so did his lungs and heart.

The adjustment was not going to be easy. One really
awesome fight was not going to clear away what was going
to be months and months of awkward learning and frustration and anger and missteps.

But he had perspective. Unlike the bloody nose he'd
gotten falling down the stairs, the one he had now didn't
seem like a symbol of all he'd lost. It was more like a representation of everything he still had.

As Wrath came back to his form in the library of the
Brotherhood's mansion, he was smiling, and when he got to
his feet, he chuckled as one of his legs hollered in pain.

Concentrating, he took two limping steps to the left
and ... found the couch. Took ten forward and ... found
the door. Opened the door, took fifteen straight ahead,
and ... found the balustrade to the grand staircase.

He could hear the meal that was being eaten in the dining room, the soft chiming of silver on porcelain filling the
void where chatter usually was. And he could smell the ...
oh, yeah, lamb. That's what he was talking about.

As he took thirty-five measured crab steps to the left, he
started to laugh, especially as he swiped his face and the
blood dripped off his hand.

He knew exactly when they all saw him. Forks and
knives dropped on plates and bounced, and chairs scraped
backward and curses filled the air.

Wrath just laughed and laughed and laughed some
more. "Where's my Beth?"

"Oh, sweet Lord," she said as she came to him. "Wrath ...
what happened—"

"Fritz," he called out as he fit his queen against him.

"Will you make me a plate? I'm hungry. And get me towel so I can mop up." He squeezed Beth. "Take me to my seat, would you, my love?"

Lots of silence that positively rang with holy-shit-what-is-this.

Hollywood was the one who asked, "Who the hell used your face as a soccer ball?"

Wrath just shrugged and rubbed his *shellan's* back. "I made a new friend."

"Hell of friend."

"She is."

"She?"

Wrath's stomach let out a grumble. "Look, can I join the meal here or what?"

Something about sustenance snapped everyone back in focus, and there was all kinds of talk and bustling, and then Beth was leading him down the room. As he sat, a damp washcloth was put into his hand, and the heavenly scent of rosemary and lamb appeared right in front of him.

"For God's sake, will you sit down," he told them as he mopped up his face and neck. When there were all kinds of chair noises, he found his knife and fork and prodded around his plate, identifying the lamb and the baby new potatoes and . . . the peas. Yup, the roly-polies were peas.

The lamb was delicious. Just as he liked it.

"You sure that was a friend," Rhage said.

"Yup," he said, squeezing Beth's hand. "I'm sure."

FIFTY-EIGHT

Twenty-four hours in Manhattan was enough to turn even the son of evil into a new male.

Behind the wheel of the Mercedes, with a trunk and backseat full of bags from Gucci, Louis Vuitton, Armani, and Hermès, Lash was a happy camper. He'd crashed at the Waldorf in a suite, fucked three women—two at the same time—and eaten like a king.

As he got off the Northway at the exit for the *symphath* colony, he checked the time on his brand-spanking-new gold Cartier Tank, the replacement for that fake Jacob & Co. bling shit, which was so beneath him.

What the hour hand was showing wasn't so bad, but the date was trouble: He was going to catch shit from the *symphath* king, but he so didn't care. For the first time since he'd been turned by the Omega, he felt like himself. He was wearing twill slacks from Marc Jacobs and an LV silk shirt and an Hermès cashmere vest and slipper loafers from Dunhill. His cock was drained, his belly was still full from the dinner he'd had at Le Cirque, and he knew he could go back to the Big Apple and do it all over again in the blink of an eye.

Provided his boys stayed tight in the game.

At least things seemed to be going along okay on that front. Mr. D had called about an hour ago and reported that product continued to move swiftly. Which was a good news/bad news sitch. They had more cash, but their supply was dwindling fast.

Lessers, however, were familiar with persuasion and that was why the last guy who'd been willing to see them for a large buy hadn't been popped, but nabbed.

Mr. D and the others were going to be working him out, and not in the gym.

Which made Lash think about his time in the city.

The war with the vampires would always be in Caldwell, unless the Brothers chose to move. But Manhattan was one of the drug capitals of the world, and it was close, very close. Only an hour's drive.

Naturally, the trip down south had been about more than the Fifth Avenue shoppies. He'd spent most of the evening going from club to club, checking the scenes, looking for patterns in who went where—because that would tell you what people were buying. Ravers liked X. Slick, twitchy new money liked coke and X. College kids preferred weed and 'shrooms, but you could also move Oxy and meth to them. Goths and emos were into X and razor blades. And the junkies who were in all the alleys around the clubs were into crack, crank, and H.

If he could make inroads in Caldie first, he could do the same for more return in Manhattan. And there was no reason not to think big.

Turning off onto the dirt lane he'd been down before, he reached under the seat and brought out the spank SIG forty he'd bought the night before on the way down to the city.

There was no reason to change into fighting clothes. A good assassin didn't need to break a sweat to do his job.

The white farmhouse still sat all lovely amidst the now-snow-covered landscape, a perfect Christmas-card candidate for humans. In the lingering night, pale smoke drifted up out of one of its chimneys, the whiffs catching and amplifying the soft moonlight, creating shadows that scampered across the roof. On the other side of the windows, the golden illumination of candles shifted as if there were a subtle breeze moving throughout all the rooms. Or maybe that was just those damn spiders.

Man, in spite of all the home-and-hearth appearance, the place really was tweaked with dread, wasn't it.

As he parked the Mercedes by the monastical order sign and got out, snow fluffed over the tops of his brand-new

Dunhills. As he shook the shit off with a curse, he wondered why in the hell the fucking *symphaths* couldn't have been quarantined in Miami.

But nooooooooo, the sin-eaters got parked an ass crack away from Canada.

Then again, no one liked them, so the logic did follow.

The farmhouse door opened and the king appeared, his white robes wafting around, his glowing red eyes oddly resplendent. "You are late. By a factor of days."

"Whatever, your candles are holding up just fine."

"And my time is not so valuable as wasted wax?"

"Didn't say that."

"But your actions, they speak loudly."

Lash mounted the stairs with his gun in his hand and felt like he wanted to double-check that his fly was up as the king watched his body move. And yet, when he was standing head-to-head with the guy, the current sparked between them again, licking in the cold air.

Fuckin' A. He didn't drive that kind of stick. Really, he didn't.

"So, we going to take care of business?" Lash murmured, staring into those bloodred eyes and trying not to be captivated.

The king smiled and raised his three-knuckled fingers to the diamonds at his throat. "Yes, I do believe we shall. Come this way and I shall take you to your target. He is abed—"

"I thought you only wore red, Princess. And what the fuck are you doing here, Lash?"

As the king stiffened, Lash shifted around, leading with his gun. Coming up the lawn was ... a massive male with glowing amethyst eyes and an unmistakable signature mohawk: Rehvenge, son of Rempoon.

Bastard wasn't at all surprised to find himself on *symphath* ground. On the contrary, he looked quite at home. As well as pissed off.

Princess?

A quick look over Lash's shoulder showed him ... nothing that he hadn't seen before. Thin guy, white robes, hair twisted up like a ... girl's, actually.

In this circumstance, it would be nice to have been snowed. Much better to want to fuck a female liar than have to confront the fact that he was a . . . Yeah, no reason to go there, even in his own mind.

Whipping his head back around, Lash knew the timing of this little weird-ass interruption was perfect. Getting Rehv out of the drug game would free up all kinds of commerce space in Caldwell.

Just as his finger squeezed the trigger, the king shot forward and grabbed the muzzle. "Not him! Not him!"

As the gunshot rang out in the night and the bullet wall-eyed into a tree trunk, Rehvenge watched Lash and the princess fight for control of the weapon. On one level, he didn't give a shit which of the two of them won, or whether he or anybody else got popped in the process, or exactly why a kid who'd been killed was still very much alive. His life was ending where it had been conceived, here in this colony. Whether he died tonight or in the morning or after a hundred years, whether he was killed by the princess or Lash, the outcome had been decided, so the particulars didn't matter.

Although maybe that laissez-fuck-off attitude was a mood thing? After all, he was a bonded male without his mate, so in traveling terms, he'd pretty much packed up his luggage, checked out of his mortal motel room, and was in the elevator going down to hell's lobby.

At least, that was the way the vampire side of him was thinking. The other half of his bloodline was doing the wakey-wakey: mortal drama was always inducement to his bad side, and he wasn't surprised as the *symphath* in him beat back the last of the dopamine he'd pumped into his veins. In a quick flash, his vision lost the full-color spectrum and flattened out, the princess's robes turning to red, the diamonds at her throat bleeding into rubies. Evidently, she dressed in white, but as he'd never seen her without his sin-eater eyes, he'd just assumed she clothed herself in the color of the vein.

But like he gave a crap about her wardrobe?

With his bad side out, Rehv couldn't help but get involved. As feeling flooded his body, pulling his arms and legs out of their numb sleeves, he jumped up onto the porch. Hatred warmed him from deep inside, and although he had no interest in aligning with Lash, he wanted the princess to get fucked, and not in a good way.

Going up behind her, he grabbed her around the waist and jacked her up off the ground. Which gave Lash an opening to yank the gun free and spin out away.

The little shit had transitioned into a big male. But that wasn't all the changing he'd been doing. He reeked of sweet evil, the kind that animated *lessers*. Evidently, he'd been brought back from the dead by the Omega, but why? How?

The questions were ones Rehv didn't care much about. He was, however, jazzed up about squeezing the princess's rib cage so hard she was struggling to breathe. With her nails biting into his forearms through his silk shirt, he was damn sure she'd have been sinking her teeth into him if she could, but he wasn't giving her a chance. He had a death grip on the back of her chignon, keeping her head under his control.

"You make a great body shield, bitch," he said into her ear.

While she tried to speak, Lash straightened his admittedly spank clothes while leveling the SIG in his hand at the Rehv's head. "Nice to see you, Reverend. I was coming after you, and you just saved me the trip. Gotta say, though, seeing you hide behind that female, male, whatever it is doesn't quite do justice to your ass-kicker reputation."

"This is not a guy, and if it wouldn't nasty me the hell out I'd rip open the front of her robe to prove it. And listen, catch me up, would you? Last time I knew, you were dead."

"Not for long, as it turned out." The guy smiled, flashing long, white fangs. "She's really a female, huh?"

The princess struggled, and Rehv subdued her by nearly snapping her skull off her spine. As she gasped and groaned, he said, "She is. Didn't you know *symphaths* are all but hermaphroditic?"

"I can't tell you how much of a relief it is to know she lied."

"You two are a match made in hell."

"I'm thinking the same. Now, how about you let my girlfriend go?"

"Your girlfriend? Moving a little fast, aren't you? And

I'll pass on the catch-and-release program. I like the idea of you shooting us both."

Lash frowned. "Thought you were a fighter. Guess you're a pussy. I should have just gone to your club and shot you there."

"Actually, as of about ten minutes ago, I'm already dead. So I don't give a fuck. Although I'm curious to know why you'd want to kill me."

"Connections. And not the social kind."

Rehv arched his brows. Lash was the one killing those dealers? What the hell? Although . . . the fucker had tried to sell drugs on ZeroSum turf a year ago and gotten kicked off the premises for it. Clearly, now that he'd fallen in with the Omega, he was resurrecting old, lucrative habits.

With the smooth logic of hindsight, things started to fall into place. Lash's parents had been the first of all those murdered last summer during the *lesser* raids. As family after family had turned up dead in their supposedly secret and protected homes, the question on the council's mind, on the Brotherhood's minds, on every civilian's mind, was how all those addresses had been found at once by the Society.

Simple: Lash had been turned by the Omega and led the charge.

Rehv cranked his hold down on the princess's rib cage a little harder as the final dregs of his numbness lifted. "So you're trying to get into my business, huh. It was you popping all those retailers?"

"Just working my way up the food chain, as it were. And with you doing the dirt nap, I'm at the top, at least for Caldwell. So let her go and I'll shoot you in the head and we can all just move along here—"

A wave of dread washed up onto the porch, cresting and falling over Rehv and the princess and Lash.

Rehv shifted his eyes and froze. Well, well, well, what do you know. This was all going to be over so much faster than he'd thought.

Coming up the snow-covered lawn, in robes of ruby red, were seven *symphaths* in arrow formation. At the center of the group, walking with a cane and wearing a headdress of rubies and black spears, was a bent branch of a male.

Rehv's uncle. The king.

He seemed much older, but however aged and weak his body, his soul was as strong and dark as before, causing Rehv to shudder and the princess to stop fighting the hold against her. Even Lash had the sense to step back.

The private guard stopped at the base of the porch steps, their robes blowing in the cold breeze Rehv could now feel against his own face.

The king spoke in a weak voice, his reedy Ss drawn out. "Welcome home, my dearest nephew. And greetings, visitor."

Rehv stared at his uncle. He hadn't seen the male for . . . God, a long time. Long, long time. The funeral for his father. Evidently, the years had not been kind, but rather a grind on the king, and this made Rehv smile as he imagined the princess having to bed that baggy-skinned, warped body.

"Evening, Uncle," Rehv said. "And this is Lash, by the way. In case you didn't know."

"I have not been properly introduced, no, although I have knowledge of his purpose on my land." The king fixed his watery red eyes on the princess. "My dear girl, did you think I was unaware of your regular visits to Rehvenge? And think you I was ignorant of your more recent scheme? I'm afraid I was rather attached to you and thus content to allow your trysts with your brother—"

"Half brother," Rehv cut in tightly.

"—however, this treason with the *lesser* I cannot allow. In truth, I am not unimpressed with your resourcefulness, given that I rescinded my bequest of the throne to you. But I am not swayed by my former adoration. You underestimated me, and for that disrespect, I shall render a punishment consistent with your wants and desires."

The king nodded, and on a sudden instinct, Rehv wheeled around. Too late. A *symphath* with a raised sword was right behind him, the guy's arm already in midswing— and although the blade wasn't in the lead, that was only a marginal improvement as the hilt of the damn thing caught Rehv right on the top of the skull.

The impact was the second explosion of the night, and unlike the first, this time he was not standing after all the light and the noise faded.

FIFTY-NINE

Ehlena was still wide-awake at ten a.m. Stuck inside by daylight, she paced around her bedroom in a huddle with her arms around herself, and her socks doing little to keep her feet warm enough.

Then again, she was so cold on the inside, she could have been wearing a pair of George Foreman Grills and still been chilly. Shock seemed to have reset her core temperature, her inner dial pointing to Refrigerator instead of Normal.

Across the hallway, her father slept soundly, and every once in a while, she ducked into his room to check on him. Part of her wished he would wake up, because she wanted to ask him about Rehm and Montrag and bloodlines and . . .

Except it was better to leave him out of it. Getting him all riled up over what could well be nothing was the last thing either of them needed. Sure, she'd gone through the manuscript and found those names, but it had been a single mention among a lot of relatives. Besides, what her father recalled wasn't material. It was what Saxton could prove.

God only knew what was going to come of it.

Ehlena stopped in the middle of her room, abruptly too tired to keep up the constant walking. Not a good plan, though. The instant she fell still, her mind shifted to Rehv, so she resumed circling on her cold feet. Boy, she wouldn't wish anyone dead, but she was almost glad Montrag had passed and created a wild distraction with all the will stuff.

Without it, she would be losing her mind right now, she was quite sure.

Rehv...

As she dragged her tired body around the end of her bed, her eyes went downward. Lying on the duvet, in nearly the same peaceful, quiet repose as her father, was the manuscript he'd written. She thought of all that he had put on the pages and knew exactly what he meant now. He'd been duped and double-crossed much in the way she had, led astray by appearances of honesty and trustworthiness because he himself wasn't capable of behaving with the kind of base calculation and cruelty others were. Same for her. Could she ever rely on her ability to read people again?

Paranoia tumbled her mind and her gut. Where was the truth in Rehv's lies? Had there been any? As images of him flickered before her eyes, she probed her memories, wondering where the divide was between fact and fiction. She needed to know more.... Trouble was, the only one who could fill in the picture was a guy she was never, ever going to get near again.

Contemplating a future full of relentless, unanswered questions, she brought shaking hands to her face and dragged her hair back. Holding the stuff hard, she pulled at it as if she could yank all the spinning, crazy thoughts out of her head.

Christ, what if Rehv's deception was the equivalent of her father's financial ruin? The thing that took her over the edge into madness?

And this was the second time a male had shown her up, wasn't it. Her fiancé had done something similar—the only difference being that he had lied to everyone else *except* her.

You'd have thought she'd learned her lesson about trust thanks to her first trip through the park. But evidently not.

Ehlena stopped pacing, waiting for ... hell, she didn't know, her head to explode or something.

It didn't. And no luck on the cognitive weeding with all her hair pulling, either. All that was getting her was a headache and a Vin Diesel 'do.

Turning away from the bed, she saw her laptop.

With a curse, she walked across the shallow space and sat down in front of the Dell. Dropping the death grip on her hair, she put her fingertip on the mouse pad and killed the screen saver.

Internet Explorer. Favorites: www.CaldwellCourier-Journal.com.

What she needed was a dose of concrete reality. Rehv was the past, and the future was not about some slick lawyer with a bright idea. Right now, the only thing she could trust was her job search: If Saxton and his papers fell through, she and her father were out on the street in less than a month unless she found employment.

And there was nothing false or misleading about that.

As the *CCJ*'s Web site loaded, she told herself that she was not her father, and that Rehv was a male she had been involved with for all of, what . . . a matter of days? Yes, he had lied to her. But he was a flashy-dressing, supersexy player, and in retrospect, she shouldn't have put any faith in him in the first place. Especially given what she already knew about males.

His bad, and her mistake. And although the realization that she'd been seduced into stupidity didn't make her pick up her pom-poms and cheer, the idea that there was an internal logic, even if it sucked, helped her feel a little less crazy—

Ehlena frowned and leaned in close to the screen. On the splash page of the Web site was a picture of a bombed-out building. The headline read: *Explosion Levels Local Club*. In smaller font beneath there was: *ZeroSum latest casualty in drug war?*

She read the article without breathing: Authorities investigating. Unknown whether there was anyone in the club at the time. Suspicion that there were multiple detonations.

A sidebar detailed the number of suspected drug dealers who had been found dead around Caldwell in the past week. Four of them. All killed in a professional way. The CPD was looking into each of the murders, and among the suspects was the owner of ZeroSum, one Richard Reynolds, a.k.a. the Reverend—who was now missing apparently. It was noted that Reynolds had been on the CPD Narcotics watch list for years, though never formally charged with any crime.

The implication was obvious: Rehv had been the real target of the blast because he'd been killing the others.

She scrolled back up to the pictures of the decimated club. No one could survive that. No one. The police were going to report that he was dead. It might take them a week or two, but they would find a body and declare that it was his.

No tears fell from her eyes. No sobs from her lips. She was too far gone for that. She just sat in silence, arms going around herself once more, eyes staring at the glowing screen.

The thought that occurred to her was bizarre, but inescapable: There was only one thing that would have been worse than what she had faced walking into that club and learning the truth about Rehv. And that would have been reading this article before she'd made that trip downtown.

Not that she wanted Rehv dead, God ... no. Even after everything he had snowed her on, she didn't want him to die violently. But she had been in love with him before she'd known about the lying.

She had been ... in love with him.

Her heart had truly been his.

Now her eyes welled and spilled, the screen growing wavy and indistinct, the pictures of the blown-out club washing away. She had fallen in love with Rehvenge. It had been fast and furious and hadn't lasted, but the feelings had bloomed just the same.

With a spearing pain, she remembered his warm, surging body on top of hers, his bonding scent in her nose, his huge shoulders bunched and hard as they'd made love. He'd been beautiful in those moments, so generous as a lover. He honestly had enjoyed pleasuring her—

Except that had been what he wanted her to believe, and as a *symphath*, he was good at manipulation. Although, God, she had to wonder what exactly he'd gotten out of being with her. She had no money, no position, nothing that benefited him, and he had never asked anything of her, never used her in any way....

Ehlena stopped herself from sliding into any kind of rosy view of what had gone down. Bottom line was, he hadn't deserved her love, and not because he was a *symphath*. Strange as it seemed, she could have lived with that—although maybe that just proved how little she knew about sin-eaters. No, it was the lying and the fact that he was a drug dealer that killed it for her.

A drug dealer. In a flash, she saw the ODs that had come through the doors of Havers's clinic, those young lives in danger for no good reason. Some of those patients had been revived, but not all and even one death caused by what Rehvenge had sold was too much.

Ehlena wiped her cheeks and rubbed her hands on her slacks. No more crying. She couldn't afford the luxury of being weak. She had her father to take care of.

She spent the next half hour applying for jobs.

Sometimes the fact that you were forced to be strong was enough to actually turn you into what you had to be.

When her eyes finally threw in the towel and started crossing from exhaustion, she turned off the computer and stretched out on her bed next to her father's manuscript. As she let her lids fall, she had a feeling she wasn't going to sleep. Her body might be calling it quits, but her brain didn't seem interested in playing follow-the-leader.

Lying there in the dark, she tried to quiet herself by imagining the old house she and her parents had lived in before everything had changed. She pictured herself walking through the grand rooms, going by the lovely antiques, pausing to sniff at a bouquet of flowers that had been cut fresh from the garden.

The trick worked. Slowly, her mind vested itself in the calm, elegant place, her racing thoughts downshifting, then braking, then parking in her skull.

Just as rest crept upon her, she had the oddest conviction strike the center of her chest, the surety of it flowing throughout her whole body.

Rehvenge was alive.

Rehvenge was alive.

Fighting against the knockout tide, Ehlena struggled for rational thought, wanting to pin down the why and what-the-hell of the belief, but sleep seeped into her, carrying her away from everything.

Wrath sat behind his desk, hands traveling gently across the surface. Phone, check. Dagger-shaped envelope opener, check. Papers, check. More papers, check. Where was his—

There was a knock and a scatter. Right, pen holder and pens.

All over everywhere. Check.

As he gathered up what he'd spilled, he heard Beth come forward to help, her footfalls soft on the rug.

"It's okay, *leelan*," he told her. "I got it."

He could sense her hovering over the desk and was glad she didn't intervene. As childish as it seemed, he needed to clean up his own mess by himself.

Patting around, he found every last pen. At least, he thought he had.

"Any on the floor?" he asked.

"One. By your left foot."

"Thanks." He ducked under, felt around the floor, and locked his fist around the smooth, cigarlike body of what had to be a Mont Blanc. "That would have been harder to find."

As he straightened, he was careful to locate the lip of the desktop and make sure his head was free of it before sitting up. Which was an improvement to what he'd done earlier in the day. Right, so, he was fucked on the pen holder, but doing better on the whole getting-upright thing. Not a perfect report card, but he wasn't cursing and he wasn't bleeding.

So, considering where he'd been hours ago on the way to Last Meal, things were looking up.

Wrath finished his hand parade across the desk, finding the lamp, which was over on the left, and the royal seal and the wax he used to mark documents.

"Don't cry," he said softly.

Beth sniffled a little. "How did you know?"

He tapped his nose. "I smelled it." He pushed his chair back and patted his lap. "Come over here and sit. Let your male hold you."

He heard his *shellan* ease around the desk, and the scent of her crying grew stronger because the closer she got to him, the more her tears fell. As he always did, he found her waist, hooked his arm about her, and pulled her onto him, the dainty chair squeaking as it accommodated the added weight. With a smile, Wrath let his hands find the waving length of her hair and he stroked the softness.

"You feel so good to me."

Beth shuddered and leaned into him, and he was glad she did. Unlike when he had to use his hands as his eyes or was picking up something he'd knocked over, with her warm body in his hold, he felt strong. Big. Powerful.

He needed all that right now, and going by the way she sagged into his chest, she needed it, too.

"You know what I'm going to do after we're done pushing papers?" he murmured.

"What?"

"I'm going to take you to bed and keep you there for a day straight." As her scent flared, he laughed with satisfaction. "You wouldn't mind that, huh. Even though I'm going to get you naked and make you stay that way."

"Not in the slightest."

"Good."

They stayed together for a long while, until Beth's head lifted from his shoulder. "You want to do some work now?"

He moved his head so that, had he had sight, he would have been looking at the desk. "Yeah, I kind of ... shit, I need to. I don't know why. I just need to. Let's start easy. ... Where's Fritz's mailbag?"

"Right here next to Tohr's old chair."

As Beth bent down, her ass drove into his cock in the most satisfying way, and with a groan, he grabbed her hips and surged upward. "Mmm, anything else on the floor that needs picking up? Maybe I should spill some more pens. Knock over the phone."

Beth's throaty laugh was sexier than lingerie. "If you want me to bend over, all you need to do is ask."

"God, I love you." As she righted herself, he turned her head and kissed her lips, lingering on the softness of her mouth, stealing a quick lick ... getting hard as a log. "Let's go through the paperwork fast so I can get you where I want you."

"And where would that be?"

"On top of me."

Beth laughed again and opened up the leather satchel that Fritz used to pick up snail-mail requests. There was a shifting of envelopes against envelopes and a deep breath from his *shellan*.

"Okay," she said. "What have we got here."

There were four mating requests that needed to be

signed and sealed, and normally that would have taken him all of a minute and a half. Now, though, the John Hancock, wax-and-press business took some coordination with Beth—but that was fun with her on his lap. Then there were a bunch of bank statements for the household. Followed by bills. Bills. More bills. All of which would go to V for online payments, thank fuck, as Wrath was not into micromanaging numbers.

"One last thing," Beth said. "A big envelope from a law office."

As she reached forward, no doubt for his sterling-silver dagger opener, he ran his hands down her thighs and up their insides.

"I love how your breath catches like that," he said, nuzzling the back of her neck.

"You heard that?"

"You'd better believe it." He continued his stroking, wondering if maybe he might just turn her around and settle her on top of his erection. God knew, he could lock the door from where he was. "What's in the envelope, *leelan*?" He slipped one hand directly between her thighs, covering her core, massaging it. This time her gasp was his name, and how sexy was that. "What you got there, female?"

"It's . . . a declaration of . . . bloodline," Beth said huskily, her hips beginning to rock. "For the purposes of a will."

Wrath moved his thumb over her sweet spot and nipped her shoulder. "Who died."

After a gasp, she said, "Montrag, son of Rehm." At the name, Wrath froze and Beth shifted, as if she'd turned her head back to look at him. "Did you know him?"

"He was the one who wanted me killed. Which means by the Old Law, everything that was his is now mine."

"That bastard." Beth cursed some more, and there was the sound of pages being turned. "Well, he's got a lot of . . . Wow. Yeah. Very wealthy—hey. It's Ehlena and her dad."

"Ehlena?"

"She's a nurse at Havers's clinic. Nicest female you ever met. She was the one who helped Phury evac the old facility when the raids were going on? Evidently, she—well, her father—is the next of kin, but he's very ill."

Wrath frowned. "What's wrong with him?"

"Says here mental incompetence. She's his legal guardian and caretaker, and that must be hard. I don't think they have much money. Saxton, the lawyer, has written a personal— Oh, this is interesting. . . ."

"Saxton? I met him the other night. What did he say?"

"He said he feels very certain that her father's and her bloodline certificates are authentic, and he's willing to put his reputation on the line to vouch for them. He's hoping you will expedite the distribution of the estate, as he's worried about the poor conditions they're living in. He says . . . he says they are worthy of the windfall that has unexpectedly presented itself. The 'unexpectedly' is underlined. Then he adds . . . they hadn't seen Montrag in a century."

Saxton hadn't struck him as a stupid guy. Far from it. Even though the whole assassination thing hadn't been confirmed back at Sal's, that handwritten note sure as hell seemed like a subtle way of urging Wrath not to exercise his vested rights as monarch . . . in favor of relatives who were shocked to find out they were on the next-of-kin list, in need of the money—and had nothing to do with the plot.

"What are you going to do?" Beth asked, drawing his hair back from his brow.

"Montrag deserved what happened to him, but it would be cool if something good came out of it. We don't need the assets, and if that nurse and her father—"

Beth pressed her mouth to his. "I love you so much."

He laughed and held her to his lips. "You want to show me?"

"After you seal this approval? You got it."

To process the will, they got to play around with the flame and the wax and his royal seal again, but he was in a rush this time, unable to wait a second longer than he had to before getting into his female. His signature was still drying and the seal still cooling when he took Beth's mouth again—

The knock on the doors made him growl as he glared at the sound. "Go. Away."

"I got news." Vishous's muffled voice was low and tight. Which added the modifier *bad* to what he'd said.

Wrath opened the panels with his mind. "Talk to me. But make it quick."

Beth's shocked inhale gave him an idea of V's expression. "What's happened?" she murmured.

"Rehvenge is dead."

"What?" they both said at the same time.

"I just got the call from iAm. ZeroSum's been bombed into dust, and according to the Moor, Rehv was in it when it went. No way there was a survivor."

There was a dead zone as the implications set in.

"Does Bella know?" Wrath said grimly.

"Not yet."

SIXTY

John Matthew rolled over in his bed and woke up when something hard poked against his cheek. With a curse, he lifted his head. Oh, right, he and Jack Daniel's had gone a couple rounds, and the aftermath of the whiskey's fists lingered: He was too hot even though he was naked, his mouth was dry as tree bark, and he needed to hit the bathroom before his bladder exploded.

Sitting up, he rubbed his hair and eyes . . . and succeeded in waking a hangover.

As his head started to pound, he grabbed for the bottle he'd been using as a pillow. There was only an inch of booze left in the bottom, but that was enough to pull a dog-that-bitcha. Ready for relief, he went to unscrew the cap to the Jack and found that he hadn't put it on. Good thing he'd passed out with the bottle upright.

Drinking hard, he pulled the shit down into his belly and told himself to just breathe through the shock waves of nausea that fired up in his gut. When there were only fumes left in the bottle, he let the dead soldier sit on the mattress and looked down his body. His cock was asleep against his thigh, and he couldn't remember the last time he'd woken up without an erection. Then again, he'd been with . . . three? four? How many women had there been? God, he had no idea.

He'd used a condom once. With the prostitute. The rest had been bareback pullouts.

In shady images, he saw Qhuinn and him two-timing some of the women, then going solo on others. He couldn't remember what it had all felt like, remembered nothing of the orgasms he'd had, knew none of their faces, barely recalled their hair colors. What he did know was that as soon as he'd come back to this room, he'd had a long, hot shower.

All that shit he couldn't recollect had left a stain on his skin.

With a groan, he shifted his legs off the bed and let the bottle fall on the floor next to his feet. The trip to the bathroom was a real party, his balance so far off that he weaved . . . well, like a drunk, as a matter of fact. And walking wasn't the only problem he had. Standing over the toilet, he had to brace himself against the wall and concentrate on his aim.

Back in bed, he pulled a sheet over his lower body, in spite of the fact that he felt like he had a fever: Even though he was alone, he didn't want to lie around like some porn star looking for a supporting actress.

Shit . . . his head was killing him.

As he closed his eyes, he wished he'd turned the light off in the bathroom.

Abruptly he stopped caring about the hangover, though. With terrible clarity, he remembered Xhex straddling his hips and riding him in a fluid, powerful rhythm. Oh, God, it was so vivid, so much more than a just a memory. As the pictures played out, he felt the tight hold of her body on his sex and the hard way she held his shoulders down, reliving that sense of being mastered.

He knew every shift and slide, all the scents, even the way she breathed.

With her, he remembered everything.

Leaning to the side, he picked the Jack up off the floor, as if by some miracle the alkie elves had refilled the fucker. No such luck—

The scream that lit off next door was the kind someone made when they'd been stabbed deep and hard, and the tearing screech sobered him like he'd been splashed with an ice bath. John grabbed his gun, shot out of bed, and hit the floor running, throwing open the door and racing into the hall of statues. On both sides of his room, Qhuinn and

Blay did the same, making the same rushed, ready-to-fight appearance he did.

Down at the end of the corridor, the Brotherhood was standing in the doorway of Zsadist and Bella's quarters, their faces dark and sad.

"No!" Bella's voice was loud as the scream had been. *"No!"*

"I'm so sorry," Wrath said.

From the knot of Brothers, Tohr looked over at John. The male's face was white and drawn, his stare hollow.

What happened? John signed.

Tohr's hands moved slowly. *Rehvenge is dead.*

John took a lot of deep breaths. Rehvenge . . . dead?

"Jesus Christ," Qhuinn muttered.

From the doorway of her bedroom, Bella's sobs tumbled into the hall, and John wanted to go to her. He remembered what that pain was like. He'd been in those horrible, numbing shoes when Tohr had taken off, right after the Brotherhood had done exactly what they were doing now—reporting the worst news that anyone could hear.

He'd screamed the same as Bella had. Wept the same as she was now.

John glanced back to Tohr. The Brother's eyes burned as if there were things he wanted to say, hugs he wanted to offer, regrets he wanted to make right.

For a split second, John almost went to the guy.

But then he turned away and stumbled into his room, shutting the door and locking it. As he sat down on the bed, he braced the weight of his shoulders against his hands and let his head hang down. Banging around in his brain was the chaos of the past, but at the center of his chest was a single, overriding word: *No.*

He couldn't go there with Tohr again. He'd been through the wringer too many times. Besides, he wasn't a child anymore, and Tohr never had been his father, so that whole daddy-save-me shit didn't apply to the two of them.

The closest they were going to get was fighter-to-fighter.

Shoving the Tohr crap out of his head, he thought of Xhex.

She was hurting right now. Badly.

He hated that there was nothing he could do for her.

Except then he reminded himself that even if there were, she wouldn't have wanted what he had to offer. She'd made that perfectly clear.

Xhex sat on the twin bed in her place on the Hudson River, head hanging low, the weight of her shoulders braced against her hands. Next to her, on the thin blanket, was the letter iAm had given her. After taking it out of its envelope, she'd read it once, refolded it along its pristine creases, and retreated into this small room.

Shifting her head to the side, she looked out through frosted windows to the sluggish, murky river. It was bitterly cold today, the temperature slowing the current of the water down and icing up the rocky shores.

Rehv was such a bastard.

When she'd sworn to him that she would take care of a female, she hadn't thought that vow through well enough. In the letter, he called her on the pledge and identified the female as herself: She was not to come for him, nor endanger the life of the princess in any way. Furthermore, in the event she did anything like that on his behalf, he would not accept her help and would choose to stay in the colony no matter what actions she took in the name of saving him. Finally, he directed that should she go against his wishes and her word, iAm was to follow her to the colony, thus endangering the life of the Shadow.

Mother. Fucker.

It was the perfect endgame, worthy of a male like Rehv: She might be tempted to can her vow, and she might think there was a way to talk sense into her boss, but she already had the burden of Muhrder's life around her neck, and now Rehvenge's. Adding iAm's to the list would kill her.

Plus Trez would go after his brother. Making it an even four.

Caged by the situation, she gripped the edge of the mattress so hard her forearms shook.

The knife got into her palm somehow; only later would she recall that she'd had to stand up and walk naked across the room to her leathers to get it out of its holster.

Back on the bed, she thought of the males she'd lost over the course of her life. She saw Muhrder's long dark hair and his deep-set eyes and the scruff he always had on his heavy jaw . . . heard his Old Country accent and recalled the way he'd always smelled of gunpowder and sex. Then she saw Rehvenge's amethyst stare and his mohawk and his beautiful clothes . . . smelled his Must de Cartier cologne and relived his chic brutality.

Finally, she pictured John Matthew's dark blue eyes and short-cropped military-style hair . . . felt him moving deep inside of her . . . heard his heavy breathing as his warrior body had given her what she'd wanted and hadn't been able to handle.

They were all gone, even though at least two of them were still alive on the planet. But people didn't have to be dead to be out of your life.

She looked down at the viciously sharp, shiny blade and angled the thing so that it caught the weak sunlight in a flash that momentarily blinded her. She was good with knives. They were her favorite weapon, actually.

The knock on her door brought her head up.

"You okay in there?"

It was iAm—who not only had acted as Rehv's mail carrier, but was evidently charged with babysitting. She'd tried to throw him out of her house, but he'd just shadowed on her, taking a form that she couldn't get hold of, much less bootlick out the damn door.

Trez was sitting in the hunting cabin's main room, as well, but talk about role reversal. When she'd locked herself in her bedroom, he'd been stock-still in a hard-backed chair, staring out over the river in a heavy silence. In the wake of the tragedy, the brothers had traded personalities, iAm being the only one who talked: As far as she recalled, Trez hadn't said one thing since the news had droppped.

All that quiet was not about Trez mourning, though. His emotional grid was marked with anger and frustration, and she had a feeling Rehv, in all his cocksucking wisdom, had found a way to trap Trez into inaction, too. Like her, the Moor was trying to find a way out, and knowing Rehv, there wouldn't be one. He was a master at manipulation—always had been.

And he'd put a lot of thought into this exit strategy. According to iAm, everything was all set up, not only on the personal levels, but the financial ones, too. iAm got Sal's; Trez got the Iron Mask; she got a chunk of cash. Ehlena was provided for as well, although iAm said he would handle that. The bulk of the family estate went to Nalla, with millions and millions of dollars passing to the young, along with all the heirlooms that, according to primogeniture, had been owned by Rehv, not Bella.

He'd exited beautifully, wiping clean ZeroSum's drug and bookie businesses entirely. The Mask still had girls for hire, but none of the other stuff was going to go down there or at Sal's. With the Reverend gone, the bunch of them were almost clean.

"Xhex, say something so I know you're alive."

There was no way iAm could get through the door or dematerialize inside to check and see if she was still breathing. The room was a steel safe, utterly impenetrable. There was even fine mesh skirting around the doorjamb so that he couldn't shadow his way in.

"Xhex, we already lost him tonight. You make it two for two and I'm going to kill you all over again."

"I'm fine."

"None of us is fine."

When she didn't reply, she heard iAm curse and move away from the door.

Maybe later she could help the two of them. They were, after all, the only people who knew what she felt like. Even Bella, who'd lost her brother, didn't know the exquisite torture the three of them were going to have to live with for the rest of their days. Bella thought Rehv was dead, so she could go through the mourning process and come out the other side and get on with her life in some fashion.

For Xhex, iAm, and Trez? They were going to be stuck in the limbo-hell of knowing the truth and being able to do nothing to change it—with the result being that the princess was free to torture Rehvenge for as long as he had a heartbeat.

As Xhex thought about the future, her grip on the dagger hilt tightened.

And got stronger as she brought the weapon downward onto her skin.

With her mouth screwed down tight to keep her pain inside, Xhex shed her own blood instead of tears.

Although what was the difference, really. *Symphaths* cried red, in the manner of the vein anyway.

SIXTY-ONE

Rehv's brain came back online in a slow wave of flickering consciousness. Awareness flared and faded and returned, spreading from the base of his skull up into his front lobe.

His shoulders were on fire. Both of them. Head was killing him from when that *symphath* had sweet-dreamed him with the sword hilt. And the rest of him felt curiously weightless.

On the other side of his closed lids, light twinkled around him and registered deep red. Which meant the dopamine was fully out of his system and he was now who he would forever be.

Breathing in through his nose, he smelled . . . earth. Clean, damp earth.

It was a while before he was ready to do a look-see, but eventually he needed some other reference point than the pain in his shoulders. Opening his eyes, he blinked. Candles as long as his legs were set up at the far reaches of what appeared to be some kind of cave, the tremulous flames atop each one bloodred and reflecting over walls that seemed fluid.

Not fluid. There were things crawling on the black stone . . . crawling all over—

His eyes shot down to his body, and he was relieved to see that his feet were not touching the moving floor. A glance up and . . . chains held him aloft from the undulating ceiling, chains that were anchored by ... bars inserted through his torso under his shoulders.

He was suspended in the midst of the cave, his naked body hovering above and below the shimmering, pulsating confines of rock.

Spiders. Scorpions. His prison was teeming with venomous guards.

Closing his eyes, he reached out with his *symphath* side, trying to find others of his kind, determined to get through the place where he was, to minds and emotions he could manipulate to get himself free: He might be in the colony to stay, but that didn't mean he had to keep hanging around like a chandelier.

Except all he could sense was a web of static.

The cast of hundreds of thousands that surrounded him formed an impenetrable psychic blanket, castrating his *symphath* side, allowing nothing into or out of the cave.

Anger rather than fear fisted in his chest, and he reached over to one of the chains and pulled on it using his massive pectoral muscles. Pain made him tremble head to foot as his body shifted in midair, but there was no budging his tether or dislodging the bolting mechanism that went through his flesh.

As he swung back to straight vertical, he heard a shifting sound, as if a door had opened behind him.

Someone came in, and he knew who, given how strong the psychic block they were putting up was.

"Uncle," he said.

"Indeed."

The king of the *symphaths* came shuffling around with his cane, the spiders on the floor breaking their quilt of bodies briefly to make way for him before swallowing up his path. Beneath those blood-colored imperial robes his uncle's body was weak, but the brain on top of that curved spine was incredibly strong.

Proof positive that physical strength wasn't a *symphath*'s best weapon.

"How fare thee in thy floating repose?" the king asked, his royal headdress of rubies catching the candlelight.

"Complimented."

The king's brows lifted above his glowing red eyes. "How so?"

Rehv glanced around. "Hell of a lock and key you've got me under. Which means I'm more powerful than you're comfortable with or you're weaker than you wish you were."

The king smiled with the serenity of someone utterly unthreatened. "Do you know that your sister wished to be king?"

"Half sister. And it doesn't surprise me."

"For a time, I gave her what she wanted in my will, but I realized that I was inappropriately swayed and I changed everything. That was what your tithes were for. She was using them to transact business with humans, of all things." The king's expression suggested this was akin to inviting rats into one's kitchen. "That alone indicates she is utterly unworthy to rule. Fear is far more useful to motivate subjects—money being comparatively irrelevant if one is looking to gain power. And killing me? She presumed she could best my succession plan that way, which vastly over-estimates her capabilities."

"What did you do with her?"

More of that serene smile. "What was fitting."

"How long are you going to keep me here like this?"

"Until she is dead. Her knowledge that I have you and that you are alive is part of her punishment." The king looked around at the spiders, something close to true affection flaring in his white Kabuki face. "My friends will guard you well, worry not."

"I'm not."

"You will be. I promise you." The king's eyes returned to Rehv's, his androgynous features shifting into something demonic. "I didn't like your father and was quite pleased that you killed him. That being said, you are not getting that chance with me. You live solely as long as your sister does, and then I shall follow your fine example and reduce the number of my kin."

"Half. Sister."

"So intent you are on distancing the ties between yourself and the princess. No wonder she adores you as much as she does. For her, that which is unattainable will always hold the most fascination. Which, again, is the only reason you live."

The king leaned on his cane and began to slowly creep

back the way he had come. Just before he got out of Rehv's sight, he paused. "Have you ever been to your father's grave?"

"No."

"It is my favorite place in all the world. To stand upon the ground where his funeral pyre burned his flesh to ash . . . lovely." The king smiled with cold joy. "That he was murdered by your hand makes it all even sweeter, as he'd always thought you were weak and worthless. Must have stung him rather badly to be bested by the inferior. Do rest well, Rehvenge."

Rehv didn't respond. He was too busy poking at his uncle's mental walls, seeking a way in.

The king smiled, as if he approved of the attempts, and headed on his way. "I always liked you. Even though you are but a half-breed."

There was a click, as if a door had closed.

All the candles went out.

Disorientation squeezed Rehvenge's throat shut. Left alone, floating in the darkness, with nothing to ground him, terror seized him hard. To be without sight was the worst—

The bolts through his upper body began to tremble slightly, as if a breeze were blowing through the chains and vibrating them.

Oh . . . God, *no*.

The tickling started on his shoulders and intensified in a rush, flowing down his stomach and over his thighs, streaming out to the tips of his fingers, covering his back, blooming up his neck to his face. He used his hands to the extent he was able, trying to brush off the horde, but as many as he cast down to the floor, more overcame him. They were on him, moving over him, coating him with a constantly shifting straitjacket of tiny touches.

The fluttering at his nostrils and around his ears was his undoing.

He would have screamed. But then he would have swallowed them.

Back in Caldwell, in the brownstone he was damn well going to move into, Lash showered with lazy precision, taking his time with the washcloth, going in between his toes and

behind his ears, paying special attention to his shoulders
and lower back. There was no need to rush.

The longer he waited the better.

Plus, what a bathroom to hang out in. Top-drawer everything, from the Carrera marble on the floors and walls to
the gold fixtures to the awesome stretch of etched mirror
over the sunken sinks.

The towels hanging from the ornate racks were from
Wal-Mart.

Yeah, and they were going to be replaced ASAP. The
fucking things were all Mr. D had had at the ranch house,
and Lash wasn't about to waste time driving around
Caldwell just to find something better to wipe his ass dry
with—not when he had his new piece of exercise equipment to put through its paces. After he got his workout in
this morning, though, he was going to get on the Internet
and order shit like furniture, bedding, rugs, kitchen supplies.

It would have to be delivered to that POS ranch where
Mr. D and the others stayed now, though. UPS men were
not welcome around here.

Lash left the bathroom light on and walked out into the
master bedroom. The ceiling was prewar height, which
meant the damn thing was so high cumulus clouds could
form and float around the hand-carved moldings if the at-
mospheric conditions were right. The floor was gorgeous
hardwood with inlaid cherry accents, and the walls were
papered in an amazing dark green swirl, like the inside covers of an antique book.

The windows had just been sealed over with cheap blankets they'd had to hammer into the moldings—a crying
shame. But like the towels, that would change. As would
the bed. Which was nothing but a king-size mattress on the
floor, its white, quilted skin laid out bare, like a Midwest-
erner trying to get a tan somewhere fancy.

Lash dropped the towel from his hips, his erection
springing forward. "I love that you are a liar."

The princess lifted her head, her shiny black hair shifting with flashes of blue. "Will you let me go? The fucking
will be better, I promise you."

"I'm not worried about how good it's going to be."

"Are you sure?" Her arms pulled against the steel chains that had been bolted into the floor. "Don't you want me to touch you?"

Lash smiled down at her naked body—which he now owned, for all intents and purposes. She was his gift, given by the *symphath* king as a gesture of good faith, a sacrifice that was also a punishment for her treason.

"You are going nowhere," he said. "And the fucking is going to be fantastic."

He was going to use her until she broke, and then he was going to take her out and make her find him vampires to kill. It was the perfect relationship. And if he got bored with her or she couldn't perform either sexually or as a divining rod? He would get rid of her.

The princess's eyes glared up at him, the bloodred color of them loud as a curse thrown at full volume. "You are going to let me go."

Lash reached down and started stroking his cock. "Only if it's to put you into your grave."

Her smile was pure evil, so much so, his balls tightened up like he was about to come. "We'll see about that," she said in a low, deep voice.

She'd been drugged by the king's private guard before Lash had left the colony with her, and when she'd been stretched out on this mattress her legs had been spread as far apart as possible.

So as her sex glistened for him, he could see it.

"I'm never letting you go," he said as he knelt down to the mattress and grabbed onto her ankles.

Her skin was soft and white as snow, her core pink as her nipples.

He was going to leave a lot of marks on her whip-thin body. And going by the way her hips rotated, she was going to like it.

"You are mine," he growled.

In a sudden flash of inspiration, he pictured his old rottweiler's collar around her slender neck. King's ownership tags were going to look great on her, and so was a dog's leash.

Perfect. Fucking perfect.

SIXTY-TWO

ONE MONTH LATER . . .

Ehlena woke up to the sound of china on china and the scent of Earl Grey tea. As her eyes opened, she saw a uniformed *doggen* struggling under the weight of a massive silver tray. On it was a fresh bagel capped by a crystal dome, a pot of strawberry jam, a scoop of cream cheese on a tiny porcelain plate, and, her favorite part, a bud vase.

Every night it was a different flower. This evening it was a sprig of holly.

"Oh, Sashla, you really don't have to do this." Ehlena sat up, pushing back sheets that were so fine and well made they were smoother than summer air against the skin. "It's lovely of you, but honestly . . ."

The maid bowed and offered a shy smile. "Madam should wake up to a proper repast."

Ehlena lifted her arms as a stand was put over her legs and the tray set on top of it. As she stared down at the lovingly polished silver and the carefully prepared food, her overriding thought was that her father had just gotten the same, served to him by a butler *doggen* by the name of Eran.

She stroked the fine curling base of the knife. "You are good to us. All of you. You've made us so welcome in this grand house, and we thank you very much."

When she looked up, there were tears in the *doggen*'s eyes, and the maid hastily patted them away with a handkerchief. "Madam . . . you and your father have transformed this house. We are of great joy that you are our masters. Everything ... is different now that you are here."

It was as far as the maid would go, but given how she and all the other staff had flinched for the first two weeks, Ehlena gathered that Montrag had not been the easiest head of household.

Ehlena reached over and gave the female's hand a squeeze. "I'm glad it's worked out for all of us."

As the maid turned away to resume her duties, she seemed flustered, but happy. At the door, she paused. "Oh, and Madam Lusie's things arrived. We've settled her in the guest suite next to your father. Also, the locksmith is coming in a half hour, as you requested."

"Perfect on both accounts, thank you."

While the door was shut quietly and the *doggen* went off humming a tune from the Old Country, Ehlena took the dome off her plate and knifed up some cream cheese. Lusie had agreed to move in with them and function as a nurse and personal assistant to Ehlena's father—which was fantastic. Overall, he'd taken to the new estate with relative ease, his demeanor and mental stability better than they had been for years, but the close supervision did much to ease Ehlena's lingering worry.

Being careful with him remained a priority.

Here in the mansion, for example, he didn't require tinfoil over the windows. Instead, he preferred to look out at the gardens that were beautiful even after having been put to bed for the winter, and in retrospect, she wondered if part of shutting out the world hadn't been because of where they'd been living. He was also much more relaxed and at peace, working steadily in the other guest bedroom next to his. He still heard the voices, though, and preferred order to mess of any kind, and he needed the medication. But this was heaven compared to what the last couple years had been like.

As Ehlena ate, she looked around the bedroom she'd chosen and was reminded of her parents' former manse. The curtains were the same kind that had hung back in her family's house, huge swathes of peach and cream and red falling from ruched headers with fringe. The walls were likewise done in luxury, the silk paper showing a pattern of roses that matched perfectly with the curtains, as well as coordinating with the needlepoint rug on the floor.

Ehlena, too, was at home in the surroundings, and yet utterly ungrounded—and not just because her life seemed like a sailboat that had capsized in cold water, only to abruptly right itself in the tropics.

Rehvenge was with her. Relentlessly.

Her last thought before she slept and her first upon waking was that he was alive. And she dreamed about him, seeing him with his arms at his sides and his head hanging down, silhouetted against a shimmering black background. It was a total contradiction, in a way, the belief that he was alive measured against that image of him—which seemed to suggest he was dead.

It was like being haunted by a ghost.

Make that tortured.

With frustration, she put the tray aside, got up, and showered. The clothes she changed into were nothing fancy, just the same ones she'd gotten from Target and on sale from Macy's online before everything had changed. The shoes . . . were the Keds Rehv had held in his hand.

But she refused to think about that.

The thing was, it didn't seem right to run out and spend a lot of money on anything. None of this felt like hers, not the house or the staff or the cars or all the zeroes in her checking account. She was still convinced Saxton was going to show up at nightfall with an oh-my-bad-all-this-should-have-gone-to-someone-else.

What a whoopsie that would be.

Ehlena took the silver tray and headed out to check on her father, who was down at the end of the wing. When she got to his door, she knocked with the tip of her sneaker.

"Father?"

"Do come in, daughter mine!"

She put the tray down on a mahogany table and opened the way into the room he used as his study. His old desk had been brought over from the rental bed, which had been placed next door, and her father was sitting down to his work as he always had, papers everywhere.

"How fare thee?" she asked, going over to kiss his cheek.

"I am well, very well indeed. The doggen *has just brought my juice and my repast."* His elegant, bony hand swept over a silver tray that matched the one she'd been brought. *"I adore the new* doggen, *don't you?"*

"Yes, Father, I—"

"Ah, Lusie, dearest!"

As her father rose to his feet and smoothed his velvet smoking jacket, Ehlena glanced over her shoulder. Lusie came in dressed in a dove gray sheath and a knobby hand-knitted sweater. She had Birkenstocks on her feet and thick, bunched-up socks that had likely been homemade as well. Her long, wavy hair was back from her face, pinned in a sensible clip at the base of her neck.

Unlike everything that had changed around them, she was still the same. Lovely and . . . cozy.

"I've brought the crossword." She held up a *New York Times* that was folded in quarters, as well as a pencil. *"I need help."*

"And, indeed, I am at your disposal, as always." Ehlena's father came around and gallantly angled a chair for Lusie. *"Ease yourself herein and we shall see how many boxes we may fill."*

Lusie smiled at Ehlena as she sat down. *"I couldn't do them without him."*

Ehlena's eyes narrowed on the female's faint blush and then shifted over to her father's face. Which was showing a distinct glow.

"I'll leave you two to your puzzle," she said with a smile.

As she left, two good-byes were given to her, and she couldn't help but think the stereo effect sounded very nice to the ear.

Downstairs in the grand foyer, she went left into the formal dining room, and paused to admire all the crystal and china that were set out on display—as well as the gleaming candelabra.

There were no candles topping those graceful silver arms, though.

No candles in the house. No matches or lighters either. And before they had moved in, Ehlena had had the *doggen* replace the gas-powered restaurant range with one that ran on electricity. Likewise, the two televisions in the family part of the house had been given to the staff, and the security monitors had been moved from an open desk in the butler's pantry to a closed room with a locked door.

There was no reason to tempt fate. Especially given that any kind of electronic screen, including those on cell phones and calculators, still made her father nervous.

The first night that they had come to stay at the mansion, she had taken pains to walk her father all around and show him the security cameras and the sensors and the beams not just in the house, but on the grounds. As she wasn't sure how he would handle the change in address or all the safety measures, she'd given him the tour right after he'd had his medications. Fortunately, he'd viewed the better accommodations as a return to normalcy, and had loved the idea that there was a system looking out all over the estate.

Maybe that was another reason he didn't feel the need to have the windows covered up. He felt as if he were being watched over in a good way now.

Pushing through the flap door, Ehlena went into the pantry and out to the kitchen. After chatting with the butler who had started cooking Last Meal, and complimenting one of the maids on how beautifully she'd polished the handrail of the big staircase, Ehlena headed for the study that was on the other side of the house.

The trip was a long one, through many lovely rooms, and as she went she trailed a gentle hand over the antiques and the hand-carved jambs and the silk-covered furniture. This lovely house was going to make her father's life so much easier, and as a result, she was going to have a lot more time and mental energy to focus on herself.

She didn't want it. The last thing she needed was empty hours with nothing but the crap in her head to keep her company. And even if she were in the running to win Miss Well-Adjusted, she wanted to be productive. She might not need the money to keep a roof over what was left of her family, but she'd always worked, and she'd loved the purpose and heart of what she'd been doing at the clinic.

Except she'd burned that bridge and then some.

Like the other thirty or so rooms in the mansion, the study was decorated in the manner of European royalty, with subtle damask patterns on the walls and sofas, plenty of tassels on the drapes, and lots of deep, glowing paintings that were like windows open to other, even more perfect worlds. There was one thing off the mark though. The floor was bare, the couches and the antique desk and every table and chair sitting directly on the polished wooden floor, the center of which was slightly darker than the edges, as if it had once been covered up.

When she'd asked the *doggen*, they had explained that the carpet had suffered a stain that was not removable, and thus a new rug had been ordered from the household's antiques dealer in Manhattan. They didn't go into any further detail about whatever had happened, but given how worried they all had been about their jobs, she could just imagine what Montrag would have done if there had been any kind of deficiency in performance, no matter how reasonable. One spilled tea tray? No doubt they'd had a big problem.

Ehlena went around and sat behind the desk. On the leather blotter, there was the day's *Caldwell Courier Journal*, a phone and a nice-looking French lamp as well as a lovely crystal statue of a bird in flight. Her old computer, which she'd tried to give back to the clinic before she and her father had come to the house, fit perfectly in the big flat drawer under the top—kept there always just in case he came in.

She supposed she could afford a new laptop, but again, she wasn't going to buy another one. As with her clothes, what she had worked just fine, and she was used to it.

Plus, maybe she was grounded a little by the familiar. And, man, she needed that.

Putting her elbows on the desk, she looked across the room at the spot on the wall where a spectacular seascape should have lain flat. The painting was angled out into the room, however, and the face of the safe that was exposed was like a plain female who'd been hiding behind a glamorous ball mask.

"Madam, the locksmith is here?"

"Please send him in."

Ehlena got to her feet, and went over to the safe to touch its smooth, matte panel and its black-and-silver dial. She'd found the thing only because she'd been so taken by the depiction of the sun setting over the ocean that she'd put her hand on the frame on impulse. When the whole picture popped forward, she'd been horrified that she'd hurt the mounting in some way, except then she'd looked behind the frame . . . and what do you know.

"Madam? This is Roff, son of Rossf."

Ehlena smiled and walked over to a male who was dressed in black coveralls and carrying a black tool case. As she went to put her hand out, he took off his cap and bowed low, as if she were someone special. Which was beyond strange. After years of being just a civilian, the formality made her uncomfortable, but she was learning that she had to let others honor the social etiquette. Asking them not to, whether they were *doggen* or workmen or advisers, just made things worse.

"Thank you for coming," she said.

"It is a pleasure to be of service." He looked over at the safe. "This is the one?"

"Yes, I don't have the combination to it." They headed for the thing. "I was hoping there was some way you could get into it?"

The wince he tried to hide was not encouraging. "Well, madam, I know this kind of safe, and it's not going to be easy. I'd have to bring in an industrial drill to get through the pins and release the door, and it would be noisy. Also, when I've finished the safe would be ruined. I mean no disrespect, but is there no way of retrieving the combination?"

"I wouldn't know where to look for it." She glanced around at the shelves of books and then over to the desk. "We just moved in, and there were no instructions."

The male followed her lead and ran his eyes around the room. "Usually owners leave such a thing in a hidden place. If you could only find it, I could show you how to reset the combination so that you could reuse the safe. As I said, if I have to drill in, it will have to be replaced."

"Well, I've been through the desk when I was exploring after we first came here."

"Did you find any hidden compartments in it?"

"Er . . . no. But I was just going through random papers and trying to make some space for my things."

The male nodded across at the piece of furniture. "In a lot of desks like that, you'll find at least one drawer with a false bottom or back that hides a small place. I wouldn't want to presume, but I could try to help you find one? Also, the moldings in a room like this might conceal spaces as well."

"I'd love another set of eyes on this, thanks." Ehlena went over and, one by one, removed the drawers of the desk, laying them side by side on the floor. As she went along, the male took out a penlight and looked into the holes that were revealed.

She hesitated when she got to the big drawer on the bottom left, not wanting to see what she'd stored there. But it wasn't as though the locksmith could see through the damn thing.

Muttering a quick curse, she pulled on the brass handle and did not look at all the sections she'd kept from the *Caldwell Courier Journal*, each folded in on itself to hide the articles she'd read and saved even though she didn't want to read them yet again.

She put that drawer as far away as she could. "Well, that's the last one."

With the male's head wedged under the desk, his voice echoed. "I believe there's a . . . I need my tape measure from my tool—"

"Here, I'll get it."

When she passed the thing over, he seemed astonished that she was helping. "Thank you, madam."

She knelt down beside him as he ducked backed under. "Is something off?"

"There appears to be . . . Yes, this is more shallow than the others. Let me just . . ." There was a squeak and the male's arm jerked. "Got it."

As he sat up, he had a rough-cut box in his workworn hands. "I believe the lid flips open, but I'll let you do it."

"Wow, I feel like Indiana Jones, just without the bullwhip." Ehlena lifted the top panel off and . . . "Well, no combination. Just a key." She took the slip of steel out, looked it over, then replaced it. "Might as well leave it where we found it."

"Let me show you how to put the hidden drawer back."

The male left twenty minutes later, after the two of them had knocked on all the walls and shelving and molding in the room and found nothing. Ehlena figured she'd search around one last time, and if she still ended up empty-handed, she'd have him come back with his big guns to bust the safe open.

Returning to the desk, she put the drawers into their slots, pausing when she got to the one that held all the newspaper articles.

Maybe it was the fact that she didn't have her father to worry about. Maybe it was the fact that she had some free time.

More likely, she was just having a weak moment in fighting back the need to know.

Ehlena took all the papers out, opening the folds and spreading them across the desk. All of the articles were about Rehvenge and the ZeroSum bombing, and no doubt when she cracked today's edition, she would find another to add to the collection. The reporters were fascinated by the story, and there had been a ton of coverage on it in the last month—not just in print, but on the evening news as well.

No suspects. No arrests. Skeleton of a male found in the rubble of the club. Other businesses he'd owned now run by his associates. Drug trade in Caldwell brought to a halt. No more murders of dealers.

Ehlena picked up an article off the top. It wasn't among the more recent ones, but she'd looked at it so much, she'd smudged the newsprint. Next to the text was a blurry picture of Rehvenge, snapped by an undercover police officer two years ago. Rehvenge's face was in shadow, but the sable coat and the cane and a Bentley were all clear.

The past four weeks had distilled her memories of Rehvenge, from the times they'd been together to the way things had ended with that trip she'd taken to ZeroSum. Instead of time dissolving the images in her head, what she remembered was becoming even clearer, like whiskey strengthening over time. And it was strange. Oddly enough, of all the things that had been said, good and bad, what came back to her most often was something that female security guard had barked at her as Ehlena had been on her way out of the club.

. . . that male has put himself in a rat-hole situation for me, his mother, and his sister. And you think you're too good for him? Nice. Where the hell do you come from that's so perfect?

His mother. His sister. Herself.

As the words banged around her head yet again, Ehlena let her gaze wander around the study until it reached the door. The house was quiet, her father busy with Lusie and the crossword puzzle, the staff working happily.

For the first time in a month, she was by herself.

All things considered, she should take a hot bath and cozy up to a good book ... but instead, she took her laptop out, cracked the screen open, and fired the thing up. She had the sense that if she followed through with what she wanted to do, she was going to end up going down into a deep, dark hole.

But she couldn't help herself.

She'd saved the clinical record searches she'd done on Rehv and his mother, and as both of them had been declared dead, the documents were technically part of public record—so she felt less as if she were invading their privacy as she called both files up.

She studied his mother's records first, seeing some familiar things from having previously scanned it, when she'd been curious about the female who had birthed him. Now, though, she took her time, searching for something specific. Although God knew what it was.

The recent notes that had been entered were nothing remarkable, just Havers's comments on the female's yearly checkups or her treatment for the occasional virus. Scrolling through page after page, she began to wonder why she was wasting time—until she got to a knee operation that had been performed on Madalina five years ago. In the pre-op notes, Havers had mentioned something about the degradation in the joint being a result of chronic-impact injury.

Chronic impact? On a female of worth from the *glymera*? That sounded more like what you'd get on a football player, for chrissakes, not Rehvenge's high-bred chatelaine mother.

Made no sense.

Ehlena went back farther and farther through more nothing-specials ... and then starting twenty-three years from the present she started to see the entries. One after the other. Broken bones. Bruises. Concussions.

If Ehlena didn't know better ... she'd swear it was domestic violence.

Each time, Rehv was the one who brought his mother in. Brought her in and stayed with her.

Ehlena went back to the last of the entries that seemed to indicate a female who was being abused by her *hellren*. Madalina had been accompanied by her daughter, Bella. Not Rehv.

Ehlena stared at the date as if some sudden break-through were about to come from the line of numbers. When she was still fixated five minutes later, she felt like shadows of her father's illness were once again moving across the floors and walls of her mind. Why the hell was she obsessing over this?

And yet even with that thought, she followed an impulse that would only make her obsession worse. She cracked open the search on Rehv.

Back, back, back through the entries . . . He'd started needing dopamine right around the time his mother had stopped coming in injured.

Maybe it was just a coincidence.

Feeling half-crazy, Ehlena shifted over to the Inter-net and went into the race's public-records database. Typing in Madalina's name, she found the registry of the female's passing, then hopped over to that of her *hellren*, Rempoon—

Ehlena leaned forward in the chair, her breath leaving on a hiss. Not willing to believe it, she went back to the re-cord on Madalina.

Her *hellren* had died on the night of the last time she'd come in hurt to the clinic.

With a sense that she was on the verge of answers, Ehlena considered the matching dates in light of what the female security guard had said about Rehvenge. What if he'd killed the male to protect his mother? What if that se-curity guard knew that? What if . . .

Out of the corner of her eye, she saw the picture of Reh-venge from the *CCJ*, his face in shadow, his fancy car and his pimp cane so very obvious.

With a curse, she slapped the laptop shut, put it back in the drawer, and got to her feet. She might not be able to control her subconscious, but she could take charge of her waking hours and not encourage this craziness.

Instead of driving herself more nuts, she was going to go

up to the master bedroom Montrag had slept in and poke around trying to find the combination to the safe. Later, she would have Last Meal with her father and Lusie.

And then she needed to figure out what she was going to do with the rest of her life.

"'...suggests that the recent killings of area drug dealers might have come to an end with the likely death of club owner and suspected drug kingpin Richard Reynolds.'" There was a rustle as Beth put the *CCJ* on the desk. "That's the end of the article."

Wrath shifted his legs around to more comfortably support his queen's weight in his lap. He'd been to see Payne about two hours ago, and his body was beat to shit, which felt really nice.

"Thanks for reading it to me."

"My pleasure. Now let me go tend the fire for a second. We've got a log that's about to roll out onto the carpet." Beth kissed him and stood up, the pansy chair creaking with relief. As she went across the study toward the fireplace, the grandfather clock started to chime.

"Oh, this is good," Beth said. "Listen, Mary should be coming in a minute. She's bringing you something."

Wrath nodded and reached forward, running his fingertips across the desk's top until he got to the glass of red wine he'd been drinking. By its weight, he knew that he'd almost finished it, and given his mood, he was going to want more. The shit about Rehv had been bothering him. Badly.

After he polished off his Bordeaux, he put the glass down and rubbed his eyes under the wraparounds he still wore. It might be weird to keep the sunglasses on, but whatever—he didn't like the idea that other people could look at his unfocused pupils and he couldn't see them staring at him.

"Wrath?" Beth came over to his side, and he could tell by her tense tone that she was trying to keep the fear out of her voice. "Are you all right? Does your head hurt?"

"No." Wrath tugged his queen back into his lap, the little chair creaking once again, its spindly legs wobbling. "I'm okay."

Her hands brushed his hair from his face. "You don't seem that way."

"I just . . ." He found one of her hands and took it into his own. "Shit, I don't know."

"Yes, you do."

He frowned hard and tight. "It's not about me. At least, not really."

There was a long pause, and then they both spoke at once:

"What is it?"

"How's Bella?"

Beth cleared her throat as if she were surprised by his question. "Bella's . . . doing the best she can. We don't leave her alone much, and it's good that Zsadist has taken some time off. It's just so hard that she lost both of them within days of each other. I mean her mother and her brother . . ."

"That shit about Rehv was a lie."

"I don't understand."

He reached around for the *Caldwell Courier Journal* she'd been reading him, and tapped the article she'd just finished. "I find it hard to believe that someone blew his ass up. Rehv was no dummy, and those Moors who guarded him? That head of security? No fucking way they'd let some cocksucker with a bomb anywhere near that club. Plus, Rhage said that he and V went to the Iron Mask the other night to drag John home, and the three of them are working there—iAm, Trez, and Xhex are still together. Usually people scatter after tragedy. Except that bunch is right where they always were, like they're waiting for him to come back."

"But there was a skeleton in the ruins, wasn't there?"

"Could be anyone's. Sure, it was male, but what else do the police know? Nothing. If I wanted to disappear from the human world—hell, even the vampire one—I'd plant a body and blow up my building." He shook his head, thinking of Rehv lying in his bed up at the Great Camp, so fucking ill . . . and yet well enough to have his assassin take care of the guy who'd wanted to kill Wrath. "Man, that SOB was there for me. He had every chance in the world to fuck me when Montrag met with him. I owe him."

"Wait . . . why in the world would he fake his own death? He loved Bella and her young so much. Hell, he practically raised his sister, and I can't believe he would ever hurt her like that. Plus, where would he go?"

The colony, Wrath thought.

Wrath wanted to tell his queen everything that was on his mind, but he hesitated, because he'd been flirting with a decision that was going to complicate the shit out of things. Bottom line was, that e-mail about Rehv? Wrath's intuition was telling him the guy had lied about it. It was just too co-incidental that the thing came in and the next night Rehv "dies." It had to have been legit. But with Montrag dead, who could have—

There was a sharp crack and a free fall and a hard-ass landing.

As Beth shrieked, Wrath cursed. *"What the fuck?"*

He patted around, feeling splinters of old, delicate French wood all around them.

"Are you okay, *leelan*?" he said sharply.

Beth laughed and got up to her feet. "Oh, my God . . . we broke the chair."

"Pulverized it might be more accurate—"

The knock on the door had Wrath struggling up to his feet with grunts of pain. Which he was getting used to. Payne always went for the shins, and his left leg was killing him. But it wasn't like he didn't return the favor. After this last session, it was quite possible that she was nursing a concussion.

"Come in," he called out.

The instant the door opened, he knew who it was . . . and that she was not alone.

"Who is with you, Mary?" he demanded, reaching for the knife he wore on his hip. The scent wasn't human . . . but it wasn't a vampire.

There was a subtle clinking and a long, lovely sigh from his *shellan*, as if she were looking at something that pleased her greatly.

"This is George," Mary said. "Please put your weapon away. He won't hurt you."

Wrath kept his dagger in the palm of his hand and flared his nostrils. The scent was . . . "Is that a dog?"

"Yes. He's trained to assist the blind."

Wrath recoiled slightly at the b-word, still struggling to accept that classification as pertaining to him.

"I would like to bring him over to you," Mary said in that level voice of hers. "But not until you put the weapon away."

Beth stayed silent, and Mary stayed back, which was smart of them. His neurons were firing in all kinds of directions, thoughts racing everywhere. The past month had had a lot of triumphs and a lot of shitty losses: Back when he'd returned from his first meeting with Payne, he'd known it was going to be a tough road ahead, but it had been longer and steeper than he'd thought.

The two biggest problems were that he hated having to rely so much on Beth and his brothers, and he found re-learning simple things was curiously exhausting. Like ... for fuck's sake, making toast for himself was now a production. He'd tried it again yesterday and succeeded in breaking the glass dish the butter was kept on. Which naturally had taken him forever to clean up.

Still, the idea of using a dog to get around was ... too much.

Mary's voice eased across the room with the vocal equivalent of an ambling, nonthreatening gait. "Fritz has been trained to handle the dog, and together he and I are prepared to work with you and George. There's a two-week trial period, after which, if you don't like it or it isn't working, we can return the animal. There is no obligation here, Wrath."

He was about to tell them to take the dog away when he heard a soft whine and more of that jingle.

"No, George," Mary said. "You can't go over to him."

"He wants to come to me?"

"We've trained him using a shirt of yours. He knows your smell."

There was a long, long period of silence, and then Wrath shook his head. "I don't know if I'm a dog person. Besides, what about Boo—"

"He's right here," Beth said. "He's sitting next to George. He came downstairs as soon as the dog entered the house, and he hasn't left George's side since. I think they kind of like each other."

Damn it, even the cat wasn't on his side.

More silence.

Wrath slowly sheathed his dagger and took two wide

steps to the left so he could clear the desk. Walking forward, he stopped in the center of the study.

George whimpered a little, and there was that quiet ringing of a harness again.

"Let him come to me," Wrath said darkly, feeling as if he were getting squeezed and not liking it in the slightest.

He heard the animal approach, the padding of paws and the chinking of the collar moving closer, and then . . .

A velvet-soft muzzle nudged at his palm, and a rasping tongue licked quickly over his skin. Then the dog ducked under his hand and eased up against his thigh.

The ears were silky and warm, the nap of the animal's fur curling slightly.

It was a large dog with a big, boxy head. "What kind is he?"

"A golden retriever. Fritz was the one who picked him."

The *doggen* spoke up from the door, as if he were afraid of entering the room, given how tense things were. "I thought it was the perfect breed, sire."

Wrath felt along the dog's flanks, finding the harness that went around his chest and the handle that the blind person would hold on to. "What can he do?"

Mary spoke up. "Anything you need. He can learn the layout of the house, and if you give him the command to take you to the library, he will. He can help you get around the kitchen, answer the phone, find objects. He's a brilliant animal, and if you two are a fit, you and he can be as independent as I know you want to be."

Frickin' female. She knew exactly what had been bothering him. But was an animal the answer?

George whined softly, as if he desperately wanted the job.

Wrath let go of the dog and stepped back as his whole body started to shake. "I don't know if I can do this," he said in a hoarse voice. "I don't know if I can . . . be blind."

Beth cleared her throat a little, as if she were choking up because he was.

After a moment, Mary, in her kind, firm way, said the hard thing that needed to be said: "Wrath, you *are* blind."

The unspoken so-deal-with-it resonated in his head, throwing a spotlight on the reality he'd been limping through. Sure, he'd stopped waking up every day hoping his vision would come back, and he'd been fighting with Payne and making love to his *shellan* so he didn't feel physically weak, and he'd also been working and keeping up with the king shit and all that. But none of it meant things were fantastic: He was hobbling around, running into shit, dropping crap . . . clinging to his *shellan*—who hadn't been out of the house for a month because of him . . . using his brothers to get him places . . . being the kind of burden he resented.

Giving this dog a chance didn't mean that he was all gung ho about being sightless, he told himself. But it might help him get around on his own.

Wrath turned so that he and George were facing the same direction, then stepped in close to the dog. Leaning to the side, he found the handle and clasped it.

"Now what do we do?"

After a shocked silence, as if he'd surprised the shit out of his peanut gallery, there was some discussion and demonstration, only a quarter of which he heard and absorbed. Evidently, though, it was enough to go with, because he and George were soon taking a trip around the study.

The handle had to be adjusted up to its limit so that Wrath didn't have to list to the side to hold on, and the dog was much better at the whole deal than his charge was. But after a while, the two of them headed out of the study and down the hall. Next trip was hitting the grand staircase and coming back up.

Alone.

When Wrath returned to his office, he faced the group that had gathered—and it was now a big one, as each of his brothers, as well as Lassiter, had apparently joined Beth and Fritz and Mary. Wrath caught the scent of each of them . . . and there was a fuckload of hope and worry in the breeze as well.

He couldn't blame them for the way they felt, but he didn't like the attention. "How'd you pick the breed, Fritz?" he said, because he needed to fill the silence and there was no reason to ignore the pink elephant in the room.

Or the blond dog, as it were.

The old butler's voice quavered, as if he, along with everyone else, were struggling with emotion. "I, ah . . . I chose him . . ." The *doggen* cleared his throat. "I chose him over the Labradors because he sheds more."

Wrath's blind eyes blinked. "Why would that be a good thing?"

"Because your staff enjoys vacuuming. I thought this would be a lovely gift for them."

"Oh, right . . . of course." Wrath chuckled a little, and then started to laugh. As the others joined in, some of the tension drained out of the room. "Why didn't I think of that."

Beth came over and kissed him. "We'll just see how you feel, okay?"

Wrath stroked George's head. "Yeah. Okay." He raised his voice. "Enough of the kibitzing. Who's on deck tonight for fighting? V, I need a financial report. Is John still passed out drunk in his bed? Tohr, I'm going to want you to contact the remaining families within the *glymera* and see if we can get any trainees to come back. . . ."

As Wrath barked out orders, it was good to have answers coming back at him and people moving around to sit and Fritz leaving to clean up after First Meal and Beth settling into Tohr's old chair.

"Oh, and I'm going to have to have something else to sit on," he said as he and George went behind the desk.

"Wow, you dusted that bitch, didn't you," Rhage drawled.

"I can make you something?" V suggested. "I'm good at carving."

"How about a Barcalounger?" Butch cut in.

"You want this chair?" Beth offered.

"If someone can just grab me that wing thing over in the corner by the fireplace?" Wrath said.

When Phury brought it over, Wrath sat down and pulled the chair forward—only to smash both his knees into the desk drawer.

"Okay, that had to hurt," Rhage muttered.

"We need something shorter," someone else said.

"This'll be fine," Wrath bit out tightly, taking his palm off George's handle and rubbing the twin pains. "I don't care what I sit in."

As the Brotherhood got down to business, he found himself putting his hand on the dog's big head and stroking the soft fur ... playing with an ear ... dipping down and finding the long waves that flowed from the animal's broad, strong chest.

Not that any of that meant he was keeping the the animal, of course.

It just felt nice, was all.

SIXTY-THREE

The following evening, Ehlena watched as her new friend, Roff the locksmith, drilled the holy hell out of the wall safe. The whine of his high-powered tool stung her ears, and the sharp smell of heated metal reminded her of the floor sanitizers that had been used in Havers's clinic. The sense that she was getting something—anything—done, however, made up for all of that.

"Almost finished," the locksmith called out over the din.

"Take your time," she yelled back.

It had become a personal thing between her and the safe, and that sucker was getting opened tonight come hell or high water. After looking all around the master bedroom with the help of the staff, and even going through Montrag's clothes, which had been creepy, she'd phoned the locksmith and was now enjoying the sight of that drill head disappearing farther and farther into metal.

Ultimately, she didn't care what was inside the damn thing, but what was critical was getting past the roadblock of not having the combination—and it was a relief to feel like herself again. She'd always been one to push through the hard stuff . . . much like that drill.

"I'm in," Roff said, retracting his tool. "Finally! Come have a look."

As the whine slowed into silence and the male took a breather, she went over and opened the panel. Inside was dark as midnight.

"Remember," Roff said as he began to pack up, "we had to cut the electricity and the circuit that tied it to the security system. There's usually a light that comes on."

"Right." She peered in anyway. It was just like a cave. "Thank you so much."

"If you'd like me to find you a replacement, I can?"

Her father had always had safes, some of them in walls, a couple down in the cellar that had been as big and heavy as cars. "I guess . . . we'll need one."

Roff glanced around at the study and then smiled at her. "Yes, madam. I think you will. I'll take care of you, though. Make sure you get what you need." ·

She turned and put her hand out. "You have been very kind."

He flushed from the collar of his coveralls up to his dark hairline. "Madam . . . you have been very nice to work for."

Ehlena saw him to the grand front door and then went back to the study with a flashlight she'd gotten from the butler.

Clicking the beam on, she peered into the safe. Files. Loads of files. Some flat leather cases she recognized from when her mother's jewels had still been around. More documents. Stock certificates. Bundles of cash. Two accounting ledgers.

Moving a side table over, she emptied everything out, making piles. When she got to the very back, she found a lockbox that she had to grunt in order to lift.

It took her about three hours to go through the paperwork, and when she was done, she was absolutely stunned.

Montrag and his father had been the corporate equivalent of mobsters.

Rising from the chair she'd tucked her butt into, she went up to the bedroom she used and pulled open the drawer of the antique bureau she'd put her clothes in. Her father's manuscript was held with a simple rubber band, which she snapped free with a flick of the hand. Leafing through the pages . . . she found the description of the business deal that had changed everything for her family.

Ehlena took the manuscript page downstairs to the documents and ledgers from the safe. Going through the set of books that recorded hundreds of transactions for business interests, real estate, and other investments, she found one

that matched the date, dollar amounts, and subject matter
that had been listed by her father.

It was there. Montrag's father had been the one who'd
double-crossed hers, and the son had been in on it.

Letting herself fall back in the chair, she took a long
hard look at the study.

Karma was indeed a bitch, wasn't it.

Ehlena went back to the ledgers to see if there were any
other people in the *glymera* who had been taken advantage
of. There hadn't been, not since Montrag and his father had
ruined her family, and she had to wonder if they'd moved
toward human dealings to decrease the likelihood of being
discovered as crooks and swindlers within the race.

She glanced down at the lockbox.

As this was clearly the night for airing dirty laundry, she
picked the thing up. It wasn't secured by a combination
lock, but a key one.

Looking over her shoulder, she stared at the desk.

Five minutes later, after having successfully pried open
the secret compartment in the lower drawer, she took the
key she'd found the night before back to the lockbox. She
had no doubt it was going to open the thing.

And it did.

Reaching inside, she found only one document, and as
she unfurled the thick, creamy pages, she had exactly the
same sense she'd had when she'd first talked to Rehvenge
on the phone and he'd asked her, *Ehlena, are you there?*

This was going to change everything, she thought for no
good reason.

And it did.

It was an affidavit by Rehvenge's father fingering his
killer, written while the male was dying of mortal wounds.

She read it twice. And a third time.

The witness was Rehm, father of Montrag.

Her mind flipped into processing mode, and she raced
for her laptop, getting the Dell out and calling up the clinical search she'd done on Rehv's mother. . . . Well, what do
you know, the date the affidavit had been dictated by the
dying male was the same as the last night Rehv's mother
had been brought into the clinic beaten up.

She took the affidavit and reread it. Rehvenge was a
symphath and a killer, according to what his stepfather had

said. And Rehm had known it. And Montrag had known it.

Her eyes went to the ledgers. Given what was in those records, father and son had been total opportunists. It was hard to believe that that kind of information wouldn't have been used at one time or another. Very hard.

"Madam? I've brought you tea?"

Ehlena looked up at the *doggen* in the doorway. "I need to know something."

"Of course, madam." The maid came over with a smile. "What may I answer for you?"

"How did Montrag die?"

There was a sharp rattle as the maid all but dropped the tray on the table in front of the couch. "Madam . . . surely you do not wish to speak of such a thing."

"How."

The *doggen* looked at all the papers that had been scattered around the disemboweled safe. Going by the resignation in the female's eyes, Sashla knew that secrets had been revealed, secrets that didn't reflect well on her previous master.

Diplomacy and deference quieted the maid's voice. "I would not wish to speak ill of the dead, nor to pay disrespect to the Sire Montrag. But you are the head of household, and as you have requested . . ."

"It's okay. You're doing nothing wrong. And I need to know. If it helps, think of it as a direct order."

This seemed to relieve the female, and she nodded, then spoke in a halting tone. When she fell silent, Ehlena glanced down at the glossy floor.

At least she knew why the rug was missing now.

Xhex was on the graveyard shift at the Iron Mask, just as she'd been at ZeroSum. Which meant as her wristwatch flashed three forty-five, it was time to do sweeps of the bathrooms while the bartenders were doing last call and her bouncers were hauling the drunk and drugged-up out into the street.

On its surface, the Mask was nothing like ZeroSum. Instead of steel and glass, it was all about the neo-Victorian, with everything black and deep blue. There were a lot of velvet drapes and private, deep couch booths, and fuck the technopop shit; the music was acoustic suicide, as depressive as anything that ever carried a backbeat. No dance floor. No VIP section. More places for sex. Fewer drugs.

But the escapist vibe was the same, and the girls were still working, and the liquor was still going fast as a mudslide.

Trez ran the place in a very low-key kind of way—gone were the days of a hidden back office and the pimptastic presence of a flashy owner. He was a manager, not a drug lord, and the policies and procedures over here didn't involve any knuckle-busting or pistol-whipping. Bottom line, there was a lot less to police because of the lack of wholesale and retail drug business—plus Goths were moodier and more introspective by nature, as opposed to the hyped-up, sparkly jackass set that had regulared ZeroSum.

Xhex missed the chaos, though. Missed . . . a lot of things.

With a curse, she hit the main ladies' bathroom, which was by the bigger of the two bars, and found a woman leaning into the darkened mirror over the sink. With an intent look, she was sweeping her fingertips under her eyes, not to clean up her eyeliner but to drag it down farther onto her paper white skin. God knew she had plenty of the Cover Girl smudgible to go around; she was wearing so much of the shit, she looked like someone had punched her twice with an andiron.

"We're closing," Xhex said.

"Okay, no problem. See you tomorrow." The girl pulled back from her *Night of the Living Dead* reflection and hustled out the door.

That was the fucked-up thing about the Goths. Yeah, they looked like freaks, but they were actually a lot cooler than the frustrated-frat-boy, wannabe–Paris Hilton types. Plus they had much better tats.

Yup, the Mask was a lot less complicated . . . which meant Xhex had more than enough time to indulge in her deepening relationship with Detective de la Cruz. She'd been down to the Caldwell police station twice already for interrogation, as had many of her bouncers—including Big Rob and Silent Tom, the two she'd sent to find Grady for her.

Naturally, both of them had lied beautifully under oath, saying they had been working with her at the time of Grady's death.

It was clear at this point that she was going to get grand juried, but the charges weren't going to stick. Undoubtedly the CSIers had gotten busy pulling fibers and hair from Grady, but they weren't going to get much on her that route as vampire DNA, like blood, disintegrated quickly. Plus she'd already burned her clothes and boots from that night, and the knife she'd used was widely available at hunting stores.

All de la Cruz had was circumstantial evidence.

Not that any of it mattered. If for some reason things got too hot, she was just going to disappear. Maybe head out west. Maybe she'd go back to the Old Country.

For fuck's sake, she should have left Caldwell already. Being so close and yet so far from Rehv was killing her.

After checking each of the stalls, Xhex went out and around the corner to the men's room. She knocked hard and put her head in.

The rustling and gasping and pounding sounds meant there were at least one woman and one man. Maybe two of each?

"We're closing," she barked.

Evidently her timing was spot-on, because a woman's high cry of orgasm echoed around the tile and then there was a lot of recovery panting.

Which she was not in the mood to listen to. It just reminded her of her short time with John.... Then again, what didn't? Since Rehv had taken off and she'd given up sleeping, she'd had many, many, many hours during the day to stare at the ceiling in her hunting camp and count the ways she'd fucked up.

She hadn't been back to that basement apartment. And was thinking she was going to have to sell it.

"Come on, move it," she said. "We're closing."

Nothing. Just that breathing.

Sick of the postcoital respiratory-theater group in the handicapped stall, she fisted up her hand and slammed the paper towel dispenser. "Getcha asses out of here. *Now.*"

That got their hustle on.

The first one out of the stall was what she thought of as a woman with crossover appeal. The female was dressed in the Goth tradition, with torn stockings and boots that weighed four hundred pounds and a lot of leather strapping, but she was Miss America beautiful and had a Barbie body.

And she'd been done but good.

Her cheeks were flushed and her overly black hair bed-headed, no doubt both effects caused by her having been worked out up against the tile wall.

Qhuinn was the next to leave the stall, and Xhex stiffened, knowing exactly who the third was in this trifecta of fucking.

Qhuinn nodded to her stiffly as he passed, and she knew he wouldn't go far. Not until—

John Matthew came out in the process of buttoning his fly. An Affliction shirt was shoved up his six-pack, and he wasn't wearing any boxers. In the glowing fluorescent lights, the smooth, hairless skin below his belly button was so tight, she could see the muscle fibers that ran down his torso and into his legs.

He did not look up at her, but not because he was shy or embarrassed. He simply did not care that she was in the room, and it wasn't an act. His emotional grid was ... empty.

Over at the sinks, John cranked the hot faucet on and pumped the soap dispenser on the wall. Lathering up the hands that had been all over that woman, he rolled his shoulders as if they were stiff.

There was stubble on his jaw. And bags under his eyes. And his hair hadn't been cut for a while, so the ends had started to curl up at the nape and around the ears. Most of all, he reeked of alcohol, the scent coming out of his very pores, as if no matter how hard his liver worked, it couldn't filter the shit from his blood fast enough.

Not good, not safe: She knew he was still fighting. She'd seen him coming in with fresh bruises and the occasional bandage.

"How long you going to keep this up?" she asked flatly. "This whole wino-slut thing?"

John turned off the water and came over to the paper

towel box that she'd just put a spectacular dent in. He was less than two feet away from her as he snapped a couple of white squares free and dried his hands as thoroughly as he'd washed them.

"Christ, John, this is a hell of a way to spend your life."

He tossed the wadded-up towels in the stainless bin. As he got to the door, he looked at her for the first time since she'd left him in her bed. There was no flicker of recognition or memory or anything in his face. The blue stare that had once sparkled was now opaque.

"John . . ." Her voice cracked slightly. "I'm really sorry."

With deliberate care, he extended his middle finger at her and left.

Alone in the bathroom, Xhex went over to the darkened mirror and leaned in just as the Goth had been doing next door. As her weight shifted forward, she could feel the cilices dig into her thighs and was surprised to notice them.

She didn't need them anymore, wearing the bands only out of habit now.

Ever since Rehv had sacrificed himself, she had been in so much pain, she didn't need the extra help to control her bad side.

Her cell phone went off in the pocket of her leathers, the beeping sound a drain on her. As she took the thing out, she checked the number . . . and closed her eyes hard.

She'd been waiting for this. Ever since she'd arranged for everything that came in to Rehv's old phone to be forwarded to hers.

Accepting the call, she said in an even voice, "Hello, Ehlena."

There was a long pause. "I didn't expect anyone to answer."

"Then why did you call his number." Another long pause. "Look, if this is about the money going into your account, there's nothing I can do about it. It was part of his will. If you don't want it, give it to charity."

"What . . . what money?"

"Maybe it hasn't kicked in yet. I thought the will had been certified by the king." There was another long pause. "Ehlena? Are you there?"

"Yes . . . " came the quiet response. "I am."

"If it wasn't about the money, then why did you call?"

The silence wasn't a surprise, given all that had come before. But what the female replied was a dead shocker.

"I phoned because I don't believe he's dead."

SIXTY-FOUR

Ehlena waited for a response from Rehv's head of security. The longer there wasn't one, the more she was certain she was right.

"He isn't, is he," she said with strength. "I'm right, aren't I."

When Xhex finally spoke, her deep, resonant voice was curiously reserved. "In the interest of full disclosure, I think you should be aware you're talking to another *symphath*."

Ehlena gripped her cell harder. "Somehow, that is not a news flash."

"Why don't you tell me what you think you know."

Interesting response, Ehlena thought. Not a he's-not-dead. Not by a long shot. Then again, if the female was a *symphath*, this could be going anywhere.

Which meant there was no reason to hold back. "I know that he killed his stepfather because the male was beating his mother. And I know that his stepfather was aware that he was a *symphath*. I also know that Montrag, son of Rehm, knew about the *symphath* thing, too, and that Montrag was ritualistically murdered in his study."

"And this math adds up to you how?"

"I think Montrag came forward with Rehvenge's identity and he had to go up to the colony. That explosion at the club was to hide the fact that he is what he is from other people in his life. I think that's why he chose to bring me to ZeroSum like he did. It was to get rid of me safely. As for

Montrag . . . I think Rehvenge took care of him on the way out." Long, long, long silence. "Xhex . . . are you there?"

The female let out a short, hard laugh. "Rehv didn't kill Montrag. I did. And it had nothing directly to do with Rehv's identity. But how do you know anything about the dead male?"

Ehlena sat forward in her chair. "I think we should meet."

Now the laughter was longer and a little more natural. "You have giant brass balls, you know that? I just told you I killed a guy and you want to hang out?"

"I want answers. I want the truth."

"Sorry to channel a little Jack Nicholson here, but are you sure you can handle the truth?"

"I'm on this phone, aren't I? I'm talking to you, aren't I? Look, I know Rehvenge is alive. Whether you're willing to admit it to me or not, it won't change a thing for me."

"Girl, you don't know shit."

"Fuck. You. He fed from me. My blood is in him. So I know he's still breathing."

Long pause and then a short chuckle. "I'm getting a picture of why he liked you as much as he did."

"So will you meet me?"

"Yeah. Sure. Where."

"Montrag's safe house in Connecticut. If you were the one who killed him, you know the address." Ehlena felt a shot of satisfaction as the line went dead quiet. "Did I forget to mention that my father and I are Montrag's next of kin? We inherited everything he had. Oh, they had to get rid of the rug you ruined. Why couldn't you have just killed the bastard out in the foyer on the marble?"

"Jesus . . . Christ. You're no little nursey, are you."

"Nope. So are you coming or not?"

"I'll be there in a half hour. And don't worry, you aren't getting a houseguest overday. *Symphaths* have no problem with sunlight."

"See you in a few."

As Ehlena hung up, energy drummed through her veins and she raced around to tidy up, gathering together all the ledgers and cases and documents and filling the now impotent safe's belly. After she put the seascape back against the wall, she shut down her computer, told the *doggen* that she was expecting a visitor, and—

The gong of the front doorbell reverberated through the house, and she was glad she was the one who made it to the door first. Somehow she didn't think the staff would feel comfortable around Xhex.

Swinging the huge panels wide, she stepped back a little. Xhex was just as she remembered, a hard-ass female in black leathers with hair cut short as a man's. Something had changed, though, since she'd seen the security guard last. She seemed . . . thinner, older. Something.

"You mind doing this in the study?" Ehlena asked, hoping to get them behind closed doors before the butler and the maids came.

"You are brave, aren't you. Considering the last thing I did in that room."

"You had your chance to come after me. Trez knew where I was living before we ended up here. If you were that pissed off about me and Rehv, you'd have come for me then. Shall we?"

As Ehlena extended her arm toward the room in question, Xhex smiled a little and headed in that direction.

Once they had some privacy, Ehlena said, "So how much of it did I get right?"

Xhex prowled around, pausing to look at the paintings and the shelved books and a lamp that was made out of an Oriental vase. "You're right. He did kill his stepfather for what that bastard was doing at home."

"Was that what you meant when you said he put himself in a rough position for his mother and his sister?"

"Partially. His stepfather terrorized that family, especially Madalina. Thing was, she thought she deserved it, and besides, it was less than what had been done to her by Rehv's father. Female of worth, she was. I liked her, even though I only met her once or twice. I wasn't her kind of chick, not by a long shot, but she was nice to me."

"Is Rehvenge up in the colony? Did he fake his own death?"

Xhex stopped in front of the seascape and looked over her shoulder. "He wouldn't want us talking like this."

"So he is alive."

"Yes."

"In the colony."

Xhex shrugged and continued her meandering, her slow, easy strides doing nothing to mask the innate power in her body. "If he had wanted you involved in all of this, he would have done things very differently."

"Did you kill Montrag to keep the affidavit from getting out?"

"No."

"Why did you kill him then?"

"That is none of your business."

"Wrong answer." As Xhex's head whipped around, Ehlena squared her shoulders. "Considering what you are, I could go to the king right now and blow your cover. So I think you need to tell me."

"Threatening a *symphath*? Careful, I bite."

The lazy smile tacked onto the words made Ehlena's heart flicker with fear, reminding her that what was staring across the room at her was nothing she was used to dealing with, and not because of the whole *symphath* thing: Those cold gunmetal gray eyes of Xhex's had looked down on a lot of dead people—because she had killed them.

But Ehlena wasn't backing off.

"You won't hurt me," she said with utter conviction.

Xhex bared long white fangs, a hiss coming up and out of her throat. "Won't I."

"No . . ." Ehlena shook her head, an image of Rehvenge's face as he held her Keds in his hand coming to mind. Knowing what he'd done to keep his mother and his sister safe . . . made her believe what she had seen in him at that moment. "He would have told you not to touch me. He would have protected me on his way out. That's why he did what he did at ZeroSum."

Rehvenge hadn't been all good. Not by a long shot. But she had looked into his eyes and smelled his bonding scent and felt his kind hands on her body. And at ZeroSum, she had seen the pain in him and heard the strain and desperation in his voice. Whereas before she had assumed all that was either for show or out of disappointment that his cover was blown, now she had a different picture of it.

She knew him, goddamn it. Even after all the shit he had left out, even after the lies of omission, she *knew* him.

Ehlena lifted her chin and stared across the study at a trained killer. "I want to know everything, and you are going to tell me."

Xhex spoke for a half hour straight, and she was surprised by how good it felt. Surprised also by how much she approved of Rehv's choice of female. The entire time she was rolling out the horrors, Ehlena sat on one of the silk sofas all calm and steady—even though there were a lot of bombs.

"So the female who came to my door," Ehlena said, "that's the one who's blackmailing him?"

"Yes. It's his half sister. She's married to his uncle."

"God, how much money did she take him for over the past twenty years? No wonder he needed to keep the club open."

"It wasn't just money she was after." Xhex looked straight into Ehlena's face. "She made a whore out of him."

Ehlena's cheeks drained of color. "What do you mean?"

"What do you think I mean." Xhex cursed and started to pace again, going around the fringes of the gorgeous room for the hundredth time. "Look ... twenty-five years ago I fucked up, and to protect me, Rehv struck a deal with the princess. Every month he went up north and paid her the money ... and had sex with her. He hated it and despised her. Plus, she made him sick, literally—she poisoned him when he did what he had to, which was why he needed that antivenin. But, you know ... even though it cost him a lot, he kept on making that trip so she wouldn't blow our covers. He's been paying for my mistake month after month, year after year."

Ehlena shook her head slowly. "Good ... his half sister ..."

"Don't you dare harsh on him for that. There are very few *symphaths* left anymore, so inbreeding happens a lot, but more than that, he didn't have a choice, because I put him in the position of being trapped. If you think for one second he would have volunteered for that shit you're out of your fucking mind."

Ehlena raised a hand up as if to calm things down. "I understand. I just ... I feel badly for you and for him."

"Don't waste that on me."

"Don't tell me how to feel."

Xhex had to laugh. "You know, under different circumstances, I could like you."

"Funny, I feel the same way." The female smiled, but it was the sad kind. "The princess has him, then?"

"Yes." Xhex turned away from the couch, because she wasn't sharing what was no doubt in her eyes. "The princess was the one who blew his cover, not Montrag."

"But Montrag was going to come forward with that affidavit, wasn't he? Which was why you killed him."

"That was only part of what he was going to do. The rest of his plans are not my story to tell, but let's just say Rehv wasn't even the bigger part of it."

Ehlena frowned and leaned back in the cushions. She'd been fiddling with her ponytail, and wisps had come free of the scrunchie she pulled it back in—so that as she sat on the silk couch in front of a lamp, she had a halo around her.

"Must the world always be so harsh, I wonder," she murmured.

"In my experience, yup."

"Why didn't you go after him?" the female asked quietly. "And this is not a criticism—it truly isn't. It just seems out of character for you."

The fact that the question was phrased like that made Xhex slightly less defensive. "He made me take a vow not to. He even put it in writing. If I go back on my word, two of his best friends are going to die—because they're going to come after me." With an awkward shrug, Xhex took the goddamn letter out of the pocket of her leathers. "I have to keep this with me because it's the only thing that helps me stay put. Otherwise, I'd be up at that fucking colony this morning."

Ehlena's eyes clung to the folded envelope. "May . . . may I please see it?" Her lovely hand shook as she reached out. "Please."

The female's emotional grid was a tangled mess, strips of desolation and fear bound in ropes of sadness. She had been through the wringer these last four weeks, and she was in extremis, stretched beyond her limit and then some . . . but at the core, at the center, at the heart of her . . . love burned.

Love burned deeply.

Xhex put the letter against Ehlena's palm and held on to it for a brief moment. In a choked voice, she said, "Rehvenge . . . has been my hero for years. He's a good male in spite of his *symphath* side, and he's worthy of what you feel for him. He deserves so much better than he's gotten out of life . . . and to be honest, I can't imagine what that female is doing to him right now."

As Xhex released the envelope, Ehlena blinked quickly, as if she were trying to keep tears from spilling.

Xhex couldn't bear to look at the female, so she went over to stand before the oil painting that depicted a beautiful sun setting over a calm sea. The colors chosen were so warm and lovely, it was as if the seascape actually projected a glowing heat you could feel upon your face and shoulders.

"He deserved a real life," Xhex murmured. "With a *shellan* who loved him and a couple of young and . . . instead he's going to be abused and tortured for—"

That was as far as she could go, her throat closing up so hard she found it difficult to breathe. Standing in front of the glowing sunset, Xhex almost broke down and wept: The internal pressure of keeping all of the past and the present and the future inside of her rose to such a foaming, sizzling combustion that she looked down at her arms and hands to see if they had expanded.

But no, they were the same as always.

Locked into the skin she was in.

There was a soft rustle of paper, the letter sliding back into its envelope.

"Well, there's only one thing to do," Ehlena said.

Xhex focused on the burning sun in the center of the painting and forced herself to pull back from the brink. "And that is."

"We're going to go up and get him out."

Xhex shot a glare over her shoulder. "At the risk of sounding like we're in an action movie . . . there's no way you and I can go up against a shitload of *symphaths*. Besides, you read the letter. You know what I agreed to."

Ehlena tapped the envelope on her knee. "But it says you can't go on his behalf, right? So . . . what if I asked you to head up there with me. Then it would be on my behalf, right? If you're a *symphath*, surely you must appreciate that loophole."

Xhex's brain churned over the implications and she smiled briefly. "Quick thinking. But no offense, you're a ci-vilian. I'm going to need a lot more backup than you."

Ehlena rose from the sofa. "I know how to shoot, and I'm trained as a triage nurse, so I can deal with field injuries. Besides, you need me if you're going to get around that vow you're stuck with. So what do you say?"

Xhex was all for the guns-blazing shit, but if she got Ehlena killed in the process of letting Rehv out, that wasn't going to go over well.

"Fine, I'm going alone," Ehlena said, tossing the letter down on the sofa. "I'll find him and I'll—"

"Hold up, hard-ass." Xhex took a deep breath, picked up Rehv's last missive, and allowed herself to be open to the possibilities. What if there were a way to . . .

From out of nowhere, purpose poured into her, her veins firing up with something other than pain. Yes, she thought. She could see how to work this.

"I know who we can go to." She started to beam. "I know how we can do this."

"Who?"

She put her palm out to Ehlena. "If you want to go up there, I'm in, but we do it my way."

Rehv's nurse glanced down before leveling toffee-colored eyes on Xhex's face. "I go with you. That's my one condition. I. Go."

Xhex nodded slowly. "I understand. But everything else is up to me."

"Deal."

When their palms met, the other female's grip was strong and steady. Which, considering everything they were contemplating, boded well for how Ehlena would hold on to the butt of a gun.

"We're going to get him out," Ehlena breathed.

"God help us."

SIXTY-FIVE

"Okay, here's the deal, George. You see these fuckers? They're trouble, straight-up trouble. I know we've done this a couple of times, but let's not get cocky."

As Wrath tapped the bottom step of the mansion's staircase with his shitkicker, he pictured the stretch of red-carpeted on-your-ass going all the way up from the foyer to the second floor. "Good news is? You can see what you're doing. Bad news is? I go down and there's a risk I might take you with me. Not what we're looking for."

He absently stroked the dog's head. "Shall we?"

He gave the forward signal and started stepping up. George stuck right with him, the dog's slight roll of the shoulder transmitted through the handle as they ascended. At the top, George paused.

"Study," Wrath said.

Together, they walked straight ahead. When the dog stopped again, Wrath oriented himself by the sound of the crackling in the fireplace and was able to walk with the dog over to the desk. As soon as he sat down in the new chair, George took a seat as well, right next to him.

"I can't believe you're doing this," Vishous said from the doorway.

"Tough shit."

"Tell me you want us in with you."

Wrath ran his hand down George's flank. God, the dog's fur was soft. "Not at first."

"You sure?" Wrath let his raised eyebrow speak for itself. "Yeah, okay. Fine. But I'm going to be right outside the door the whole time."

And V wasn't going to be alone, no doubt. When the call to Bella's phone had come through in the middle of Last Meal, it had been a surprise: Everyone who could have been hitting her up was in the room. She'd answered the ring, and after a long silence, Wrath had heard a chair get pushed back and soft footsteps approach him.

"It's for you," she had said in a tremulous voice. "It's . . . Xhex."

Five minutes later, he'd agreed to see Rehvenge's second in command, and though nothing specific had been discussed, it didn't take a genius to figure out why the female had called and what she was going to want. After all, Wrath wasn't just king, he was gatekeeper to the Brotherhood.

Who all thought Wrath was nuts to see her, but that was the great thing about being the ruler of the race: You could do what you wanted.

Down below, the vestibule's door opened and Fritz's voice echoed up as he escorted the two guests into the mansion. The old butler was not alone as he came in with the females, having himself been escorted by Rhage and Butch when he took the Mercedes out for the pickup.

Voices and many feet came up the stairs.

George tensed, his haunches pulling up, his breathing changing subtly.

"It's okay, my man," Wrath murmured to him. "We're cool."

The dog eased immediately, which made Wrath look over at the animal even though he couldn't see anything. Something about that unconditional trust was . . . very nice.

The knock on the door brought his head back around. "Enter."

His first sense of Xhex and Ehlena was that they emitted grim purpose. His second was that Ehlena, who was on the right, was particularly nervous.

Going by the slight shifting of clothes, he imagined they were bowing to him, and the pair of "Your Highness"es that came his way confirmed the intuition.

"Take a seat," he said. "And I want everyone else out of this room."

None of his brothers dared to throw out a grumble, because the protocol button had been punched: If they were around outsiders, they treated him as their sovereign lord and king. Which meant no fucking around and no insubordination.

Maybe they needed visitors more often in the fucking house.

When the doors were shut, Wrath said, "Tell me why you're here."

In the pause that followed, he imagined the females were probably looking back and forth at each other to decide who went first.

"Let me guess," he cut in. "Rehvenge is alive, and you want to get him out of the shithole."

As Wrath, son of Wrath, spoke, Ehlena wasn't at all surprised the king knew what they'd come for. Sitting on the other side of a delicate and lovely desk, he was exactly what she remembered from when he'd nearly plowed her down back at the clinic: both cruel and smart, a leader in his physical and mental prime.

This was a male who knew how the real world worked. And was used to having the kind of muscle you needed to get hard things done.

"Yes, my lord," she said. "That's what we want."

His black wraparounds shifted over to her. "So you're the nurse from Havers's clinic. Who turned out to be Montrag's kin."

"I am, yes."

"Mind if I ask how you got involved in this sitch?"

"It's personal."

"Ah." The king nodded. "Got it."

Xhex spoke up, her voice grave and respectful. "He did a good thing for you. Rehvenge did a very good thing for you."

"You don't have to remind me. It's the reason you two are sitting here in my home."

Ehlena glanced over at Xhex, trying to read in the female's face what they were referring to. She got nothing. Not a surprise.

"Here's my question," Wrath said. "We bring him back, how are we going to get around the e-mail that came in to us? He said it was nothing, but clearly he lied. Someone from up north threatened to ID your boy, and if he gets loose . . . that trigger's going to be pulled."

Xhex spoke up. "I will personally guarantee that the individual who made that threat will not be able to use a laptop after I'm through with her."

"Niiiiiiiiiiiiiiice."

As the king smiled and drawled out the word, he leaned to the side and seemed to be stroking . . . With a start, Ehlena realized there was a golden retriever seated next to him, the dog's head just barely peeking up over the top of the desk. Wow. Odd choice of breed, in a way, as the king's companion was as kind-looking and approachable as its owner was not—and yet Wrath was gentle with the animal, his big, broad palm moving down its back slowly.

"Is that the only hole that needs to be plugged in his identity?" the king asked. "If that leak is eliminated are there any other parties who could threaten to expose him?"

"Montrag is good and dead," Xhex murmured. "And I can't think of anyone else who would know. Of course, the *symphath* king could come after him, but you can stop that. Rehv is one of your subjects as well."

"Damn fucking straight, and let's hear it for the whole 'possession is nine-tenths of the law' thing." Wrath's smile returned briefly. "Besides, the leader of the *symphaths* is not going to want to fuck with me, because if I get testy, I could take away his happy little home up there in freeze-your-nuts-off territory. He's under my privilege, as they used to say in the Old Country, which means he rules only because I let him."

"So are we going to do this?" Xhex asked.

There was a long silence, and as they waited for the king to speak, Ehlena looked around the pretty, French-inspired room to avoid Wrath's eyes. She didn't want him to know how anxious she was, and was afraid her face reflected weakness: She was totally out of her element here, sitting before the race's leader, presenting a plan that involved going into the very heart of an incredibly dark place. But she couldn't risk his doubting her or excluding her, because no matter how nervous she was, she wasn't backing down. Fear didn't mean you turned away from a goal. Hell, if she believed that, her father would be institutionalized right now, and she might well have ended up as her mother had.

Doing the right thing was scary sometimes, but her heart had taken her here to this place and was going to carry her through . . . whatever came next, and whatever it took to get Rehvenge out.

Ehlena . . . are you there?

Yes, she sure as hell was.

"Couple of things," Wrath said as he shifted around with a wince, like he had a fighting injury. "The king up there— he's not going to like us coming onto his turf and walking off with one of his own."

"With all due respect," Xhex cut in, "Rehv's uncle can go fuck himself."

Ehlena's brows popped up. Rehvenge was the nephew of the king?

Wrath shrugged. "I happen to agree, but my point is, there's going to be conflict. Armed conflict."

"I'm good with that," Xhex said evenly, like they were talking about nothing more than what movie to go see. "Very good."

Ehlena felt the need to interject herself into the conversation. "And so am I." As the king's shoulders stiffened, she tried not to be too forceful, because the last thing they needed was to get booted out the door for disrespect. "I mean, I would expect nothing more, and I'm prepared for it."

"You're prepared for it? No offense, but a civilian hanger-on is not a good thing if there's going to be fighting."

"With all due respect," she echoed Xhex's words, "I'm going."

"Even if it means I pull my men out?"

"Yes." There was a long inhale, as if the king were thinking of how to shut her down nicely. "You don't understand, my lord. That's my . . ."

"Your what?"

On impulse, to give her position some added weight, she said, "That is my *hellren*." In her peripheral vision, she caught Xhex's head whipping around toward her, but she'd jumped into the pool and couldn't get any wetter. "That's my mate and ... he fed from me a month ago. If they've hidden him, I can find him. Also, if they've done what they"—oh, Jesus—"probably have to him, he's going to need medical attention. And I'm going to give it to him."

The king played with his dog's ear, rubbing his thumb on the soft, pale brown flap. The animal clearly liked the way it felt, and leaned into his master's leg with a sigh.

"We have a medic," Wrath said. "And a physician."

"You don't have Rehvenge's *shellan*, though, do you."

"My brothers," Wrath called out abruptly. "Getcha asses in here."

When the study doors opened wide, Ehlena stared over her shoulder, wondering whether she'd pushed it too far and was about to be "escorted" out of the mansion. Sure as hell, any one of the ten tremendous males who came in would be up to the task. She'd seen them all before at the clinic, except for the one with the blond-and-black hair, and she was not at all astonished to find that they were fully armed.

To her relief, they did not perform a cash-and-carry on her, but settled around the dainty, light blue room, filling the place up to the rafters. It seemed a little odd that Xhex did not look at any of them, staying focused on Wrath instead—although maybe that made sense. As hard-core as the Brothers were, the king was the only one whose opinion truly mattered.

Wrath looked around at his warriors, his wraparounds shielding his eyes so that there was no way to tell what he was thinking.

The silence was a killer, and Ehlena's heart thundered in her ears.

At last, the king spoke. "Gentlemen, these lovely ladies want to make a trip up north. I'm prepared to let them go up there to bring Rehv home to us, but they're not going in alone."

The response was immediate from the Brothers.

"I'm in."

"Sign me up."

"When do we go."

"About fucking time."

"Oh, man, there's a marathon of *Beaches* running tomorrow night. Can we go after ten so I can see it once all the way through?"

Everyone in the room turned to the blond-and-black haired guy, who was propped up in the corner, massive arms over his chest.

"What," he said. "Look, it's not *Mary Tyler Moore*, 'kay? So you can't give me shit."

Vishous, the one with the black glove on his hand, glared across the room. "It's *worse* than *Mary Tyler Moore*. And to call you an idiot would be an insult to half-wits around the fucking world."

"Are you kidding me? Bette Midler rocks. And I love the ocean. Sue me."

Vishous glanced at the king. "You told me I could beat him. You promised."

"As soon as you come home," Wrath said as he got to his feet, "we'll hang him up by his armpits in the gym and you can use him as a punching bag."

"Thank you, baby Jesus."

Blond-and-Black shook his head. "I swear, one of these days I'm just going to leave."

As one, the Brothers all pointed at the open door and let silence speak for itself.

"You guys suck."

"Okay, enough." Wrath came around the desk and—

Ehlena sat up sharply. His palm was gripping the handle of a harness that went around the dog's chest, and the king's face was forward, his chin held high, so that he couldn't have been looking at the floor at all.

He was blind. And not in the sense of being unable to see very clearly. Given the way he was now, he couldn't see anything at all. When had this happened, she wondered. He'd appeared to have some vision when she'd last seen him.

Respect rolled through Ehlena's chest as she and everyone else in the room looked up at him.

"This is going to be tricky," Wrath said. "We need to send in enough fighters to provide both cover as well as search and rescue, but we don't want to create more disturbance than absolutely necessary. I want two teams, with the second on standby. We're also going to need car support in the event Rehvenge is incapacitated and we have to transport him back—"

"What are you talking about?" came a female voice from the doorway.

Ehlena glanced over her shoulder and recognized who it was: Bella, mate of the Brother Zsadist, who frequently helped with Safe Place patients. The female was standing between the ornate jambs with her young in her arms, her face drained of color, her eyes hollow.

"What about Rehvenge?" she demanded, voice rising. "What about my brother?"

As Ehlena started to connect the dots, Zsadist went to his *shellan*.

"I think you two need to talk," Wrath said carefully. "In private."

Z nodded and escorted his mate and young from the room. As the pair went down the hall, Bella's voice could be heard still, her questions peppered with increasing panic.

And then there was a *"What?!"* that seemed to indicate a bomb had just been dropped on the poor female.

Ehlena stared down at the lovely blue carpet. God . . . she knew exactly what Bella was going through right at this moment. The ripples of shock, the recasting of what she knew, the feeling of betrayal.

Hard place to be in. Hard to get out of, too.

After a door shut and the voices were dimmed, Wrath looked around the room as if giving everyone a chance to measure his resolve.

"Tomorrow night is showdown, because there isn't enough daylight left now to get a car up there." The king nodded to Ehlena and Xhex. "You both are staying here until then."

So that meant she was going? Thank the Virgin Scribe. As for the overday, she would have to call her father, but given that Lusie was in the house, she wasn't worried about being gone. "No problem for me—"

"I have to go," Xhex said tightly. "But I'll be back at—"

"Not an invitation. You are staying here so that I know where you are and what you are doing. And if you're worried about weapons, we have plenty of them—hell, we got a whole crateful off the *lessers* just last month. You want to do this? You're under our roof until nightfall."

It totally was obvious that the king didn't trust Xhex,

given the mandate and the way he smiled at her so fiercely.

"So what's it going to be, sin-eater?" he said smoothly. "My way or the highway?"

"Fine," Xhex shot back. "Whatever you want."

"Always," Wrath murmured. "Always."

An hour later, Xhex stood with her arms out straight in front of her and her boots planted eighteen inches apart. In her hands was a SIG Sauer forty that reeked of baby powder, and she was squeezing off rounds at a man-shaped target twenty yards down the Brotherhood's shooting range. In spite of the stench, the weapon was superlative, with a sweet kick and excellent aim.

While she put the gun through its paces, she could feel the males behind her staring hard. To their credit, it wasn't at her ass.

Nah, the Brothers weren't interested in her tail. None of them particularly liked her, although, given their expressions of grudging respect as she'd reloaded the gun, they were viewing her spot-on aim as an asset.

In the shooting stall next door, Ehlena was proving she hadn't lied about being good with a gun. She'd chosen an autoloader with a little less firepower, which made sense, given that she didn't have the upper-body strength that Xhex did. Her aim was awesome for an amateur, and what was more, she handled the weapon with the kind of quiet confidence that suggested she wouldn't mistakenly cap someone's knees.

Xhex took off her ear protection and turned around to the Brotherhood, keeping her weapon down by her thigh. "I'll want to try the other one out, but the pair of these should do me just fine. And I want my knife back."

The weapon had been taken from her before she and Ehlena had been driven to the mansion in that black Mercedes.

"You'll have it," someone said, "when you need it."

Against her will, her eyes did a quick check of who was kibitzing. Same cast of muscle. Which meant John Matthew hadn't sneaked in.

Given how big the Brotherhood's compound seemed to be, she figured he could be anywhere, including the next town, for chrissakes: When the meeting in the king's study had finished, he'd just walked out, and she hadn't seen him since.

Which was good. Right now she needed to be focused on what was looming over them all tomorrow night, not her crappy, castrated love life. Fortunately, everything seemed to be falling into place. She'd called iAm and Trez and left voice mails that she was taking a day off, and they'd phoned back saying it wasn't a problem. No doubt they were going to check in with her again, but hopefully with the Brothers' backing, she would be in and out of the colony before their babysitting impulses overwhelmed them.

Twenty minutes later, she finished trying out the other SIG and was not at all surprised when both guns were confiscated. The trip back to the mansion was long and tense, and she looked over at Ehlena to see how the other female was faring. It was hard not to approve of the resolute strength in that nurse's face: Rehv's female was going after her male, and nothing was going to get in her way.

Which was great . . . but the determination made Xhex twitchy nonetheless. She was willing to bet Muhrder had had the same kind of resolve in his eyes when he'd gone up to that colony to get her.

And look at how well that had gone.

Then again, true to his character he'd gone in rogue, without backup. At least she and Ehlena had been smart enough to get some serious-ass help, and one could only pray that made all the difference.

Back at the mansion, Xhex grabbed some food from the kitchen and was shown to a second-floor guest room that was down a long hall of statues.

Eat. Drink. Shower.

She left the light in the bath on because the room was unfamiliar, got into bed naked, and closed her eyes.

When the door opened some half an hour later, she was both shocked and unsurprised at the big shadow standing in the lee of the hallway light.

"You're drunk," she said.

John Matthew came inside without an invitation, and he locked the door without permission. He was indeed drunk, but that was not a news flash.

The fact that he was sexually aroused was also not front-page material.

As he put the bottle he was carrying down on the bureau, she knew his hands were headed for the fly of his jeans, and there were roughly a hundred thousand reasons why she should tell him to cut the shit and get the hell away from her.

Instead, Xhex tossed the duvet off her body and put her hands behind her head, her breasts tingling from the chill and so much more.

Of all the justifications for not doing what they were going to, there was one overriding reality that crumbled the foundations of healthy choice: By the end of tomorrow night, there was a chance one or both of them might not be coming home.

Even with the Brotherhood as support, going to the colony was a suicide mission—and she was willing to bet there were a lot of people having sex under the mansion's roof right now. Sometimes you had to have a taste of life right before you knocked on the Grim Reaper's front door.

John took off his jeans and his shirt and left his clothes right where they landed. As he came over to her, his body was magnificent in the glowing light, his cock hard and ready, his heavily muscled form everything a female would want in her bed.

But all that oh-yeah wasn't what she focused on as he got up on the mattress and mounted her. She wanted to see his eyes.

No luck, though. His face was in shadow, the light from the bathroom coming from directly behind him. For a moment, she almost turned on the lamp next to them, but then realized she wouldn't want to catch a load of the numb coldness that was no doubt in his stare.

She wasn't going to get what she was looking for from this, Xhex thought. This was not going to be about living.

And she was right.

No prelude. No foreplay. She opened her legs and he pushed in and her body loosened and accepted him because of biology. As he fucked her, his head was by hers on the pillow, but it was turned away.

She didn't come. He did. Four times.

When he rolled off her body and lay on his back, breathing heavily, her heart was thoroughly and completely broken: There had been a crack in the damn thing after she'd left him in her basement apartment, but with each pounding stroke he'd taken just now, more and more of it splintered and fell from the core of her.

A few minutes later, John got up, put his clothes back on, palmed his liquor bottle, and left.

As the door clicked shut, Xhex pulled the duvet over herself.

She did nothing to try to control the shakes that rattled her body, and didn't attempt to stop herself from crying. Tears left both of her eyes at the far corners, slipping out and flowing over her temples. Some landed in her ears. Some eased down her neck and were absorbed by the pillow. Others clouded her vision, as if they didn't want to leave home.

Feeling ridiculous, she put her hands to her face and captured them as best she could, wiping them on the duvet.

She cried for hours.

Alone.

SIXTY-SIX

The following evening, Lash was about fifteen miles south of Caldwell when he eased the Mercedes onto a dirt lane and turned off the sedan's headlights. Driving slowly along a bumpy dirt lane, he used the rising moon to navigate, cutting through a scruffy, debrided cornfield.

"Get your weapons out," he said.

In the passenger seat, Mr. D palmed his forty, and in the back, the pair of slayers cocked the shotguns they'd been given before Lash had taken them all out of town.

A hundred yards later, Lash hit the brakes and ran his gloved hand around the leather-wrapped steering wheel. The good thing about a big-ass black Mercedes was that when you got out of it you looked like a businessman, not a flashy drug thug. Plus you could fit your guard in the backseat.

"Let's do this."

In a synchronized punch, they popped the latches on their doors and got out, facing off across the snowy earth at another big-ass Mercedes.

Maroon AMG. Nice.

And Lash wasn't the only one to bring guns-and-ammo accessories to the meeting. As all the AMG's doors opened, three guys with forties and one who appeared to be un-armed got out.

Whereas the sedans suggested civility, or at least the appearance of it, all the men in them represented the violent side of the drug trade—which had fuck-all to do with calculators and offshore accounts and money laundering.

Lash approached the man who didn't have a weapon with both his hands out of the pockets of his Joseph Abboud coat. As he came forward, he searched the mind of the South American importer, who, at least according to the drug dealer they had tortured for fun and profit, had sold bulk product to Rehvenge.

"You wanted to meet with me?" the guy said with an accent.

Lash put his hand into the breast pocket of his coat and smiled. "You are not Ricardo Benloise." He glanced to the other Mercedes. "And I do not appreciate you and your boss fucking around with me. You tell that motherfucker to get out of the car now, or I'm walking—which means that he will not be doing business with the guy who cleared the decks in Caldwell and who will be servicing the market the Reverend used to handle."

The human seemed nonplussed for a moment; then he glanced back at the three comrades who were standing behind him. After a moment, his eyes finally shifted to the maroon Mercedes and he subtly shook his head.

There was a pause and then the passenger-side door opened and a smaller, older man got out. He was impeccably dressed, his black coat fitting his slight shoulders perfectly, his glossy loafers leaving a shuffling path in the snow.

He came forward with total calmness, as if he were a thousand percent sure that his men could handle whatever happened.

"You will understand my caution," Benloise said with an accent that seemed part French and part Latin American. "It is a good time to be of care."

Lash removed his hand from his jacket, leaving his gun where it was. "You got nothing to worry about."

"You sound very sure."

"As I'm the one who's been knocking off the competition, I am very sure."

The old man's eyes traveled up and down Lash, taking stock, and Lash knew he was going to see nothing but strength.

Figuring there was no time to waste, Lash laid it all out.

"I want to move what the Reverend did in terms of volume, and I want to do it now. I have plenty of men and the territory is mine. What I need is a good, steady professional supplier of powder, and that's why I wanted to meet with you. It's simple, really. I'm stepping into the Reverend's shoes, and as you were the one he worked with, I want to do business with you."

The old man smiled. "Nothing is simple. But then, you are young and will discover that for yourself if you live long enough."

"I'm going to be around for plenty of time. Trust me."

"I do not trust anyone, even my family. And I'm afraid I don't know what you are talking about. I am an importer of fine Colombian art, and I have no idea how you got my name or why you connected it to anything of an illegal nature." The old man bowed slightly. "I bid you good evening and suggest that you find legitimate pursuits for your no doubt many talents."

Lash frowned as Benloise returned to the AMG, leaving his men behind.

What the fuck? Unless this was going to turn into a lead shower . . .

As Lash went for his gun, he braced for a shoot-out . . . but no. The man who'd tried to pass himself off as Benloise just stepped forward and extended his hand.

"Nice to have met you."

As Lash looked down, he saw there was something in the guy's palm. A card.

Lash did the shake thing, took what he'd been given, and went back to his own Mercedes. As he got behind the wheel, he watched the AMG amble off down the lane, its tailpipe smoking in the cold.

He looked down at the card. It was a number.

"Whatchu got there, suh?" Mr. D asked.

"I think we might be in business." He got out his cell phone and dialed, then put the car in gear and went in the opposite direction from Benloise's crew.

Benloise picked up the call. "So much more comfortable to speak in a warm car, is it not?"

Lash laughed. "Yeah."

"Here is what I shall offer you. A quarter of the product

that I shipped monthly to the Reverend. If you are able to safely move it on the streets, then we shall look at increasing the trade. Are we in accord?"

It was such a pleasure dealing with a professional, Lash thought. "We are."

After they discussed the money and the delivery side of things, they hung up.

"We're good," he said with satisfaction.

As all kinds of backslapping went on in the car, he allowed himself to grin like a motherfucker. The prospect of setting up labs was proving more difficult than he'd expected—although he was still moving forward on that, he needed a big-league, reliable supplier and this relationship with Benloise was the key to that. With the cash it was going to generate, he could recruit, acquire state-of-the-art weapons, buy more real estate, target the Brothers. As it stood now, he felt like the Lessening Society had been in neutral since he took over, but that was over, thanks to the old man with the accent.

Back in Caldwell proper, Lash dumped Mr. D and the other *lessers* off at that nasty-ass ranch and then proceeded across to the brownstone. As he parked in the garage, he was flushed from possibilities of the future, the buzz making him aware of how fucking bummed out he'd been. Money mattered. It was freedom to do what you wanted, buy what you needed.

It was power stacked in orderly piles and rubber-banded with authority.

It was what he required to be who he was.

As he came in through the kitchen, he took a moment to savor the improvements he'd already been able to make. No more empty counters and cabinets. There were espresso machines and Cuisinarts and dishes and glasses, none of which had been purchased from Target. There was also gourmet food in the refrigerator and fine wines in the cellar below and top-shelf booze at the bar.

He walked out into the dining room, which was still bare, and hit the stairs two at a time, loosening his clothes as he went, his cock getting stiffer with every step. Upstairs his princess was waiting for him. Waiting for him and ready. Bathed and oiled and perfumed by two of his slayers, prepared for his use like the sex slave she was.

Man, he was glad all *lessers* were impotent; otherwise there would have been a rash of castrations in the Society.

As he hit the first of the landings, he unbuttoned his shirt, revealing the scores of scratches that ran across his chest. They had each been made by his lover's nails, and he smiled, ready to add to the collection. After about two weeks of having her tied down completely, he'd started releasing one of her hands and one of her feet. The more they fought the better.

God, she was a hell of female—

He froze as he got to the top of the stairs, the scent coming down the hall stopping him dead. Oh . . . God, the sweet saturation was so heavy, it was as if a hundred perfume bottles had been smashed open.

Lash raced for the door to the bedroom. If anything had happened to—

The carnage was stunning, black blood staining the new rug and the fresh wallpaper: The two *lessers* he'd left to guard his female were propped up on the floor across from the canopy bed, each with a knife in his right hand. Both had multiple, glistening gashes to their necks, having stabbed themselves over and over again until they lost so much blood, they went lax.

His eyes shot to the bed. The satin sheets were rumpled, and the four chains the *symphath* king had given him to subdue her were lying slack from their corners.

Lash wheeled on his men. Slayers didn't die unless you got them in the chest with some stainless steel, so both were incapacitated, but still alive.

"What the fuck happened?"

Two mouths worked, but he couldn't understand a thing—the bastards had no air supply to their voice boxes, thanks to the shit escaping out of all the holes they'd made in themselves.

Weak-minded fools—

Oh, hell no. Oh, no, she didn't.

Lash went over to the messy sheets and found the collar of his old dead rottweiler. He'd put the thing on his princess's neck to mark her as his, keeping it on her even when he took her vein during sex.

She'd slit it up the front instead of unbuckling the thing. She'd ruined it.

Lash tossed the collar on the bed, rebuttoned his shirt, and shoved the silk tails into his slacks. Over at the antique Sheraton bureau he'd bought three days ago, he took out another gun and a long knife to add to what he'd worn to meet Benloise.

There was only one place she would go.

And he was going up there and bringing his bitch back.

With George guiding the way, Wrath left his study at ten p.m. and hit the stairs with a confidence that surprised him. The thing was, he was starting to trust the dog and anticipate the signals that George transmitted through the harness handle: Each time they got to the head of the stairs, George would stop and allow Wrath to find the first step. And as they came to the bottom, the dog would pause again so that Wrath was aware they'd reached the foyer. And then there would be a wait until Wrath announced what direction they would go in.

It was . . . a very good system, actually.

As he and George descended, the Brothers gathered down below, checking their weapons and talking. In the midst of the group, V was smoking his Turkish tobacco and Butch was saying some Hail Marys under his breath and Rhage was unwrapping a Tootsie Pop. The two females were with them, and he recognized them by their scents. The nurse was nervous, but not hysterical, and Xhex was itching for a fight.

When Wrath stepped off onto the mosaic floor, he gripped the handle in his palm hard, the muscles in his forearm cranking tight. Shit, he and George were staying behind. And that just sucked.

Ironic, wasn't it. Not so long ago, he'd been upset about leaving Tohr home like a dog. What a role reversal. The Brother was the one going out into the night . . . and he was the guy staying behind.

A sharp whistle from Tohr shut everyone up. "V and Butch, I want you with Xhex and Z on team one. Rhage, Phury, and I are on team two and will be backing up you four with the boys. According to the text I just got from Qhuinn, he and Blay and John have arrived up north and are in position about two miles from the entry to the colony. We're ready to go—"

"What about me," Ehlena said.

Tohr's voice was gentle. "You're going to wait with the boys in the Hummer—"

"The hell I am. You're going to need a medic—"

"And Vishous is one. Which is why he's going in first with the others."

"Along with me. I can find him—he fed from—"

Wrath was about to jump in when Bella's voice cut through the argument.

"Let her go in with the others." There was a quick, breathless silence from everyone as Rehvenge's sister spoke sharply. "I want her to go in."

"Thank you," Ehlena said in a small voice, like it had been decided.

"You're his female," Bella murmured. "Aren't you."

"Yes."

"You were on his mind the last time I saw him. It was clear how he felt about you." Bella's voice grew even stronger. "She has to go. Even if you can find him, he'll live only for her."

Wrath, who'd never really been on board with that nurse joining the team, opened his mouth to can the idea . . . but then he thought back a year or two, remembering when he'd been shot in the stomach and Beth had been beside him. She had been the reason he'd survived. Her voice and her touch and the power of their connection had been the only things that had pulled him through.

God knew what the *symphaths* had been doing to Rehv up there in the colony. If he was still breathing, chances were good he was hanging by a thread.

"She should go," Wrath said. "It might be all that gets him out alive."

Tohr cleared his throat. "I don't think—"

"That's an order."

There was a long, disapproving pause. Which was broken only when Wrath raised his right hand and flashed the massive black diamond that had been worn by every king of the race.

"Okay. Fine." Tohr cleared his throat. "Z, I want you guarding her."

"Roger that."

"Please . . ." Bella said roughly. "Bring my brother home. Bring him back where he belongs."

There was a beat of silence.

Then, Ehlena vowed, "We will. One way or the other."

No clarification was needed for that. The female meant alive or dead, and everyone, including Rehvenge's sister, knew it.

Wrath said some things in the Old Language, things that he could remember hearing his father speak to the Brotherhood. Wrath's voice had a different tone to it, though. His father hadn't minded staying home to be on the throne.

It ate Wrath alive.

After some good-byeing, the Brothers and the females left on a chorus of boots hitting the mosaic floor.

The vestibule's door shut.

Beth took his free hand. "How you doing?"

By the tightness of her voice, she knew exactly how he was, but he didn't begrudge her the question. She was concerned and worried, just as he would have been in her position, and sometimes the only thing you could do was ask.

"I've been better." He pulled her against him, and as she fit her body to his, George pressed his head in for a stroke.

Even with both of them, Wrath was lonely.

It seemed to him, as he stood in the grand foyer whose depths and colors and wonder he could no longer see, that he had ended up in the very place he hadn't wanted to ever find himself: Going out to fight even though he was king had not been just about the war and the species. It had been for himself, too. He'd wanted to be more than a paper-pushing aristocrat.

Evidently, however, fate was bound and determined to shove him in that peg hole of a throne one way or the other.

He squeezed Beth's hand, then released it and gave the command to move forward to George. When he and the dog got to the vestibule, he opened the way through the various doors until they stepped free of the house.

Facing the courtyard, Wrath stood in the cold wind, his hair getting swept out and away from his head. Breathing in, he smelled snow, but felt nothing on his cheeks. Just the promise of a storm, apparently.

George settled into a sit as Wrath searched the sky he could not behold. If it was going to snow, was it cloudy yet? Or were the stars still out? What phase was the moon in?

The yearning in his chest made him strain his dead eyes

in an attempt to pull out shapes or forms from the world. It used to work . . . gave him a headache, but it used to work.

Now he just got the headache.

From behind him, Beth said, "Do you want me to get you a coat?"

He smiled a little and looked over his shoulder, imagining her standing in the mansion's great portal, the glow of the lights from inside framing her.

"You know," he said, "this is why I love you so much."

Her tone was heartbreakingly warm. "What do you mean?"

"You don't ask me to go inside because it's cold. You just want to make it easier for me to be where I want to stand." He shifted around to face her. "To be honest, I ask myself why the hell you stay with me. After all the shit . . ." He motioned around at the facade of the mansion. "The constant interruptions of the Brotherhood, the fighting, the kingship. My being an asshole about keeping things from you." He briefly touched his wraparounds. "The blindness . . . I swear, you're going for sainthood."

As she came over, the night-blooming rose of her scent grew stronger even in the stiff breeze. "That's not it."

She touched both his cheeks, and as he leaned in to kiss her, she stopped him. Holding his head steady, she lifted his sunglasses off his face and caressed his brows with her free hand.

"I stay with you because, whether you have sight or not, I see the future in your eyes." His lids fluttered as she brushed gently across the bridge of his nose. "Mine. The Brotherhood's. The race's . . . such beautiful eyes you have. And you're even braver to me now than ever before. You don't need to fight with your hands to have courage. Or be the king your people need. Or be my *hellren*." She put her palm in the center of his broad chest. "You live and lead from here. This heart . . . here."

Wrath blinked hard.

Funny, transformative events were not always scheduled and not always expected. Yeah, sure, your change turned you into a male. And when you went through the mating ceremony, you were part of a whole, no longer just yourself. And the deaths and births around you made you view the world differently.

But every once in a while, from out of the blue, someone reaches the quiet place where you spend your private time and changes the way you see yourself. If you're lucky it's your mate . . . and the transformation reminds you once again that you are absolutely, positively with the right person: because what they say doesn't touch you because of who they are to you, but because of the content of their message.

Payne nailing him in the face woke him up.

George brought him back his independence.

But Beth handed him his crown.

The thing was, if she could reach him in the mood he was in, she proved that it could be done. You could tap into what others needed to hear when they needed to hear it. The heart was the answer. She proved her own point.

He had ascended to the throne and done some things since then. But in his soul, he had been a fighter stuck in a desk job. Resentment had made him edgy, and even though he hadn't been aware of it, he had had his eye on the exit every single night.

No sight. No exit.

And what if that was actually . . . okay. What if those Hallmark motherfuckers were right. Door closes, window opens. What if losing his vision was exactly what he needed in order to be . . . the true king of the race.

Not just a son bearing the obligations of his father.

If it was true that the loss of sight heightened other senses, maybe his heart was what made up the difference. And if that were true . . .

"The future," Beth whispered, "is in your eyes."

Wrath snatched his *shellan* to him hard, holding her so close he absorbed her all the way inside his body. As they stood together, united against the winter wind, the darkness in his body was pierced by a warm glow.

Her love was the light in his blindness. The feel of her was the heaven he didn't need to see to know. And if she had this much faith in him, she was his courage and his purpose, too.

"Thank you for staying with me," he said hoarsely into her long hair.

"There is no place I would rather be." She put her head on his chest. "You're my man."

SIXTY-SEVEN

As Ehlena materialized up north along with the Brothers, she couldn't get Bella out of her mind. The female had seemed strangely transparent as she'd stood in that grand, regal foyer, surrounded by males who were strapped with weapons. Her eyes had been vacant, and her cheeks pale and hollow, as if her will had been tested horribly.

But she wanted her brother back.

The nature of lying was such that its working components were always the same: The objective truth was twisted or hidden or downright overwritten with the intent to deceive. What was murkier were the motivations behind the falsifications, and Ehlena thought of what she'd done in getting those pills for Rehvenge. She had intended to do good, and although that didn't make her actions right or proper or get her out of deserving the consequences, at least she hadn't had malice in her heart. The same was true with Rehvenge's choices. They weren't right or proper, but he'd been protecting Ehlena and his sister and the other people in his life, given what the Old Law mandated and how destructive the princess was.

This was why Ehlena chose to forgive Rehvenge—and she hoped his sister would do the same.

Of course, that forgiveness didn't mean Ehlena was going to end up with the male—the stuff about Rehv being her *hellren* had been to make sure she went to the colony;

it didn't reflect reality. Besides, who knew whether they were even going make it back to Caldwell in one piece.

Lives could be lost tonight.

Ehlena and the Brothers took form in the lee of a thick stand of pines, a protected spot chosen after Xhex had detailed the area. Up ahead, just as the female had described, was a picturesque white farmhouse with a sign that read, TAOIST MONASTICAL ORDER, EST. 1982.

On the surface, it was hard to believe anything other than jam and quilt making went on inside those pristine clapboard walls. Harder still to think that the charming place was the entry to the colony of *symphaths*. But there was something very wrong about the whole setup, as if a force field of dread surrounded all the come-on-in.

As Ehlena looked around, she could feel that Rehv was close, and just before Xhex spoke, she focused on an outbuilding that was about a hundred yards away from the farmhouse. There ... yes, he was *there*.

"We'll enter through that barn," Xhex said quietly, pointing where Ehlena was drawn to. "It's the only way into the labyrinth. Like I said last night, they'll already know we're here, so when we go face-to-face, our best shot is to approach this in an ostensibly diplomatic fashion— we're merely taking back what is ours and want no bloodshed. They'll understand and respect the reasoning—before they start fighting—"

A stench of sweetness drifted over on the cold breeze.

As all heads turned, Ehlena frowned at the sight of the male who had appeared out of nowhere on the farmhouse lawn. His blond hair was slicked back from his forehead, and his eyes glowed with an odd shining blackness. As he strode toward the front porch, his gait was anger in motion, his powerful body tight, as if he were ready for battle.

"What the fuck," V breathed. "Is that Lash I'm looking at?"

"Apparently," Butch answered.

Xhex cut in. "You didn't know?"

All the Brothers stared back at her as V said, "That he was alive and a *lesser*? Er, that would be a hell no. And why are you not surprised?"

"I saw him a couple of weeks ago. Just assumed the Brotherhood knew."

"Ass. You. Me."

"That would be just you—"

"Cut the crap," Z hissed. "Both of you."

Everyone went back to focusing on the male, who by now had leaped up onto the porch and was banging on the door.

"I'm calling the others in," V whispered. "The *lesser* presence has to be neutralized before we can go in."

"Or it could create a diversion that helps us," Xhex said with a lot of *duh*.

"Or we could call for backup and not be idiots," V snapped.

"That would be tough for you."

"Fuck y—"

Z forced a phone into V's gloved hand. "Dial." Then he pointed at Xhex. "Stop pushing his buttons."

As V talked and Xhex shut up, daggers and guns were unsheathed, and a moment later, the others appeared.

Xhex stepped over to the Brother Tohrment. "Look, I really think we should split up. You guys take care of Lash and I'll go in for Rehv. The chaos of the fighting will split the colony's attentions. It's better this way."

There was a pause as everyone looked at Tohr. "I agree," he said. "But you don't go in alone. V and Zsadist are with you and Ehlena."

There was a collective nod and . . . holy shit, they were on the move, out in the open, jogging across the snow.

As Ehlena headed for the barn, the boots she'd been given crunched over the ground, her palms sweated in her gloves, and the backpack full of medical supplies she wore grabbed at her shoulders. She did not arm herself, having agreed not to draw her gun unless there was a good reason to. Made sense. You wouldn't want an amateur manning an emergency room; there was no reason to complicate the situation with her trying to pretend she was as comfortable at the trigger as Xhex and the Brothers so clearly were.

The barn was a good-size one, with a pair of front doors that slid back on well-oiled runners. Xhex didn't take the obvious way in, though, leading them around the side to a squat door instead.

Just before they filed into the lofty, empty space, Ehlena glanced back at the farmhouse.

The blond male was squared off at a circle of Brothers, the guy as calm and cool as someone at a cocktail party might be, his smug smile suggesting big trouble, in Ehlena's opinion: Only somebody with a lot of weapons at his disposal looked like that when he was confronting a wall of muscle.

"Hurry up," Xhex said.

Ehlena ducked inside and shivered, even though she was out of the wind. Man ... this was all wrong. Like the farmhouse, there was something off about everything: no hay, no feed, no harness or tack. There was no horse in the stall, either. Natch.

The urge to flee choked her, and she clawed at the collar of her parka.

Zsadist put his hand on her shoulder. "It's their equivalent of *mhis*. Just breathe. It's an illusion that stains the very air, but what you're feeling is not real."

She swallowed and looked up into the Brother's scarred face, drawing strength from how steady he was. "Okay. Okay ... I'm all right."

"Good girl."

"Over here," Xhex said as she headed for the stall and opened its two-part door.

The floor inside was concrete and marked with an odd geometric pattern.

"Open sesame." Xhex bent down and lifted what turned out to be a slab of stone, the Brothers coming forward to help her with the weight.

The staircase that was revealed was lit with a soft red glow.

"I feel like I'm walking down into a porn movie," V muttered as they took the steps with care.

"Wouldn't that require more black candles for you," Zsadist cracked.

At the bottom of the landing, they looked left and right down a corridor carved out of stone, seeing nothing but row after row of ... black candles with ruby-colored flames.

"I take that back," Z said, eyeing the display.

"We start hearing chick-a-wow-wow shit," V cut in, "can I start calling you Z-packed?"

"Not if you want to keep breathing."

Ehlena turned to the right, overwhelmed by a sense of urgency. "He's down here. I can feel him."

Without waiting for the others, she took off at a jog.

Of all the miracles that could have been granted on the planet, of all the, *OMG, you're alive!*s, or, *Thank you, Scribe Virgin, he's cured!*s, the resurrection John was staring at was a total nut-buster.

Lash was standing in front of a Martha Stewart white colonial, dressed in slick clothes, looking like he was not only perfectly alive and as impressed with himself as ever, but as if he'd been turbocharged somehow: He smelled like a *lesser*, but as he stared down from the porch it was as if he were the Omega itself—nothing but evil power that was unimpressed by any mortal displays of strength.

"Hey, John-boy," Lash drawled. "I can't tell you how great it is to see your pansy-ass face again. Almost as good as my rebirth."

Jesus . . . Christ. Why couldn't Wellsie have been the recipient of this kind of gift? But no . . . psychotic ass-wipe with the narcissistic disorder got fingered to do the Lazarus shuffle.

The irony was that John had prayed for this. Shit, immediately after Qhuinn had sliced the guy's throat, John had prayed that somehow Lash would live through the massive blood loss. He could remember getting down onto the wet tile in the training center's shower and trying to plug up the wound with his shirt. He'd begged God, the Scribe Virgin, whoever would listen, to somehow fix the situation.

Lash's becoming the vampire equivalent of the Antichrist was not exactly what he'd been going for, however.

As snow started to ease down from the cloudy sky, some words were exchanged between Rhage and Lash, but the buzzing in John's head drowned most of them out.

What he did hear clearly was Qhuinn's voice right behind him: "Well, look at it this way. At least we get to kill him again."

Then the world exploded. Literally.

From out of nowhere, a meteor formed in Lash's palm and went flying, coming straight at John and the Brothers, a metaphysical bowling ball from hell. As it made contact, its glowing shock waves knocked all of them off their feet, a full strike.

Flat on his back with the others, John struggled to catch his breath as flakes settled softly on his cheeks and lips. The next blast was coming. Had to be.

Either that or something worse.

The roar that lit off across the landscape originated from in front of him, and at first he assumed Lash had transmogrified into some kind of five-headed horror that was going to eat them all alive.

Except . . . well, it was a beast, but as purple scales flashed and a barbed tail swept through the air, John was relieved. It was their Godzilla, not the Omega's: Rhage's alter ego had come out of him, and the massive dragon was good and pissed off.

Even Lash seemed a little surprised.

The dragon inhaled with a great dragging pull on the night air, and then it stretched its neck forward and let out a burst of fire that was so intense the skin on John's face tightened like shrink-wrap—even though he was well out of range.

When the flames dissipated, Lash was standing between porch supports that were singed, his clothes steaming, his body otherwise unharmed.

Great. Fucker was flame-retardant.

And ready to serve up another round of H-bomb. Like something out of a video game, he palmed up another serving of hot-and-heavy and sent the energy rolling right at the beast.

Who took it like a man. Rhage's other half stayed strong against the onslaught and gave the rest of them the break they needed to get on their feet and be ready to shoot. It was a bold, sweet move—but then again, when you could spit out a bonfire, you had to be able to stand the heat or your burps were going to immolate your ass.

John started shooting, as did the others, even though he suspected that they were going to need more than bullets to take down the new and improved Lash.

He was slipping another clip in when two carloads of *lessers* showed up.

SIXTY-EIGHT

Xhex was willing to follow Ehlena directionally, but she didn't feel comfortable having the female in the lead as they hotfooted along. In a burst of speed, she overtook Rehv's mate.

"You tell me if we take a wrong turn, 'kay?" As Ehlena nodded, the Brothers fell in behind her to guard against a rear ambush.

As they went down the rock corridor, Xhex didn't have a good feeling about any of this. She couldn't sense Rehv at all, which from a vampire standpoint was not surprising—Ehlena had been the last female he'd fed from, so her blood superseded Xhex's. The problem was that *symphath* to *symphath* she couldn't get a bead on him. In fact, she was unable to pinpoint where he or anyone else in the colony was. It didn't compute. *Symphaths* could pick up on anything with emotions, anywhere. So she should have been finding all kinds of grids.

She glanced at the wall as she hurried along. When she'd been here last, it had all been rough-cut stone, but now it had a smooth surface. Guess they'd improved things over the decades.

"The corridor is going to branch out in another hundred yards," she whispered over her shoulder. "They keep the prisoners to the left, and their quarters and common rooms are all to the right."

"How do you know?" Vishous asked.

She didn't answer the Brother. No reason to mention she'd been in one of their jail cells. She just kept going, following the rows of black candles, going deeper into the colony, closer to where its inhabitants slept and ate and played with one another's minds. And still she sensed nothing.

No, that wasn't quite true. There was a strange kind of static. At first she'd assumed it was the softly flickering red flames atop all that black wax, the subtle currents in the air fluffing the lit wicks. But no ... it was something else.

When they got to the hall's three-way branch, she automatically headed to the left, but Ehlena said, "No, straight ahead."

"Doesn't make sense." Xhex stopped and kept her voice down. "That's where the HVAC rooms are."

"That's where he is."

Vishous shoved his way to the front. "Look, let's go where Ehlena says. We need to find him before the battle going on outdoors ends up down here."

As the Brother shot off, Xhex's ass was frosted that he was out in front. But short of throwing down over it, which was a waste of time, she was in the number two position and that was that.

They went at a clip, going into a network of smaller tunnels that led to the heating system and the air draw and all the blowers. The colony was built along the lines of an ant farm, a sustainable, underground living environment that had grown and expanded over time, with more offshoots burrowing deeper and deeper through the earth. The construction and the upkeep rested on the backs of the working class of *symphaths*, who were nothing more than slaves who were encouraged to breed so their numbers doubled over time. There was no middle class. Next up from the servants was the royal household and the aristocrats.

And never the twain would meet.

Xhex's father had been of the servant class. Which made her beneath Rehvenge, and not just because he was royal. Technically, she was one step up from dog shit.

"Stop!" Ehlena called out.

They pulled up short, facing ... the stone wall.

As one, they reached forward, running their hands over the smooth surface. Zsadist and Ehlena found fissures at the same time, the nearly hidden seam forming a tall square.

"How the fuck do we get in here," Z said as he prodded the rock.

"Move back," Xhex barked.

When they were out of the way, and clearly expecting something fancy, she hauled back, slammed her shoulder against the thing, and got nothing but molars that rattled like marbles in a box.

"Fuck," she breathed with a wince.

"That had to hurt," Z muttered. "You okay—"

The wall started to vibrate and they all jumped aside, training their weapons on the door that emerged from the stone and slid out of the way.

"Guess it was scared of you," Vishous said with a hint of respect.

Xhex frowned, as the humming static suddenly increased until her ears rang. "I don't think he's in there. I can't sense him at all."

Ehlena stepped forward, clearly prepared to plunge into the darkness that was revealed. "I can. He's right—"

Three sets of hands grabbed her and held her back.

"Hold up," Xhex said, unclipping a Mag-Lite from her belt. As she hit the beam, a thin hall about fifty yards long was revealed. At the end, there was a door.

Vishous went first, and Xhex was right on his ass, with Ehlena and Z coming quickly behind.

"He's alive," Ehlena said as they came to the end of the corridor. "I can feel him!"

Xhex expected trouble at the steel panel—but no, it swung right open, revealing a room that . . . shimmered?

V cursed as Xhex's light sliced into the chamber. "What the . . . *fuck*?"

Hanging in the midst of a room with liquid walls and flooring was a massive cocoon shape, the black outer wrapping of which moved and glistened.

"Oh . . . God," Ehlena breathed. "*No.*"

Lash had been practicing his gifts at the Omega's lair, and man, didn't all that work come in handy on a night like tonight. As the two squadrons of *lessers* he'd called in from the neighboring town got to work fighting with the Brothers, he faced off against a beast the size of a Ford Expedition—and traded fireballs with the motherfucker.

Jumping away from the house, because the last thing this situation needed was a visit from the Plattsburgh Fire Department, he caught sight of a splinter group of vampires heading for the outbuilding across the way. They went inside, and when he didn't see them again, he had a feeling that was the way you got into the colony.

Which meant that as nice as it was to play volleybomb with Puff the Magic, he needed to stop fighting and start going after his female. He had no clue why the hell the Brothers showed up at exactly the same time he had, but when it came to *symphaths*, he was willing to bet there were no coincidences. Had the princess known he was coming up here and tipped off the Brotherhood?

The dragon spat out another barrage of flames, and the blast illuminated the fighting that was going on all around the farmhouse's lawn: Everywhere he looked there were Brothers squaring off against slayers with bare knuckles swinging, and daggers flashing and shitkickers flying. The symphony of grunts and curses and pounding, cracking impacts made him feel stronger, more powerful.

His troops were fighting his teachers.

How fucking poetic was that?

But enough with the nostalgia. Concentrating on his hand, he created a whirlwind of molecules, spinning them with his mind faster and faster until the centrifugal force spontaneously combusted. As the whirling mass of energy pulled together, he kept it palmed and raced forward toward the purple-scaled beast, knowing the damn thing had to take an inhale break after it threw out its bombs.

The dragon was no dummy and crouched down, viciously clawed arms coming up to defend itself. Lash stopped just out of swiping range and didn't give the bastard a chance to pounce. He threw the energy ball right into the beast's chest, plowing it over, knocking it out cold.

He didn't hang around to roast s'mores over the smoking carcass. Sure as shit, after some deep-breathing recovery that dragon was going to pop up off the ground like the Energizer Bunny, and at the moment the coast was clear between Lash and the barn.

In a tearing rush, he raced for the outbuilding and burst into the empty, unremarkable space. In the far corner, he saw a horse stall, and he followed damp footsteps over to it. The treads disappeared into a black square.

Lifting the slab was grunt work and then some, but the sight of more prints down a set of stone steps got him juiced. Tracking them all the way to the bottom, he found himself in a stone corridor, and thanks to the red glow from black candles, he was able to follow their wet path— although his road map didn't last forever. With all the warmth being thrown off, water dried fast, and by the time he got to a three-way branch, he had no clue which way the bunch had gone.

Inhaling, he hoped to catch a scent, but all his nose picked up on was burning wax and earth.

Threre was nothing else. No sounds. No rustle of movement. It was as if the four he'd seen going down here had disappeared.

He looked left. Right. Straight ahead.

On impulse, he went to the left.

SIXTY-NINE

Ehlena's eyes refused to process what she was looking at: They just flat out no-way'd the situation.

It couldn't possibly be spiders. She couldn't possibly be looking at thousands upon thousands of spiders . . . oh, God, spiders and scorpions . . . covering not just the walls and floors, but . . .

In horror, she realized what was hanging in the center of the room. Hanging from ropes or chains. Hanging and covered with the teeming masses that blanketed every square inch of the cell.

"Rehvenge . . ." she moaned. "Dearest Virgin . . . Scribe."

Without thinking, she lurched forward, but Xhex's strong hand pulled her back. "No."

Struggling against the iron band locked on her upper arm, Ehlena shook her head violently. "We have to save him!"

"I'm not suggesting we leave him," the other female said tightly. "But if we go in there, we're going to be attacked like something out of the Bible. We have to figure out how to—"

A brilliant glow flared, cutting off Xhex and bringing Ehlena's head around. Vishous had removed the glove on his right hand, and as he lifted his palm up, the planes of his harsh face and the swirls of the tattoo around his eye stood out in sharp relief.

"Bug Be Gone." He flexed his illuminated fingers. "The

Orkin man only wishes he had this kind of shit on his truck."

"And I have a buzz saw," Z said, grabbing a black tool from his belt. "If you can clear the way, we'll get him down."

Vishous crouched by the sharp edge of the swirling insects, his hand spotlighting the tangling, surging horde of small bodies and twitching, spinning legs.

Ehlena clapped her palm over her mouth, trying not to gag out loud. She couldn't imagine that all over her body. Rehvenge was alive . . . but how had he survived? Without being stung to death? Without going mad?

The light from the Brother's hand spiraled out in a straight line, singeing its way to where Rehv hung, leaving nothing but ashes and a burning, wet stench that made her pray for nose plugs. Once extended, the burning illumination split and spread, creating a path.

"I can hold it, but move fast," Vishous said.

Xhex and Zsadist leaped out into the cave, and the spiders on the ceiling responded by spinning threads and dripping down like blood seeping from a deep wound. Ehlena watched the two of them bat the invaders away for only a moment before she whipped off her backpack and dug in.

"You smoke, right?" she said to Vishous as she unwrapped her scarf and put it over her head. "Tell me you brought your lighter."

"What the hell do you . . ." V smiled when he saw the aerosol spray can of topical antibiotic in her hand. "It's in my ass pocket. Right side."

He shifted so she could work the heavy gold weight free, and as soon as she got the thing, she stepped out into the chamber. The can wasn't going to last long, so she didn't use it until she was standing right behind Xhex and Zsadist.

"Duck!" she said just as she depressed the spray button and fired up the lighter.

The two of them went low and she vaporized the air guard from above in a blast of flame.

With the way momentarily clear, Xhex got up on Z's shoulders and reached forward toward the chains with the buzz saw. As a high-pitched whirring noise filled the cave, Ehlena kept up her offensive, letting out bursts of fire that kept most of the bastards on the ceiling and not on the pair's heads and necks. The saw helped as well, sending sparks that further repulsed the arachnid guard, but as if in payback, spiders landed on the sleeves of Ehlena's jacket and crawled upward.

Rehvenge jerked. Then moved.

One of his arms reached out toward her, scorpions dropping off of it, spiders shuffling to stay on. The limb lifted slowly, as if the burden of its second skin of insects made it nearly too heavy to move.

"I'm here," Ehlena said roughly. "We're here for you—"

From over where they had come in, there was a thud. And abruptly the light Vishous was emitting went out, plunging the chamber into total darkness.

Giving what jailed Rehvenge free access to everyone in the cave.

From beneath the horrid masses that covered him, Rehvenge's fragile consciousness woke him the moment Ehlena came into the chamber's doorway. At first, he didn't trust what he sensed, however. In the thousand years he'd spent suspended in a living hell, he'd had many dreams of her, his brain hanging on to its memories, using them as food and water and air.

But this felt different.

Maybe it was just the break with reality he had been praying for? After all, although he had lamented that things had to come to an end when his mother had passed, he wanted only an end now—whether that was mental or physical, it didn't matter to him.

So perhaps he'd finally been granted one mercy in his wretched, fucked-up life.

Besides, the idea that Ehlena had actually come to get him out scared him more than where he was or what other tortures the future held.

Except ... no. It was her, and there were other people with her.... He could hear their voices. Then he caught a glow of light ... and smelled some kind of rancid stench that reminded him of the nasty smell of a beach at low tide.

A high-pitched whine followed. Along with a series of ... popping blasts?

Rehv had been unable to move since those first couple of days, his body growing weak fast, but he needed to reach out now and try to communicate, try to tell Ehlena and whoever she had come with to go away from this terrible place.

Focusing all his strength, he managed to lift his arm to wave her back.

The light was extinguished as quickly as it had appeared.

Only to be replaced by a red glow that meant his beloved was in mortal danger.

Fear for Ehlena made him panic, his body spasming on its tethers, flopping like an animal in a trap.

He needed to wake the fuck up. He needed to . . . wake the *fuck up*!

SEVENTY

Nothing. Fucking nothing.

Lash paused and looked inside another cell that was made up of an odd kind of glass. Empty. Just like the other three.

Inhaling deeply, he closed his eyes and held still. No sounds. No smells other than the beeswax-and-fresh-dirt combo that had been there all along.

Wherever that group had gone, it was not down here, goddamn it.

Retracing his steps, he returned to where the corridor branched into three directions, and looked down. Someone had just been by: A trail of dark blue dots stretched off in two directions, to the right and straight ahead, meaning someone had come from one of those compass points and gone toward the other.

Bending down, Lash dragged his forefinger through the viscous dribble and rubbed the substance with his thumb. *Symphath* blood. God knew he'd spilled enough of his female's to know exactly what the shit was.

Lifting his hand to his nose, he inhaled. Not his female's. Someone else's. And it was unclear which way they'd been and where they were headed.

With nothing to go on, he was about to jog right when a bright red flare boiled out of the smallest of the three off-shoots, the one that was in front of him. Jacking to his feet, he ran in that direction, following the trail of blood.

As the corridor eased into a turn and the glow intensified, he had no idea what the hell he was going to interrupt
and didn't care. His princess was here, and someone was
going to tell him where the fuck to find the bitch.

A hidden hallway appeared with no warning, breaking
from the corridor without a jamb or doorstop. From down
at the end of it, the red light was brilliant enough to sting
the eyes, and Lash headed for the source.

He walked into a whole lot of . . . *What the fuck?*

Crumpled at the entrance of a chamber was the Brother
Vishous, and beyond him was a tableau that made no sense
at all:

The princess was standing in what he'd dressed her in the
night before, her bustier and thigh-high stockings and stilet-
tos looking ridiculous out of the context of the bedroom.
Her blue-black hair was a shaggy mess, her hands were dripping blue blood, her wild, red eyes the source of the glow
that had guided him. In front of her, captivating her, was
something like a gigantic side of beef that was covered in
what appeared to be a lottery-winning load of insects.

Shit, those things were everywhere.

And clustered around the airborne body was that
scarred Brother Zsadist, Xhex the security dyke, and some
female vampire with a lighter in one hand and an aerosol
can in the other.

That bunch weren't long for this world. Spiders and
scorpions were on full advance, gunning for the trio who'd
invaded their territory, and Lash had a brief, gory premoni-
tion of raw skeletons cleaned of meat.

But that wasn't his concern.

He wanted his female.

Who had ideas of her own, evidently. The princess lifted
her bloody hand, and in a flash, the crawling bastards that
papered the walls and the ceiling and the floor retreated
like floodwaters sucked up by the thirsty earth. In their
wake, Rehvenge was revealed, his heavy, naked weight
strung up by bolts set into his shoulders. It seemed like a
miracle that his skin wasn't pitted with a million bites, but
it was almost as if he'd been preserved beneath that carpet
of eight-legged and two-clawed monstrosities.

"He is mine," the princess shouted at no one in particular. *"And no one takes him but me."*

Lash's upper lip curled back, his fangs elongating in a rush. She did not just say that. She so totally did not just say that.

That was *his* woman.

One look at her face, though, and he knew the truth. That sick fixation as she stared at Rehvenge had never shined back at Lash, no matter how intense the sex had been.... Nope, that single-minded obsession had never been trained on him. She'd just been marking time with him, waiting to get free—not because she didn't want to be held against her will, but because she wanted to get back with Rehvenge.

"You fucking cunt," he spat.

The princess wheeled around, her hair swinging in an arc. "How dare you address me like—"

Shots rang out in the stone room, one, two, three, four, loud as planks falling on the hard floor. The princess went rigid in shock as bullets plowed into her chest, tearing through her heart and lungs, blue blood bursting out of the exit wounds and splattering on the wall behind her.

"No!" Lash screamed, racing forward. He caught his lover as she fell, holding her gently. "No!"

He looked across the chamber. Xhex was lowering a gun, a slight smile on her lips, as if she'd just enjoyed a good meal.

The princess gripped the lapels of Lash's singed coat, the sharp yank on the fabric bringing his eyes back to her face.

She was not looking at him. She was staring at Rehvenge ... reaching out to him.

"My love ..." The princess's last words drifted up into the room.

Lash snarled and threw her body against the nearest wall, hoping the impact was what killed her, needing the satisfaction of knowing he was the one who'd fucked her up last.

"You"—he pointed to Xhex—"owe me *twice* now—"

The chanting was quiet at first, nothing but an echo reverberating down the corridors outside, but it grew louder and more insistent, louder ... and more insistent, until he heard each syllable spoken by what had to be a hundred mouths. He understood nothing, the language not one he knew, but the shit was reverent, that was for sure.

Lash turned and faced the direction from which the chant came, being careful to get his back against the wall. He had a vague sense that the others were likewise bracing themselves for what was coming.

The *symphaths* arrived in two-by-two formation, their white robes and long, thin bodies not so much walking as swaying along. They were each wearing a contoured white facial mask, the kind that gave them black holes to see through and left their chin and jaws free. As they entered the chamber and began to circle Rehvenge, they didn't seem concerned in the slightest about the vampires or the princess's body or Lash himself.

Filing in, they gradually filled up the room, forcing the others to step back until all the interlopers were up tight against the walls, as Lash and the dead princess's body already were.

Time to get the fuck out of Dodge. Whatever this was wasn't something he needed to be involved with. Anger made his powers weaker, for one thing. For another, this situation could spiral out of control in an instant, and only part of it was his fight.

He wasn't leaving alone, though. He'd come for a female and he was leaving with one.

In a quick burst, he cut through one of the precise breaks in the *symphaths'* front-to-back ranks and came around to where Xhex stood. The female was looking up at Rehvenge all awestruck, like the assembly meant something. Which was just the kind of distraction a guy needed at a time like this.

Putting forward both his hands, Lash summoned a shadow out of thin air and spread it wide until it fell to the floor like a cloak.

With a quick sweep, he cast it up and over Xhex's head, disappearing her though in fact she was still in the room. As expected, she struggled, but one sharp fist to the head and she went lax, making the exodus so much easier.

Lash just dragged her out of the cave, right from under everyone's noses.

Chanting . . . chanting that rose up and filled the air with a rhythmic drumming.

But first, there had been gunshots, too.

Rehvenge peeled open his eyelids and had to blink his red vision clear. The spiders were gone from his body, gone from the chamber . . . replaced by the assembling masses of his *symphath* brethren, their ceremonial masks and robes making their features anonymous so that the power of their minds could shine through all the more clearly.

There was fresh blood.

His eyes shot over to— Oh, thank you, Virgin Scribe, Ehlena was still standing, and Zsadist was on her tight as Kevlar. That was the good news. Bad news? The pair was directly opposite the door, with, oh, maybe a hundred sin-eaters between them and the safe way out.

Although given the way she held his eyes, she wasn't leaving without him.

"Ehlena . . ." he whispered hoarsely. "No."

She nodded and mouthed, *We're getting you free.*

He looked away in frustration, watching the sway of the robes, knowing more than Ehlena could about what exactly this procession and the chanting meant.

Holy . . . shit. But how?

The question was answered as he saw the dead body of the princess against the wall. Her hands were stained blue, and he knew why: She had killed his uncle, her mate . . . the king.

Shaking himself, he wondered how she had done it. It couldn't have been easy—getting past the royal guard would have been nearly impossible and their uncle had been a crafty, suspicious piece of work.

Payback had been a bitch, however. Although she hadn't found death in the manner of *symphaths*, who preferred making their victims commit involuntary suicide. She'd been shot through the chest four times, and going by the accuracy of the cluster of wounds, he figured Xhex had done the shooting.

She always marked her victims, and the N, S, E, and W of the compass was one of her favorites when she was using a gun.

He refocused on Ehlena. She was still staring up at him, her eyes impossibly warm. For a moment, he allowed himself to get lost in the compassion, but then his vampire side took over. As a bonded male, the safety of his mate was his first and greatest priority, and weak though he was, his body jerked against the chains that held him aloft.

Go! he mouthed. When she shook her head, he glared at her. *Why not?*

She put her hand over her heart and mouthed back, *Because.*

He let his head fall loose on his stiff neck. What had changed her mind? he wondered. How was it possible she'd come for him after everything he'd done to her? And who had cracked and told her the truth?

He was going to kill them.

Assuming anyone got out of this alive.

The *symphaths* stopped chanting and fell still. After a moment of silence, they turned to face him with military precision and bowed low.

Their grids registered in a rush as each one of them presented him- or herself to Revhenge. . . . It was everyone he remembered from long ago, his extended family.

They wanted him as their king. Regardless of his uncle's will, they were choosing him.

The chains he hung from jerked and then started to lower him, the pain in his shoulders roaring, his stomach rolling in agony. But he couldn't let on how weak he was. Surrounded by his sociopathic brethren, he knew this respectful-prostration bit wasn't going to last long, and if he looked vulnerable in any way, he was fucked.

So he did the only thing that made sense.

As his feet touched the cool stone floor, he allowed his knees to buckle smoothly and forced his upper body to sit up straight—as if the classic contemplative pose of the king were exactly what he chose to assume, instead of the best he could do considering he'd been suspended by his clavicles for . . .

How long had it been? He had no idea.

Rehv glanced down at his body. Thinner. Much. But his skin was intact, which, given all the creepy-crawly crap was a fucking miracle.

He took a deep breath . . . and drew strength from his vampire side in order to fuel his *symphath* mind: With his *shellan*'s life at stake, he had reserves he wouldn't be able to call on for anyone else.

Rehvenge lifted his head, lit the chamber with his amethyst eyes, and accepted the adulation.

As the candles out in the hall flared brilliantly, power surged through him, a great wave of command and domination rising, his vision shifting past red and into purple. In the base of his gut, he grounded himself and branded every single *symphath* in the colony with the knowledge that he could make them do anything. Slit their own throats. Fuck one another's mates. Hunt down and kill animals or humans or anything else with a heartbeat.

The king was the CPU for the colony. The head brain. And these citizens of the race had been taught that lesson well by his uncle and his father: *Symphaths* were sociopaths with a deep sense of self-preservation—and the reason they chose Rehvenge, a half-breed, was because they wanted to keep the vampires away. With him at the helm, they could continue to live among themselves, sequestered in the colony.

From over in the corner, there was a sloppy shifting and a growl.

The princess rose to her feet in spite of her wounds, her hair a tangled mess around her maniacal face, her lingerie glossy with her own blue blood.

"They are mine to rule." Her voice was reedy, but determined, her obsession sufficient to reanimate what was or should have been dead. "It is my rule, and you are *mine*."

The assembled masses lifted their bowed heads and looked over. Then stared back at Rehv.

Fuck, the mind spell had been broken.

Rehv shot quick thoughts to Ehlena and Zsadist to block their cerebral cortexes by thinking of something, anything, the more clearly the better. Immediately, he sensed them changing their patterns, with Ehlena picturing . . . the oil painting from Montrag's study?

Rehv refocused on the princess.

Who had noticed Ehlena and was lurching over with a dagger in her hand.

"He is mine!" she gurgled, blue blood dripping from her mouth.

Rehvenge bared his fangs and hissed like a great snake. With his will, he barreled into the princess's mind, plowing through even the defenses she was able to marshal, taking

over, popping open the lids on her lust to rule and to have
him as a mate. Her desires made her stop and turn to him, her
mad eyes full of love. Overcome with what she wanted, trembling in ecstatic visions, at the mercy of her weakness ...

He waited until she was good and worked up.

Then he slammed her with one single message: *Ehlena is
my revered queen.*

The five words shattered her. Broke her down more
surely than if he had taken out a gun and shot another compass into her chest.

He was what she wanted to be.

He was what she wanted to have.

And she was getting the shaft.

The princess put her hands to her ears, like she was trying to stop the buzzing in her head, but he just spun her
mind faster and faster and faster.

With a raw scream, she took the knife in her hand and
thrust it into her gut all the way to the hilt. Unwilling to let
her stop there, Rehv made her turn the weapon with a
quick jerk to the right.

And then he called on a little help from his friends.

In a black tide, from out of small fissures in the walls, the
multitude of spiders and scorpions returned. Once controlled by his uncle, the hordes were now under Rehvenge's
dominion, and they swelled forward, encompassing her.

He told them to bite and they did.

The princess screamed and clawed at them and suc-
cumbed, falling over onto a mattress of what would destroy
her.

The *symphaths* watched it all.

While Ehlena turned her head into Zsadist's shoulder,
Rehv closed his eyes and sat still as a statue in the center of
the room, promising each and every one of the citizens before him something worse if they did not obey him. Which,
in the twisted value system of *symphath*s, only confirmed
their choice of ruler.

When the princess ceased her sobs and fell still, Rehv
lifted his lids and called off the insect guard. In their reces-
sion, they revealed her swollen, pitted body, and it was clear
she wasn't getting up again—the venom in her veins had
stopped her heart and clogged her lungs and shut down her
central nervous system.

No matter how great her desire, there was no reanimating that corpse.

Rehv calmly told his robed and masked subjects to retreat to their quarters and meditate on the display. In response, he got back the *symphath* version of love: They feared him totally and therefore respected him.

At least, for the time being.

As one, the *symphaths* stood and filed out, and Rehv shook his head at Ehlena and Z, praying they did what he needed them to—which was stay right where they were.

With any luck, his brethren in the masks would assume he'd kill the interlopers at his leisure.

Rehv waited until the last sin-eater was gone not just from the chamber, but the halls beyond. And then he released the hold on his spine.

As his body slammed into the floor, Ehlena rushed over to him, her mouth working like she was speaking to him. He couldn't hear her, though, and her toffee-colored eyes seemed all wrong viewed through the rose lenses of his *symphath* eyes.

I'm sorry, he mouthed. *I'm sorry.*

Something fucked-up happened to his vision at that point, and Ehlena was suddenly rifling through a backpack brought over by . . . Christ, was Vishous here, too?

Rehv faded in and out as things were done to him and shots given. A little later, the whirring sound started up again.

Where was Xhex? he wondered dimly. Probably gone to clear the way out after she killed the princess. She was like that, always with the exit strategy. God knew the practice had defined her life.

As he thought about his head of security . . . his comrade . . . his friend . . . he was pissed off that she'd broken her vow to him, but not all that surprised. The real question was how she'd managed to get up here without the Moors. Unless they'd come as well?

The whirring sound stopped, and Zsadist sat back on his heels, shaking his head.

In slow motion, Rehv looked down at himself.

Ah, he was still tethered by his shoulders, and they weren't having any luck cutting through the chains. Knowing his uncle, those links were made of something stronger than any saw could get through.

"Leave me . . ." he mumbled. "Just leave me. Go . . ."

Ehlena's face came back in front of his, and her lips moved with deliberation, as if she were trying to explain things to him—

Abruptly, having her so close triggered the bonded male in his blood and caused some of his depth perception to return—and he was relieved as her face started to assume its normal contours . . . and colors.

Rehv lifted a shaking hand up, wondering if she would let him touch her.

She did more than that. She clasped his palm hard and brought it to her lips for a kiss. She was still talking to him, not that he heard what she was saying, and he tried to concentrate. *Stay with me.* That was what it looked as if she were trying to communicate to him. Or perhaps he was picking up on that through the way she held on to his hand.

Ehlena reached out and stroked his hair back, and he got the impression she mouthed, *Breathe deep for me.*

Rehv inhaled to make her happy, and as he did, she glanced at something or someone behind him. She gave a quick nod to whoever it was.

At then pain exploded in his right shoulder, his whole body torquing, his mouth cracking wide to let out the scream.

He didn't hear himself yell. Didn't see anything else. Agony knocked him out cold.

SEVENTY-ONE

Ehlena rode home in the back of a black Escalade with Rehv curled up in her lap. The two of them were mashed into the rear section, but she didn't care that there was barely enough room for his huge body alone. She wanted him this close.

Needed to put her hands on him and keep them there.

As soon as they'd torn the hooks out of his shoulders, she'd done the best she could with the horrible wounds left behind, quickly packing them with sterile gauze that she taped in place. The second she was done, Zsadist had picked him up and carried him out of that godforsaken chamber, with her and Vishous providing guard.

Xhex had been nowhere to be found on the trip out.

Ehlena tried to reassure herself that the female had gone to join the above-ground fight with the slayers, but the rationalization didn't stick. Xhex never would have left Rehvenge until he was safely free from the colony.

As fear flickered through Ehlena's chest, she tried to calm herself by stroking the stripe of thick dark hair that ran down Rehvenge's head. In response, he turned his face into her, as if needing the comfort.

God, he might have *symphath* in him, but he had proven where his heart was: He had destroyed the princess and protected them all against those terrifying creatures in the masks and robes. Which said everything about whose side he was on, didn't it? Without him somehow taking control of the colony, there was no way any of them, including the Brothers who'd been fighting *lessers* on the lawn, would have gotten out of there safely.

She glanced up at the others in the SUV. Rhage was wrapped in leather jackets, naked and shivering, the color of congealed oatmeal. They'd had to pull over twice so he could throw up, and given the way he was swallowing with such force, they were going to have to do that again soon. Vishous was next to him and didn't look much better. The guy's heavy legs were draped over Rhage's lap—and with his head turned to the side and his eyes squeezed shut, it was pretty obvious that he had a concussion from where the princess had struck him. And way up front, Butch was in the passenger seat, reeking of a sickly sweetness that was no doubt making Rhage's stomach worse.

Tohrment was behind the wheel, driving steadily and smoothly.

At least she didn't worry about how they were getting home.

Rehvenge stirred and she immediately focused on him. As his amethyst eyes struggled to open, she shook her head.

"Shh . . . just lie there." She stroked his face. "Shh . . ."

He shifted his shoulders and abruptly winced so hard his neck cracked. Wishing there were more that she could do for him, she retucked the blanket that had been wrapped around him. She'd given him as many painkillers as she dared, as well as antibiotics for the shoulder wounds, but she'd held back on antivenin, as he didn't appear to have been bitten.

Given the way the princess had been carnaged, apparently those spiders and scorpions stung only on command, and Rehv had been spared that for some reason.

Abruptly, he grunted and strained, his hands pushing into the floor beneath him.

"No, don't try to sit up." She gently held his chest down. "Just lie with me here."

Rehvenge collapsed back against her lap and brought one of his hands forward. As he found her palm, he mumbled, "Why . . . ?"

She had to smile. "You ask that a lot, you know."

"Why did you come?"

After a moment, she said quietly, "I followed my heart."

Evidently, that didn't make him happy. On the contrary, he grimaced as if in pain. "Don't ... deserve ... your ..."

Ehlena stiffened in alarm as he started bleeding from his eyes. "Rehvenge, stay still for me." Trying not to panic, she reached for her backpack full of supplies, wondering what kind of medical crisis he was having.

Rehvenge caught her hands. "Just ... tears."

She stared at what appeared to be blood on his cheeks. "Are you sure?" When he nodded, she took a Kleenex out of her parka and dabbed his face carefully. "Don't cry. Please don't cry."

"You shouldn't ... have come for me. You should have ... left me there."

"I told you," she whispered, wiping away more. "Everyone deserves to be saved. It's the way I look at the world." As she met his beautiful, iridescent eyes, they seemed even more magical as they shimmered with their wash of red tears. "It's the way I look at you."

His lids squeezed shut, as if he couldn't bear her compassion.

"You tried to protect me from all this, didn't you," she said. "That was what the showdown at ZeroSum was about." When he nodded, she shrugged. "So why don't you understand my need to save you, if you did the same for me?"

"Different ... I'm a ... *symphath*. ..."

"You're not all *symphath*, though." She thought of his marking scent. "Are you."

Rehvenge shook his head reluctantly. "But not enough ... vampire ... for you."

The sadness in him welled up, a rain cloud condensing over them both, and as she struggled for words, she touched his face again—and found that his skin was too cold for her liking. Shit ... she was losing him in her arms. With every mile that took them closer to safety, his body was giving out on them both, his respiration growing logy, his heart rate slowing.

"Can you do something for me?" she said.

"Please ... yes," he replied roughly, even though his eyes fluttered shut and he started to shiver. As he curled into a tighter ball, she could see his spine jutting through the skin of his back even through the blanket.

"Rehvenge? Wake up." When he looked at her, the purple in his eyes was that of a bruise, opaque and pained. "Rehvenge, would you please take my vein?"

In a rush, his lids peeled wide as though along with, *We're going to Disneyland!*, and, *How about some drive-thru for dinner?*, what she'd said was the last thing he'd expected to come out of her mouth.

As his lips parted, she stopped him before he spoke. "If you ask me why, I'm going to be forced to give you a time-out."

A small smile quirked the edge of his mouth, but then was lost. And even though his fangs had dropped down, their sharp tips suddenly revealed, he shook his head.

"Not like you," he murmured, touching his tattooed chest with a weak hand. "Not good enough . . . for your blood."

She shrugged out of one half of her parka and yanked up the sleeve of her turtleneck. "I'll be the judge of that, thank you very much."

As she put her wrist over his mouth, he licked his lips, his hunger rising so much, so fast, that color returned to his pale cheeks. And yet still he hesitated. "Are you . . . sure?"

She had an odd memory of the two of them in the clinic forever ago, jousting, circling each other, wanting and not taking. She smiled. "Absolutely. Positive."

She dropped her vein onto his lips and knew he wouldn't be able to resist her—sure enough, he tried to fight it . . . and lost. Rehvenge bit clean and sucked deep, a moan bubbling up as his eyes rolled back in bliss.

Ehlena stroked the hair that had grown out on either side of his mohawk and rejoiced quietly as he fed.

This was going to save him.

She was going to save him.

Not her blood, but her heart was going to save him.

As Rehvenge fed from his love's wrist, he was overwhelmed and overwrought, at the mercy of emotions more powerful than his mind. She had come for him. She had gotten him out. And even knowing all she did about him, she was letting him feed and staring down at him with kindness.

But wasn't that more a measure of who she was as a person than what she felt for him as a male? Wasn't this duty and compassion instead of love?

He was too weak to read her grid. At least at first.

As his body revived though, so did his mind, and what she felt became known to him ...

Duty. Compassion.

And love.

A complex joy flared in his chest. Part of him felt like he'd won the lottery against crippling odds. But the core of him knew that what he was would drive them apart even if the rest of the vampire population never found out about his mixed blood: He was supposedly the head of that colony.

Which was no place for Ehlena.

He released her vein and licked his lips. God ... she tasted good.

"Do you want more?" she asked.

Yes. "No. I've had enough."

She resumed stroking his hair, her nails rasping against his scalp. Closing his eyes, he felt his muscles and bones strengthen as what she had so graciously given him revived his body.

Yeah, it wasn't just his arms and legs coming to life. His cock swelled and his hips surged forward, even though he was half-dead and his shoulders were on fire. But hard-ons were what happened to male vampires when they'd taken the vein of their mate.

Biology. He couldn't help it.

As his body temperature stabilized, he uncurled from the heat-conserving crouch he'd been in, and in the process kicked off part of the blanket that was around him. Worried that he was flashing his cock, he reached down to pull the thing back into place.

Ehlena got there first.

And her eyes flared in the darkness as she tugged the cover back where it had been.

Rehv swallowed a couple of times, her taste still on his tongue and down the back of his throat. "Sorry about that."

"Don't be." She smiled and stared into his eyes. "You can't help it. Besides, it means you're probably out of the danger zone."

And into the erotic one. Great. Nothing like extremes to spice life up.

"Ehlena . . ." He released a long, slow breath. "I can't go back to the way things were."

"If you mean being a drug lord and a pimp, somehow I'm not crushed."

"Oh, that shit would be over with anyway. But no, I can't return to Caldwell."

"Why not?" When he didn't respond right away, she said, "I hope you do. I want you to."

The bonded male vampire in him was all, *Yeehaw, sign us up.* But he had to be practical.

"I'm different from you," he said again, like it was his theme song.

"No, you're not."

Because she needed convincing and he could think of no better way of proving the point, he took her hand and moved it under the blanket, putting it on his cock. The contact made him shudder from pleasure, his hips bucking, but he reminded his libido that he was doing this to show her exactly how different he was.

He guided her to his barb, to the place at his base that was slightly uneven. "Do you feel that?"

She seemed to work for control for a moment, as if she were struggling against the same erotic current he was. "Yes . . ."

The husky way she drew out the word made his spine lift and recede, making his arousal slide in her palm. As his breath got short and his heart pounded, his voice grew deeper. "It locks in place when I . . . when I come. I'm not like what you've had before."

As she explored him, Rehv tried to remain still, but the power in his body from the feeding, coupled with where her hand was, proved to be too enticing. He moved against her hold, arching in her lap, feeling strangely at her mercy.

Which was just another huge turn-on.

"Is that why you pulled out of me?" she said.

Rehv licked his lips again, remembering the feel of her core surrounding his—

The Escalade went over a bump in the road and he was abruptly reminded that the dark haven of the far back of the SUV was only semiprivate: They were not, in fact, alone.

But Ehlena didn't remove her hand. "Is that why?"

"I didn't want you to know about any of this. I wanted to ... be normal for you. I wanted you to feel safe around me ... and I wanted to be with you. That's the why of the lying. I didn't mean to fall in love with you. I didn't want that for you—"

"What did you say?"

"I ... I'm in love with you. I'm sorry, but that's the way I feel."

Ehlena grew so quiet, he worried that in his delirium he had seriously misread everything between them. Had he merely projected onto her grid that which the weak part of him had needed to find?

Except then she dropped her mouth to his and whispered, "Don't hide from me ever again. I love you the way you are."

A rush of gratitude and *holy shit* and *OMG* and *thank you, manna from heaven* overrode everything logical, and Rehv reached up for her, holding her head with care as he kissed her. At that moment, he didn't give a fuck that there were complications way above and beyond their control, things that would drive them apart again as sure as the burning sun would rise at the end of the night.

To be accepted, though ... to be accepted and loved for exactly who he was by the one he loved in return was too great a joy to be capsized by cold reality.

As they kissed, Ehlena started moving her hand under the blanket, her palm going up and down his hard shaft.

When he tried to pull back, she recaptured his mouth with hers. "Shh ... trust me."

Rehvenge collapsed into the passion, riding the wave she called out of his body, letting her do exactly what she wanted to him. He tried to keep quiet, not wanting the others to know, and prayed that at least the two in the seats in front of them had passed out.

It didn't take long for his balls to cinch up tight and for his hands to crank down on her hair. Gasping against her mouth, he gave one last great thrust and came hard, soaking her hand and his stomach and the blanket.

When her touch drifted down to his barb and she felt the extension, he froze, praying she wasn't disgusted by the way he was built.

"I want to feel this inside me," she groaned against his lips.

As her words sank in, Rehvenge's body exploded in orgasm again.

Man . . . he couldn't wait for them to get wherever they were going.

SEVENTY-TWO

The following morning, Ehlena woke up naked in the bed she'd slept in before they'd all gone up to the colony. Next to her, Rehvenge's huge, warm body was as close to her as it could get, and he was awake.

At least in one sense of the word.

His erection was hot and hard against the back of her thigh, and he was rubbing it against her. She knew what was coming next, and she welcomed him as he rolled on top of her, mounted her, found his way between her legs. As he sank in deep and moved with sleepy instinct, her body echoed his rhythm and her arms went around his neck.

There were bite marks on his throat. A lot of them.

Bite marks on hers as well.

She closed her eyes, losing herself once again in Rehvenge . . . in them.

The day they had passed together in this guest room of the Brotherhood's hadn't just been about sex. There had been a lot of talking. She'd explained to him everything that had happened, including the inheritance and how she'd figured it all out, and how Xhex had not technically broken her vow to him when the female had headed for the colony.

God . . . Xhex.

No one had heard from her. And whatever joy and relief and triumph might have been felt at all of the Brothers and Rehvenge coming home without mortal injury was dimmed to the point of regret.

Rehvenge was going to go up to the colony at nightfall and search, but Ehlena could read in his face that he didn't think that was where she was.

It was just too odd and scary. No one had seen her body, but they hadn't seen her leave. Or caught sight of her outside of that chamber. It was as if she had just disappeared.

"Oh, God, Ehlena . . . I'm coming. . . ."

As Rehv's body jackhammered against her, she held on to her mate and let the sex take over, knowing that hard thoughts and sharp anxiety would be waiting for her on the other side of the orgasm. She heard her name being called out as Rehv released and then felt that exciting, rushing grab as he engaged deep within her.

All she had to do was think of it and her own orgasm erupted, carrying her over the edge.

When they were both satiated, Rehvenge rolled to the side, being careful not to try to separate them too soon. As his amethyst eyes focused properly, he brushed her hair back from her face.

"Perfect way to wake up," he murmured.

"I agree."

Their eyes met and held, and after a while, he said, "Can I ask you something? And it's not a why, it's a what."

"Hit me." She leaned up and kissed him quickly.

"What are you doing for the rest of your life?"

Ehlena's breath caught. "I thought . . . you said you couldn't stay in Caldwell."

His massive shoulders, which were still bandaged, shrugged. "Thing is, I can't leave you. Just isn't going to happen. Every hour next to you just makes that reality all the more clear. I literally . . . can't go unless you make me."

"Which is isn't going to happen."

"It . . . isn't?"

Ehlena framed his face with her palms, and the instant she did, he stilled. Which was something that happened every time she touched him. It was as if he were perpetually waiting for some kind of command from her . . . but then, that was what bonded male vampires were like, weren't they. Yes, they were stronger and more physically powerful than their mates, but the *shellans* ran the show.

"Looks like I'm spending my future with you," she said against his mouth.

He shuddered, as if he were letting his last doubts go. "I don't deserve you."

"Yes, you do."

"I'm going to take care of you."

"I know."

"And like I said, I'm not going back to what I did before here in town."

"Good." He paused, as if he wanted to reassure her even more and was searching for words. "Stop talking and kiss me again. My heart's made up and so is my mind, and there's nothing more you need to tell me. I know who you are. You're my *hellren*."

As their mouths met, she was well aware that there was a lot to sort out. If they lived among the vampires, they were going to have to continue protecting his *symphath* identity. And she didn't know what he was going to do about the colony up north—she had a feeling all that circling and worshiping business meant that he was in some kind of leadership role there.

But they were going to face all that and more together.

Which was the only thing that mattered.

Eventually, he pulled back. "I'm going to shower and go see Bella, okay?"

"Good, I'm glad." He and his sister had had only a brief, awkward hug before everyone had gone to bed. "Let me know if there's anything I can do."

"I will."

Rehvenge left the bedroom a half hour later, dressed in a pair of sweats and a thick sweater that one of the Brothers had given him. With no clue where to go, he tagged a *doggen* who was vacuuming in the hall and asked for directions to Bella and Z's bedroom.

It wasn't far. Just a couple of doors down.

Rehv went to the end of the hallway full of Greco-Roman statuary and knocked where he'd been told to. When there was no answer, he tried the next door up, through which he could hear Nalla's soft crying.

"Come in," Bella called out.

Rehv opened the way into the nursery slowly, unsure of the welcome he was going to get.

Across a room that had bunnies stenciled on the walls,

Bella was sitting in a rocking chair, her foot working against the carpet, her young cradled in her arms. In spite of the tender treatment, though, Nalla was not happy, her fussy, whimpering dissatisfaction at the world painfully apparent.

"Hi," Rehv said before his sister looked over. "It's me."

Bella's blue eyes rose to meet his, and he watched her face go through all kinds of emotions. "Hi."

"Mind if I come in?"

"Please do."

He closed the door behind himself and then wondered if she wouldn't feel safe shut in with him. He went to reopen it, but she stopped him.

"It's okay."

He wasn't so sure of that, so he stayed across the room from her, watching as Nalla registered his presence. And reached out for him.

A month ago, a lifetime ago, he would have gone over and taken the young into his arms. Not now. Probably not ever again.

"She's so fussy today," Bella said. "And once again my feet are tired. I can't walk around with her in my arms for even a minute longer."

"Yeah."

There was a long silence as they both focused on the young.

"I never knew about you," Bella said eventually. "I never would have guessed."

"I didn't want you to know. Neither did *Mahmen*." As the words left his lips, he said a quick, silent prayer for their mother, hoping that she would forgive him for the fact that the dark, horrible secret was now known. The thing was, though, life had played out as it had, the revelation not his to control.

God knew he'd taken his best shot at keeping the veil of lies in place.

"Was she . . . How did it happen?" Bella asked in a small voice. "How did . . . you . . . happen?"

Rehvenge thought about how to phrase things, tried out some lines in his head, changed words and added new ones. The image of his mother's face kept intruding, though, and in the end he just looked at his sister and slowly shook his head from side to side. As Bella paled, he knew she had guessed the gist of it all. *Symphaths* had been known to snatch females from the general population before. Particularly the beautiful, refined ones.

That was part of the reason the sin-eaters ended up in that colony.

"Oh, God . . ." Bella closed her eyes.

"I'm sorry." He wanted so badly to go to her. So very badly.

When she opened her lids again, she brushed away tears and then straightened her shoulders as if she were gathering strength.

"My father . . ." She cleared her throat. "Did he mate her knowing the truth about you?"

"Yes."

"She never loved him. At least, not that I saw." When Rehv stayed silent, because he was not going to go into that mating if he could help it, she frowned. "If he knew about you . . . did he threaten to expose her and you unless she committed to him?"

Rehv's silence seemed to be enough of an answer, because his sister nodded tightly. "That makes more sense to me. It makes me very angry . . . but I can see why she stayed with him now." There was a hard pause. "What else aren't you telling me, Rehvenge."

"Listen, what happened in the past—"

"Is my *life*!" As the young squawked, Bella lowered her voice. "It's my life, goddamn it. A life that everyone else around me knew about than I did. So you'd better fucking tell me everything, Rehvenge. If you want us to have any relationship at all, you'd better tell me *everything*."

Rehv exhaled hard. "What do you want to know first."

His sister swallowed hard. "That night my father died . . . I took *Mahmen* to the clinic. I took her because she had fallen down."

"I remember."

"She didn't fall down, did she."

"No."

"Not once."

"No."

Bella eyes shimmered, and as if to distract herself, she

tried to capture one of Nalla's falling fists. "Did you . . . that night, did you . . ."

He didn't want to answer the unfinished question, but he was through with lying to his nearest and dearest. "Yes. Sooner or later he would have killed her. It was him or *Mahmen*."

A tear trembled on Bella's lashes and fell off, landing on Nalla's cheek. "Oh . . . God . . ."

As he watched his sister's shoulders huddle in, as if she were cold and in need of shelter, he wanted to point out that she still had him to turn to. That he would still be there for her if she wanted him to be. That he remained her Rooster, her brother, her protector. But he wasn't the same to her and never would be again: Though he hadn't changed, her perception of him had been completely altered, and that meant he was a different person.

A stranger with a shockingly familiar face.

Bella swiped under both her eyes. "I feel like I don't know my own life."

"Can I come a little closer. I won't hurt you or the young."

He waited forever.

And still longer.

Bella's mouth compressed into a tight line, as if she were trying to keep soul-racking sobs in. Then she reached out to him, taking the hand that had wiped away her tears and extending it to him.

Rehv dematerialized across the room. Because running would have taken too long.

Crouching down next to her, he took that palm of hers between both his hands and brought those cold fingers to his cheek.

"I'm so sorry, Bella. I'm so sorry about you and *Mahmen*. I tried to apologize to her for my birth . . . I swear to you I did. It's just . . . talking about it was too hard for her and me."

Bella's luminous blue eyes rose to his, the tears in them magnifying the beauty of her stare. "But why would you apologize? None of this was your fault. You were innocent . . . utterly innocent. This was not your fault, Rehvenge. Not. Your. Fault."

His heart stopped as he realized . . . that was what he

had needed to hear. All his life he had blamed himself for being born and wished he could make amends for the crime against his mother that had resulted in . . . him.

"It wasn't your doing, Rehvenge. And she loved you. With everything she had, *Mahmen* loved you."

He didn't know how it happened, but suddenly his sister was in his arms, up tightly against his chest, she and her young in the haven of strength and love he offered.

The lullaby left his lips on nothing more than breath— there were no words to the gentle tune because his throat refused to let them through. The only thing that came out of him was the rhythm of the old ancient rhyme.

It was all they needed, though—that which couldn't be heard was enough to pull the past into the present and unite brother and sister once again.

When Rehvenge could go on no longer, even with as little as he was doing, he rested his head on his sister's shoulder and hummed to keep it going. . . .

As all the while the next generation slept soundly, surrounded by her family.

SEVENTY-THREE

John Matthew lay in the bed that Xhex had used, his head on pillows and his body on sheets that carried not just her scent but that of the cold, soulless sex they'd had when he'd come to her. In the chaos of the night, the *doggen* had yet to clean the room, and when the maid finally arrived to do it, he was going to turn her away.

No one was touching this place. Period.

Stretched out where he was, he was fully armed and dressed in the clothes he'd gone up to the colony to fight in. He was cut in a number of places, one of which was still bleeding, judging by the fact that his sleeve was wet, and he had a headache that was either a hangover or another battle wound. Not that it mattered.

His eyes locked on the bureau across the way.

The vicious cilices Xhex had insisted on wearing around her thighs sat on top of the dresser very much in the same way he lay on the bed—they were out of place, having nothing to do with the silver brush set they were next to.

The fact that she'd left them behind gave him hope. He was assuming that she used the pain they caused to control her *symphath* urges, so if she didn't have them on, that meant she had another weapon at her disposal to fight with.

And she would be fighting. Wherever she was, she would be in battle, because that was her nature.

Although, man, he wished he had fed from her. That

way ... maybe he could have sensed where she was. Or known for sure that she was still alive.

To keep himself from getting violent, he reviewed what he'd learned from the various field reports that had come in when everyone had gotten back to the mansion.

Zsadist and V had been with her and Ehlena in the chamber where Rehvenge had been found. The princess had shown up, and so had Lash. Xhex had shot the *symphath* bitch ... right before the entire colony had decided to pull a worshipful routine around Rehv, their new king.

Princess had then made a *Night of the Living Dead* reappearance. Rehv had fucked her up. Dust had settled ... and Lash and Xhex hadn't been seen again.

That was all anyone knew.

Evidently Rehv planned on heading up to the colony at nightfall to look for her ... but John knew the guy was going to come up with nothing. She wasn't with the *symphaths*.

Lash had snatched her. It was the only possible explanation. After all, her body hadn't been found on the way out, and there was no way in hell she would have taken off without making sure everybody else got to safety first. And the thing was, according to everyone who'd been in that chamber, Rehv had owned the will of all of those *symphaths*. So it wasn't like any of them could have broken free and overpowered her mentally.

Lash had her.

Lash was back from the dead and aligned with the Omega somehow, and on his way out of the colony, he had taken her with him.

John was going to kill that motherfucker. With his bare hands.

As anger rose in him until he was choking on all the pissed-off, he rolled away from what was on the bureau, unable to bear the idea that Xhex might be in pain.

At least *lessers* were impotent, though. If Lash was a *lesser* ... he was impotent.

Thank God.

With a plaintive sigh, John rubbed his face in a spot that smelled particularly strong of Xhex's gorgeous, dark scent.

If he could have, he would have gone back to the day before and ... he still wouldn't have walked past her door. No, he would have come in here again. But he would have been kinder to her than she had been to him that first time they'd been together.

And he also would have forgiven her when she had said she was sorry.

Lying in the dark with his regrets and his fury, he counted the hours until nightfall and made plans. He knew Qhuinn and Blay were going to go out with him—not because he asked them to, but because they weren't going to listen to him when he told them to mind their own business.

But that was it. He wasn't telling Wrath or the Brothers a thing. He didn't need them putting all kinds of safety features on this runaway carnival ride. Nope, he and his buddies were going to find Lash where he slept and slaughter him once and for all. If this got John kicked out of the house? Fine. He was on his own anyway.

Here was the thing: Xhex was his female, whether she wanted to be or not. And he was not the kind of male who was going to sit on his ass when his mate was out there in a world of hurt.

He was going to do exactly what had been done for Rehvenge.

He was going to avenge her.

He was going to bring her home safe . . . and make sure that the one who had taken her ended up in Hell.

SEVENTY-FOUR

When Wrath heard the knock on the study door, he stood up from behind the desk. It had taken an hour for him and Beth to empty the dainty thing out, which had been a surprise. Fucker had held a lot in its tiny drawers.

"Is it here?" he asked his *shellan*. "Is it them?"

"Let's hope so." Beth's footsteps sounded out as the door opened, like she was trying to get a good look. "Oh . . . it's beautiful."

"Try heavy as fuck," Rhage grunted. "My lord, didn't you think there was a middle ground somewhere?"

"This coming from you?" Wrath said as he and George took two steps directly to the left and one back. With his hand, he felt for the drapes and anchored himself as the fringe brushed his palm.

The sound of people milling around in heavy boots got louder and was accompanied by a shitload of cursing. And more grunting. A lot more grunting. As well as some slurs about kings and their royal prerogatives being a pain in the ass.

Then there were a pair of *boom*s as a pair of heavy things hit the floor, the sounds kind of like what you'd hear when two safes fell off a cliff and landed.

"Can we burn the rest of this nancy shit?" Butch muttered. "Like the sofas and the—"

"Oh, everything else is staying," Wrath murmured, wondering if the path was clear to the new furniture. "I just needed an upgrade."

"You're going to keep shafting us?"

"The sofa has already been reinforced for your fat ass. You're welcome."

"Well, you got an upgrade, all right," Vishous said. "That shit . . . is pretty boss."

Wrath continued to hang back, standing to the side as Beth told his brothers exactly where the furniture needed to be rearranged.

"Okay, you want to give this a shot, my lord?" Rhage said. "I think it's ready."

Wrath cleared his throat. "Yeah. Yeah, I do."

He and George went forward, and he put out his hand until he felt . . .

His father's desk was hand-carved out of ebony, the fine filigree work around the edge done by a real master craftsman.

Wrath leaned down, feeling his way around, remembering what it had looked like to his young eyes, recalling how centuries of wear had only increased its imposing beauty. The massive legs of the desk were actually statues of males depicting the four seasons of life, and the smooth top they supported was marked with the same symbols of lineage that had been tattooed on the insides of Wrath's forearms. As he traced along farther, he found the three wide drawers that ran beneath the surface and remembered his father sitting behind the thing with papers and edicts and feather quills all around.

"It's extraordinary," Beth said softly. "Good God, it's—"

"The size of my frickin' car," Hollywood muttered. "And twice as heavy."

"—the most beautiful desk I've ever seen," his *shellan* finished.

"It was my father's." Wrath cleared his throat. "We got the chair, too, right? Where is it?"

Butch groaned and there was some heavy shuffling. "And . . . here . . . I . . . thought this . . . was an . . . elephant." The sound of the thing's legs hitting the Aubusson carpet was thunderous. "What is this fucker made out of? Reinforced concrete painted to look like wood?"

Vishous exhaled Turkish tobacco. "I told you not to try that one on your own, cop. You want to cripple yourself?"

"I did just fine. Stairs were a piece of cake."

"Oh, really. So why are you bent over and rubbing your lower back?"

There was another groan, and then the cop muttered, "I'm not bent over."

"Anymore."

Wrath ran his hands up the arms of the throne, feeling the symbols in the Old Language that pronounced it not a mere chair, but a seat of leadership. It was exactly how he remembered . . . and, yes, at the pinnacle of the tall back he found cool metal and slick stones, and recalled the shimmering sight of gold, platinum, diamonds . . . and a rough, uncut ruby the size of a fist.

The desk and throne were the only surviving things from his parents' house, and they had been brought over from the Old Country not by him, but by Darius. D had been the one who'd found the human who'd purchased the set after the *lessers* had sold it as loot, found them and brought them back.

Yeah . . . and Darius had also cared enough to make sure that when the Brotherhood had come across the ocean, the race's throne and the king's matching desk had come with them.

Wrath had never expected to use either.

But as he and George took up res and sat down . . . it felt right.

"Shit, does anyone else feel the need to bow?" Rhage asked.

"Yes," Butch said. "But then again, I'm trying to take pressure off my liver. I think it got wrapped around my spine."

"Told you you needed help," V quipped.

Wrath let his brothers go on, because he sensed they needed the release and the distraction of verbal sparring.

Things had not gone well during the trip up north to the colony. Yes, Rehv was out, and that was great, but the Brotherhood did not leave fighters behind. And Xhex was nowhere to be found.

The next knock that came was another one Wrath had been waiting for. As Rehv and Ehlena came in, there was a lot of oohing and ahhing from the pair, and then the Brotherhood filed out, leaving Wrath and Beth and George alone with the couple.

"When are you going back north?" Wrath asked the male. "To find her."

"Second I can stand the fading light in the sky."

"Good. Do you want backup?"

"No." There was a soft rustling, as if Rehv had drawn his mate to his side because she was uncomfortable. "I go alone. It's better. Apart from looking for Xhex, I'm also going to tap a successor, and that means things could get dicey."

"A successor?"

"My life is here. In Caldwell." Even though Rehv's voice was steady and strong, the guy's emotions were bouncing all over the place, and Wrath was not surprised. The blender of life had been spinning the motherfucker but good the last twenty-four hours, and if there was one thing Wrath knew firsthand, rescue was sometimes just as disorienting as a capture.

Of course, the outcome of the former was far more palatable. May the Virgin Scribe grant such a thing to Xhex.

"Look, about Xhex," Wrath said. "Anything you need to find her, any kind of support we can offer, you have it."

"Thanks."

As Wrath thought about that female and realized it would be kinder to wish her dead rather than alive at this point, he reached out and put his arm around his *shellan's* waist so he could feel Beth safe and warm beside him.

"Listen, about the future," he said to Rehv. "I need to throw my hat in the ring on that one."

"What do you mean?"

"I want you to lead up there."

"What?"

Before the male could get rolling with the NFWs, Wrath cut in. "The last thing I need right now is instability in the colony. I don't know what the fuck is going on with Lash and the *lessers*, or why he was up there, or what the hell he was doing messing around with that princess, but I'm sure about this—from what Z told me, that group of sin-eaters is scared to death of you. Even if you don't live up there full-time, I want you in charge of them."

"I get where you're coming from, but—"

"I agree with the king."

It was Ehlena who spoke, and evidently she surprised the shit out of her mate because Rehv's speech devolved into a whole lot of stuttering.

"Wrath is right," Ehlena said. "You're the one who needs to be king."

"No offense," Rehv muttered. "But that wasn't the kind of future I had in mind for you and me. For one thing, if I never go up there again, it's too fucking soon. For another, I'm not interested in leading them."

Wrath felt the hard throne under his ass and had to smile. "Funny, sometimes I feel the same way about my citizens. But destiny has other plans for the likes of you and me."

"The hell it does. I got no clue how to do the king thing. I'd be flying blind—" There was a quick pause. "I mean . . . shit . . . not that being unable to see is . . . Damn it."

Wrath smiled again, imagining the chagrin on the guy's face. "Nah, it's cool. I am what I am." As Beth's grip found his hand, he gave her a squeeze to reassure her. "I am what I am, and you are what you are. We need you up there taking care of business. You didn't let me down once before, and I know you won't disappoint me now. As for the leading thing . . . news flash—all kings are blind, buddy. But if you get your heart in the right place, you can always see your way clear."

Wrath lifted his sightless eyes to his *shellan*'s face. "An extraordinarily wise female told me that once. And she was very, very right."

Son of a bitch, Rehv thought as he stared at the vampire race's great, revered Blind King. The guy was jacked into the kind of old-school throne you'd expect a leader to be in. . . . The thing was a hell of a piece of hardware, and the desk wasn't shabby either. And what do you know, while sitting all regal and shit, the motherfucker dropped bombs with the casual surety of a monarch whose demands were always met.

Christ, it was like he expected to always be obeyed, even if he were talking out his ass.

Which meant ... well, he and Wrath kind of had shit in common, didn't they.

For no particular reason, none at all, whatsoever, Rehv pictured where the king of the *symphaths* ruled from. Just a white marble pedestal seat. Nothing special, but then, what was respected up there were the powers of the mind—external shows of authority were not viewed as that impressive.

The last time Rehv had been in the throne room had been when he'd slit his father's throat open, and he remembered how the male's blue blood had dripped down the fine-grained, pristine stone like an ink bottle that had been spilled.

Rehv didn't like the image, although not because he was ashamed of what he'd done. It was just ... if he caved in to what Wrath wanted, would that be his future? Would one of his extended family someday slice him down?

Was that the fate that waited for him?

All in his head, he looked at Ehlena for help ... and she gave him precisely the kind of strength he needed. She stared up at him with such a steady, burning love that he decided maybe he shouldn't take such a dim view of destiny.

And when he glanced back over at Wrath, he saw that the king had the same kind of hold on his *shellan* as Rehv did on his.

That was the model to work off of, Rehv thought. Right in front of him was who and what he wanted to be: a good, strong leader with a queen who stood beside him and ruled as much as he did.

Except his civilians were nothing like Wrath's. And Ehlena could have no part up in the colony. Ever.

Although she would be great at advising him: There was no one he'd rather seek counsel from ... except for the vampire motherfucker in that throne across the room.

Rehv took his mate's hands in his. "Listen to me carefully. If I do this, if I rule, I interact with the colony by myself. You cannot go up there. And I promise you, there are going to be ugly parts. Really ugly parts. Things are going to happen that might change your opinion of me—"

"'Scuse me—been there, done that, got the T-shirt."

Ehlena shook her head. "And no matter what happens, you're a good male, and that's always going to win out—history's proven it over again and over again, which is the only guarantee anyone's ever going to get."

"God, I love you."

And yet even as she beamed up at him, he felt the need to double-check. "Are you sure, though. Once we jump—"

"I'm absolutely, positively"—she lifted up onto her tiptoes and kissed him—"sure."

"Hot damn." Wrath clapped his hands like the home team had just scored. "I love a good female."

"Yeah, me too." With a small smile, Rehv gathered his *shellan* into his arms, feeling like the world had righted itself in so many ways. Now if they could just get Xhex back—

Not *if*, he told himself. *When.*

As Ehlena laid her head against his chest, he rubbed her back and stared over at Wrath. After a moment, the king's face shifted away from his queen, like he knew that Rehv was looking at him.

In the quiet of the lovely, pale blue study, an odd communion was struck between them. Even though they were so different on so many levels, even though they shared little and knew each other even less, they were united by a commonality that neither had with any other person on the planet.

They were rulers who sat alone on their thrones.

They were . . . kings.

"Life is such a glorious trauma, is it not," Wrath murmured.

"Yeah." Rehv kissed the top of Ehlena's head, thinking that before he had met her, he would have cut the *glorious* out of that statement. "That's exactly what it is."

Read on for a sneak peek at *Lover Mine*,
J. R. Ward's next hardcover in the
#1 *New York Times* bestselling
Black Dagger Brotherhood series,
on sale in April 2010—featuring
one of the most beloved
Brothers of all time, John Matthew.

"Okay, I think we're done."

John felt a last dragging swipe on his shoulder and then the tattoo gun went silent. Sitting up from the rest he'd been curled against for the last two hours, he stretched his arms over his head and pulled his torso back into shape.

"Gimme a sec and I'll clean you up."

As the human male headed for a stainless-steel sink, John settled his weight on his spine once again, and let the tingling hum that stretched across his upper back reverberate through his whole body.

In the lull that followed, an odd memory came to him, one he hadn't thought of for years. It was from his days of living at Our Lady's orphanage, back when he hadn't known what he truly was. One of the benefactors of the place had been a rich man who owned a big house on the shores of Saranac Lake. Every summer, the kids had been invited to go up for a day and play on his football field-sized lawn and go for rides on his beautiful wooden boat and eat sandwiches and watermelon.

John had always gotten a sunburn. No matter how much goo they slathered on him, his skin had always burned to a crisp—until they finally relegated him to shade on the porch. Forced to wait things out on the sidelines, he'd watched the other boys and girls do their thing, listening to the laughter roll across the bright green grass, having his food brought to him and eating alone, witnessing the party instead of being a part of it.

Funny, his back felt now as his skin had then: tight and prickly, especially as the tattoo artist came back with a wet cloth and made circles over the fresh ink.

Man, John could remember dreading that annual ordeal at the lake. He'd wanted so badly to be with the others ... although if he was honest, that had been less about what they were doing, and more because he was desperate to fit in. For fuck's sake, they could have been chewing on glass shards and bleeding down the front of their shirts and he still would have been all *sign-me-up*.

Those six hours on that porch with nothing but a comic book or maybe a fallen bird's nest to inspect and reinspect had seemed as long as months: Too much time to think and yearn. He'd always hoped to be adopted, and in lonely moments like that, the drive had consumed him. The thing was, even more than being one among the other little boys, he'd wanted a family—a real mother and a father, not just guardians who were paid to raise him.

He'd wanted to be owned. He'd wanted someone to say *you're mine*.

Of course, now that he knew what he was ... now that he lived as a vampire among vampires, he understood that "owning" thing much more clearly. Sure, humans had a concept of family units and marriage and all that shit, but vampires were more like pack animals. Blood ties and matings were far more visceral and all-consuming.

As he thought about his younger, sadder self, his chest ached—although not because he wished he could reach back in time and tell that little kid that his parents were coming for him. Nope, he ached because the very thing he'd wanted had nearly destroyed him. His adoption had indeed come, but the "owning" hadn't stuck. Wellsie and Tohr had waltzed into his life, told him what he was and shown him a brief glimpse of home ... and then disappeared.

So he could say categorically, it was far worse to have had and lost parents, then to have not had them at all.

Yeah, sure, Tohr was technically back in the Brotherhood's mansion, but to John he was ever away: Even though the guy was now saying the right things, too many takeoffs had occurred such that now that a landing might actually have happened, it was too late.

John was done with that whole Tohr thing.

"Here's a mirror. Check 'er out, my man."

John nodded a thank-you and went over to a full-lengther in the corner. As Blay came back in from his cigarette and Qhuinn emerged from behind the side room's curtain, John turned around and got a look-see at what was doing on his back.

It was exactly what he wanted. And the scrollwork was boss.

He nodded as he moved the hand mirror around, checking out every angle. God, it was kind of a shame that no one other than his boys were ever going to see this. The tat was spectacular.

Xhex's name was in his skin. Ever a part of him. 'Til death did his flesh decay off his bones.

No matter what happened next, whether he found her dead or alive, she would always be with him.

The sight of those four Old Language characters eased him. Which was more than he could say of anything else he'd tried. Drinking, working out to exhaustion, fighting *lessers* until they weren't the only ones bleeding . . . nothing gave him any peace.

These last two weeks since her abduction had been the longest of his life. And he'd had some pretty fucking long days before this shit.

Christ, to not know where she was. To not know what had happened to her. To have lost her . . . he felt as if he'd been mortally injured though his skin was intact and his arms and legs unbroken and his chest unpenetrated by bullet or blade.

She hadn't wanted him, true. She had shut him out, true. But here was the deal. After having become toxic over the rejection, it had dawned on him that although she didn't feel the same way he did, he could still own his own emotions.

He could still pledge his life to her. And kill to find her. And bring her home in whatever condition she was in— whether it was to heal her or bury her.

She was his. And the lack of reciprocation didn't change that reality. Even if he got her back just so she could live a life that didn't include him, that was okay. He just wanted her safe and alive.

Guess that was how he knew he really did love her.

John looked at the artist, put his hand over his heart and bowed deeply. As he rose from his position of gratitude, the man stuck his palm out.

"You're welcome—means a lot that you approve. Now let me cover it up with some wrap."

Except John signed and Blay translated, "Not necessary. He heals lightning quick."

"But it's going to need time to—" The tattoo artist leaned in and then frowned as he inspected where he'd worked.

Before the guy started asking questions, John stepped back and grabbed his shirt from Blay. The fact was, the ink they'd brought with them had been lifted from V's stash— which meant part of its composition included salt. So that name and those fabulous swirls were in John's skin permanently—and his skin had already recovered.

Which was one advantage of being a nearly pure-bred vampire.

While Blaylock handed over John's jacket, the woman Qhuinn had balled came out from behind that curtain and it was hard not to notice Blay's pained expression. As someone who also had their shorties in a pinch over the whole unrequited-love thing, John's first impulse was to reach out to his buddy, but he held off.

Sometimes all a guy had going for him was his dignity.

"The tat rocks," Qhuinn said.

As the woman nodded, she slipped a piece of paper into Qhuinn's back pocket, but John wanted to tell her not to get her hopes up. Once the guy had someone, that was it— kind of like his sex partners were disposable razors he used to shave off the edges of his aggression. Unfortunately said Kat von D look-alike had stars in her eyes.

"Call me," she whispered to him with a confidence that would fade as the days passed.

Qhuinn smiled a little. "Take care."

At the sound of the two words, Blay relaxed, his big shoulders easing up. In Qhuinn-landia, "Take care" was synonymous with "I'm never going to see, call or fuck you again."

On that note, John took out his wallet, which was stuffed with tons of bills and absolutely no identification, and peeled off four hundreds. Which was twice what the tat cost. As the artist started shaking his head and saying it was too much, John nodded at Qhuinn.

The two of them lifted their right palms at the humans, and then reached into those minds and covered up the memories of the last couple hours. Neither the artist nor the receptionist would have any concrete recollection of what had been done. At the most, they might have hazy dreams. At the least, they'd have a headache.

As the pair slipped into trances, John, Blay and Qhuinn walked out of the shop's door and into the shadows. They waited until the artist shook himself into focus, went over and flipped the lock . . . and then it was time to get back to business.

"Sal's?" Qhuinn asked, his voice a little lower than usual, evidence of postcoital satisfaction.

As Blay lit up a Dunhill, John nodded and signed, *They're expecting us.*

One after the other, his boys disappeared into the night, but John paused for a moment before ghosting out, his instincts ringing.

Looking left and right, his laser-sharp eyes scanned Trade Street. There were a lot of neon lights and a number of cars going by because it was only two a.m., but he wasn't interested in the lit parts.

The dark alleys were the thing.

Somebody was watching them.

He put his hand inside his leather jacket and closed his palm around his dagger's hilt. He had no problem killing the enemy, especially now when he knew damn well who had his female . . . and he truly hoped something that smelled like a week-old dead deer stepped up to him.

No such luck. Instead, his cell phone went off with a whistle—no doubt Qhuinn and/or Blay wondering where the fuck he was.

He waited a minute more and decided the information from the Shadows was more important than throwing down with whatever slayer was hanging around. Xhex was the focus. She was the only thing that mattered in his whole world.

Getting her home safe was the be-all and end-all.

With vengeance flowing thick in his veins, John dematerialized into thin air, leaving nothing of himself behind.

"**S**he wants you."

Jim Heron lifted his eyes from his Budweiser.
Across the crowded, dim club, past bodies that were clad in
black and hung with chains, through the thick air of sex and
desperation, he saw the "she" in question.

A woman in a blue dress stood beneath one of the few
ceiling lights in the Iron Mask, the golden glow floating
down over her Brooke Shields brown hair and her ivory
skin and her banging body. She was a revelation, a standout
slice of color among all the gloomy, neo-Victorian Prozac
candidates, as beautiful as a model, as resplendent as a
saint.

And she *was* staring at him, though he questioned the
wanting part: Her eyes were set deep, which meant as she
looked over, the yearning that stalled out his lungs could
just be a product of the way her skull was built.

Hell, maybe she was simply wondering what he was doing in the club. Which made two of them.

"I'm telling you, that woman wants you, buddy."

Jim glanced over at Mr. Matchmaker. Adrian Vogel was the reason he'd ended up here, and the Iron Mask was definitely the guy's scene: Ad was dressed in black from head to toe and had piercings in places most people didn't want needles anywhere around.

"Nah." Jim took another swig of his Bud. "Not her type."

"You sure about that."

"Yup."

"You're a fool." Adrian dragged a hand through the black waves on his head and the stuff eased back into place like it had been trained well. Christ, if it weren't for the fact that he worked construction and had a mouth like a sailor, you'd wonder whether he trolled the women's mousse and spray aisles.

Eddie Blackhawk, the other guy with them, shook his head. "If he's not interested, that doesn't make him foolish."

"Says you."

"Live and let live, Adrian. It's better for everyone."

As the guy eased back on the velvet couch, Eddie was more Biker than Goth in his jeans and shitkickers, so he looked as out of place as Jim did—although given the hulking size of the guy and those weird-ass red-brown eyes of his, it was hard to imagine him fitting in with anyone but a bunch of pro wrestlers: even with his hair in that long braid, nobody razzed him at the construction site—not even the meathead roofers who gave the biggest lip.

"So, Jim, you don't talk much." Adrian scanned the crowd, no doubt looking for a Blue Dress of his own. After focusing on the dancers who writhed in iron cages, he flagged their waitress. "And after working with you for a month, I know it's not because you're stupid."

"Don't have a lot to say."

"Nothing wrong with that," Eddie murmured.

This was probably why Jim liked Eddie better. The SOB was another member of the Spare Club for Men, a guy who never used a word when a nod or a shake of the head could get his point across. How he'd gotten so tight with Adrian, whose mouth had no neutral on its stick shift, was a mystery.

How he roomed with the fucker was inexplicable.

Whatever. Jim had no intention of going into all their hows, whys and wheres. It was nothing personal. They were actually the kind of hardheaded smart-asses he would have been friends with in another time, on another planet, but here and now, their shit was none of his business—and he'd only gone out with them because Adrian had threatened to keep asking until he did.

Bottom line, Jim lived life by the code of the disconnected and expected other people to leave him to his I-am-an-island routine. Since getting out of the military, he'd been vagabonding it, ending up in Caldwell only because it was where he'd stopped driving—and he was going to hit the road after the project they were all working on was finished.

The thing was, given his old boss, it was better to stay a moving target. No telling how long it was going to be before a "special assignment" popped up and Jim got tagged again.

Finishing off his beer, he figured it was a good thing he owned only his clothes, his truck, and that broken-down Harley. Sure, he didn't have much to show for being thirty-nine—

Oh, man . . . the date.

He was forty. Tonight was his birthday.

"So I gotta know," Adrian said, leaning in. "You have a woman, Jim? That why you're not picking up Blue Dress? I mean, come *on*, she's smokin' hot."

"Looks aren't everything."

"Yeah, well, they sure as hell don't hurt."

The waitress came over, and while the others ordered another round, Jim shot a glance at the woman they were jawing about.

She didn't look away. Didn't flinch. Just slowly licked her red lips like she'd been waiting for him to make eye contact again.

Jim refocused on his empty Bud and shifted in the booth, feeling like someone had slipped lit coals into his shorts. It had been a long, long time for him. Not a dry spell, not even a drought. Sahara Desert was more like it.

And what do you know, his body was ready to end that stretch of nuthin' but left-handers.

"You should go over there," Adrian said. "Introduce yourself."

"I'm cool where I am."

"Which means I may have to reassess your intelligence." Adrian drummed his fingers on the table, the heavy silver ring he wore flashing. "Or at least your sex drive."

"Be my guest."

Adrian rolled his eyes, clearly getting the picture that there was no negotiating when it came to Blue Dress. "Fine, I'll lay off."

The guy sat back into the sofa so that he and Eddie were striking similar sprawls. Predictably, he couldn't stay silent for long. "So did you two hear about the shooting?"

Jim frowned. "There another one?"

"Yup. Body was found down by the river."

"They tend to turn up there."

"What is this world coming to," Adrian said, throwing back the last of his beer.

"It's always been this way."

"You think?"

Jim leaned back as the waitress planted freshies in front of the boys. "Nope, I know."

"No offense, but I think I'm going to take off."

Jim put down his empty and grabbed for his leather jacket. He'd had his two Buds, and one more was going to put him into DUI territory, so it was time to pull out.

"I can't believe you're leaving alone," Adrian drawled, his eyes going over to Blue Dress.

She was still standing beneath that ceiling light. And still staring. And still breathtaking. "Yup, just me, myself, and I."

"Most men don't have your kind of self-control." Adrian smiled, the hoop in his lower lip glinting. "Kind of impressive actually."

"Yeah, I'm a saint, all right."

"Well, drive home safe so you can keep polishing that halo. We'll see you tomorrow at the site."

There was a round of palm slapping and then Jim was making his way through the crowd. As he went, he drew looks from the black-chained and spike-collared, probably in the same way all these Goths did when they were out at a mall: *What the hell are you doing here?*

Guess Levi's and a clean flannel shirt offended their leather-and-lace sensibilities.

Jim chose a path that kept him far away from Blue Dress, and once he was outside, he took a deep breath like he'd passed some kind of test. The cold air didn't bring quite the relief he wanted, though, and as he walked around to the back parking lot, his hand went to the pocket of his shirt.

He'd quit smoking, and yet a year later, he was still reaching for the Marlboro Reds. His frickin' habit was like having an amputated limb with phantom pain.

As he made the corner and walked into the lot, he went past a row of cars that were parked grilles-in to the building. All of them were dirty, their flanks spackled with salt from the road treatments and months-old white-snow grime. His truck, which was way down at the end of the third row in, was exactly the same.

He looked left and right as he went. This was a bad part of town, and if he were going to get jumped, he wanted to see what was coming at him. Not that he minded a good fight. He'd gotten into a lot of them in his younger years, and then been trained properly in the military—plus, thanks to his day job, he was in rock-hard shape. But it was always better to—

He stopped as a flash of gold winked at him from the ground.

Crouching down, he picked up a thin gold ring—no, it was a hoop earring, one of those guys that plugged into itself. He cleaned the grunge off and glanced over at the cars. Could have been dropped by anyone, and it wasn't very expensive.

"Why did you leave without me?"

Jim froze.

Shit, her voice was as sexy as the rest of her.

Straightening to his full height, he pivoted on his work boot and stared across the trunks of the cars. Blue Dress was about ten yards away, standing under a security light—which made him wonder if she always chose spots that illuminated her.

"It's cold," he said. "You should go back inside."

"I'm not cold."

True enough. *Hot as fuck* would cover it. "Well . . . I'm leaving."

"Alone?" She came forward, her high heels tracking across the pitted asphalt.

The closer she got, the better-looking she became. Shit, her lips were made for sex, deep red and slightly parted, and that hair of hers . . . All he could think about was it falling over his bare chest and thighs.

Jim shoved his hands into the pockets of his jeans. He was much taller than she was, but the way she walked was a sucker punch to the solar plexus, immobilizing him with hot thoughts and vivid plans: Staring at her fine pale skin, he wondered if it was as soft as it seemed. Wondered a whole hell of a lot about what was under that dress. Wondered what she would feel like beneath his naked body.

As she stopped in front of him, he had to take a deep breath.

"Where's your car?" she said.

"Truck."

"Where is it?"

At that moment a cold breeze rolled in from the alley and she shivered a little, raising thin, lovely arms to wrap herself in a hug. Her dark eyes, which had been seductive in the club, abruptly became pleading . . . and made her nearly impossible to turn away from.

Was he going to do this? Was he going to fall into this warm pool of a woman, if only for a short time?

Another gust came barreling in, and she stamped one stiletto, then the other.

Jim took off his leather jacket and closed the distance between them. With their eyes locked, he encircled her with what had warmed himself. "I'm over here."

She reached for his hand and took it. He led the way.

Ford F-150s were not exactly great for hooking up, but there was enough room if you needed it—and more to the point, the truck was all he had to offer. Jim helped her inside and then went around and got behind the wheel. The engine started quick and he turned the fan off, halting the blast of frigid air until things heated up.

She moved across the seat to him, her breasts rising above the tight bands of her dress as she got closer. "You're very kind."

Kind was not the way he saw himself. Especially not now, given what was on his mind. "Can't have a lady cold."

Jim ran his eyes all over her. She was huddled in his beat-to-shit leather jacket, her face turned down, her long hair falling over her shoulder and curling up into her cleavage. She might have come across as a seducer, but the truth was she was a good girl who was in over her head.

"Do you want to talk?" he said, because she deserved better than what he wanted from her.

"No." She shook her head. "No, I want to do ... something."

Okay, Jim was definitely not kind. He was a man who was a palm's reach away from a beautiful woman, and even though she was giving off vulnerable vibes, playing therapist with her was not the sort of horizontal he was after.

As her eyes lifted, they were orphan sad. "Please ... kiss me?"

Jim held back, her expression putting the brakes on him and then some. "You sure about this?"

She swept her hair over her shoulder and tucked it behind her ear. When she nodded, the dime-size diamond in her lobe flashed. "Yes ... very. Kiss me."

When she held his stare and didn't look away, Jim leaned in, feeling ensnared and not minding in the slightest. "I'll go slow."

Oh ... God ...

Her lips were every bit as soft as he'd imagined, and he stroked her mouth carefully with his own, afraid he would crush her. She was sweet, she was warm, and she trusted him to set the careful pace, welcoming his tongue inside of her, then later shifting back so that his palm could ease down from her face to her collarbone ... to her full breast.

Which changed the tempo of things.

Abruptly, she sat up and took off his jacket. "Zipper's in the back."

His rough workman's hands found it quick, and he worried about marring the blue dress as he drew the fastening downward. And then he stopped thinking as she took the top from her breasts herself, revealing a satin-and-lace bra that probably cost as much as his truck.

Through the fine material, her nipples were peaked, and in the shadows thrown by the dim light of the dash, they were feast-for-the-starved spectacular.

"My breasts are real," she said softly. "He wanted me to get implants, but I ... I don't want them."

Jim frowned, thinking that whatever pig asshole had

come up with that one deserved an eye operation—performed by a tire iron. "Don't do it. You're beautiful."

"Really?" Her voice wavered.

"Truly."

Her shy smile meant too much to him, piercing through his chest, going too deep. He knew all about the ugly side of life, had been through the kinds of things that could make a single day feel like it lasted a month, and he wished her none of that. Seemed, though, she'd had plenty of hard cracks herself.

Jim reached over and turned the heater on to warm her.

When he eased back, she swept aside one of the bra's cups and framed herself with her hand, offering the nipple to him.

"You're amazing," he whispered.

Jim bent down and captured her flesh with his lips, sucking on her gently. As she gasped and thrust her hands into his hair, her breast cushioned his mouth and he had a moment of raw lust, the kind that turned men into animals.

Except then he remembered the way she'd looked at him, and he knew he wasn't going to have sex with her. He was going to take care of her, here in the truck cab, with the heater going and the windows fogging up. He was going to show her how beautiful she was and how perfect her body looked and felt and . . . tasted. But he wasn't taking anything for himself.

Hell, maybe he wasn't all bad.

You sure about that? his inner voice cut in. *Are you really sure about that?*

No, he wasn't. But Jim laid her down on the seat and wadded his leather jacket into a pillow for her head and vowed to do the right thing.

Man . . . she was drop-dead gorgeous, a lost, exotic bird who'd found a chicken coop for shelter. Why on God's green earth did she want him?

"Kiss me," she breathed.

Just as he braced his weight on his heavy arms and leaned over her, he caught sight of the digital clock on the dash: 11:59. The very minute he had been born forty years before.

What a happy birthday this had turned out to be.